J.A. Symonds

Miscellaneous Writings of John Conington Vol. 1

J.A. Symonds

Miscellaneous Writings of John Conington Vol. 1

ISBN/EAN: 9783742820648

Manufactured in Europe, USA, Canada, Australia, Japa

Cover: Foto ©Andreas Hilbeck / pixelio.de

Manufactured and distributed by brebook publishing software
(www.brebook.com)

J.A. Symonds

Miscellaneous Writings of John Conington Vol. 1

MISCELLANEOUS WRITINGS

OF THE LATE

JOHN CONINGTON.

MISCELLANEOUS WRITINGS

OF

JOHN CONINGTON,

LATE CORPUS PROFESSOR OF LATIN IN THE
UNIVERSITY OF OXFORD.

EDITED BY

J. A. SYMONDS, M.A.

LATE FELLOW OF MAGDALEN COLLEGE,
OXFORD.

WITH A MEMOIR

BY

H. J. S. SMITH, M.A. LL.D. F.R.S.

FELLOW OF BALLIOL COLLEGE; SAVILIAN PROFESSOR OF GEOMETRY, OXFORD.

IN TWO VOLUMES—VOL. I.

LONDON:
LONGMANS, GREEN, AND CO.
1872.

EDITOR'S PREFACE.

The REPUTATION of Professor CONINGTON as a scholar will rest upon his editions of the Choephoroe and of the works of Virgil and of Persius. As a translator he will continue to be known by his verse renderings of Horace, of the Æneid, and of the Agamemnon. In the Miscellanies now offered to the public he appears both as a scholar and a translator; but their distinctive mark is what, for want of a better phrase, may be styled literary versatility. Professor Conington approached scholarship from the point of view of literature, rather than of philology. As a scholar he was drawn to literature; as a man of letters he inclined to scholarship. Throughout the Miscellanies we trace this blending of his two main interests.

By the arrangement I have adopted in this book, the articles on English literature are followed by what will appear the most important section of the work, the Lectures on the History of Latin Poetry. To these succeed a few papers of pure scholarship. The first volume is completed by two essays on Liturgical questions, which during the last years of his life greatly occupied Mr. Conington's mind.

In making this collection I have availed myself of nearly everything in print or MS., with the exception of a few early contributions to the *Edinburgh Review*. These, I believe, Mr. Conington would not himself have wished to reprint.

The second volume consists almost entirely of a prose translation of Virgil. I have reason to know that Professor Conington contemplated the publication of this translation as a supplement to his edition. Yet he has not left it in a state of entire completion; and it is clear from the rapidity with which the MS. is written, as well as from the minute alterations which have been made in the more studied passages, that this portion of his work suffers severely from posthumous publication.

In conclusion, I have only to add that in collecting and editing these Miscellanies, I have to the best of my ability performed what I regarded as a sacred duty to the memory of a friend from whom I received more than I find it possible to express.

Thanks must be rendered to the proprietors of the *Quarterly*, *Edinburgh*, *North British*, *Contemporary*, and other reviews, for their kind permission to reprint articles published by them.

CLIFTON: April 1872.

CONTENTS

OF

THE FIRST VOLUME.

———

MEMOIR.

THE LIVES of literary men do not often offer any considerable
variety of incident, and that of Professor Conington was far
from being an exception to this general rule. The habits of a
student and a scholar were formed in him at an unusually early
age; he showed at all times a marked distaste for any change in
his way of life, or for adventure of any kind; and though during
a great part of his life he took a keen interest in political and
social questions, he never cared to mix with a larger world than
that offered to him by his own circle of family and university
friends. There is little, therefore, for a biographer to do but
to attempt to convey to the readers of these miscellaneous
writings something of the impression which the character of
their author, by its simplicity and force, its gentleness and purity,
made on all who had any opportunities of knowing him
intimately.

The following particulars relating to his parentage and early
boyhood have been communicated by his family:—

His father, the Rev. Richard Conington, was at first curate of the
parish church of Boston, and afterwards incumbent of the Chapel-of-
Ease in the same town. This incumbency he held till the year 1827,
when he was presented to the Rectory of Fishtoft, a retired village
in the neighbourhood. In 1823 he married his cousin, Jane Thirkill,
and their eldest son John was born on August 10, 1825. John was
from his birth a grave, quiet child, preferring books to play, and, as
he grew older, he always chose the society of grown-up people in
preference to that of children of his own age. He knew his letters
when he was fourteen months old, and could read well for his own

amusement at three and a half. From his earliest years until he
went to school he was his father's constant companion, and under
his careful training was laid that solid foundation of reverence for
the Word of God, which was the safeguard of his after-life amidst
the snares of an intellectual career. Before he was six years old he
was well acquainted with the historical parts of the Scriptures, and
it was his constant habit to sleep with a Bible under his pillow, that
he might read it as soon as he awoke in the morning. Books, and
especially poetry, were over his delight, and the greatest treat that
could be given was to allow him to go into the study and choose a
book for himself. When he was eight years old he would in this
way amuse himself by comparing different editions of Virgil, and
even before he was eight he repeated 1,000 lines of Virgil to his
father. Even at that early age, in all his varied reading, the purity
and refinement of his taste was remarkable. In 1834 he was sent
to a small school at Silk Willoughby, where the Rev. J. Sanders
became his tutor. The trial of leaving home for the first time was
great, but his spirits were cheered by the promise of being allowed
to go into the study when he liked. At the end of two years he was
removed to the Beverley Grammar School, under the care of the
Rev. Mr. Warren.

At Beverley he appears to have acquired the love of letter-
writing, which he retained through his whole life, and which
formed a marked peculiarity in his tastes in an age which is
said to have almost forgotten the art. His early letters to his
father are characterised by an ease and freedom from stiffness,
which tell not only of the affectionateness of his temper but
also of the command over expression to which he had already
attained. The following is a fair specimen :—

March 12, 1838.

My dear Papa,
    I received your kind letter about a fortnight ago. I am very
glad to hear that Henry has obtained the half-holiday, and that
Frank has begun Euclid *with a relish*. I am sorry to hear that you
must postpone sending the books I requested, since the third volume
of Valpy's Greek Testament is requisite to my at all understanding
the meaning of the Epistle to the Hebrews, or cutting anything like
a respectable figure in the class. I hope you will not think me idle
when I tell you that the five librarians, in which number I am of

course included, have been reading by ourselves, independently of
the subjects we prepare for Mr. Warren, some extracts from
Theocritus. We have also agreed that every one of our number
should devote an hour on Saturday afternoon to the reciting of a
lecture on some art or science, the composition of some one or other
of the librarians. None but us five know anything of the scheme,
so that, between ourselves, you are the only one to whom these
arcana have been communicated. My finances are at present reduced to a very low degree; but they have not been expended in
any eatables, or anything like that. Two or three weeks ago,
seeing a copy of Sotheby's Homer, I resolved to make myself master
of it. It was quite new, uncut, unsullied; its publishing price is
3*l.* 12*s.*, this one cost me 1*l.* 15*s.* It is accompanied with seventy
illustrations by Flaxman. As soon as Mr. Warren saw it, he told
me that I had made a very excellent bargain, and soon after procured one himself, but I should hardly think at the same low price.
There will then be an additional reason for sending me a parcel;
but perhaps you will say you never take hints. I can only hope
that this one will not be lost on you. In your next would you be so
kind as to send me the last stanza of the parody on Roderick Dhu.
Please remember that the books in request are three volumes of
Valpy's Greek Testament and Mr. Gee's Virgil. The smallest
donations will be thankfully received.

  With love to all, I beg to subscribe myself

  Your affectionate son,

  J. Conington.

P.S. A certain person, whose name I do not care to mention, told
me to inform you that he was a good boy. I have written a poem
of 104 lines on the Witch of Endor. I have shown it to Mr.
Warren, who has as yet given no decision concerning it, so that I
am on the ove of expectation.

It may gratify some youthful students of Latin to know that,
in the postscript to another letter of about the same date,
the future commentator of Virgil observes—' Memorandum :
My head was tapped yesterday morning for not perfectly understanding a passage of Virgil. The accompanying words' (some
customary formula which, it may be presumed, was not very
complimentary) ' were however dispensed with.'

In 1838, at the age of thirteen, he was sent to school at Rugby,

then at the height of its fame under Dr. Arnold. He was placed
in the house of Mr. Cotton (afterwards successively Head Master
of Marlborough School, and Bishop of Calcutta), to whom he
became strongly attached, and whom he regarded through life
as one of his most valued friends. But the earlier part of his
time at Rugby was not a very happy one. His near-sightedness
unfitted him for the active amusements of a public school, and
he probably never took part in a game of cricket or football
except against his will. The old custom of the school by which
all the boys, with hardly any exceptions, were compelled to join
in certain football matches, or big-sides, was singularly irksome
to him as a young boy, and never found much favour with him
when he was older. Indeed, the first recollection of him which
I myself retain, is that of seeing him wearily pacing to and
fro inside the goal at the sixth form match. But, besides the
continual feeling of being out of place which must haunt the
mind of every schoolboy who cares for books and does not care
for games, there were other and more positive causes of dis-
comfort. The Rugby of those days still retained some of its
primæval roughness, and though it may be hoped that even
then all the worst forms of bullying had already disappeared,
enough of the spirit of it remained to interfere seriously with
the comfort of a sensitive boy, whose character and tastes were
so much in advance of those around him. But these comparatively evil days were not of long duration, and might have left
no deep impression on his memory, if it had not been for the
gratitude with which he always remembered any kindness shown
to him at this period by his older schoolfellows. Writing in
1859 to a young friend, he says :—

Another man there is who has just had his life written as an
Indian hero—Hodson, of Hodson's Horse—but I have not seen the
book yet, though I am anxious to do so. He was at Rugby years
ago with me, though my senior, and for the last half year was head
of Cotton's House, to which he had been sent to restore law and
order—a sort of patron of mine, having considerable literary taste,

while he was a great athlete, so that I used to have the privilege of
going to see him in his study and hearing him talk about eminent
persons in and out of Rugby, and in return used occasionally to do
him a copy of verses, both before and after I got into the sixth
form, a piece of compliance which as you know I do not approve of
now. I felt quite inclined to regard him as a hero then, and am
proud to think that he proved himself so on a wider stage to the
world at large.

Conington had never been a fag, having been placed on
first coming to the school in the fifth form. By the end of
1839 he was already at the top of the twenty, and in after years
he could still remember with pleasure 'the second Sunday in
Advent 1839, when I got perhaps my greatest κῦδος at Rugby,
being thanked for my examination by Price' (the present Professor of Political Economy at Oxford) 'before the form, as
having beaten everybody by 1,300 marks.'

The work of the school had at no time (as may easily be
believed) been too hard for him, and in the sixth form which
he now entered, and in which, as in most public schools, the
boys did not change places, he sometimes found the incentives
to exertion insufficient to induce him to put any great strain on
his faculties. But he was never idle, and at the times when he
was least absorbed in the work of the form, he read largely for
himself. Dr. Arnold's estimate of his powers may be gathered
from the following passages in letters addressed to his father :—

Ambleside, June 20, 1840.

I spoke to him a little before he left Rugby, advising him rather
to read during the holidays any good works in English literature,
than to work at Latin or Greek. He has an immense advantage
in his good scholarship, which will tell with double effect when his
general powers of mind are more developed, and his knowledge
becomes more extensive.

Fox How, Ambleside, December 26, 1840.

In his work I observe with great pleasure his remarkable memory
and very good scholarship; his general knowledge is deficient, and
his powers of thought or fancy are not in proportion to his memory;
but this is the right order in which the faculties should develope

themselves, and I have no doubt that his compositions will regularly improve in point of matter, when his great facility and correctness of language will be an immense advantage to him.

Rugby, Nov. 2, 1841.

I have the greatest pleasure in telling you that your elder son's mind seems to me to have grown very considerably during the long holidays, and I find a great improvement in the matter of his compositions, which used to be unequal to the exceeding goodness of his scholarship.

One cannot help feeling that in these remarks due allowance is hardly made for the immaturity of a very young pupil. But Dr. Arnold's own earnestness and intensity of purpose led him to expect even from the very young a high degree of intellectual as well as moral excellence; and there can be no doubt that the powerful influence for good which he exercised over the minds of the boys of his sixth form was owing in great measure to the severe justice of his criticisms, and to the high standard by which he judged their work and their conduct. It is probable that, in the case of Conington, the strong contrast between the natural boyishness of his thoughts and the extraordinary command over language which he sometimes displayed, may have occasionally led the masters of the school to under-estimate the force and originality of his reasoning powers and of his imagination. If it were so, his schoolfellows judged differently. To us his conversation was delightful, and was certainly as instructive as it was entertaining. In the long summer walks, which then as now were one of the chief pleasures of Rugby boys, he would sometimes, if we pressed him to do so, awaken our admiration with some marvellous display of his powers of memory, repeating to us, for instance, our own unsuccessful and forgotten prize poems. But he would much oftener interest us in a discussion relating, it might be, to some incident of our school life, or to some question of literary or poetical criticism, or perhaps to matters of graver import; and to these discussions his genial wit and pleasant fancies, and above all his varied stores of knowledge, which to us seemed inexhaustible, gave a perpetual charm.

One unfortunate event in his school history it may be proper to mention here, as it was not without influence on the formation of his character. He may be allowed to tell the story as he told it to his father at the time :—

Rugby, Nov. 8, 1811.

You have, I suppose, ere this received a letter from Dr. Arnold, informing you of my recent degradation. I was doubtful at first whether you would expect to hear from me before you wrote yourself, but on consideration I thought you would be better pleased if I wrote forthwith, without waiting to hear from you. The facts of the case are these. Friday being the 5th of November, preparations were made as usual for a display of fireworks. Mr. Cotton happened to find a parcel containing the greater part of the purchases, which, to use his own expression, he confiscated as contraband goods. However, as there were still a few left, they were discharged forthwith, partly in the open air, and partly in the passage. Mr. Cotton, instead of coming out himself, which would have been the natural course to pursue, sent for me, as being the then head of the house (a title of ostensible responsibility, though in reality it confers no actual power), and told me to send up those who had discharged the fireworks in the passage. I accordingly represented the matter to the rest, and the consequence was that two out of the fifth form (over whom we have no power, and consequently could only *recommend* them to surrender themselves) gave themselves up as having taken a part in the affair. I was then sent for again, and desired to ask a number of boys, whom he named, if they were guilty or not guilty. The question having been put, three out of the number were sent up. On the next morning we (i.e. the whole sixth form in our house, being five in number, —— having been absent that evening) were unexpectedly charged by the Doctor for not having stopped the fireworks as they were going on. Having nothing to say in exculpation of ourselves, sentence was pronounced upon me, to take my place below —— (who, as I told, was not implicated, owing to absence), and moreover a severe punishment was threatened to myself and the rest, which was to be considered of. This evening we were accordingly desired to translate Cicero de Republicâ, lib. ii. as a penalty.

I do not wish to say anything in self-vindication, but merely to

give a statement of facts which may speak for themselves. I am at
a loss to think how you will regard the part I took in this unpleasant
affair. I took care of course not to participate in the discharge of
fireworks myself, and also not to be a looker-on, lest my presence
might be interpreted into countenancing the proceeding . . . . I do
not think that if you had been informed of my conduct without
reference to punishment, you would have been very seriously dis-
pleased; so I cannot believe that the magnitude of the punishment
will aggravate the offence in your eyes, as the case would have been
different had we known the penalty, and done the thing (I should
say, left it undone) knowing what we should incur by so doing.

The loss of a few places in the sixth form was not in itself a
matter of any great consequence, and it speaks well for the
discipline of the school that this should have been considered
so severe a punishment. It must be remembered that great
importance was attached by Dr. Arnold to the position and
duties of the Præpostors, upon whom he relied to no in-
considerable extent for the discipline and good management of
the school. While, therefore, he was always ready to support
their authority to the utmost, he regarded any remissness in the
discharge of their duties as a matter for the very gravest re-
prehension. In the present case, however, after a little time had
passed, he intimated to Conington that he no longer took so
severe a view of the matter as he had done at first. The pre-
vailing opinion in the school was that Conington had been
treated with some harshness, but that it was on the whole a
fortunate thing for him to be relieved from the irksome respon-
sibilities attaching to the position of head boy in his boarding-
house. He himself always maintained that more had been
expected from him than was possible under the circumstances,
and that the punishment inflicted on him was excessive. But
he was too generous to allow this feeling to interfere for one
moment with the sentiments of veneration and affection with
which he regarded the 'Doctor;' and it was always a great
pleasure to him to remember that, before Dr. Arnold's death,
which took place in the following midsummer, he had been

completely restored to the confidence and favour of one to whose
teaching he owed so much. It is right to add, that if the lesson
was a rough, and to a great extent, an undeserved one, it was
certainly not lost upon him; for few men in later life would
have been less likely to show weakness or irresoluteness in the
presence of any public duty.

His father had originally intended that he should go to Cambridge, being partly influenced by dislike to the Tractarian
movement, which seemed at that time to be dominant at
Oxford. But the son's own prepossessions were strongly in favour
of Oxford, and his wishes found a warm advocate in Dr. Tait,
who urged with great justice that, as he had confessedly no taste
for mathematics, if he should go to Cambridge he would in
all probability devote himself exclusively to Greek and Latin
scholarship; whereas at Oxford, the reading of Aristotle and
of Moral Philosophy would form the best supplement to the
study of language, and would prevent it from degenerating into
mere verbal criticism. A letter of his own to his father, written
while this question, to him so important, was still unsettled,
will show how seriously he reflected on it himself, and how far
he was from wishing to have it decided on the simple ground of
his own personal preference. His comparison between the
courses of study at the two Universities, in which he appears
to give the palm to Cambridge, is remarkable for its clearness
of insight and breadth of view, while it shows all the 'courage
of criticism' which is seldom wanting in young men brought
up under the modern system of education. It must be remembered, however, that in the last thirty years both Oxford and
Cambridge have undergone great changes, and that the points
of contrast which were so prominent in 1843 have been since
to a considerable extent softened down.

Rugby, May 19, 1843.

. . . . I have been led from attentive observation lately to look
upon the two rival systems of Oxford and Cambridge as being
neither of them perfect in themselves, from their being each con-

fined to one part of education. Cambridge, I should say, from its
verbal criticism and philological research, as well as its mathema-
tical studies, imparts a system of education, valuable not so much
for itself, as for the excellent discipline which prepares the mind to
pass from the investigation of abstract intellectual truth to the contemplation of moral subjects. Oxford, on the contrary, seeks
without any such medium to arrive at the higher ground at once,
without passing through the lower, leading the mind, before it has
been sufficiently disciplined, to investigate the highest and most
sacred subjects at once. Cambridge men too often view the intellectual exercise as sufficient in itself, instead of as a preparation for
higher things; Oxford men, without any such preparation, which
they affect to despise, proceed to speculate on great moral questions
before they have first practised themselves with lower and less
dangerous studies. And this, I look upon it, is the cause of the
theological novelties at Oxford—men apply to the most sacred
things powers which ought first to have been disciplined by purely
intellectual exercise. The one, if I may so express myself, raise a
scaffolding, and too often rest contented with that; the other endeavour to build the house either with no scaffolding at all, or at least
a very slight one—and a most unsubstantial structure it generally
proves. The fault of Cambridge, you see, is not the fault of the
system, but its abuse; in Oxford, the plan seems to me radically
wrong, and consequently, if followed out to the full, cannot do much
good. Cambridge appears to have seen that the province of a
university is not to give a complete education, but to furnish the
mind with rules drawn from lower subjects to be applied in after
life to higher; Oxford wishes to give a complete education, and by
attempting too much, does the whole very imperfectly.

As might have been expected, his strongly-felt wishes (rather
perhaps than his carefully-balanced reasons) were allowed by
his father to prevail, and he matriculated at University College,
Oxford, on June 30, 1843. But he did not commence residence at that College. In midsummer of the same year he
offered himself as a candidate for a demyship at Magdalen,
and was successful. The demyships at that time were filled up
by nomination, there being always, however, an examination of
a more or less competitive character. It was understood that
the venerable President of the College, Dr. Martin Routh,

made it a rule never to pass over any young man of eminent
merit; and in this instance he gave his first nomination to the
Rugby candidate, unsupported as he was by any private interest
or influential recommendation.   Dr. Routh's advanced age at
this time prevented him from seeing much of the undergraduate
members of his College, or from exercising any important influence on the course of their education.   Conington was much
impressed by his kindness and old-world courtesy on all occasions
when he had to call on him officially; and it would seem that
the old man had no difficulty in discerning the true character
of his visitor; for instead of exhortations to steadiness of conduct, or encouragement to diligent study, he would give him
shrewd lessons of worldly wisdom, and hints as to the best way
of succeeding in life.

Conington now finally quitted Rugby, where he had been
elected an Exhibitioner for three consecutive years, and commenced residence at Oxford in the October term.   In the
following Lent he succeeded in carrying off both the Hert-
ford and Ireland scholarships, which are looked upon as the
highest classical distinctions attainable by any undergraduate
in the University.   It was the custom then, much more than
it is at present, for young men to read with private tutors;
and soon after coming up to Oxford he had the good fortune
to become the private pupil of a justly eminent scholar, the
Rev. W. Linwood, of Christ Church; and no doubt his early
success in these two examinations is in great measure to be
attributed to the good use he made of this advantage.   He
had been unusually anxious about the result; and, conscious
that he would not win without a great effort, he had taxed his
strength of mind and body to the utmost in order to secure
his victory.   It is not, therefore, very surprising to find that,
when the contest was over, his energies somewhat flagged so
far as his university work was concerned.   The course of reading required for the final examination was far from enough to
find him occupation for the whole of his time.   The Greek

and Latin scholarship, which at that time was an essential
requisite for a first class, was already at his command in an
abundant measure.   For history he never had any special predilection, and he used often to say regretfully that he considered
himself to be without any natural aptitude for that study.
But his gift for reading rapidly, and remembering accurately
after the most cursory perusal, made it very easy for him to
acquire as much knowledge of ancient history as he needed
for the purposes of the schools.   In Moral Philosophy, which
formed the third, and perhaps even then the most important
subject of the examination, he took a livelier interest.   His
love for the discussion of political and moral questions had
here full scope ; and under the skilful training of another
excellent tutor, the Rev. C. P. Chretien, of Oriel, he soon
became a fair Aristotelian.   Still, neither Plato nor Aristotle
were ever genuine favourites with him ; in later years he
would refuse to see any merit, sometimes indeed to find any
sense, in the Metaphysics of Aristotle ; and he used steadily to
maintain that the study of ancient philosophy was by no means
a necessary, and perhaps not even a desirable, preparation for
the pursuits of a scholar.

Before offering himself for his final examination, he quitted
Magdalen, having been elected in March 1846 to a scholarship
at University, thus returning to the college at which he had
been originally matriculated.   He took this step, because,
having already determined not to take holy orders, he found
that there was only a very remote prospect of succession to a
lay fellowship at Magdalen.   ‘ I shall never fail,’ he wrote, ‘ to
speak of the authorities there as having been very kind to me
personally, and as having made my residence there as comfortable as they could ; and it is a satisfaction to me to think that
in leaving them I acted with their entire concurrence.’   He
obtained his first class in December 1846, and his fellowship at
University fourteen months later, in February 1848.

In competing for the University Prize Poems and Prize

Essays he was less immediately fortunate than he had been in the examinations for the University Scholarships. The New-degate Prize for English Verse he never obtained at all, and the Prize for Latin Verse not till 1847, after two unsuccessful efforts. The subject set for the poem in that year was 'Turris Londinensis,' and, perhaps owing to its somewhat trite character, it failed to interest him seriously. There is consequently a certain want of life about his composition, which prevents it, notwithstanding its correctness, from being a very favourable specimen of his powers of Latin versification. He regarded it himself in this light, and thought it not so good as some of his own unsuccessful poems, while with his usual candour he placed it much below the brilliant 'Numa Pompilius' of his friend, Mr. Goldwin Smith, which he always looked on as one of the very best among recent pieces of Latin verse. Something of the same ill fortune attended him with regard to the English and Latin Essays—the prizes for which he obtained in the years 1848 and 1849, and in each case on his first attempt. But the subjects of these essays, 'The Respective Effects of the Fine Arts and Mechanical Skill on National Character,' and 'Quænam fuerit Platonis idea in republicâ suâ conscribendâ?' were neither of them exactly suited to him, and did not excite in his mind that sort of enthusiasm without which he found it difficult to put forth his full powers. Thus his essays, though they do not fall below, do not rise very much above the standard of merit usually found in compositions of this kind.

During his undergraduate career, and for two or three years after taking his degree, he took an active part in the discussions of the Union Society, of which he was secretary in 1845, president in 1846, and librarian in 1847. He had not in those days as yet abandoned the ambitious desire—a desire which is probably never wholly absent from the mind of any young Englishman—of entering some day on public life; and he naturally regarded the Union as the best available school of preparation for such a career. The debates of that society, though never at any time intermitted, have not always been equally popular with the undergraduate members of the university. In Conington's time they were in great favour, and it was quite the fashion to attend them. The 'House,' always crowded, was often stormy and uproarious, and, not unfrequently, it required some tact and management to get a hearing from it at all. It had strong Tory convictions, which it did not like to have contradicted; it exhibited an intolerance of bores which cannot be too strongly commended to the imitation of other popular assemblies; and altogether it presented as good a praetising ground for mimic political warfare as a young orator could desire. Conington had some personal difficulties to contend against, among which his near sight, and an occasional hesitation in speaking, were not the least. But, in spite of them, he soon established for himself a good position with his audience; and obtained as much control over them as any of his contemporaries. There was sense and sound reasoning even in his most unprepared speeches; and he always, in speaking no less than in writing, had at his command a copious supply of polished language. His delivery was never free from embarrassment; but, notwithstanding this, there was something fine and classical in his way of speaking. Unlike some orators of much greater note, he finished every sentence which he began; and, in his speeches, just as in his conversation, or in his most careless and hastily written letters, it would have been hard to find an ungrammatical turn of expression, or a phrase of questionable English.

Some of the subjects which were uppermost in his mind during this period are referred to in the following extracts from letters to his father and mother:—

Magd. Coll., November 7, 1844.

The favourite passage of Arnold, I suppose, is Ἐχθίστη ὀδύνη πολλὰ φρονέοντα μηδένος κρατέειν, which occurs several times in the course of his correspondence. It may mean either that it is a most grievous curse for a man, who sees much truth, to influence no one, or (instead of the last four words) to realise nothing. Either way the sense is the same—the question is whether μηδίνος refers to a person or a thing. Apart from verbal points, the observation is most true, and most painful, and must come home to every one who thinks at all.

Magd. Coll., April 30, 1845.

I scarcely know how the Maynooth question is regarded among us. The opinion of the generality of the undergraduates is, as you may imagine, not worth having, and even if it were, it would still be a difficult matter to test it. In February I brought forward a motion against the grant at the Union, which I carried after an animated debate by about three to two, in a house of about forty members. At present, however, we have a debate pending, which has already continued a fortnight—'That Sir Robert Peel's Government has forfeited the confidence of the country,' and the question of Maynooth of course enters very largely into it. There have been several good speeches both from the friends and the enemies of the grant; nor can I tell from the feeling expressed which way the general opinion really is. The attendance is much larger, averaging, I believe, between 200 and 300 each night. Even after the division has taken place, it will be hard to tell the feelings of the men on this particular subject, as many who would oppose the Government thereon, will vote for them on a broad general question, myself among the number.

Magd. Coll., May 3, 1845.

The question now before the Union is not the grant to Maynooth, which, as I told you, was discussed last term under my auspices, but the confidence of the country in Sir Robert Peel's Government, and this is what I mean to affirm by my vote, as I suppose you would do yourself. My objections to the Maynooth grant continue in full force, and had I had a seat in the House of Commons I should have certainly voted against it, though I knew that my vote would endanger Peel's continuance in office; but as to objecting to his continuance in office, when that is the question to which you must say aye or no, I should be one of the last persons in the world to do so. I do not agree with many of his opinions, but I respect him nevertheless. A statesman, according to my view, ought to make right his exclusive standard of action; but the man who makes expediency his exclusive standard—expediency, I mean, in the wide

sense of the term—is, in my opinion, second best. The generality
of statesmen are guided by expediency in a very low sense—the
expediency of party, not the expediency of the nation. I do not
withdraw my confidence from Sir Robert Peel, simply because I
know no one better to whom to give it. You would not trust the
Whigs. Ward's motion for robbing the Irish Church to pay Maynooth was supported by Lord J. Russell. The agriculturists and
old Tories could never raise an administration. Young England,
even were it practical enough, is divided against itself, and I should
hardly think you would wish to see Cobden First Lord of the
Treasury, with Roebuck for a Lord Chancellor. In Gladstone, I
had real confidence, previous to the change of his opinions on the
Maynooth grant. I could scarcely understand his speech in the
papers, so I got the published copy, and cannot call it in any way
satisfactory, so that I am constrained to own that there is no help
in him. Now the country must have confidence in some one, and
there being no other conceivable administration in which it could so
confide, I argue that its confidence must still be possessed by Peel.

Oxford: The Union, February 17, 1846.

I glance over the debates each day, just to keep up with the
news; but I do not learn enough to enable me to form an opinion.
Peel's speech last night seems a good one, especially the first part,
where he speaks of the accusation of having broken up his party.
What will the state of parties be in ten years' time? It passes my
power of guessing; in fact, I should doubt whether anyone now
living could tell. That the Free Traders will split up into parties
on different questions, I suppose there can be no doubt. Partisan-
ship is too deeply engrafted in the heart of man to be rooted up
by the vicissitudes of a Corn Law battle.

Magd. Coll., February 21, 1846.

I can tell you very little about Pusey's sermon, as I did not hear,
and have not read it. It excited great expectation, and there was a
tremendous crowd to hear it, as the newspaper accounts will
doubtless have informed you. The first sentence was, I should
think, well calculated to work up the attention of all to the highest
pitch, opening with a direct mention of the last occasion on which
he filled the University pulpit. As a point of controversy, it does
not seem to have been much talked of, as he appears not to have
committed himself doctrinally, so as to be liable to University penal-

ties. Men spoke of it, however, in the spirit of those who had witnessed a great historical event, and the general feeling was certainly in favour of the preacher.

Next in general interest to Pusey's sermon, was one the next Sunday from Stanley, who you know is select preacher, and then delivered the first of a course on the distinctive characters of the Apostles Peter, Paul, and John. It was very eloquent and imaginative, and, as I think, very good, though many Oxford men attacked it as being the very essence of rationalism, fixing mainly on two points: first, his plan of recognising the distinct *human* characters of the Apostles as remaining visible amid their common inspiration; secondly, one of the practical inferences which he drew from such a recognition, that good may present itself under different forms of character and shades of opinion within the Church. I do not undertake to subscribe to every expression he used, but generally I thought, so far from being rationalistic, it furnished the true means of meeting rationalism—taking a middle line between rationalism on the one hand, and superstition on the other. I am sure it is a good thing to have theology presented to the mind of Oxford in other than a controversial aspect; it may, if followed up, do much to allay the present unwholesome excitement on such matters, and besides has a work of its own, as the explanation or exegesis of Scripture is much neglected here, no one being more behindhand in it generally than practised disputants.

Magd. Coll., March 17, 1846.

About great men, I am inclined on the whole to agree with what you say about Cobden. A very great man I should scarcely call him, as that is a name which you would hardly give to one or two in a century; but a great man I think he must be, whether you sympathise with his Free Trade schemes or no. His speech on the Corn Law Debate showed his greatness; there was throughout a calmness and self-possession, a consciousness of power, and a disposition, I should hope, to use it with moderation and firmness which told on me considerably.

Oxford: The Union, May 6, 1846.

I cannot enter into the Corn Law question, because as a matter of fact I do not understand it. What you say about the burdens pressing almost exclusively on the landed proprietor would be a strong argument, if it were clearly made out; but I have certainly seen counter-statements in the *Times* to prove that a small trades-

man is much more burdened than a farmer. So between statement
and counter-statement I really do not know what to think. I
merely say on general grounds that the rise of a new power ought
always to be recognised, and that the same reason which led to the
ennobling of the landed proprietor in the first instance now points
out that their honours ought to be shared with a new claimant. I
have never heard anything to shake me in this, if I had I should be
glad to give it up. The fact is that neither party will bear
analysing in point of worth; but an aristocracy of worth you cannot
have, so you must fall back upon some principle like that of property or power of commanding labour.

The summer preceding his election to his fellowship he
spent at Dresden with his friends, Mr. Goldwin Smith and Mr.
Philpot. This was the only visit he ever paid to the Continent,
and though he retained some pleasant recollections of it he
never ventured on another. The discomforts and small annoy-
ances of foreign travel were so repugnant to him, that he felt
they were but poorly compensated by the wider opportunities
of observing men and things. His truly English preference
for home to a strange country, combined with the tendency to
attach himself to any place even after a very short residence
in it, find a not unpleasing expression in a letter written to his
mother shortly before leaving Dresden :—

Dresden, September 21, 1847.

I am sorry that Papa and Frank should have been forced to part
company, though I have no doubt it was better that it should be so.
The latter appears to be having a regular outing, and will probably
have seen more during his three weeks than I shall be able to give
an account of when my eight have come to an end. N'importe, it
is my way, and in my way I hope I have picked up something in
consequence of leaving England; indeed it would be a pity if it were
not so, as it is really the only thing to my mind which can justify
going abroad at all, considering the superiority in almost every way
of what one leaves behind. Nevertheless, though heartily glad to
be at home again, I shall be sorry, yes certainly sorry, to leave
Dresden, putting the annoyance of moving out of the question. Six
weeks do a great deal to attach one to a place, and I shall carry

with me many pleasant memories of persons and things which I do
not like to think that I am not likely to see again. And yet,
whether I shall see the persons or things again is more than
doubtful; in the little amount of travel which I shall probably
accomplish one year with another there will hardly be time to visit
the same place a second time. And this strikes upon me as rather
a melancholy thought. Well, I suppose it must be so in life over
and over again, and I will not indulge in myself a feeling which I
should snub as sentimental in J——.

Before quitting the Continent he did not fail to visit
Leipsic, in order to see Godfrey Hermann, the veteran chief of
Greek Philology. Hermann received him very cordially, and
talked freely with him on literary subjects. But the visit,
embarrassed as it was by difficulties of language (they had to
talk in Latin, and each of course pronounced it after the
manner of his own country), did not lead to any further intercourse or correspondence.

The years which elapsed between his election to his Fellowship and his appointment to the Professorship of Latin were
the most unsettled of his life; and although the restless activity
of his mind prevented them from being fruitless, there was a
want of definite purpose in his efforts at this time which was
a cause of some regret to him afterwards. The Oxford institutions of that day offered but few inducements to a clergyman,
and none whatever to a layman, to devote himself to the study
of philology, or indeed to any study at all. There seemed to
be no 'carrière ouverte aux talents,' and there were certainly
very few University offices to which a layman could look forward as affording extended opportunities of usefulness, or a
just reward for services already rendered. There was as yet no
Professorship of Latin at all, and the Regius Professorship of
Greek (then held by Dr. Gaisford, the Dean of Christ Church)
still retained its ancient endowment of 40l. a year. Under
these circumstances, it is not surprising to find that Conington
determined (though not without much anxious deliberation) to
abandon his favourite studies and his Oxford life, and to try his

fortune in a more active profession. He accordingly applied
for and obtained the Eldon Law Scholarship, which is awarded
by its trustees to the candidate whose University distinctions
have in their judgment established the best claim to it. The
Eldon Scholar is required to keep his terms regularly at
one of the Inns of Court, and, during his tenure of the Scholarship, is considered bound in honour to be a *bonâ fide* student
of the law. In compliance with these regulations Conington
gave up residence at Oxford in Michaelmas 1849, and, establishing himself in London, began to read in chambers, and
for some time used his best endeavours to transfer his affections from the Greek poets to jurisprudence. Fortunately the
experiment proved a complete failure before too much time
was wasted on it. He found that he disliked, or more properly
detested, the work he had to do in a lawyer's chambers; and
such ambition as he had was too fitful and uncertain to be
maintained in permanent activity by the far-off prospects of
great success which form the day-dreams of many a young
lawyer. What he really longed for was some recognised and
permanent position, of which the duties might be congenial to
him, and in which he could conscientiously feel himself of use.
His wishes were certainly not immoderate in their range, but
on the other hand he was somewhat impatient for their immediate fulfilment. To a man in such a temper the hope of
becoming in twenty years' time an eminent leader at the
chancery bar had very little charm; and the aimlessness of an
Oxford life might well seem better than the faint chance of obtaining at a remote period what after all he did not very much
care for. But, even more perhaps than by the change in his
occupations, or the uncertainty of his prospects, he was rendered
uncomfortable by the loss of intimate companionship with his
friends. His nature was so affectionate and expansive that the
comparative isolation, in which young men from the Universities often find themselves when they first enter on a London
life, seemed chilling and even insupportable to him, when

contrasted with the easy ways of society at Oxford, where men who wish to meet without inconvenience or interruption to the regular course of their occupations can do so almost daily, in the college halls or common rooms, in country walks, or in transacting the public business of the University. After six months' trial of the law, during which he became very dissatisfied with himself, and more or less dissatisfied with everything about him, he wisely gave up a useless and irritating struggle against the natural bent of his genius; and resigning the Eldon Scholarship, he returned, with a sense of extreme relief and thankfulness, to the quiet of his rooms in University College.

During his stay in London he formed a connection with the *Morning Chronicle*, and became for a time a regular contributor to that journal. But, notwithstanding all his fluency in writing, it may be doubtful whether he would ever have developed the somewhat peculiar talent which is required for the daily production of first-rate leading articles. He never could write his best except when he wrote from strong conviction, or, at least, when he wrote upon matters which interested him deeply, and which had been present to his mind long enough for him to know what attitude he could conscientiously take up with regard to them. But the journalist has sometimes to write at a few hours' notice on a subject with which, to say the least, he is only superficially acquainted, and has to advocate a view which is indicated to him in advance by party or editorial exigencies, and which may not be the same as that which the facts, when he begins to examine them, would of themselves have suggested to his mind. These difficulties were keenly felt by Conington, and when it fell to his lot to do one of the rough-and-ready pieces of work which are necessary to the successful conducting of a newspaper, there was a sort of timidity in the execution of his task, a conscientious balancing of the two sides of the question, and a hesitation in pressing his point, which was very unlike the vigorous way in which he could lay about him when writing upon questions with regard to which his mind

was made up. The articles in the *Morning Chronicle* of
1849–50 which relate to University Reform, a topic then
attracting much attention in the Liberal press, are chiefly from
his hand; and these certainly will not be found to exhibit any
indecision of purpose or any want of incisive expression.

Before he went to London he had already (in 1848) edited
the Agamemnon of Æschylus, with English notes, and an
interleaved translation into English verse. With this, his first
effort, both as a translator and editor of a classic author, he
was never thoroughly satisfied, even at the time of its publication; and later, when he had to consider the advisability of
republishing it, he determined not to do so, saying that he
should have to rewrite the whole commentary and to suppress
the translation altogether. Of the translation he probably
judged too hardly, for though as a whole it is inharmonious, and
is blemished here and there with harsh and even infelicitous
renderings, it is not wanting in vigour nor in poetic feeling, while
it hardly needs to be said that it is scholarlike and accurate.
After his return to Oxford Æschylus continued to be his
favourite. He knew the whole of the seven plays by heart,
and lavished time and thought upon the criticism and explanation of their text. His 'Choephoroe' appeared in 1857, and is
one of the best editions of that play in existence, contributing
only a little, it is true, to the settlement of the text, but very
much to its right interpretation. He had also collected the
materials (chiefly, however, storing them in his memory) for a
similar edition of the 'Supplices.' But he was prevented from
carrying out this design, in the first instance, by his undertaking in conjunction with Mr. Goldwin Smith to edit Virgil,
and afterwards by his appointment to the chair of Latin. From
a conscientious motive, which it is difficult not to think over-
strained, he was unwilling after he became Professor of Latin
to devote any considerable portion of his time to Greek, and
when pressed, as he often was, to prepare his edition of the
'Supplices' for publication, he would always say that he must let

it wait until he had done what he could with Latin. The
edition of Virgil was begun in 1852, and the first volume, containing the Eclogues and Georgics, was published in 1858. The
greater part of the work had to be done alone, as Mr. Goldwin
Smith, on becoming secretary to the Oxford University Commission, was obliged to retire from the joint editorship. The
transition from the absorbing study of Æschylus to that of
Virgil was an abrupt one, as it would be difficult to find two
poets whose merits and imperfections are more absolutely
unlike. Thus, when he began working on Virgil he was not
indisposed to sympathise with much of the depreciatory
criticism of which that poet has been the object during the
present century. Traces of this want of admiration are by no
means unfrequent in his earlier notes, though even these are
much softened down from what they were in their first rough
drafts. But to all lovers of Virgil it is pleasant to see how
the beauties of the poet, though they grew upon him only
gradually, proved irresistible in the end ; and if he was guilty,
when comparatively a beginner, of finding a certain clumsiness
in the construction of the first Eclogue, he made ample amends
by the genuine and hearty admiration which he afterwards
bestowed upon other writings of its author. The lecture 'On
the style of Lucretius and Catullus as compared with that of
the poets of the Augustan age,' which is printed in this volume,
expresses the judgment at which he finally arrived, and contains
some fine criticism of the minuter details of Virgil's consummate
art, as well as an earnest vindication of his claim to genuine
originality.

The election to the Professorship of Latin took place in 1854.
The Chair was a new one in the University, having just been
founded by Corpus Christi College to carry out a provision in
the statutes of their founder, which had been allowed to fall
into abeyance during the long torpor which had crept over the
professorial system in Oxford. As Conington was opposed by
more than one distinguished competitor, whose merits he most

fully recognised, and as he was himself better known as a Greek
than as a Latin scholar, he did not expect a favourable result with
any great confidence, and his anxiety was in proportion to his
uncertainty. His success gave him all the external advantages that he desired in life ; and, if in the few preceding years
his mind had been sometimes disturbed by an under-current of
restlessness and discontent, these feelings passed away at once
and for ever.

But this was not the only change that his friends observed in
him at this time. During the Long Vacation, which intervened
between his election to the Professorship and his entrance upon
the discharge of its duties, he passed through a mental conflict
which left a deep and permanent impression upon his character,
and which, even in this brief memoir, it would be inconsistent
with truthfulness to leave unmentioned. The liveliness and
sincerity of the religious impressions of his childhood have
been already noticed; and these impressions had at no subsequent time faded from his mind. At Rugby they had grown
with his growth, and had been widened as well as deepened by
the teaching and the example of Dr. Arnold, to whom the discharge of every duty, however secular, seemed a direct religious
service, and who had the gift of communicating something of
this sacred earnestness to those immediately around him. At
Oxford, in a larger world, Conington was exposed, as his father
had anticipated, to influences of a more varied and unsettling
kind. It would have been strange if, with his powers of sympathy, and with his unfeigned reverence for every manifestation
of intellectual or moral greatness, he could have remained wholly
unaffected by either of the two tendencies of thought which
divided the Oxford of his day between them, although neither
of them were in unison with the early teachings of his home,
or perhaps with his own most deeply-rooted convictions. As an
undergraduate he became a disciple, though by no means an
advanced one, of the Oxford high church theology, combining
it, as many others have done, with a sort of political radicalism,

which with him was never very extreme, though it sufficed to
obtain for him, at least with the young Tories of the Union,
the reputation of being a very dangerous and revolutionary
character. But, living as he did in a society which might
have taken for its adage the words of Ecclesiastes, *Mundum
tradidit disputationi eorum*, and which assuredly believed
that animated conversational discussions are as effectual for the
discovery of truth as they unquestionably are for the sharpening of the wit, he gradually formed the habit of submitting the
varying opinions of men on religious questions, as on all other
subjects of human interest, to a keen intellectual criticism;
and, though it is likely that he never adopted any conclusions
of a rationalistic kind, he acquired a distaste for all dogmatic
definiteness, and a warm sympathy with the spirit of free
enquiry in theology. But at the time at which he had now
arrived, a change passed over the tenor of his thoughts in relation to these subjects—a change, which was as sudden as it
was complete and enduring. As he described it himself, a sense
of the reality of eternal things was instantaneously borne in
upon him, while he was engaged in one of his ordinary occupations. For some weeks his mind was agitated and unstrung
by this overwhelming consciousness of the immediate presence
of the terrors of the unseen world. He was unable to take any
interest in, or even to give any sustained attention to, any
subject not directly affecting the momentous questions which
engaged his thoughts. He would not even read the New Testament in Greek, apparently because the very language suggested
associations which for the time had become repugnant to him.
When he emerged from this state of depression, it was with the
fixed determination to make the obligations of religion, as he
had learned them in his childhood, the sole governing principle
of his life; and to this determination he consistently adhered.
It was some little time before his mind completely recovered
its calmness and energy, and before a settled and cheerful piety
replaced the gloom which had for a while overshadowed him.

There is a perfect love which casts out fear; but it is not in
every saintly life that this perfection is realised, and perhaps of
Conington it may be true to say that his mind was at all times
too prone to dwell on the awfulness of eternity, and not ready
enough to take comfort in the thought of eternal love. Perhaps, also, he never again allowed himself the same range of
sympathy with all matters of human concern in which he had
previously indulged. In after years he used not to advert to
the circumstances of the change that had taken place in him;
at the time he spoke of it to his intimate friends—unre-
servedly, it is true, but in the simplest language, and without
any unnecessary dwelling on details. It cannot be wrong to
record that he counted among his many friends some to whom
that which had befallen him was unintelligible, except when regarded as the passing weakness of an overworked brain, and
to whom it was as unwelcome as it was unintelligible. But the
deep affectionateness and sincerity of his character prevented
any one of his friendships from being broken, or even strained
by such a divergence of sentiment; he was, in fact, incapable of
losing a friend whom he had once made. And if his interests
were somewhat narrowed, they became even more intense; nor
were they in any manner limited to sacred subjects. His enjoyment of philology, of poetical criticism, and of literature
became keener than ever; and, if he cared less than formerly
for social and political questions, he took an eager and prominent part in the ever-recurring discussions relating to the
studies and the reform of the University.

The general character of his professorial teaching is described
by anticipation in his inaugural lecture. 'The way,' he says,
'to study Latin literature is to study the authors who gave it
its characters; the way to study those authors is to study them
individually in their individual works, and to study each work
as far as may be in its minutest details. . . . . The peculiar
training which is sought from the study of literature is only to
be obtained, in anything like its true fulness, by attending not

merely to each paragraph or each sentence, but to each word, not merely to the general force of an expression, but to the various constituents which make up the effect produced by it on a thoroughly intelligent reader.' He was not insensible to the advantages to be derived by a scholar from a widely extended, and therefore a necessarily rapid, perusal of ancient writers, in such a manner as to fill the mind almost unconsciously with the spirit of antiquity. But he felt strongly that the greatest danger of a young student is to pass too lightly over what he reads, and to rest content with ascertaining the general meaning of a passage, without stopping to examine closely those fine shades of expression which are often the source of all its force and beauty. The foreign literature of modern times bears so great a resemblance to our own, and is the work of minds moulded by influences so entirely the same as those to which we are ourselves subject, that the meaning of each sentence is apprehended with the utmost fulness, as soon as it is apprehended at all, by any intelligent person having even a moderate acquaintance with the language he is reading; and to consider each line minutely, in the hope of extracting more from it, would be as great a waste of labour as to apply a similar process to a paragraph in the *Times*. But in the case of works which have come down to us in a dead language, and from a world of which the civilisation has long since passed away, it requires an unusual familiarity with ancient forms of thought to be sure that in a hasty reading some considerable part of the impression which the author intended to convey has not escaped us altogether. And if this be true to a certain extent of all ancient literature, it is emphatically true of works like those of the tragic poets in Greek, or of Virgil in Latin, which are composed in a style of which a peculiar and essentially un-modern subtlety is the chief characteristic. In the preface to the 'Choephoroe,' Conington had insisted strongly on the necessity of examining Æschylus 'line by line and word by word;' and the main object that he proposed to himself in his lectures was to

promote the study of Latin in the same spirit of elaborate
and even microscopic enquiry. It was in accordance with this
general purpose that in a course of lectures he never made his
class travel over very much ground; he aimed rather at teaching them how to read a little aright, than how to read much
or easily. This limitation in the scope of his lessons did not
make them less interesting to the best scholars in his audience,
but it certainly rendered them less attractive to the generality
of students. Nor was he unconscious of the inartistic and confused effect produced by massing together in one discourse a
great number of minutiæ of interpretation, with but rare opportunities of relieving their monotony by grouping them with reference to some wider and more generally important principle.
But to this disadvantage he deliberately submitted himself,
believing it to be inseparable from the method which he regarded as the only right one. For the more public and formal
lectures required by the statute of his Chair, he either chose
some subject connected with Latin literature, and capable of a
treatment more satisfactory to his sense of artistic completeness, or else he read a portion of the prose translation of
Virgil, which is placed in the second volume of this collection.
His lessons on Latin Verse Composition are thus characterised
by Mr. Nettleship:—

Mr. Conington's lectures on Latin verse deserve, I think, some
special notice on account of the thoroughness of their method. He
always began with an analysis of the piece of English set, comparing
it sentence by sentence with any passages of the Latin classics which
occurred to him as similar either in spirit or expression, and taking
especial care to point out anything modern or unclassical, and to
show the nearest approximation to it which was likely to have
occurred to a Roman poet. The remainder of the hour he took up
with reading out and criticising a selection of the best pieces sent
in by the pupils, and a dictation of his own translation. The last
part of the lecture, though dry, was yet serviceable in thoroughly
sifting the piece and giving the students an idea of the manifold
possibilities of Latin expression; the pre-eminently original and
suggestive portion, however, if I may be allowed to judge by my

own experience, was the preliminary analysis.   To a student fresh
from school, and perhaps from a comparatively conventional system
of correction, it was a new light to have set before him, by one
whose memory was stored with reminiscences of the best Latin and
English literature, and who touched all poetry with an innate tact
and sense of its meaning, a detailed comparison between modern and
ancient poetical feeling and modes of utterance.   Just as the best
teachers of ancient philosophy are careful to exhibit a historical or
comparative view of the relations between ancient and modern
embodiments of thought, so Mr. Conington in these lectures did
much towards opening up to the student a historical view of poetry.

As has been already said, he continued to take an active part
in all public questions relating to the University. His opinions
on the changes introduced by the Act of 1854, are clearly
stated in the following letter addressed by him in 1861 to
Mr. Grant Duff:—

April 17, 1861.

There can be no doubt that Oxford has already gained very substantially from the effects of the University Commission, and will
gain still more when the changes introduced have had time to
work.

One of the most obvious benefits is the opening of the Fellowships
to the free competition of all undergraduates. Ten years ago, as
you know, there were scarcely any open Fellowships except those
at Baliol and Oriel, and to a certain extent at University—two or
three colleges out of nineteen; the rest being limited, in various
ways, chiefly to persons born in certain counties, founders' kindred,
and scholars of the College. Now, with one or two exceptions, all
have been, or will be, thrown open. Vested interests have been
allowed to remain, but these are gradually disappearing, and at the
present time half, or nearly half, of the Colleges are in a condition
to hold open elections. In former times the best men very often
succeeded in getting Fellowships, but this was by no means always
the case; and when they did succeed they owed their success to
some accident over and above their merit, such as those which I
have named—birthplace, founders' kinship, or previous connection
with the College. Under the changed system, the stimulus is applied equally, and every undergraduate knows that what he has to
look to is his own industry, ability, and good conduct.

Another benefit has been the modification of the restriction, which obliged Fellows to take orders sooner or later. Ten years ago a lay fellowship was almost as rare as an open fellowship, and unfortunately the two did not generally coincide, the open colleges being as a general rule clerical colleges. Now a proportion, varying in different Colleges from one half to one third or one fourth, may be held by laymen. This makes the field of choice greater, removes the temptation to take orders for the sake of retaining the Fellowships, and, in some cases, enables a College to reward men who are likely to do good in some lay profession away from the University; this last being a provision capable of abuse, but capable also of being turned to good.

Another great boon has been the foundation of Professorships, out of the surplus revenues of Colleges. The Colleges had for two or three centuries virtually superseded the University; and though in many respects they had performed their functions well, the loss of efficient University teaching had begun to be seriously felt. In some subjects there was no teaching at all, in others the teaching was too elementary and schoolboy-like. There were professorships in existence, but the professorial system had but little life. On my first coming to Oxford in 1849, I remember asking an older friend what Professors' lectures he would recommend me to attend. His answer was, 'You will soon find that you need not care about any.' As a matter of fact, I believe that during the whole of my under-graduate time I attended none whatever; certainly I did not attend any consecutive course. Had the undergraduates with whom I lived attended, I should have attended; but they did not, and I did not. Attention had been drawn to the subject before the appointment of the Royal Commission in 1850, and changes were in progress which have since borne fruit. But there can be no doubt that the most powerful impulse that has been given in that direction is due to the University Reform Act. Money was required to augment old Professorships and endow new ones, and the operation of a Parliamentary Commission was needed, partly to compel, partly to enable the Colleges to give. We have now a body of working Professors, whose lectures are in some cases numerously, in others respectably, attended; and gradually funds are becoming available for securing them competent incomes. Able men are retained in the University who might otherwise be lost to it; University society gains by their presence, and the literary world may hope in time to gain by their published works.

The last great benefit I shall name is the reform of the University Constitution. Previous to the change the initiative in all legislation was in the hands of a body composed almost entirely of Heads of Colleges—men chosen by their own small societies, not on broad academical grounds, but simply to preside over those societies, and in general prevented by age and isolation from sympathising with the mass of students. Now the Constitution is a representative one; the Council, as it is called, is elected by the votes of the residents, who are only restricted so far that they have to choose in equal proportions from three orders—the Heads of Colleges, the Professors, and the whole body of M.A.'s. Again, under the old system, the measures of the initiative body could not be discussed; all speaking in academical meetings was required to be in Latin, and in consequence it very rarely happened that anybody cared to speak at all. Now every statute, before being finally submitted to the general body of the University, is promulgated at a previous meeting of the residents, who may discuss it in English, and hand in amendments to the initiative body, though they have no power of putting those amendments to the vote, or of voting at all on the same day on which the discussion has taken place. The results even of this modified freedom have been very considerable. Previously but little interest was felt by the mass of the residents in the business of the University; not living in familiar intercourse with members of the initiative body, they knew little or nothing of a measure before it was proposed, had no power of discussing it when it was proposed, and so either allowed it to pass out of simple indifference, or were tempted, in many instances, by party feeling or class jealousy, to vote against it. Now the proceedings of Council are known and canvassed among the residents, the discussions on the promulgation of a statute are not unfrequently interesting and valuable; unintelligent votes are fewer. I do not say that there is not great room for improvement, both in our constitution and in its working; but much has already been done, and the operation of time will do more. And for all this we are indebted to the Act of 1854.

I might also touch on the augmentation which has taken place in the number and value of the scholarships in most of the Colleges—in itself a very great boon to education; but here, though the Commission has done something both to compel and to enable, the changes have generally been such as the Colleges themselves were able, and probably would have been willing, to originate.

Generally I cannot doubt that the mere fact of an extensive
enquiry, followed by a reform from without, has greatly quickened
the zeal for improvement. The simple publication of the Blue
Book of the Royal Commission was itself a great event; it popu-
larised important information hardly accessible till then, and gave
to the world the views of many able and practical men which
might not otherwise have been expressed. May the Public School
Commission be as successful.

In the agitation for the repeal of University Tests, which
resulted, after his death, in the passing of the University Tests
Abolition Act, he took but little part. In point of fact he was
unable to sympathise entirely with either side. He felt on the
one hand the injustice, or at least the impolicy, of excluding
nonconformists from the emoluments and dignified offices of
the University; but on the other hand he entertained the
utmost aversion for a measure which seemed to dissociate the
Universities from religion, and which proposed to admit
persons who might profess no form of Christian belief, on the
same footing with Churchmen or orthodox dissenters. He did
not approve of the use made of the Thirty-nine Articles as a
test to be applied to the laity as well as to the clergy. But he
thought it indispensably necessary in the interest of religion
that some sort of declaration of faith should be required from
every person admitted to a share in the government of the
University. And though he would have been contented with
the simplest and most comprehensive formula of subscription
that could well be devised, yet, when he found that no such
proposal was likely to be accepted by either side, he could not help
drifting, somewhat to his regret, into an attitude of defence of
the *status quo*, as being the less of two evils, between which no
middle course was possible. This attitude on his part produced a partial separation, so far as public matters were
concerned, between him and some of the friends of University
Reform, a separation which was still further widened by the
feeling which he entertained that many educational reformers,

both in Oxford and out of it, were anxious in various ways to disparage the classics as the basis of the higher education of the country, and in Oxford itself unduly to subordinate the study of Language to that of History and Philosophy. Indeed, the place assigned to the higher Greek and Latin Philology in the studies of the University was far from giving him complete satisfaction, and he did not often miss an opportunity of asserting its claim to a still larger recognition in the public examinations. His warm interest in all that tended to the advancement of classical learning, as well as his sense of what was right, led him to join actively in the long contest relating to the Regius Professorship of Greek; and even to write a pamphlet in support of its endowment by the University. But he exerted himself to the utmost in opposition to the proposal of Lord Westbury to annex a canonry to the Chair, because that proposal would have had the effect of rendering the office tenable by clergymen only.

In the last two or three years of his life his interest in academic discussions became even more prominent. He gave but a qualified approval to the proposals relating to the admission of unattached students; fearing, in common with many others (though happily the fear has not been justified by the event), that such students would be dangerously exposed to temptations, from which students living within the walls of a college are to a certain degree protected. But he was an earnest supporter of the establishment of a School of Theology, as an independent branch of the final examination. He was himself slowly but steadily acquiring a large amount of theological knowledge, and he naturally thought highly of a scheme which had for its object the encouragement of sacred learning; and which was also a step towards that specialisation of University studies which he believed to be essential to the right development of any one of them. He had always been a regular attendant at the debates in the Congregation of the University; and the proposal to increase the power of that body, by conceding to it the right of amending measures submitted to it by the Hebdomadal Council, gave him the greatest satisfaction. During the summer term of 1869—the last of his life—the subject was considered in a committee appointed by the University, and those who served on it with him can well remember the lively pleasure which the progress of its deliberations gave him, and the almost boyish freshness with which he entered into every detail of the plan.

During the whole of the fifteen years for which he held the Professorship of Latin, his intellectual activity may be fairly described as unceasing. Upon his edition of Virgil he spared no time or labour; indeed, he found the demands it made upon him so exacting, that in order to get leisure for other work, he was glad, in the latter half of the Æneid, to obtain the assistance of his friend, Mr. Nettleship, by whom the third volume of the work, the result of their joint labours, was brought out shortly after his death. His study of Virgil made him turn to the English translators of Virgil; and thus the old love—dating at least as far back as the purchase of Sotheby's Homer in his schoolboy days at Beverley—for poetical translations of the classics revived within him. He had become so dissatisfied with his Agamemnon that he hesitated a little before a second venture; but when at last he did give way to the strong inward impulse he chose no task less difficult than the Odes of Horace. Probably no translation of Horace has any chance of obtaining a very extensive popularity, and Conington confessed that if he had no other means of subsistence the 'Odes' would not keep him. But he nevertheless had the pleasure of finding his work received with a large measure of approbation by the most competent judges. His success determined him to proceed. The Odes had appeared in 1863; they were followed by the Æneid in 1866, by the last twelve books of the Iliad in 1868, and finally by the Satires, Epistles, and Ars Poetica of Horace in 1869, the last appearing at the very time of his death. The discovery that he could translate his

favourite poets in a manner which gave some satisfaction
to himself and others was like finding a new vocation, and was
the source of intense enjoyment to him. With all his love for
the details of philology, he could not help feeling that they
detained him in regions somewhat remote from human
sympathy. But now, without quitting his own domain of
classical literature, he had found an attentive and sympathetic
audience, and had become an interpreter of the ancient world
to his own generation in a larger sense than he ever could have
been as a mere commentator. His manner of translating was
characteristic. He used to learn some couple of hundred lines
of his original by heart (if indeed they were not already present to his memory), and then work out his version in his head,
sometimes in hours regularly set apart for the purpose, but often
at odd times, as in a solitary walk, or on a railway journey, or
before he rose in the morning. He used in this way to get
through his work with great rapidity, sometimes not writing
down each batch of verses till it was quite ready for the press.

The translation of the last twelve books of the Iliad was
undertaken in order to complete the unfinished work of the
lamented Mr. Worsley, during whose last illness he had promised
to discharge this office of piety and affection. It was a labour
of love in every sense of the term; it was a pleasure to him to
have to translate Homer, and almost an equal pleasure to have
to attempt the management of the Spenserian stanza. Nor did
he feel it any constraint to be obliged to regulate his treatment
of that stanza by Mr. Worsley's. In his preface he half apologises for his hasty mode of composition, pleading that experience
taught him that he could not improve his first drafts by
retouching them. And probably this extreme facility of production is the source of the graceful fluency which characterises
his versions both of the Æneid and the Iliad, and which makes
the reader at times forget that it is not an original work which
he has before him.

The following letter from the late Earl of Derby, then Chancellor of the University, and himself a distinguished translator of Homer, will be read with pleasure :—

St. James's Square, April 5, 1868.

Dear Sir,

I have delayed thanking you for your obliging letter of the 2nd inst. till I had time, I will not say to read through your translation of the twelve last books of the Iliad, which your publisher had sent me on the previous day, but to look so far into it as to form in my own mind some opinion as to your execution of your difficult task. You will not expect me to abandon my preference for the metre which I had myself adopted; but I may say with truth that I have seen with equal admiration, how readily, in your hands and those of Mr. Worsley, the Spenserian stanza accommodates itself to the text of the original. Here and there no doubt the exigencies of rhyme have led to the introduction of what we used to call at Eton (forgive the expression) a 'botch;' but taken as a whole, you move in your self-imposed trammels with an ease and freedom which excite my astonishment; and, so far as I have yet been able to examine your work, the fidelity of your adherence to the original is very remarkable. I must examine a little into your secret of compression, by which you have brought your version into so much a smaller compass than I was able to accomplish; but in the meantime I hope you will allow me to offer you my congratulations on the general success you have achieved. I must however ask you to forgive me if I enter my protest (notwithstanding your vindication of the practice in your preface) against the liberties which you have taken with the quantities of the proper names, of which I must do you the justice to say that you have selected as an illustration (pp. xix.-xx.) one of the most striking examples.

Requesting you to excuse the freedom of my remarks, I have the honour to be

Dear Sir,
Yours faithfully,
Derby.

Professor Conington.

The version of the Æneid has acquired a very considerable popularity. In adopting the octosyllabic metre, familiar to the readers of Scott and Byron, he hazarded a bold experiment, but his boldness has been justified by the event. He was well

aware that this metre could but ill represent the majesty of
the Virgilian numbers, and that thus one important characteristic of the great poet must be imperfectly rendered. But
he also felt that by means of it he could convey to English
readers a just impression of the movement and life of the whole
poem, and of the continued variety of its cadences, as well as
some faint echo of its pathetic undertones. Thus it has come
to pass that—while many great scholars have been unable to
forgive the degradation of the Latin hexameter into the metre
of Marmion—the book has been a favourite with the world at
large—with the *virgines* and *pueri*—and probably has been
read through by some who never did as much for any other
original or translated epic.

Of all his versions, that of the Satires and Epistles of
Horace would seem to have attracted the least attention. This
cannot be attributed to any inferiority of execution; for its
pages sparkle with wit, and preserve to a surprising extent the
tone and spirit of the original. But it would seem that only
those strains of the ancient world which are of a higher mood
have a chance of making themselves heard in our day; the
'sermo pedestris,' and the 'mitis sapientia' of the Satires and
Epistles have counterparts, and no mean ones, in our own
literature, and, when presented in an English dress, do not
seem to rise above their rivals.

When he had sent the last sheet of the Ars Poetica to the
press he would gladly have begun to occupy himself in the
same way with some other Latin poet. But neither with Lucretius nor Catullus did he feel any deep sympathy. In the case
of Juvenal, he considered the ground pre-occupied by Gifford,
and the obscurity of Persius called for a commentary rather
than a poetic version. On the whole, therefore, he determined
to give up translating for a while, and to take for the subject of
his next task the history of Latin literature, or at least of
Latin poetry, during the silver age. Though no transcendent
interest attaches to any poet of that age, he was of opinion

that not enough had yet been done by English scholars to
direct attention to a group of writers whose very faults are
instructive to us, from their belonging to a time the circumstances of which are in some respects comparable to our own.
One other work he had marked out for himself, but as one
which he desired rather than hoped to accomplish—a complete
edition of Tacitus. Unlike many great scholars, he took less
pleasure in the criticism of classical texts, than in their interpretation. He was by no means without the gift of conjectural criticism, as even his early attempts in the *Epistola
Critica* to Dean Gaisford prove, nor was he disposed to underrate the results which have been obtained by means of it. But
his long devotion to Virgil, whose text is better ascertained
perhaps than that of any other classic, had given him an
increased distaste for the uncertainties of emendation; and
in his choice of Tacitus he was partly guided by the circumstance that the text of that author is based upon the authority
of only one or two MSS., and that consequently conjectural or
palæographical criticism must be supposed to have already
done for it as much as can be expected. On the other hand,
the condensed eloquence of Tacitus, which suggests so much
that is not expressly said, seemed to invite the same kind of
minute analysis which had yielded such good results in the case
of the Greek and Latin poets. Conington used to say that he
seldom opened Tacitus without finding something which, as far
as he could make out, had either not been explained at all, or
had been explained amiss. The vast extent and difficulty of the
work, which, as he well knew, if he once undertook it, must
occupy him for many years, was one reason for his giving it only
the second place in his plans of future employment; another
was his want of interest in history itself, which he felt to be a
great drawback on his fitness to be the editor of a historian.
But, whether this diffidence on his part was well or ill founded,
it is difficult not to feel that the loss of this meditated work
is the greatest of the many losses which Latin scholarship has
sustained by his death.

His activity as a correspondent kept pace with his activity
as an author. He liked to write of what occupied him at the
moment, and thus, the more work he was doing the more letters
he wrote. And in truth they cost him but very little trouble,
for they were as free and unrestrained as his conversation.
Unfortunately, they are often not well suited for publication,
dealing as they do with the intimacies of private life, or with
more public matters of very temporary importance. But they
are models of the 'familiar style,' if this expression may be
allowed; and they exemplify a still higher sort of excellence,
for it would be difficult to find in them a trace of unkindness
towards any human being. His wit had at all times been free
from the slightest tinge of bitterness, and in his later years he
was, from conscientious motives, almost morbidly apprehensive
of saying or writing anything, even in the most good-humoured
way, which could put another person in a disadvantageous light.
Some of his longest letters are addressed to his younger friends,
of whom he had many; for generally in each successive generation of undergraduates he would attach to himself one or two
of the most promising scholars, and would exert himself inde-
fatigably for their improvement. It was his custom for many
years to spend a portion of every long vacation with a reading
party of young friends, not acting in any formal manner as
their private tutor, but often giving them as much of his
time as if he had undertaken that duty. There are not a few
who look back upon the days they thus spent with him as
among the happiest in their lives, and who regard the university
successes which they obtained as the least of the advantages
which they derived from the instruction and assistance which
he so freely gave. Latterly, indeed, he gave up his yearly
reading parties; not that the society of young men had grown
less congenial to him, but because a nearer duty claimed him
elsewhere. His father had died in 1861, his brother Frank in
1863, his brother Henry early in 1868; his still surviving sister
was settled in the south of England. Thus the care of his aged

mother devolved very mainly upon him; and, in order to be
with her as much as possible, he never stayed in Oxford a day
longer than the statutes of his Chair required.   To his mother
he had always been most devotedly attached; his letters to
her at all times of his life breathe a spirit of the most intimate
confidence; and now, the thought that in consequence of so
many bereavements he had become the chief stay of her declining years, gave a new impulse to his feelings, and inspired
his affectionate nature with a still deeper tenderness.

The following selection of passages from his letters has been
made somewhat casually, and the names of many of his most
favoured correspondents are absent from it.   Still these extracts
will be found to bear the impress of his simple and amiable
character, and to give some evidence of his critical acuteness
and sound judgment in literary questions.

To C. CHOLMELEY PULLER, ESQ.

Boston, August 23, 1858.

It is perhaps a pity that you are reading 'King Lear' in a variorum
Shakspere.   I bought a copy a year ago, not wishing to be ignorant
of what the various commentators have said, but it is weary work,
wearier than any good commentary on a classical author.   Your
plan of reading Sophocles by your own light, before resorting to
notes, might, I think, be transferred to Shakspere with more advantage.   Indeed, in the passages where the thought is difficult, one
generally has to be one's own guide, though notes are sometimes
wanted to explain obsolete terms, old customs, &c.   I think,
perhaps, I could generally help you to a meaning if you would send
the passages to me as they occur; at least I found that, with the
helps we have here and my own wit, I made it all out to my own
satisfaction when I had to give my lectures.   What am I to say to
you about the tragedy itself—so overwhelmingly tremendous—so
true to nature—and so full of things from which every one may
learn?   Study the characters as they evolve themselves, observing,
e.g., the relation between Edmund and Gloster in the first scene,
the way in which the old man speaks of the sin of his youth, and
the kind of influences under which the base-born son has evidently
been reared.   Observe again how the two tragedies of filial ingrati-

tude play into each other, and how Gloster is deceived by
Edmund all the more readily because he sees Lear to have been
deceived by his daughters. Ask yourself what it is that makes
the conduct of Goneril and Regan appear so monstrous, while so
much that they say about their father's irritating changefulness of
mood is shown to be just by the play itself. Try and make out—I
have scarcely made it out to my own satisfaction—why Cordelia,
seeing Lear's state of mind, does not humour it, but deliberately
says less than she feels. These are some of the points that will
meet you in the earlier part of the play; as you get on, I can easily
suggest others if you think well.

I am myself reading Dante, in Carlyle's prose translation, which
is, I should think, as good as a prose translation can be. I don't
know Italian—and Dante's Italian is peculiar—but I am glad to
have it at the bottom of the page to compare every now and then
with the English, by the light of one's knowledge of the cognate
languages. I began it about a year ago, for the first time, but
dropped it, and now I have got nearly to the same point, and hope
to go on. I can see enough to satisfy me that it is very great—a
simpler and severer Milton—Homeric in its *naïveté*, but not
garrulous as Homer is, and as full of the learning and thought of
its time, I should think, as the Paradise Lost, while there is a
spirit of intense patriotism pervading the whole. I was very much
struck with a passage where he makes Virgil speak of 'that low
Italy ("humilem Italiam"), for which the virgin Camilla and
Euryalus, and Turnus, and Nisus died of their wounds;' a view of
the latter part of the Æneid which Virgil never dreamed of, but
appealing profoundly to the spirit of Italian nationality.

Boston, September 6, 1859.

. . . . Again, I can understand the impatience with which, as
you say, you regard this prolonged arming for the battle of life.
I can understand it, having felt it, or something like it, myself at
one time. Now I fear I am in the other extreme, shrinking from
anything which involves action or struggle, and fancying that the
time for them is not come yet. But I suppose a man who goes on
residing at Oxford may be excused for not recognising any broad
differences between the time during which he was educating himself,
and the time after which he is supposed to have completed his education. Meantime there are perhaps one or two things which you
scarcely bear in mind enough. Metaphors are apt to mislead, and

though there is a distinction undoubtedly between the time of
pupilage and the time of independent action, it is not quite the
same as that between arming and fighting. A good deal of fighting
goes on during the process which you designate as arming, and
each stage is an arming for a further stage. At Eton you have
been arming for a battle at Oxford, which is only just beginning,
and when you enter on life you will still have to arm yourself as
well as to fight. Remember too that in Oxford a great portion of
your work will be entirely new. You already see that there are
intellectual worlds of which you scarcely dreamed at Eton, and you
will hardly doubt that to explore them will be a worthy object for
those coming three years. Would you be nearer to real life, think
you, if you were to begin to read law now, leaving speculative
politics, moral philosophy, works of imagination, and 'things in
general,' to take their chance? If so, fortunate are they who
become clerks in attorneys' offices as soon as they leave school,
though it is not on them that Fortune is commonly supposed to
smile most. I could lecture you too for saying that it is better to
be base than not to be free, and tell you (what would be true) that
liberty which does not obey some kind of law is a very base thing
indeed. I could point to your own programme of work as a
standing witness in favour of external law, but instead of that I will
show you that at one time I used to indulge in the same strain, by
quoting some stanzas of a poem which I wrote while under pressure
of working for the schools in 1846 :—

(Metrum Barrett Browningianum.)

Aye, routine may do for planets, and the stars may have their
   courses,
But we are no planet-system, we are living, thinking men ;
Framed with higher aspirations, and impelled by other forces,
Than the bodies which are measured by the telescopic ken.

Both alike are bound by nature in one vast harmonious concord ;
   We and they move on together, but move on in different ways :
For the human spirit's music is not played alone on one chord,
But results at once from many—it is free while it obeys.

Lo, the chains with which you bind it, it has cast them far
   behind it,
Owing, paying no allegiance, save to Truth's eternal laws :
Drawn by them, it hastens onward, like an eagle soaring sunward,
And through infinite successions, gazes ever on a cause.

There, if that does not show that I can sympathise with you, I don't know what should. But I fear it is rather stuff, never-theless.

Boston, September 13, 1868.

. . . . I am gratified by your eldest brother's good opinion of the preface to Virgil. I do not myself think it a very remarkable or satisfactory piece of work, and perhaps the expunctions which I had to make have rendered it less so than it might otherwise have been, though on this point, as you may remember, Froude and H. Smith are at issue. If I might venture to recommend any other part of the volume to your brother, it would be the two introductions to the Eclogues and Georgics, which seem to me by far the best things in the book for a general reader. It is hard to judge of one's own things, and I find that even when I seem to myself to have striven most successfully to be popular, people complain of me as abstruse and ponderous, as in the case of my Oxford Essay; but the introductions were found interesting by serious persons who heard them as lectures, and my *Spectator* critic seemed to think that I had succeeded, as I certainly tried to do, in combining actual infor-mation about Virgil with such broad and general views as would interest those accustomed to general literature. But enough of this—only one occasionally indulges in such self-approving, self-excusing remarks to one's self, and so every now and then they become audible to one's friends as well. . . . . . To your remarks on literary and general matters I have two or three exceptions to make, though you will not believe that they interest me less because I cannot agree with them. I am not sure that you are regarding Carlyle altogether from the point of view from which he wishes to be regarded. You ask 'Does he mean us to admire A., to condemn B., and so on?' whereas I fancy that he means his reader to give no such unqualified verdict. History with him, I take it, is a thing to understand and to accept, rather than to judge; to a certain extent he seems to regard it as beyond human judgment. Without being a fatalist, he evidently looks upon the course of events as a thing which cannot be influenced by one man, scarcely by a generation of men; even the evil-doers are not responsible for all the evil that is brought about through their means, as, but for generations of previous evil-doers, they would not have had the same power for mischief; so that wonder and pity come in as well as blame, say for Lewis XV.; much more for the

c 2

Sans Culottes, whom, without admiring, he evidently thinks very
little short of an inevitable fact. I do not at present say whether he
is right or wrong, I merely explain what I take his view to be.
Judging after the event, we may very likely see that the government
ought to have coerced the noblesse; but—judging before it—the
noblesse had not shown their weakness, that was a thing to be
learnt. They had stood in the forefront of other civil wars. They
must still have had a great prestige—in fact, a France in which
they should not have the upper hand had not yet made itself
conceivable. . . . . . To what I said about a man's being practically
acquitted who follows the general opinion of his time I quite
adhere. I do not see how anybody who reads history can deny
that morality is, to a certain extent, progressive. Surely to say
that persecution was at one time not thought a vice, and toleration
not recognised as a virtue, is to state a truism; and there is no
want of scriptural authority for allowing, within limits, the plea of
ignorance. Indeed, what do you gain by disallowing it? You
condemn a whole age; then you have to take the condemnation for
granted, and try the different individuals anew. No doubt it would
be simpler if we could apply the same rule to everything and everybody; but the complexity is one which meets us in every case
where circumstances have to be taken into account, and to deal
with a complex case simply is neither philosophical nor just. Of
course there is a unity which runs through our judgment even of
the most different men and the most different things, but it is a
unity which is compatible with almost infinite diversity, and so far
from 'destroying the interest of historical discussion,' I cannot
doubt that it greatly enhances it. My space obliges me to be
brief, and so I cannot avoid the appearance of contradicting you
rather than of arguing with you, but you will pardon me. I shall
be very glad to return to the subject if you will restate your case,
as I feel I could say a good deal more about it.

September 20, 1858.

I am very glad that you like my introduction to the Eclogues.
If you will turn to p. 8, beginning 'Nor would it be just,' you will
find a passage which was intended to apply not only to Virgil, but,
'mutatis mutandis,' to myself. Curiously enough I find a similar
remark in Deerbrook, where a character, into whose mouth Miss
Martineau evidently puts many of her own thoughts, says, 'I saw

plenty of summer sunrises, but none of them gave me a feeling like
the two lines—

> " Now morn, her rosy steps in the Eastern clime
> Advancing, sowed the earth with orient pearl." '

. . . . When I talk of morality being progressive, I do not mean
exactly that a steady approach to the Christian standard has been
making during the eighteen Christian centuries. There is a fashion
in vices, and if in some respects we are better than our fathers, I can
well believe that in others we are worse. But there are certain
questions where morality seems to have advanced simply by the
widening of thought; persecution is one, slavery is another.
Would you condemn a Christian slave-owner under the Roman
empire as you would condemn a Christian slave-owner now? ' We
have no right now to excuse ourselves by comparison with our
neighbours.' True, but have we no right to excuse our neighbours
in comparison with ourselves? It is the self-excusation which is
the evil; we are not fair judges in our own case, and it is our duty
to strive against our faults instead of palliating them. But where
we can judge fairly, there surely we may and ought to take
difference of circumstances, antecedents, traditional opinions, and
the like, into account.

P.S. Did you see an impertinent large-type letter in Friday's
Times, comparing a kennel to a Greek play, and especially to the
'Choephoroe'? It made me feel a kind of brotherhood with the
sporting world, which I had certainly never expected to feel.

Boston, October 4, 1858.

The article on the first volume of the Virgil in the *Saturday
Review* is really a very skilful one, if you come to examine it:
it has the appearance of strong eulogy, but it is really very guarded
and qualified in its language. I fancy it nearly hits the mark in
speaking of the class of the edition, though vanity winces a little
at being told that it is merely a student's book. But I do hope, if
I live, to be able to show that I can do something more than ' clear
the whole ground for the literary critic.' 'An examination into
Virgil's place in literature, and into the modes in which he appeals
to our imagination and taste,' is quite within the scope of an edition
like mine, as I conceive it; and if I have not regularly attempted
it as yet, it is because I thought I should be better qualified for it
in a later volume, when I have studied the whole of him as I have

now studied a part. I have read also the review in the *Press*, and find there is hardly anything in it of which I can really complain, except it be an inference that, as I have chosen to comment on Virgil and Pope, my bias is all for refinement of execution as against grandeur of design, and that any admission I make in favour of the latter is extorted from me by the spirit of the time, which will not let me be so *born* as I should have been 100 years ago—just what Macaulay says of Gladstone's admissions in favour of toleration. If I am to be judged by the subjects I have chosen, surely the 'Agamemnon' and 'Choephoroe' ought to be allowed to count. . . . I fear my chance of finding favourable dispositions at Youngsbury would be damaged irreparably, if I were to confess to anyone but you how little interest I take in the comet; and even you, perhaps, will not be able to forgive me without an effort, and a conscious reflection on some of my countervailing good qualities. In justice to my people here, I must observe that I stand quite alone; my father and mother both watch it with lively interest, so that I really fancy at times that my own apathy must be something more than a mere defect. But a comet with me awakens no train of associations; its laws belong to astronomy, of which I know nothing. This year at least it has not formed the nucleus of superstitious anticipations, which might compel one's interest from the very fact of their having taken so strong a hold of our common humanity, however far one might be from sharing them one's self, while the mere sight of it affects me but little. I suppose I do not see it very distinctly, and it appears to me different indeed from the stars, but yet not wholly unlike them, and altogether not so completely *sui generis* but that it can be remembered sufficiently after it has been once or twice seen. You will understand that I am not reflecting on the interest taken by others, but simply explaining the grounds of my own insensibility. It is doubtless one of my intellectual faults that my sphere of knowledge is so narrow; and it may be a fault, too, that where I have not knowledge I have not interest, not caring for things on a broad popular ground. There is probably the counterbalancing advantage that my interest is worth more when I do feel it. I take in the various bearings of an object that I care for. Still I believe that I am wrong, and that it would be better for me if my feelings were more frequently enlisted on matters which I am not likely to have much to say about, either in talking or writing. As I am scribbling I get a letter from one of my few lady correspondents, containing the following passage:

'I wonder whether you have looked at the comet—seeing it you
could hardly escape; but I suppose you make a point of "not encouraging that phenomenon." '

. . . , Besides, I have been reading, or dipping into, various
other books. My brother Frank has got Buckle at home, and I
have been looking more at him, though still not consecutively. Do
you know an exceedingly impertinent note of his about scholars,
and the harm they have done to their own language, where he goes
so far as to say that the reason why women confessedly write and
speak their own language so much better than men is, that they
have had no classical training? I suspect it is a sample of his one-
sided and random way of writing. He is right in attacking Parr,
who did corrupt his mother tongue, certainly; but Bentley's Milton
is not a case in point, while Bentley's own English was exceedingly
good and vigorous. As for the scholars of the present day, their
English style is not more Latinised or foreign than Buckle's own;
in fact the very passage in which Buckle makes the attack is anything but free from Latin or technical terms.

On the whole, my recollections of him [Hallam] are exceedingly
pleasing. He was full of conversation on all literary subjects, and
his manner was very amiable and courteous, in talking as well as
writing. The *Times* I have no doubt speaks truly of the softening
effect produced on him by his great sorrows. I suppose it may be
long before we see another historian or critic gifted with the same
thorough good sense and impartiality. Certainly there is nothing
like it in those who have since risen up. His Whig sympathies you
will value more than I do. I think, however, I had heard that he
rather recoiled before the Reform Bill of 1832, and thought things
were going too far. I remember, in the supplemental notes to his
' Middle Ages,' published soon after the Revolution of 1848, he took
occasion to compliment Guizot as one whom ' Non civium ardor
prava jubentium . . . , Mente quatit solida,' when a reviewer remarked that he had not dared to quote the intervening line ' Non
vultus instantis tyranni.' Generally he dealt out scant justice to
characters that had anything extreme or excessive about them.
Tait, I recollect, used to say to us when we were reading the
' Constitutional History ' in form : ' He evidently thinks Luther mad.'

To W. J. COURTHOPE, ESQ.

Boston, January 15, 1864.

I expected that my Statius article would be simply a matter of copying; the publisher, however, who seems to be editor also, was of opinion that it was too short and too little critical; and as that was at bottom my own opinion also, and I knew it was shared by others who had heard the lecture, I conquered my indisposition to reconstruct a thing already finished, and have added four or five pages on the poet's style and mode of narration, which, if not as elaborately written as the earlier part, will, I hope, be lively enough. I suppose it will appear about the end of the month. All else that I have done has been revising some of my Persius notes. Perhaps I may have to do more than I bargained for in the way of collating MSS., as it appears that the English MSS. have been a good deal neglected hitherto, and there are some at Cambridge and in the British Museum, besides five or six at Oxford.

Boston, June 28, 1866.

I am grooving down into work here, though I have hardly taken as kindly to my real business, the commentary on Virgil, as I ought to do. Of translation I have done a fair quantity, chiefly outstanding fragments of Greek poets for Miss Winkworth's 'Bunsen,' remnants from last year. These are mostly elegiac—Callinus, Tyrtæus, Solon—and I have rendered them line for line in elegiac quatrains, I hope with some terseness, and some of the simplicity of the original. They come very easily, so that I got through about 170 lines between Monday afternoon and Tuesday evening. And now I am trying Homer. At first he was very difficult, quite baffling my railway-carriage efforts last week. Now he is easier, but it is still rather like dancing in fetters. What sort of jingle I make I scarcely know. I write plenty of rough lines in the hope of avoiding monotony, and sometimes fancy that the effect is not bad; but of the hidden soul of Spenserian melody I have no notion. In the main I aim at giving the Greek line for line, with a simplicity which I allow to run into uncouthness. The labour of finding four similar sounds for each stanza is considerable, and for the present at least prevents anything like spontaneity. But I seem to find it easier as I go on; only I have a constant sense of twisting and torturing the language, which a translator of Homer, I take it, ought not to have.

This morning I hope to make some return for your two letters. As usual, I have found a good deal to occupy me since my return, and though my evenings are oftener vacant than they used to be, I don't like to scribble off a few lines to you when I am half asleep.

I understand, I think, pretty well what you say about the experiences that you have gone through. No doubt your 'Greats' reading, aided by the Oxford atmosphere, was likely to introduce you to a new world; it is natural also that you should feel that, being introduced to it, you have some duties to it—that you cannot ignore it and write as if it were not. Those little expressions of imaginative feeling that you used to throw off, doubtless seem to you very inadequate now—'major rerum tibi nascitur ordo,' and you are perplexed and confounded by it. Probably you make too much of the time that you have lost. A poet need not so completely absorb the culture of his age as to make it necessary that he should be posted up to twelve o'clock on the day that he begins to write. You have lost nothing that you may not make up if life be given you; and the 'sensations and fancies' to which you have surrendered yourself have been helping to give your thoughts the body, the artistic form, without which intellectual impressions are not poetry at all. My metaphor may be ill chosen; but you will see what I mean. Your first thing, it seems to me, ought to be to determine, on as probable grounds as you can, what you can do intellectually and what you cannot. *Intellectually*, I say, distinguishing again the intellect from the imagination and artistic powers. How much of the intellectual culture of your time can you reasonably hope to realise and appropriate? Very few poets can appropriate all the culture of their time, or anything like all. If you form your plans with a view to realising more of this culture than you are likely to realise, your work, I suppose, will be an ambitious failure; if you calculate accurately, then, though you may not achieve all that at times you may have hoped, you will achieve something real. Are you likely, think you, to contribute anything to the solution of the theological and philosophical problems of the time *directly*? If not, do not trouble yourself about them as matters for poetry; use them if you like as materials for illustration and ornamentation, but not further. That your poetry, if it is good for anything, will contribute something indirectly to the strengthening, quieting, and clearing of men's minds you may be sure. Aim at something certain, however limited. I don't mean that you are to

go after the first little thing that comes uppermost, but that you are
to choose something which, being in itself large enough to give
occupation to the mind, is likely in reason to be accomplished. I
was miserable till I found my *métier*—kept wasting myself in efforts
which I could not myself approve, or get others to approve; and
at last, in despair, I returned to scholarship as something which I
know I could do, though as my world widened I had come to
despise it as inadequate. Now I am reaping, I hope, the reward
of those stormy turbid years in a way that I had ceased to expect.
I find that, though I cannot write any original verse, I can translate well enough to make it worth while continuing to do so. But
this came to me, as you know, 'longo post tempore,' when I had
ceased for years to entertain the hope of being able to write anything
but prose. I am not of course comparing our two cases except in
the most general way; your natural element is probably poetry, and
the question is simply between the more and less ambitious sorts of
it. Again, I am not recommending μικροψυχία as such. I am only
saying that if you *cannot* strike the mean it may be the better extreme. By all means keep your mind open, and be ready to
recognise any way in which God may be drawing you, anything to
which your powers and circumstances seem to point. But remember
that in this as in higher matters it is well not to 'seek great
things,' but to be content if 'your life is given to you as a prey.'

Perhaps I may seem to wander from your real case, and to use
language inapplicable to you. You know that I am not likely to
warn you of vanity or self-conceit, for I don't think you want any
such warning; if I did, I would. But a person honestly seeking
to employ his powers properly may be led wrong by aiming at too
much—by thinking small beginnings unworthy; and the new-born
sense of infinite possibilities about you is peculiarly likely to foster
that feeling. I have spoken as if your difficulty were about
subjects, and did not extend to style; but I can well believe that to
be a difficulty also. All I can say, then, in the absence of anything
definite from you to guide me, is that while I would not have you
sacrifice any of the peculiar charm which belongs to almost everything that I have seen of yours, I would have you remember that
you must look to as wide a circle of readers as you can; readers who
may not be in sufficient sympathy with you to detect what you
mean without trouble, and who naturally wish to take no trouble
that they can help—readers of another generation than this, who
will naturally find pleasure, not in what is temporary and special,

but in what is permanent and general. 'And of these things let so
much be said for the present;' but I will return to them whenever
you ask me. Your confidence in me, you may be sure, is very
pleasant.

To J. A. SYMONDS, Esq.

March 24, 1866.

The saddest thing this term is the news about Worsley, who is, I
fear, at length dying. He had an attack of hæmorrhage at
Christmas, was in imminent danger for four or five days, then for
ten days or a fortnight seemed to be rallying, but has since gone
back, so that now no hope seems to be entertained. I have had one
or two notes from him, very kind and affectionate; but when I last
heard, he could scarcely even dictate, for fear of bringing on
coughing. He expressed regret at having to leave his Iliad unfinished. This set me thinking whether I could do anything, and
at last, after much doubt, I tried to translate the beginning of the
Eighteenth Iliad in something like his style, and succeeded better
than I had expected. So now I have undertaken to take up the
work after he is gone, simply in order that his copyright may not
suffer. I need not say that I do not hope to attain the higher
qualities of his version; but the outward appearance is easier to
catch than I thought. I think I can manage to keep pretty close
to the Greek, and perhaps my name may be worth something with
the translation-buying public. This accordingly will be my *horæ
subsecivæ* occupation when the translation of Virgil is done. That
work is nearly *in statu quo*. After leaving you I did a little, then it
went to sleep for the time, now it is reviving again. I am still
dissatisfied with myself at the present moment (you know I fluctuate very much), and the discovery that I can do Spenser stanzas
better than I thought rather cuts away my ground for adopting
the Walter Scott metre, that it was the only one I could manage
for long together.

Talking of translations, I found my first impression of Milman
confirmed. The book is very unequal, in parts (the passage about
Helen and about the urns in the second chorus especially) very
good, though even then not Æschylean, in parts exceedingly indifferent. The inaccuracies are great and glaring, sometimes
owing to obsolete interpreters, which one can excuse; sometimes
resulting from carelessness, which is less excusable. One wonders

that he did not get some one to look through the translation for
him. The Bacchae looked to me the better of the two, but that
may be because one is not saturated with the original, and because
the existing translations, Potter and Wodhull, are poor enough.
Like all the world, I have been reading 'Ecce Homo,' which I
admire, but not enthusiastically. My difficulties are not those
which it professes to meet; our Lord's character does not require
credibilising to my mind, and any attempt to do so under the
circumstances is almost sure to appear worse than useless. The
most interesting part I thought the latter chapters, where the evan-
gelical virtues are translated into their modern equivalents. But it
is no doubt a very considerable effort, and would, I should think, do
something to the 'restoration of belief.'

August 2, 1866.

After a little stiffness I soon found that I could write the Spenser
stanza even more easily than the Walter Scott. For this I see two
reasons: 1, that the stanza itself gives swing, so that one has not to
think so much how to create it; 2, that the style one adopts in
Homer is more incondite than that in Virgil—'did say,' and the like.
Everything considered, the rhymes have really given me very little
trouble. I keep closer to Homer than Worsley, it is 'my nature
to,' and I feel it is my one chance, as I have not his native vein to
fall back upon; perhaps, too, though I say it very doubtfully, I may
have a greater command of poetical commonplaces, and so am less
put about. The result is, I hope, fairly good on the whole. I am
nearly as close as the blank verse translators; in about three-fourths
of my work, even closer than (say) Lord Derby, and the metre
makes me (me judice) more pleasing than they. Almost all the
credit of this is due to Worsley, as the inventor of the style which
I have endeavoured to follow; but, as aforesaid, I think the style a
success. The difficulty is not so much in finding rhymes as in
breaking up the original into stanzas. Sometimes there is a convenient lump of nine lines, in which case I generally manage to
render line for line with very little sacrifice; but more commonly
the cleavage comes at the tenth, eighth, or seventh, and then I have
to contract or expand as the case may be. The proper names are a
difficulty. I do a good deal in the way of anapæsts for iambuses
—'Polydamas spoke,' 'Deiphobus slew,' &c.—which perhaps may
give my English readers some trouble.

To A. O. PRICKARD, ESQ.

Boston, October 9, 1868.

. . . . All Oxford, I presume, is talking about Mansel's elevation. Many things occur to me to say on the subject. So far as
he is concerned I don't grudge it, though I had rather hoped they
might have taken Merivale, who is a better *analogon* of Milman,
and a more obvious person for a metropolitan deanery. But
Mansel has deserved well of science and learning, and not wholly ill of
theology, let alone Conservative principles. To the University the
thing is rather humiliating. It seems to justify what was said when
he was transferred from Philosophy to Ecclesiastical History—that
in a university where the dignity of knowledge was properly
valued no one would accept an exchange from a subject which he
had properly studied to a subject which he had not studied merely
because the latter was better endowed. And now, before he has
had time to leave any mark on Ecclesiastical History, the Government which appointed him whirls him off in a different direction.
I don't blame him—possibly, under the same circumstances, I might
do the same thing—give up Latin (say) and go into Parliament;
but it certainly shows that the appreciation of knowledge in
England is not in a satisfactory state, and it shows also, I think,
that the Crown is not absolutely fitted to look after the interests of
the University. To the Conservative body in Oxford it must be a
considerable blow. I don't suppose that for some time past he had
been very available for active party purposes; but he was beyond
all question their most considerable man with the world at large.
Resident Liberals might not appreciate him (one of their most
patent weaknesses, I have long thought), but the intellectual public
outside knew that his was one of the chief Oxford names. I suppose
now the Conservatives have no one, at least of this generation, who
has really made himself a name. I mean, of course, the Conservatives proper, not Pusey and his party. All this is of good augury
for the Liberals, at least for the next few years; what monsters
may rise up from the deep during that time one cannot say.
Magee's appointment is a curious one. I suppose it may either be
taken as a slap in the face to those who are attacking the Irish
Church, in which case it is rather plucky, or as an instinctive movement like that of rats leaving a falling house. In himself I should
think he was a very good man to choose; he is said to have great
pulpit powers, and a paper of his in defence of the Irish Church in
the *Contemporary*, early in the year, was not only well written,

but showed much good humour and play of mind.　Ditto an extract I saw the other day from a speech of his at the Dublin Congress.

To the Rev. E. H. BRADBY.

Boston, June 30, 1868.

I, as I dare say you may have seen, have been relieving my mind by denouncing ritualist interpretations of the Communion Service in the *Contemporary Review*, and I am following up the blow this month by a similar demolition of similar explanations of the Articles, where the case, as might be expected, is still grosser than in the Prayer Book.　I have begun to print Vol. III. of Virgil, and hope to get on pretty fast with it this summer; but it will not be out before next year.　The volume of the translation of the Iliad is out, though the Reviews have scarcely shown themselves conscious of its existence.　Private judges seem to speak favourably of it, and I think myself it is as good as anything I have done.

To W. J. COURTHOPE, Esq.

Boston, January 16, 1869.

. . . . This will show you that your advice has begun to bear fruit.　I tried the first few lines [of the First Satire of Horace] in a solitary walk after you were gone on Monday, as usual without much hope of making anything of them, and though they did not come very well at first, as I got further I found myself better pleased with them.　I shall be very anxious to hear what you think. The style aims at what I told you, an imitation of Cowper.　I indulge in colloquial abbreviations more than he does, and have more inversions of verbs, a thing from which he is, I find, singularly free, more so than Pope in his 'Imitations of Horace'; but I don't think either of these matters (at least as I practise them) really involves a deviation from the easy colloquial style of good society, which is what I suppose answers in English to Horace in Latin. The two translations I have by me are Francis and a certain Howes. The first I have no doubt I have beaten, and on the whole I hope the second, though he has a great many good lines, and in some cases has anticipated me, if indeed I have not reproduced him unconsciously.

Oxford, January 20, 1869.

I confess I am disappointed at your opinion of 'Horace,' not so much at the opinion itself (so far as you express it) as at the grounds on which you put it. When we talked about the matter at Boston, I thought you distinctly urged me to undertake the work on the ground that a translation was wanted. Now you seem to say that no translation can be successful, because of the dimness and coldness of the time-basis, as Dr. Carlyle calls it in speaking of Dante, and that imitations are the only things. These, of course, we have, therefore there is no want. All that I can infer from this is that you have changed your opinion since we spoke of the thing, and that my translation has been the unlucky means of your doing so—a sufficiently likely, but not a flattering conclusion.

My own opinion, so far as I can take an external view of the question, is this. To all that you have said about the reasons for imitation I entirely subscribe; it is just what impresses itself on me in every paragraph which I translate. The 'time-basis' becomes very cold indeed at times, names are meaningless and even jokes have sometimes to be dodged, not met fairly. But an imitation cannot do all that a translation might, and the question is whether there is not room for a translation, allowing for all inevitable imperfections. Did the existence of 'London' and the Vanity of human wishes, cut the ground from under Gifford's Juvenal? I cannot think it did. Whether people would care for Gifford apart from the Latin I don't know. I only know that I care for it a good deal, and I trust there are others who feel with me. There is to me a distinct pleasure in seeing an author whom I know transfused well into English—a sense of correspondence and fitness which appeals to me strongly. Two questions then remain, Is Horace less translatable than Juvenal? and am I hopelessly inferior to Gifford? The first may be the case to a certain extent, but I think the extent may easily be exaggerated. The real difficulty is in writing easily and idiomatically in any particular style. One who tends to passionate declamation may write in the style of Juvenal, one whose manner is more level in the style of Horace. But there is much in Juvenal which is as colloquial as anything in Horace, and some of Gifford's most successful bits are in passages of this sort. On the whole, I don't think Horace less translatable than any writer of original power must necessarily be. This is of course an opinion formed on a week's experience, and I may hereafter see reason to change it. Now for myself. The counts that I could bring against myself are heavy enough, but the question is, Can I do the Satires and Epistles as well as I have done the Odes, the Æneid, and the Iliad? My own belief (founded on the same limited experience, and contrary to what I expressed when talking to you) is, I confess, that I can. I am not sanguine of obtaining a great success, but I don't think I ought to lose reputation, and meantime the occupation will be pleasant.

This is how the case seems to me to stand; if you will give me your judgment from that point of view, I shall be very grateful. Don't fear speaking out. If you say anything unfavourable, of course I shall feel it; I value your opinion too much not to do so, but I shall be grateful all the same. What are we meant for except to criticise each other for our good to the best of our ability?

Oxford, January 27, 1869.

I have been going on with the translation, and have done the third Satire and the greater part of the fourth. I don't suppose they would materially alter your opinion, but perhaps they do to some small extent meet by anticipation one of your objections to what you have seen. I think I have introduced into them a certain number of lines which may fairly be called *points*, so that the reader is rewarded from time to time for the dead level he goes over. Sometimes I have been antithetical where Horace is straightforward; sometimes I have brought into prominence an image at which he has only hinted. I scarcely knew why I began to do this, I suppose from some sense of the exigencies of composition; but I have continued it deliberately, on a sort of principle of compensation on which I occasionally acted in Virgil—that where one was obliged from time to time to rub off a little from the point of the Latin, one might from time to time give the Latin a point which it was without. I think the composition is improved in strength and vigour by it, without losing much of its character. However, I will not praise myself beforehand. I am only too fond of my last baby, whatever it happens to be, and possibly when you see the new work on your next visit here, you will think it substantially the same as you have already seen. My chief difficulty is about the rhythm. I don't like not to run the couplets into each other occasionally, as otherwise I make no attempt to reproduce Horace; but I scarcely ever do so without a suspicion of discord, especially since I have taken to writing antithetically.

*   *   *   *   *   *   *   *

A difficulty which seems to me greater than that about the names (though it is in fact only the same difficulty in another form) is about the social customs. Translate them verbally, they are nu-

meaning; paraphrase them, they lose all point; substitute modern customs for them, and of course the thing becomes an imitation. Names can be taken on trust because they are names; at all events they don't lose in translation, though they cease to have associations; but significant words have the fate of all significant words when you change them, they become significant of something else. I doubt whether, when I started, I was sufficiently alive to this difficulty, and it is quite possible that before I get much further I may find myself shipwrecked by it altogether. As yet I seem to myself still above water. The very fact of there being a choice of evils gives me some help. Sometimes I translate closely, sometimes paraphrase, sometimes modernise cautiously, while I try occasionally to give Horace a little point which he has not. I could give you instances of each, but I fear I should be ruining what little chance I have of producing any effect on you when I come to read what I have written to you continuously, which is of course the real test. This, I suppose, is a difficulty which presses equally on a translator of Juvenal; and Gifford seems to have met it, as I am trying to meet it, by varying his expedients. I will just give you a few instances where I think he succeeds in this or other matters, as it will show you what I aim at myself:—

> Sed Rufum atque alios credit sua quemque juventus,
> And *boys with bibs* strike Rufus on his chair.

Here the *bibs* are of course modern, and no detail at all was needed; but he doubtless felt he wanted to get more point than he could get by a simple rendering, so he got the thought of the bibs and also the alliteration.

> Cede, Palæmon!
> Et patere inde aliquid decrescere, non aliter quam
> Institor hibernæ tegetis, niveique cadurci.

> Courage, Palæmon! be not over nice,
> But suffer some abatement in your price,
> As those who deal in rags will ask you high,
> And sink by pence and half-pence till you buy.

The 'hibernæ tegetis niveique cadurci' are huddled up into 'rags,' but you get the detail of 'pence and half-pence' in their place.

> Occidit miseros crambe repetita magistros.

> Till like hashed cabbage served for each repast,
> The repetition kills the wretch at last.

Here he partly translates simply, partly amplifies—both weak of course, but he recovers himself by the vigour of his second line, which gives a notion of worn-out patience.

I broke off to read Gifford, and as I was carried along by the flow of his rhetorical passages, I became disgusted with myself; so I have just been reading my two last satires again to reassure myself, with tolerable success. There are fairly long reaches of quasi-rhetoric in each, in which I think I show movement, and on the whole I find I give myself something of the notion of Horace. But a good deal of it has been far from easy work. It certainly would be worth while translating Horace, *if* he can be translated, for only a translation can give Horace as Horace. Horace as Pope is a different thing; you think of the points in which Pope as a man did (or did not) resemble Horace, but you don't think of Horace as a man. 1¼ A.M.—I must go to bed.

To A. O. PRICKARD, ESQ.

August 5, 1869.

By the way, you will be amused at an ingenious misprint in the proof of 'Ibam forte viâ sacrâ.' I had written—

> ' 'Tis a Jews' fast to-day :
> Affront a sect so tonchy ? Nay, friend, nay.'
> 'Faith, I've no scruples.' 'Ah ! but I've a few—
> I'm weak, you know, and do as others do.'

The printer *ex ingenio* emended, 'Ah ! but I'm a Jew.' . . . . Who is the resident at Winchester who communicates to the *Times* his experience about bathing with a dog? History has repeated itself more nearly than he would have people think, as I had an experience twenty-nine years ago still more like the story which he tries to cap, being half drowned by a dog that jumped in after me at Rugby, and tried to drag me to shore, when I was swimming in perfect comfort; but then, it did not occur to me to write to the *Times*. I remember poor Cotton quoted, 'Invitum qui servat idem facit occidenti.'

I hope to try, at any rate, to know your young friend when he comes up, but for the last two or three years I have not taken so much hold on New College as aforetime. Perhaps as I get older I lean more to the Graces than to the Muses—and yet I hardly know that I can say that—but the modern Muses are apt to be rather like Courthope's Cornelia.

To W. J. COURTHOPE, Esq.

Scarborough, August 23, 24, 1869.

As you anticipate, I am not willing to accept all the flattering unction you give my Æneid, though I am, of course, pleased by what you say. I think I see plainly that such canons of criticism, if pushed a little further, would make short work of all translation; and I am not minded to confess the inutility of an art which I have practised so much during the last seven years. If Dryden and Pope really are the last word on the subject, 'cadit quæstio.' You can never have a good translation, unless the natural language of the period in which the translation is made is analogous to that of the period in which the original was written. Homer had his one real chance in England in the Elizabethan period and lost it. I have always clung to the hope that a writer of our period might be able, to a certain extent, to reproduce the style of another, just as he may enter into it thoroughly as a reader; so that, granting sufficient force on his part, he may hope to please not only the critic but the general reader, that is, if such general reader knows anything beyond the literature of his own time. One of my quarrels with Lord Derby is that he has translated an archaic poem into the language of the nineteenth century; one of my quarrels with the English hexameter is that it has no literary associations at all, but simply belongs to the time at which it happens to be written. All this, I dare say, is delusion; but I am not inclined to surrender it just yet, merely to save the credit of my Æneid.

I am reading very skimmingly the 'Ring and the Book,' which Strachan happens to have with him. There is infinite ability about it, quantities of subtle thought cleverly expressed—a good deal which I suppose is natural, not a little which is really poetical as well as ingenious or profound—yet it certainly seems to me ability misapplied. I have no great belief in the possibility of striking out new types in poetry; old types, no doubt, may be so manipulated in detail as to have the effect of now; witness the difference between the modern and the ancient drama; but in the main old types represent what poetical experience has proved to be possible, and an attempt to strike out anything beyond or by the side of them in poetry seems to be a mistake. I remember remarking the same thing to you this time last year about the 'Spanish Gipsy,' which seems to me to be a hybrid between the epic and the drama. The 'Ring and the Book' I

d 2

suppose is an attempt to create a new dramatic species, what may
be called a number of monologues bound together by a common
purpose. I cannot say that I think the gain is sufficient to justify
the deviation from received forms. The story is not worth viewing
in all these different relations, the different relations are by no
means all equally important, and yet, for artistic purposes, they
have to be all treated as if they were so; each occupies a book, and
takes up something like the same number of lines. Then I think
Browning's dramatic method is a mistake. Scarcely one of the
speakers could be imagined really to say what he is made to say;
no one, however rambling, would go off at so many tangents in
talking, much less in pleading or making a statement. What it
really resembles is thinking aloud, such thought being expressed
not as the thinker would express it in his own unassisted way, but
by the help of a clever interpreter. That is my judgment of the
work : I must look back at some of the reviewers to see whether
they agree with me. Some would doubtless tell me I ought to take
what is given me and be thankful, not grumble that it is not something else; but I cannot consent to let criticism surrender at dis-
cretion in this way, and, till better instructed, I shall persist in
regretting that a man who could do so much, should spoil what he
does by waywardness and eccentricity.

To A. O. Prichard, Esq.

Boston, September 4, 1869.

I have been reading the 'Ring and the Book' very skimmingly,
yet I think I have arrived at something like a critical judgment of
it. I don't think the plan a very happy one in itself, though it is
ingenious enough. With the execution of the plan I quarrel a good
deal. The speeches are not really speeches, but thinkings aloud;
no one ever rambles so much in talk as all Browning's personages
do ; while on the other hand no one ever thinks aloud meaning to
be overheard. These people follow out, not the thoughts which
really occur to them, as they would if they were thinking to themselves, but the thoughts which they wish their readers to think
occur to them. Surely this is a fatal blunder, destroying all
dramatic effect. Again, though the speakers are made to differ a
good deal from each other in what they say, they are all of them
intellectual and subtle—you wonder at their powers of analysis and
exposition—which again is undramatic, as, granted that three or

four of them might be people of that calibre, it is to the last degree
unlikely that all would be so.   Again, I doubt whether the story
itself is sufficiently considerable to bear being regarded from all
those different points of view.   Suppose one had the story of the
Agamemnon told by the chorus, and by one of Ægisthus' λοχῖται,
and by Clytemnestra, and by one of her waiting-maids, and by the
ghost of Agamemnon, and by the ghost of Cassandra, and by
Strophius, with a conclusion by Apollo, should not we rather tire of
it ? and yet it is surely the greater story of the two.

To the Rev. G. D. Boyle.

Boston, September 8, 1869.

. . . . I don't see how the Eucharistic doctrine can avoid being
brought to some sharp issue.   After all, the English Church *cannot*
leave it an open question whether it differs from Transubstantiation
by more than a verbal distinction.   The utmost Pusey and Bennett
can expect from a judicial decision must be that they will be left,
like the Evangelicals in the Baptismal Controversy, just inside the
Church, but not on its high road.   I have been reading Coleridge's
Keble aloud to my mother, and am rather dissatisfied with its tone
on questions of the kind.   Surely the simple fact is this—Keble
when he wrote the Christian Year, whatever his tendencies may
have been, had not formed definite views on various points; so he
was able to produce a book with which the vast mass of Churchmen
sympathised.   Afterwards his views developed, and though he
became dear to a party, he was less dear to the Church at large.
Those who represent him now must choose one thing or the other ;
if they wish to conciliate general sympathy they must keep his
later views in the background ; if they set store by his later views,
they must be content to abandon general sympathy.

It only remains to record the closing scene of this uneventful
but busy life.   For two or three years Conington's health had
given his friends some slight uneasiness.   Continued work,
rather than overwork, had begun to tell on him ; and he found
himself at times suffering from headache and a sense of oppres-
sion, the natural consequences of a too sedentary life, and of a
mental activity too uninterrupted.   But there was no symptom
of any alarming kind ; it seemed as if the simplest change in his

habits would be sufficient to restore him to full vigour; and it
is probable that these slight indications of constitutional weakness had no connection with his sudden and fatal illness.   He
spent the Long Vacation of 1869, as usual, with his mother, and
was described as having completely recovered his health and
spirits, and as looking forward with pleasure to the recom-
mencement of his work at the University.   But just before he
was to leave Boston for Oxford, a pimple appeared on his lip,
which soon assumed all the deadly characters of a malignant
pustule.   His illness began on Friday, October 15, and did not
appear to be serious until Wednesday night.   On Thursday all
hope of his recovery was over.   The eminent surgeon, who was
summoned from London to see him, and whose painful duty it
was to confirm the worst fears of his friends, wrote to Oxford:
'I am on my way home from a sad visit to Boston, where I
have left Professor Conington, apparently dying quickly. . . .
He is the last son of his mother, who is a widow, blind, and
past eighty.   It would have been nearly the saddest sight I
have ever seen, but for his calmness and resignation.'   The
whole truth was communicated without reserve to the sufferer,
who even knew how many hours he had to live.   As soon as
some necessary business was done, he dismissed all earthly cares,
and set himself to prepare for the immediate presence of death.
Not in the remembrance of a life useful and innocent as his
must be accounted among men, but only in the simplest teachings of his childhood could he find any comfort.   And even as
he listened anew to these, his mind was harassed by the terrible
doubt, whether indeed they had any personal interest for him.
While his consciousness remained unimpaired by the poison
which was working in his blood, this state of anxiety and depression lasted; but those who watched by his bedside observed
that it vanished at the first approach of the delirium which was
to end in death.   His utterances were now full of triumph;
and, so long as any faint light of reason was left unquenched,
his wandering words seemed to tell of a divine ecstasy.   At one

time he would again and again repeat the lines, whence taken, none of the listeners knew—

> Now the vision is complete;
> That is the way they speak in heaven;

while again a little later his thoughts seemed to turn once more to earth, or at least to her who on earth was dearest to him— 'There was God, and me, and my mother, and I was her guardian angel.' He breathed his last in the early morning of Saturday, October 23, and was buried on the following Tuesday by the side of his father and his brothers, in the churchyard at Fishtoft.

MISCELLANEOUS WRITINGS

OF THE LATE

JOHN CONINGTON, M.A.

———

THE POETRY OF POPE.[1]

IT is not my intention to attempt an investigation of
any of the incidents in the life of Pope. Anyone who is
acquainted with the discussions to which that biography
has given rise, and has observed the proportions which
they have lately assumed, as conducted in the book or the
pamphlet, in the weekly newspaper or the bookseller's
catalogue, will see that an independent judgment on their
various details could scarcely be pronounced without a
special study, not of months, but of years. Who were
Pope's parents? Who was the Unfortunate Lady that he
celebrates? Was he justified in his breach with Addison?
What was his real share in the translation of the 'Odyssey'?
What was his relation to the Misses Blount? What is
the history of the publication of his 'Letters,' and how far
did he tamper with them in preparing them for the press?
Was the 'Dunciad' provoked or unprovoked? What was
his quarrel with Lady Mary Wortley Montagu, and how
far did he go in avenging himself? Did he mean to

---

[1] Reprinted from *Oxford Essays*, contributed by Members of the University, 1858.

satirise the Duke of Chandos? Can he be acquitted of
disingenuousness in his correspondence with Aaron Hill?
Was he bribed by the Duchess of Marlborough to suppress
what he afterwards printed? How far was he to blame in
the posthumous quarrel fastened on him by Bolingbroke?
Such are some of the questions, of greater or less importance, which are sure to be raised by the casual reader,
and not sure to be answered by the best-informed writer.
Other literary men have been the subjects of equal or
greater mystery as regards some single event or trans-
action in their lives. The cloud which rests on the birth
of Savage is apparently still undispersed. If we now
know Chatterton to have been his own Rowley, and
Ireland his own Shakspeare, we are perhaps hardly in a
condition to speak definitely of Macpherson as his own
Ossian. But there is probably no English author whose
life can be compared with Pope's, as a succession of petty
secrets and third-rate problems. The fact itself is significant, and can scarcely fail to bias the opinions even of
one who expressly absolves himself from forming a judgment on the particular points at issue. A man whose
actions were generally blameless would not have left so
many things for his apologist to explain. A man whose
character was truthful and simple would not have been
the hero of so many enigmatical narratives. I mention
this in order to excuse myself, if, in making remarks on
the poet, I occasionally imply a judgment on the man.
My object is to produce a critical estimate of Pope's
several poems in themselves, with some prefatory remarks on his poetry generally, in one of its relations to
English literature ; but the writings must necessarily bear
some impress of the writer, and it is hardly possible to
take a survey of the one which shall not reflect more or
less definitely on the other.

That Pope is the most correct of English poets is a notion which of late years various eminent critics have been at considerable pains to explode. The opinion is one which has the advantage of prescription, having apparently been a received doctrine for many years after the poet's death. Yet, if a question can be decided by the authority of great names, it would seem necessary at once to abandon such a position. Hazlitt, in his ' Lectures on the English Poets,' [1] mentions particular instances of incorrectness which are to be found in Pope; and an article in the ' North British Review,' for August 1848, attributed to Mr. de Quincey, analyses one or two passages in the poems at considerable length, with a view to prove that the belief, in which it is admitted that the poet himself shared, is a gross popular error. Lord Macaulay, in his ' Essay on Byron,' is equally strenuous on the same side, though the ground which he takes up is somewhat different. According to him, what Pope and the post-Restoration poets aimed at and realised was not real correctness, which, with him, is synonymous with excellence and truthfulness to nature, but the pseudo-correctness of conformity to an utterly artificial and illusory standard. It appears to me, however, that the old view was substantially a just one, that there is a legitimate and intelligible sense in which Pope may be said to have especially earned the praise of correctness, and that this praise discriminates him, not only from his predecessors, but also to some extent from subsequent poets. The ideal which he laboured to attain was a reasonable one, and his efforts were sufficiently, though not wholly, successful. The question will, perhaps, be found to be partly a question of words; but the right understanding

<hr>

[1] Page 148 (first edition). The whole lecture contains much discriminating criticism, frequently expressed in very felicitous language.

of it is, I think, important, if we wish really to appreciate the position which Pope occupies as a poet.

It is worthy of remark that, as the 'North British' Reviewer admits, correctness is a thing on which Pope is known to have especially valued himself. He had scarcely commenced authorship when it was placed before him by one of his earliest critical friends as the principal object after which he was bound to strive. 'Walsh,' he told Spence, 'used to encourage me much, and used to tell me that there was one way left of excelling; for, though we had several great poets, we never had any one great poet who was correct; and desired me to make that my study and aim.'[1] It is easy to smile at this criticism, and to ask what is the worth of a canon which thus summarily condemns Shakspeare, Spenser, and Milton as alike deficient in the particular requirement sought. These writers, it is now generally acknowledged, far transcend Pope in grandeur and comprehensiveness of conception; they have achieved triumphs of expression to which he was unequal, and struck chords of melody of which he never dreamed. Yet it is possible that he may have been conscious of something in himself which they had not, and possible, too, that this special acquirement may have been a thing of real and enduring value. That he and his contemporaries should have overrated it is only too likely; that they should have been altogether wrong in their estimate of its nature and importance is far from probable.

Perhaps there is no better help towards a true apprehension of the English poetry of the eighteenth century than a knowledge of the poetry of Augustan Rome. The similarity of the two periods, as phases of national literature, has often been pointed out: it would be easy, if

[1] Spence's *Anecdotes*, Malone's edition, p. 52.

this were the case, to pursue the parallel into detail.
Now, it is curious that what Walsh said to Pope is precisely the same as what Horace said to his countrymen.
He tells them, almost in so many words, that, though they
had had several great poets, they never had any one great
poet who was correct. Speaking of Roman genius, in its
application to tragedy, he says :—

> Tentavit quoque rem si digne vertere posset,
> Et placuit sibi, natura sublimis et acer :
> Nam spirat tragicum satis, et feliciter audet,
> Sed turpem putat inscite metuitque lituram.[1]

In another passage he extends the censure to Roman
poetry in general :—

> Nec virtute foret clarisve potentius armis
> Quam lingua Latium, si non offenderet unum
> Quemque poetarum limae labor et mora.   Vos O
> Pompilius sanguis, carmen reprehendite, quod non
> Multa dies et multa litura coercuit, atque
> Perfectum decies non castigavit ad unguem.[2]

What it was that Horace quarrelled with in the poetry of
his predecessors may be seen more at length in those passages of his Satires where he speaks of Lucilius.[3]   It was,
in short, that they did not spend sufficient pains upon their
poetry ; that they did not make it as good as they might
have done.   Their treatment of a subject was not sufficiently varied ; their language was not sufficiently elegant ;
their versification was not sufficiently polished.   This may
at first sight seem to be a charge not against the individual
poets, but against the age in which they lived.   Ennius
and Lucilius may have been as laborious as Horace ;
Shakspeare and Spenser may have polished as assiduously

---

[1] 2 *Epist.* i. 164 foll.   [2] *De Arte Poetica*, vv. 280 foll.
[3] *Satires* 4 and 10 of Book i.

as Pope; and any superiority in finish that may be conceded to the later poet may be simply owing to his
having had the advantage of living after the earlier. But
it will commonly be found that the necessity of careful
elaboration, though implicitly recognised more or less by
every one who practises composition as an art, is not
strongly felt in the earlier periods of literature. In such
times a man of genius speaks at once, out of the fulness
of his own ebullient heart, or in the fervour of his admiration of the great writers of another age and country:
he is eager to communicate what he has felt and read,
rather than solicitous about the manner in which the
communication should be made. So, if I may borrow an
humbler illustration from the childhood of the individual,
it is hard to teach a boy to labour at his composition
beyond a certain point; he may feel that his verses are
inferior to a classical model, but it is utterly incomprehensible to him how by any expenditure of time he should
be able to make them better. As a matter of fact, we
find Horace distinctly asserting that Lucilius thought more
of quantity than of quality; the old bard, he tells us,
considered it a great feat to pour out two hundred verses
in an hour *stans pede in uno*; at the same time that he
bore witness against himself by laughing at the verses of
Attius and Ennius as less correct than his own. Even if
we had no express testimony on the subject, what we know
of the pre-Augustan poets would certainly lead us to think
that they were inferior to their successors in the labour
which they bestowed upon their pieces. Let us hear how
Mr. de Quincey, in one of his acknowledged writings,
decides the question as between Horace and Lucretius:[1]—

The *curiosa felicitas* of Horace in his lyric composition, the

---

[1] *Sketches, Critical and Biographic*, pp. 271, 273.

elaborate delicacy of workmanship in his thoughts and in his style, argue a scale of labour that, as against any equal number of lines in Lucretius, would measure itself by months against days. There are single odes in Horace that must have cost him a six-weeks' seclusion. . . . . . Let the proportions of power between Horace and Lucretius be what they may, the proportions of labour are absolutely incommensurable; in Horace the labour was *directly* as the power, in Lucretius *inversely* as the power.

If we compare Virgil with his hexametrical predecessors, the result is the same. Take any paragraph in Lucretius, or in the 'Peleus and Thetis' of Catullus; there may, perhaps, be some conceptions there which Virgil's less vigorous genius could not have entertained, some daring felicities of language which his more timid judgment would have rejected; but what remains will be seen to be characterised by a carelessness and want of art, both in style and versification, to which they yielded, but over which he triumphed. We can imagine, that if by any chance the first draft of any part of Virgil's poems had been preserved, we should find traces of prosaic redundancy in expression and monotonous uniformity in metre which would remind us forcibly of Lucretius. On the other hand, it is difficult to conceive that the 'De Rerum Natura,' as we now have it, could have been produced by a man who even in his own time realised the ideal which Horace has so well described,[1] sitting down to write in the spirit of a candid censor, removing undignified words from their place in the language of poetry, retrenching luxuriant redundancies, softening harshnesses, and exhibiting the plastic flexibility of a well-trained performer of several parts. This was the service which the great writers of the Augustan age rendered to the poetry of their country.

[1] 2 *Epist.* ii. 100 foll.

If we cannot give them the praise which, in a different
application, was bestowed on their master, and say that
where they found brick they left marble, we may say that
where they found a rough-hewn and rudely-carved block
they left a finished statue. They may have done injustice
to their materials by cutting away more than was needed:
but they were the first workmen who showed their
countrymen that they knew the more delicate uses of the
chisel.

Such a metaphor would, of course, convey a very exaggerated notion of what was done for English poetry by
Pope. The difference between him and his predecessors
would be more nearly represented by one of Dr. Johnson's
tropes,[1] which contrasts a genius cutting a Colossus from
a rock with an artist carving heads on cherry-stones. The
excellences of the school of English poetry which came
in with the Restoration appear to sink into absolute insignificance compared with that utterly incommensurable
with anything known or surmised to have existed in
republican Rome, which gave form and spirit to the poetry
of the preceding century. Yet what has been said of the
Augustan poets is substantially true of those whom I have
fixed on as their English representatives, and of Pope in
particular. Even Shakspeare, if we analyse him calmly,
cannot be said to have the characteristics of a finished
writer. It is true that his obedience to the eternal laws
of truth and beauty was infinitely more comprehensive in
its range, infinitely higher in its quality, than Pope's. But
it is no less true that there are rules of style and versification, not arbitrary, but grounded on those very laws, which
Shakspeare neglected and Pope observed. We know, in
fact, that Shakspeare's habits of composition were unfavourable to the attainment of that faultless propriety

[1] Boswell, vol. viii. p. 306 (Croker's ed. 1835).

which is the reward of long-continued labour. Pope, as was to be expected, has noted this in his imitation of one of those passages from Horace which I quoted in the last paragraph :[1]—

> Otway failed to polish or refine,
> And fluent Shakspeare scarce effaced a line :
> E'en copious Dryden wanted, or forgot,
> That last and greatest art, the art to blot.

What is to be said of such expressions as '*reverbs* no hollowness,' '*exsufflicate* and blowed surmises,' where a word is formed, in contempt of analogy, more gross than when Lucretius talks of *differitas* for *differentia*, *pestilitas* for *pestilentia* ? If we turn to the passages where Shakspeare and Pope may properly be brought into comparison, the rhyming couplets in the plays, the minor poems, and the sonnets, can it be maintained that there is no weakness, no redundance, such as might have been avoided by an exacting self-criticism? The last stanza of the 'Rape of Lucrece' will give an instance of what I mean :—

> When they had sworn to this advised doom,
> They did conclude to bear dead Lucrece thence,
> To show her bleeding body thorough Rome,
> And so to publish Tarquin's foul offence :
> Which being done with speedy diligence,
> The Romans plausibly did give consent
> To Tarquin's everlasting banishment.

This is, of course, no fair specimen of the beauties of the poem ; but even were it more exceptional than it is, it would still illustrate the proposition that its author is frequently unequal to himself. There is something not ineffective in the monotony of the lines and the simplicity of the expression ; but it can hardly be doubted that the

[1] Book ii. ep. l. vv. 279 foll.

one might have been varied and the other rendered less
prosaic, without striking a note out of harmony with the
natural conclusion of a story so melancholy. ' *Did* conclude,' ' *did* give consent,' were too common in Shakspeare's time to offend a critical reader; but Pope surely
did good service in expelling them, by precept and
ridicule,[1] from the ordinary language of poetry. ' Which
being done with speedy diligence,' may remind us of the
prosaic style—half oratorical, half conversational—in
which Lucretius is apt to pass from sentence to sentence.
Altogether, the passage does not seem to conform to
Coleridge's definition of poetry, which is at bottom much
the same as the demand for correctness, ' the *best* words
in their right places.' The language and metre of Spenser
will still less bear to be examined strictly according to
such rules as a modern critic is accustomed to recognise.
There are, I need not say, innumerable instances of
felicitous diction and musical versification; but our feeling for both is apt to be overpowered by the general
sense of redundance on the one hand, and of long-drawn
uniformity on the other. It is doubtless this sense that
even in our day, when the appreciation of the elder
poetry has so greatly revived, prevents his writings from
enjoying anything that can fairly be called popularity.
Of Milton it is far more difficult to speak. His blank
verse unquestionably shows marks of an art more ex-

---

[1] ' Another nicety is in relation to expletives, whether words or syllables,
which are made use of purely to supply a vacancy. *Do*, before verbs plural,
is absolutely such, and it is not improbable that future refiners may explode
did and *does* in the same manner, which are almost always used for the sake
of rhyme.' (Pope to Walsh—Bowles, vol. vii. p. 75.) So the well-known
' Expletives their feeble aid do join,' of the *Essay on Criticism*. The ridicule
of expletives, like that of the lines of ten monosyllables, is taken from a
passage in Dryden's *Essay on Dramatic Poesy*, as Malone remarks; the
expletives, however, which Dryden singles out for censure are ' for to,' and
' unto.'

quisite, though less obvious, than that which Pope employed in the elaboration of the rhyming heroic. So far, however, the two cannot be said to be on common ground. It was one of the characteristics of the poetry which came in with the Restoration—a characteristic doubtless attributable to the French affinities of the school—that it discouraged the cultivation of blank verse. Rhyming tragedies, indeed, did not long remain the fashion; but those which succeeded them cannot be classed among the most successful poems of their time. Dryden might express his regret that he had chosen rhyme for his translation of Virgil,[1] and Pope might select blank verse for an epic which never was written; but such afterthoughts cannot be accepted in contradiction of the testimony of a whole poetical life. Of the blank-verse poems which that school produced, only two—Thomson's 'Seasons,' and Young's 'Night Thoughts'—are much known to the readers of the present day; and no one will pretend that, as blank verse, they have any points of superiority to the great Miltonic master-works. On the other hand, in rhyme Milton can hardly be said to have put forth his strength, though what he has done—if we except his more juvenile pieces—certainly shows felicity of execution, as well as force of imagination. On the whole, however, Milton lived too much in an atmosphere of his own, too little in sympathy with the generation in which his greatest works were produced, to impart to English poetry that correctness of which it was beginning to find its need. He might have led it by a steeper and more rugged way to a higher point of exaltation; but other

---

[1] The story rests on the authority of the elder Richardson, who heard it from the person to whom Dryden made this confession, 'a north-country gentleman,' supposed to be Sir Wilfred Lawson.—See Scott's *Life of Dryden*, p. 351, ed. 1834.

guides were preferred, and it was not till they had had
their day that his influence came to be really felt. These
writers were, as might be expected, themselves incum-
bered more or less, especially at first, with the faults of
carelessness and roughness, against which it is their praise
to have protested. As compared with Pope, Dryden is
certainly an incorrect poet. He is full of inequalities—
at one time polished and vigorous, at another flat and
slovenly. Yet his felicities are of a kind which can
hardly have been attained without some use of the file,
some conscious imitation of classical models. As a prose
writer, he may perhaps be called the father of English
criticism ; and it is not likely that his practice should
have been uninfluenced by his precepts. In his ' Defence
of the Essay on Dramatic Poesy,' he says of himself,

> As for the more material faults of writing which are properly
> mine, though I see many of them, I want leisure to amend
> them. It is enough for those who make one poem the business
> of their lives to leave that correct ; yet, excepting Virgil, I
> never met with any which was so in any language.

It is of this spirit of criticism that Pope's poetry is the
triumphant embodiment. He appears to have been the
first English writer possessed of high poetical power
(Milton I have already intimated that I should wish to
except) who addressed himself to the composition of
poetry with the full determination to do his best. He
occasionally published poems which he afterwards found
himself able to improve ; that, so far from proving that
he acquiesced in imperfection, is really an evidence to
the contrary : but we may be sure that he never published his first draft.[1] Even in his most finished pieces

[1] ' The only poems which can be supposed to have been written with
such regard to the times as might hasten their publication, were the two
satires of " Thirty-eight," of which Dodsley told me that they were brought

there may be occasionally something that more study
might have mended—an ill-turned thought, an inaccurate
expression, a bad rhyme. So much may be readily conceded to those who, like Hazlitt and Mr. de Quincey,
think the praise of his correctness exaggerated. But are
there no blemishes of a similar kind in writers who are
commonly allowed in these respects to come little short
of perfection—in Virgil or Horace, for example? The
point is not that Pope was universally correct, but that
correctness, in the sense in which I have attempted to
explain it, was at any rate one of his leading characteristics, and that the instances of carelessness which can be
quoted from his works are not sufficiently numerous or
important to disturb the general impression. Nor do I
think it can be maintained that such a praise is slight or
nugatory. It is the praise which is given to a schoolboy
for a good exercise; but it goes along also with that
schooling to which a wise man will be willing to submit
all his life. If we ignore it, we must ignore nearly the
whole of what criticism has done for literary composition
from the days of Horace downwards. It must, perhaps,
be admitted that this zeal for correctness operates on the
higher functions of the poet rather negatively than positively, rather by restraining him from an untrue or
exaggerated conception than by suggesting others of
greater reality or beauty. Such is doubtless the tendency of all endeavours to act by rule, though there may
seem no sufficient reason why the fear of failure should
not act as a stimulus to the attainment of success. But
if the patient pursuit of excellence is not uniformly

to him by the author that they might be fairly copied. "Almost every
line," he said, "was then written twice over. I gave him a clean transcript,
which he sent some time afterwards to me for the press, with almost
every line written twice over a second time."'—Johnson, *Lives of the Poets*
(Cunningham's edition), vol. iii. p. 114.

rewarded in the wider circles of poetical activity, it
meets with its recompense in the narrower. In avoiding
minor faults, the poet is led on to perceive and appropriate minor beauties. There, at all events, the result of
an exacting self-criticism is not barrenness, but increased
fertility. The mind rejects many thoughts, but only that
it may produce others of a higher and rarer quality.
The conception may be inadequate, but it is adequately
represented; and as it has to be represented by the aid
of subordinate and ancillary conceptions, there is still
room for the presence of that seeing and shaping power,
without which poetry can scarcely be said to exist. It
is quite possible that a poet of this class, in refining his
country's language and versification, may cast away much
that is at least of equal value with what he preserves,
simply because he has not the insight to perceive its
latent capabilities. He may close his eyes to the complex graces of Shakspearian diction, and regard the
varieties of Miltonic rhythm as things forbidden. Even
then, however, it may be doubted whether he does not
gain far more than he loses by these self-imposed
restraints. To expect that the taste of such a man will
be infallible, teaching him always, or even generally,
what to take and what to leave, would be to expect
more than is authorised by our knowledge of human
nature. It is enough that he acquires himself, and leads
others to acquire, the habit of judging according to fixed
rules—that he puts an end to an anarchy which, though
harmless while the national mind is in a state of comparative unconsciousness, becomes pernicious as soon as
it is felt and recognised. Such, at any rate, is one of the
stages through which it would seem that the poetical
literature of a nation must ordinarily pass. It may be
only the prelude to a final decay of creative power; but

even then it is entitled to the respectful consideration of
the critic or the literary historian, not only as a legitimate development of previous conditions of the national
mind, but for the sake of its own intrinsic worth.

If this view of Pope's position be the true one, it need
not surprise us that no subsequent writer should be found
to dispute with him the boasted pre-eminence in correctness. That a period like that which his poetry symbolises
should be short-lived is only what experience would lead
us to expect. The Athenian drama, as a work not of
genius but of self-conscious art, attained its culminating
point in Sophocles, and its subsequent development,
though full of significance and promise in relation to
dramatic literature generally, was in itself undoubtedly
a corruption. Virgil and Horace are the sole representatives of that perfection of poetic style which is commonly
associated with the Augustan age ; in Ovid the declension
has already begun ; melodious versification has passed
into unvarying smoothness, and polish of language into
epigram and antithesis. The writers who succeeded
Pope attempted to pursue the same course of refinement,
but they had not the same true instinct to guide them,
and the material which they strove to elaborate gave
way under their hands. They either repeated the more
obvious features of his language and his rhythm, or, in
endeavouring to improve upon them, ran into that excess
which it was the very object of his chastened taste to
restrain. A spirit of reaction became apparent : Churchill
endeavoured to return to the negligent vigour of Dryden ;
Cowper, Churchill's schoolfellow and admirer, went
further, not only making the heroic couplet less mellifluous, but reviving the fashion of blank-verse writing,
which he learned to use as it had not been used by
Thomson or Young ; till at last the springs of new life

in taste and opinion which arose in the great political
convulsion of those days burst up to the surface, and the
literary traditions of a century and a half were sub-
merged or swept away. Since then it may be almost
said that correctness such as Pope's is to be numbered
among the lost arts; the leaders of the revolution, like
Coleridge, Wordsworth, and Keats, disdained it as the
badge of an unimaginative and artificial school; the Conservatives, like Rogers and Campbell, were scarcely
strong enough to realise in practice what they upheld
in theory; while Byron, who, as Lord Macaulay happily
remarks, belonged to both parties, not by turns but
simultaneously, bears probably more marks of slovenliness
and haste than any great poet of the time. But the
importance of form in poetry is not a doctrine which can
long be lost sight of while any feeling for art survives;
and though the circumstantial differences between Mr.
Tennyson and Pope are too many and too great to justify
any parallel of the one with the other, we may rejoice in
the possession of a writer whose self-criticism is as exacting
as Pope's own, and who has taught us once more that
high poetry will not lightly tolerate a trivial phrase or a
tuneless line.

I now proceed to notice Pope's several poems, classi-
fying them, as nearly as may be, according to the order
in which they appeared.

I. '*The Pastorals.*'

It seems at one time to have been considered a
natural thing that a young poet should make his *début*
by writing pastorals. This notion was supposed to
find its justification in the example of Virgil, who represents himself as a shepherd warned by Phœbus to

abstain from heroic song and be content with meditating the woodland muse while feeding his flocks. Virgil, however, if not a shepherd, was certainly a countryman during the early part of his life; and though his rural pictures are mere fancy pieces, where the scenes portrayed, so far as they are pastoral at all, are as much Sicilian as Italian, no very violent allegory was involved in this mode of describing the condition from which he was raised by his patron's favour. But the fiction was taken up by men whose circumstances had as little in common with Virgil's as Virgil's had with those of the shepherds whom he professed to personate. Spenser introduces his ' little booke ' to Sir Philip Sidney as the offspring of ' a shepheard's swaine, all as his straying flocke he fedde;' and the commendatory epistle addressed to Gabriel Harvey says that therein he followed ' the example of the best and most ancient poets, which devised this kinde of writing, being so base for the matter and homely for the maner, at the first to trie their habilities.' And Philips, Pope's rival, in expressing his wonder that, ' in an age so addicted to the Muses, pastoral poetry comes to be never so much as thought of,' reminds his contemporaries that ' Virgil and Spenser made use of it as a prelude to epic poetry.' Johnson has perhaps gone nearer to the truth when he suggests[1] that the utter unlikeness of the pastoral Arcadia to anything in real life would naturally recommend it as an easy subject of composition to those who had had no experience of real life themselves. Pope, however, in his after years, was pleased to think[2] that he had done just what Virgil says of himself—trying his boyish hand on an epic, and then turning to pastoral poetry as his first serious work.

[1] *Lives of the Poets*, Cunningham's edition, vol. iii. p. 110. Compare vol. ii. p. 207.
[2] Spence's *Anecdotes*, Malone's edition, p. 40.

It is not surprising that Pope's 'Pastorals' should have
been received at the time of their appearing with almost
unbounded favour. His friendly correspondent Walsh,[1]
in language which, to persons acquainted with the life of
the Roman poet, will seem either an unmeaning truism or
a blunder, observed that it was no flattery at all to say
that Virgil had written nothing so good at his age: the
critic might have said, with as little fear of being thought
a flatterer, that no English poet, old or young, had produced anything bearing such proofs of finish in its language and its versification. Further than that commendation cannot fairly go; but it may well seem wonderful
that such powers should have been exhibited by a boy of
sixteen. Yet it would be a great mistake to suppose that
Pope's 'Pastorals' are worthy of being mentioned in the
same day with any genuine work of Virgil's. A comparison of any one of the English pastorals with any one
of the 'Eclogues' would soon show where the difference
lies. It is not merely that Pope appears throughout as
the imitator of Virgil, the copyist of one who is himself
a copyist; the disparity is shown not in the greater or
less degree of imitation, but in the manner of imitating.
Virgil transcribes Theocritus with a fidelity which makes
him sometimes appear confused and unskilful; but all
the while there are under-currents of thought and feeling
which are peculiarly his own. The image which he uses
may be trite, but you can trace in it some subtle relation,

---

[1] Walsh to Wycherley, in Bowles' *Pope*, vol. vii. p. 00. It used to be
supposed that Walsh was the author of the *Life of Virgil* and the preface
to the *Pastorals* prefixed to Dryden's translation. Malone, however (*Life
of Dryden*, vol. i. of *Prose Works*, p. 232), on the authority of Dryden's
letters to Tonson, attributes them to Dr. Knightley Chetwood, afterwards
Dean of Gloucester. Walsh's pastoral eclogue on Mrs. Tempest (for which
see Tonson's *Miscellany*, vol. v.) supplied something more than the general
thought to Pope's fourth pastoral.

if not to the subject treated of, at least to the poet's
mind. So there is an artificial delicacy of texture about
his language which defies analysis.   In Pope, on the
contrary, the results are obvious—they can be understood
and appreciated at once.   We are astonished at the skill
which has enabled him to command and produce them;
but they do not themselves astonish us, though they give
us sufficient pleasure.   He has not indeed exhausted the
subject of his own versification in his letter to Walsh
(the sixth and last of the series); but he tells us, at any
rate, part of the secret of his success, and we feel the
difference between a secret and a mystery.   Nor did he
approach nearer to Virgil when six years later he appeared as the poet of the Messiah.   He had the language
of Jewish prophecy at his disposal, and he has translated
it into classical equivalents, which are marshalled into
sonorous lines.   But he has missed the art which under-
lies the 'Pollio'—the art which makes the regenerating
change in the order of nature proceed step by step with
the progress of the child from infancy to maturity, each
event being at once a stage in the gradual emancipation
of the universe, and a tribute specially appropriate to the
young deliverer.

A few words may be said about the controversy between
Pope and Philips. The pastorals of the latter are probably
best known through the celebrated article in the 'Guardian,'[1] if indeed they can be said to be known at all; but
there was a time[2] when Pope thought them deserving of
a more favourable notice. So far as the theory of pastoral
poetry is concerned, a modern reader will most likely
give the victory to Philips. If shepherd life is to be
written about at all, it seems clear that the proper style
for it is the simpler style, not the more artificial. But

---

[1] *Guardian*, No. xl.   [2] Pope to Cromwell, Bowles, vol. ii. p. 136.

Philips' attempts to realise simplicity are not always satisfactory. Where his language deviates from that of ordinary poetry, it generally becomes not rustic, but obsolete. His model is not the English of the rural districts of his own day, but the English of Spenser; and in the names of his *dramatis personæ* Hobbinol, Cuddy, and Colin Clout are strangely mingled with Myco and Menalcas. On the other hand, in the structure of his poems, he follows not Spenser, but Theocritus and Virgil; his shepherds not only talk in heroics, but sing in the same metre; so that, in fact, it is only by a conventional fiction that they can be said to sing at all. Thus anyone who takes the trouble to peruse his pastorals will probably pronounce them to be compositions of the same class with Pope's, but of course infinitely inferior. Those, however, who read Gay's 'Shepherd's Week' with pleasure as a natural picture of rustic life,[1] may, I think, extend some of their approbation to the poet whom Gay was employed to parody. If Philips, while endeavouring to be natural, has omitted the coarser features of shepherds' society, Gay has run, as he intended to run, into the opposite extreme. Gay's style is as conventional as Philips', and if the work has any merit beyond that of a clever burlesque, it is as representing the same life in a lighter aspect which Philips has described more sentimentally.

II. *The ' Essay on Criticism.'*

Pope had already given some proof of his judgment and knowledge as a critic in a 'Discourse on Pastoral Poetry,'

---

[1] 'But the effect of reality and truth became conspicuous, even when the intention was to show them grovelling and degraded. These pastorals became popular, and were read with delight as just representations of rural manners and occupations by those who had no interest in the rivalry of the poets, nor knowledge of the critical dispute.'—Johnson's *Lives*, vol. ii. p. 285.

prefixed to his ' Pastorals '—an essay which has received
high and not wholly undeserved praise. Like all Pope's
more serious prose compositions, it is written with elegance, though with some stiffness; and if his precepts are
drawn not from nature, but from the most artificial specimens of an artificial school, the fault must rest mainly
with the authorities from whom he borrowed them.
There were not wanting precedents for his next attempt,
a didactic poem on poetical criticism. Four poems of
this sort, three of them by patrons of Pope's, had been
produced within a short period previously—Sheffield's
' Essays on Satire and on Poetry,' Roscommon's ' Essay on
Translated Verse,' and Granville's ' Essay on Unnatural
Flights in Poetry ; ' and the poem to which they doubtless
owed their impulse, Boileau's ' Art of Poetry,' had appeared
in an English version, to which Dryden was known to
have lent a helping hand. We might have expected that
Dryden himself, so eminent as a prose critic, and so
didactic in the style of his poetry, would have undertaken
a similar work ; and indeed there are many of his occasional poems, prologues and epilogues, and epistles to
friends, which may not unfairly be classed under this
head. Pope had prepared himself for the task, as he told
Spence,[1] by devouring as a boy all the best critical works
that came in his way; and his early letters show that
when he read the poetry of his predecessors he read it as
a critic. Spence is the authority for a statement,[2] once
questioned by Johnson, but surely possessing intrinsic
probability, that the essay was originally written in prose ;
and those who would examine it must subject it to something like the reverse process, and turn it back into prose
again. As a preceptive work, its merits have, I think,
been exaggerated. Johnson certainly goes too far when

[1] Malone's Spence, p. 10.   [2] Ibid. p. 3.

he says that it 'displays such extent of comprehension, such nicety of distinction, such acquaintance with mankind, and such knowledge both of ancient and modern learning, as are not often attained by the maturest age and the longest experience.' Without endorsing Lady Mary Wortley Montagu's vindictive assertion [1] that it is 'all stolen,' we may question whether there are many of the precepts which might not be traced to their source in some earlier writer. That a boy should be able to master and appropriate criticism of the dogmatic and conventional sort—and the essay can hardly be said to have advanced beyond this—is not surprising. Johnson's own 'Lives' are precisely the book which an intelligent schoolboy may appreciate and make his own. So again, worldly remarks on life and manners may be picked up at second-hand and retailed by one who has had no reason to find them true. As to the method, no one but Warburton ever pretended that the essay was thoroughly systematic, though Pope himself appears to have censured the absence of a regular plan in the work which is the prototype of his and all similar attempts, Horace's 'Art of Poetry.' [2] Warburton admits that many of the directions are as much addressed to poets as to critics; but though he shows without difficulty that the arts of poetry and criticism are cognate subjects, he does not prove the poem to be regular. When we come to examine the execution, we find much that can only be called commonplace. In the first two paragraphs, for example (eighteen lines), there is nothing remarkable but the witty comparison of judgments to watches. These short pointed illustrations constitute, in fact, one main source of the attractiveness of the poem; but they are not always equally happy, and they are not scattered about in any great profusion. They furnish a sufficient

---

[1] Malone's *Spence*, p. 30.   [2] Spence.

number of lines for quotation to keep the essay in the
mouths of men, if not in their minds; but they are
rather foreshadowings of that eminence which Pope was
to attain as a sparkling and epigrammatic writer than
actual contributions towards it. To a modern reader
probably the acceptability of the poem rests chiefly on
those longer passages which elaborate versification and a
certain elevation of sentiment are evidently intended to
lift above the level of the rest. Such are the tribute to
the great classic poets which concludes the first part, the
comparison of progress in learning to the ascent of the
Alps, the reflection on the short duration of modern
poetry, the lines on the revival of learning, and the
apostrophe to Walsh with which the poem is brought to
an end. Yet it may be doubted whether any of them
approaches the beauty of that digression in Horace,
almost the only thing of the kind in the 'Ars Poetica,'[1]
where an observation on the mutability of language is
drawn, though but for a moment, into a general moral.
There is, however, one passage in the essay which is
worthy of higher praise than any of those which I have
enumerated. I allude of course to the famous lines
where keen and graceful ridicule of common faults in
versification is followed by an enforcement and exemplification of the doctrine that the sound should seem an
echo to the sense, and the whole culminates in an eulogy
of Dryden's magnificent 'Ode on the Power of Music.'
Johnson has attempted to break down the doctrine of
representative harmony by a rigorous examination of
Pope's endeavours to produce the effect of swiftness and
slowness. But in the lines where he has, as he says, set
the numbers used in describing the labour of Sisyphus to

[1] A. P. vv. 60 foll.

another sense, the numbers are not really the same;[1] and he forgets, too, that a poet is not bound to produce a line where the sound of the words shall tell its own tale quite irrespectively of the sense, but only one where the sound will assist the impression which the sense is already making. Whether, as he asserts elsewhere, there is no particular heaviness, obstruction, or delay in the lines which mention the effort of Ajax, is a question for the ear; and the ear too will, I think, decide that there is a reason why a line, constructed so as to be pronounced rapidly, will give an additional notion of speed if it happens to be an Alexandrine. Altogether, the passage is an eminently happy instance of criticism conveyed in a delicate artistic form, and passing into poetry of a higher, though not the highest, sort. The only drawback to its excellence is the

---

[1] Pope's lines are—

> With many a weary step, and many a groan,
> Up the high hill he heaves a huge round stone:
> The huge round stone, resulting with a bound,
> Thunders impetuous down, and smokes along the ground.

Johnson's parody is—

> While many a merry tale and many a song
> Cheered the rough road, we wished the rough road long:
> The rough road then, returning in a round,
> Mocked our impatient steps—for all was fairy ground.

It is obvious to remark that 'merry' has a much less tedious sound than 'weary;' that the sense of panting occasioned by the five aspirates in Pope's second line is not analogous to anything in Johnson's; and that 'thunders impetuous,' which is nearly equivalent to two dactyls, has a more rapid movement than 'mocked our impatient.'

The Eleventh Book of the Odyssey was translated by Broome; Pope, however, speaks of the lines as his own, having perhaps made them so by alteration. The last line is taken from one of Dryden's plusquam-Alexandrines in his version of the end of the Third Book of Lucretius.

> What is it but, in reason's true account,
> To heave the stone against the rising mount,
> Which urged, and laboured, and forced up with pain,
> Recoils, and rolls impetuous down, and smokes along the plain?

resemblance of the last line to another in the poem which occurs exactly a hundred lines later. Two such verses as —'And what Timotheus was is Dryden now,'and 'And such as Chaucer is shall Dryden be '—ought not to have occurred in a single composition of no immeasurable length.

On the whole, while the 'Essay on Criticism' may be readily allowed to be superior in execution, as it certainly is in compass, to any work of a similar nature in English poetry, it can hardly be said to redeem the class of didactic poems on æsthetics from the neglect into which it has now fallen, or to make us regret that the critical ability of our own day should prefer to follow the path which Dryden marked out when he chose to discourse of poetry in his own vigorous and flexible prose.

III. *The Lyric Poems.*

If there is any kind of composition which Pope can be said to have cultivated without success, it is lyric poetry. His minor pieces, indeed, such as the boyish 'Ode to Solitude,' are not unpleasing; and the 'Dying Christian to his Soul' might, perhaps, call for some praise, in spite of its utter conventionality, if the verses, which, as he tells his correspondent Steele, came to him the first moment he waked in the morning, had not presented themselves in the borrowed plumes of Flatman. But it was in an evil hour that he listened to the entreaties of the same correspondent, at that time probably busied in the management of a public concert, and accepted the perilous service of writing an 'Ode for St. Cecilia's Day.' The result is a poem which, as Gray justly observes, is not worthy of so great a master. While challenging comparison but too evidently with the unapproached grandeur of Dryden's

second ode, it hardly rises to the height of the first and
much slighter effort, and is perhaps less pleasing than the
forgotten attempt of Congreve. The opening stanza is an
experiment in imitative versification, which succeeds
where it is confined to the iambic or trochaic rhythm,
but fails when it passes into a different measure. What
harmony can be extracted from lines like these :—

> Let the loud trumpet sound
> Till the roofs all around
> The shrill echoes rebound,

which are evidently meant to run in the same measure,
but really oscillate between two distinct rhythms, the
cretic and the anapæstic? or can an ear which has been
accustomed to the unforced flow of Moore's anapæstic
dimeters (metrical questions can hardly be treated with
precision except in a pedantic terminology), find any
pleasure in such cadences as the following :—

> Exulting in triumph now swell the bold notes,
> In broken air trembling the wild music floats?

Johnson remarks that the second stanza consists of hyper-
bolical commonplaces ; he might have added that some of
them are peculiarly unhappy, as anticipating in the comparatively weak language of metaphor the images which
appear a stanza or two afterwards in the bolder form of
personifying fable. When we are told that ' Melancholy
lifts her head, Listening Envy drops her snakes,' the effect
is to prevent any vivid impression which we might have
received from the dancing spectres and listening Furies
in the story of Orpheus. The conclusion of the third
stanza is musical, and there is vigour of expression in the
line ' And men grew heroes at the sound ;' but the images
are again trite. The stanzas about Orpheus and Eurydice,
with their ' Dreadful gleams, Dismal screams, Fires that

glow, Shrieks of woe,' their iteration of Virgil's thoughts in numbers which, if sometimes marked by melancholy sweetness, too often affect a rapidity of movement which is simply grotesque and undignified, have just now been characterised, not more strongly than they deserve, by the author of 'Merope.' It is curious that Johnson should consider the form perfect and lay all the blame on the matter, as if the sorrows of the bereaved husband had not been made interesting by Virgil, and could not be made interesting again by a poet who should realise them by his own power of independent sympathy. The conclusion is an unhappy imitation of an unhappy thought of Dryden's, whose ode ends, as Johnson remarks, with a false antithesis. Dryden balances Timotheus, who metaphorically ' raised a mortal to the skies,' against Cecilia, who, according to the legend, literally ' drew an angel down.' Pope contrasts the power of Orpheus, which literally ' raised a shade from hell,' with that of Cecilia, which metaphorically ' lifts the soul to heaven.' Both are unfortunate, but Pope the more so, as he gives the weaker, the metaphorical attribute, to the power which he is anxious to show to be the stronger. It may be observed, too, that Pope's epigram is more gratuitous than Dryden's, as, while the power of Timotheus is the one subject of ' Alexander's Feast,' Orpheus is the hero of only part of Pope's performance, and so need not have been recalled to the stage at the falling of the curtain. Pope might probably have done better if he had followed Dryden's example more closely, and made his ode turn entirely on the Orphean story, which he might then have related with greater fulness; though his subject would have been less suitable to his purpose than Dryden's, as being calculated to bring out only a single effect of music, its power to soothe and soften, not that universal mastery over the various forms

of human emotion which the tale told by Dryden so glo-
riously embodies.   Of course Pope is not to be compared
with any ideal standard, or to be blamed because he could
not philosophise on music like Wordsworth in his 'Ode on
the Power of Sound,' or make us feel the spell which it
lays on a reveller as intuitively as Mr. Tennyson has done
in the earlier part of his 'Vision of Sin.'   All that could
be asked of him was that he should exhibit his own
strength; and this he has certainly failed to do.   The
cause of this inequality is doubtless to be found in his
inaptitude for lyric metres.   The beaten track of the
heroic couplet he knew; but, in attempting the wider
and more complex harmonies of the ode, he was venturing on a region which, though visited by many, had
been fully explored by none, and from which only one
had returned with anything like adequate success.[1]   He
knew his failure, and never repeated the experiment.   I
need say nothing of his attempts to imitate the Greek
chorus, which Mr. Arnold has lately had occasion to notice.
Warburton thinks them 'enough to show his great talents
for this species of poetry, and to make us lament he did
not prosecute his purpose in executing some plans he had
chalked out;' but the reconciliation between the two
contending branches of the drama was not to be accomplished by the insertion of choruses about 'Moral truth
and mystic song,' 'Guilty joys, distastes, surmises, ...

[1] I see that Dryden uses the same image in speaking of the Pindaric ode
in a letter to Dennis (Malone, vol. i. part 2, p. 35):—' I could wish you
would cultivate this kind of ode, and reduce it either to the same measures
which Pindar used, or give new measures of your own. For, as it is, it
looks like a vast tract of land newly discovered: the soil is wonderfully
fruitful, but unmanured; overstocked with inhabitants, but almost all
ravagers, without laws, arts, arms, or policy.' Anyone who has glanced at
the Pindaric compositions of the seventeenth century will see that Dryden's
language is amply merited. Dennis wrote a Pindaric ode to Dryden on his
translation of the Third Georgic.

False tears, deceits, disguises, Dangers, doubts, delays, surprises,' in tragedies altered from Shakspeare by the Duke of Buckingham.

IV. ' *Windsor Forest.*

The poems from which Pope is supposed to have drawn hints for ' Windsor Forest' are Denham's ' Cooper's Hill,' Waller's ' Verses on St. James's Park,' and Addison's ' Epistle from Italy.' The two former belong to a different period, and so are to be contrasted rather than compared with Pope's poem, though the first has sense, vigour, and some force of imagination, and the latter fancy and a turn for courtly compliment : but the third affords a better analogy, not only in versification and language, but in the treatment of the subject, where local description is intermixed with reflections on politics. Here, however, as elsewhere, Pope's command of diction and harmony give him an unquestionable pre-eminence. His poem is also distinguished from those of his predecessors by a number of descriptive touches, though it may be doubted whether they are of the kind which is most proper for poetry. We see not only the fisher and his angle, but the different colours of the various fish—not only the sportsman and his gun, but the several parts of the pheasant, discriminated according to the hues of their plumage. The description is sufficiently minute ; but little or no imagination seems to have presided over it, and the emotions which it raises are not much more elevated than the childish wonder with which a savage regards a picture simply because it is a picture. Add to this that the poet is led to compensate for the want of imagination in his manner of conceiving the object by a stilted magniloquence which is meant to do duty as the language of

poetry. The barrel of the gun becomes ' the tube,' the
report ' a short thunder,' the shot the ' leaden death,' the
fishing-rod ' the reed.' It would be a little unfair to
parallel the description of the pheasant with that of the
phœnix in Whitbread's Rejected Address for the opening
of his own theatre, which, according to Sheridan's report,
was a regular poulterer's description, beak, feathers, and
all ; but though the reader's eye may be supposed to rest
on the beauty of the plumage as he sees the bird on the
ground, it would hardly take in all the various particulars ;
and there is something ludicrous in supposing them to be
severally pleading for the creature's life.   Johnson blames
Warton for comparing Pope's description of the stag-chase
disadvantageously with Somerville's, alleging that they
stand on different grounds, the latter being the author's
main subject, the former an incidental feature, to be
briefly despatched ; but if Warton had chosen to amend
his plea, and point to the stag-chase in ' Cooper's Hill,' he
might, I think, have shown that Denham has given more
poetical interest to the object than Pope. Denham does
not describe the antlers or quarters of the stag, but he
awakens human sympathy for the hunted animal, whose
race for life is represented in language which may remind
us of the human colouring of the picture of the bull-fight
in the Third Georgic, or of the more pronounced pathos
of Wordsworth's ' Hart-leap Well.'   The passage is too
long, not merely for quotation, but for the propriety of
the poem ; but I extract a few lines :—

> Betrayed in all his strengths, the wood beset,
> All instruments, all arts of ruin met,
> He calls to mind his strength, and then his speed,
> His winged heels, and then his armed head,
> With these to avoid, with that his fate to meet ;
> But fear prevails, and bids him trust his feet.

So fast he flies, that his reviewing eye
Has lost the chasers, and his ear the cry ;
Exulting, till he finds their nobler sense
Their disproportioned speed does recompense ;
Then curses his conspiring feet, whose scent
Betrays that safety which their swiftness lent :
Then tries his friends ; among the baser herd,
Where he so lately was obeyed and feared,
His safety seeks ; the herd, unkindly wise,
Or chases him from thence, or from him flies.
Like a declining statesman, left forlorn
To his friends' pity and pursuers' scorn,
With shame remembers, while himself was one
Of the same herd, himself the same had done.[1]

Pope's minuteness of description, however, does not extend to the main features of the forest, which, as Warton points out, are mostly described in language that would apply to almost any other place. 'He' (the critic), retorts Johnson, 'must inquire whether Windsor Forest has in reality anything peculiar ;'[2] a remark which will appear in its true light when illustrated by another Johnsonian dictum—'Sir, when you have seen one green field, you have seen all green fields : Sir, let us walk down Cheapside.' Mr. Carruthers reminds us that we have another poem in our language which was composed 'under the oak-shades of Windsor Great Park,' Shelley's 'Alastor ;' and though it does not profess to represent the spot, its pictures of forest scenery are anything rather than vague or generalised.

'Windsor Forest' contains some happy imitations of passages in the Latin classics, and one so unhappy as almost to extinguish the merit of the rest. In the story

[1] Thomson, in his description of the stag-hunt, may have had his eye on Denham.
[2] Review of Warton's Essay.

of Lodona, Pope has shown that he can tread in the
steps of Ovid; but it is difficult to estimate the want of
poetical feeling which, even to compliment a patron, could
so travestie those noble but melancholy lines in which
Virgil gives the palm of happiness to an insight into the
causes of things, and the next place to rural enjoyments,
as to make an award assigning the first prize to a life at
Windsor Castle, the second to a life in Windsor Forest.

V. *The 'Rape of the Lock.'*

If we need not spend much time over the 'Rape of the
Lock,' it is only because there can be little to say about a
poem so exquisite in its peculiar style of art as to make
the task of searching for faults almost hopeless, that of
commending beauties simply impertinent.   Here, indeed,
Pope was on his own ground, and his progress from first
to last is a continued triumph.   His marvellous polish of
language and metre, his exuberant liveliness of fancy, his
fondness for classical imitations, which are too often only
parodies, may occasionally appear unseasonable elsewhere;
but here they are thoroughly in place.   The air of studied
stiffness, which is apt to spoil the effect of his prose compliments to his female correspondents, is carried off and
disappears in the atmosphere of a poem the metre and
conduct of which proclaim it to be designedly artificial.
Where no warmth is expected or desired, we do not feel
frigidity; where there is no work for imagination to do,
we do not complain that her place should be supplied by
fancy.   That the machinery is borrowed, Pope himself
confesses; but Warton testifies that the debt extends to
nothing more than the general idea of the existence of
these sylphs and gnomes: and though, to take another
instance, all honour is to be given to Dryden for the sub-

lime conception of employing the guardian angels of
kingdoms as the supernatural motors of an epic, scarcely
less would have been due to Pope had he introduced
them, as he hoped to do, in his own projected poem
without the sacrifice of dignity or propriety. Many will
doubtless agree with Cowper that

> The man that means success should soar above
> A soldier's feather, or a lady's glove ;

but while such regrets may affect our estimate of the poet,
they are out of place in considering the poem. In an
artistic sense, the labour is not misapplied, for it accom-
plishes its result, and there is no reason to think that the
same thing could have been produced at less cost. Pity
as it may be that so slender a pillar should have to bear
so large a part in sustaining the weight of so great a reputation, no one can say that the consummate art of its
workmanship would not render it a conspicuous object in
any palace which has ever been reared for the Muses
under our own or any other sky.

VI. The 'Temple of Fame.'

It is not strange that in an age when translations from
the classics seem to have been as popular among the
writers and readers of poetry as original compositions,
men should have attempted to modernise the earlier
authors of their own language. Dryden had published
adaptations from Chaucer in his 'Fables,' the work of his
old age, which had attained, as it deserved, splendid
success; the story of 'Palamon and Arcite,' as rewritten
by him, being a sort of specimen of his powers in the
minor epic. To modernise Chaucer accordingly was one
of the exercises proposed to himself by the youthful Pope.

The 'Temple of Fame,' however, the only one of these displays of talent which need be noticed here, exceeds the
ordinary license of a modernised imitation. Chaucer's
'House of Fame' consists of three books; Pope has almost
wholly confined his attention to one of them, the last.
His omissions are more extensive than his alterations; but
in a poem of which every part is characteristic, to omit
largely is in effect to alter largely. The change in the
versification produces a change in the whole external
form of the work. Dryden had substituted his own
vigorous heroics for the ruder ten-syllable lines of Chaucer;
but the measure was really the same, and the infusion of
a little new blood in the shape of one or two more modern
or more full-sounding words was frequently all that was
wanted to make the old verses such as a later age might
read with pleasure. But the seven-syllable or eight-
syllable metre of the 'House of Fame,' running on from
line to line without balance and without pause, had no
parallel in Pope's time to plead for its retention; and the
heroic in Pope's hands is much less Chaucer-like than in
Dryden's. The step in the one case is from the hexameter
of Ennius to that of Lucretius or Catullus; the step in
the other is from the Saturnian measure of Naevius to
the hexameter of Virgil. The Gothic house is pulled
down, and a temple of the Composite order erected on its
site. Few things, certainly, can be less like the manner
of Pope than Chaucer's opening ejaculation, 'God turne
us every dreme to goode!' followed as it is by above
sixty lines of disquisition on the material or supernatural
character of dreams, by way of introduction to the dream
which is the subject of the poem; or than the eagle's
somewhat unreasonable attempt to extract a compliment
from the poet at the end of the long discourse with which
he has enlivened their aerial journey—

Telle me this now faythfully,
Have I not preved thus symply,
Withouten any subtilite
Of speche, or grete prolyxite
Of termes of philosophie,
Of figures of poetrie,
Or coloures of retorike?

Pope preferred, as he tells us himself, to take a hint for
his opening from other poems of Chaucer which begin
with a description of some season of the year. One of
these poems—'The Flower and the Leaf'—is included
among Dryden's paraphrases; and Pope's exordium shows
that he had his eye on his master. But his language and
versification, finished as they are, have not the spring and
life of Dryden's; and, after a few lines, he wisely declines
the contest with one of the most musical and energetic
passages of description which are to be found in that great
poet's works. The picture which he raises in the next
paragraph seems open to an obvious objection. Standing
between earth, seas, and skies, he sees the globe below
him hanging self-balanced in air, with its rising mountains,
circling oceans, naked rocks, empty wastes, towering cities,
green forests, sailing ships, trees, temples, and alternations
of sunshine and cloud. A poet's fancy is not to be circumscribed; but we may perhaps question whether Pope had
reflected that he is supposing himself to take a very distant
and a very close view of the earth at one and the same
time. Chaucer's eye rolled in no such fine frenzy. Borne
in the talons of his eagle, he rises gradually. On first
looking down he sees the various objects which Pope has
enumerated, but on a second view these have vanished,
and the earth is just recognisable, not as a self-sustained
ball, but as something no bigger than a point. In Pope's
account of the temple, and throughout the poem, we may

observe an intermixture of the moral with the allegory,
which in Chaucer is mere simplicity, but in a more
artificial poet is unpoetical and tasteless. Thus, we are
told that the ice-palace is impaired alike by storm and
sun, *for* fame decays both by envy and by excess of
praise—that the wall has the multiplying effect of glass,
for romantic fame increases all—that crowds of all degrees
bend before the goddess, *for* good and bad alike are fond
of fame. Nor is there much to commend in the manner
in which the heroes and kings are for the most part represented. Some notion is given to us of what they were
historically; but we do not see their statues, or, if we do,
the marks of likeness are generally commonplace. What
conception of sculptured imagery do we gain from being
told that Scipio was great in his triumphs and great in
retirement, that Aurelius had a well-balanced mind, that
Agis was not the last of Spartan names? or from the negative statement that ' Brutus his ill genius meets no more '?
In the six primary columns the representation is addressed
more directly to the eye, but in general it is poorly
imagined, though the language is ornamental and the lines
sonorous. The best of the figures is Pindar; the worst,
Horace, who is hardly described at all, unless by the
epithet ' happy,' and the mention of his lyre, though we
see the accessory sculptures round his column, and are
told that he imitated Alcæus and Sappho. Chaucer, it is
true, is not more graphic; but he apparently means us to
think not so much of the bodily similitude of the individual poets as of the office which they perform, each
standing on his pillar and supporting the fame of some
grand historical event. Nothing need be said of Pope's
selection of the six great names of ancient literature,
except that it illustrates the range of his own reading and
of that of his time, when Plato and the Greek dramatists

were all but unknown to the general student, and the
poets had thrown the historians completely into the shade.
The conclusion of the poem, which is Pope's own, reminds
the reader gracefully enough of the individuality of the
author : it is awkwardly placed, however, as the subject
has shifted from the temple of Fame to that of Rumour ;
and, if the criticism is not too microscopic, the last couplet
is blemished by a rhyme—*unknown* and *none*—which is
either no rhyme at all, or the rhyme of a word rhyming
to itself.

VII. *The Elegiac Poems.*

The ' Elegy on the Memory of an Unfortunate Lady ' has,
I venture to think, been a little over-praised. The pre-
vailing sentiment of the piece is one which calls out but
a very qualified sympathy, and the images by which it is
advanced approach too nearly to poetical or rhetorical
commonplace to excite any warmer feeling than that of
admiration for the beauty and ingenuity of their expression. Our sense of the ' striking abruptness' of the
opening is materially diminished when we find that both
thought and language are taken from the commencement
of another elegy on a lady, by Ben Jonson. Nor does
it seem possible to abate the censure which the great
moralist passes on ' the illaudable singularity of treating
suicide with respect.' Pope, who was always more or
less of the critic and the reasoner, does not merely commend the lady's death to our feelings, but argues in its
praise ; and by argument he must accordingly be judged.
He pleads for her as a lover, and he pleads for her as a
Roman—two characters which might possibly be found
capable of reconciliation if we knew the secret of her
personal history, but which certainly do not amalgamate
readily in our thoughts. A Roman death was frequently

proposed as an object for the enthusiasm of the last century; but there probably was never a period in which fewer Roman spirits walked on the earth; and it would require strong evidence to make us believe that this heroine, as she appears to have been, of an attachment to one who was her superior in rank, was animated by anything like the spirit of the daughter of Cato and wife of Brutus. The very address to the 'Powers' is a piece of unreality in a serious poem; and it is strange recklessness, if not something worse, to talk of heaven as the origin of that ambition which was 'the glorious fault of angels and of gods.' The poet's teaching might have been immoral, yet he might have found his way to our feelings; but what feeling can be touched by a vindication of ambition as having originated with the fallen angels, and having thence passed into the breasts of kings and heroes, who are called 'their images on earth'? The contrasted picture of the meaner souls is striking, but perhaps too satirically ingenious for elegy; the image of the sepulchral lamps is spoiled by the less appropriate one which follows, of the Eastern kings; and a modern reader may be excused for preferring 'the long mechanic pacings to and fro, The set grey life, and apathetic end,' of 'Love and Duty.' The 'ruby lips,' the breast that once warmed the world, and the 'love-darting eyes,' are somewhat commonplace in themselves, and, in the connexion in which they stand, affect the fancy rather than the feelings. A set appeal to them can hardly suggest the thoughts which the poet would have to knock at the heart of the 'false guardian.' The words with which Lear's agonised soul expires, though apparently similar, are really different: in his mind, if in anyone's, the thought of the soul which is gone must have been undistinguishably blended with that of the form which he clasps in his arms; yet all is contained in a single word —'her lips'—with not even an epithet to indicate the mysterious union of beauty and death.· The rest of the paragraph, however, is grand in its way—a denunciation of the terrible revenges of Greek legend in the majestic style of the translation of Homer. In the lines on her funeral, I conceive, with submission, fancy is again predominant over feeling. The first few couplets are admirable; but when he comes to disparage the ceremonial observances of which she has been deprived, he passes into an enumeration which is too much of a *locus classicus* of the funeral honours usual among Englishmen, more judicious, because shorter, than Lucan's catalogue of the rites which were dispensed with at the marriage of Pompey and Cornelia. The remainder of the poem is graceful, and not unaffecting, though the tone seems to vary a little between that of the admirer and that of the lover. There is something ungracious in pointing out what appears to be the defects of a work that has had so many eulogists, but I trust that it may be possible to do so in the present day without becoming obnoxious to the language with which Warburton crushed a similar attempt by Lord Kaimes, and being reminded of the difference between 'the candour of a sensible and reflecting judge,' and 'the malice of every short-sighted and malevolent critic.'

The Ovidian Epistle is one of those artificial kinds of composition which can hardly hope to retain permanent favour. Horace and his imitators might write to their friends in familiar verse, as poets to readers of poetry; but there is something undramatic in representing the letters of lover to lover, even in the heroic age, by the studied elaboration of the modern elegiac couplet. If Pope's Eloisa does not talk in the language of epigram, there is something in her utterances which seems too

stately and rhetorical for the occasion that calls them
forth. The fact that we have her letters to refer to, and
can see that Pope, has followed them more or less closely
throughout his poem, only makes us feel the contrast
between the more natural and less natural forms of expression more strongly. Every point that is selected has
the most made of it : the artist goes to work, and ex-
amines the turns which can be given to the thought, the
possible felicities of the language, the charms of which
the versification is capable; inquiring, not as a great
dramatist would inquire of himself, in what manner his
heroine would most naturally express her feeling, but
how he can express it most finely as a poet. Taken as a
poem, it is undeniably marked throughout by great vigour
and sweetness : line follows line, each more forcible and
musical than the last, till we are lost in wonder at the
patient strength of execution that could sustain itself so
long. But it would be vain to pretend that every part
of the poem is calculated to give the same pleasure. The
contrast between the heavenly and the earthly love is
meant to be broadly marked, and the distinction is effected
by stripping the latter of anything approaching to ethereal
purity, and reducing it to merely sensual desire; while
even there, as in the 'Elegy,' Pope's argumentative vein
breaks out, and immoral doctrines are put forward in a
tersely dogmatic form. To say that the coarseness of
some of the expressions of passion is rendered from
Eloisa's own letters,[1] is only to say that Pope ought never
to have chosen the subject, especially as his plan has led
him to amplify and embellish every detail, throwing no
part of his heroine's feelings into the shade, but exhibit-

---

[1] Eloisa's letters I only know from the extracts given in Warton's *Essay*;
but it appears from an article on Pope in the *Quarterly Review*, vol. xxxii.,
that Pope has aggravated coarseness into licentiousness.

ing each emotion, whether virtuous or criminal, in all the
light that poetical diction and harmony can shed over it.
The passages which speak of cloistral solemnities, of the
neighbouring scenery and its effect on the mind, and
of the details of Catholic worship, are in general eminently beautiful, though the researches of the critics or
Pope's own admission have shown that for some of his
most striking expressions or lines he has been indebted
to predecessors who are now only known to travellers
along the byeways of English poetry.   The egotism of
the conclusion is artfully introduced, and additional interest is lent to it by the mystery that hangs over the
attachments which Pope appears to have felt; but with
the 'Temple of Fame' and the 'Elegy' fresh in our memory,
we rather resent a third attempt to make the feelings
with which we lay down a poem rest not on the subject,
but on the writer.

VIII. *The Translation of Homer.*

To censure Pope's ' Homer' as un-Homeric has now become a cheap and easy task.   It was always known not
to be a close rendering of the original; and the difference
of centuries between the manner of the pre-historic age
of Greek literature and the manner of the English poetry
of Queen Anne's reign has at last made itself felt by readers
of every sort.   Whatever errors there may be in the conceptions of style which prevail in the present day, there
can be no doubt that a keen appreciation of the characteristic style of different periods, a perception of the
historical analogies of different manners of writing, are
more generally diffused now than was the case even thirty
years ago.   The various translators of Homer, as a general
rule, have simply rendered him into the style in which

they were themselves accustomed to write—some with
greater, some with less fidelity to the words of the Greek,
but none of them paying any special attention to the
Homeric manner. Chapman's early English fortunately
happens to coincide to some extent with Homer's early
Greek; but though his simplicity strikes us in contrast
with the conventional art of a modern poet, he is an Elizabethan writer all over, continually running off into quaint
conceits, forced metaphors, and a philosophical jargon, for
which it is needless to say that his author affords no warrant. Ogilby and Hobbes simply fashioned ' Homer' into
such English as they could command ; and if their language is mean and their metre rugged, it is because they
had not the genius or the skill to do better. Dryden,
indeed, in the preface to his ' Fables,' dwells at some length
on the difference between Homer and Virgil, asserting that
the former is more congenial to his own temperament, and
consequently more pleasant to translate, than the latter ;
but his general notion is that Homer is more rapid and
careless, Virgil more slow and careful ; and he shows his
sense of the distinction when he passes from one to the
other, simply by throwing off restraint, disdaining to correct
his language, and taking liberties with versification : he
imitates the simplicity of the old Greek garb merely by
appearing in public in his own dressing-gown and slippers.
Cowper, writing after Pope, had the advantage of knowing what to avoid ; but he was misled by a false analogy,
and seeing in Milton a great epic poet, austere in his
manner and repellent of meretricious ornament, attempted
to force on Homer a style which, rightly considered, is
almost as artificial as Virgil's, and which, moreover, he
was himself unequal to wield. Sotheby is the last whom
I need name ; and his translation, though welcomed with
enthusiastic encomium by Professor Wilson in a series of

brilliant articles, which it is a satisfaction to see reprinted, is really, as Christopher North's friend Tickler observes in another part of the same magazine, only Pope spoilt, closer to Homer in words, and with fewer additions of the translator's own, but in all its essentials as much a poem of 1834 as Pope's is a poem of 1715–1725, with all the difference between them which existed between the two men as poetical artists. Errors of this kind we can now understand, and it is perhaps a wonder that they should not have been understood sooner. In one sense we may very probably be losers by the discovery; in another we shall certainly be gainers. A future Pope is not unlikely to be deterred from attempting Homer at all; but should he make the experiment, he will hardly be satisfied with merely giving a new nib to the pen which executed the boyish version of the 'First Book of Statius his Thebais.'

So much it was necessary to say on the theory of translation; and now we are free to do justice to the extraordinary and unrivalled excellence of the poem, as a product of Pope's peculiar power. Probably no other work of his has had so much influence on the national taste and feeling for poetry. It has been—I hope it is still—the delight of every intelligent schoolboy: they read 'of kings, and heroes, and of mighty deeds,' in language which, in its calm majestic flow, unhasting, unresting, carries them on as irresistibly as Homer's own could do, were they born readers of Greek; and their minds are filled with a conception of the heroic age, not indeed strictly true, but almost as near the truth as that which was entertained by Virgil himself. Their imagination is refined, exalted, satisfied. All the felicities of Pope's higher style are concentrated in this translation. It occupied ten of the best years of his life, and it adequately represents the fruits which powers like his were sure to produce by the mere

force of constant exercise. The peculiarities of his own
mind, which sometimes offend us when exhibited on a
small scale, do not appear equally unpleasing when we see
them more at large. It may be only an arbitrary fancy,
but I do not find the modernisation of Homer nearly so
frigid as the modernisation of Chaucer. The language
which Achilles and Agamemnon are made to talk seems
less inappropriate than the words which are put into the
mouth of Eloisa. One cause doubtless is, that Pope was
compelled to allow himself less latitude and exhibit himself less. His ' Homer,' though a sufficiently free translation, is a translation after all. It was on this limited
neutral ground, I incline to think, that his genius as a
writer on heroic or ideal subjects was best qualified to
expatiate. For such themes it was well that others should
find the thoughts, he undertaking to supply the manner,
the diction, and the numbers. Marvellous as his ' Pastorals '
are, as I have said, as a feat of youthful dexterity, he
would probably have done more justice to his own gifts
had he merely given a translation of the ' Eclogues.' We
should then have had a version which, though inferior to
Dryden's in freedom, facility, and dauntless vigour, might,
even at that early time of Pope's life, have shown marks
of a skill resembling, however faintly, the exquisite delicacy of Virgil's own touch. As it is, we have poems
which, while owing nearly all their merit to the passages
in which they remind us of Virgil, have not the substance
and texture of independent works—Virgil's images and
Virgil's thoughts, but not strung together in Virgil's order.
From such an attempt his reverence for Dryden, whom
even then he doubtless aspired to succeed, would alone
have been sufficient to deter him. It was, on the whole,
fortunate that the same feeling, aided by the inducements
of interest and the solicitations of friends, led him to under-

take the great work which Dryden had hoped to compass,
but had left unaccomplished.

But whatever may be thought of the wisdom of his
engaging in such a task at a time so critical for his fame,
there can be no doubt that the applause with which his
contemporaries almost unanimously greeted the appearance
of his translation was richly deserved.   It was not to be
expected that they should weigh Chapman's merits against
his in a goldsmith's scales ; Chapman must have been
already half obsolete, and would naturally appear to them
only as one of the representatives of a state of literary
barbarism, from which it was their glory to have at last
completely emerged.   Hobbes' 'unstudied and unpre-
tending language,' which Sir William Molesworth thought
might give the reader a better notion of Homer's style
than Pope, was estimated by them as what in fact it is,
merely a piece of bald writing, which would be poetry if
it could ; and Ogilby, the favourite of Pope's schoolboy
days, and the banker on whom he not unfrequently drew
for rhymes while composing his own translation, though
a faithful interpreter of the Greek, ranks as an epic poet
below Sir Richard Blackmore.   Dryden, as was just now
observed, from his incredible carelessness and rashness,
fails just where he might have been expected to succeed ;
he sees that factitious dignity is no longer required, and
therefore takes out a license to be vulgar ; and in the
very same volume, where he shows, in his adaptations of
Chaucer and Boccacio, how well he could write while on
his good behaviour, Jupiter is made to call Juno his
'household curse,' his ' lawful plague,' his ' other squint-
ing eye ; ' and the gods are sent off to bed ' drunken and
drowsy,' even the Thunderer applying ' his swimming head
to needful sleep.'   Tickell's version of the First Book of

the ' Iliad,' which appeared within a day or two of Pope's,[1]
and was the cause of the rupture with Addison, though

[1] It appears from advertisements quoted in Nichols's *Literary Anecdotes*
(vol. i. p. 100), that Pope's first volume was due June 6, 1715; Tickell's,
June 8. In one passage Pope afterwards condescended to borrow from his
rival—that describing the abduction of Briseis by the heralds. Pope's lines
at first were—

> She in soft sorrow, and in pensive thought,
> Supported by the chiefs on either hand,
> In silence passed along the winding strand.

For the two latter of these we now have—

> Past silent, as the heralds held her hand,
> And oft looked back, slow moving o'er the strand.

Tickell's lines being—

> Sore sighed she, as the heralds took her hand,
> And oft looked back, slow moving o'er the strand.

It is curious that this circumstance of Briseis's looking back, which is
not in Homer, but was apparently first introduced by Dryden, perhaps from
the picture of Andromache's departure from Hector in *Iliad* vi., should have
become so identified with Homer as to be reproduced not only by Sotheby,
who is in general faithful enough, but by Cowper, who, contrasting his
treatment of the original with Pope's, says, ' I have omitted nothing; I
have invented nothing.' Other coincidences between Pope and Tickell
seem to be merely fortuitous; as when Pope (in the first, as well as in
subsequent editions) renders

> Φάσγανο δ' ἐκ κολεοῖο μέγα ξίφος,

> While half unsheathed appeared the glittering blade,

Tickell—

> And half unsheathed he held the glittering blade;

the picture, though not the words, having been doubtless taken from
Dryden's

> Half shone his falchion, and half sheathed it stood,

as that may have been from Ogilby's

> His sword half out.

I had hoped to have been able to present those who may be curious, as I
am myself, about this passage in literary history, with a specimen, if not an
entire transcript, of the MS. remarks which Pope at one time (see Johnson's
Lives, Cunningham's edition, vol. iii. pp. 43, 44) thought of publishing on
Tickell's version. It appears from Nichols's *Anecdotes* (vol. v. p. 640) that
this volume (a copy of Tickell with remarks in Pope's handwriting), having
been accidentally separated from Pope's other books, fell into the hands of
Isaac Reed; and that Hurd, to whom Warburton had given the rest of

hailed by the Whig coterie as 'the best that ever was made,' is really a performance of no remarkable merit; a respectable production of the Addisonian school, with far less vigour than Dryden's, and far less splendour than Pope's; and the passages in which, as his friend Young told him, he was allowed even by partial judges to have outdone his rival, can only be called inferior, though meritorious, specimens of the heroic style of which that rival proved himself so great a master. There is another translation of the greater part of the First Book, by Maynwaring, now so completely forgotten, that probably scarcely a single reader of Johnson's 'Life of Pope,' where it is casually mentioned, knows where it is to be found, as it was published anonymously in the fifth volume of Tonson's 'Miscellany,' and is not included in the author's 'Remains'—a level, matter-of-fact, business-like composition, never rising into high poetry, and sometimes sinking into low prose.[1] Pope, while smarting under the non-recog-

---

Pope's library for the collection belonging to the see of Worcester, wished to purchase it, when Reed generously presented it to the collection, observing that such treasures should not be made a matter of bargain and sale. I accordingly applied to the Bishop of Worcester, who kindly threw open to me the library at Hartlebury; but I found that the volume was missing. Its existence being vouched for by a catalogue dated May 28, 1808, as the fact of its absence is recorded in pencil on the margin of the same catalogue by some later hand, probably within the last few years. Nichols, however, says that Reed, before sending the book to Hurd, caused a transcript to be made, and that this transcript was afterwards in the possession of Alexander Chalmers; so that it is possible that some one may be able to point out the copy, even if the original should prove to have been irrecoverably lost. Since the above was written, my attention has been called to the *Gentleman's Magazine* for 1830, p. 349, where the author of an article on Pope speaks of a copy of Tickell containing Pope's MS. remarks as in his own possession.

[1] Pope, and, I think, Tickell are under some slight obligations to Maynwaring, as all three of them doubtless are to Dryden. Compare the following:—

Thou glorious light! whom Tenedos obeys.—*Maynwaring.*
Thou source of light; whom Tenedos adores.—*Pope.*

nition of his own superiority, had thoughts of republishing
this version, together with Dryden's and Tickell's, side by
side with his own, that the public might judge more
readily of their respective merits. Let us do him some
portion of that justice which booksellers' difficulties prevented him from doing to himself, by setting down in
juxtaposition a short passage from each of the four translations. The specimens I have selected are, so far as I
can judge, adequate representatives of the average quality
of each ; though Dryden in particular, along with some
worse passages, contains some better. Those who care to
compare them with the Greek, which is not my present
object, may turn to ' Iliad,' i. vv. 233—247.

DRYDEN.

But by this sceptre solemnly I swear
(Which never more green leaf or growing branch shall bear,
Torn from the tree, and given by Jove to those
Who laws dispense and mighty wrongs oppose),
That when the Grecians want my wonted aid,
No gift shall bribe it, and no prayer persuade.
When Hector comes, the homicide, to wield
His conquering arms, with corps to strew the field,
Then shalt thou mourn thy pride, and late confess
Thy wrong repented, when 'tis past redress.
He said, and with disdain, in open view,
Against the ground his golden sceptre threw ;

Encouraged thus, the blameless prophet spoke.—*Maynwaring*.
Encouraged thus, the blameless man replies.—*Pope*.

Till prosperous gales, no bribe or ransom paid,
To longing Chryses bear the black-eyed maid.—*Maynwaring*.
Till the great king, without a ransom paid,
To her own Chrysa send the black-eyed maid.—*Pope*.

Black choler boiling in his manly breast.—*Maynwaring*.
Black choler filled his breast that boiled with ire.—*Pope*.

Maynwaring intervened between Dryden and Pope and Tickell, the
date of the fifth volume of the *Miscellany* being 1704.

Then sate : with boiling rage Atrides burned,
And foam betwixt his gnashing grinders churned.

MAYNWARING.

But by this awful sceptre now I swear
(Which ne'er again will happy branches bear,
Nor native bark, nor growing leaves will shoot,
But left on distant hills the kindly root,
And now with Grecian judges must remain,
Who right dispense, and sacred laws maintain),
Hear what I swear : whence'er the Greeks shall want
My needful aid, destruction to prevent,
And with regret their lost Achilles mourn,
No prayers nor gifts shall bribe me to return :
Hector shall strew with slaughtered foes the field,
And no relief thy impotence shall yield ;
But, torn with deep remorse, thy heart shall break
For wronging thus in arms the bravest Greek.

    The speech concluded, in disdain he tossed
His sceptre down, with golden studs embossed :
Atrides also stormed.

TICKELL.

But thou my fixed, my final purpose hear :
By this dread sceptre solemnly I swear,
By this (which, once from out the forest torn,
Nor leaf nor shade shall ever more adorn,
Which never more its verdure must renew,[1]
Lopped from the vital stem whence first it grew,
But given by Jove the sons of men to awe,
Now sways the nations and confirms the law),

---

[1] Tickell seems in this couplet to have been indebted to the *Rope of the Lock*, Canto iv. vv. 135, 6 :—

> Which never more its honours shall renew,
> Clipped from the lovely head where late it grew.

Such an appropriation would hardly have been made by one who translated Homer with the express object of injuring Pope by his rivalry. Pitt has borrowed from one or other of the couplets in his version of the sceptre-passage in the Twelfth Æneid.

A day shall come when for this hour's disdain
The Greeks shall wish for me, and wish in vain;
Nor thou, though grieved, the wanted aid afford,
When heaps on heaps shall fall by Hector's sword:
Too late with anguish shall thy heart be torn
That the first Greek was made the public scorn.

He said, and mounting with a furious bound,
He dashed his studded sceptre on the ground;
Then sat: Atrides, eager to reply,
On the fierce champion glanced a vengeful eye.

POPE.

Now by this sacred sceptre hear me swear,
Which never more shall leaves or blossoms bear,
Which, severed from the trunk (as I from thee),
On the bare mountains left its parent tree;
This sceptre, formed by tempered steel to prove
An ensign of the delegates of Jove,
From whom the power of laws and justice springs
(Tremendous oath! inviolate to kings):
By this I swear, when bleeding Greece again
Shall call Achilles, she shall call in vain.
When, flushed with slaughter, Hector comes to spread
The purpled shore with mountains of the dead,
Then shalt thou mourn the affront thy madness gave,
Forced to deplore, when impotent to save:
Then rage in bitterness of soul, to know
This act has made the bravest Greek thy foe.

He spoke, and furious hurled against the ground
His sceptre, starred with golden studs around:
Then sternly silent sat. With like disdain
The raging king returned his frowns again.

This will enable us to measure Pope's superiority to
his predecessors. What they did with more or less
success, he did excellently. Dryden was the only one of
them that could have stood the competition with him;
and Dryden was exposed to defeat by his own disdainful

security. Pope's lines are, indeed, a memorable comment
on what was urged in the early part of this essay about
the exactingness of his self-criticism. We feel that the
passage could not have been written at once—that his
first thoughts must have more nearly resembled those of
his competitors, and that it can have been only after
many reconsiderations that they assumed their present
form. I do not know what evidence would be furnished
by the famous MS. of Pope's 'Iliad' in the British Museum,
which I have never had the opportunity of consulting;
but the specimens of other passages quoted by Johnson
and by Disraeli the elder are enough to show what it
probably would be; and we must not forget that there
are such things as mental erasures, effacing first draughts,
which have never been written down.[1]

Perhaps there will be no more convenient place than
the present for speaking of the epic poem, which was the
project of Pope's latest years. He told Spence[2] that he
should certainly have written an epic poem if he had not
engaged in the translation of Homer, so that it is perhaps
to that cause that we owe the non-fulfilment of a dream
which actually took substance in his early boyhood, and
towards the end of his life was regarded as a thing half
accomplished already.[3] Yet, though it is no wonder that
he should have entertained a thought which had filled
Dryden's mind, it seems not unlikely that distrust of his
own genius might have prevented him, even in his hot

---

[1] 'One must tune each line over in one's head, to try whether they
go right or not.'—Pope, speaking of pastoral versification (Malone's Spence,
p. 72).

[2] Malone's Spence, pp. 34, 54.

[3] ("Though there is none of it writ as yet, what I look upon as more
than half the work is already done, for it is all exactly planned." . . . "It
would take up ten years?" "Oh, much less, I should think, as the matter
is already quite digested and prepared."'—Malone's Spence, p. 56.

youth, from executing a work for which English poetry
supplied no model within the reach of his imitation; while
we can scarcely doubt that his reading, multifarious, but
not profound, would not have stood in the place of
invention, and supplied him with the substance without
which an undertaking of that compass would have been
sure to collapse. Nor were the changes which took place
in his taste and feelings, as he receded from youth, such as
were likely to be favourable to epic inspiration. His
early aptitude for criticism and argumentative writing had
developed into an inclination for philosophical study and
didactic exposition.

'The idea that I have for an epic poem of late,' were his
words to Spence, 'turns wholly on civil and ecclesiastical
government. The hero is a prince, who establishes an empire;
that prince is our Brutus from Troy, and the scene of the
establishment, England. . . . . What was first designed for an
epistle on Education, as part of my essay-scheme, is now
inserted in my fourth "Dunciad;" as the subject for two other
epistles there (those on civil and ecclesiastical government)
will be treated more at large in my "Brutus."'

Possibly another poet, of profounder philosophic insight
and stronger imagination, might have accomplished the
task, even under this view of it, without investing the
heroic ideal with unseasonable modern associations; but
Pope was not likely to do so. The government introduced by Brutus was to have been the early English constitution; the religion, that Deism which Pope seems to
have embraced in his heart as the real truth which
underlay his hereditary Catholicism. 'Brutus is supposed to have travelled into Egypt, and there to have
learnt the Unity of the Deity and the other purer doctrines afterwards kept up in the Mysteries.' The prose
draught itself of the plan of 'Brutus,' which is given in

Ruffhead's 'Life,' and reprinted in Mr. Dyce's Memoir
prefixed to the Aldine edition, as it ought to be in all
biographies of the poet, is not very promising. Brutus
is a philanthropist, who thinks not merely of settling the
countrymen he has ransomed from slavery in an appropriate spot, but of planting pure manners in a virgin
soil; he argues against the avarice and effeminacy of his
less enlightened followers, who wish to settle in rich and
fertile districts, 'as incompatible' (I quote Ruffhead's
words) 'with his generous plan of extending be-
nevolence, by instructing and polishing uncultivated
minds.' His followers are alarmed by an Aurora
borealis; he admits that he is as ignorant of it as they,
but calms their terrors by the general reflection that
Heaven never works miracles but for the good; and
accordingly, when they are attacked by barbarians the
same night, the light proves serviceable for their defence.
He lands in Britain, partly for the purpose of confounding the credulity which represented our island as in-
habited by demons. He encounters giants who symbolise superstition, anarchy, and tyranny, and priests and
magicians, whose supposed supernatural powers resolve
themselves into the possession of natural secrets, such as
the use of gunpowder. Then there were the guardian
angels of kingdoms; and what proof had Pope shown of
his capability, as Dryden expresses it, of managing anything so ponderous? Nor were these somewhat naked
conceptions to have been clothed in the dress which
mantles so proudly round the 'Homer,' and fits so gracefully to the 'Essay on Man.' He had adopted blank
verse, as Johnson says, 'with great imprudence, and I
think without due consideration of the nature of our
language'—of that part of our language, at least, which
was understood and wielded by himself and his great

critic. Some lines with which he appears to have
enriched the description of 'the lovely young Lavinia'
in Thomson's 'Seasons' are graceful enough; but they
afford no proof that he had the real command of a
measure which he appears never to have practised, and
which appears in the eighteenth century to have been all
but a lost art. On every account there seems reason to
rejoice that Pope's epic never came to the birth. What
Lord Macaulay is in prose, that Pope was in poetry.
Each affords an exemplification of the truth of an acute
remark made by the former,[1] that 'the world generally
gives its admiration, not to the man who does what
nobody else even attempts to do, but to the man who does
best what multitudes do well.' Each has won, and justly
won, almost unbounded applause by a number of comparatively short pieces, where any defect in the matter
is neutralised by the transcendent skill of the manner.
Each has been led, and fortunately led, to concentrate
the full force of his genius in setting forth and adorning
a story which, though doubtless standing in need of
appreciation, repels the aid of invention. Had Lord
Macaulay's judgment been less sound, he might have
possibly been induced to expend the prodigal wealth of
his historical knowledge, his extraordinary narrative skill,
and the exuberance of his power of vivid illustration, on
an attempt to rival the creations of Sir Walter Scott.
It was Pope's happiness, when still meditating epic song,
to find himself condemned 'ten years to comment and
translate.' Dr. Henry, in his commentary on Virgil,[2]
aptly remarks on 'the resemblance between these professedly original poems, but really semi-translations of the
"Æneis"'[1] (such as Ronsard's 'Franciade,' of which he
happens to be speaking), 'and our modern professed

---

[1] *Essay on Addison.*   [2] *Classical Museum*, vol. vi. p. 39.

translations, but really semi-original poems.' Pope was, in fact, realising his own dream without knowing it, in a better way than if he had worked on his own plan. His greater epics are the English 'Iliad' and 'Odyssey,' as his lesser are the ' Rape of the Lock ' and the ' Dunciad.'

IX. *The 'Dunciad.'*

The 'Dunciad' is unquestionably a very great satire. As in so many of Pope's works, the conception may be found elsewhere, but the execution is pre-eminently his own. The empire of Dulness had been described by Dryden in ' Mac-Flecknoe,' but ' Mac-Flecknoe ' is to the ' Dunciad ' what a masterly sketch is to a finished painting. Satire had been conducted in heroic pomp through six cantos, by Garth, in his ' Dispensary ; ' but though there are good poetry and good sarcasm in the ' Dispensary,' they are not the poetry and the sarcasm of Pope. The same power which in the ' Rape of the Lock' was employed to give pleasure, is employed in the ' Dunciad ' to give pain. It is precisely because, as I have said, he was qualified to succeed in the heroic vein, not as an original inventor, but as a translator or close imitator, that he succeeds so admirably in the mock-heroic. His sympathy with epic grandeur is the sympathy of art, not of kindred inspiration ; he can catch the tone of the grand style, but he is never so identified with its spirit as to be unable to contemplate it *ab extra* ; he can see how it may be employed to burlesque the mean as well as to extol the lofty, nor is he in any danger of forgetting that the more than royal honours which he pays to his hero are paid only as a refinement of insult. There is a felicitous appropriateness, too, in the scope of his satire, at least as originally conceived. It is an involuntary

comment on one of Aristotle's definitions, which perhaps
has never received so strong a light from the best intentions of any commentator—that in which he erects the
absence of art into a kind of positive quality, and calls
it intellectual creation under the guidance of false reasoning. Just as Pope's own art was a power of which he
was able, in whole or in part, to explain the mystery,
admitting the public into the workshop, and displaying
the secrets of the machinery, so the blundering which
he chose to satirise was not simply capricious or inscrut-
ably abstruse, but had intelligible laws of its own—it
was, in fact, if we may so paraphrase Aristotle's word
ἀτεχνία, an art of no art. The treatise on the Bathos
had unfolded this method of going wrong in burlesque
prose ; the ' Dunciad ' was to exemplify it in burlesque
verse. The lines on false description, near the opening
of the First Book, are an admirable specimen of Pope's
power of illustrating absurdities, and show, moreover,
how much his hand had gained in strength and delicacy
since the ' Essay on Criticism ':—

> Here gay Description Egypt glads with showers,
> Or gives to Zembla fruits, to Barca flowers ;
> Glittering with ice, here hoary hills are seen,
> There, painted valleys of eternal green ;
> In cold December fragrant chaplets blow,
> And heavy harvests nod beneath the snow.

Yet we may be struck here with the same thing which I
noticed in speaking of ' Windsor Forest '—a tendency to
dwell on the mere obvious externals of description. He
takes no note of deeper offences against the truth of
nature, as he had shown no deep sense of that truth in
his own practice. Glittering hills and green valleys in
their right places are what he praises ; glittering hills

and green valleys in their wrong places are what he blames.

But, however strong the admiration with which we may regard the 'Dunciad,' heavy deductions remain to be made. Pope himself spoiled it, by the confession of all, when, to gratify the pitiful spleen of his latest years, he changed the hero from a dull plodding scribbler to a lively caterer for the popular taste; retaining, nevertheless, as he could hardly avoid retaining, most of the accessories of the original poem. Individual passages are made more brilliant—indeed, how could a fresh touch from Pope fail to communicate fresh brilliancy?—but the intellectual consistency of the poem, so far as it depends on its central figure, is gone. Nor was the previous addition of a Fourth Book—the 'New Dunciad,' as it was at first called—a happy thought. The arrow was aimed too high, and so, though, like that of Acestes in Virgil, it displayed the art of the veteran and his sounding bow, it struck no mark. The splendid passage which once contained its anticipation, and now forms its conclusion —that passage which Pope himself could not repeat without a faltering in the voice, which Johnson recited with a kindred emotion, and which, in Mr. Thackeray's judgment, shows the author to be the equal of all poets of all times—is, I venture to think, incommensurate with its subject. An artist may describe the corruption of art: to speak adequately of the great twilight of the gods, when truth and wisdom shall be vanquished by falsehood and ignorance, requires an understanding that can comprehend, an imagination that can grasp, the several branches of knowledge. The general part of the description is, perhaps, worthy of the theme. The mythological image of Medea blighting the stars is grand; the sacred image of Chaos uncreating the universe is

sublime. But the extinction of the individual lumin-
aries is not pursued with uniform success. Physic, Meta-
physic, and Mathematics perish as they might be expected to perish ; but the lines in which Faith and Philosophy decay are inadequate ; those in which Religion
and Morality expire, almost trivial. Great as were
Pope's peculiar powers, it was not for him to make his
intellect the standard of measurement for the generation
in which he lived. He had read widely, but to erect
himself into an arbiter of learning, and affect to discriminate true knowledge from false, was the mere insanity of presumption, as one memorable instance shows.
Bentley had wielded his Thor's hammer against an army
of puny assailants ; Pope hailed the defeated pigmies as
his brethren, and placed the conquering giant among the
dunces. Even in those cases where the poet was intellectually competent to award praise or censure, his
private enmities often made him grossly unjust. Several
of those who are held up to scorn as miserable poet-
asters, seem in reality to have been humbler fellow-
labourers with himself in the work of giving strength
and sweetness to English versification. Take, for instance, some of the lines which he has quoted in the
preface to the poem as tributes to his merit extorted
from his opponents. Lastly, where the intellectual de-
merits of the persons attacked appear to have been real,
it is but very seldom that our moral feelings can go
along with the inflictor of the chastisement. 'Its victims,' to borrow the words of Sir William Hamilton on
another occasion, ' are treated like vermin ; they are
hunted without law, and exterminated without mercy.'
They are lashed for their vices by one who, for his love
of filthy and revolting images, as shown in this very
poem, might well be called upon to strip his own back.

The Roman satirist could speak feelingly of the poverty
of his literary brethren, and lament the cruel ridicule
which attended it; the English humourist gibbets it as a
crime.   Such inhuman, unpitying animosity cannot be
justified, even on the plea of retaliation; and the plea of
retaliation, though elaborately urged, seems not to have
been always true.   *This* is not 'heroic courage speaking,
a splendid declaration of righteous wrath and war.'[1]   It
is rather an unblessed contest, undertaken in the spirit of
Persian tyranny against those who would not propitiate
the arrogance of one man, and waged partly with weapons
of the keenest edge and finest temper, but partly also
with noisome implements of offence, and inventions of
gratuitous barbarity.

X. *The Moral Epistles and ' Essay on Man.'*

The ambition of being a philosopher was a feeling not
unknown to the poets of Augustan Rome.   It would be
too much to say, with the 'learned and every way excellent ' person who gave Dryden a life of Virgil, that the
subject of his biography wrote poetry to get a fortune on
which to live as a philosophical student; but many
passages in Virgil's poems prove that he dabbled in
physical speculations, and lead us to receive with attention,
if not with implicit credence, the story that, after finally
polishing his ' Æneid,' he meant to devote the rest of his
life to science.   Propertius expressly holds out to himself
the prospect of retiring after a youth of pleasure into an
old age of study, to be passed in inquiring into the
changes of the moon, the origin of wind and rain, the
reason why the four seasons are no more than four, the

[1] I quote Mr. Thackeray, who seems, however, to be speaking only of the
conclusion of the poem.

probability of a final dissolution of the universe, and the
truth of the legends about Tartarus.   It is not probable
that Pope thought of either of these parallels ; but in his
case, as in theirs, the same causes seem to have produced
the same effects.   Further prosecution of knowledge had
led to a sharper division of the several sciences from each
other, so that Pope's speculative interests are not as wide
in their range as those of Propertius ; they appear, however, to have included ethics, political philosophy, natural
theology, and an inquiry into the limits of the human
intellect.   His ' Brutus,' as we have seen, was to have been
philosophical ; his ' Essay on Man,' like the ' Excursion,'
was but part of a cathedral that was never completed.   It
would have been better if he had taken pattern by the
Augustan poet whom he knew best and imitated most
successfully, confining his philosophy to practical observations on the conduct of life, and leaving more recondite inquiries without a sigh to any noble or reverend
Iccius whom he might number among his friends.   That
he should have occupied his mind with such thoughts at
times is not unnatural, and, in fact, highly commendable ;
that he should have digested them into verse is, on the
whole, to be regretted.   The former half of the first and
most ambitious of the ' Moral Essays ' consists of remarks
of no great depth, expressed in couplets such as those
which form the staple of the ' Essay on Criticism,' neatly
rather than felicitously worded.   The worldly observer,
who despises book-philosophy, is told that his tendency
may be pushed to an extreme, and apparently blamed as
if he were apt to overlook the fact that men not only
differ from each other, but are inconsistent with themselves —certainly not the error into which a sage of this
class might be expected to fall.   We are then instructed
that actions are no sure test of character, that the observer's

prejudices often vitiate his judgment, that passion often overpowers reason, and so action is determined by chance ; that some men are uniformly intelligible, others uniformly inscrutable, but that most completely baffle observation by their inconsistency, right actions sometimes arising from wrong feelings, and character being generally determined by education. The sum of all is, that there is nothing in which a man cannot change :—

> Manners with fortunes, humours turn with climes,
> Tenets with books, and principles with times.

But there is a way to educe Cosmos from this Chaos, and that is by finding out the ruling passion. This doctrine announced, Pope leaves an element for which he is not fitted, and passes into one which is all his own. He forgets his philosophy, does not prove his great principle, but takes it for granted, and proceeds to illustrate it with a series of brilliant and spirited sketches, known doubtless to every reader of poetry. As we see Dryden's 'Zimri' revived in the elaborate portrait of Wharton, and smile and wonder at the skill which tells so well, though so briefly, the anecdotes of Helluo, Narcissa, the courtier, and Euclio, we are willing to forget that the epistle consists of anything else but such triumphs of dexterity as these. The remaining three essays are, happily, not constructed on so philosophical a basis. Pope's opinion of women must have been contemptuous indeed, if he thought he had given a really exhaustive analysis of the female character in the 'Epistle to Martha Blount ;' but, taken as a jest, his theory may pass, and its lightness is redeemed by the heavier metal of the lines on Atossa, and the four or five concluding paragraphs, some of the most delicate, wise, and feeling verses that Pope ever wrote, where he specially addresses the lady of his love. It is

the same with the third epistle, on the ' Use of Riches,'
which Pope told Spence he had laboured as much as any
of his works.   To dilate on the extremes of avarice and
prodigality requires a rhetorician rather than a philosopher; to exhibit them in the concrete is work for a
humourist rather than for a dramatist.   The humour of
conceiving bribery to be carried on without a circulating
medium perhaps wears out when protracted through
seven illustrations ; nor is there much to console or edify
in the thought that hoarding and squandering are as much
parts of the general balance of the universe as drought
and rain, or the ebb and flow of the sea.   But though
the truths which the pictures embody are not of the pro-
foundest, the pictures themselves will not be willingly let
die while the language lives—the Villiers, the Cutler, the
Sir Balaam, and even the less delicate and more obvious
delineation of the Man of Ross.   Taste is a subject more
congenial to an artist than the doctrines of morality, and
accordingly, if there is not more to admire in the fourth
epistle than in the rest, there is less to question.   If it is
a subject that has its limits, it must be owned that within
those limits justice has been done to it.   Whether Timon's
mansion was intended for Canons, is a question unhappily
of serious significance to the author's character ; but it
does not affect our sense of the variety, vividness, and
energy of his poetry.

If we must trust a letter from Bolingbroke to Swift,
the task of writing the ' Essay on Man ' was not only not
sought spontaneously by Pope, but, when urged upon
him, accepted with considerable reluctance.   The applause
with which the poem was received may have led him to
think that his genius had been more truly estimated by his
friend than by himself, and to entertain those further
projects for the union of philosophy with poetry at which I

have already glanced; but his natural instinct seems to
have told him that he was unqualified for the undertaking.
Brilliant in many respects as the result of the experiment
has been, I cannot but think that his hesitation was right,
and his compliance ill-judged. Bolingbroke was of opinion
that the subject was one on which he and Pope might
advantageously labour side by side, pursuing the same end
by different means. 'The business of the philosopher,'
he writes, 'is to dilate, if I may borrow this word from
Tully, to press, to prove, to convince; and that of the
poet to hint, to touch his subject with short and spirited
strokes, to warm the affections, and to speak to the heart.'
These words, though apparently just, are somewhat
vague; but we may, I presume, interpret them in the
light of the approbation which he gave to Pope's poem
when written. Can it be said, however, that the 'Essay
on Man' is really what Bolingbroke seems to have wished
it to be?—that it brings out the poetical or imaginative
aspect of the subject, and discards the philosophical or
argumentative? The work is cast into a form nearly
resembling that of a prose treatise of the more rhetorical
sort; appeals to the imagination and the feelings are
introduced not sparingly; but the staple of the poem is
argument, or what is intended to be such. Not far from
the beginning we meet these lines:—

> Of systems possible, if 'tis confessed
> That wisdom infinite must form the best,
> Where all must full, or not coherent be,
> And all that rises, rise in due degree;
> Then in the scale of reasoning life, 'tis plain,
> There must be, somewhere, such a rank as man;
> And all the question (wrangle e'er so long)
> Is only this—if God has placed him wrong?

Johnson has shown that this passage is not good philosophy; it remains to ask, Is it good poetry? What is there in the language or the thought which gains from the metrical form into which they are thrown? The lines are somewhat bold, and the expression is far from clear. Pope did not generally condescend to the artificial inversion which places the adjective after the substantive. Here, in a passage where simplicity was an object, we have 'systems possible' followed by 'wisdom infinite'—combinations, too, which have the effect of producing a disagreeable monotony, occurring in the same part of the lines to which they respectively belong. Nor is it easy to collect from the mere words of the third line that Pope meant, as Warburton expresses it in his prose, 'that the best system cannot but be such a one as hath no inconnected void, such a one in which there is a perfect coherence and gradual subordination in the parts.' It would not be difficult to point out other passages which are not poetry, but simply argument in metre. Pope says himself, in the 'Design' prefixed to the poem :—

I chose verse, and even rhyme, for two reasons. The one will appear obvious—that principles, maxims, or precepts so written both strike the reader more strongly at first, and are more easily retained by him afterwards; the other may seem odd, but it is true. I found I could express them more shortly this way than in prose itself; and nothing is more certain than that much of the force as well as grace of arguments or instructions depends on their conciseness.

In other words, he chose metre, not from any consideration of the fitness of the subject for poetry, but partly for his reader's convenience, partly for his own : he knew how much he could pack into a single line or couplet, and he knew that verse is useful as a *memoria technica*. And yet, with all this, he has not produced, I do not say a philosophical, but a strictly argumentative work. We are not carried on regularly from stage to stage of the discussion as we should be carried on by any prose treatise of merit, or as we are carried on by the powerful flow of versified reasoning, the combined logic and rhetoric of the 'Religio Laici.' We stop to admire the neatness and terseness of particular lines, the vivid and harmonious language of particular paragraphs; but we do not at once see the connexion of thought, though we are every now and then reminded that we have been making progress, and are expected to admit some new point on the strength of what has gone before. In fact, the sentences which I quoted just now from Pope's preface contain an involuntary confession. He busies himself chiefly with 'principles, precepts, or maxims,' not with consecutive reasoning. The effect on the reader is what might be anticipated. A multitude of isolated lines have imprinted themselves on the public memory, and form part of the public stock of quotation. But it may be doubted whether, of the thousands that have read the poem, there is one who could sit down without consulting it afresh, and give anything like a connected sketch of the argument.

It is a great mistake to imagine that thoughts which can be expressed with force and beauty in prose can be expressed with greater force and greater beauty in verse. On the contrary, it will often happen that a very perceptible loss is occasioned by the transference. Something will probably be omitted, either from the mechanical difficulty of bringing it into metrical shape, or from deference to the dignity of poetry, and thus there will be a loss of perspicuity. Even where a conception has been safely transferred, it is likely to have sustained a further loss—a loss of propriety. The dignity of poetry may have been consulted, even to the sacrifice of clearness of expression,- but it will probably not have been wholly propitiated.

The conception, as it would be naturally worked out in prose, will doubtless present various features, some of a more, others of a less elevated character. The former may perhaps be improved by the embellishment of verse; the latter will certainly be injured. Prose is, in fact, the more plastic material of the two—capable of being better accommodated to the various gradations of thought and feeling. As an instance of what I mean, I will take leave to transcribe a fine passage from Shaftesbury, quoted in one of Warton's notes on the 'Essay on Man':—

Imagine only some person entirely a stranger to navigation, and ignorant of the nature of the sea or waters, how great his astonishment would be when, finding himself on board some vessel anchoring at sea, remote from all land prospect, whilst it was yet a calm, he viewed the ponderous machine firm and motionless in the midst of the smooth ocean, and considered its foundations beneath, together with its cordage, mast, and sails above! How easily would he see the whole one regular structure, all things depending on one another, the uses of the rooms below, the lodgments, and the conveniences of men and stores! But being ignorant of the intent, or of all above, would he pronounce the masts and cordage to be useless and cumbersome, and for this reason condemn the frame and despise the architect? O my friend! let us not thus betray our ignorance, but consider where we are, and in what universe. Think of the many parts of the vast machine, in which we have so little insight, and of which it is impossible we should know the ends and uses, when, instead of seeing to the highest pendant, we see only some lower deck, and are in this dark case of flesh confined even to the hold and meanest station of the vessel.

Warton justly remarks that this is a noble and poetical illustration of many passages in Pope's essay. It seems to me that it is nobler and more poetical in its present form than it would be if turned, even as Pope would have turned it, into verse. The description contained in the first sentence would not have really gained much from

being associated with a more measured cadence, a more
regular recurrence of sounds.   It would then have provoked comparison with other passages more truly imaginative; as it is, we have the feeling of poetry without the
pretension.   The second sentence would certainly have
suffered.   We might have retained the cordage, mast, and
sails: we should inevitably have had to part with the
uses of the rooms below, the lodgments, and the conveniences of men and stores, which would either have been
slurred over in some general expression or exaggerated
into something unseasonably picturesque.   So on through
the rest of the passage: in return for a slight increase of
beauty in one or two of the parts, we should have sacrificed the propriety of the whole.   Even if the thoughts
and language were preserved nearly intact, the uniform
elevation of the metre would be a misfortune.   It would
be raising the lower parts on stilts, in order to bring them
to a level with the higher.   Yet this imaginary case is
precisely what we see realised in the ' Essay on Man,' with
all the adroit cleverness of its ordinary manner, all the
sonorous grandeur of its occasional bursts of eloquence.
Johnson says of the blank-verse poem of one of the
subjects of his biographies, that he wishes it well enough
to wish it were in rhyme.   A well-wisher to Pope's essay
would, I think, wish it were in prose.   Perhaps one
who has felt the power of Plato, and read the ' Essay
on Epitaphs,' might be tempted to wish the same for the
' Excursion.'

XI. *The Imitations of Horace, &c.*

Pope's predilection for ethical poetry grew on him, as
I have said, in his later life.   In his last illness he compared himself to Socrates, dispensing his morality among
his friends just as he was dying.   His last compositions,

however, were rather satiric than strictly ethical. But
satire and ethics had come to be associated in his mind as
two aspects of the same thing. Even the ferocity of the
' Dunciad ' he wished to be regarded as virtuous indignation, the natural feeling of one whose life was a ' more
endearing song' than his poetry, against scribblers, who
had not only wounded his taste by their dulness and his
just self-love by their unprovoked libels, but outraged his
moral sense by the scandalousness of their lives. On the
other hand, the exordium of the ' Essay on Man,' with
its sporting metaphors of ' shooting folly as it flies,' and
' catching the manners living as they rise,' and its proposal
' to laugh where we must,' and ' be candid where we can,'
promises us satire as well as ethics. Again, in the ' New
Dunciad,' the last substantive work which he seems to
have written, he uses up materials which had been
intended to appear in a new series of ' Moral Epistles.'
His ' Imitations of Horace,' of which it now remains to
speak, extend over several years, a period partially coin-
ciding with that during which the works mentioned in
the preceding section were composed or published. Like
the ' Essay on Man,' they were suggested to him by
Bolingbroke, and the suggestion was this time an eminently fortunate one. The thought of pointing an ancient
satire with modern applications had occurred to others.
Rochester had made Dryden the hero of an experiment
of this sort; Dryden, while stigmatizing[1] those who, as
he says, persecute Horace ' by their ignorant and vile
imitations of him, by making an unjust use of his authority and turning his artillery against his friends,' himself
went a step further, introducing his enemy Shadwell into
what professed to be a translation of ' Juvenal ; ' and his
own name, along with that of Roscommon, takes the

---

[1] Preface to All for Love.

place of Orpheus in a version of the Eighth Eclogue by
his ally Dr. Chetwood.[1]   But Pope's imitations, it is needless to say, are so excellent of their kind as to obscure all
previous attempts, and constitute, as it were, a class by
themselves.   As in the translation of Homer, he has the
advantage of being able to superadd his own terseness and
brilliancy to Horace's sense, while he can afford to allow
himself more freedom, and keep with safety at a greater
distance from an original whose genius and literary position
were in many respects nearly akin to his own.   Johnson,
perhaps, thinking of his own 'Juvenal,' and writing in one
of those gloomy fits of self-depreciation of which we have
a specimen in the opening of the celebrated preface to
the 'English Dictionary,' observes that 'such imitations' as
Pope's 'cannot give pleasure to common readers: the
man of learning may be sometimes surprised and delighted
by an unexpected parallel; but the comparison requires
knowledge of the original, which will likewise often detect
strained applications.'   Yet I am mistaken if a common
reader may not enjoy these imitations nearly as much as
any of Pope's more original satires—if they have not, in
fact, yielded nearly as large a percentage of familiar quotations; while those who read Horace certainly have the
additional pleasure of seeing how dexterously the English
poet pursues the track of the Latin, now striking out a
happy translation, now an unexpected analogy, sometimes
deviating from the way, but never losing it.   We have
none of those elaborate characters in the delineation of
which Pope shone so much; but there is the same power
of touching contemporary events gracefully, the same nod
of easy recognition for a passing friend, the same transient
flush as an opponent crosses his path, while the texture of
the whole poem is generally stronger than what Pope

---

[1] Published in vol. I. of the *Miscellany*.

cares to employ in his own occasional pieces. They are
like a felicitous quotation, which is often worth more than
an independent *bon mot*, having all its own wit and
wisdom, and all the associations of the original passage
besides. The one point in which Pope differs most
markedly from Horace is his versification. It has been
said [1] that the Roman poet wilfully untuned his harp
when he commenced satirist; Pope, without attempting
to import into satire the sonorous cadence of the epic,
polishes and points the lines which are to reproduce
Horace as scrupulously as those which are to render
Homer. It is what Roman satire would have been had it
accepted the regulating mechanism of the elegiac couplet—
an epigram, as one of the writers in the Greek anthology
expresses it, prolonged into a rhapsody. Each form has
its advantage for what is, in fact, an embodiment of
sparkling social talk, witty and wise—the loose fireside
robe as well as the trim evening dress—and we need not
adjust their claims to preference.

The 'Epistle to Arbuthnot,' which comes under notice
here from having been finally made the Prologue of the
'Satires,' is justly characterised by Johnson as 'a performance consisting of many fragments wrought into one
design, which, by this union of scattered beauties, contains
more striking paragraphs than could probably have been
brought together into an occasional work.' This plan of
utilizing pieces formerly written was a favourite one with
Pope, and throws some light on his theory of composition,
accounting for the want of connexion which I have noticed
in the 'Essay on Man,' and for what, I think, may be
observed in some of his other poems, the superiority of
parts to the whole. Thus in the Prologue there are plain

---

[1] The expression is quoted by Scott—*Life of Dryden*, p. 230 (ed. 1834)
—but I do not know where it is to be met with.

marks of joining—signs that the poem was written up to some of the fine passages which form its glory. It would read, for instance, equally well as a whole if the unrivalled character of Atticus were omitted. We can see indeed that the name of Addison in the previous line was intended to prepare us for it; still, it breaks in some measure the continuity of the satire, which had been treating of scribblers before, and (not very consistently with the emphatic ' Peace to all such !') goes on to treat of them afterwards. It is easy to see, too, that though the mention of the supposed injury done by Addison to Pope naturally forms a part of this apologetic autobiography, it would have been differently and more clearly indicated if Pope had not had the portrait already finished and lying by him, and had not felt, justly enough, that such brilliant and vigorous drawing might be spoilt by any touch which could be regarded as an alteration. The picture of Bufo has every appearance of being a separate sketch of the same kind. It has no real relation to the context, as Pope does not speak of himself as aggrieved by Bufo, but only affects to contrast him with himself; while the fact that Pope had some kind of grudge against Halifax only makes it less likely that the grudge should not have been hinted at if these lines had been actually written for the occasion. I may add, too, that this view of their insertion will meet the objections to identifying Bufo with Halifax which have been found in the fact that Halifax had been dead nineteen years when the satire was published, and in the honourable mention which Halifax receives in the Epilogue to the ' Satires' four years later. The lines on Bufo, like the lines on Atticus, were doubtless in the poet's desk; the feeling which prompted the one, like that which prompted the other, had doubtless cooled to a great extent, but the lines themselves were not to be lost ;

while after their publication the satirist was at liberty to
say a good word for Halifax, as he has said a good word
for Addison. But whatever skill has been shown in the
framing or hanging of the pictures, this Prologue or
Epistle must be always regarded as a splendid gallery;
though we may question whether the likenesses are not
idealised throughout, by self-flattery where he talks of his
own life, as by animosity where his subject is Atticus,
Bufo, or Sporus. The Epilogue is not equal to the
Prologue. The satire is transient, not concentrated; and
the grand passage about the triumph of Vice— ' perhaps
the noblest,' according to Warton, ' in all his works,
without any exception whatever'—is, I think, one of those
where Pope does not rise to the full height of his subject.
An allegorical picture might doubtless be founded on the
hints there given; but the attitude of most of the figures,
and the expression of their features, would have to be
the painter's own; and the conception which is most carefully elaborated, that of England's genius dragged at the
chariot-wheels of the victorious power of evil, would be
but too susceptible of a commonplace rendering.

But it is time to conclude a task which it is perhaps
presumptuous to have undertaken. I should be glad to
think that what has been here attempted insufficiently
would be adequately performed by some other writer.
Pope's poetry has hardly received yet the careful critical
examination which it deserves. The last century, indeed,
can boast of Johnson's masterly critique, and the more
elaborate, though less penetrating, survey by Warton.
But I am not aware of anything in our own day which
meets the requirements of the subject. At one time it
was made a battle-field for rival poets—Bowles, Campbell,
and Byron—to fight out their contending theories; but
no poet has done for Pope what Scott has done for

Dryden, producing a biography which is a real contribution to the history of English poetry.   Parts of his works have been examined effectively by Professor Wilson and Mr. de Quincey; but there is no single judgment of his various writings worthy of being named with those articles on Dryden with which the 'Edinburgh Review' has been successively enriched by two of its most distinguished contributors.[1]   But the union of great knowledge of literary history with great power of poetical criticism is rare; where those qualities exist together there are other fields to invite them; and it is possible that we may have to wait some time before our literature receives the desired accession.

[1] Vols. xiii. and xlvii.   There are some valuable remarks in a third article on Dryden in the volume for 1855.   The article on Pope, in vol. xxxii. of the *Quarterly Review*, contains some just criticism.

LECTURE ON 'KING LEAR.'[1]

In proposing to speak of one of the greatest works of
England's greatest poet, I have chosen a subject which
cannot have much recommendation on the ground of
novelty.   Where, however, there is so much power and
beauty, there is sure to be novelty enough.   We can never
be certain that we apprehend that power and beauty fully
—rather, we may be certain that we never can fully apprehend them ; and so, regarding our wealth as inexhaustible, we may well expect that each successive visit to
the treasure-house will only enable us to carry away more.

Most of us know the story of King Lear too well to
need being reminded of it at any great length.   We know
how the king, feeling old age increase upon him, resolves
to disburden himself of his royalty, and share his kingdom
among his three daughters—how the two elder, in return
for their large professions of love, receive their portions,
while the third, not caring to vie with them in lip-service,
is excluded from her inheritance—how the king finds his
elder daughters grudge him the entertainment they had
promised him at their courts—how he expostulates till impatience turns to madness, and he breaks away, a houseless
wanderer, seeking refuge, as it were, in the storm without
from the storm within—how his discarded daughter levies
an army to reinstate her father in his kingdom—how she
is vanquished and put to death in spite of those who

---

[1] This Lecture was delivered at the Boston Athenæum, the Oxford
Working Men's Association, and the Woodstock Night Schools in 1857 and
1858.   In printing this and the following Lecture the Editor has made but
few verbal alterations.

would have saved her—and how the worn-out thread of
his life is snapped by the shock, and he dies upon her
body. We are acquainted, too, with the by-plot, if such a
name can properly be given to what is really an integral
part of that grand complex unity—the second story of filial
ingratitude and filial love, of the base-born son who sup-
plants his brother and his father, and the lawful son who,
himself an outcast, attends on the father who had wronged
him, as he wanders helpless and blind. After this preliminary recapitulation we may proceed to the play
itself, which I shall attempt to recall to recollection by
the quotation of the more striking passages.

In the opening of the play we have a conversation
between two noblemen, the Earl of Kent and the Earl of
Gloster, on the partition of the kingdom, which has
been already announced, though not formally carried into
effect. So far the dialogue would seem to be merely a
simple and natural introduction to the play, in which no
more is meant than meets the eye. But this is not all.
Gloster has with him his base-born son, Edmund, and
the conversation happens to turn on him, when it is conducted, on the part of the father at least, in a vein of levity
which passes into grossness. Readers of Shakspeare
will be apt to conclude that this is no more than the ordinary manner of speaking, such as is unhappily only too
common in the works of the poet and his contemporaries.
But I believe that in this case at least Shakspeare meant
much more. Gloster has a terrible future in store for him,
and that future is to be brought about through the instrumentality of that very son of whose birth he now speaks
so lightly. When we see him the sufferer in a scene
which for its combination of physical and moral horror is
probably unmatched in any of Shakspeare's undisputed
works, the victim of a fate which, however softened and
alleviated, renders life henceforth a blank and a desola-

tion, we feel indeed the deepest pity; but we cannot help recurring in thought to the original fault which in the order of Providence has been destined so to avenge itself. This is no mere imaginary connection of sin and suffering: it is what Shakspeare himself intended us to observe. When Edmund is dying, in the Fifth Act, Edgar speaks to him of their father:—

> The gods are just, and of our pleasant vices
> Make instruments to plague us.
> The dark and vicious place where thee he got
> Cost him his eyes.

With this connection before us, we cannot doubt that there is a real significance in the lightness with which Gloster in this first scene is made to speak of the sin of his youth. It shows us that he has yet to be taught by suffering; it projects, as it were, the dark shadow of the event. Further, it affords a glimpse of the kind of influences that have been allowed to work on Edmund's own mind. He is the child of a shame which he knows is thought no shame; and so it is scarcely more than natural that he should plot against a brother to whom he deems himself unjustly postponed, and even against a father who, though he ought to have inspired love, can hardly have established a claim to respect. Thus in the compass of a short and seemingly slight dialogue, we are already made acquainted with one of the chief agencies which is to bring about the catastrophe.

The force of the scene of the giving away of the kingdom is patent to everybody. In saying that Lear resigns his power to those who love him not, and excludes her who alone truly loves him, we have in effect said all. The error and injustice have been committed once for all, and the object of the rest of the play is simply to bring their punishment. I will only touch on one or two things which seem to call for notice. How is it that the king, having arranged, as we know from the previous dialogue, not only the partition itself, but its actual details, now makes it conditional on the warmth of his daughters' professions of love? The answer is to be found, as a great modern critic has seen, in that complexity of character which makes the Lear of Shakspeare what he is to us. He has already taken the resolution on more ordinary grounds, considerations of state policy and regard to his own infirmities; but he has a nature of feminine susceptibility, craving for sympathy and affection, and apt to estimate their reality by their signs, and so in performing an act which is recommended by other reasons, he will indemnify himself for any sacrifice that it may cost him by anticipating the love and gratitude of those who are to profit by it. Probably there is no way in which this complication of motives could have been better expressed than by making this trial of his daughters' affections a kind of afterthought—his 'darker purpose,' as he himself seems to call it—a species of ulterior kingcraft, in his estimation, though in reality it is only the exacting fondness of the father interfering in the king's province. A second point to observe upon is the conduct of Cordelia, which may perhaps appear to some here, as I confess it has at times appeared to myself, to carry sincerity to the very border of perverseness. Why should not she have given her feeling its full and true expression, instead of extenuating it and making it appear to her father's distorted apprehension the very opposite of what she knew it to be? Possibly, if she could have had a knowledge of the future, of her father's misery, her ineffectual attempt to reinstate him, and her own death, dragging his along with it, it might have been her duty to use more conciliatory

language; but it would be hard to say that she ought to
have been influenced by the mere prospect of his immediate displeasure falling on herself. She felt his test to be
an utterly bad one; the answers which it drew forth from
her sisters showed it to be so; and it must have seemed
incumbent on her to repudiate it as firmly, though as
modestly, as she could. Their large assurances compelled
her, as it were, to bring down her own language to the
lowest point consistent with truth. Regan had expressly
adopted and endorsed Goneril's professions, with the addition of a fresh hyperbole; it remained for Cordelia to
separate herself as far as possible from both. She knew
that she should be misunderstood for the moment; but
she trusted that, in her own words, 'time would unfold
what plighted cunning hides.'

And now the award is over: Kent is banished, Lear
and his train have withdrawn, and Cordelia has taken
leave of her sisters and followed her royal consort.
Goneril and Regan remain, to say a few words to each
other on what has passed. It is worth while attending to
what they say. There is no exultation in their own good
fortune, no triumphing in their sister's disgrace, though
from their answer to her farewell, it is clear that they have
no sympathy with her. All their feeling is concentrated
in a care for self-preservation. They have been greatly
struck with this new instance of their father's uncertainty
of temper, and their sole thought is that if they do not
take measures in time, and act in concert with each other,
they may themselves be the next to suffer from it. It is
evident that the fear they express is really felt by them,
not only from the tenor of their language here, but from
other parts of the play. Goneril towards the end of the
Act expresses her apprehension that the size of her father's
train will enable him to hold her life and her husband's at

the mercy of a momentary caprice.   In the next Act,
when he has flung himself out of Gloster's castle, Regan
is anxious that the gates should be shut upon him, for fear
of any desperate attempt which his followers may make
in his behalf.   We may notice, too, that their language
has a show of justice; in fact, it is the natural language
for them to hold, from their point of view.   They simply
drop out of sight all consideration of love for their father,
and think merely of the annoyance and danger which his
infirmities may cause.   The fruits of this temper are indeed monstrous; but the temper itself is easily conceivable, perhaps not unusual.   It is only selfish coldness,
reasoning accurately from its premises—the inexorable
logic of a heart without love.

The next scene shows us Edmund's successful attempt
to abuse his father's ear and supplant his lawful brother.
I have already spoken of the feelings with which he views
his own illegitimacy; so I need merely point out the art
with which his plot is framed.   Gloster has come from
Lear's trial of his daughters astonished at the king's weakness in surrendering his power so easily; Edmund takes
advantage of the jealousy thus aroused, and makes him
fancy that his own rights as a father are threatened similarly, not by his own credulity, but by treachery from
without:—'I have heard him oft maintain it to be fit that,
sons at perfect age, and fathers declined, the father should
be as ward to the son, and the son manage his revenue.'
And so the old man at once swallows the bait and puts
the two things together:—'This villain of mine comes
under the prediction: there's son against father; the king
falls from bias of nature; there's father against child.'
He has had eyes to see Lear's infatuation, and for that
very reason he is blinded to his own.

The remaining scenes of this Act, in which the king

finally breaks with Goneril, may be taken together.
Here, again, there is doubtless reason in her complaints:
the enormity is that she should not have that natural
affection which would cast all such reasons out of sight :—

> By day and night he wrongs me : every hour
> He flashes into one gross crime or other
> That sets us all at odds : I'll not endure it :
> His knights grow riotous, and himself upbraids us
> On every trifle.

And so she resolves that this shall go on no longer, and
orders her servants to be disrespectful to him, that matters
may come to a crisis—an intelligible course enough, if
she owed him no duty, or if a child's forbearance, carried
beyond a certain point, passed into weak subserviency.
The crisis is brought about by the arrival of Kent,
who has disguised himself in order that he may enter his
old master's service, and at once resents the insolence
of Goneril's menials. And now comes the explosion.
Goneril enters, high in anger, and takes her father to
task about the misconduct of his followers, in stately,
measured language—intimating, moreover, that he con-
nives at the evil, and that he must expect to be made
responsible for it. Lear is so astounded at this reversal,
as he considers it, of their mutual relations that he can
scarcely bring his senses to credit it :—' Are you our
daughter? . . Does any here know me? This is not
Lear: Does Lear walk thus? speak thus? Where are
his eyes? Either his notion weakens, his discernings are
lethargied. Ha! waking? 'tis not so. Who is it that
can tell me who I am? . . Your name, fair gentle-
woman?' This, she tells him, is merely of a piece with
the rest of his strange conduct; he had better be advised
' by her that else will take the thing she begs,' and reduce
his retinue. Stung to madness, he calls his attendants,

and gives instant orders for their journey; he will not remain in her court a moment longer. Albany enters; Lear turns on him, but will not hear or give an explanation: tossed on the waves of his own passion, he vindicates the honour of his followers, parallels Goneril's ingratitude with Cordelia's, and at last bursts out into that terrific prayer, which, though it is doubtless known to many of you, I must quote nevertheless :—

> Hear, nature, hear! dear goddess, hear!
> Suspend thy purpose, if thou did'st intend
> To make this creature fruitful!
> Into her womb convey sterility!
> Dry up in her the organs of increase;
> And from her derogate body never spring
> A babe to honour her! If she must teem,
> Create her child of spleen; that it may live,
> And be a thwart dismatur'd torment to her!
> Let it stamp wrinkles in her brow of youth;
> With cadent tears fret channels in her cheeks;
> Turn all her mother's pains and benefits
> To laughter and contempt; that she may feel
> How sharper than a serpent's tooth it is
> To have a thankless child!—Away, away!

And so he sweeps away; half maddened by this new wrong, but clinging to the assurance that he will find in Regan's love a compensation for what he has suffered from his other two daughters. Goneril remains with her husband, who questions her part in the breach, but is for the time induced to acquiesce.

One word I must say about the fool, who is introduced in these scenes for the first time. There can be no doubt that he is a specimen, though somewhat idealised, of those strange compounds of lightheadedness and shrewdness whom it was the fancy of the great men of Shakspeare's time to encourage and cultivate. But he is not brought

into the play merely as a comic element, a concession to
those of the audience who might not have a relish for
deep tragedy. He does, indeed, in some way relieve the
feeling which the tragedy excites; but he also deepens it.
Our sympathies cling round Lear: we cannot separate
ourselves from him; yet we know him to be the victim
of a miserable delusion. But there is one person from
whom he can bear to hear the truth; and it is in keeping
with the utter derangement of men and things about him
that that one person should be the fool. Since Cordelia
went to France the fool has much pined away, and Lear
has noted it well. The spectator or reader feels that the
fool is the interpreter of his own thoughts—all the truer,
perhaps, because the mode of interpretation is so
fantastic.

The Second Act destroys Lear's last remaining hope, the
affection of Regan. She and her husband, Cornwall, have
left their palace and come to Gloster's castle—partly, perhaps, to avoid a visit from the king; partly, it would seem,
to confer with Gloster on business of various kinds. This
precipitates Edmund's intention, and he proceeds at once
to accomplish his treacherous purpose against his brother,
who is made to fly, while the old earl, their father, causes
a price to be set on his head. Lear and Goneril have
both sent messengers to Regan; his being Kent, hers the
very servant whose insolence Kent had resented: and on
their arrival at the same time at Gloster's castle, Kent
immediately renews the quarrel. The appearance of the
duke and his party does not pacify him, and at last he
provokes them to order him to be set in the stocks,
Regan especially showing her anger, and accepting his
conduct as a confirmation of her sister's version of the
breach with their father. At this juncture Lear arrives,
and his indignation at finding his servant maltreated

swells into a tempest when he hears that Cornwall and
Regan refuse to see him.   Cornwall and Regan appear,
and the old man's rage melts into tenderness as he sees
her who is now, in his eyes, the only one that loves him
as a daughter.   Whether Regan was originally dearer to
him than Goneril, we cannot tell; at any rate, we find
that while he never attempts to conciliate the elder, to
the younger he is at first all fondness and forbearance.
Perhaps we may say that though Goneril's demeanour
has rendered the breach irreparable, he feels that he may
have been too hasty, and is resolved not to err a second
time in that extreme.   Kent's disgrace he passes by: his
one thought is to tell Regan of his wrongs, to crave her
sympathy, and to assure himself of her affection. Fortified
against all appeals to tenderness, she answers coldly,
vindicating her sister, and, like her, reminding him of his
infirmities; but though he cannot follow her counsel, he
receives it with gentleness, and will not be convinced
that she really means to be so cruel.   The entrance of
Goneril revives in him the passionate sense of wrong;
but though he will hold no terms with her, he still remonstrates and reasons temperately with Regan, till at
last the long-suppressed emotion forces its way to the
surface, and all self-control is at an end :—

> O, reason not the need; our basest beggars
> Are in the poorest thing superfluous;
> Allow not nature more than nature needs;
> Man's life is cheap as beast's: thou art a lady;
> If only to go warm were gorgeous,
> Why, nature needs not what thou gorgeous wear'st,
> Which scarcely keeps thee warm.   But, for true need—
> You heavens, give me that patience, patience I need!
> You see me here, you gods, a poor old man,
> As full of grief as age; wretched in both!
> If it be you that stir these daughters' hearts

Against their father, fool me not so much
To bear it tamely; touch me with noble anger,
And let not women's weapons, water-drops,
Stain my man's cheeks! No, you unnatural hags,
I will have such revenges on you both,
That all the world shall—I will do such things—
What they are, yet I know not; but they shall be
The terrors of the earth. You think I'll weep;
No, I'll not weep:
I have full cause of weeping; but this heart
Shall break into a hundred thousand flaws
Before I'll weep.—Oh, fool, I shall go mad!

After he is gone, we have a few words from Regan,
Goneril, and Cornwall, the last of whom, unlike Albany,
agrees with the course which his wife has thought proper
to adopt. Without formally justifying themselves, they
show us that they feel no compunction. They have made
the old man a reasonable offer: he has refused it, and
must take the consequences which the storm, already
heard at a distance, threatens to travellers journeying on
such a night without shelter.

Everyone who knows even the name of Lear knows
him as he is seen at the opening of the Third Act, contending bare-headed with that fearful storm. We are
prepared for his appearance by a conversation held by a
gentleman of his retinue with Kent, which also serves the
purpose of advancing our knowledge of the plot, telling
us, what in part we knew already, that Kent has communications with Cordelia, that she is informed of her
father's wrongs, and that an army is expected from France
to avenge and restore him. And then the scene changes
to another part of the heath, and, as the stage direction
informs us, the storm continues. Then it is that we see
how weak is the most powerful narration of an action as
compared with the action itself—that action which is

indeed the very essence, as it is involved in the very name, of the drama. The speech of the gentleman to which I have just adverted would rank as one of the finer speeches in the play; yet how inadequate is the notion that it gives us of the tremendous depth and intensity of the scene which succeeds it! We learn, indeed, that the king is 'contending with the fretful elements,' 'bidding the wind blow the earth into the sea,' 'tearing his white hair,' and 'striving in his little world of man to outscorn the to-and-fro-conflicting wind and rain.' But what is this to the marvellous reality—to the surging tumult of Lear's emotions, as he braves, invokes, or pleads with the storm—now half exulting in the elemental war, as if it were a second deluge sent down to avenge the sin of human ingratitude, and offering his own white head to the stroke which he trusts is to annihilate the whole race of mankind—now exclaiming against the elements as accomplices in his misery, less criminal than his human tormentors, and yet guilty in that they have lent themselves to aid in the work of cruelty—and now, again, passing from the thought of indiscriminate vengeance to that of discriminating justice, and bidding the sinners of the earth tremble at the expectation of the impending doom, which he can contemplate calmly, as being a man more sinned against than sinning? I feel that I am myself weakening the effect of the scene sadly: it is indeed one which had better be read than criticised or characterised; but it would be too long to quote, and no quotation would be complete which did not include the wild accompaniment of the fool, with its bursts of grotesque pathos, and its snatches of stinging satire. It is one of the most touching circumstances in Lear's extremity that he is not so wholly absorbed in the maddening thought of his own wrongs, nor so completely

carried away by his half-savage sympathy with the storm
as a judgment on collective humanity, but that he can
feel for the sufferings of others in that dreadful night—for
the fool, his one inseparable companion—for the unknown
and nameless poor, once his subjects, the thought of whom
reminds him of his past shortcomings as a king, and for
the mad beggar who has taken possession of the hovel in
which he is himself obliged to seek shelter. Thus, when
Kent first mentions the hovel to him, he turns to the fool:—

> Come on, my boy. How dost, my boy? art cold?
> I am cold myself. Where is this straw, my fellow?
> The art of our necessities is strange,
> And can make vile things precious. Come, your hovel.
> Poor fool and knave, I have one part in my heart
> That's sorry yet for thee.

And again, in a subsequent scene, when they come to
the door of the hovel:—

> Prithee, go in thyself; seek thine own ease:
> This tempest will not give me leave to ponder
> On things would hurt me more. But I'll go in:
> In, boy: go first. You houseless poverty—
> Nay, get thee in. I'll pray, and then I'll sleep.
> Poor naked wretches, wheresoe'er you are,
> That bide the pelting of this pitiless storm;
> How shall your houseless heads, and unfed sides,
> Your loop'd and window'd raggedness, defend you
> From seasons such as these? Oh, I have ta'en
> Too little care of this! Take physic, pomp;
> Expose thyself to feel what wretches feel,
> That thou may'st shake the superflux to them,
> And show the heavens more just.

In the same spirit, even after his brain has begun to turn,
he interests himself to know what has brought the mad
beggar, as he thinks him, to his present plight—at first, in
the intensity of his self-concentration, assuming that it

must be a case like his own, and that the same suffering can have been produced only by the same maddening injury; but afterwards apparently pitying him for his own sake, enquiring into his past history, and finally concluding, in what perhaps may be called the last words of sanity, ' Thou wert better in a grave, than to answer with thy uncovered body this extremity of the skies.'

Of Lear's madness I cannot trust myself to say anything. When I read the scene, I feel that I can in some measure appreciate its marvellous power; but no one can speak of it profitably who has not some knowledge of the actual phenomena of insanity. It has been pronounced by Coleridge to be the one successful attempt at representing madness throughout the whole range of the drama: all others produce the effect, not of madness, but of mere lightheadedness. The same high authority calls attention to Edgar's assumed madness as serving the great purpose of taking off part of the shock which would otherwise be caused by the true madness of Lear, and further, as displaying the profound gulf which separates the one from the other. In Edgar's ravings, he says, Shakspeare all the while lets you see a fixed purpose, a practical end in view: in Lear's there is only the brooding of the one anguish, an eddy without progression.

The interest of this tremendous Act, the central and culminating point of the tragedy, now shifts from Lear to Gloster. Gloster has expostulated with his guests, Cornwall and Regan, on their treatment of the king, without any result but that of provoking them to threaten him with their displeasure; he now resolves to do what he can himself to alleviate the sufferings of his old master, having first taken counsel with Edmund, whom he further informs of a communication he has received relating to the movement about to be made on behalf of Lear by the

army of France and their English adherents. Edmund
has now got the opportunity he looked for: he has
supplanted his brother in his father's affections, and he
can now supplant his father and obtain, not the prospect
of an inheritance merely, but the actual possession.
Accordingly he goes to Cornwall, while Gloster seeks out
the king, takes him and his companions from the hovel
on the heath, and lodges them in an outhouse adjoining
his castle. Gloster is himself, as he tells Kent, half mad
with misery :—

> Thou say'st the king grows mad: I'll tell thee, friend,
> I'm almost mad myself. I had a son,
> Now outlaw'd from my blood ; he sought my life,
> But lately, very late: I loved him, friend—
> No father his son dearer: true to tell thee,
> The grief hath crazed my wits.

Except that he is not houseless, his sufferings appear to
be as great as Lear's ; yet how much has he still to
undergo, and how far is his cup from being full! He
returns to his castle, not as yet to find out what has been
resolved against himself, but to learn that a plot has been
laid against the life of the king. How it is that Regan
and her husband and sister, whom we left at the end of the
Second Act destitute, indeed, of any sentiment of tenderness towards their father, but apparently not indisposed
to render him the offices of hospitality if he would submit
to their terms, should have risen so soon to the monstrous
wickedness of compassing his death, is a question which
we can only answer inferentially. Shakspeare may have
meant merely to show how easily a callous nature can be
brought to hate intensely where it has injured deeply ; but,
though such a cause might of itself be adequate to effect
the change, we can hardly do wrong in supposing their
minds to have been worked on further by jealousy of

Gloster's interference, which would make them feel their
own criminality, and produce, moreover, a sense of inse-
curity, and also by the actual dread of the French
invasion, which they would learn from Edmund's disclosure. Gloster is just able to save the king, who is sent
off under an escort of his knights to Dover, there to join
his adherents; but he has himself to feel the vengeance
of the fiery Cornwall. The scene that follows is, as I have
already intimated, probably the most horrible in Shakspeare's undisputed works; and yet I hardly know how the
poet could have spared us a particle of the horror, though
it undoubtedly overpasses the bounds which dramatic
writers have generally, and wisely, imposed upon themselves. The mere announcement of an action, as I said
just now, affects us infinitely less than the action itself as
performed in our presence. It was necessary, in order to
fill to the full our conception of Lear's sufferings, that we
should know of what fiendish cruelty his enemies are
capable; and this is impressed on us far less vividly when
we simply hear that they have laid a plot against his life,
than when we actually see a venerable nobleman, who
has rescued him from them, bound in his chair in his own
castle, and having his eyes torn out by the duke's hand.
Thus we may feel that Shakspeare has really exercised
forbearance, and consulted how to spare the sensibilities
of the spectator or the reader: he has not shown us the
father actually exposed to the white heat of his children's
hatred, but has left us to estimate its intensity for ourselves
from the manner in which they deal with his preserver.
But the scene itself is one at which we can only hold our
breath, and hope that it may pass as speedily as possible.
Meantime, it is a consolation to feel that what we witness
is not the pure and absolute triumph of wickedness.
Cornwall is struck down in the middle of his barbarity,

though he has still time to consummate it ; and the sorrow
that we feel for the servant, who so generously throws
away his life, is swallowed up in our satisfaction at the
thought that the tide of iniquity has at last been in some
measure stayed. 'This shows you are above,' is Albany's
exclamation when he hears what has happened :—

>   This shows you are above,
> You justicers, that these our nether crimes
> So speedily can venge !

Hitherto the course of the play has been such as to make
us almost doubt the reality of retribution ; now, for the
first time, we are reassured.

In the Fourth Act the painful strain which had been
put upon our sympathies is gradually relaxed. The shock
of horror is over, and it is succeeded by a calm, which,
while it gives us leisure to realise the sufferings of Lear
and Gloster, yet, from the mere absence of harrowing
excitement, can hardly have other than a soothing effect.
It is only a consequence of the frightful cruelty which
we have just seen perpetrated on Gloster that our
thoughts should turn, in the first instance, to him, rather
than to the king his master, who would otherwise, of
course, be the principal object of our interest ; accordingly,
it is of Gloster that we first hear. Edgar, whom we see
alone for a few moments communing with himself in his
own proper character, makes no reference to Lear, from
whom he had recently parted ; he merely moralises on
his own condition, as one who is now at the worst, and
can fall no further. The next moment shows him the
rashness of his conclusion. He sees his father approach,
under an escort provided for him by the servants of the
castle, who pity their blind master, and have thought of

the mad beggar as a person who might be induced to act
as his guide. ' O Gods,' he exclaims :—

> Who is't can say, I am at the worst ?
> I am worse than e'er I was—
> And worse I may be yet : the worst is not
> So long as we can say, This is the worst.

The father blinded—the son proscribed, and compelled
to adopt the condition of a mad beggar—both victims of the
same conspiracy, and now suddenly thrown together, such
is the spectacle that now meets us. Yet, though for the
moment we feel with Edgar, and think only of the depth to
which both are fallen, we are soon made sensible that there
is compensation for both in the mere fact of their meeting.
Gloster sees in it only the times' plague, when madmen
lead the blind ; we know that the heart of the father has
been turned again to the child, and that the child, so disguised, will be able to protect the father. Why Edgar,
who is no stranger to his father's change of feeling, does
not throw off his disguise and make himself known, is one
of several questions connected with the economy of the
play which I do not feel myself able to answer with confidence. From a passage in the Fifth Act, where Edgar
tells his brother and Albany of his attendance on his
father, it would seem that he himself, at least, in the freshness of his grief for the old man's death, regards the
concealment as a fault ; but this is clearly no explanation
of Shakspeare's motive. Nor is it sufficient to say that if
Edgar had been made to reveal himself, we should have
lost the well-known scene that follows later in the Act,
where Gloster is deluded into thinking that he is standing
on the verge of Dover cliff, and afterwards that he has
actually thrown himself down. Great as is the power of
that scene for mingled terror and pathos, it would be an

insult to Shakspeare to imagine that he would have pur-
chased its achievement at the price of what he knew to
be an error in the conduct of the play, or that if he had
chosen to make Edgar adopt a different course, the
exhaustless wealth of his creative energy would not have
enabled him to produce another scene, worthy in all
respects to stand by the side of that which we now
admire so justly. The question, I repeat, is one which I
do not presume to settle; but it seems possible that Shakspeare may have felt that the old man could at no time
have survived the effect of a disclosure which, when it
takes place at last, makes, as we are told—

> His flawed heart,
> Alack! too weak the conflict to support
> 'Twixt two extremes of passion, joy and grief,
> Burst smilingly.

Or, perhaps we may say, with more probability, that
the complete preservation of Edgar's disguise would be
likely to make him of more use to his father, whose interest in him might otherwise have broken out in the
presence of any of their common enemies. This last consideration Edgar himself would naturally feel at the time
with more or less definiteness, while he would no less
naturally lose sight of it afterwards, while speaking of his
father's death, and blame himself for not having made the
acknowledgment earlier, when the old man, as it might
appear, had yet sufficient energy to sustain the shock of
joy.

For Lear also we feel that the day of consolation has
dawned. The same Act that brings Gloster into companionship with his discarded son reunites Lear to his discarded daughter. Cordelia, though cast off, has not been
exposed to want or privation; on the contrary, she has
been advanced to a condition which now gives her the

means of succouring her father; and her only suffering
has been in the thought of the contumely and hardship
which he has had to endure. Accordingly, when we read
of her grief, we are not pained, but rather soothed and
softened. It is a picture of grief, not in its wild intensity,
but in its tender beauty :—

> Now and then an ample tear trill'd down
> Her delicate cheek : it seem'd she was a queen
> Over her passion, who, most rebel-like,
> Sought to be king o'er her.
>
>   O, then it moved her.
>
> Not to a rage : patience and sorrow strove
> Which should express her goodliest.   You have seen
> Sunshine and rain at once : her smiles and tears
> Were like a better day.   Those happy smilets,
> That play'd on her ripe lip, seem'd not to know
> What guests were in her eyes ; which parted thence
> As pearls from diamonds dropp'd.

For the moment she is separated from him. He is in
Dover; but, in his intervals of reason, the thought of his
past unkindness to her overpowers him with shame, and
he will not see her.   At other times he wanders about—

> As mad as the vex'd sea, singing aloud ;
> Crown'd with rank fumiter and furrow weeds,
> With harlocks, hemlock, nettles, cuckoo flowers,
> Darnel, and all the idle weeds that grow
> In our sustaining corn.

It is in this plight that he falls in with Gloster, is recognised by him, and half recognises him in turn, when a
party of Cordelia's followers appear, and he is carried off
by gentle violence.   So, as the Act closes, we leave him
in the French camp, just recovering from the heavy sleep
into which exhausted nature has thrown him, and exhi-

biting the proofs of returning reason in the consciousness
of past derangement :—

> Where have I been ?   Where am I ? fair daylight ?
> I am mightily abus'd.   I should e'en die with pity
> To see another thus.   I know not what to say.
> I will not swear these are my hands—let's see :
> I feel this pin prick.   Would I were assur'd
> Of my condition !

And again :—

>   Pray, do not mock me :
> I am a very foolish, fond old man,
> Fourscore and upward ; not an hour more nor less ;
> And, to deal plainly,
> I fear I am not in my perfect mind.
> Methinks I should know you, and know this man ;
> Yet I am doubtful, for I am mainly ignorant
> What place this is ; and all the skill I have
> Remembers not these garments ; nor I know not
> Where I did lodge last night.   Do not laugh at me ;
> For, as I am a man, I think this lady
> To be my child Cordelia.

Meanwhile, at intervals during this Fourth Act, we hear
of the preparations that are being made by the two
English courts to oppose the invaders.   Edmund had left
Gloster's castle with Goneril, just before the close of the
Third Act, as it was not thought decent that he should
witness the execution of the cruelty to which his perfidy
had consigned his father, and they arrive in company at
Albany's palace.   From his conversation with the lady,
we find that she has conceived a passion for her companion,
while she regards her husband with coldness and contempt, as possessed of no true manliness, and altogether
unworthy of a mate like her.   But Albany's own feelings
have also undergone a change.   The mistrust with which
he has long viewed his wife's conduct to her father is no

longer put aside as easily as in the First Act. He has heard of the effect of her cruelty: he taxes her with it in a tone that will not be gainsaid, and as she meets his reproofs with scorn, he bursts into a strain of execration and menace, which at any rate gives the lie to her assertion that he bears ' a cheek for blows, a head for wrongs.' No doubt Shakspeare intended us to notice the sluggishness of his nature, which does not take fire till after long exasperation and repeated outrages to his sense of right. The same hesitation shows itself in the next Act, where he appears, an undecided general, at the head of his army; so that we conclude that the success of the battle is owing rather to Edmund than to him. On the whole, however, his is a character which must command a considerable portion of our respect. ' Where I could not be honest, I never yet was valiant,' is what he says of himself, and there seems much justice in the self-description. In the first instance he feels himself bound to his wife; she dwells, apparently with sincerity, on the fears she entertains from the king's uncertainty of temper, and he is willing to think that all that is needed is to caution her against the extreme of ' fearing too far.' And now, though his eyes are opened to the ' proper deformity' of her real character, it does not follow that he is to give way to or make terms with the invaders: in his wife's right, he is sovereign of one half of England; and in spite of the provocation which she and Regan have given, he may reasonably doubt whether he and his subjects are to submit to the dictation of a foreign army. So the preparations for war go on—on his side with misgiving and vacillation, on Regan's with a vigour and energy due not merely to her own indomitable spirit, but to Edmund's superintendence. She, too, cherishes an affection for the young earl, whom she regards as the natural successor to her dead husband's.

place; and she makes him commander of her forces, as a preliminary step to honouring him with her hand. Thus, we have a further prospect of retribution opened, both in the aroused indignation of Albany, and in the seed of jealousy sown between the two sisters, which easily overpowers the sympathy they have hitherto manifested towards each other, as embarked in the same selfish cause. The miscarriage of their messenger, who, attempting Gloster's life, falls by the hand of Edgar, is another movement in the same direction. We rejoice in the extinction of so much baseness, and we conceive new hopes as we see Edgar armed with the proofs of his brother and Goneril's treachery, which he may use as an instrument for working on the ' death-practised duke.'

So we are brought at length to the Fifth and last Act, in which the problem is to be solved, and the web unravelled. About the first question, the event of the battle, we are not left long in doubt. Regan arrives first with Edmund, on whom she presses her love and her jealousy; and they are speedily joined by Goneril and Albany. As they are going out to marshal their forces, Albany is stopped by Edgar, who, being still in disguise, gives him the paper which proves Goneril's and Edmund's guilt, promising that if the combined armies win the battle, a champion shall appear on his part to substantiate the charge. In a very short time we find that they have won the battle; Lear and Cordelia are taken, and brought in as prisoners by Edmund. Cordelia is resigned to her fate, but grieves for her father, and asks, 'Shall we not see these daughters and these sisters?' But the old king has no such thoughts: he can only think of a life in prison as a life with Cordelia, where they may be happy in each other's company, withdrawn from the flux and reflux of their former fortune, and regard the world from which they are cut off merely as a theme for pleasant discourse :—

> No, no, no, no! Come, let's away to prison :
> We two alone will sing like birds i' the cage :
> When thou dost ask me blessing, I'll kneel down
> And ask of thee forgiveness. So we'll live,
> And pray, and sing, and tell old tales, and laugh
> At gilded butterflies, and hear poor rogues
> Talk of court news : and we'll talk with them too;
> Who loses, and who wins : who's in, who's out ;
> And take upon us the mystery of things,
> As if we were God's spies : and we'll wear out,
> In a wall'd prison, packs and sects of great ones,
> That ebb and flow by the moon.

Edmund, however, has no intention that they shall have a long captivity. He professes to reserve them for Albany's judgment, but gives secret orders to an officer to have them put to death in prison. So they are carried out, and Albany enters with his wife and her sister and the rest of the forces. Albany, after a compliment to Edmund's valour, asks for the prisoners. Edmund excuses himself for their non-appearance, alleging that it is best to keep the king out of sight at a time when public feeling might be stirred in his favour. Albany resents this independence of action, and replies that he holds Edmund 'as a subject of the war, not as a brother.' This calls forth Regan, who intimates her intentions in favour of her lover—at first indirectly, afterwards, in reply to Goneril's questions and taunting comments, by a direct announcement. While the two sisters, not yet avowed rivals, are retorting on each other, and Edmund doubtless in perplexity at being thus called upon to make his election, Albany cuts the knot by producing Edgar's paper, and proclaiming the treachery of his wife and Edmund. He then bids the trumpet sound for the champion who is to prove the charge, offering himself, if need be, as a substitute. Meanwhile Regan is carried out sick, a whisper from Goneril informing us that she has been poisoned by her sister. The trumpet sounds, and at the third blast it is answered by Edgar himself. Though he will not give his name he is accepted as an antagonist by Edmund, and the two brothers join in mortal combat, in which the traitor falls. Edmund admits his guilt, while Goneril flies from the scene in desperation. Edgar makes himself known, exchanges forgiveness with his brother, and tells how he has tended his father till the old man expired in his arms, and how Kent has been discovered in Lear's faithful servant. And now the strokes of retribution fall thick. An attendant of Goneril's rushes in with a bloody knife, which his lady has just plunged in her own heart, confessing in death that she has poisoned Regan. 'I was contracted to them both,' says Edmund; 'all three now marry in an instant.' One only anxiety remains. If but Lear and Cordelia can be saved, all will be well. Edmund acknowledges that his writ is on their lives, and prays that it may be at once countermanded. But it is too late. Edgar goes, only to return with Lear, who is carrying Cordelia dead in his arms :—

> Howl, howl, howl ! O, you are men of stones
> Had I your tongues and eyes, I'd use them so,
> That heaven's vault should crack ! She's gone for ever
> I know when one is dead, and when one lives :
> She's dead as earth. Lend me a looking-glass ;
> If that her breath will mist or stain the stone,
> Why, then she lives.

The three friends ask each other whether the end of the world is indeed come. Lear thinks he spies a ray of hope :—

This feather stirs: she lives! If it be so,
It is a chance which does redeem all sorrows
That ever I have felt.

Kent presses himself on his old master. The father
thinks himself baffled in his attempt to restore his
child:—

A plague upon you, murderers, traitors all!
I might have sav'd her; now she's gone for ever!
Cordelia, Cordelia! stay a little. Ha!
What is't thou say'st? Her voice was ever soft,
Gentle, and low—an excellent thing in woman.—
I killed the slave that was a hanging thee.

He then recognises Kent, but cannot identify him with
the servant that followed him so faithfully. He is told
of the deaths of his elder daughters, but the news
makes no impression on him. And then, just as Albany
is announcing his intention to resign the crown to him
during his life, that life gives way:—

And my poor fool is hang'd! No, no, no life!
Why should a dog, a horse, a rat have life,
And thou no breath at all? Thou'lt come no more;
Never, never, never, never, never!
Pray you, undo this button: thank you, sir.
Do you see this? Look on her—look—her lips—
Look there, look there!

I have been unwilling to interrupt my brief sketch of
this, the concluding part of the play, with anything in
the shape of criticism. The crowd of incidents naturally
hurries us along with it, without giving us breathing
time or pause for thought. Now, however, that it is
over, we may be allowed to stop and raise a question.
The old story on which Shakspeare founded his tragedy
is known to have had, at least in one of its versions, a

м 2

very different termination. The triumph of right over
wrong is not, as here, chequered and saddened, but pure
and unmixed. Lear and Cordelia are not the conquered,
but the conquerors in the battle ; the old king lives, and
is restored to his throne. This version, if not the only
one known when Shakspeare wrote, seems at any rate to
have been the more popular one. Not only is it found in
Holingshed's 'Chronicle,' and in Spenser's 'Faery Queen,'
but it forms the subject of a play which was printed in
Shakspeare's time, and which seems, as was the case in
so many other instances, to have held possession of the
theatre till he came to supersede it. Nor is this all.
Even after Shakspeare had put forth his conception of the
story of Lear, the other version was still found to be
congenial to the English taste. About the time of the
Revolution, Nahum Tate, a person of some reputation in
his day, known to us by his share in the New Version of
the Psalms, published a tragedy altered from Shakspeare's
'King Lear,' where, though the battle goes against the
king and his daughter, Cordelia is rescued in time and
given in marriage to Edgar, who has been her lover
throughout. Its success was complete. It superseded
the Shakspearian original, and, either in its own form, or
in a modification introduced, I believe, by Garrick, was
the accepted version at the theatres through the whole of
the eighteenth century, and indeed, down to a comparatively late period, in our own. It was, in fact, the form
in which I myself, as a boy, first became acquainted with
the play. The change pleased not only the people but
the critics. Dr. Johnson avows his sympathy with it.
'Cordelia,' he says, 'from the time of Tate, has always
retired with victory and felicity. And if my sensations
could add anything to the general suffrage, I might relate, I
was many years ago so shocked by Cordelia's death, that

I know not whether I ever endured to read again the
last scenes of the play till I undertook to revise them as
an editor.' With such a consent of authorities on the
other side, we may fairly ask why Shakspeare chose to
forsake the more popular and acceptable version of the
story and follow or invent the more painful. Here, as
before, it is not a sufficient answer to point to the alteration, and show, as might easily be done, how far it falls
short of the original. Nor is it enough, though the
answer is one which goes far more deeply into the merits
of the question, to show how Shakspeare has prepared
us for the catastrophe, and how impossible it would be
to conceive a mind like Lear's, maddened and unhinged
by wrong, as brought to any other issue than a comparatively placid and soothing euthanasia. We may be confident that had Shakspeare thought it right that the story
should have a happy conclusion, all the lustre of his
genius would have been employed to gild the mild
evening of the old king's days; nor would he have
dreamed, as an inferior writer might, of wounding the
sympathies of a rightly-tempered mind merely in order
to exhibit the natural evolution of a powerfully-drawn
character. No; it was because he knew that the sorrow
with which we regard such deaths as Cordelia's and
Lear's is really a deeper and nobler feeling than any joy
which could be excited by the triumphant conclusion of
a story like theirs. It would not be fair, as I have said,
to institute a formal comparison between Tate's last
scene and Shakspeare's: but we may justly point to the
words with which the two respectively conclude, and ask
which conveys the higher lesson: Edgar's speech which
assures us—

> Whatever storms of fortune are decreed,
> That truth and virtue shall at last succeed;

or Albany's—

> The weight of this sad time we must obey;
> Speak what we feel, not what we ought to say.
> The oldest hath borne most : we that are young
> Shall never see so much, or live so long.

As they are carried off to prison, Lear says to Cordelia :—

> Upon such sacrifices, my Cordelia,
> The gods themselves throw incense.

And how much would the sacrifice have lost if it had
not been consummated? She has given up not only her
father's favour and her third of the kingdom, but her
life : he has paid the penalty of his miserable error in
madness and agony, and death comes to him, not only as
his appointed repose, but as the completion of the expiation. Nay, we feel that such a death as theirs is needed, as
the only perfect contrast to the doom which falls on the
guilty. Cornwall, Regan, Goneril, and in a less degree
Edmund, are dead by a judgment which, as Albany says,
makes us tremble, but touches us not with pity. Cordelia,
Lear, Gloster, and Kent are taken away not in anger but
in mercy. Had they lived, their triumph would have
been more palpable to apprehension, but less real. By
their death, they point the moral of a Providence which,
while it frequently visits the guilty with punishment
even here, would not have us look upon worldly
honours as the most appropriate reward of long-suffering
virtue.

It has not seldom been asked, whether or no Shakspeare
can be called a Christian poet. So far as the term can be
used with any strictness, the answer given, I fear, cannot
be in the affirmative. It is not Shakspeare's way to teach
anything pointedly or directly: he teaches as life itself

teaches, by example and experience; but the general
effect of his plays, though partaking of the Christian
atmosphere which may be said more or less to pervade
the whole of modern society, stands in no marked relation to the characteristic teaching of the New Testament.
But if he cannot be called the Poet of Revelation, he may
be spoken of as the Poet of Natural Theology. He shows
life as it appears to the unwarped and unperverted observer who loves the right and hates the wrong. There
have been writers of power and genius who have deliberately lent themselves to making wickedness attractive;
there have been others who, not being themselves masters
of the experience of life, have enlisted their readers' feelings on the side of criminal weakness, and requested
sympathy for struggles in which failure has been a foreseen
thing from the first. Such is not Shakspeare's practical
philosophy. Villany and heartlessness with him are objects
of abhorrence, generally punished, always represented in
their native hideousness; even error and infirmity, though
they may excite compassion, do not escape without censure or penalty. These, at any rate, are some of the
lessons which we learn from 'King Lear.' It is a school
for parents and children, for husbands and wives, for
sovereigns and subjects. There is no one-sidedness in
its teaching. Those who are under reciprocal obligations are not left to imagine that the failure of either
party in his duty exonerates the other. All is impartial,
even-handed justice, as if it had been the moral law itself.
I do not mean to say that this directly didactic purpose
ought to be our only, or even our main, object in the study
of Shakspeare. We read his plays ordinarily with a moral
purpose, but it is one less directly obviously moral—the
purpose of enlarging our conceptions of power, beauty,

and truth—and thus cultivating, as far as its capability extends, that complex nature which God has given us. But there are times when in the course of our general culture it is well that we should be reminded more distinctly and definitely of practical objects, and I am not sorry in closing my lecture to have directed attention for a while to the lessons of moral truth which may be obtained from the study of so great a work of art as 'King Lear.'

THREE YEARS ago, when I chose Shakspeare's 'King Lear' as the subject of a lecture, I sincerely felt my choice to be an adventurous, not to call it a presumptuous, one. What, then, must be said of my present subject, which is no other than the play of 'Hamlet?'

I am not intending to undertake, even cursorily, what in itself perhaps would be scarcely a modest attempt, a comparison of two of the greatest works of our great dramatist. I would not venture to assert that the entire tragedy of 'Hamlet' is a nobler, and consequently a less measurable, a more incomprehensible creation than the entire tragedy of 'Lear.' But I believe I am in no danger of being contradicted when I say that of all Shakspeare's characters, Hamlet is the one of which it is hardest to speak worthily. The old joke, so old that it has passed into a proverb, about 'Hamlet' with the part of Hamlet left out, represents the feeling of which I speak. We feel that in the play of 'Hamlet,' more than in any other play, the grand, the commanding interest of the whole, centres in a single character. There is probably no character in the whole range of poetical creation which has tasked so often the utmost resources of the highest criticism. The great poet of modern Germany, himself an eminent critic ; the great critic of modern England, himself an eminent poet —Goethe and Coleridge—have each elaborated theories of a conception which, more perhaps than any other,

[1] Delivered at the Boston Athenæum January 4, 1800, and repeated January 6.

seems as if it must have proceeded from a conscious artist, from a genius who was critic and poet in one. Nay, it is possible that there may be a yet deeper interest connected with the character—an interest beyond any which can attach to any mere effort of poetry or criticism. Persons who have wondered, as reflecting persons may well wonder, that Shakspeare should have drawn so many characters and yet have never drawn his own, have thought that Hamlet may perhaps be an exception, and that in the character of the young Hamlet we may have something like the character of the young Shakspeare, as he appeared to himself in that troubled period of thought and feeling of which the 'Sonnets' are doubtless the authentic exhibition. Certainly there is no character which seems so completely to include all others, while it is itself included by none, and consequently in its mysterious complexity to approach so nearly to that yet more complex mystery which imagined not only 'Hamlet' but the entire world of the Shakspearian drama. But I will not proceed with observations the effect of which can only be to set in a clearer light the presumption of which I confess myself guilty in venturing to choose a subject like this. My excuse is the surpassing interest of the play.

Coleridge remarks that of all Shakspeare's plays 'Hamlet' is the slowest in movement, as 'Macbeth' is the most rapid. The observation is meant to apply to the prolonged agony of vacillation and mental irresolution which it is the chief business of the play to exhibit; but it is equally true as applied to one of the most obvious external characteristics of the play—its extraordinary length. The fact is one of which anyone who has been in the habit of reading Shakspeare aloud must be sufficiently aware, and of which anyone may satisfy himself by comparing the pages of 'Hamlet' in any printed volume with those of any other play. Three or four others come within a page or two of it, but 'Hamlet' is the longest of all. This I mention as a reason for moving myself as rapidly as I can, and without further preamble entering upon the play itself.

In the first scene we have a platform in front of the royal castle of Elsinore, and soldiers walking up and down, one relieving the other in their nightly guard. It is precisely an opening of that quiet everyday kind which the Roman poet and critic recommended fifteen hundred years before as the only proper way of commencing a great work, and which Shakspeare, led doubtless not by any regard to the precepts of Horace, but by his own sense of fitness, almost habitually affects. We hear the ordinary remarks about the hour, the coldness of the night, the perfect stillness—'not a mouse stirring'—before we are made sensible that anything extraordinary is at hand. And when we *do* get an intimation of what we are to expect, it is made in the most simple and natural manner possible: one asks another, 'What! has this thing appeared again to-night?' We may observe, too, the judgment shown in the gradual process by which the credibility of the vision is brought home to us. The object is to make us see it with the same eyes as the personages in the drama, and especially as Hamlet himself. Consequently our suspicions must be laid artfully to sleep; we must be made to feel that reasonable as they may be in other cases, they would be unreasonable in this. That the sentinels who are keeping guard are convinced would not be enough to convince us. Nor should we, I think, be satisfied by simply finding that their convictions were shared by Hamlet, when he came to see for himself. They are credulous from ordinary superstition; he, we might well think, is credulous from over-inquisitiveness; their prejudices are common and trivial to him, but the doubts

by which those prejudices are usually assailed are common
and trivial too.   One who already finds 'all the uses of
this world weary, stale, flat and unprofitable' would be
unduly predisposed to accept with favour an alleged
message from the other world.   It is precisely here that
Horatio comes in.   He is not a common man—he is a man
of education, and has been Hamlet's fellow-student; and
so when he first hears of the supposed apparition, his impulse is to doubt it, just as ours would be.   Those well-
known words in which Hamlet addresses him after both
are convinced of the reality of what they have seen :—

> There are more things in heaven and earth, Horatio,
> Than are dreamt of in your philosophy—

those very words show us that Horatio is precisely such
a person as most of us would wish to be thought—a
person who takes a calm, rational view of things, removed
from all extravagance of speculation, and that which
triumphs over his doubts may well triumph over ours.
This, then, seems to be the great purpose answered by the
opening scene.   Quietly and without effort, we are led to
be as thoroughly convinced of the truth of the Ghost's
appearance as the less enlightened persons who first saw
it; and instead of being prepared to treat Hamlet as a
dreamer who would naturally acquiesce in an impression
of anything preternatural, we simply look forward to the
effect which a thing confessedly transcending all our experience may be expected to produce on a nature more
powerful and deeper than our own.

The next scene introduces us to the king and queen,
and to Hamlet himself.   The king has lately succeeded
his brother, and has married his brother's widow; and
we now see him entering on the duties of royalty, providing for State emergencies, and giving audience to

private suitors. With his character and the queen's we
need not trouble ourselves at present; they will come
before us as the play proceeds. Laertes, too, the young
nobleman, and his father, the old politician, will meet us
again : at present we need only note, as others have noted,
that Shakspeare, intending afterwards to bring Laertes and
Hamlet into collision, has taken care at the moment of
their first introduction to indicate the opposition between
the natures of the two men : both anxious to be allowed
to leave the court; the one that he may get back to his
pleasures in France, the other that he may return to his
studies at Wittenberg. In the case of Hamlet, however,
we have little need to dwell, even for a moment, on such
slight indications, valuable as they are in illustrating subordinate characters like that of Laertes. Hamlet has but
to open his mouth in order to show us that he is unlike
those with whom we have hitherto been conversing. As
he says of himself, he has 'that within which passeth
show.' He is not acquiescent in the state of things about
him ; he is not even, like Horatio, simply observant and
suspicious; he is profoundly distrustful. The great German poet whom I mentioned a short time since has
endeavoured to ascertain what was Hamlet's natural temperament—what he was previously to the death of his
father and marriage of his mother, and would probably
have continued had nothing happened to convulse his
being. The question may or may not be a profitable one ;
at any rate, it is one which Shakspeare does not enable us
to approach otherwise than indirectly, as we only see
Hamlet after the shadow of that great event has passed
over him. But there is a comparison which we are enabled
and intended to make—a comparison of Hamlet when he
has not yet heard of the Ghost, and Hamlet when he has
seen and talked with it. What we observe, indeed, is not

so much the unlikeness as the likeness of the two states of
mind.   The discovery that in losing his father he has lost
his mother too—that she, being apparently anxious merely
to preserve her queenly state, has passed lightly and
almost without an interval from the arms of a worthy
king to those of his unworthy successor—has engendered
in him already a weariness of life, a world-sickness, if I
may use the expression, which it requires no supernatural
communication to aggravate.   What he learns from the
Ghost afterwards is not so much that he has to suffer,
though there *is* an additional ingredient thrown into his
cup of suffering, as that he has to *act*.

Hamlet has been told by Horatio of the appearance of
the Ghost, and he wishes the night were come, that he
might see for himself.   It might naturally be supposed
that the impatience of the reader or spectator would keep
pace with that of the actor, and that the poet would be
ready to gratify it.   Shakspeare is not circumscribed by
any law of unity of time—the action of the play is
extended over a number of days; and, so far as its
requirements are concerned, he was perfectly free to
annihilate the intervening space, and bring Hamlet at once
face to face with his father's spirit.   Or, if he did not
wish to precipitate the crisis, he might have allowed us to
accompany Hamlet, and enter with him into all the horror
of strained and excited expectation.   Instead of this, he
introduces us again to Laertes, who, as we have just seen,
has obtained leave to go back to France; we are present
at the preparations for his journey, hear his parting
counsels to his sister, and the other parting counsels
which his father, in his turn, administers to him.   We are
thus made acquainted with a family which, having been
long attached to the fortunes of the royal family of Denmark, is doomed, in the sequel, to be involved in the

tragic destiny which drags them down. But this object would not be sufficient to redeem the scene, standing where it does, from the charge of inappropriateness. Its real justification lies even nearer to the surface. We are called off from Hamlet and his expectation precisely because it is well that we should be called off. We obtain that relief without which the contemplation of a work of art would give us more pain than pleasure; and we are also made to realise life as it is. While we acknowledge Hamlet to be the centre of the piece, it is well that we should feel that there are other minor centres, even within the limits of the Danish court. Everyday life cannot stand still, even during those few agonising hours which separate Hamlet from the object of his expectation. The ship is waiting for Laertes, and he must sail whether there be anything rotten in the state of Denmark or no; and our presence at his preparations makes us acknowledge the fact that he has interests as well as Hamlet. We also see something of what Hamlet himself has been, apart from the terrible responsibility which is being now laid upon him. He is not only a prince and a student, but a lover; and though, in the course of the play, we are not made very sensible of his love, we are intended to take notice of it as one of the influences acting on his nature. To what extent it has already mastered him is not easy to say. I do not pretend to reconcile the utter sickness of heart which makes Hamlet cry out on the unprofitableness of all the uses of the world with the tenders of affection which he has of late made to Ophelia, supposing these last to have taken place after his father's death and his mother's marriage. At any rate, the passion is one which cannot but be overpowered by the sense of his situation, as 'the son of a dear father murdered,' the duty of setting right a time

that is out of joint; though he may afterwards feel painfully that Ophelia, too, should have turned against him;
may tell her that he loved her once, may taunt her with
the brevity of woman's love; and when she is dead, assert
that he loved her more than forty thousand brothers. So,
perhaps, we may say that there is something tragical in
the old man cautioning his daughter against listening to
Hamlet's love, just when Hamlet has entered the cold
shadow in which all love's blossoms are doomed to wither
and die.

And now midnight has come: the watch is set, and
Hamlet is with them. At the very outset of the scene
there is a contrast, which the poet certainly intended, and
we shall do well to observe. While they are in the cold
biting air, they hear a flourish of trumpets, and a discharge
of cannon, and Hamlet remarks that his uncle is holding
a carouse, and drinking deep. The king is at the height
of his revelry; his nephew is expecting a communication
from the other world. The contrast is the same which
the reader of English history will remember, on the night
before the battle of Hastings, when the Normans prayed
and fasted, and the Saxons ate and drank—an omen, as
we instinctively feel it, of the event of the coming day.
Shakspeare loses no opportunity of pointing the opposition
between this grossness of carnal excess and the purity enforced by the world of spirits. Hamlet's father, as he tells
us, was ' cut off in the blossom of his sin '—' grossly, full of
bread, with all his crimes broad blown '—and so, in his
disembodied state, is condemned ' to fast in fires ' till the
stains contracted in life 'are burnt and purged away.'
The late king was a noble and worthy monarch, yet he
has given way to the national vice of intemperance, and
so he suffers: what is to be looked for by him whose
nature, as deeply, or more deeply steeped in the same

'gross mud-honey,' has on it the far blacker taint of
fratricide? As yet, however, the veil has not been lifted
up, and Hamlet can speak soberly and calmly about the
'heavy-headed revel,' as a feature lowering to the national
character. The speech is one of that numerous class
which have made Shakspeare's plays celebrated as a storehouse of moral wisdom; yet it is perfectly in keeping:
it shows us Hamlet in his sane and more self-contained
mood, conversing with a friend whom he loves and
esteems, not abandoned to his own despair; and it makes
the impression more striking when, just as he ceases,
Horatio says, 'Look, my lord, it comes!' Hamlet's tone
changes in an instant; his whole nature is called forth to
address the spirit, and reflective philosophy is lost in a
strain of the loftiest and most impassioned poetry :—

> Angels and ministers of grace defend us!
> Be thou a spirit of health, or goblin damn'd;
> Bring with thee airs from heaven or blasts from hell;
> Be thy intents wicked or charitable,
> Thou com'st in such a questionable shape
> That I will speak to thee: I'll call thee Hamlet,
> King, Father, Royal Dane: Oh, answer me!
> Let me not burst in ignorance; but tell
> Why thy canonised bones, hearsed in death,
> Have burst their cerements! why the sepulchre
> Wherein we saw thee quietly in-urn'd,
> Hath op'd his ponderous and marble jaws
> To cast thee up again! What may this mean,
> That thou, dread corse, again, in complete steel,
> Revisit'st thus the glimpses of the moon,
> Making night hideous: and we fools of nature,
> So horridly to shake our disposition,
> With thoughts beyond the reaches of our souls?
> Say, why is this? wherefore? what should we do?

His companions would fain hinder him from following
the Ghost; but he will not hear them :—

> I do not set my life at a pin's fee :
> And for my soul, what can it do to that,
> Being a thing immortal as itself?

The dialogue between Hamlet and his father I will not dwell on ; everybody that knows anything of Shakspeare is familiar with it already.   I will merely notice one or two points which throw light upon Hamlet's character.   The whole scope of the play is to represent Hamlet as irresolute : ' from thinking too precisely o'er the event,' he lets the time for action go by; yet he believes himself to be ready to avenge his father's murder the instant he has been informed who the murderer is :—

> Haste me to know it, that I with wings as swift
> As meditation, or the thoughts of love,
> May sweep to my revenge.

So it doubtless is : in his first impulse he is rapid and lightning-like (though even here we are, perhaps, intended to note the two things uppermost in his mind, ' meditation and the thoughts of love'): then the intellectual power wakes, and thought overcrowds and stifles action. Again, when the Ghost leaves him alone, and his tumultuous feelings first find words, he appears vividly conscious of the obstacles he is likely to meet with in his own nature and temperament.   It is the dreamy, meditative student that is speaking when he promises :—

>   Remember thee ?
> Yes, from the table of my memory
> I'll wipe away all trivial fond records,
> All saws of books, all forms, all pressures past,
> That youth and observation copied there ;
> And thy commandment all alone shall live,
> Within the book and volume of my brain,
> Unmix'd with baser matter—yes, yes, by heaven.

Whether it is to record the Ghost's charge, or the

generalised observation that he draws from what he has just heard, 'that one may smile, and smile, and be a villain'—for whichever of these two purposes it is that he takes out his tables, Coleridge is equally justified in his profound remark that 'Shakspeare alone could have produced the vow of Hamlet, to make his memory a blank of all maxims and generalised truths . . . followed immediately by the speaker noting down a generalised fact '—a subtle inconsistency, which shows, indeed, how thoroughly the creator of the character had realised his own creation. So, too, there can be no doubt that Coleridge is right in saying that when Hamlet resolves, as he does immediately, to counterfeit madness, ' he plays the trick of pretending to act only when he is very near really being what he acts.' Hamlet's feigning madness, indeed, is a sort of instinct of self-preservation. He resolves not to speak of what he has seen; and if he is to keep it to himself, his only chance lies in not brooding over it, but diverting himself from it—not shaping his language cautiously, but flashing out his thoughts as they rise to his lips, and running an intellectual riot, such as only the supposition of madness could justify in the eyes of the world. At the first moment he seems to think of telling the secret to Horatio and Marcellus; but his mind changes: he attempts to generalise, to say something which shall yet be nothing; he falls into a truism and owns it, laughing apparently at himself; ' and so, without more circumstance at all, he holds it fit that they shake hands and part.' These, as Horatio tells him, ' are but wild and hurling words;' but it is only in some such words as these that the overwrought spirit can find natural vent.

In the Second Act we see much of a personage who has hitherto played but a subordinate part in the drama. I mean Polonius, an old and trusted counsellor of State,

father of Laertes and Ophelia. His is a character which
presents a good deal of difficulty. Hamlet dislikes and
contemns him; but if we judge him by his own speeches,
as Shakspeare must have intended us to do, we shall find,
setting aside a certain tedious formality on the one hand,
and traces of superannuation on the other, that he is a good
specimen of a type which is unquestionably entitled to our
respect, the old practised politician. The first writer who
set his character in a true light was, I believe, Dr. Johnson, whose remarks, truly called by a subsequent critic
'just, judicious, and masterly,' I will venture to quote at
length :—' Polonius is a man bred in courts, exercised in
business, stored with observation, confident in his knowledge, proud of his eloquence, and declining into dotage.
His mode of oratory is truly represented as designed to
ridicule the practice of those times, of prefaces that made
no introduction, and of method that embarrassed rather
than explained. This part of his character is accidental :
the rest is natural. Such a man is positive and confident,
because he knows that his mind was once strong, and
knows not that it is become weak. Such a man excels in
general principles, but fails in the particular application.
He is knowing in retrospect, and ignorant in foresight.
While he depends on his memory, and can draw from his
repositories of knowledge, he utters weighty sentences,
and gives useful counsel; but as the mind in its enfeebled
state cannot be kept long busy and intent, the old man is
subject to sudden dereliction of his faculties : he loses the
order of his ideas, and entangles himself in his own
thoughts, till he recovers the leading principle, and falls
again into his former train. This idea of dotage encroach-
ing upon wisdom will solve all the phenomena of the
character of Polonius.' In the first scene he is sending a
messenger to his son, with secret instructions to enquire

about his way of life in Paris; and there we see the old
man trusting partly to his memory, partly to a certain
formal sequence of thoughts, to supply the failing of his
faculties, while the general result, allowance being made
for a little pomp and self-consciousness, is wise and
sagacious.   Ophelia enters, and the question of Hamlet's
relation to her is resumed.   His madness, real or supposed, has shown itself in a strange interview with her;
the old man is alarmed, and fears that the course of
conduct which he had prescribed on the supposition that
the prince's passion was a momentary fancy has had the
effect of inflaming that passion into an insanity of which
he now sees the cause.   The next scene shows us the king
and queen, who have been pondering on the same subject
of Hamlet's madness, now evident to the whole court.
They have sent for two of Hamlet's friends, Rosencranz
and Guildenstern, and are receiving from them assurances
that they will do their best to trace the evil to its source.
After these noblemen have been dismissed, Polonius
comes in with the announcement of his discovery, which
is gladly welcomed.   His self-importance is considerable,
and the absurdity of his methodical style of oratory rather
irritates the queen, who exclaims, 'More matter with less
art;' while we may smile at the pardonable vanity which
makes him suppose he understands Hamlet's madness,
not only in the general, but in detail :—

> And he, repulsed (a short tale to make),
> Fell into a madness; then into a fast;
> Thence to a watch; thence into a weakness;
> Thence to a lightness; and by this declension,
> Into the madness wherein now he raves,
> And all we wail for.

Hamlet appears, and the old politician begs to be left
alone with him : he is no match, however, for the 'wild

and hurling words ' in which Hamlet, using a madman's privilege, expresses his contempt for him, and he retires ; not, however, without doing justice to the pregnancy of the prince's replies, in which, he observes, madness often has the advantage of reason and sanity. Rosencranz and Guildenstern are introduced. Hamlet is at first inclined to welcome them on the score of old friendship, and seems even to be preparing to take them into his confidence : —' O God ! I could be bounded in a nutshell, and count myself a king of infinite space, were it not that I have had bad dreams.' They misunderstand him, and he begins to see that they are set as spies upon him. Yet, though he does not tell the cause of his melancholy, he gives a picture of it, in words which, though Shakspeare has chosen to throw them into prose, have all the character- istics of the highest poetry :—' I have of late (but where- fore I know not) lost all my mirth, forgone all custom of exercises ; and, indeed, it goes so heavily with my dis- position, that this goodly frame, the earth, seems to me a sterile promontory ; this most excellent canopy, the air, look you, this brave o'erhanging firmament, this majes- tical roof fretted with golden fire, why, it appears no other thing to me than a foul and pestilent congregation of vapours. What a piece of work is a man ! how noble in reason ! how infinite in faculty ! in form and moving, how express and admirable ! in action, how like an angel ! in apprehension, how like a god ! the beauty of the world ! the paragon of animals ! And yet, to me, what is this quintessence of dust? Man delights not me ; no, nor woman neither, though by your smiling you seem to say so.' They tell him his old favourites, the players, are on their way to court : Hamlet shows that his interest in them is not dead ; and a conversation ensues which is curious for its obvious reference to the caprices of the popular taste about actors in Shakspeare's own time. Polonius returns, bringing the same information about the players, which he flatters himself will be welcome. Hamlet is more disrespectful to the old man than ever— interrupts him, mimics his words, twits him with his stale intelligence, and plies him with scraps of songs glancing indirectly at his daughter. The players enter: Hamlet welcomes them, and calls for a favourite speech about the sack of Troy and the murder of Priam, which is given with great effect, partly by himself, partly by one of the actors. A thought strikes Hamlet: he knows a play on a subject closely resembling his father's murder, and he will have it performed the next night. The thing is arranged, and he is left alone, and then his pent-up thoughts break out :—

> Oh, what a rogue and peasant slave am I!
> Is it not monstrous, that this player here,
> But in a fiction, in a dream of passion,
> Could force his soul so to his whole conceit,
> That, from her working, all his visage wann'd;
> Tears in his eyes, distraction in his aspect,
> A broken voice, and his whole function suiting
> With forms to his conceit? and all for nothing!
> For Hecuba!
> What's Hecuba to him, or he to Hecuba,
> That he should weep for her?   What would he do
> Had he the motive and the cue for passion
> That I have?   He would drown the stage with tears,
> And cleave the general ear with horrid speech;
> Make mad the guilty, and appal the free;
> Confound the ignorant, and amaze indeed
> The very faculties of eyes and ears.

He contrasts his own miserable apathy, execrates his uncle, and then upbraids himself again for 'unpacking his heart with words,' when he ought to be doing.

Summoning his thoughts, he thinks the play may be
made a good expedient for bringing out his uncle's guilt.
After all, a supernatural appearance is no absolute proof
of the truth of its own communication.   It may be a
spirit of evil, working on that weakness and melancholy
of which Hamlet is but too conscious.   Far better to
take the opportunity, thus accidentally presented, of
arriving at the truth : —

> The play's the thing
> Wherein I'll catch the conscience of the king.

And so the Act ends, leaving Hamlet satisfied with his
own procrastination, which has thus brought him the
means of feeling his way before he acts.

Rosencranz and Guildenstern inform the king and
queen of their ill success with Hamlet, telling them also
of his wish to see the players perform.   They gladly
clutch at this disposition, as they think, to seek relief
in amusement, and promise to be present themselves.
Meanwhile the truth of Polonius' theory, that it is love
of Ophelia that has driven Hamlet mad, is to be put to
the test.   Ophelia is to be thrown in Hamlet's way, her
father and the king being hidden where they can make
their own observations, while the queen expresses her
gracious wish that Ophelia's beauties may prove the happy
cause of her son's wildness.   They retire, leaving Ophelia.
Hamlet enters, talking to himself.   I need not relate
what he is saying: it is that marvellous speech, the best
known in the whole play, perhaps in the whole of Shakspeare, where he raises the question ' to be or not to be.'
I shall neither quote it nor abridge it, but merely make
one or two remarks on it by way of comment.   Hamlet, in
his very first soliloquy, had wished ' that the Everlasting
had not fixed his canon 'gainst self-slaughter.'   This was

when, as I said a short time ago, he was wholly absorbed
in the thought of suffering, and did not know that there
was a call on him to act. But the occasion for acting is
a new cause of grief, and so, to his tortured and agonised
mind, is the call itself: the procrastination, which appeared to ease it, has in reality made it more painful. He
seeks to escape from the burden; and accordingly once
more he considers the question of self-murder, approaching it this time in a spirit of profound, and, so far as his
nature will allow, calm meditation, and enquiring into
the reasons why men do not commit a crime that they
are so often tempted to. We all know the answer to
which he comes—an answer, I may remark in passing, all
the more significant as coming, not from a moralist, but
from a sufferer at the height of his suffering, But the
answer is one which reaches beyond its original application. In saying that 'conscience does make cowards
of us all,' Hamlet, as has been well remarked by a recent
critic, comes upon 'the key to the tendency to hesitation,
where momentous action is' required, 'in every other
case.' 'He has at last' (I am quoting the same authority) 'got the clue to his own state of mind, or rather to
his whole being:'—

> Thus the native hue of resolution
> Is sicklied o'er with the pale cast of thought;
> And enterprises of great pith and moment,
> With this regard, their currents turn awry,
> And lose the name of action.

As he is speaking, he sees Ophelia: his first words are
those of tender regard; but he immediately suspects that
she, like the others, is set on to spy him, and he lets
loose against her the same tongue which he had let loose
against her father.   There is sincerity in each case: feel-

ing, as he does, that the uses of the world are weary,
flat and unprofitable, and the time out of joint, he sees as
keenly the frivolities of young women as he sees the
infirmities of old men ; and when he says—' I have heard
of your paintings too, well enough : God hath given you
one face, and you make yourselves another: you jig,
you amble, and you lisp, and nickname God's creatures,
and make your wantonness your ignorance. Go to ; I'll no
more on't : it hath made me mad '—when he says this, it
is simply the outcome of an experience which weighed
little or nothing with him so long as he could allow
himself to be a happy lover, but now oppresses and re-
volts him.   Ophelia, conscious of her innocence, receives
his words only as so many proofs of the utter completeness of a calamity which she bewails most touchingly, not
for her own sake, but for his.   The scene has had a
different effect on the king: he sees nothing of love in
Hamlet's words, and no madness either, and so purposes
to send him on a mission to England.   The old counsellor
assents, though with a reserve in favour of his own
opinion about the origin of the distemper, suggesting as
a previous step that after the play the queen shall be
closeted with Hamlet, he himself being set to watch the
conversation.   The players come on, and Hamlet, who
has been instructing them in their parts, delivers some
injunctions about acting generally, which are doubtless
the result of Shakspeare's own judgment and dramatic
experience, and have been household words with English
critics ever since.   Then they are dismissed to get the
exhibition ready, and Hamlet has a few words with
Horatio in anticipation of the play. ' Horatio,' he tells
him, in a speech which is a model of what friend may
say of friend, testifying to the worth of him who gives
the praise as much as to that of him who receives it :—

Horatio, thou art e'en as just a man
As e'er my conversation coped withal.

. . . .

Since my dear soul was mistress of her choice,
And could of men distinguish, her election
Hath seal'd thee for herself: for thou hast been
As one, in suffering all, that suffers nothing;
A man that fortune's buffets and rewards
Hast ta'en with equal thanks: and blest are those
Whose blood and judgment are so well commingled
That they are not a pipe for fortune's finger
To sound what stop she please. Give me that man
That is not passion's slave, and I will wear him
In my heart's core—aye, in my heart of heart,
As I do thee.

Being such as he is, he has been taken into Hamlet's
confidence about the murder, and now promises to
observe the king's behaviour. The royal party enter:
Hamlet taunts the king with having done nothing to
advance him, jeers at the old counsellor to his face, and
finally gives himself up to Ophelia, on whom he vents a
wayward and, as we must consider it, a coarse humour.
The play commences—a somewhat stilted and unnatural
performance to our tastes; the player-king and queen
making love to each other in long rhyming speeches, full
of antithetical sentences; but we must remember that it
is a play within a play, and that Shakspeare had to
discriminate it from the free natural dialogue of his
own characters by artificial language and an obviously
balanced metre. Then comes the crisis: as the player-
king is asleep, his nephew pours poison into his ears;
Hamlet, who professes to have studied the story, taking
care to inform the spectators what the action is, in case
it should not speak for itself. The real king rises: the
spectacle is broken up; and Hamlet is left with Horatio.

Hamlet has, as it were, attained an intellectual triumph, which he is disposed to enjoy, and Horatio humours him. They are interrupted by Rosencranz and Guildenstern, who come to report that the king is in high displeasure, and that the queen is anxious to see Hamlet in her own chamber. Hamlet answers them lightly; and on Guildenstern's pressing to be admitted into his confidence, intimates in plain terms that he will not let himself be made an instrument for pretended friends to play on. Polonius enters with the same message: Hamlet answers by pointing to a cloud, which he makes him admit successively to be like a camel, a weasel, and a whale. He has apparently two objects in this, not strictly consistent with each other, but both consistent with the bitterness of his own spirit: to make the old man eat his own words, showing him thus that he thoroughly understands his courtier-like nature, and to evidence to himself how he himself is regarded as a lunatic whom no one contradicts: 'They fool me to the top of my bent.' And now he believes himself wrought up to the deed of vengeance; but first he must see his mother. Meantime the king arranges to send Hamlet to England with Rosencranz and Guildenstern, Rosencranz accepting the charge in a speech which I have not time to quote, but which is well worthy of your attention, both for its own sake—for it is a splendid acknowledgment of the paramount importance of royalty, soaring far above anything like vulgar flattery—and as affording an instance of what I may call the fearless justice and truthfulness of Shakspeare, who, while preserving the prominence of one commanding character, is not afraid to give others their full scope, but allows them to utter noble sentiments in noble language, even though he does not mean us, on the whole, to respect or approve them. Hamlet is on his

way to the queen; the king, conscience-stricken, attempts
to pray before he goes to rest. I cannot stop to point
out the marvellous power shown in pourtraying the
agonising self-conflict of the guilty man, knowing that
mercy is infinite and may extend even to him, but feeling
that he cannot place himself within the range of that
mercy by repentance and restitution. I will only say
how thoroughly I agree with Coleridge that Hamlet's
unwillingness to kill his uncle while praying, which must
have shocked many readers, as it certainly once shocked
me, is not really a deliberate expression of fiendish
malice, but the result of irresolution seeking an excuse
for itself in a thought which, however frightful, is never
intended to be more than a thought. Hamlet's interview
with his mother has a very different ending from that
which she and her advisers anticipated. It opens with
the death of the unfortunate old counsellor, who, having
ensconced himself behind the tapestry, suffers by mistake
the death which Hamlet, as able to act on impulse as he
is unable to act on deliberation, intends for the king.
The queen had flattered herself that she should be able
to command Hamlet and bring his unreasonable conduct
home to him; in an instant she finds her nature cowed and
subjected by his, and has to sit and listen to representations of her unworthy life with her new husband, which
pierce her to the heart and call forth her better self.
Altogether, the effect of this scene is to make us feel
kindly and compassionately towards the queen, and induce us to be glad that the Ghost enjoined Hamlet to
spare her. Whether she was really cognisant of her
first husband's murder, either before or after the fact, is
not altogether easy to say. We know that in Shakspeare's original draught she was made to avow her
innocence and co-operate with Hamlet in taking measures

against the king; so that the omission may seem as if
on second thoughts it was intended that she should be
implicated in the crime. On the other hand, there is
strong evidence for her in the fact that, except a single
expression, which shocks and astonishes her, Hamlet's
reproaches are entirely directed to the infamy of her
second marriage; though this is perhaps counterbalanced
by the fact that, in a former speech, Hamlet appears
distinctly to warn himself against the temptation to kill
her, which could hardly have entered his mind if her
only crime had been accepting the hand of an unworthy
successor to her husband. Again, it is hard to say
whether Shakspeare is chargeable with inconsistency in
not allowing her to see the Ghost, which has already been
shown not to be the mere coinage of Hamlet's brain by
appearing to others besides him. But whatever may be
the physical explanation of this apparent inconsequence,
there can be no doubt that Shakspeare is justified
morally in excluding her from the sight of what has
stirred Hamlet so powerfully. What he evidently intends
is that she should be left to the operation of her own
conscience, acting, not on what she does not know, but
on what she knows only too well. That is the way in
which her moral deliverance is to be accomplished, if at
all :—' If they hear not Moses and the prophets, neither
will they be persuaded, though one rose from the dead.'

The king finds the queen deeply agitated; but she
simply tells him that Hamlet is mad, and that he has slain
the poor old man. The king is troubled—troubled at
what may happen to himself from Hamlet's real or feigned
wildness, and troubled at the possible consequences of
the murder of an officer of State within the royal house.
He concludes to carry out at once the resolution he had
formed, and to send Hamlet to England, with secret in-

structions, of which we now hear for the first time, to
have him put to death on landing.   Hamlet has already
suspected that the king may intend some treachery by
this mission to England, and, characteristically enough,
accepts the charge on that very account, seeing in it an
opportunity of a fresh intellectual triumph for himself,
as he has no doubt that he shall be able 'to delve one
yard below their mines and blow them at the moon.'
Accordingly, while taunting Rosencranz to his face as
the king's sponge, and hurling sarcasms against royalty
at the king himself, he simply asks whither he is to go,
and then sets about the journey cheerfully and eagerly.
All this is of course mere irresolution, taking refuge from
the great duty which presses on it in a new display of
ingenuity, as if he wished that his enemies should afford
him some sport before he destroys them.   This is not as
apparent to himself as it is to us ; but he is nevertheless
pricked by a sense of his own procrastination, in an
incident which happens to him as he is going.   It is
doubtful whether the scene is or is not part of the play
as Shakspeare finally left it, as it is omitted in the first
folio, the edition which appeared immediately after
Shakspeare's death ; but there is no doubt that it proceeded from Shakspeare's hand.   As Hamlet is going, he
meets with a Norwegian army, which has obtained leave
to march through the Danish territory on an expedition
against Poland.   On enquiry, he learns that the prize of
war is ' a little patch of ground, which hath no profit in it
but the name ;' yet both sides are going to squander
blood and treasure in attacking or defending it.   Hamlet,
moralising as usual, at first treats a war like this, as well
he may, as ' the imposthume of much wealth and peace ;'
but as he goes on he is led to admire the daring of
these men and their leader, and to contrast it with

his own supineness, though he has far stronger reasons
for action :—

> Rightly to be great,
> Is not to stir without great argument,
> But greatly to find quarrel in a straw,
> When honour's at the stake.   How stand I, then,
> That have a father kill'd, a mother stain'd,
> Excitements of my reason and my blood,
> And let all sleep? while, to my shame, I see
> The imminent death of twenty thousand men,
> That, for a fantasy and trick of fame,
> Go to their graves like beds—fight for a plot
> Whereon the numbers cannot try the cause ;
> Which is not tomb enough and continent
> To hide the slain? Oh, from this time forth
> My thoughts be bloody, or be nothing worth!

Meantime, the deed of blood which Hamlet has already
committed is breeding misery to friend and enemy alike.
The plague of madness, in counterfeiting which he has
found a refuge for his own wild thoughts, has seized on
her whom he loved and whom he has just made father-
less. We see her 'fantastically dressed with straws and
flowers,' and hear her singing snatches of songs in which
the loss of her father blends strangely with her love for
Hamlet, and with the warning, so harsh to the ears of
a pure-minded maiden, which she received from her
father and her brother about the possible consequences
of that love to herself. Her brother is brought back
from Paris by the news of their father's death, and the
popular feeling of Denmark, which had gathered round
Hamlet while he was in the country, now attaches itself
to him. While the king is conferring of these troubles
with the queen, a noise is heard at the gates, and Laertes
presents himself, at the head of a rabble. It is then that
we see that the king is something more than a mere

sensualist, usurper, and murderer. He is all these; but
Shakspeare, with that fearless justice of which I spoke a
short time back, has allowed him the royal virtue of
dignified intrepidity; and, as he confronts Laertes, he
utters one of those sentences about the essential sacred-
ness of the monarch which have made Shakspeare dear
to all loyal enthusiasts, from the old cavalier in 'Woodstock' downwards. Confident in his power to satisfy
Laertes, he lets his expressions of indignation have their
way before he proceeds to show him by calm reasoning
that the fault is Hamlet's, and that he, no less than
Laertes, is interested in Hamlet's punishment. While he
is hinting to him how he has contrived to have Hamlet
taken out of the way, unexpected news arrives from
Hamlet himself, who has met with an adventure on his
voyage, and returned to Denmark. Astonished as the
king is, he takes advantage of the occasion to show his
confidence in Laertes, whose advice he asks under these
new circumstances. Laertes, confused, and thinking only
of his own revenge, can originate nothing; and so the
king proceeds to unfold a plan which has suggested itself
on the moment to his cooler brain. He lets Laertes
know that Hamlet is jealous of his reported skill in
fencing, taking care, with masterly adroitness, to speak of
the real or supposed occasion of that jealousy in a way
which shall at once seem most credible to Laertes and
most flatter his vanity. Laertes is led on to convert his
wild thoughts of indefinite vengeance into a deliberate
scheme for murdering Hamlet in a fencing match. He
even improves upon the king's suggestion, by proposing
to poison his rapier; and the king, not to be outdone,
says that he will have a poisoned cup ready for Hamlet
to drink when he is tired of the sport. Perhaps it is
to soften these horrors and recall our minds to Laertes'

grounds of provocation, that we, like them, are interrupted by the news of the death of poor Ophelia, who,
having gone with her fantastic garlands to the brook and
attempted to hang them on a willow, has fallen into the
water, and, after floating awhile, been drawn under and
drowned, with the 'snatches of old tunes' still in her mouth.
Laertes breaks away in a passion of tears, and the king
follows, fearing that his rage will blaze out again. And
so we come to the end of the Fourth Act. We know
that Hamlet has returned without his watchers, and guess
that he has found some means of accomplishing his plan,
and 'hoisting them with their own petard;' but we
know that his enemies, old and new, have been acting
in concert, and that the snare is again set for his life.
The sky is heavy with thunderclouds, and we wait anxi-
ously to see whether they will burst or pass over.

The Fifth Act opens with the preparations for the funeral
of Ophelia, which is intended not to be hurried over, like
her father's, but performed with more or less of solemn
ceremony. Yet in the preparations, at all events, Shakspeare may seem to have done his utmost to disregard and
set at nought our notions of tragic solemnity. It is the
celebrated grave-digging scene, much hated of Voltaire
and his school of criticism, and omitted by Garrick in his
representation of the play. Properly considered, it is
only an additional instance of Shakspeare's intense reality
and depth of feeling. The two clowns are discussing
'crowner's quest law' with an absurd formality which, as
the commentators show us, is only a caricatured imitation
of the style of their superiors, the old lawyers, and plying
each other with riddles about their own trade. Hamlet
enters with Horatio, and is at once struck by this
apparently gross insensibility: 'Hath this fellow no
feeling of his business, that he sings at grave-making?'

He is reminded of the power of custom to dull and deaden impressions, and is led to think of the terrible equality introduced by death : sculls of those who were esteemed in life—politicians, courtiers, lawyers—tossed about by the spade of an ignorant sexton : 'How the knave jowls it to the ground, as if it were Cain's jawbone, that did the first murder!' He bandies jokes with the clown, from whom he hears the popular version of his own madness. He is shown a scull of one whom he used to play with as a child, the court jester, and realises yet more keenly the havoc made by death : 'To what base uses we may return, Horatio! Why may not imagination trace the noble dust of Alexander till we find it stopping a bung-hole?' This is the moral of the scene, the ruth-less levelling of worldly distinctions in the grave, and no tragic pomp of language could have conveyed it half so forcibly. All this time Hamlet is unaware whose grave is being got ready. The funeral procession advances, and from the abridgment of the ceremonial he gathers that the corpse is one of a suicide who in life enjoyed some worldly consideration. He recognises Laertes, who at last speaks of his sister, and then the truth breaks on Hamlet : 'What, the fair Ophelia!' The sight of the passionate grief of Laertes, who leaps madly into the grave, provokes Hamlet : he will not have it supposed that a brother could have so much right in the dead as a lover; so he follows the example, and a scuffle ensues. The king parts them with some trouble, solacing himself and Laertes by a reference to their last conversation, which gives a hope shortly of 'an hour of quiet.'—When we next see Hamlet, he has been talking to Horatio, whom he now tells, what we have for some time been anxious to hear, the story of the interruption of his voyage. The night of their starting he was troubled

with restlessness—a providential restlessness, as he himself regards it; finding Rosencranz and Guildenstern
asleep, he opened their commission, and learned what
was intended against himself; whereon he sat down and
wrote a commission, substituting their names for his own,
and sealed it with a copy of his father's royal signet,
which providentially, as he again says, he happened to
have by him. The next day they were attacked by a
pirate: during the fight, Hamlet boarded the enemy
alone, and was carried off by them, when he induced
them to land him in Denmark. 'So,' as Horatio observes,
'Guildenstern and Rosencranz go to 't.' Here, then, is
another reason to stir Hamlet to vengeance against his
uncle: and accordingly he is minded to strike before the
news from England shows that the treachery has been
penetrated. Meanwhile the king on his part is preparing
to strike at once. One of the courtiers is sent to Hamlet
to arrange about the fencing match with Laertes—an
office which he performs in the most approved euphuistic
style of the day. Hamlet plays upon him, as usual; jeers
him; overwhelms him with euphuism of a yet choicer
absurdity than his own, but eventually consents to the
match—all the more readily, perhaps, as he feels that he
has done Laertes some wrong by his violence at the grave.
Left alone with Horatio, Hamlet expresses his confidence
of success, adding, however, ' But thou would'st not think
how ill all's here about my heart; but it is no matter.'
Horatio urges him to yield to the presentiment, offering
to make his excuses to the king; but Hamlet will not:
' Not a whit; we defy augury: there's a special providence
in the fall of a sparrow. If it be now, 'tis not to come;
if it be not to come, it will be now; if it be not now, yet
it will come: the readiness is all. Since no man has
ought of what he leaves, what is 't to leave betimes?'

The king, queen, and courtiers enter the hall, and the preparations are made for the match. It is to be a courteous and chivalrous trial of skill, and so the king commences by reconciling the combatants. Hamlet offers his apologies to Laertes, which Laertes accepts, with a reservation about the point of honour. The rapiers are chosen, Laertes of course taking care to choose the one which has been prepared for his purpose. The king performs his part, ordering cups of wine to be set on the table, that, if Hamlet should obtain any advantage, he may pledge him royally, the event being announced to the city by the firing of cannon. They play, and the advantage is soon gained; the king drinks, but Hamlet will not yet. A second bout is called for : Hamlet again has some superiority ; and the queen, interested in the game, offers to pledge her son. He still will not drink ; but she has drunk already : the king, who has in vain tried to hinder her, exclaiming aside, ' It is the poisoned cup.' At the third bout, Laertes, who has hitherto reserved himself, puts forth his skill : Hamlet is not only touched, but wounded : a scuffle ensues : the rapiers are exchanged, and Laertes is wounded too. And now the crisis comes, all in a moment. The queen falls, crying out that she is poisoned. Hamlet orders the door to be locked. Laertes, who has fallen himself, in a very few words explains that the queen is poisoned and himself and Hamlet mortally wounded, and that the king is at the bottom of it all. Hamlet, with Laertes' rapier in his hand, stabs the king. The queen is dead already; the king dies almost instantly; Laertes follows them in a few moments, having begged Hamlet to exchange forgiveness. Hamlet would fain explain the whole tragedy to the horror-stricken spectators, but he finds himself dying, and commits the charge to Horatio, conquering his wish

to follow his friend in death by reminding him that, if
Horatio dies, no one will be left to tell the story and clear
Hamlet's name. Even while Hamlet is dying, the noise
of cannon announces that the ambassadors from England
and the Norwegian army from Poland have returned at
the same moment. But the poison is too swift, and he
dies, recommending with his last breath that the Norwegian prince, who has already some claim, be chosen as
his successor to the Danish crown. The Norwegians and
the English ambassadors enter, to find that the ears which
should give them hearing are senseless. Rosencranz and
Guildenstern are dead; but we hear the fate of the tools
with unconcern, now that we have lost those who played
with them. Horatio undertakes to explain all, begging
that the bodies may be placed on a conspicuous stage, that
all may see. The Norwegian prince, who already assumes
the command, gives orders accordingly, and directs that
Hamlet's body in particular be carried with martial
honours, paying a brief tribute to the virtues which he
would have shown, had he lived to wear the crown.
And so ' exeunt, with a dead march.'

Such is the end of what is most truly called ' the
tragical history of Hamlet.' As in the last scene of ' King
Lear,' we are stunned and confounded by the number of
deaths, crowding on each other in the space of a few
moments. The blood-guilty and the avenger of blood,
the traitors and their victim, fall one after another, till
the survivors seem all too few to bury the dead. 'This
quarry,' cries the Norwegian Prince :—

> This quarry cries on havoc. Oh, proud death!
> What feast is toward in thine eternal cell,
> That thou so many princes at a shoot
> So bloodily hast struck?

The general result of the play is summed up by Horatio

himself, when he offers to 'speak to the yet unknowing
world, how these things came about ':—

> So shall you hear
> Of carnal, bloody, and unnatural acts ;
> Of accidental judgments, casual slaughters ;
> Of deaths put on by cunning, and forced cause ;
> And, in this upshot, purposes mistook,
> Fallen on the inventors' heads : all this can I
> Truly deliver.

Yet this, though expressing, as I have said, the general
result of the action, as it appears to one who has
been half actor, half spectator, is far from expressing
the interest which the play has for us. What gives
this terrible story of crime upon crime, avenged by
chance medley, its profound importance in our eyes, is
its connexion with the character of Hamlet. We see a
strong nature paralysed in action by an intellect of extraordinary subtlety and a sensibility of extraordinary
keenness ; unbounded fertility of resource is employed
not to expedite the doing of the great deed, but to retard
it, by discovering other things, invisible to a less acute
perception, which must apparently be done first : that
energy which should have thrown off the burden is expended in estimating its weight and realising its pressure ;
and when the spell is broken—as it is at last—it is broken
by the sudden discovery that the time for deliberation is
past for ever, and the time for action all but over. It is
from Laertes, a dying man, that Hamlet, a dying man,
learns what he has to do :—

> It is here, Hamlet. Hamlet, thou art slain ;
> No medicine in the world can do thee good ;
> In thee there is not half an hour of life :
> The treacherous instrument is in thy hand,
> Unbated and envenom'd ; the foul practice

Hath turn'd itself on me.   Lo, here I lie,
Never to rise again: thy mother's poison'd—
I can no more—the king, the king's to blame.

Those few seconds, aided by the working of the poison,
have done what could not be done by days of self-
communing and parleying with others. Yet, nevertheless,
it is that self-communing and parleying with others that
have made Hamlet what he is to us. I will not attempt
to draw out the lessons which may be learnt from this
wonderful exhibition of human character and human life.
It would be vain to enumerate where the features are so
many and complex; vain to classify where each reader is
likely to form a different estimate of their relative importance.   Let it suffice to say, that probably there is no
play of Shakspeare which requires study so much and
repays it so well.   It is the opportunity which I have had
for such study that has been my chief satisfaction in the
composition of the lecture which I now bring to an end.

THE ENGLISH TRANSLATORS OF VIRGIL.[1]

To attempt an exhaustive account of all the translations
of the whole or parts of Virgil which have been made in
English is a task which would exceed our own opportunities, as it probably would the wishes of our readers.
Many of these productions are doubtless unknown to us:
with others we are acquainted by name or by character,
but they do not happen to be within our reach. It is
obvious, too, that there must be a considerable number
which do not deserve even the slender honour of a
passing commemoration. Here, as elsewhere, something
will depend on the date and consequent rarity of the
book. A worthless translation of the nineteenth century
calls for no mention at all; the work can be procured
without difficulty, or the reader, if he pleases, can himself
produce something of the same character. A worthless
translation of the sixteenth century has an adventitious
value: it is probably rare, and, at any rate, the power of
producing anything similar is gone for ever. While,
therefore, we do not cater for professed antiquaries, we
may, perhaps, hope to interest those who care to see how
Virgil has fared at the hands of writers, great and small,
belonging to the various schools of English poetry—who,
for the sake of a few instances of beauty and ingenuity,
will pardon a good deal of quaintness, and even some
dulness, and are not too severe to smile at occasional

[1] Reprinted from the *Quarterly Review*, July 1861.

passages of rampant extravagance and undisguised absurdity.

A very few words are all that need be spent on the first translation of Virgil into English by Caxton. The title, or rather tail-piece, runs as follows : ' Here fynyssheth the boke of Eneydos, compyled by Vyrgyle, whiche hathe be translated oute of latyne in to frenshe, And oute of frenshe reduced in to Englysshe by me Wyllm Caxton the xxii. daye of Iuyn, the yeare of our lorde m. iiii. clxxxx. The sythe yeare of the Regne of Kynge Henry the seuenth.' Some account of the original work (by Guillaume de Roy) may be found in Warton's ' History of English Poetry,' Section xxiv. It seems, in fact, to be a romance made out of the ' Æneid ' by numerous excisions and some additions, the bulk of the whole being comparatively small. We have only glanced at the translation, the printing as well as the language of which is calculated to repel all but black-letter students; but its chief characteristic seems to be excessive amplification of the Latin. This is apparently the version of Virgil's two lines (' Æn.' iv. 9, 10):—

> Anna soror, quæ me suspensam insomnia terrent ?
> Quis novus hic nostris successit sedibus hospes ?

Anne my suster and frende I am in ryghte gret thoughte strongely troubled and incyted, by dremes admonested whiche excyte my courage tenquire the maners & lygnage of this man thus valyaunt, strong, & puyssaunt, whiche deliteth hym strongely to speke, in deuysing the hie fayttes of armes and perillys daungerous whiche he sayth to haue passed, neweli hither comyn to soiourne in our countreys. I am so persuaded of grete admonestments that all my entendement is obfusked, endullyd and rauysshed.

It was not long before Caxton was to meet with one

who proved himself both a severe critic and a successful
rival. This was 'the Reverend Father in God, Mayster
Gawin Douglas, Bishop of Dunkel, and unkil to the Erle
of Angus,' whose 'xiii Bukes of Eneados of the famose
Poete Virgill translatet out of Latyne verses into Scottish
metir,' though not published till 1553, was written forty
years earlier. In the poetical preface to this work—a
composition of some five hundred lines—there is a long
paragraph, entitled in the margin 'Caxtoun's faultes,'
which passes in review the various delinquencies of the
father of printing; his omission of the greater part of the
'thre first bukis,' his assertion that the storm in Book I.
was sent forth by Æolus *and Neptune*, the 'prolixt and
tedious fassyoun' in which he deals with the story of
Dido, his total suppression of the Fifth Book, his ridiculous
rejection of the descent into the shades as fabulous, his
confusion of the Tiber with the Tover, his substitution of
Crispina for Deiphobe as the name of the Sibyl, the whole
being summed up by the assurance that—

> His buk is na mare like Virgil, dar I lay,
> Than the nyght oule resemblis the papingay.

The Bishop's own version has been highly praised by
competent judges, and we think deservedly. One specimen we will give, and it shall be from the exordium of
Book I.:—

> The battellis and the man I will discriue,
> Fra Troyis boundis first that fugitiue
> By fate to Italie come and coist lauyne,
> Ouer land and se cachit with meikill pyne
> By force of goddis aboue fra euery stede
> Of cruel Iuno throw auld remembrit feid:
> Grete payne in batelles sufferit he also
> Or he his goddis brocht in Latio

And belt the clete, fra quham of nobil fame
The latyne peopill taken has thare name,
And eke the faderis, princis of Alba,
Come, and the walleris of grete Rome alsua.

The reader of these lines will not fail to remark their
general closeness to the original, at the same time that he
will be struck with a certain diffuseness, such as seems to
be an inseparable adjunct of all early poetry. To expect
that such rude and primitive workmanship should represent adequately Virgil's peculiar graces would, of course,
be absurd; but the effort was a great one for the time
when it was made, and our northern neighbours may well
be proud of it.

Not less marked, though not altogether of the same
character, is the interest attaching to the next translation,
or rather fragment of translation. The Earl of Surrey
may or may not have died too soon for the political
well-being of England, but his fate was undoubtedly an
untimely one for her literature, and the historian who
denies his claim to our sympathy expressly acknowledges
his 'brilliant genius.'[1] His version, which embraces the
Second and Fourth Books of the 'Æneid,' deserves attention, not only for its own sake, but as the first known
specimen of English blank verse. As might be expected,
the versification is not entitled to any very high positive
praise. It is languid and monotonous, and sometimes unmetrical and inharmonious; but the advance
upon Gawin Douglas is very perceptible. The language
is chiefly remarkable for its purity and simplicity; occasionally there is a forcible expression, but in general a
uniform medium is kept, and a modern reader will still
complain a little of prolixity, though he will acknowledge

[1] Froude's *Hist. of England*, vol. iv. p. 500.

that the fault is being gradually corrected.   Dr. Nott has
remarked that some parts of the translation are more
highly-wrought than others; and while he draws attention
to the fact that Surrey has frequently copied Douglas,
whose work must have been known to him in MS., he
notes that these obligations are much more frequent in
the Second Book than in the Fourth.   The following
extract (we quote from Dr. Nott's edition) will, perhaps,
give an adequate notion of Surrey's manner (' Æn.' ii. 228,
'Tum vero tremefacta,' &c.):—

> New gripes of dread then pierce our trembling breasts.
> They said, Lacon's deserts had dearly bought
> His heinous deed, that pierced had with steel
> The sacred bulk, and thrown the wicked lance.
> The people cried with sundry greeing shouts
> To bring the horse to Pallas' temple blive,
> In hope thereby the goddess' wrath to appease.
> We cleft the walls and closures of the town,
> Whereto all help, and underset the feet
> With sliding rolls, and bound his neck with ropes.
> This fatal gin thus overclamb our walls,
> Stuft with arm'd men; about the which there ran
> Children and maids, that holy carols sang;
> And well were they whose hands might touch the cords.

The next translator, like Surrey, only lived to accomplish a portion of the ' Æneid;' but it was a much larger
portion, and it had the good fortune to be completed by
another hand.   Thomas Phaer, at one time ' sollicitour to
the king and quene's majesties, attending their honourable
counsaile in the marchies of Wales,' afterwards ' doctour
of physike,' published seven Books of the ' Æneid' in 1558.
At his death, two years afterwards, he left a version of
the Eighth and Ninth Books, and a part of the Tenth;
and in 1573 ' the residue' was ' supplied and the whole

worke together newly set forth by Thomas Twyne, gentleman.' This translation is in the long fourteen-syllable
or ballad metre, which had then come into vogue, being
used even in versions from the drama,[1] and which was
afterwards adopted by Chapman in rendering the ' Iliad.'
It is of Chapman, indeed, that the ordinary reader will
most naturally think in turning over Phaer's pages. Not
to dwell on the essential difference between the two
involved in the choice of subject, the ballad-measure of
Queen Mary's time being as ill suited to the Virgilian
hexameter as the ballad-measure of King James's may be
well suited to the Homeric, we shall probably be justified
in saying that Phaer's inferiority in original power makes
him more faithful as a translator, though less interesting
as a writer, and that his greater prolixity gives him a certain advantage in dealing with a measure which, from its
enormous length, can hardly be made attractive, when
written, as Chapman has written it, in couplets closely
interlaced and complicated with each other. But Phaer
has little or nothing of that ' daring fiery spirit ' which, as
Pope says, made Chapman write like an immature Homer ;
and though his language is not without merit, not many
expressions can be quoted from him which would appear
felicitous to a modern taste. His greatest eulogist is
Godwin,[2] who pronounces his book ' the most wonderful
depository of living description and fervent feeling that is
to be found, perhaps, in all the circle of literature ; ' and,
after quoting various passages with the highest commendation, says that whoever shall read his version of
Anchises's speech about Marcellus, at the end of the Sixth

---

[1] See Warton's account of ' Seneca his tenne Tragedies translated into
English,' 1581 (*Hist. of Eng. Poetry*, § lvii.).
[2] *Lives of Edward and John Philips* (London, 1815), pp. 247 foll.

Book, will cease to wonder that the imperial court was
dissolved in tears at Virgil's recital.   Let us see if we can
transcribe it dry-eyed:—

Æneas there (for walke with him he saw a seemly knight,
A goodly springold yong in glistring armour shining bright,
But nothing glad in face, his eyes downcast did shewe no
          cheere),
O father, what is he that walkes with him as equall peere ?
His onely son ? or of his stock some child of noble race ?
What bustling makes his mates ? how great he goth with
          portly grace ?
But cloud of louring night his head full henuy wrappes about.
Then lord Anchises spake, and from his eyes the teares brake
          out,
O son, thy peoples huge lamented losse seeke not to knowe.
The destnies shall this child onto the world no more but
          showe,
Nor suffer long to liue: O Gods, though Rome you think to
          strong
And ouermuch to match, for enuie yet do us no wrong.
What wailings loude of men in stretes, in feeldes, what
          mourning cries
In mighty campe of Mars, at this mans death in Rome shall
          rise ?
What funeralls, what numbers dead of corpses shalt thou see,
O Tyber flood, whan fleeting nere his new tombe thou shalt
          flee ?
Nor shall there neuer child from Troian line that shal proceede
Exalt his graunsirs hope so hie, nor neuer Rome shal breede
An impe of maruel more, nor more on man may iustly bost.
O vertue, O prescribid faith, O righthand valiaunt most !
Durst no man him haue met in armes conflicting, foteman
          fearce,
Or wold he fomy horses sides with spurres encountring pearce.
O piteous child, if euer thou thy destnies hard moist breake,
Marcellus thou shalt be.   Now reatche me Lillios, Lilly flours,
Giue purple Violetts to me, this nouews soule of ours

With giftes that I may spreade, and though my labour be but
   vayne,
Yet do my duety deere I shall.   Thus did they long com-
   playne.'

   The remaining attempts in the sixteenth century deserve
registering, chiefly as curious and grotesque experiments.
Abraham Fleming, indeed, gave promise of something
better in his ' Bucolikes of Publius Virgilius Maro, with
alphabeticall Annotations upon proper nams of Gods,
Goddesses, men, women, hilles, flouddes, cities, townes,
and villages, &c., orderly placed in the margent. Dravvne
into plaine and familiar Englishe, verse for verse ' (London, 1575), which is in rhymed fourteen-syllable measure
in the style of Phaer.   But in 1589 he published another
version of the ' Eclogues,' along with one of the ' Georgics,'
in which he discarded ' foolish rime, the nise observation
whereof many times darkeneth, corrupteth, peruerteth,
and falsifieth both the sense and the signification,' in favour
of unrhymed lines of fourteen or fifteen syllables, not very
graceful in themselves, and rendered additionally quaint
by a strange fashion of introducing into the middle of the
text explanatory notes, which form part and parcel of the
metre. Thus he makes Virgil compliment his patron on—

                        Thy verses, which alone are worthy of
The buskins [brave] of Sophocles [I meane his stately stile],

and mentions, among the prognostics of fair weather—

And Nisus [of Megera king and turned to a falcon]
Capers aloft in skie so cleore, and Scylla [Nisus daughter
Changed into a larke] doth smart for [his faire] purple haire.

   The prevalent mania, too, for reviving classical metre,
which infected even Sidney and Spenser, took hold, as
might be expected, of the would-be translators of Virgil.

Webbe, in his 'Discourse of English Poetrie' (London, 1586), 'blundered,' as he aptly as well as modestly expresses it, upon a hexametrical version of the two first 'Æglogues,' in which Melibœus tells his 'kidlings':—

Neuer again shall I now in a greene bowre sweetlie reposed
See ye in queachie briers farre a loofe clambring on a high hill,
Now shall I sing no Iygges, nor whilst I doo fall to my iunkets,
Shall ye, my Goates, cropping sweete flowers and leaues sit
    about me.

But the most considerable, and by far the most extraordinary feat of this nature was performed by Richard Stanyhurst, in his 'First Foure Bookes of Virgil's Æneis translated into English Heroical Verse, with other Poëticell deuises thereto annexed' (London, 1583). His remarks on his own translation are a curiosity in themselves, and may remind us of Chapman's 'Mysteries revealed in Homer.' 'Virgil,' he says, 'in diuerse places inuesteth Iuno with this epitheton, Saturnia. M. Phaer ouerpasseth it, as if it were an idle word shuffled in by the authour to damme vp the chappes of yawning verses. I neuer to my remembrance omitted it, as indeed a terme that carieth meate in his mouth, and so emphaticall, as that the ouerslipping of it were in effect the choaking of the Poets discourse, in such hauking wise as if he were throtled with the chincoughe. And to inculcate that clause the better, where the mariage is made in the fourth boke betwene Dido and Aeneas, I adde in my verse Watry Iuno. Although mine Author vsed not the epitheton, Watrye, but onlye made mention of earth, ayer, and fier, yet I am well assured that word throughly conceiued of an hedeful student may giue him such light as may ease him of six moneths trauaile; whyche were well spent, if that Wedlocke were wel vnderstoode.' His practice was not

less remarkable than his theory. Phaer had talked of
' Sir Gyas ' and ' Sir Cloanthus,' made Isis masquerade as
' Dame Rainbowe,' and turned ' Gallum rebellem ' into
' rebell French.'   Stanyhurst (we take the instances given
by Warton) calls Corœbus a ' bedlamite;' arms Priam
with his sword ' Morglay,' a blade that figures in Gothic
romance; makes Dido's ' parvulus Æneas ' into ' a cockney,
a dandiprat hop-thumb,' and says that when Jupiter
' oscula libavit natæ ' he ' bust his pretty prating parrot.'
But he shall exhibit himself more at length, and somewhat
more favourably, in a passage from the end of the First
Æneid (v. 736, ' Dixit, et in mensam,' &c.):—

Thus sayd, with sipping in vessel nicely she dipped.
Shee chargeth Bicias: at a blow bee lustily swapping
Thee wine fresh spuming with a draught swild up to the
    bottom.
Thee remnaunt lordings him pledge: Then curled Iöppas
Twang'd on his harp golden what he whillon learned of Atlas.
How the moone is trauers'd, how planet soonnie reuolueth,
He chaunts: how mankind, how beasts dooe carrie their off-
    spring:
How flouds be engendered, so how fire, celestial Arcture,
Thee raine breede sev'n stars, with both the Trionical orders:
Why the sun at westward so timely in winter is housed,
And why the night seasons in summer swiftly be posting.
The Moores hands clapping, thee Troians plaudite flapped.

In passing to the seventeenth century we feel that a
change has already set in. The metres adopted are such
as commend themselves to modern ears; the language,
though varying according to the greater or less skill of
the individual writer, is not in general marked by much
quaintness or redundancy.   Let us take a specimen from
the earliest version with which we are acquainted[1]—

[1] When we wrote the above, we had not met with a translation of the
Second Æneid published in 1620 by Sir Thomas Wroth, under the title of

'Dido's Death : Translated out of the best of Latine
Poets into the best of vulgar Languages. By one that
hath no name' (London, 1622). 'Præterea fuit in tectis,'
&c. (Book iv., v. 457) :—

> In her house of alone
> A temple too she had, of former spouse,
> By her much Reuerenc't, with holy bowes
> And Snowwhite Wooll adorn'd, whence oft she hears
> A voice that like her husbands call appeares,
> When darke night holds the world. The ellenge Owle
> Oft on her housetop dismall tunes did houle,
> Lamenting wofull notes at length outdrawing :
> And many former Fortune-tellers' awing
> Forewarnings fright : AEneas too in Dreames
> Makes her runne mad : left by her selfe, she seemes
> Alone some vncouth foule long way to haue taken,
> Tyrians to seeke in desert Land forsaken.

The vogue which these translations obtained does not
seem always to have been proportioned to their merits.
In 1628 were published ' Virgil's Georgicks Englished by
Thomas May, Esq'.,' and 'Virgil's Eclogves translated
into English by W. L.' (William Lisle). The former, if
little read, has been not unfrequently mentioned since ;
the very existence of the latter has been forgotten.[1] Yet

The Destruction of Troy, or the Acts of Aeneas, a copy of which is in the
British Museum. Our space will only allow us to say that the metre is
Phaer's, but the style more modern.

[1] An account of Lisle, who was an Anglo-Saxon scholar and antiquary, is
given in Chalmers's *Biographical Dictionary* ; but nothing is said of this
translation. He appears, however, to have dedicated an edition of a treatise
by Ælfric to Prince Charles in a copy of verses ' by way of Eclogue, imitating
the 4th of Virgile,' besides being the author of a version from Du Bartas,
and of *The Fair Ethiopian*, which Chalmers calls a long poem of very
indifferent merit.

Benson, whom we shall have occasion to mention below, says that almost
100 of May's lines are adopted by Dryden with very little alteration. The
first two lines of May seem to have been copied by Ogilby.

> What makes rich crops, what season most inclines
> To plowing th' earth, and marrying elms with vines.—*May.*

our readers, if we mistake not, will peruse the following
extract from May's heroics with comparative indifference,
while they will thank us for selecting two of Lisle's
stanzas. (' Felix qui potuit,' &c., ' Georg.' ii. 490) :—

> Happy is he that knowes the cause of things,
> That all his feares to due subjection brings,
> Yea, fate itselfe, and greedy Acheron !
> Yea, happy sure is he, who ere has knowen
> The rurall Gods, Sylvanus, and great Pan,
> And all the sister Nymphs ! that happy man
> Nor peoples voices, nor kings purple moue,
> Nor dire ambition sundring brothers loue,
> Nor th' Istrian Dacians fierce conspiracies,
> Nor Romes estate, nor falling monarchies.

' Quem fugis, ah demens,' &c. (' Ecl.' ii. 60) :—

> (Ah foolish Fon) whom dost thou seek to shun ?
> Why, Dardan Paris (that same shepheard knight).
> Yea, e'ne the gods themselves, the woods did woon :
> Let Pallas praise her Towres goodly hight,
> And in her pompous Palaces delight
> Which shee hath builded : but of all the rest,
> In my conceit, the Forrest-Life is best.
> The crewell grim-faced Lionesse pursues
> The bloody Woolfe : the Woolfe the kid so free
> The wanton capring kidd doth chiefly chuse
> Amongst the flowring Cythisus to bee :
> And Corydon (Alexis) followes thee :
> So each thing as it likes : and all affect
> According as their nature doth direct.

We must confess, however, that Lisle's ' Eclogues,' which
are in a variety of metres, contain other passages less

What makes Rich Grounds, in what Cælestial Signs
'Tis good to Plow, and marry Elms with Vines.—*Ogilby.*

Dryden borrows also once at least from Lisle. But of his plagiarisms more
below.

attractive than this. Nor should it be forgotten that much
of the charm of these stanzas consists in their reminding
us of strains which, when Lisle wrote, already belonged
to the past—the pastoral poetry of Spenser. May's notes
are less sweet, but they are probably more his own;
they reach forward, not backward; they contain not an
echo of Spenser, but a prophecy of Dryden.

The year 1632 saw a complete version of the ' Æneid '
by Vicars,[1] and a translation of the First Book by Sandys.
Vicars, a Parliamentary fanatic, is known to the world as
a poet only by the savage lines in ' Hudibras,' where he is
coupled with Withers and Prynne as ' inspired with ale
and viler liquors to write in spite of nature and his stars.'
Sandys is celebrated as the author of the translation of
Ovid which Pope read as a child and (not an invariable
consequence with him) praised as a man. There seems to
be no merit in Vicars. Sandys is perhaps superior to May,
but, like him, he pleases chiefly as the harbinger of better
things in language and versification. Here is a favourable
specimen (' Est in secessu,' &c., ' Æn.' i. 159) :—

> Deepe in a Bay an Ile with strecht-out sides
> A harbor makes, and breakes the justling tides :
> The parting floods into a landlockt sound
> Their streams discharge, with rocks invirond round,
> Whereof two, equal lofty, threat the skies,
> Under whose lee the safe Sea silent lies :
> Their browes with dark and trembling woods arayd,
> Whose spreading branches cast a dreadfull shade.

Sir John Denham's translation of the Second Æncid is
said to have been made in 1636. We know not whether

---

[1] The title of Vicars's work is *The XII Æneids of Virgil, the most
renowned Laureat-Prince of Latine Poets, translated into English deca-
syllables, by Iohn Vicars.* Sandys's is added to an edition of his translation
of Ovid's *Metamorphoses* (1632), and entitled, *An Essay to the Translation
of Virgil's Æneis.*

his ' Passion of Dido for Æneas' was written at the same
time, but it seems rather the better of the two.   In both,
however, Denham is very unequal ; 'a series of vigorous
couplets will be followed by passages written in ' con-
catenated metre,' as Johnson calls it, and disfigured by
bad or feeble rhymes.   He is fond, too, of engrafting
comments and conceits upon his original, as when Dido
tells Æneas—

> Thou shouldst mistrust a wind
> False as thy Vows, and as thy heart unkind.

The Queen's dying speech is a fair example of his better
manner ('Dulces exuviæ,' &c., ' Æn.' iv. 651) :—

> Dear Reliques whilst that Gods and Fates gave leave,
> Free me from care, and my glad soul receive :
> That date which fortune gave I now must end
> And to the shades a noble Ghost descend :
> Sichæus blood by his false Brother spilt
> I have reveng'd, and a proud City built :
> Happy alas! too happy I had liv'd,
> Had not the Trojan on my Coast arriv'd :
> But shall I dye without revenge ? yet dye,
> Thus, thus with joy to thy Sichæus flye.
> My conscious Foe my Funeral fire shall view
> From Sea, and may that Omen him pursue.

A better translation of this Fourth Book appeared in
1648 by Sir Richard Fanshaw, a friend of Denham's, who
does justice to his powers in an excellent copy of verses
recommendatory of his version of Pastor Fido. Fanshaw's
case is not unlike Lisle's : instead of prosecuting the
cultivation of the heroic, he revives that of the Spenserian
stanza.   The choice was not a happy one under the circumstances : Virgil did not write in periods of nine lines,
and Fanshaw, not being a diffuse writer, is led in consequence to run stanza into stanza, so that the versification

does not enable us to follow the sense. Where, however, sense and metre happen to coincide, he may be read with real pleasure, as in the following passage ('Dissimulare etiam sperasti,' &c., 'Æn.' iv. 305):—

> Didst thou hope too by stealth to leave my land,
> And that such treason could be unbetrayed,
> Nor should my love, nor thy late plighted hand,
> Nor Dido, who would die, thy flight have stayed?
> Must too this voyage be in winter made?
> Through storms?   O cruel to thyself and me!
> Didst thou not hunt strange lands and sceptres swayed
> By others, if old Troy revived should be,
> Should Troy itself be sought through a tempestuous sea?

We now come to the first translation of the whole of Virgil, 'The Works of Publius Virgilius Maro, Translated by John Ogilby, and Adorn'd with Sculptur,' first published in 1649-50, and afterwards, we believe, three times reprinted. This indefatigable adventurer, who practised successively or simultaneously the callings of dancing-master, original poet, translator from the classics, and literary projector, frequently ruined, but always recovering himself, learnt Latin in middle life, and proceeded to translate Virgil, as he afterwards learnt Greek and translated Homer. In his way he must be pronounced successful ; he was ridiculed, but his version continued to be bought till Dryden's came into the market ; and the 'Sculpturs' (engravings), which form a prominent feature in this, as in his other books, were considered good enough to be borrowed by his rival, who did not like to go to the expense of new plates. Nay, he seems to have found admirers still later : his work heads the list of the Lady's Library in the 'Spectator,' Dryden's 'Juvenal' coming second ; and we happen to know that it not only is included among the books recommended for examina-

tion to the fraternity of labourers whom the Dean of
Westminster is marshalling with a view to the production
of a new English dictionary, but that a member of the
band has undertaken to study it. In its day it was
doubtless a useful and—in the absence of anything better
suited to the taste of that generation—even a readable
book. It is sufficiently close to the words of Virgil —
much more so than Dryden. Its margin is furnished with
a collection of notes from the old commentators, done in
a tolerably business-like style; and though the author
shows no trace of poetical feeling, no real appreciation of
poetical language, he writes in general fair commonplace
prosaic English, while his mastery over the heroic couplet
will probably be pronounced creditable by those who,
like our readers, have the means of comparing him with
his predecessors and contemporaries. Ad aperturam
libri, we select the opening of his Sixth Æneid :—

> Weeping he said : at last with Sails a-trip,
> To the Euboick Confines steers his Ship :
> Then sharpflook'd Anchors they cast out before,
> And the tall Navy fring'd the edging Shore.
> To Latian Shores the youthful Trojans leap'd :
> Some seek the hidden Seeds of Fire that slept
> In Veins of Flint ; Beasts shadie Holds, the Woods
> Others cut down, and find concealed Floods :
> But those high Tow'rs pious Æneas sought,
> Where Phœbus reign'd, dread Sybils spacious vault,
> Whom Delius had inspired with future Fates.
> They enter Trivia's Grove, and Golden Gates.
>   Dædalus leaving Crete (as Stories say)
> Trusting swift Wings, through skies, no usual way,
> Made to the colder north a desperate Flight,
> And did at last on Chalcis Tow'r alight :
> There he his Wings to thee, O Phœbus, paid,
> And wide Foundations of a Temple laid.

> The stately porch Androgeus death adorn'd,
> Then the Athenians, punish'd, early mourn'd
> For seven slain children : there the Lottery stood :
> High Crete against it overlook'd the Flood.

Ogilby's elaborate work may possibly have stood in the way of other attempts on a large scale, but it did not deter 'holiday-authors,' as Dryden calls them, who felt they could do better, from exhibiting specimens of their powers in translating portions of Virgil. The Fourth Book of the 'Æneid' still continued to be popular with this class of writers, three or four of whom attempted it about this time—Edmund Waller and Sidney Godolphin (1658), Sir Robert Howard (1660), and Sir Robert Stapylton. None of them are memorable ; but as some slight interest may be felt in comparing them, we give their versions of the end of the book in juxtaposition :—

> From heaven then Iris with dewy wings,
> On which the Sun a thousand glories flings,
> Flies to her head: This to the dark abode
> I bear, and free thee from this body's load,
> She said : then with her right hand cuts her hair,
> And her enlarged breath glides into air.—*Howard.*

> So dewy rose-winged Iris,[1] having won
> Thousand strange colours from the adverse Sun,
> Slides down, stands on her head : I bear this, charged,
> Sacred to Dis: be from this flesh enlarged.
> Thus says, and cuts her hair : together slides
> All heat, and into air her spirit glides.—*Stapylton.*

Godolphin makes such short work of Dido's death, that we are compelled to begin our extract from him some lines earlier :—

> Then Juno, looking with a pitying eye
> Upon so sad and lasting misery,

---

[1] ' Dewy rose-winged Iris' also appears in Ogilby, who resembles Stapylton likewise in his version of 'teque isto corpore solvo.'

> Since deepest wounds can no free passage give
> To self-destroyers who refuse to live,
> Sent Iris down to cut the fatal hair;
> Which done, her whole life vanished into air.

Waller's work merely embraces about a hundred lines, which were not translated by Godolphin. The following lines will show that it is well for him that his reputation as an English poet does not rest on his translation. 'Tu lacrimis evicta meis' (v. 548).—

> Ah sister! vanquished with my passion, thou
> Betrayedst me first, dispensing with my vow.
> Had I been constant to Sychæus still
> And single-lived,[1] I had not known this ill.
>   Such thoughts torment the Queen's enraged breast,
> While the Dardanian does securely rest
> In his tall ship, for sudden flight prepared:
> To whom once more the son of Jove appeared.

More remarkable than any of these experiments on Dido's story is 'An Essay upon Two of Virgil's Eclogues, and Two Books of his Æneis (if this be not enough) towards the Translation of the whole. By James Harrington, 1658.' The author, Sir James Harrington, better known by his 'Oceana,' is compared to Vicars by Butler, who, disliking his politics, chose to sneer at his poetry; but those who have seen his Essay will feel that the sneer falls pointless. Unequal, and occasionally grotesque, he yet shows undeniable signs of vigour and ability, reminding us of Cowley both in his better and his worse manner. His felicities are not indeed Virgilian, as when he translates 'Oscula libavit natæ'

> Jove, with the smiles that clear the weather, dips
> His coral in the nectar of her lips,

---

[1] 'Single-lived' is the spelling of the copy before us (1658); but it may be doubted whether the writer did not intend 'lived' for a verb. In that case the compound adjective would be rather a felicitous blunder.

or speaks of Æneas among the paintings at Carthage as

> wandering through a world the pencil struck
> As out of Chaos with stupendous luck:

but they are felicities nevertheless: nor need we deny him
the praise of ingenuity when he tells us that Dido

> brings the Trojan to her court,
> And sends a royal present to the port,
> A hundred ewes and lambs, a hundred sows;
> And Bacchus rides upon a drove of cows.

The first simile in the 'Æneid' is rendered thus:—

> As when some mighty city bursteth out
> Into sedition, the ignoble rout
> Assault the palaces, usurp the street
> With stones, or brands, or anything they meet
> (For Fury's armoury is everywhere):
> But, if a man of gravity appear
> Whose worth they own, whose piety they know,
> Are mute, are planted in the place, and grow
> Unto his lips, that smooth, that melt their souls:
> So hush the waves where Neptune's chariot rolls.

As might be expected, the number of holiday-authors
increased formidably after the Restoration—so formidably
that it would be impossible within our present limits to
give any adequate account of their several performances.
Not one of the six volumes of Tonson's 'Miscellany' is
without some pieces of Virgilian translation: one of them,
the first, contains a complete translation of the 'Eclogues'
by various hands; a collection which Dryden enriched by
two of his own versions, and from which he afterwards
did not disdain to borrow.[1]   Of these studies by far the

---

[1] Dryden's chief plagiarisms are from the version of Eclogue I., 'by John
Caryll, Esqre,' twenty-four of whose lines he appropriates, with slight
changes. But there are cases of obligation in subsequent Eclogues which a
future editor of Dryden's Virgil will do well to note.

most noteworthy is 'The Last Eclogue, translated, or rather
imitated, in the year 1666, by Sir William Temple, Bart.,'
a remarkably flowing and vigorous paraphrase, some lines
of which might challenge comparison with Dryden's own.
As it appears now to be quite forgotten, we shall not
apologise for extracting from it rather copiously :—

> One labour more, O Arethusa, yield,
> Before I leave the shepherds and the field:
> Some verses to my Gallus ere we part,
> Such as may one day break Lycoris' heart,
> As she did his. Who can refuse a song
> To one that loved so well, and died so young?
> Begin, and sing Gallus' unhappy fires,
> While yonder goat to yonder branch aspires
> Out of his reach. We sing not to the deaf:
> An answer comes from every trembling leaf.
>
> .   .   .   .
>
> Under a lonely tree he lay and pined,
> His flock about him feeding on the wind,
> As he on love : such kind and gentle sheep
> E'en fair Adonis would be proud to keep.
>
> .   .   .   .
>
> What shakes the branches ? what makes all the trees
> Begin to bow their heads, the goats their knees?
> Oh! 'tis Silvanus, with his mossy beard
> And leafy crown, attended by a herd
> Of wood-born satyrs : see ! he shakes his spear,
> A green young oak, the tallest of the year.
>
> .   .   .   .
>
> Would it had pleased the Gods I had been born
> Just one of you, and taught to wind a horn,
> Or wield a hook, or prune a branching vine,
> And known no other love but, Phyllis, thine,
> Or thine, Amyntas : what though both are brown?
> So are the nuts and berries on the down ;
> Amongst the vines, the willows, and the springs
> Phyllis makes garlands, and Amyntas sings.

No cruel absence calls my love away
Further than bleating sheep can go astray:
Here, my Lycoris, here are shady groves,
Here fountains cool and meadows soft: our loves
And lives may here together wear and end:
O, the true joys of such a fate and friend!

Meantime, while veteran diplomatists, rising peers, and future secretaries of state were employing themselves with these occasional performances, the whole of Virgil was being undertaken by a patrician author, Richard Maitland, Earl of Lauderdale. Unfortunately for his reputation, his lordship appears to have hesitated about publishing, and, while he hesitated, the time went by. The version of the First Georgic appeared in the third volume of the 'Miscellany,' in 1694: the 'Æneid' was communicated to Dryden before he had embarked in his own great undertaking, and suffered to remain in his hands afterwards. At length it was resolved that it should be given to the world, but the design was prevented by the author's death. Two years later Dryden took his place as the translator of Virgil, and the chance was gone for even a temporary occupation of the throne. When the great poet, in the preface to his 'Æneid,' complimented his noble friend's work, acknowledging some of his obligations to it, and concealing others, he spoke as if he did not expect that it would ever see the light. Eventually, however, the entire translation found an editor, who supposed, or affected to suppose, that if it could no longer reign alone, the crown might at any rate be divided. 'They who do not place my Lord Lauderdale upon the same foot with Mr. Dryden,' says this friendly critic, 'must be equally injurious to the one's judgment and to the other's translation; for t' will be easy to find upon the parallel that the poetry of South and North Britain is no more incompatible than the constitu-

tion.' But the union did not extend to translations of
Virgil. The North British version seems to have attracted
no attention: Trapp praises it, and Martyn and Davidson
quote it; but it probably was never read. Anyone who
will now take the trouble to look at it will see that it is
not without merit. But though the noble translator was a
better versifier and a greater master of English than Ogilby,
he had studied in a school which is on the whole less
favourable to a writer of limited powers: instead of copying his original closely, he sometimes transforms and adds
to it; and his transformations and additions are hardly,
in Denham's language, true to Virgil's fame. The following is an extract from the version of the 'Georgics,' which
is more flowing than that of the 'Æneid' ('Nocte leves
melius stipulæ,' &c. 'Georg.' i. 289):—

> Parched meadows and dry stubble mow by night:
> Then moisture reigns, which flies Apollo's light.
> Some watch, and torches sharp with cleaving knives
> Till late by winter fires: their careful wives,
> To ease their labour, glad the homely rooms
> With cheerful notes, while weaving on their looms,
> Or else in kettles boil new wine, and skim
> The dregs with leaves, when they o'erflow the brim.
> But reap your yellow grain with glowing heat,
> And on your floor with scorching Phœbus beat.
> When days are clear, then naked till and sow:
> In lazy winter labourers lazy grow:
> For that's a jovial time, when jovial swains
> Meet, and in feasting waste their summer gains,
> As seamen, come to port from stormy seas,
> First crown their vessels, then indulge their ease.

In 1690, as we have already intimated, Dryden's translation was published. Of its surpassing merits we must
defer speaking till we have finished our chronological
enumeration, as they are not of a nature which will bear

dismissing in a few sentences. Standing as it does nearly midway in the history of Virgilian translations, it throws into the shade not only all that preceded, but all that have followed it. If Dryden's successors are less incapable of being put into comparison with him than his predecessors, it is to Dryden himself that the advantage, such as it is, is in some measure due.

Dryden's successors did not, in the first instance, attempt to meet him on his own ground. He had himself expressed an opinion, whether deliberately formed or not, in favour of translations into blank verse; and translations into blank verse soon became as popular among writers, if not among readers, of poetry as translations into rhyme. The illustrious examples of Shakspeare and Milton, long slighted, had at last done their work, the one restoring blank verse in tragedy, the other reinstating it in epic poetry : the new measure was doubtless felt to be easier than the old ; and criticism was beginning to find out that a translation which should represent the words as well as the general meaning of an author could hardly be executed in such rhyme as the literary public of the eighteenth century would care to read. Accordingly, when Dr. Brady, Nahum Tate's coadjutor in the New Version of the Psalms, turned to translating the 'Æneid' (1716–1726), he translated it into blank verse. His attempt is characterised contemptuously enough by Johnson, whose opinion we do not feel inclined to dispute. The next blank verse experiment is better known to ourselves, and probably to our readers also. In the last volume of Tonson's 'Miscellany,' Trapp appeared as a translator of the Tenth Eclogue into rhyme, and of the end of the First Georgic into blank verse : he was afterwards to execute a blank version of the whole of Virgil's three poems, publishing the 'Æneid' in 1717 or 1718, the 'Bucolics' and 'Georgics' about 1731.

We may perhaps speak of his work more in detail hereafter; for the present it is sufficient to say, that whether owing to the University reputation of the author, who was the first Oxford Professor of Poetry, or to the more substantial recommendations of a version which, as Johnson says, might serve as the clandestine refuge of schoolboys, and of a commentary containing a good deal of information and not a little prosaic good sense, the book reached the honours of a third edition in 1735.

In 1764 Trapp's example was followed by another ex-Professor of Poetry, Hawkins by name. If we are unable to give any account of his version of the 'Æneid,' we may plead as our excuse that it is not to be found in the library of the University of which the translator was a professor, nor in that of the college (Pembroke) of which he was a Fellow, nor again in that of the British Museum. By way of amends, however, we can tell our readers something of the translation which appeared next in order of time, 'The Works of Virgil Englished by Robert Andrews, 1766.' The author, who was fortunate enough to secure Baskerville for his printer, and thus to make his work externally, at any rate, a most attractive one, imputes the shortcomings of former translators to their adoption of rhyme. 'The best of 'em had not doft their Gothic shackles when they dared to the race the most rapid of the poets: how then should they save their distance?' Here is this unshackled runner's own start :—

> M. You, Tityro, lolling 'neath the spreading beech,
> Muse on your slender straw the sylvan song.
> We leave our country, our sweet meadows quit,
> Our country fly. You, Tityro, soft imbowered,
> Prompt fair Amarilla to the echoing woods.
> T. A God, Meliboe! gave us these calm hours.

This singular fashion of manipulating proper names runs

through the book, and is indeed one of its chief characteristics. Thus we have Daphny, Alexy, Mopsy, Philly, Lycid (a name which may perhaps show that Mr. Andrews conceived himself only to be taking a Miltonic liberty), Thyrse, Menalca, Paleme, Cloanth, Helnor and Lyke (for Helenor and Lycus), Mezente, and Jutna (for Juturna).

In 1767 was published 'The Æneid of Virgil, translated into Blank Verse by Alexander Strahan, Esq.,' who had already twice before attempted portions of the poem. He professes to have 'kept as close to his author as the late Dr. Trapp in respect of his sense, but to have taken a little more compass for the sake of harmony.' The experiment issues in lines like these ('Quæ te tam læta tulerunt,' 'Æn.' i. 605):—

> What happy ages gave you to the world?
> What parents such perfection could produce?
> While to their mother sea the rivers flow,
> While mountains cast their spreading shadows round,
> While Æther feeds the stars, your sacred name,
> Your bright idea shall for ever last,
> Where'er my fate may bear me o'er the globe.

The Tenth and Twelfth Books were contributed by Dobson, the same who gave a Latin dress to the 'Paradise Lost.'

More than thirty years remained to the end of the century; but it was not till 1794 that another blank verse translator of Virgil showed himself. This was the Rev. James Beresford, Fellow of Merton College, otherwise known as the author of a popular *jeu d'esprit* called the 'Miseries of Human Life,' and of a less successful polemic against Calvinism. Cowper's 'Homer' had recently appeared, and had been recognised to be, what it certainly is, a work of real merit; and it was tempting to try whether the same process could not after all be made to

answer with Virgil. But Cowper's success, whatever it
may have been, was due, not to the theories of his preface,
but to his practice as an original poet : it established a
case for blank verse as wielded by Cowper, not as wielded
by Mr. Beresford. As usual, we give a specimen of his
translation (' Tempus erat, quo prima,' 'Æn.' ii. 268) :—

> 'Twas at the hour when first oblivious rest
> To care-sick mortals comes, and, gift of gods,
> Of all their gifts best welcome, steals unfelt,
> When, as I slept, before my eyes, behold,
> Hector, all woe-begone, appeared to come
> In present sight, and pour down copious tears,
> As dragged erewhile fast by the chariot wheels
> Sordid with bloody dust, his big-swoln feet
> With thongs transpierced. Ah me! what seemed he then!
> How from that Hector changed, who late returned
> Clad in the glorious spoils of Peleus' son,
> Or fresh from hurling on the barks of Greece
> His Phrygian fires! Now—squalid was his beard,
> His locks blood-knotted, and those gashes too
> Were seen, which round his parent country's walls,
> In fights of yore, he, numberless, had borne.
> Melting in tears, I seemed to accost the shade
> Spontaneous, and these mournful words draw forth.

Dr. Symmons—who speaks of blank verse rather
happily,[1] as ' only a laborious and doubtful struggle to
escape from the fangs of prose,' adding that, ' if it ever
ventures to relax into simple and natural phraseology, it
instantly becomes tame, and the prey of its pursuer '—has
passed a censure which, inapplicable to Cowper, for whom
it was intended, is not more than a just description of
what has been accomplished by Cowper's Virgilian
follower.

The rhyming translators of Virgil during the eighteenth

---

[1] Preface to *Æneid*, p. 22 (2nd edition).

century were fewer, but they were men of more mark.
Some portion of their success is doubtless due to the
vehicle which they chose. The heroic couplet, as
managed by Dryden, is far more open to imitation than
the blank verse of the ' Paradise Lost; ' the sources of
the pleasure which it creates lie nearer to the surface,
and are more accessible to an ordinary writer. And if
Dryden is more imitable than Milton, Pope is more
imitable than Dryden. Dryden was essentially capricious:
sometimes vigorous and splendid, at others flat and
slovenly. He was a critic, but his canons of criticism are
constantly varying, and the astonishing effects which he
at times produces are due to ear and natural instinct
rather than to deliberate judgment. With Pope, on the
other hand, all was conscious art; he took his measure,
such as it was, of the capabilities of the heroic couplet,
and with steady and unwearied patience set himself to
realise them in his practice; and his successors, after
admiring the marvellous result, might reasonably hope,
by the exertion of moderate powers of analysis, to attain
to some notion of the process. In or before 1724, after
the completion of the English ' Iliad,' Benson, celebrated
by Pope as the admirer of Milton and Johnston's Psalms,
being dissatisfied with the way in which Dryden had
dealt with the poetry and the agriculture of Virgil, published ' Virgil's Husbandry ; or an Essay on the Georgics; '
a version of the Second Book, with explanatory notes,
following it up next year with a similar ' Essay ' on the
First. The subjoined extract, if it has no other interest,
will show, at any rate, that Pope's influence was already
beginning to tell (' Nec requies quin aut pomis,' ' Georg.'
ii. 516) :—

> Nor rests the year, but still with fruit abounds
> Or vast increase of herds, or loads the grounds

M 2

With piles unnumbered of promiscuous grain,
Subdues the barns, and triumphs on the plain.
A storm descends: Sicyonian berries feel
The nimble poundings of the clattering steel:
The falling acorns rustle in the wood,
And swine run homeward cheerful with their food:
The copse her wildings gives from shattered bowers,
And teeming autumn lays down all her stores,
Whilst high on sunny rocks the clustered vine
Boils into juice and reddens into wine.

A much more memorable attempt to beat Dryden with
Pope's weapons was made by Pitt, who, after dallying for
some time with a new version of the ' Æneid,' completed it
at last, and published it in 1740.   Pitt was intimate with
Spence, the friend of Pope; and the great poet, in words
which seem not to have been preserved, signified his
approval of an experiment which but for him would
scarcely have been possible.   After the author's death,
Joseph Warton, a brother Wykehamist, completed the
translation by the addition of the ' Eclogues ' and ' Georgics,'
and republished it with a dedication to the first Lord
Lyttelton, in which he finds fault with Dryden, and asserts
Pitt's superiority: a judgment, the merits of which, as
well as those of Warton's own translation, we hope shortly
to consider.   Sotheby's version of the ' Georgics,' the first
edition of which (1800) is just included in the eighteenth
century, will come in for its share of notice most appro-
priately at the same time.   All three were conspicuously
inferior to Dryden, but they were in some sense foemen
worthy of his steel, and it is well that they should have
an opportunity of exhibiting themselves along with him.
We have been in some doubt whether to reserve our
judgment of Beattie's ' Eclogues;' but a comparison of his
translation with Dryden's and Warton's, by a favourable
though not undiscriminating judge, is included in his

Life by Sir William Forbes, and may be consulted there.
The translation seems not to have been greatly valued by
the author, who apparently did not reprint it, nor is it to
be found in all collections of his poems.   In his original
compositions Beattie is pleasing rather than vigorous, and
this is very much the character, both positively and
negatively, of his translation, which is freely executed,
and contains at least as much of the author as of his
Latin model.   The following lines will exhibit at once
his better and his worse qualities (' Muscosi fontes,' &c.
' Ecl.' vii. 45):—

Corydon.   Ye mossy fountains, warbling as ye flow,
            And, softer than the slumbers ye bestow,
            Ye grassy banks ! ye trees with verdure crowned,
            Whose leaves a glimmering shade diffuse around !
            Grant to my weary flocks a cool retreat,
            And screen them from the summer's raging heat !
            For now the year in brightest glory shines,
            Now reddening clusters deck the bending vines.

Thyrsis.   Here 's wood for fuel : here the fire displays
            To all around its animating blaze ;
            Black with continual smoke our posts appear,
            Nor dread we more the rigour of the year
            Than the fell wolf the fearful lambkins dreads
            When he the helpless fold by night invades,
            Or swelling torrents, headlong as they roll,
            The weak resistance of the shattered mole.

The one other translator of the eighteenth century whose
work has fallen in our way, is a Mr. John Theobald,
whose ' Second Book of Virgil's Æneid, in Four Cantos,
with Notes '—a handsome quarto—bears no date, but has
the appearance of having been published some time after
the middle of the century.   His lines are such as Surrey
or Phaer would doubtless have envied for their smoothness
and finish ; but a reader of the present day will hardly

regret that the four cantos were not extended to forty-eight.

The course of Virgilian translation in the nineteenth century is as illustrative of the general literary history of the period as the corresponding phase in the eighteenth. In the first thirty years several translations appeared, marked more or less by the characteristics of the preceding century : since that time, the old notion of translation—that which aims at substituting a pleasing English poem for an admired original—has been well-nigh abandoned, and experiments as multiform as those practised by the Elizabethan scholars and poets have become the order of the day. We are reminded, not of Dryden or Warton, but of Webbe, Fleming, and Stanyhurst. These revolutionary aspects constitute a new division of our subject, and call, in fact, for a separate discussion. Of the translations that remain, by far the most considerable is the ' Æneis ' of Dr. Symmons, which appeared in 1816, and was reprinted in 1820. It is worth reserving for further notice, and we reserve it accordingly.

The only other attempt we need mention is the version of the ' Eclogues ' made about 1830 by Archdeacon Wrangham, an accomplished scholar and versifier, whose name has not yet died out of remembrance. His lines are elegant, but artificial and involved ; they show the man of taste, not the genuine poet or the master of vigorous English. Take the end of the ' Pollio ' (' Aggredere, O magnos,' ' Ecl.' iv. 48) :—

> These honours thou—'tis now the time—approve,
> Child of the skies, great progeny of Jove !
> Beneath the solid orb's vast convex bent,
> See on the coming year the world intent :
> See earth and sea and highest heaven rejoice :
> All but articulate their grateful voice.

O reach so far my long life's closing strain!
My breath so long to hymn thy deeds remain!
Orpheus nor Linus should my verse excel,
Though even Calliope her Orpheus' shell
Should string, and (anxious for the son the sire)
His Linus' numbers Phœbus should inspire!
Should Pan himself before his Arcady
Contend, he'd own his song surpassed by me.

Know then, dear Boy, thy mother by her smile:
Enough ten months have given of pain and toil.
Know her, dear Boy,—who ne'er such smile has known,
Nor board nor bed divine 'tis his to own.

Thus far we have seen what has been accomplished by
the different translators of Virgil, down to a few years
from the time at which we are now writing. Their
object, in general, has been, as we said just now, to
substitute a pleasing English poem for an admired
original. This being the case, it was naturally to be expected that the one who happened to be the best English
poet should be the best translator. Perhaps it might be
necessary to stipulate that there should be some similarity
between the genius of the poet translating and that of the
poet translated. A 'Virgil' by Shelley would have been
un-Virgilian, though scarcely more so than Pope's 'Homer'
is un-Homeric; but where any scope is given for the
exhibition of native poetical power, a true poet, however
careless, is sure to please more than the most fastidiously
elegant versifier. And this is just what has happened.
Whatever a few critics may have thought and said,
Dryden's is the only English 'Virgil' of which the bulk of
English readers know anything.

It is doubtless true, as a critical theory, that a translator ought to endeavour not only to say what his author
has said, but to say it as he has said it. In the greatest
writers, thought and language may possibly be distinguished,

but can scarcely be dissociated. Every true poet has a
style of his own : a style which probably forms half of
what makes him please, and more than half of that which
makes him remembered. And if this be true of other
writers, it is especially true of Virgil. He has chosen to
trust, as scarcely anyone else has done, to expression—
to the preference not merely of one word to another, but
of one arrangement of words to another. He insinuates
new thoughts through the medium of apparent tautolo-
gies ; he calls in old phrases, recasts them, and produces
new effects. On the other hand, it cannot be denied that
few of the translators of Virgil have trusted to themselves
so entirely as Dryden. He worked hurriedly and under
pressure ; he was hardly likely to be more attentive to
his author's language than in his original compositions ;
nay, the very vigour of his genius required that he should
abandon himself to his own impulses and express himself
in his own way. He was constantly adding to his original, and that in the most wilful and reckless manner.
There were elements in his nature peculiarly repugnant
to the Virgilian ideal, and those elements he was at no
great pains to conceal. When he chose he could be not
only careless and slovenly, but offensively coarse and
vulgar, and he is so in his ' Virgil ' a hundred times. From
the very first he made himself fair game for his rivals and
critics, and they have taken their full advantage. From
Milbourne and Trapp down to the Messrs. Kennedy,
every aspiring translator has been able to quote a long
list of passages where Dryden has failed grossly, and has
argued in consequence that a true translation of Virgil
has yet to be made. Yet their case, as we venture to
think, easily proved in theory, has uniformly broken
down in practice. The fact is, that what they have proved
has been proved not merely against Dryden, but against

themselves.   The question of fidelity of rendering, in the case of a writer like Virgil, can hardly be made one of degree.   It is idle to discuss who has come nearest to the style and language of Virgil, when no one has come within any appreciable distance.   A blank versifier may flatter himself that he can do more than a rhymer, but it will probably be because he is less capable of producing something which may be read with pleasure as an original poem.   The rhymers, at any rate, are placed *ipso facto* on terms of virtual equality so far as resemblance to Virgil's manner is concerned.   They are compelled to sacrifice all that makes that manner what it is, and the one thing that the public has to care for is the goodness or badness of the substitute they offer.   Here it is that Dryden's greatness comes out.   Compare him with other translators, and it will be seen that while none of them have anything of Virgil's individuality, he alone has an individuality of his own of sufficient mark to interest and impress the reader.   Let us make our meaning clear by an instance or two.   We will take four lines near the opening of the First Æneid, and see how they have been dealt with by the chief rhyming translators :—

> Musa, mihi causas memora, quo numine laeso,
> Quidve dolens regina Deûm tot volvere casus
> Insignem pietate virum, tot adire labores
> Impulerit.   Tantæne animis cœlestibus iræ ?

DRYDEN.

> O Muse ! the causes and the crimes relate ;
> What goddess was provoked, and whence her hate ;
> For what offence the queen of heaven began
> To persecute so brave, so just a man,
> Involved his anxious life in endless cares,
> Exposed to want, and hurried into wars.
> Can heavenly minds such high resentment show,
> Or exercise their spite in human woe ?

PITT.

Say, Muse, what causes could so far incense
Celestial powers, and what the dire offence
That moved heaven's awful empress to impose
On such a pious prince a weight of woes,
Exposed to dangers, and with toils opprest.
Can rage so fierce inflame a heavenly breast?

SYMMONS.

Speak, Muse! the causes of effects so great:
What god was wronged? or why, incensed with hate,
Should Heaven's high queen with toils on toils confound
The man for piety to heaven renowned,
And urge him with a ceaseless tide of ills?
Ah! can such passions goad celestial wills?

Here, if we make it a question of degrees, there is doubtless much to be urged against Dryden, who has expanded
into eight lines what the others have been content to
express in six, and a closer pressure, such as Sotheby
occasionally practised, might possibly have reduced to
four. But if we look closely at the original, we shall
see that its peculiar characteristics have really been preserved by none of the three. Which of them gives any
conception of the Virgilian rhythm? and yet what would
a passage of Virgil be without this? Who has imitated
the peculiarity of 'quo numine læso'—that expression
which still continues to be the *crux* of commentators?
Or, if it be thought too much to expect that a translator
should adumbrate what no annotator has succeeded in
fixing, what have we in any of the three to represent
that most Virgilian of phrases—half-inverted, half-direct
—'tot volvere casus'? Dryden has 'involved;' Pitt
talks of 'a weight of woes;' Symmons of 'confounding
with toils on toils;' but none of these is what Virgil has
said, though any of them will serve to express roughly

what be meant.   Looking to Virgil's general meaning, we
see no reason to doubt that it is fairly conveyed by
Dryden's eight lines—eight lines which seem to us the
very perfection of clear unaffected musical English.   It is
needless to compare them in detail with those of Pitt and
Symmons; they are obviously such as only a master like
Dryden could have written :—

> Haec miscere nefas: nec cum sis cetera fossor,
> Tres tantum ad numeros Satyrum moveare Bathylli.

The same easy strength is observable throughout Dryden's version of the 'Georgics.'   Even where it is evident
that he is not putting forth his full power, he will
generally be found to distance his competitors.   Let us
try them in a tolerably simple passage from the Second
Book (v. 362):—

> Ac dum prima novis adolescit frondibus aetas,
> Parcendum teneris: et dum se laetus ad auras
> Palmes agit, laxis per purum immissus habenis.
> Ipsa acies nondum falcis tentanda, sed uncis
> Carpendae manibus frondes interque legendae.
> Inde ubi jam validis amplexae stirpibus ulmos
> Exierint, tum stringe comas, tum brachia tonde:
> Ante reformidant ferrum: tum denique dura
> Exerce imperia, et ramos compesce fluentes.

DRYDEN.

> But in their tender nonage, while they spread
> Their springing leaves, and lift their infant head,
> And upward while they shoot in open air,
> Indulge their childhood, and the nursling spare:
> Nor exercise thy rage on new-born life,
> But let thy hand supply the pruning-knife,
> And crop luxuriant stragglers, nor be loth
> To strip the branches of their leafy growth.

But when the rooted vines with steady hold
Can grasp their elms, then, husbandman, be bold
To lop the disobedient boughs, that strayed
Beyond their ranks: let crooked steel invade
The lawless troops which discipline disclaim,
And their superfluous growth with rigour tame.

WARTON.

The new-born buds, the tender foliage spare:
The shoots that vigorous dart into the air,
Disdaining bonds, all free and full of life,
O dare not wound too soon with sharpened knife!
Insert your bending fingers, gently cull
The roving shoots, and reddening branches pull.
But when they clasp their elms with strong embrace,
Lop the luxuriant boughs, a lawless race:
Ere this they dread the steel: now, now reclaim
The flowing branches, the bold wanderers tame.

SOTHEBY.

When the new leaf in Spring's luxuriant time
Clothes the young shoot, oh! spare its tender prime:
And when the gadding tendril wildly gay
Darts into air and wantons on its way,
Indulgent yet the knife's keen edge forbear,
But nip the leaves, and lighten here and there:
But when in lusty strength the o'ershadowing vine
Clings with strong shoots that all the elm entwine,
Range with free steel, exert tyrannic sway,
Lop the rank bough, and curb the exuberant spray.

As usual, Dryden allows himself more license than the
rest, and his freedom has led him into a misconception of
the meaning of the first sentence, which the other two,
owing to their greater fidelity, avoid, or appear to avoid.
He confuses the earliest stage, when the leaves are not to
be touched at all, with the second, when they are not to
be touched by the pruning-hook. But in spite of this,

and in spite of the general latitude of his rendering, we
are mistaken if our readers fail to perceive his great superiority.   Sotheby keeps much closer to Virgil, but it is a
closeness by which we set very little store, failing, as it
does, to bring out the chief points of his author's lan-
gunge,—the ' laxis per purum immissus habenis,' and even
the ' tum—tum—tum denique.'   The military metaphor
in Dryden's last lines may seem rather a bold expansion
of ' dura exerce imperia ;' but it is thoroughly in the
spirit of the original.   Every line of Virgil shows that he
regarded the vine-branch as a living thing ; that is the
key-note of the paragraph, and no one has seen this so
clearly or brought it out so vividly as Dryden.

Our judgment then is, that Pitt and Warton, Symmons
and Sotheby, fail as translators precisely because they fail
as original poets.   They cannot help being more or less
original, substituting, that is, their own mode of expression
for Virgil's ; and their originality is comparatively uninte-
resting.   They are not great poets, but simply accomplished
versifiers.   Each has his own merits ; each shows his
weakness in his own way.   Pitt wrote with the echoes of
Pope in his ears, and may remind his readers of the
English ' Homer' as long as they have not the English
' Homer' by them.   Those who wish to estimate his real
relation to his master may compare a translation of his
from the Twenty-third Odyssey, printed in ' Pope's
Letters,' [1] with Pope's own.   His chief fault is a general
mediocrity of expression : a monotonous level, which is
neither high poetry nor good prose.   Dryden's narrative
is easy and straightforward ; Pitt's indefinite and conventional.   He has, as it were, a certain cycle of rhymes

---

[1] Pitt to Spence in Pope's Letters (*Works*, by Bowles, vol. viii. p. 352).
The Twenty-third Book was translated by Broome, but Pope doubtless
altered it.

which Pope has made classical, and he rarely ventures to
deviate from it. We open his translation at random,
glance down a page, and find the couplets end as follows:
*Tyre, fire; round, crowned; joy, Troy; hour, o'er; grace,
race; glows, rows; delay, way; designed, mind; come,
room; inspire, fire; place, race; rest, address; above,
Jove; implore, adore; tost, coast; know, woe.* Ex pede
Herculem, when we see *tost* and *coast, inspire* and *fire,* in
a writer of the school of Pope, we know pretty well what
the rest of the line is likely to have been. One of Pitt's
most enthusiastic admirers observes, not without truth,
that he is peculiarly unfortunate in his versions of similes.
A simile is one of those things in which weakness of
handling is most likely to come out; as managed by
Virgil it is commonly a description in itself, and the features in it which are not intended to be made prominent
will often escape an inattentive reader. Warton was
heavier and more prosaic than Pitt, without being much
less conventional. His ear was worse, his command of
poetical language more restricted; yet he sighs, in his
dedication, over the necessity of using ' coarse and common
words' in his translation of the ' Georgics,' viz. *plough* and
sow, wheat, dung, ashes, horse, and *cow,* &c.; words
which he fears ' will unconquerably disgust many a delicate reader.' When Virgil rises, Warton does not rise
with him; his version of the ' Pollio ' and of the Praises
of Italy may be read without kindling any spark of
enthusiasm. Who, with genuine poetry in his soul, could
have thus rendered ' Salve, magna parens frugum,' &c.
(' Georg.' ii. 173)?—

> All hail, Saturnian soil! immortal source
> Of mighty men and plenty's richest stores!
> For thee my lays inquisitive impart
> This useful argument of ancient art:

> For thee I dare unlock the sacred spring,
> And through thy streets Ascræan numbers sing.

Sotheby and Symmons may be contrasted as well as
paralleled with Warton and Pitt. When they wrote, the
language of English classical poetry had become still more
artificial, the structure of the heroic couplet still more
conventional. Sotheby's 'Georgics' run, in fact, to the tune
of the 'Pleasures of Hope.' It would be too much to
ascribe any very direct influence to a poem published only
a year previously. Still the secret of their weakness could
hardly be better described than in the words which
Hazlitt applies to Campbell's poem. 'A painful attention
is paid to the expression in proportion as there is little
to express, and the decomposition of prose is substituted
for the composition of poetry.'[1] There are many well-
wrought lines; sometimes we may find a whole passage
which has been successfully laboured; but we miss
throughout that pervading vigour which works from
within, not from without—which expresses itself poeti-
cally, because it has first learned to express itself in
English. Nowhere is the power of writing English more
needed than in translating the 'Georgics.' Even as it is,
Virgil's didactics are well nigh crushed under a load of
ornament: there is everything to tempt a translator not
to say a plain thing in a plain way; and the slightest
additional bias in favour of the indirect chicaneries of
language is sure to be fatal. Here are Sotheby's directions for the construction of bee-hives ('Ipsa autem, seu
corticibus tibi suta cavatis,' &c. 'Georg.' iv. 33):—

> Alike, if hollow cork their fabric form,
> Or flexile twigs enclose the settled swarm,

---

[1] *Lectures on the English Poets*, p. 204 (1st edition).   Hazlitt censures
Rogers—who, as he truly says, is a poet of the same school—in language
still more severe, but, with all its exaggeration, not wholly undeserved.

With narrow entrance guard, lest frosts congeal,
Or summer suns the melting cells unseal.
Hence not in vain the bees their domes prepare,
And smear the chinks that open to the air,
With flowers and fucus close each pervious pore,
With wax cement, and thicken o'er and o'er.
Stored for this use they hive the clammy dew,
And load their garners with tenacious glue,
As birdlime thick, or pitch, that slow distils
In unctuous drops on Ida's pine-crowned hills.
And oft, 'tis said, they delve beneath the earth,
Hide in worn stones and hollow trees their birth :
Aid thou their toil : with mud their walls o'erlay,
And lightly shade the roof with leafy spray.

Every line here gives evidence of taste and refinement : some of them show considerable power of condensed expression, yet who would care to read page after page of poetry of this sort, apart from the associations of the Latin? 'Decipit exemplar vitiis imitabile.' Sotheby knew and felt that one of Virgil's greatest charms was his diction ; he was doubtless conscious that his own strength lay in elegance of expression ; and he may not unreasonably have been led to believe that he was well qualified to succeed in a translation of the 'Georgics.' But though his 'Virgil,' the task of his youth, is very superior to his 'Homer,' the labour of his old age, not only from the greater congeniality of the subject, but in itself, as an original poem, few, we apprehend, would be found now to endorse the opinion expressed by several of his contemporaries, that he has contrived to occupy a place which the carelessness and slovenliness of Dryden had left vacant. One cause of the want of interest with which we read his 'Georgics' may be the wearying monotony of their versification. The heroic couplet is there as it passed from Pope to Darwin, and from Darwin to Campbell; but an unbroken series of such couplets is a poor substitute for the interwoven harmonies of Virgil. When a strong or even a rough line is wanted, Sotheby has no objection to introducing it, any more than Pope had before him; but to fuse couplet into couplet, varying the cadences till the entire paragraph becomes a complex rhythmical whole, was a gift which nature denied him, and art did not supply.

Symmons is, as we have intimated, a writer of the same school as Sotheby, preferable in some respects, inferior in others. Probably he has not as many good lines, but he produces less the effect of sameness: he is not so conventional, but he is more of a pedant. On the whole, however, the family likeness between them is considerable, as will be seen from the following extract from the boat-race in the Fifth Æneid ('Quo diversus abis,' &c. v. 166):—

> Why thus, Mencetes, still licentious stray?
> Keep to the rock! be frugal of the way!
> Gyas again exclaims: and close behind
> Beholds Cloanthus to the rock inclined.
> He 'twixt the ship of Gyas and the steep
> Steers with nice judgment, and attains the deep:
> Then, as he there in fearless triumph rides,
> From the late victor and the goal he glides.
> But rage and anguish swell in Gyas' breast,
> Nor stands within his eye the tear repressed.
> His rank forgetting, and the care he owes
> To his ship's safety, from the stern he throws
> The tardy master headlong on the tide,
> And his own hands the vacant steerage guide.
> Become the pilot and the captain too,
> Landward he turns the helm and cheers his crew.
> But, scarcely rising from the deep at length,
> With his drenched clothes and age-diminished strength,
> Mencetes to the rock with labour swims,
> And on its sunny forehead dries his limbs.

> Him in his plunge, and in his dripping plight,
> The Trojans view, diverted at the sight,
> And, as the briny draught his breast restores,
> Loud peals of laughter rattle through the shores.

This is carefully done, and undoubtedly keeps closer to the
Latin than Dryden's version; but it is not the narrative of
Virgil; nor was it likely to make the readers of 1816
forget the 'Corsair' and 'Lara.'

The moral which we would draw from this part of our
criticism is, that no one is likely to attain as a poetical
translator the excellence which would be denied to him as
an original writer. In prose the case is different, as there
the translator has to draw far less on his own powers;
though even there it will be true that a man who is best
able to express his own thoughts will be best able—we
do not say most willing—to express the thoughts of
another. But the poetical translator is really an original
poet; and the stream cannot rise higher than its source.

One great poet there has been who once conceived the
thought of disputing Dryden's supremacy as a translator of
the 'Æneid.' Wordsworth saw, as many others have seen,
that Dryden's genius did not correspond to Virgil's—that
there is no analogy between the Latin and the English
'Æneid,' the peculiar charm of the one being different from
the peculiar charm of the other; and he thought that, by
submitting to a more exacting self-criticism than Dryden's,
he might produce something more Virgilian. But he
found himself surrounded with difficulties. In his own
mind he was convinced that the proper equivalent to the
hexameter of Virgil was the blank verse of Milton, which he
conceived to have been actually modelled upon it; but he
did not venture to adopt it, feeling that a poem so remote
in its whole complexion from the sympathies of modern

England would not be read with interest without the obvious attractions of rhyme.   He found, too, that in spite
of the resolution with which he had set out, not to introduce anything for which there was no warrant in the
original, he had to admit the rule of compensation—a
give and take principle, conferring on Virgil some new
beauty in return for having deprived him of an old one.
His sense of the discouraging nature of his task at last
made him give it up, but not before he had accomplished
several books.   One or two passages from his translation
are given in letters quoted in his Life, the source to which
we are indebted for the facts we have just mentioned; but
by far the most satisfactory specimen is a long extract of
one hundred lines, published in the 'Philological Museum'
(vol. i. pp. 382 fol.), to which he was induced to communicate it by his friendship to the editor, the late Archdeacon
Hare.   Judging from this sample, we incline to think that
he acted wisely in retiring from the contest.   He may
have had a more delicate sense of language, and perhaps a
subtler feeling for metre, than Dryden, but his own poetical
art was scarcely equal to his power of conception; and
the philosophical and reflective character of his genius,
which could not but be impressed on everything he wrote,
was quite unlike the reflectiveness of Virgil.   In particular,
he wanted that rapidity of movement which is absolutely
necessary to an epic narrative, and which Dryden possessed
to a degree greater perhaps than any other English poet.
We give one passage—the one where it appears to us
Wordsworth has succeeded best in representing what, as
he justly observes, Dryden habitually neglects, the peculiar
rhythm of his original: and we subjoin to it Dryden's
lines, that the two may be compared as pieces of independent poetry ('Præcipue infelix,' 'Æn.' i. 712):—

N 2

WORDSWORTH.

But chiefly Dido, to the coming ill
Devoted, strives in vain her vast desires to fill;
She views the gifts: upon the child then turns
Insatiable looks, and gazing burns.
To ease a father's cheated love he hung
Upon Æneas, and around him clung:
Then seeks the queen: with her his arts he tries:
She fastens on the boy enamoured eyes,
Clasps in her arms, nor weens (O lot unblest!)
How great a god, incumbent o'er her breast,
Would fill it with his spirit.   He, to please
His Acidalian mother, by degrees
Blots out Sichæus, studious to remove
The dead by influx of a living love,
By stealthy entrance of a perilous guest
Troubling a heart that had been long at rest.

DRYDEN.

But, far above the rest, the royal dame,
Already doomed to love's disastrous flame,
With eyes insatiate and tumultuous joy
Beholds the present, and admires the boy.
The guileful god about the hero long
With children's play and false embraces hung:
Then sought the queen: she took him to her arms
With greedy pleasure, and devoured his charms.
Unhappy Dido little thought what guest,
How dire a god, she drew so near her breast.
But he, not mindless of his mother's prayer,
Works in the pliant bosom of the fair,
And moulds her heart anew, and blots her former care:
The dead is to the living love resigned,
And all Æneas enters in her mind.

Dryden is here not at his strongest; while Wordsworth,
as we think, has succeeded better than in any other part
of the specimen.   Yet we should not wonder if the English

reader should like Dryden best. He has fewer delicate touches, and generally preserves less of Virgil's manner; but he is as usual easy, vigorous, and masterly: his language is what Wordsworth wished the language of poetry to be, the language of good prose; *mutatis mutandis*; and the measure, if not Virgilian, has at any rate the same effect as Virgil's, carrying the reader along without anything to interrupt the sense of intellectual satisfaction.

Here accordingly we leave the question of the translation of Virgil into verse, its practice and its theory. England, we think, is to be congratulated on the possession of one really fine poem, not more unlike Virgil than its rivals in external feature, while possessing to an infinitely greater degree than any of them that 'energy divine' which constitutes the essence of all poetry, ancient or modern. That a better version—one more Virgilian, and not less attractive—might not conceivably be produced, we do not say. Mr. Tennyson is yet among us, and we would not presume to limit the capabilities of so great a master of language and metre. But the change which has taken place in literary taste forbids us to think it likely that any great poet will ever make the attempt. The work of translation was found irksome even by Pope; it would be doubly irksome now, when imitative classical poetry has ceased to be the order of the day; and the advance in critical perception, which has raised infinitely the ideal of what a translation should be, in perfecting the theory has removed the practice to an indefinite distance. In the meantime we may congratulate ourselves on the possession of a splendid English epic, in which most of the thoughts are Virgil's, and most of the language Dryden's.

But a further inquiry remains behind. If in one sense the demand for translations of the classics has greatly diminished, in another it has increased. The success of

Mr. Bohn's Classical Library—success attained against considerable disadvantages, the authors in many cases being far from popular, while the translators are not always absolutely competent—is a proof that a considerable portion of the reading public, for different reasons, desires to have the classics made accessible in English. Schoolboys are as fond of 'clandestine refuges' now as they were in Trapp's days; schoolmasters are, we fancy, beginning to tolerate, under certain modifications, what they cannot exterminate, while they see that among their elder pupils at any rate the practice of translation into English—one of the most valuable parts of a classical education—may be greatly facilitated by the use of good models; those who acquire the classical languages with little or no help from masters—probably an increasing class—find the book a natural substitute for the living teacher; and there is a large class of readers to whom Latin and Greek are as unattainable as Coptic, yet who are interested in knowing what the ancients thought and said.[1]   The question, How may classical poetry be best represented in English? which had long been supposed to be confined to the single issue of Rhyme v. Blank Verse, has come in again for hearing, and has been found to open into numberless ramifications. The case for translation into prose, once contemptuously dismissed, has been brought on again by such writers as Mr. Hayward, and has proved to be at least worthy of discussion.   Writing prose is now pretty well understood to be as much an art as writing verse; and it is seen consequently that a prose translator does not *ipso facto*

---

[1] In Germany, where translations of the classics are far more numerous than in England, as may be seen from the fact that Seneca's Tragedies have been three times translated since the beginning of the present century, the demand is said to arise to a great extent from ladies' schools, where girls are taught to read in the vernacular what their brothers are reading in the original.

abandon all pretension to grace and elaboration of style. Blank verse is cultivated for purposes of translation, not by imitators of Milton and Thomson, but by writers who wish to unite the fidelity of a prose version with something of metrical ornament. Attempts are made to cut in between prose and blank verse by the introduction of a sort of rhythmical prose, which again subdivides itself into prose written as prose with a rhythmical cadence, and irregular verse, rather rhythmical than metrical, but still more or less uniform in its structure. Lastly, the old fashion of imitating ancient metres is revived, and the English hexameter in particular is practised with an assiduity worthy of a more promising object, though as yet its fanciers seem scarcely to have extended their experiments from Homer to Virgil. This part of the subject accordingly requires a few remarks from us. As before, we shall speak not only of what may be done, but of what has been done, holding ourselves absolved, however, by the circumstances of the case, as well as by the scantiness of our own knowledge, from saying more than a very few words on the antiquarian part of the question. A portion of the ground, indeed, has been previously travelled in what we said of the translations of the sixteenth century. There was then no sharp line of demarcation between the two kinds of literary activity—that which aspires to poetical honours, and that which aims at producing translations for practical objects. All readers, in one sense or another, were learners; and the office of the translator was virtually that of the commentator, to give his countrymen the means of entering into a new world. But, as time went on, the division of labour came in. The only translation of the kind in the seventeenth century which we happen to have met with, is entitled ‘Virgils Eclogves, with his Booke De Apibus, concerning the Governement and Ordering of Bees : Translated Grammatically, and also according to the proprietie of our English tongue, so farre as Grammar and the verse will well permit. Written chiefly for the good of Schooles, to be used according to the directions in the Preface to the painfull Schoole-Master, and more fully in the Booke called *Ludus Literarius*, or the Grammer-Schoole, *Chap.* 8.   London, 1633.'   In its full form the page consists of four columns, containing respectively an analysis of the sense, a translation of the words, a verbal commentary, and notes on matters of fact, points of rhetoric, &c.

What precise chronological place among the prose translators of Virgil is occupied by Davidson we cannot say, but there can be no doubt that he has been the most popular. His work was published as early as 1754, if not earlier, and it still continues to be reprinted, even Mr. Bohn being content with presenting it to the world in a revised edition.   In its complete form it may certainly claim the praise of comprehensiveness, containing, as it does, not only a translation, 'as near the original as the different idioms of the Latin and English languages will allow,' but 'the Latin text and order of construction on the same page, and critical, historical, geographical, and classical notes, in English, from the best commentators, both ancient and modern, beside a very great number of notes entirely new;' a most ample provision 'for the use of schools, as well as of private gentlemen,' especially if we throw in some seventy-five pages of prefatory matter. Its literary characteristics are such as will sufficiently account for its success, though they are not of that rare order which might have been expected to place it beyond the reach of future rivalry.   It keeps fairly close to the Latin, at the same time that it is written in a fluent, respectable English style, such as might easily commend

itself to a person without much poetical taste—the style
of an ordinary newspaper or of a Polite Letter-writer.
Sometimes the verbiage is too glaringly anti-poetical, and
may move even a prosaic reader to a smile, as where
' fœdera jungi ' is rendered ' the formation of an incorpo-
rative alliance,' or ' heu miserande puer ' ' Ah, youthful
object of sincere commiseration ;' but in general there is
not much to find fault with in the language as tried by an
ordinary standard.   Here is Davidson's version of a
famous passage in the Sixth Æneid (' Quis te, magne
Cato,' &c., v. 841):—

Who can in silence pass over thee, great Cato, or thee,
Cossus, who the family of Gracchus, or both the Scipios, those
two thunderbolts of war, the bane of Africa, and Fabricius, in
low fortune exalted? or thee, Serranus, sowing in the furrow
which thine own hands had made? Whither, ye Fabii, do ye
hurry me *already* tired?   Thou art that Fabius, *justly styled*
the greatest, who alone shalt repair our *sinking* state by *wise*
delay.   Others, I grant indeed, shall with more delicacy mould
the breathing *animated* brass; from marble draw the features
to the life: plead causes better: describe with the *astronomer's*
rod the courses of the heavens, and explain the rising stars:
but to rule the nations with imperial sway be thy care, *O*
Roman ! these shall be thy arts; to impose terms of peace, to
spare the humbled, and crush the proud *stubborn foes.* (The
italics, which are the translator's, represent his additions to the
original.)

There is not much rhythm here, not much of strictly
poetical expression, and no attempt to preserve the
peculiar character of Virgil's style; but the language is
such as an Englishman might speak or write, and we
appeal to the class to whom Davidson dedicates his
labours, ' those gentlemen who have the immediate care
of education,' whether that is not something.

But it is in the last few years, as we intimated a short

time ago, that these more practical and closer versions of
Virgil have chiefly been attempted.

In 1846 Dr. Sewell published a blank version of the
'Georgics,' intended as a help to teachers and pupils in the
practice of translation.   His object is to make a practical
protest against the habit of bald prosaic rendering so
common in schools, by substituting a mode of translating
which shall be sharply discriminated from prose, both in
metre and in language.   For this purpose he adopts the
ordinary measure of blank heroic verse, and chooses
words which are expressly intended to recall, not the
ordinary conversational style of the present day, but the
distinctive phraseology of the Elizabethan and sixteenth-
century writers.   In 1854 he brought out a second
edition, in which the translation, as he tells us, is entirely
rewritten.   We have not the means of comparing the
two; but it strikes us that, as usual, second thoughts are
best.   Some expressions, which we remember as uncouth
in the first edition, we are glad to find effaced from the
second, such as 'pacts eterne,' a version of 'æterna
fœdera,' now exchanged for 'changeless pacts;' but the
fault of which the word 'eterne' is a symbol may still be
observed—a tendency to use words simply because they
happen to have the sanction of one or other of the great
English poets, without considering whether they harmonise with the general style of the translation, or whether
the effect they produce is analogous to anything in
Virgil's own language.   In attempting, too, to bring out
the force of expressions in Virgil, Dr. Sewell is too apt to
exaggerate them, as when he renders 'magnos canibus
circumdare saltus,' 'vasty lawns with hounds to *belt*,' or
'atræ picis' '*inky* pitch.'   The following version of part
of the storm in the First Georgic is, we think, a favourable
specimen.   'Implentur fossæ' (v. 326):—

The dykes are brimming high, and hollow floods
Are swelling with a roar, and ocean seethes
With steaming friths.   The sire himself of gods,
Throned midst a night of storms, launches his bolts
With red right hand.   Commotion, wherewithal
Quakes the huge earth : fled have the forest tribes,
And through the nations grovelling panic fear
Low hath laid mortal hearts.   With blazing bolt
He doth or Atho or Rhodope or heights
Ceraunian dash on earth.   Peal upon peal
Follow south blasts, and thickest sheeted showers.
Now groves, now strands, roar 'neath the tempest wild.

The next version which we have to note is one which
perhaps in strictness should have been mentioned earlier
in the article, as it is professedly a blank version of the
same sort as those which were produced in the eighteenth
century—in theory opposed to Dryden, but aiming at the
same object—the production of a readable English poem.
But, though the Messrs. Kennedy may belong rather to
the conservative than to the revolutionary school of
translators, we think we are not disparaging their labours
in exhibiting them in connection with those of others,
who, like them, desire to adhere to the letter of the
original, where such adherence can be made not less
poetical than a deviation from it.   Their translation shows
what blank verse is likely to be in fairly competent hands
—how far it is likely to give us such a representation of
Virgil as cannot be attained by a method like Dryden's.
At the same time, as the passage which we intend to
examine will be taken from the part of the work performed by Mr. Kennedy sen., we may say at once that we
think Mr. Charles Kennedy the superior artist, more terse
and forcible than his father, without being less poetical.[1]

---

[1] Mr. Charles Kennedy has since translated the whole of Virgil on his
own account (Bohn, 1861); but we have no space to examine his version.

What measure of absolute success he has achieved may be seen from the following passage from the Fifth Eclogue, v. 56, 'Candidus insuetum,' &c. :—

> New wonders now fair Daphnis doth behold,
> The Olympian threshold, and beneath his feet
> The clouds and stars. Therefore doth new delight
> Exhilarate the woods and rural scenes,
> Pan and the shepherds, and the Dryad maids:
> Wolves prowl not for the flock, nor toils intend
> Harm to the deer: peace gentle Daphnis loves.
> The unshorn mountains joyful to the stars
> Send a spontaneous cry: the rocks, the groves
> Unbidden sing: a God, a God is he.

A version of the whole of Virgil, on a plan substantially the same as Dr. Sewell's, has just been completed by his predecessor at Radley, Mr. Singleton, the first volume having been published in 1855. The chief difference lies in the somewhat greater flexibility of the form, which is rhythmical rather than metrical; but, even in this respect, the two versions are not easily distinguishable, as, while Dr. Sewell has not been concerned greatly to elaborate his blank verse, Mr. Singleton's is in reality blank verse with occasional licenses, a syllable or foot being sometimes added to, sometimes deducted from, the ordinary heroic standard. Mr. Singleton's theory is expounded, not, like Dr. Sewell's, in a short advertisement, but in a long and interesting preface; and he consults further for the poetical taste of his readers by subjoining in foot-notes parallel passages 'from British poets of the sixteenth, seventeenth, and eighteenth centuries.' What his success has been we shall see by and bye; meantime, we must mention a translator whom he has honoured with his approbation—Dr. Henry Owgan, of Trinity College, Dublin, whose prose version of the

whole of 'Virgil' he classes with Dr. Isaac Butt's prose
version of the 'Georgics' as 'very far the most poetical' of
all those which he has had an opportunity of seeing. Dr.
Butt's we have unfortunately been unable to procure. To
Dr. Owgan's we shall return presently. Last on the list,
though not last in order of time, comes a translation of
the First Six Books of the 'Æneid,' by Dr. James Henry,
also an Irishman, under the quaint title of 'Six Photo-
graphs of the Heroic Times.' This work again is not
metrical, but rhythmical, its peculiarity being that the
rhythm is changed from time to time to suit the translator's convenience, pages of trochaic time being succeeded
by others where anapæsts are predominant, and these
again by ordinary blank verse, a measure which is preserved through the whole of the Fourth Book. The
translator had made many experiments before he satisfied
himself; and this somewhat heterogeneous assemblage of
varieties is the result. If we cannot praise it very highly,
we are glad to be able to add that Dr. Henry's labours
have been far more successful in another part of the
Virgilian field. About the same time with his translation
appeared a commentary on the same portion of the
'Æneid,' to which he has given a title not less quaint—
'Notes of a Twelve Years' Voyage of Discovery in the
First Six Books of Virgil's Æneis'—a work which,
though somewhat cumbrous in its form, and disfigured by
too frequent an obtrusion of the author's individuality,
contains a very great deal that appears to us at once new
and true. A writer who has shown himself one of the
best commentators on Virgil's poem need not repine that
he has not the additional honour of being one of its best
translators.

We are now in a position to test these different modes
of translation by a comparison of some of their results.

Let us take a passage from the Second Æneid, that in
which the bursting of the Greeks into Priam's palace is
described with so much power and energy. We give the
Latin, as our intention is to scrutinise closely the conformity of the translations. Our list will be headed by
an extract from Trapp, of whom we promised to speak
again :—

> Fit via vi : rumpunt aditus, primosque trucidant
> Immissi Danai, et late loca milite complent.
> Non sic aggeribus ruptis cum spumeus amnis
> Exiit, oppositasque evicit gurgite moles,
> Fertur in arva furens cumulo, camposque per omnes
> Cum stabulis armenta trahit. Vidi ipse furentem
> Cæde Neoptolemum, geminosque in limine Atridas :
> Vidi Hecubam, centumque nurus, Priamumque per aras
> Sanguine fœdantem quos ipse sacraverat ignes.
> Quinquaginta illi thalami, spes tanta nepotum,
> Barbarico postes auro spoliisque superbi,
> Procubuere. Tenent Danai qua deficit ignis.
>
> vv. 494-505.

TRAPP.

>   A spacious breach
> Is made : the thronging Greeks break in, then kill
> The first they meet, and with armed soldiers crowd
> The rich apartments. With less rapid force
> A foamy river, when the opposing dams
> Are broken down, rolls rushing o'er the plain,
> And sweeping whirls the cattle with their folds.
> These eyes saw Pyrrhus raging, smeared with gore,
> And both the Atridæ in the entrance storm,
> Amidst a hundred daughters saw the queen,
> And Priam on the altars with his blood
> Pollute those hallowed fires, which he himself
> Had consecrated. Fifty bridal rooms,
> So great their hopes of numerous future heirs,
> The posts, with trophies and barbaric gold
> Magnificent, lay smoking on the ground :
> Where the flames fail, the Greeks supply their place.

KENNEDY.

An ingress made by force,
The Greeks admitted slay the first they meet,
And crowd the places all around with troops.
Not with such rage a river pours o'er lands
A swollen flood, and herds with stalls bears down
Through all the plains when it has burst away
From broken banks, and with a foamy whirl
O'ercome opposing mounds.   These eyes beheld
Pyrrhus with slaughter rage, and at the gates
The two Atridæ. Hecuba I saw,
Wives of her sons a hundred, and at shrines
Priam the king, defiling with his blood
The fires which he himself had sacred made.
The fifty bridal chambers, which had raised
Hopes of a long posterity, their posts,
Proud with barbaric gold and spoils, fall down.
Greeks plant their footsteps where the flames relent.

SINGLETON.

A way is made by force : the Greeks poured in,
Burst passage, and the foremost massacre,
And wide with soldiery the places fill.
Not so [resistless] when from bursten dams
The foamy river hath escaped away,
And mastered in its eddy barrier mounds,
'Tis carried in a pile upon the tilths
In frenzy, and throughout the champaigns all
The cattle with their cotes it sweepeth off.
I Neoptolemus beheld myself
Raving with butchery, and in the gate
Atreus' twain sons ; I Hecuba beheld
And her one hundred daughters ; Priam too
Among the altars staining with his blood
The fires which he himself had sanctified.
Those fifty nuptial couches, hope so great
Of children's children, doors with foreign gold
And trophics haught, down tumbled to the earth.
Possess the Danai where fails the flame.

Owgan.

A path is cleared by force : the thronging Greeks force their way and massacre the foremost, and fill the open space with soldiers. Not so resistless the foaming torrent, when it o'erflows its broken banks and washes down with its flood the obstructing dams, rushes upon the fields in a mass, and from every plain sweeps herds and stalls. I saw myself Neoptolemus revelling in slaughter, and the two Atridæ in the gate : I saw Hecuba and her hundred daughters-in-law, and Priam amid the altars staining with blood the fires his hands had consecrated. Those fifty chambers, so rich a promise of descendants, the doorways rich with barbaric gold, lay prostrate. The Greeks are masters where the fire dies out.

Henry.

Main strength bursts a passage,
The entrance is forced,
In rush the Danai,
Slaughter the foremost,
And the whole place with soldiery
Fill far and wide.

Less furiously the foaming river,
Whose gushing flood has overcome
And burst the dam's opposing mass
And left its channel, on the fields
Rushes aheap, and drags along
Cattle and stall o'er all the plain.

Myself have seen upon the threshold
Neoptolemus and the twain Atridæ,
Furious and reeking slaughter :
Hecuba and her hundred daughters
Myself have seen, and midst the altars
Priam defiling with his blood
The fires himself had consecrated.
Low lie those fifty sponsal chambers,
So rich hope of a teeming offspring,
Low lie those fifty doors superb
With conquered spoils and gold barbaric :
The Danai or the fire have all

Of the three blank versions of this passage we incline to put Mr. Singleton's first. It does not pretend to Miltonic grandeur, but it is not worse versified than its rivals, and its language gains strength from its closeness to the original. 'Tilths,' a word by which he pregnantly renders 'arva,' is quaint; but it is important here that we should conceive of the fields as tilled, so we prefer it to Mr. Kennedy's 'lands,' or the simple 'fields' of other translators. 'I Neoptolemus beheld myself' is ambiguous, and therefore awkward. 'Couches' is of course a mistranslation for 'chambers.' 'Possess the Danai where fails the flame' is needlessly harsh, though it preserves something of the epigrammatic character of the Latin. Trapp perhaps comes next, as he has more rapidity than Mr. Kennedy; and in a passage like this rapidity is indispensable. But he has various shortcomings, and not a few blemishes. 'Fit via vi,' which he tells us in his note is no pun, but a likeness of sound, which sounds prettily, he practically slurs over altogether. 'The rich apartments' is a poor substitute for 'loca,' and 'late' is left out. The simile is shortened by being stripped of two pieces of Virgilian iteration, 'aggeribus ruptis' being fused with 'oppositas evicit gurgite moles,' and 'campos per omnes' dropped after 'in arva.' 'Nepotum,' which is meant especially to fix our thoughts on Priam and Hecuba, is lost in the generality of 'numerous future heirs,' and the precise meaning of 'spes tanta' apparently misunderstood. 'Raging, smeared with gore,' is very far from 'furentem cæde,' which is best rendered by Mr. Singleton's 'raving with butchery.' Mr. Kennedy seems to us to fail in strength throughout. He is injudicious in his management of the simile, reversing the order of the clauses, so as to put the triumph of the torrent in the foreground, and its struggle with obstacles

afterwards; whereas Virgil evidently intended us to
pause awhile on the struggle, like the torrent itself, and
then to hurry along—like the torrent itself, stronger for
the delay. 'These eyes beheld' should not have been
exchanged for 'I saw,' thus ignoring Virgil's emphatic
repetition of 'vidi.' 'Which had raised hopes of a long
posterity' is not poetry, but prose. 'Fall down' does not
give the force of the perfect 'procubuere.' 'Greeks plant
their footsteps where the flames relent' is pointless where
point is wanted: 'plant their footsteps' does not answer
to 'tenent,' nor 'relent' to 'deficit.'

Dr. Owgan's translation is respectable, but there is
nothing in it which can be called striking; and the exact
force of the Latin is not always given any more than in
the metrical versions. 'Open space' is poor for 'late
loca,' which is doubtless meant to give us a vague, illi-
mitable notion of the royal palace. 'O'erflows' and
'washes down' miss the tense, which Virgil evidently
meant to discriminate from that of 'fertur' and 'trahit.'
Nor does 'washes down' represent 'evicit.' 'Herds and
stalls' hardly gives the sense of 'cum stabulis armenta,'
not indicating the close connection between the two,
'the herds and their stalls,' or 'herd, stall, and all.'
'From every plain' seems to us an unhappy use of the
distributive; and we see no reason for changing 'per'
into 'from.' 'Descendants' is not 'nepotum;' and whether 'postes' are the doorposts or the doors, they are
certainly not the doorways, which could not have been
'rich with spoils.' 'Lay prostrate' turns the perfect into
an aorist. The best part of the version is the last sentence,
where 'tenent' and 'deficit' are both well rendered.

Putting aside the question of the propriety of its
Pindaric rhythm, we must allow that Dr. Henry's version
has its merits. The first strophe (so to call it) is well

done; the second not so well; the third worst of all.
' Myself have seen ' is, we think, a mistake, as the sense
seems to require the past, not the perfect; at any rate we
may say that the former is the predominant notion.
' Furious and reeking slaughter ' is a most unfortunate
dilution. ' So rich hope of a teeming offspring ' is another
instance of blindness to the real force of ' nepotum.'
' The Danai or the fire have all ' gives the epigram, but
we are not told, what Virgil certainly intended us to
understand, that of the two enemies the Greeks were the
more indefatigable.

Were it not for fear of tiring our readers, we would
gladly continue our examination of these competing
translations, feeling as we do that to produce a single
passage from each is a little like the uncritical procedure
of the man who brought a brick as a specimen of his
house. Perhaps, however, we have quoted enough, if not
to determine the rank of the translators, at any rate to
justify our opinion of the various styles which they have ·
attempted. Not wishing to prejudge the success of any
coming poet, who may reclaim for Virgil the rhythm for
which Milton it seems is indebted to him, we cannot
think blank verse well chosen as a vehicle for close
rendering. It has, perhaps, its advantages as an exercise
for boys, who may be supposed to be unacquainted with
the possible harmonies of poetical prose, and to be incapable of recognising anything as poetry which does not
run to the eye in measured lines. But one who can
really wield prose will, we think, find it beyond comparison the better instrument. We do not of course deny
that English verse *per se* is a better representative of
Latin verse than English prose. Mr. Singleton may be
right in saying, that if Virgil and Cicero could be got to
translate Homer closely into Latin, Virgil's translation

would be the one we should prefer. But we are dealing
with those who are neither Virgils nor Ciceros, but simply
men of culture, with a good command over their own
language, and a good eye for the beauties of their author ;
and such men, we conceive, will do wisely to try the yet
unexhausted resources of prose.   Only a great master can
handle blank verse so as to give real pleasure to his
readers. A versifier of very moderate pretensions may
write it with ease, but no one will thank him for it.
Blank verse, like other verse, presupposes and promises a
certain sustained pitch of poetical elevation, and any
descent from it is felt and resented at once. Prose, on
the other hand, promises far less ; and anything which it
gives beyond its promise is accepted with pleasure and
surprise. The indeterminate character of its rhythm,
which does not require that emphasis should be placed
on this or that word, much less on this or that syllable,
allows to admit unhesitatingly words which, if introduced
into blank verse at all, would be felt to be feeble and
burdensome. The passage which we have just been
examining supplies an instance in point. Virgil talks of
‘ Hecubam centumque nurus.’ A prose translation need
not shrink from the word ‘ daughters-in-law,’ nor from
the use of many words which embarrass the writers of
verse, and which, though essential to a lucid representation of the sense, add nothing to the poetical dignity
of the passage. Thus a vigorous Latin line is turned by
Mr. Singleton into two feeble lines of English :—

> Si'qua est cælo pietas quæ talia curet

becomes—

> If any righteousness exist in heaven
> Which may concern itself about the like.

If the writer of rhythmical prose cannot be said to be

free either from the temptation or from the compulsion
to expand himself, he does himself and his author far less
harm by yielding to them. No doubt, as Sydney Smith
said, a prose style may often be greatly improved by
striking out every other word from each sentence when
written; but there are occasions where diffuseness is
graceful, and a certain amount of surplusage may sometimes be admitted into harmonious prose for no better
reason than to sustain the balance of clause against clause,
and to bring out the general rhythmical effect. Brevity
is of course the preferable extreme; but redundancy has
its charms if a writer knows when to be redundant, as
the readers of Mr. De Quincey and Mr. Ruskin are well
aware. On the other hand, such rhythmical writing as
Dr. Henry's, or Mr. Singleton's, where he is not actually
metrical, has no real advantage that we can see over more
recognised modes of composition. It gives up the benefits of association, no one in reading it being reminded of
anything already existing in English, while the uniformity
of its structure imposes virtually as great a restraint on a
writer as actual metre. Johnson advised poets who did
not think themselves capable of astonishing, and hoped
only to please, to condescend to rhyme. Translators who
despair of imitating Virgil's diction, and are ambitious
only of giving his meaning in a pleasing form, may
reasonably be content with prose.

THE ACADEMICAL STUDY OF LATIN.[1]

[2]I TRUST I may be allowed to say that, had I felt myself
free to follow my own wishes, I should have inclined to
dispense with the custom which prescribes that a Professor, on his inauguration, should deliver an introductory
lecture.   I do not mean to press the parallel between

[1] This address, which was delivered by Professor Conington in the
Theatre, Oxford, December 2, 1854, as his inaugural lecture, has been been
reprinted without alteration from the edition published for him in 1855.

[2] The Professorship of the Latin language and literature was constituted
by a statute passed by Convocation, March 14, 1854.

Its establishment had been contemplated by the authorities of the University as early as the spring of 1851, and a statute respecting it was put forth
in the Easter Term of 1853, proposing to endow it with 300l. per annum
from the surplus funds of the University press, and in other points somewhat differing from that which has since been sanctioned.   Its promulgation, however, was prevented by a proposition from the Society of Corpus
Christi, which offered to increase the endowment to 600l., promising ultimately to take the whole charge upon itself, with the view of carrying out
the intentions of its founder, referred to in the text of this lecture.   A new
statute was consequently framed, accepting the liberality of the College, and
providing that it should have a voice in the appointment of the Professor;
and this was confirmed by Convocation, as mentioned above.

The main provisions of the statute are, that the Professor shall be at least
of the degree of M.A., B.C.L., or B.M.; that he shall reside for eight weeks
in each of the three academical terms, giving at least two public lectures
gratis in each year, and twenty-four private lectures, to be divided, if he
pleases, into two equal courses, in each term, these last being for the benefit
of junior members of the University, who are to pay the statutable fee, with
the exception of those belonging to Corpus Christi College; that he shall
explain the language philologically and philosophically, and expound the
best authors, using means to test the proficiency of his hearers; and that he
shall be liable to dismissal for neglect of duty or immorality by the electing
body.   This is an official board, consisting of the Vice-Chancellor, the two
Proctors, the President, and one of the Fellows of Corpus Christi College,
the Regius Professor of Greek, the Camden Professor of Ancient History,
the Public Orator, the Professor of Poetry, the Senior Examiner in the
School of Literæ Humaniores, and the Senior Moderator in the School of
Greek and Latin Literature.

The first election was made June 14, 1854.

such a lecture and the preface to a book, which, as we all know, though intended to be the first thing read, is the last thing written, as I am aware, without entering into the various differences involved in the distinction between reading and hearing, that the greater width and indeterminateness of the field which lies before a lecturer, in leaving it to him to choose what he should say on commencing his work, only renders it more obligatory that he should say something. Still, it seems no more than natural that one who has been placed here, not to communicate the results of a past life of study, but to devote a life only just opening to that learning which goes along with teaching, should shrink from a task which appears to contradict the facts of his position, as implying that he has already surveyed the province on which he is but now entering. Such hesitation, however, though most sincerely felt, would, I fear, be unsuited to an occasion like the present. We are met to-day to inaugurate, not merely a Professor, but a branch of professorial study—one which, though as old as the University itself, is to be calculated henceforward in Oxford with new appliances and under new auspices. The very consideration that the institution of the professorship is an experiment at once enhances the difficulty, and enforces the duty of looking forward. I propose, then, to offer a few remarks on the Academical Study of Latin, disposing them so as to touch chiefly on its history and position, the reasons for promoting it, and the manner of pursuing it.

The history of the cultivation of Latin in Oxford is a subject deserving a more elaborate commemoration than the few sentences which I am able to give to it. In the earlier times of the University we see Latin not so much a branch of study as the instrument of study itself—the

common academical language, the medium through which
knowledge was communicated and received—enjoying
the dubious honours of a vernacular, used, but not analysed, or if analysed at all, tested not by a comparison
with other tongues, which were then virtually unknown,
but by the rules of an arbitrary grammar. This suicidal
supremacy was successfully attacked towards the end of
the fifteenth century by the naturalization of Greek in
the University, the work of men who were themselves
distinguished Latinists, interested not so much in the advancement of one language over another as in the intelligent cultivation of both.[1] Soon after, Wolsey, who
had constituted himself the patron of academical progress,
sought to give Latin a more solid, though a less invidious,
position, by the endowment of a public lecture in Humanity, which took its place along with the newly-
introduced language[2] and several of the old sciences.
About the same time Bishop Fox included in the
foundation of Corpus Christi College a public readership
of Latin, first held by the celebrated Ludovicus Vives,

---

[1] Perhaps the most illustrious of them was Linacre, whose treatise, *De
Emendata Structura Latini Sermonis*, long continued a text-book.

[2] The lectures were in Theology, Civil Law, Physic, Philosophy, Mathematics, Greek, and Humanity. The Humanity Lecture is also spoken of as
a lecture in Rhetoric (Fiddes' *Life of Wolsey*, p. 216, &c.), and the two
subjects are likely enough to have been connected in teaching. Fox,
however, enjoins that *his* Humanity reader shall lecture exegetically on
approved Latin authors, whom he specifies, allowing him to read later
works on style, such as Valla's *Elegantiæ* and Politian's *Miscellanea*, only in
vacations (*Statutes*, c. 21). As Vives held both offices, we may conclude
that the duties of the two would be understood in substantially the same
manner, though he was a person of various gifts, and is believed to have
also been Wolsey's Reader in Civil Law. It is remarkable that in founding
Cardinal College, Wolsey made no provision for Greek either in his public
or domestic lectureships, while including Humanity in both. He had shown
his zeal for Greek, not only in establishing the University lecture, but in
interfering to protect the first lecturer in 1519 against the Trojans, whom he
seems to have been mainly instrumental in putting down.

the ‘mellifluous doctor,’[1] the member of a triumvirate where wit, eloquence, and judgment were said to combine

[1] The statement that the University styled Vives ‘the mellifluous doctor’ in writing to Wolsey, repeated by Fuller (Worthies, Co. Oxon), Plot (Oxfordshire), Gutch, and Ingram, seems ultimately traceable to Butler’s *Female Monarchie, or the Historie of Bees* (p. 23, ed. 2, 1634), which Plot quotes—a strange work, printed in reformed spelling. The letter itself appears to be that marked No. 22, Ep. 76, in Fiddes’ *Collection*, and the part referred to runs thus: ‘Omnes denique omnium studentium animos mellifluis tuis lectionibus in dies quam optime reficis, auges, et illustras, nec ab incepto tua clementia desistit, sed nova potius nobis parare studes. Retulit enim nobis tuus excellaaus et Oxon. commissarius quam optime meritus novum rhetoricæ artis lectorem et virum disertissimum ab Hispaniâ te nobis comparasse.’ This shows not only that the epithet in question was not applied to Vives’ lectures in particular, but that at the time of its application Vives had actually not entered upon his office, or begun to reside regularly in the University, so that it could have had no reference to him whatever. The legend of his bees may have had some foundation in truth, though its coincidence with the metaphor of the apiary, which runs through the Corpus statutes in general, and that about the prælectors in particular, is curious, and perhaps suspicious; while the success of his lectures appears to be attested by the facts that the King and Queen attended him in 1523, and the University began to revive the disused degrees in Grammar, Rhetoric, and Poetry. It is not easy, however, to ascertain how long he resided in Oxford, or in what capacity. His name appears in the original list of Fellows of Corpus named by the founder, July 4, 1517; and there is no doubt that he was their first Humanity lecturer; but it does not appear whether he received the two appointments simultaneously, or when he began to exercise the latter. The above-cited letter of the University, evidently written, as has been remarked, before he had come among them, is dated two years later, 5 Id. Jul. 1519. Wood says that he did not arrive in Oxford till 1523—a statement not shaken by Fiddes (p. 210 sqq.), who misunderstands the letter to Wolsey, and confirmed both by the fact that he had two predecessors in Wolsey’s chair, Clement and Lupsett, and also by his own letters, some of which are published in his works (Basle, 1555), others referred to in Folman’s MS. collections in the library of Corpus Christi College. Thus he writes from Louvain, August 15, 1522, that he is thinking of visiting Britain; May 10, 1523, that he is going into Spain by way of Britain; June 16, 1524, that he has left Britain to get married, but means to return at the end of September, which he appears to have done from other letters (Epp. 3 and 13); March 12, 1525, he writes from Oxford, and November 13, 1525, from London: after which he appears to have left England again, but to have returned, though not for any lengthened stay. The notices also do not determine whether he held the Corpus readership and Wolsey’s lectureship at once: they speak of him, however, as giving Wolsey’s lectures in the dining-hall of Corpus Christi College, which may

in the service of learning. But Wolsey's benefaction was
as short-lived as his greatness; and when at last Henry
VIII. came to carry out a portion of the intentions of his
fallen minister, he did not extend to the old language the
encouragement which he bestowed on the new. The
colleges, indeed, appear to have taken up the work ;[1] and
the institution of private lectureships in other societies
may have been one reason why the Corpus readers ceased
to lecture to the University, and confine their instructions
to members of their own body. Still, the position of
Latin in the University would seem to have been an
anomalous one : English had supplanted it in the services
of the Church, and Greek divided with it the attention
of the scholar ; yet it continued to be the official voice
of the University, the common speech of learned men,
and refused to abdicate its dignity by becoming a subject
of special academical study. We may readily understand how the benefactors who arose from time to time,
proportioning their bounty according to the needs of the
recipient, chose to associate their names with other departments of professorial teaching : but it is remarkable that
more than a century after Wolsey and Bishop Fox, the
Laudian system, while including Greek and Hebrew in
its elaborate course of study, should only have recognised

admit of various explanations, even if it be not attributed to a confusion by
the narrator.

The other members of the triumvirate were Erasmus and Budæus, the
latter of whom was praised for wit or genius, the former for eloquence,
leaving judgment to Vives. Dupin (xiv. 90, quoted by Jortin, *Life of
Erasmus*, p. 207) mentions this as a common saying, but thinks it too complimentary to Vives, whom he will allow to have surpassed the others only
in his knowledge of grammar, logic, and rhetoric.

[1] Henry the Eighth's Commissioners in 1535 found a Latin lecture
already established in Magdalen College, and established others themselves
in New College, All Souls, Merton, and Queen's, which were to serve, not
for those colleges alone, but for other societies where there was no such
provision.

Latin in the shape of grammar and rhetoric.[1] Yet we
can scarcely treat the assumption as an unfounded one,
when we recollect the practical familiarity with Latin
attained by Addison as a poet, and by Lowth as a prose
writer: nor should we forget the direct influence of the
University prizes in stimulating the scholarship of Gren-
ville and Wellesley, of Canning and Copleston. At any
rate, no one can mistake the attitude of the University
since the beginning of the present century : and various
examination statutes require proficiency in the study of
Latin authors as well as in Latin composition : the scholarships for the encouragement of Latin literature is a
University foundation ; and in the professorship which is
now being inaugurated, the result at once of University
and of Collegiate bounty, the objects of the two great
revivers of learning in Oxford are at length fulfilled by
the union of Wolsey's Humanity lectureship with the
institution for the 'sowing and planting' of the Latin
language, contemplated by the founder of Corpus.

Brief and imperfect as this sketch has been, I venture
to think that it has its purpose, not only as a tribute to
the past, such as on an occasion like this it would have
been injurious to withhold, but as a help to the right appreciation of our present position. The complaint has
recently been made by Cambridge scholars,[2] whose judg-

---

[1] The conceptions formed of grammar and rhetoric are explained by the
statutes which regulate the duties of the Praelectors of the two subjects
(Stat. Tit. 4. 2 and 3) : 'Praelector Grammatices publice Grammaticam legat
lingua Latinâ, vel technice a Prisciano, Linacro, aliove probato Grammatico
auctore vel critico seu philologico selectos aliquos titulos de antiquitatibus
Graecis aut Romanis explicet. . . . Praelector Rhetorices publice exponat
Rhetoricam Aristotelis, Ciceronis, Quintiliani, aut Hermogenis, quos ita
inter se conferat ut ex his artis praecepta in unum corpus redigat.' Compare
with these the statutes of the Greek and Hebrew Professorships, where the
study of the literature is enjoined.

[2] The writers alluded to are Dr. Donaldson (Varronianus, ed. 2, pp. xiv.
sqq.) and Mr. Paley (Propertius, p. xxii.).

ment I am bound to respect on private no less than on public grounds, that the study of Latin is not flourishing in England; and I have reason to believe that it finds an echo in the convictions of some among ourselves. We have abandoned, it is said, the old appliances without taking up the new: the standard of Latin writing in University examinations is confessedly low: ignorance of Latin is tolerated by those who require an exact acquaintance with Greek; Greek literature has of late been successfully cultivated by Englishmen, while in Latin we have still to depend on the Continent. I should be sorry to underrate our national shortcomings in scholarship as contrasted with the attainments of the Germans; but I believe that some at least of the facts which seem to show that there has been a peculiar falling off in the study of Latin have not been rightly interpreted. We are hardly entitled to assume a uniformity in the experience of the two Universities; still less may we argue from one public school to another, as it is notorious that while some are supposed to cultivate Greek to the prejudice of Latin, others, and those by no means the least distinguished, have the reputation of preferring Latin to Greek. In the practice of Latin, as of Greek, verse composition, our education is allowed to be greatly superior to that which can be obtained on the Continent; and *if* the Latin prose written now-a-days be worse than that which was produced in the last generation, it certainly is not because the imitation of Cicero has given place to that of Plato or Demosthenes. Nor can I admit, so far as my own experience goes, that the rule of attainment in Latin is less exacting than that which we apply to Greek. It is no reproach to the requirements of our system that we have nothing in Latin answering to the canons of Porson and Elmsley. Their discoveries reflect not only on the sagacity and

industry which effected them, but on the ignorance of
transcribers and previous scholars, which for centuries
confounded the language of Homer with the language of
the Attic writers, and the metre of tragedy with the metre
of comedy.   In a word, it is not that Greek is better understood than Latin, but that Latin, till a comparatively short
time ago, had always been better understood than Greek.
Our Latin dictionaries, indeed, are still unfortunately com-
pilations from foreign works, and the only history of
Roman literature on a considerable scale which we possess
is meagre and unsatisfactory: but the last few years have
produced at least one Latin grammar of authority, and
we may hope, ere long, to see the fragment which Arnold
left completed by the publication of standard histories of
republican and imperial Rome.   The general neglect in
this country of the antiquarian part of philology involves
the sources of the Greek language no less than the early
languages of Italy.   Meantime, we may not unreasonably
hope that the advance of our philosophical education is
gradually introducing an appreciation of the true nature
of language sufficient to compensate for those losses, more
apparent than real, but in any case inevitable, which the
practical disuse of Latin may entail on the University.
We cultivate Latin not as the vernacular of a supposed
commonwealth of scholars, but for the historical value
which attaches to it, both in itself, and as containing the
records of the thought and feeling of a large section of
the ancient world ; and while we retain the practice of
imitative composition as a means of realising to ourselves
the form as well as the spirit of that majestic literature,
we need not be anxious in our own criticisms to clothe
the mind of the nineteenth century in the body of the
first, or expect that we can apprehend the civilisation of
the past through any other medium than that in which we

ourselves live and breathe. The tendency of our academical history throughout has been to assimilate more and
more the study of Latin to the study of Greek ; and we
shall do well to accept its guidance.

But though in the present condition of the study of
Latin, I see no signs of decay or depreciation, but simply
the natural effect of the introduction of our own language
as the instrument and Greek as a rival object of knowledge, I cannot say that the reasons for promoting it, as
generally apprehended, are as strong now as they were,
or as, in my judgment, they ought to be. Now that the
incontestable advances made in Greek scholarship have
awakened our minds to a sense of the power and beauty
of the poetry, the oratory, the history, and the philosophy
of the Hellenic race, such as was not possible in the
education of the last century, it is not to be wondered at
that there should be a disposition to repudiate the traditional admiration of Roman literature as misplaced or
excessive—to discriminate sharply between the masters
and their imitators, between the intellectual conquerors
and those who submitted to receive a culture which they
could not have originated, and were not even able fully to
appropriate. It may, perhaps, be conceded that the language of Rome is not inferior in educational value to that
of Greece. An inflected language with a highly elaborate
syntax, Latin may challenge comparison with any, as a
means of mental discipline. On historical grounds, no
tongue can possess stronger interests for civilised humanity
than the speech of that victorious city, which, beginning
with almost daily struggles for life with the petty tribes of
its own narrow peninsula, succeeded in breaking to pieces
the power of one nation after another, and finally in its
imperial decline gave laws to the world. Language is
always more truly national than literature : they act and

re-act on each other, but the broad distinction remains, that one is the spontaneous product of the nameless many, the other the artificial creation of the illustrious few ; and though the remnants of early Latin are scanty and imperfect, its formal part—that which makes it what it is—was in being long before the days when, as Horace expresses it, the Roman sat down to rest after the Punic wars, and speculated what might be made out of Sophocles, and Thespis, and Æschylus. But it is too late to expect that any single language, except it be the vernacular, will continue to be studied for educational purposes apart from its literature, at a time when comparative philology is exhibiting to us the structure of articulate human speech in all its world-wide extent, and a more profound psychological analysis is searching for the principles of universal grammar in the unfathomed depths of the individual mind. What, then, are the grounds for recommending the minute study of Roman literature to one who has been taught truly to estimate the literature of Greece?

The answer, I believe, lies on the surface : it is to be found in the historical position actually occupied by Roman literature, in relation both to that which went before and to that which has followed it.

In speaking of Roman literature as imitative, it must not be forgotten that the reproach is not peculiar to it, but attaches to the whole of the literature of modern Europe.[1] Greece, in its independent, instinctive development, set the example which subsequent nations have followed with more or less of distinct consciousness. Even if we choose to consider this conscious effort after an external standard as fatal alike to national and individual genius, we must admit it to be an inevitable evil, involved

---

[1] Compare Mure's *History of Greek Literature*, I., pp. 139 sqq., 135 sqq., 142 sqq.

in the very position of those who have a preceding civilisation to reflect upon. Rome may seem to have been
more of a copyist than any of its successors, partly as
being actually more indebted to Greece, partly from the
lateness of its intellectual growth, which suggests the
notion of rational deliberation rather than of creative
energy; but the difference must not be exaggerated in
either case. If modern nations have followed Greece less
closely than Rome did, it is attributable to the fact, among
other causes, that they have had Rome as well as Greece
to follow; nor will the long barrenness of the Roman
intellect prejudice the judgment of those who bear in
mind that the Punic wars were in the life of the Eternal
City only what the war with Persia was in the briefer
history of Athens, and that even now the true literature
of modern Germany, though one of the richest that Europe
can boast, is scarcely more than a century old. Roman
literature is not without its interest for the enthusiastic
student, even where it is purely imitative. A skilful artist
will often be more honourably employed in copying a
great work, than in labouring on his own account. What
he gives is his interpretation of the original—far inferior,
no doubt, even in the sight of the shallowest perception, to
that which he represents, but sure to reveal beauties which
might otherwise have concealed themselves from a more
observant eye. It is this principle which constitutes the
true value of a really good translation—not as superseding
the original, even to the worst scholar, but as explaining
it, even to the best: and the greater freedom allowed to
an imitator only enhances the critical importance of his
labours, as he need not simply copy, but may amplify and
illustrate. Thus an imitative literature is peculiarly
adapted, by the determinateness of the art employed, for
showing what literature really is: the intense conscious-

ness of the writer can hardly fail to communicate itself to
his readers; and the very narrowness of his conception
is in some sort an advantage, as enabling them more
successfully to disentangle the confused mass of their
impressions. No one would now think of seriously comparing the 'Iliad' and the 'Æneid;' but the latter affords
the better study of the laws and conditions under which
epic poetry is produced.

Yet it would be a great mistake to suppose that imitation is the only characteristic of post-Grecian literature,
or that it furnishes any exception to the uniform law of
progress and development which appears to govern everything realised in time. Perfect as it is in its own symmetry,
the literature of Greece was not only subject to critical
changes, but itself formed a stage in a process yet unfinished, and that not as a golden age, followed by a
succession of baser metals, but rather as a heroic fore-
time, ushering in periods of historical life, which, though
constantly looking back to it as the source of light and
inspiration, have yet a purpose and a being of their own.
Few, indeed, are disposed to deny the originality of much
of the literature which they see daily living around them;
but it is not generally felt that what appears so fresh and
new is in large measure due to modifications introduced
by the great writers of the later Republic and the Empire.
In spite of the various causes which tended to assimilate
the literary character of the two nations—causes each of
which would well bear the burden of a separate discussion
—the animating principle of kindred though not identical
mythologies, the influence of like conceptions of politics
and society, the common peculiarities of a hearing as
opposed to a reading age, as seen in their effects on the
form of composition, the similarity of pronunciation, leading the Latin poets to discard any attempts at originality

in their metres, there were features in the intellectual culture of Rome which might fairly be called national, if a more careful observation did not lead us to regard them not as characteristic of this or that people, but as marking the general progress of letters. One of the most noticeable facts in literature is the gradual encroachment of prose upon poetry—a change which has been going on from the first, and of which evidently we do not yet see the end. In later times it has received a mighty impulse from the invention of printing, as it probably did before from the discovery of the art of writing: but its process has not been less certain, mechanical appliances remaining the same, and it may fairly be accepted as a test of literary development. That Rome affords an instance of it may be inferred at once from the fact, which most would admit, that its prose writers are on the whole superior in excellence to its poets. Epistolary composition, which in Greece appears scarcely to have been studied at all as an art, except by the Sophists and forgers of the later schools, in Rome is cultivated by the most accomplished men of the best ages. Satire, the one kind of poetry to which Quintilian could point as the indigenous growth of his country, is seen, in the hands of its most finished artist, to be closely allied to prose; just as under the altered circumstances of the present day it finds its representative in the pamphlet, the article, or the moral essay. The same advance in the power of adapting the form to the matter may be seen in the Roman treatment of history. Thucydides knew no better way of exhibiting his consummate knowledge of character, than by inventing long speeches such as his historical personages *might* have spoken—in other words, by confounding history with the drama. In Tacitus, on the other hand, the analysis of human actions and motives is carried on much more directly   the two

elements, the narrative and the philosophical, were felt
each to have its proper place; and the same scheme embraces both as such in their individual distinctness. Again,
we perceive in Rome, more definitely than in any of the
centres of Grecian life, the gradual withdrawal of literary
men into a separate class, which, though in some respects
prejudicial to themselves, as well as symptomatic of intellectual deterioration in the community at large, is a natural
consequence of an increasing devotion to literature ; while
it may co-exist, as our own experience shows, with extensive progress in popular education. The causes which
contributed to this result were various—the possession of
a borrowed culture, which had to be mastered by the
knowledge of technical rules—the constitution of society,
encouraging a relation which we actually express by a
metaphor borrowed from Roman civil usages, that of
patronage ; but the fact is palpable, and the picture of
things in the Seventh Satire of Juvenal, anticipating so
vividly the condition of letters in the London of the
eighteenth century, is one to which we should in vain seek
a precise parallel at Athens, or even, perhaps, at Syracuse
or Alexandria.   On the one hand, the division of labour
tends to shut men up into particular departments, and we
hear of the historian by profession as well as of the poet,
the rhetorician, and the grammarian : on the other, the
increase of skill in composition, as such, leads a writer to
attempt the union of qualifications hitherto kept distinct,
and Cicero aims at being at once the Roman Plato and
the Roman Demosthenes, not to speak of his less successful efforts after the crown of poetry.   Both were signs of
the same general tendency, and mark a peculiar conception of literature as an art, itself the result of that advance
in self-consciousness which distinguishes a later period

from an earlier, and is in fact a condition of mental progress in humanity as in individuals.

But if these indications of growth seem slight and almost imaginary in themselves, there is a light in which they may be seen to be real and striking. We are entitled, as has been before intimated, to claim as belonging to Rome, not only what it did for itself, but what it has wrought in the nations which succeeded it. What Greece was to Rome, Rome has been to modern times—the great educator, the humanizer of its barbarous conqueror, the mother of intellect, art and civilisation. That part of our culture which we have not worked out for ourselves, or received from contemporary nations, we owe almost wholly to Rome, and to Greece only through Rome, just as our language, saturated throughout with Latin, has assimilated but few particles of Greek. If the Romans viewed the great works of Greece through the medium of Alexandrian criticism, our fathers viewed them through the medium of Roman imitation. 'Paradise Lost' may ascribe its form, and much of its detail, to the conception of Homer framed by the educated men of later Greece, accepted by Virgil and the epic writers of Augustan Rome, and finally sanctioned by the heroic muse of modern Italy. The foreign element of the Shaksperian drama is traceable, ultimately, not to Æschylus and Aristophanes, but to Plautus and Seneca. The tragedy of the Restoration period is formed on the model of the French, which itself copies the declamatory dialogues of the Roman sophist. In the eighteenth century, the influence of Rome is yet more direct and exclusive: in fact, we may say that an acquaintance with the principal Latin writers is the only way to a literary appreciation of that phase—the most brilliant, as some may still esteem it—of English authorship. The position

of the Augustan era is reversed: it had openly rivalled
Greece, and it is now itself openly rivalled by England.
There is the same consummate dexterity which is characteristic of all high imitation, the same universal ambition
to be eminent not only in one department of imaginative
composition, but in several. The great Augustan artist
would be Theocritus, Hesiod, and Homer in one: the
poet of the reigns of Anne and George I. aspires to unite
the features of Ovid, Horace, and Virgil. The two forms
of composition which have been mentioned as the peculiar property of Rome are precisely those which are most
congenial to this Roman period of the English mind.
Pope and Swift recal Cicero and Atticus; nearly every
wit, whatever his intellectual temperament, writes a satire
or an epistle; and two of the greatest not only follow
Horace and Juvenal, but expressly and directly copy
them. This may now be, to many of us, merely a thing
of a bygone time: the deliberate imitation of Latin models
was impossible after men became alive to the power and
beauty of earlier and later literature. But development
does not cease with imitation; and the features which I
mentioned just now as showing that Roman literature
was growing and advancing, are coincident, at least, with
some of those which would at once be pointed to as the
effects of the revolt of the past and the present generation of Englishmen against the eighteenth century
and its classical superstition. In literature, as in history
and actual life, no effort can set us free from the laws and
conditions of our being: the direction of the will may
be changed, but it is determined, not the less, by the
causes which were appointed to preside over the formation of the character at the outset.

It is on these grounds that I would venture to recommend the study of Latin literature, as such, to anyone

inclined to question its value, as I believe that to neglect it would be to neglect a whole epoch in the history of letters, most important intrinsically, and most unequivocal in its influence on ourselves. As the first to feel and obey the impulse given by Greece, Rome might well excite our attention ; as the communicator of that impulse to modern Europe, it sublimates attention into sympathy and earnest regard. That which has actually had so much to do with the formation and discipline of a culture which the lapse of many generations of men has proved to have been no weakling, but a vigorous birth, can never cease to be studied wherever that culture is made an object of paramount interest. To allow it to pass into the shade because we have come to appreciate its relation to Greek literature more truly than heretofore, is as idle a thought as it confessedly would be to speculate on the larger results, as we may deem them, which would have accrued to humanity if Greece had been permitted to influence later ages without any interposing medium. Indeed, the historical position of Roman literature enables it to vindicate itself. We are not left to our own choice whether or no we should study that which, being as we are, we cannot afford to forget. The scholar may feel that Latin, as compared with Greek, is but ' moonlight unto sunlight ;' but if the time should come when those who wish to preserve a classical education for the generality of instructed Englishmen find it necessary to abandon one of the classical languages in order to save the other, it is not difficult to foresee that practical convenience will overturn other considerations, and plead for the language which for so many centuries has been held in England to be the symbol of cultivation, against one of whose existence there is scarcely anything in our daily speech to remind us, and whose very alphabet has to be made a matter of learning. Happily, to us in this place the alternative does not present itself; we have not to choose between a distant and a proximate benefactor—between originality and utility. Homer and Virgil, Pindar and Horace, Thucydides and Tacitus, Demosthenes and Cicero, may be studied side by side: we may acknowledge the commanding pre-eminence of the master, at the same time that we admire the skill and discrimination which the pupil has shown, not only in following, but in deviating from his model. The same method of study will enable us to acquire both: the specific differences of the knowledge to be realised will occasionally involve a difference in the manner of knowing; but the powers of mind called forth are the same, and the discipline administered to them partakes of the same character, though it may be not always in the same degree. Of this part of the subject I have now to speak.

The object which the study of literature proposes may be described as the entering into the mind of men eminent in thought and in power of expression. It may seem hardly worth while to note that it is requisite not only that the student should gain certain conceptions of power, beauty, and the like, but that they should be such as the writer intended to convey. In the case of other things of a similar nature, the distinction is one which scarcely occurs to us. When we look at a painting, we seldom set ourselves deliberately to discover the intention of the artist; we know, that though we may fail to understand all that was meant, we are not liable to substitute a wrong meaning for the right, much less to perceive graces which really result from accident or exist only in our own lively fancy. Words are acknowledged to be a more palpable and less transparent medium than forms or colours: still, in the average course of a vernacular literature, the instances are comparatively rare where a man has to ask himself whether he comprehends what he is reading; and even then the knot is generally solved, not by investigation and study, but by reflection and an appeal to common sense. Truth, as such, seldom or never has to be made a distinct object of pursuit : it seems to come unasked, and so rarely obtains even a passing glance of recognition. But when we approach the literature of another country, our view is at once changed, if not reversed. Then the difficulty of the medium is seen to be such that the thoughts which lie beyond are apt to appear easy in comparison. If the language is a modern one, the labour will be more or less mechanical. The method of discovering truth consists chiefly in looking out words in the dictionary; that done, a little experience of idiom and style supplies the rest. The trouble may be considerable for the time, but it is short, and the student soon comes to read a foreign work as he would read one written in English, and finds the process of interpretation go on intuitively. It is precisely here that the real difficulty of studying an ancient language begins. To the schoolboy reading Latin and Greek is virtually the same as reading French or German; to the scholar there is all the difference in the world. The books of reference which he uses, the lexicons and the grammars, are far more elaborate and more helpful than anything which he could obtain for studying a modern language; but they remind him that the need of assistance is far greater. They furnish him not solely or principally with patent and unquestioned facts, such as a few days' travel might verify, and the slightest authority may consequently guarantee; the certainties in which they deal are frequently such as it requires the toil of months or years to discover, and perhaps the reputation of a life to accredit. He finds that others have thought and investigated, not that he may be spared the trouble of thought or investigation, but that he may think and investigate for himself. The sense of many of the words before him is to be made out, not on direct evidence, but by a long induction of instances; the full appreciation of an idiom or construction has often to be gained by the inward exertion of sympathetic thought, as well as by wide reading; nay, the very text of the author is often itself a matter of doubt, so that the critic has, as it were, to tell both the dream and the interpretation. History has to be ransacked in the hope of finding the key to an indirect allusion in a single line; the windings of a writer's mind have to be tracked not only in his own works, but in those of the contemporaries with whom he lived familiarly, or the predecessors whom he regarded with filial reverence; the arrow, like that in the fable, has to be aimed at a mark which the archer's eye is allowed to see only as reflected in some other substance. In a word, he is constantly brought to feel that the language with which he has to do is a *dead* language, buried under the weight of interposed centuries, and only to be reached by one who has skill and resolution to penetrate through their manifold incrustations.

There are, I know, persons to whom the enumeration of the obstacles to the understanding of the classics suggests regretful, if not contemptuous, feelings. They lament the waste of labour spent, not in the discovery of the unknown, but in the recovery of the lost, and make light of divinations of truth which the unrolling of a single new manuscript may supersede or disprove. The complaint is the same which is put so epigrammatically by the author of Hudibras,' where he says of Time and his daughter Truth,

'Twas he that put her in the pit
Before he pulled her out of it.

I need hardly say, that if valid at all, it is valid, as Butler
doubtless intended it, against all historical research.
There, as here, we have the spectacle of human thought
toiling painfully to repair the losses caused by human
thoughtlessness, as well as by the unavoidable chances of
time : there, as here, the utmost that can be done may
disappear before the contradiction or the fuller affirmation
of an accidental discovery.   But is the case so different
as regards other parts of knowledge ?   Is not the attainment of all intellectual truth a labour which might have
conceivably been spared to us ; nay, which doubtless
would have been spared, had the mere possession and enjoyment of truth been the end which we were meant to
compass ?   Even the very word enjoyment, so used, implies a misconception.[1]   The intellect enjoys truth, not by
simply contemplating it, but by feeding on it, by assimi-
lating it, and thus making it instrumental to the perception
of further truth, which in its turn ministers to other and
higher realisations.   The toil of getting and the joy of
using are not, as in other things, separate, but identical :
if distinguishable in common speech, it is only as we may
choose to distinguish parts of a process which is really
uniform and indivisible.   In this sense, no one need hesitate to join in Lessing's celebrated profession, that if called
upon to choose between truth and the search after truth,
he should prefer the latter.   It is not hard to see that, the
constitution of our minds remaining as it is, the immediate
communication of all knowledge would not be a blessing,

---

[1] Compare Bp. Butler, *Sermon* xv. (*Works*, vol. ii. p. 253.   Oxford ed. of
1835.)   'Whoever will in the least attend to the thing will see that it is
the gaining, not the having of it (knowledge), which is the entertainment of
the mind.' So Sir W. Hamilton (*Discussions on Philosophy*, &c., p. 39) :
Speculative truth is subordinate to speculation itself; and its value is
directly measured by the quantity of energy which it occasions—immediately
in its discovery, mediately through its consequences.'

but an incalculable curse. 'There is,' indeed, 'nothing better for a man than that he should make his soul enjoy good in his labour'—that he should accept the knowledge and discipline which each day brings, instead of deferring his satisfaction to the end of a pursuit which, rightly understood, never can be ended on earth, and which, if followed only in the hope of some ulterior reward, even though that reward be truth itself, will but yield 'vanity and vexation of spirit.' Thus the question is, not whether we *must* seek for truth, but whether we *may*; not whether the child can be excused his task, but whether he is to be allowed the gratification of guessing the riddle. Whoever may complain of the difficulties which beset the pursuit of classical scholarship, assuredly it will not be the scholar himself. He knows it is precisely by means of these difficulties that he is made perfect in his work. If he is led to repine at times that knowledge should be hidden, it is not as wishing to evade the pains of searching, but because he is already longing to bestow his labour on some other part of the field. It is nothing to him that his time has often to be spent on minute and seemingly trivial points, for he feels that the smaller is to be estimated by the standard of the greater, and that in accepting his calling he has accepted a duty, more or less defined, to everything that appertains to it. The task of recovering a lost word or allusion is not resented as a gratuitous hardship, but embraced as a welcome boon, which compels the student, as it were, to enter the author's laboratory, not as a spectator, but as a fellow-worker, and rewards the restoration with something of the same delight which must have attended the original invention. It is his labour that he has to go down among those who have long been dead ; but there is conscious pleasure in every step of the way, and it is his glory that he can break their

sleep and revive them, that he can make them drink the
blood of life and speak living words, that he can endow
them, if not with the gift of prophecy, at least with the
human power of memory.

I have anticipated much of what I had to say about the
manner of studying Latin literature; but I feel that if my
conception of it be a true one, its worth is to be appreciated, not by generalities, but by a more detailed account.
There is something ambitious in the term 'method,' as
applied to so simple and obvious a process; and yet,
when we think of its capabilities as an intellectual discipline, we shall hardly be able to find a more appropriate
name for it. I cannot hope to explain it so that the
statement shall not appear the merest truism; indeed, I
hardly wish to do so. The way to study Latin literature
is to study the authors who gave it its characters: the
way to study those authors is to study them individually
in their individual works, and to study each work, as far
as may be, in its minutest details. For other purposes,
we may be satisfied with a general view of an author's
mind, or with a cursory perusal of some one or more of
his writings; but the peculiar training which is sought
from the study of literature is only to be obtained, in
anything like its true fulness, by attending, not merely to
each paragraph or each sentence, but to each word, not
merely to the general force of an expression, but to the
various constituents which make up the effect produced
by it on a thoroughly intelligent reader. Nothing but
practical experience can give any notion of the number
and variety of the subjects of knowledge and thought
presented by the careful study even of a small portion of
a work, without travelling beyond those considerations
which properly belong to the particular passage, as having
been present, consciously or unconsciously, to the mind of

the author. Perhaps it will not be thought tedious or inappropriate if I venture, for the sake of clearness, as well as of variety, to analyse, in this spirit, a very short passage, which must be familiar to us all—the first seven lines of the First Æneid of Virgil. I am not sorry to choose one upon which I have myself scarcely anything to offer beyond what may be found in the ordinary commentators, such as Wagner or Forbiger, because my object is to show the improvement which may be derived from this study at any time, as an every-day exercise, not the discoveries to which it may occasionally conduct us, interesting and encouraging as these undoubtedly are.

The first inquiry respects the four lines which in many copies are prefixed to the 'Æneid.' We examine the external evidence, and are struck by one fact, among others, that the testimony which would exclude them tells still more forcibly for excluding the passage about Helen in the Second Æneid: nor can we well escape without gaining some rough notion about the authorities for the text of Virgil. We examine them internally, noting not only their own peculiarities of expression, but their relevancy to the passage which they are intended to introduce. We discuss the probability whether Virgil in particular, or any poet of the Augustan age, would begin by a reference to himself, or rush at once upon his subject and his hero. We estimate the collateral testimony of those contemporary or subsequent writers who mention the words *Arma virum*, as if they were the key-note to the whole 'Æneid.' After thus pausing on the threshold, we proceed to the work itself. We ask whether the word *Arma*, bursting thus suddenly on the ear, may not be meant to imply the contrast between this and Virgil's other poems, which the interpolated lines so clumsily endeavoured to express. We compare Virgil's opening with Homer's, and

with the apparently parallel passage in one of the Cyclic
writers, noting that he begins in the first person, like the
poet ridiculed by Horace, and defers his invocation of
the muse till afterwards. We observe that Virgil himself
uses the words *Arma virum* together elsewhere in the
'Æneid,' as if he intended them to be linked by a real
connection. We remark on the sense of *primus*, not as
excluding an earlier journey, but as pointing to the beginning of Roman history, and thus reminding us of the
purpose of the Augustan epic. The word *Italiam* opens
another question, having actually given rise to a treatise
by a German scholar,[1] which is highly spoken of, on the
anomalies of quantity introduced by the Roman epic
writers. *Fato* leads us to inquire into Virgil's conception
of destiny and of its relation to the power of the gods,
in short into his theological belief. We then come to a
question of reading between *Larina* and *Lavinia*, when
we have to consider the imitation of the passage by Propertius, and to observe the circumstances under which
Virgil elsewhere employs a synizesis. In the third line,
we note the rhetorical pleonasm of *ille*, established by
other passages of Virgil, remarking on the use of pronouns,
both in Greek and Latin, to express other than pronominal
relations, and on the grammatical considerations involved
therein. The fourth line presents a difficulty of interpretation in the words *Vi superum*, the common rendering of
which has recently been disputed as implying that Juno
acted in concert with the gods, whereas the whole tenor
of the 'Æneid' represents her as Æneas' sole enemy.
Thus we have to examine Virgil's theology again, as well
as to decide on the possible meaning of the words, considered grammatically. *Memorem iram* recals us to
Homer, and reminds us also of the μνάμων μῆνις of

---

[1] Köne: *Ueber die Sprache der Römischen Epiker.* Münster, 1840.

Æschylus. In the next line, the construction of *dum* with the imperfect conjunctive opens a subtle grammatical question, the answer to which is to be sought in a consideration of the nature and force of the conjunctive mood. The two remaining lines introduce us to questions of mythology and antiquities:—what the *Penates* were, how they differed from the *Di Magni*, why the *Albani patres* are so called, and, generally, what was Virgil's view of the beginnings of Rome—all to be settled by a careful reference to other passages of the 'Æneid,' which in their turn frequently start fresh questions, even when discussed only so far as is necessary for purposes of illustration. Lastly, we are led to regard the exordium as a whole, admirably adapted as it is throughout to express the poet's full sense of the greatness of his subject—a broad and striking contrast to the unconsciousness of Homer, who presents himself as the teller of a wonderful story, not as the author of a grand national poem.

Those who are accustomed to a careful study of the classics, will see that I have by no means exhausted all that could fairly be said on these lines, or in other words, all that is required for a complete appreciation of them, at the same time that I have been careful not to make them mere pegs on which to hang irrelevant questions in philology or æsthetics. Yet, surely the amount of education which such a study pre-supposes or imparts is very considerable. In considering his author's general character in itself, or in contrast with that of another, the student is led to take broad views of rhetorical or poetical art: in analysing particular expressions, and disclosing the images which they involve, he is made to trace that art in its details. He has to skirt the undefined bounds which separate rhetoric from grammar, and ascertain the conditions under which words, grammatically appropriated to one conception, can be put for those denoting another. He is frequently called to investigate grammar itself, by the occurrence of constructions which have to be explained by some general law, or left unexplained under the shelter of some unquestionable idiom. At other times, he will have recourse to comparative philology, to illustrate a word or usage, of the true nature of which the writer himself, learned as he may have been in the antiquities of his country's language, had but a dim confused consciousness. The casual allusions scattered through the work will familiarise him with much historical knowledge: the subject of the work, even though it may have no direct bearing on history, with much also. This enumeration is a very imperfect one, even as compared with my own conception and experience; yet it will be seen that it includes many of the elements which are usually held to constitute a general cultivation, thus ensuring a discipline of the various parts of the mind, more comprehensive, probably, than can be afforded by any other single subject of knowledge. But this is not all. These several lines of thought and research are not followed for themselves, but as means for something further: they make up the method by which the truth of the writer's meaning is to be attained. However great their heterogeneity in relation to each other, in this point they all converge. It is difficult to secure anything like completeness in the method, as no man can hope to realise all the aspects in which a word or conception has appeared to the mind of another, especially when separated from him by a gulf of centuries: it is seldom that we can expect to make the best even of our incompleteness, as in any single track of investigation we are liable to meet with failure, or, at any rate, with only partial success. Such defects, however, do not destroy the value of the results which *can* be obtained; and it

only requires a careful use of the various means in our
power to convince us that the method of interpretation is
one that really deserves the name, leading not to specious
plausibilities, but to substantial truths. I know not how
it may be in the case of other sciences, but I can testify
to the genuine intellectual satisfaction which the mind
receives when some discovery, in itself, perhaps, of quite
minor importance, a latent metaphor, a concealed imitation, the substitution of one insignificant word or inflexion
of a word for another, or even the mere position of a
word, hitherto overlooked, and now noticed accidentally,
has flashed light on an entire passage, and a vague sense
of disproportion has given place to a clear perception of
harmonious symmetry. Or again, where the lighting up
has been not sudden, but gradual, it is not the less reassuring to recall the first aspect of a sentence, seemingly
complete in itself, and sufficient to the eye of the ordinary
reader, and compare it with the full appreciation which
is gained at last, when every point has been accurately
scrutinised, and the student once more comes to survey it
as a whole. Thus the exegetical study of the classics, as
it appears to me, fulfils the two great conditions of an
educational instrument: it gives at once a general and a
special discipline: it encourages exuberant variety of interest along with severe precision of aim. I do not say
that it has always had this effect on the mind of the
student, but I believe that where it has failed to do so, the
fault has not been in the method, and that if even really
great scholars have sometimes been narrow and one-sided,
they have been so far less complete, not only as men, but
as scholars. I believe also that, like all methods,[1] it has

---

[1] 'Nostra enim via inveniendi scientias exæquat fere ingenia, et non
multum excellentiæ eorum relinquit, cum omnia per certissimas regulas et
demonstrationes transigat.'—Bacon: *Nov. Org.*, lib. 1., aph. cxxii.

a salutary tendency to equalise human capacities, so that
though the greatest reward will always fall to his lot who,
having the greatest natural powers, economises them most
prudently and disposes them to the best advantage, there
will yet be an abundant harvest which inferior minds are
certain to reap, by the mere fact of their honest compliance with prescribed rules ; while those who go out in
their own strength, disdaining all labour that appears
uncongenial, find for the most part barrenness and comparative scarcity.

Such a mode of reading, I need hardly say, cannot but
be a work of time ; even a professed teacher can scarcely
expect to attain so close a familiarity with more than a
very few authors ; for a learner, who does not intend to
pursue the study, a thorough mastery of one or two books,
or parts of books, is perhaps the utmost that can be proposed.   But I am sure that a single work, studied in this
manner, may be of indefinite use to the mind ; and though
of course he who has read much will have an advantage,
in explaining a text, over him who has read little, yet, on
the other hand, under the treatment of a diligent student,
an author becomes, to a great extent, his own interpreter,
and the various books of reference which come into requisition will indicate collateral sources of information,
which may obviate, if they cannot supply, the want of
strictly independent research.   It need not, it ought not
to exclude the more rapid and cursory reading of the
principal classics.   What I have said of the peculiar value
of Roman literature as a regularly developed whole, will
show that I would have the student's acquaintance with
it general, as well as particular ; extended, as well as intimate ; but no diffusive reading, however it may expand
the views, can be accepted as a substitute for that scrupulous training in the minutiæ of thought and feeling, of

grammar and rhetoric, of historical allusion and textual criticism, all rigorously directed to one end, which it is my present object to set forth.   And I must express my pleasure that the statute which prescribes the duties of my professorship gives me peculiar facilities for promoting this special kind of study in the courses of private lectures which I am required to deliver terminally.   I think I can hardly be wrong in adopting a line of teaching which appears not only desirable in itself, but peculiarly open to me in the present circumstances of the University, when the many different duties which press upon the tutors of colleges, and, though in a less degree, upon private tutors, are not likely to leave them time or inclination for following out so elaborate, and, as it may appear, so tedious a process.   And if this mode of instruction be found to have its use, as I trust it will have, in spite of the deficiencies of the teacher, in cultivating those who are designed for practical life, as well as in raising up scholars able and willing to criticise and investigate on their own account, it may perhaps suggest the expediency of some more direct provision than at present exists for encouraging it by means of examinations and University distinctions.   In the examination before Moderators, the number of books presented by candidates for honours is too great to admit of a thorough and searching study of the details of each, not to mention the impossibility of setting up so high a standard in an examination which so many are expected to pass.   In the examinations for the University scholarships, though the general demands are more severe, the entire want of prescribed books renders any requirement a matter of uncertainty, the candidate being ignorant whether it is likely to be made, the examiner whether it is likely to be responded to.   The ideal of an examination in classical scholarship appears to me to be one which,

while encouraging general reading, by allowing an examiner to select any passage he pleases from any author,
should, at the same time, stimulate special study, by pre-
scribing two or three books, or parts of books, to be
prepared with the most minute critical accuracy. It
might be well that one, at least, of these should have been
studied under the professor; but the real gain would be
in the acquirement, by whatever means, of the habit of
thorough and genuine study.

In closing this introductory lecture, I will not attempt
to conceal my mistrust of my own sufficiency for the work
which lies before me. One whose business it is to be
conversant with a heathen literature can hardly fail to be
sensible of his need of that purity without which nothing
is holy, as well as of that power without which nothing
is strong. I feel, too, that there is likely to be much, very
much, which will compel me to look to the co-operation
and sympathy of those who now hear me. I am not
apprehending any collision between rival systems of instruction, but it is plain that when an experiment has to
be tried on a considerable scale in one of the principal
departments of University study, its success must depend
not only on the individual more especially charged with
the duty of carrying it out, but on those under whom,
among whom, and for whom, he has to labour. And
when I think both of the kind and flattering confidence
which has placed me here, and also of the many expressions of unexpected interest and regard which I have
since received, I am assured that my hopes of consideration and support will not be in vain.

ELEVEN years ago[2] the appearance of an article on
Lucretius by Mr. Munro in a classical periodical led us to
express a confident hope that the great Latin poet would
ere long find an English editor not unworthy to follow
in the steps of Lachmann. That hope has at last been
fulfilled. In 1860 Mr. Munro gave to the world a new
recension of the text of his author, with a critical preface
in Latin; and he has now published a revision of that
recension, with an English prose translation of the poem
at the foot of the page, and a volume of English commentary, consisting of two sets of notes, the one critical,
the other explanatory. To say that nothing of the same
importance has ever been done for Lucretius in England
is unfortunately to say but little. But we shall be greatly
surprised if it is not welcomed by the scholars of the
Continent as an accession of singular value to Lucretian
literature. As regards the text, indeed, Mr. Munro, like
Dr. Bernays, must rank as a follower of Lachmann.
That great man performed so much that subsequent
critics, for a long time to come, are likely to be spoken of
simply as disciples in his school. But to find an explanatory commentary on Lucretius equal in importance, in
relation to its own period, to Mr. Munro's, we must go
back exactly three hundred years, to the edition of
Lambinus, in 1564. There is simply nothing in the
intervening time, either at home or abroad, which will
bear to be named along with it. For that class of

---

[1] Reprinted from the *Edinburgh Review*, No. cexlix.
[2] *Edinburgh Review*, No. cviii. p. 80.

readers, again, which is interested not so much in the
criticism or interpretation of Lucretius as in the Latin
language and literature in general, it possesses unusual
attractions. No English work within our recollection, of
at all a recent date, contains so much of genuine yet not
trite learning, so much of ingenious yet sober speculation
on questions connected with Latin philology and the
mechanism of Latin poetry. Altogether we think we may
safely say that it is the most valuable contribution to
Latin scholarship made by any Englishman in the present
century.

To justify our opinion in detail would require an exhibition of particulars far beyond our own means and
opportunities, and not likely, we suspect, to be gratefully
received by any large number of our readers. We can
only afford to venture a few cursory remarks on the several features of Mr. Munro's edition before we proceed to
say something of the author whom he has edited. In
speaking of Lucretius, however, we shall have occasion
not unfrequently to mention his editor; and even when
we do not discuss Mr. Munro's views we shall gladly avail
ourselves of his information.

When we speak of the critical part of Mr. Munro's
commentary as less important than the explanatory part,
we by no means intend any disparagement of the former.
No conscientious student of Lucretius can afford to dispense with either of them. The critical notes, so far as
we are able to judge of them, are marked by the same
accuracy, sobriety, and, to sum up many merits in one
word, thoroughness, as the rest of the book. The
omissions of Lachmann are supplied, his occasional inaccuracies corrected, his opinions reviewed. There is also
a most elaborate introduction of twenty-eight closely-
printed pages on the formation of the text, much more

copious than Lachmann's, yet without being in any way
redundant, at the same time that it includes a sketch of
the history and a discussion of the principles of Latin
orthography. Perhaps the point on which labour and
ingenuity have been least successfully bestowed is the
emendation of corrupt passages. Yet this is no more
than may be said of Lachmann's own performances. One
whose conceptions of the remedial powers of emendatory
criticism have been formed on a study of the brilliant
restorations which it has effected in the text of the Greek
poets will be surprised to find how many of the conjectures of this 'second Bentley' fail to carry absolute
conviction. This inferiority we incline to ascribe not so
much to the critic himself as to the subject-matter on
which he was engaged. No scholar, so far as we are
aware, for the last two centuries at least, has done for any
Latin poet what Bentley did for the fragments of Greek
poetry, what Porson did for the Greek drama. Bentley
himself was far more occupied with Roman authors than
with Greek, but his reputation as a restorer of classical
text rests mainly on his epistle to Mill and his emendations
of Menander. It is not, as his biographer thinks,[1] that
'his knowledge and perception of the latter language were
incomparably better than of the former.' No one who
reads his notes to Horace can doubt the completeness of
his acquaintance with Latin poetry, or his power of
suggesting words not unworthy of his author. Nor is it,
we think, wholly or principally that he chose to correct
passages which did not need correction. Whether, as in
Horace, he substitutes a good word for a good, or, as in
Manilius, a good word for a bad, the critical reader
equally fails to find the substitution which criticism requires, the substitution of a true word for a false. Where

[1] *Monk's Life*, 8vo ed., vol. L p 168.

Bentley has failed, no subsequent Latin scholar has
succeeded. It would be difficult to name a Greek poet
who presents a fairer field for conjectural skill than
Catullus, Propertius, and Lucretius himself. There are
manuscripts of each enough to stimulate critical ingenuity,
not enough to supersede it; and, as might be expected,
there are corrupt passages enough in the text of each to
make the fortune of any scholar who should be able
successfully to restore them. Lachmann has edited all
three, and his editions show abundant marks of sagacity
and really high ability. Each of the three poets is now
made to say a great deal which he probably might have
said, in place of a great deal which he never could have
said. But conjectures where probability rises into de-
monstrative certainty—conjectures which, in restoring the
words of the author, establish at the same time the truth
of the method of conjectural restoration—are comparatively few. Into the causes which lie at the root of this
great difference between the results of criticism as applied
to Greek and to Latin writers, we do not profess to
inquire. Several considerations occur to us which might
lead to a solution of the question; but none of them
strikes us as so free from possible exception as to make it
worth while to state it here. It is enough to note the
fact, as we believe it to be, and to point out the importance of bearing it in mind in judging of a new critical
edition of a Latin author. One great qualification for
conjectural criticism—one in which English scholars as a
body greatly surpass the scholars of the Continent—Mr.
Munro has in abundant measure, the power of Latin verse
composition. Those who know the manly and vigorous
translations in hexameter verse which he has contributed
to the 'Sabrinæ Corolla' will not question that he could,
if he chose, produce whole paragraphs of philosophical

poetry of which Lucretius himself would not have been ashamed. If they think, as we are inclined to think, that in attempting to restore the corrupt passages in his author he has frequently failed to hit on the words which his author is likely to have used, they will conclude, as we are inclined to conclude, that the task of recovering those words is really beyond the reach even of high critical power.

But whatever may be the special impracticability of the text of Latin authors, there are no exceptional circumstances affecting the interpretation of that text. There, at any rate, the battle is to the strong; learning, acuteness, sobriety, and taste will have their full reward. Lucretius may keep the precise words which he used in many cases concealed from the most sagacious observer; the general meaning of his sentences, and the precise signification of that infinitely large proportion of his words which has been transmitted to us in an uncorrupted state, he will surrender to anyone who comes to the quest properly equipped with a knowledge of the Latin language, and especially of the earlier authors, an acquaintance with the Epicurean philosophy, and a relish for ancient poetry. The fault is not his if such a champion has been long in coming. Mr. Munro possesses all, and more than all, the qualifications we have named, and consequently his success is signal and complete. In fact, we know scarcely any editor who has done so much for the interpretation of any author. Very few persons indeed seem to be aware how much is required to make an explanatory commentary on an ancient writer really satisfactory. We might almost say that the knowledge of what has to be done is only to be bought by experience like Mr. Munro's own—the experience not only of editing an author, but of translating him. But, however it is to be attained, there can be no question but that it has been attained in the work before us. An intelligent reader may peruse page after page of Lucretius with the help of Mr. Munro, and find every inquiry that can reasonably occur to him, even on collateral subjects, satisfied by the commentary, at the same time that many questions which might not have occurred to him are suggested and answered. By way of example, let us take the first few lines of the poem. In the initial words, ' Æneadum genetrix,' the editor points out a contrast between the peculiar relation in which Venus stands to the children of Æneas, and that which she bears to all animate and inanimate nature ; he also notices a possible imitation of Ennius and two undoubted imitations by Ovid. He next discusses the orthography of ' genetrix,' adducing various considerations drawn from analogy and authority, and finally deciding for that mode of spelling the word as against the rival ' genitrix.' In verse 2 he explains the force of the epithet ' alma,' showing, by quotations from Macrobius, Plautus, Appuleius and the cosmographer Æthicus, that ' alma Venus ' was not only familiar to poets, but had passed into the language of the people. Following Bentley, he notes Lucretius' obligation, in the subsequent description of Venus' influence over the several parts of Nature, to two passages in the ' Hippolytus ' of Euripides, and adds *de suo* that both Euripides and Lucretius were indebted to the Homeric Hymn to Aphrodite. He comments on the epithet ' labentia,' applied to the stars, and notices, in connexion with it, the attention paid by Lucretius to Cicero's translation of Aratus—a fact of which, in a latter part of his commentary, he produces numerous instances. In verse 3 he speaks of the circumstances under which Lucretius uses the plural of ' terra ' oftener than the singular, noticing the curious fact that this use of the plural is almost confined to three cases

out of the five.   In verse 4 he illustrates the use of ' con-
celebrare ' from Lucretius himself and from Cicero, and
discusses, on poetical grounds, the precise meaning of
the word as here employed.   In verse 5 he notices that
Lucretius is fonder of using ' lumina ' in the nominative
and accusative than ' lumen.'   In the four following lines
he comments on the long-drawn stateliness of ' te adven-
tumque tuum,' explains ' dædalus ' from a passage of the
glossarist Paulus, and notes its different uses in Lucretius,
decides that ' rident,' as applied to the sea, refers to its
appearance to the eye, not to the ear, and illustrates from
Virgil the use of ' placatus ' in the sense of relief from
storms.   This summary of a couple of pages of closely-
printed annotation will show how large and comprehensive
a scope Mr. Munro gives to the interpreter's duty.   There
is minute study of his author's peculiarities of usage, however trifling ; there is a large acquaintance with other
parts of Latin literature, the less known as well as the
more known ; and there is, besides, a constant recollection
that the editor is commenting on a poet, and that inquiries
into the signification and usages of words are to be conducted in subordination to the general object of bringing
out the meaning which was in that poet's mind.   To this
part of the commentary also, as well as to the critical part,
an introduction is prefixed.   In it the chronology of the
poet's life, the circumstances of the publication of the poem,
the success with which the subject is handled, the character of Lucretius' style, the peculiarities of his versification as compared with that of his predecessors and that
of his successors, the opinion entertained of him by his
countrymen, are all examined carefully and thoroughly.
Of these divisions, the one which strikes us as most novel
and most interesting is that which treats of Lucretius'
versification, detailing as it does the principal points in

which the Lucretian hexameter differs from the Virgilian.
Few critics who are themselves accomplished versifiers
would have taken so much trouble in analysing impressions which must have come to them rather by
habituation than by distinct apprehension; few who would
have had the patience to collect the statistics of metrical
composition would have known so well what value to
assign to each item in the result.

If any exception is to be taken to the general execution
of Mr. Munro's book, it is, we think, that he has scarcely
been studious enough of literary conventionalities. His
style is lively and diversified, but it is *sui generis*; and
we often seem as if we were listening to a Latin commentator through the medium of an English interpreter.
Thus in the critical notes (Book IV. v. 594), he notices a
conjecture of Bentley's, introduced into the text by
Lachmann: '*nimis auricularum. nimi' miraclorum* Lachm.
after Bentl.: this is now the third time he has introduced
into his text the form *miraclum*, which is not once found
in the mss. of Lucr.: whence got the scribe such a hatred
of the word?' It is a style which reminds us not a little of
that of Bentley's English works; and this, in some respects,
is no mean praise, as Bentley's style is vigorous enough. But
Bentley wrote before English criticism had acquired a definite style of its own; and his English style suits the character of his critical works, which is polemical, not to say
personal.   The only thing which he produced in the shape
of an English commentary is the commentary appended
to his strange edition of Milton; and there he exhibits all
the qualities of his ordinary controversial style, railing at
the imaginary editor whom he supposes, or pretends to
suppose, to have depraved the text of the 'Paradise Lost,'
with far less self-restraint than he had showed in his contest with Boyle, and almost as little as he preserved in
his brawl with Middleton.   Mr. Munro has none of this

acrimonious temper: he speaks occasionally with just
severity of the negligence of some of his predecessors, and
considerately extenuates the Bentleian atrocities of censure
in which Lachmann not unfrequently indulged; but he
is himself perfectly good-humoured and genial, and his
quaintnesses of expression commonly produce the effect of
a pleasant freshness and individuality. On the whole, however, we can scarcely doubt that now that criticism on the
classics is passing out of the hands of Latinists and becoming
a branch of English literature, it ought to express itself as far
as possible after the manner of English literary precedents;
that an editor of the ancient classics ought to aim at a style
as classical as that of the historian of the ' Decline and Fall
of the Roman Empire,' to study the critical manner of a
writer like Mr. Hallam, and even at times to dress himself
by the glass of Lord Macaulay. The same individuality
appears even in the mechanical part of Mr. Munro's commentary. He prints his Latin with that paucity of stops
which has now become almost the established fashion
among scholars; and he apparently thinks that parity of
reasoning requires him to introduce the same custom into
English. Thus we have: ' By *pecudes ferae* Varro means
tame animals or *pecudes* found in a wild state, viz. sheep
goats swine bulls asses horses; Columella goats deer
boars, which though wild may yet be kept in herds on an
estate;' and again, ' Tantalus Tityos Sisyphus, the daughters of Danaus, are but types of people tormented here by
various lusts and passions: Tartarus too Cerberus the
furies have no existence; but are pictures of the various
punishments of crime in this world.' We are not sure,
indeed, that this parsimonious punctuation is not becoming
a point of honour among Cambridge scholars; at least we
fancy we have noticed symptoms of the same thing in other
works by eminent members of that University which have

appeared within the last few months. Yet we cannot say
that we like the fashion ; ' they will say it is Persian attire ;
but let it be changed.' As we are commenting on these
things, we may as well notice also that Mr. Munro is as
sparing of capital letters as of stops, printing for instance
' the birth-favouring breath of favonius,' 'Ritschl pref. to
trinummus,' and that in referring to notes of other editors
on other authors, he says, ' Oudendorp to Lucan x 491,'
which reads rather like a bald version of the Latin ' ad.'
We are ashamed to dwell on these things, which in
relation to so great a performance as Mr. Munro's are
mere spots in the sun ; but it appears to us that all such
peculiarities give a needlessly technical and repellant
character to the work, and we regret them accordingly.
We confess that we have ourselves not unfrequently felt
provoked by the sciolism which dogmatises about scholarship on the strength of a grammar-school knowledge of
Latin and Greek, and writes about Cicero as familiarly
as it would about Lord Derby, and have been tempted to
wish that the mystery of the craft were locked up in
algebraic symbols ; but we cannot seriously doubt that on
the whole it is fortunate for classical scholarship that it
admits of being exhibited in a form intelligible to men of
ordinary culture, and that it is worth while to make an
occasional sacrifice which is not absolutely fatal to accuracy in order to prevent the reader from being startled by
strange nomenclatures and unfamiliar appearances.

But we must leave the editor and speak of the author.
Of the translator we hope to say a few words before we
conclude our notice.

The poem of Lucretius is one of those which in modern
times at least have had many admirers, but comparatively
few readers. Of the impression which it made on its own
generation and generations near its own we know but

little.   Cicero, who, according to a tradition mentioned
by Jerome, edited it after the author's death, said something about it in a letter to his brother; but what that
something was, critics are not agreed.   Either it had
many flashes of genius, yet much art beside; or many
flashes of genius, but not much art; or not many flashes
of genius, but much art.   Lachmann takes one view of
Cicero's words, Mr. Munro another; they differ about the
meaning of the word which we have rendered genius, nor
are they agreed what is meant by art.   Ovid, borrowing
the poet's own words, says that the poem will only perish
on the day which brings the world to an end: Statius
talks of his learning, and of his lofty inspiration: but the
strongest testimony to his power is to be found in the
influence which he exercised on Virgil, who, though he
never mentions him explicitly, imitates him not only
throughout the 'Georgics,' but in not a few passages of
the ' Æneid,' and even of the ' Eclogues.'   On the whole,
however, the conclusion of one of his most enthusiastic
modern admirers, Professor Sellar of Edinburgh,[1] appears
to be that he did not count among his own countrymen
for as much as he is really worth.   Since the revival of
letters, the eulogies bestowed upon him have been numerous and emphatic.   Joseph Warton, following an ingenious analogy in use among Oriental critics, declares
that as a descriptive poet he is more than a painter—he
is a sculptor.   Byron, in a petulant and not very discriminating passage, asserts that his poem, as mere poetry,
is the first of Latin poems.   These and similar eulogies,
however, would be more valuable if they were accompanied with evidences that the eulogists had studied the
whole poem, and were not merely acquainted with the
occasional brilliant passages—perhaps seven hundred lines

[1] *Roman Poets of the Republic*, p. 313.

out of as many thousand—with which all lovers of Latin
poetry are familiar. As a matter of fact, Professor Sellar
is almost the only modern writer, not being himself an
editor of Lucretius, who, in praising the author's genius,
gives proof that he has really surmounted the difficulties
of the work in which that genius is exhibited. And
though we think that Mr. Sellar has done good service to
Latin literature in the chapters which he has devoted to
Lucretius, no less than in the rest of his book, we question
whether, even after his and Mr. Munro's labours, this great
poet is likely to become in any sense popular among
readers of Latin. There are, and always will be, two
drawbacks to his general attractiveness : first and foremost,
the nature of his poem, as an exposition of the Epicurean
system ; secondly, and in a less degree, the imperfection
of his language and rhythm, as compared with the more
finished specimens of Augustan poetry.

Didactic poetry is in fact an anachronism. Verse naturally preceded prose as a form of composition ; and so at
first everything which was thought of sufficient dignity to
be treated at all was treated in verse. When Hesiod wished
to discourse on farming operations, and lucky and unlucky
days, he naturally chose verse for his vehicle. And
though prose had been employed for philosophical writing
before the time of Xenophanes and Empedocles, it was
perhaps not unnatural that they, living when the echoes
of Orphic poetry had hardly died out, and themselves
taking an ideal and enthusiastic view of nature rather than
one based on experience and observation, should throw
their doctrines into a poetical form. But as soon as the
different types of composition came to be properly understood and discriminated, the occupation of the didactic
poet was really gone. However great his powers might
be, the result of his labours could only furnish one more

instance of genius misapplied. The Greeks seem to have felt this instinctively: their great poets did not aspire to tread in the steps of Hesiod; and it was only when the creative spirit of Greek literature had decayed, and the faculty of clever imitation was rising up in its place, that writers like Nicander and Aratus began to come to the front among their contemporaries. The literary development of Rome followed the type of Alexandria rather than that of Greek proper; and so it was natural that Roman writers should mistake where their models had mistaken.

But in their case the mistake was a most serious one. It mattered little whether the dregs of the Greek intellect were poured into new or into old bottles; but 'the first sprightly runnings' of Roman genius could not but suffer from being allowed to flow into an improper receptacle. This misdirection of power has operated in different ways to the injury of Lucretius and Virgil. The 'Nature of Things' is didactic, but much of it is scarcely poetry. The 'Georgics' are poetry, but much of them is scarcely didactic. Yet a student of philosophy, coming to Lucretius for instruction about the Epicurean system, will probably regret that the exposition is not more strictly methodical, and the language chosen in all cases with a view to philosophical significance rather than to poetical beauty or metrical convenience; while a lover of poetry will find much in the 'Georgics' which he is glad to pass over lightly as not in any true sense poetical, though he may well afford a transient feeling of admiration for that marvellous dexterity, that delicate artistic susceptibility, which even in precepts about placing stones and broken pots at the roots of vines, and directions for the construction of bee-hives, can discover an occasion for graceful expression and rhythmical felicity.

The poem of Lucretius then fails, as in our judgment

all didactic poetry must fail, because it is really an attempt
to combine incompatibilities. It was a choice between
Scylla and Charybdis; and if he had escaped the monster
he must have been drawn into the whirlpool. But we
suspect his readers would have been better pleased if he
had avoided the grim shape and allowed himself to be
carried off by the vertiginous eddy. They would have
condoned what is merely vague and uncertain, if he would
have spared them what is actually repulsive. As it is,
they are expected to face long arguments proving that
everything is either Body or Void, that the Homœomery
of Anaxagoras is a baseless theory, and that the totality
of things is infinite, and their courage fails them. We
are willing to concede to Mr. Munro that any other system of the universe would have been equally uninviting
as the subject of a poem. We have not a word to say
for the Stoics, 'with their one wretched world, their
monotonous fire, their method of destroying and creating
anew their world.' If we question the poetical success of
Lucretius, it is not in the interest of 'the leaden dulness
and tedious obscurity of the Stoic Manilius.' Perhaps
even if we had heard the discourse which the Goddess
Justice addressed to Parmenides, when the coursers of
thought brought him to the gates of day and night, or
listened to Empedocles, as he accomplished his expiation
for the murder which he had committed in the divine
fore-time, our attention might occasionally have flagged a
little. It is in a spirit of strict impartiality towards the
rival Greek systems that we venture to deny that any of
them could advantageously have been made the subject of
a didactic poem, properly so called. We do not question
that the contemplation of nature inspired Greek philosophy—the Epicurean school, if Mr. Munro wishes, in an
unusual degree—with grand and sublime conceptions,

appealing powerfully to the imagination, and as such well
calculated to be embodied in poetry. But to admit this
is very different from admitting that a thorough exposition of any philosophical system is possible in any
poetry which deserves the name. Imagination may direct
the man of science to conclusions, but the links between
them and truths already ascertained must be supplied by
reasoning. Whether these intermediate steps could possibly be represented in an imaginative form we do not
pretend to say; we only maintain that didactic poets,
as a matter of fact, do not so represent them. Certainly
Lucretius does not; he has reasoned out his argument,
and he gives friend and foe the benefit of the process. How
does he combat objections to the doctrine that atoms do
not move downwards in straight lines? We will give
his words in Mr. Munro's version, which being in prose
will show better the really prosaic character of the argument :—

But if haply anyone believes that heavier bodies, as they
are carried more quickly sheer through space, can fall from
above on the lighter, and so beget blows able to produce
begetting motions, he goes most widely astray from true
reason. For whenever bodies fall through water and thin air,
they must quicken their descents in proportion to their weights,
because the body of water and subtle nature of air cannot
retard everything in equal degree, but more readily give way,
overpowered by the heavier: on the other hand, empty void
cannot offer resistance to anything in any direction at any
time, but must, as its nature craves, continually give way; and
for this reason all things must be moved and borne along with
equal velocity though of equal weights through the unresisting
void.

It is true that this severity of reasoning is not unfrequently relieved by illustrations longer or shorter, and
that these illustrations, regarded separately, may give

R 2

pleasure to the reader who reads for pleasure. In the next page the same doctrine, that there must be deviations from the straight line of motion, is enforced by an illustration from horses, which, when the barrier of the racecourse is thrown open, cannot start forth as instantaneously as they wish: a page or two further on another part of the general argument gives occasion to the well-known descriptions of sheep seen at a distance and looking like a white spot on a hill, though really in motion, and of armies in the act of executing movements, yet appearing from a particular point of view to be at rest. Even in the original of the passage which we have just extracted, there are one or two slight things which may remind the reader that he is reading poetry. There is a rhythmical effect in the line, 'sed citius cedunt gravioribus exsuperata,' in the alliteration in the former part, and in the polysyllabic weight of the latter, which seconds the thought intended to be conveyed; while the expression 'inane quietum' affects the imagination more than Mr. Munro's 'unresisting void'—the one indicating rather the nature of the void in itself, the other, its relation to the bodies which move through it. Yet we are much mistaken if these occasional flashes of imagination, though quite sufficient to prove the writer to be a poet, will be sufficient to make his argument attractive to any reader who is not already interested in the argument for its own sake. No doubt to Lucretius himself the interest of his subject was one and indivisible. It kindled his whole nature, imagination, heart, intellect, alike. He enters as keenly into the task of proving that the mind 'must consist of bodies exceedingly small, smooth, and round,' as into that of singing the triumphant progress of his master through the universe; because he knows that if he were to fail in demonstrating the former, the latter would be

mere windy declamation. But though this does much
to make the poet the interesting figure that he is, it does
not make his poem readable. Even if it were true that
Epicureanism made him a poet, it would still be true that
Epicureanism prevented him from turning his poetical
faculty to account. It was Apollo who gave Cassandra
the power of prophecy; but it was Apollo who provided
that no one should pay attention to what she said.

But the unattractiveness of Lucretius' poem is not due
solely to its inexorably didactic character. Even if he had
sacrificed the claims of scientific exposition to those of
poetical embellishment, with as little compunction as
Virgil has done, he would still be less popular than Virgil,
because he has not Virgil's style. Of late years, indeed,
there has been a tendency among certain critics to deny
that Virgil has any poetical advantage over Lucretius—
any literary superiority which is not countervailed by
literary superiority of another kind. We suspect ourselves
that this creed is chiefly confined to those who study the
poem of Lucretius in extracts. They dwell on isolated
passages, call attention to the boldness of the imagery and
the solemn march of the versification, and ask whether
there is not something there beyond what the art of
Virgil can produce. But the question between the 'Nature
of Things' and the 'Georgics' is a question not about isolated
passages, but about the entire contexture of the two poems.
We are not speaking of the proportion of purely didactic
(and therefore, as we have been contending, unpoetical)
matter in each; that we have already considered. We
speak of the language and the metre in which Lucretius
and Virgil respectively clothe what they have to say,
whether didactic or otherwise. Comparing them from
this point of view, we find the elder bard apt to be prolix
and incondite in diction and monotonous in versification,

where the language of the younger is terse and elegant,
and his rhythm varied and effective. This is merely
tantamount to saying that Lucretius wrote before the
style and cadence of Latin poetry had been cultivated to
perfection. Mr. Munro is too good a composer himself to
contend that his author is to be compared to Virgil in
power of handling the hexameter. ' It must not be questioned,' he says candidly, ' that in the construction of
single verses, and still more in the rhythmical movement
which he impresses on a whole passage, Lucretius is a far
less careful and skilled artist than Virgil.' Yet he does
not admit as explicitly as we could wish that the Augustan
school of poetry was an advance on that which preceded
it. After conceding that the Augustan writers ' obtained
the unanimous suffrages of the best critics of the empire,
at the head of whom stood Quintilian,' he goes on to
remark that ' the reaction in favour of the older literature seems to have been headed by unskilful and too
zealous leaders, and thus to have exposed itself to
the shafts of satire :' thus implying, if we understand
him correctly, that more judicious generalship might
have changed the fortune of the day. To us, we confess,
it appears that the difference between Lucretius and
Catullus on the one hand, and Virgil and Horace on the
other, is a difference not so much between individuals as
between two periods of the poetical development of the
national mind—between immaturity and maturity. It is
true that the maturity lasted but a very short time—that
it soon became over-ripeness. But the shortness of its
duration does not make it less a real fact, or abate its
superiority to the earlier and imperfect stage. That
superiority is shown in nothing more than in uniformity
and equality of workmanship. By uniformity we do not
mean monotonous sameness, but sustained excellence. It

is this that writers of an immature period, like Lucretius, especially lack. As Miss Edgeworth says of the hospitable preparations at an Irish mansion, everything there is sumptuous and unfinished. You have a marble chimney-piece fixed to a bare wall. One of Lucretius' most justly admired lines is that which characterises the two great autumnal winds, 'Altitonans Volturnus et Auster fulmine pollens.' How many of those who quote it remember the line which immediately precedes it, ' Inde aliæ tempestates ventique sequuntur '? If the one has a grandeur hardly to be found in Virgil, the other has a triviality which would suit Lilly or Dean Aldrich. And it is needless to say that the number of lines of the latter stamp very greatly exceeds the number of lines of the former. To a certain extent this may be imputed to the unfinished state of the poem; but not, we think, wholly. The imperfection we complain of is discernible in Catullus' 'Peleus and Thetis,' though in that case there is nothing in the nature of the subject to force it into such glaring prominence. In Lucretius and Catullus alike we see that kind of garrulity which is delightful in Homer, but in almost every other poet is more or less tedious and ungraceful—the utterance of a child impeding the thoughts of the growing or grown man. Lachmann may call it ' lactea ubertas ; ' but to our taste it savours too much of the bread and milk of the nursery. The child has realised the fact that the fields are green and the sand yellow, that the sea can carry ships, and that cattle part the hoof, and it is anxious to proclaim its discovery to all the world. We are interested in observing the development of its intelligence, but after a certain time we are tempted to bid it hush, and reserve our attention for communications more absolutely novel.

If, however, we may regard Lucretius not as a finished

artist, but as the writer of a period when poetical art was
immature, we are quite ready and desirous to do justice
to his extraordinary powers. Whether any altogether
definite notion of the poet can be formed from his poem
we are not sure. Those who have attempted such a
realising process have obtained somewhat different results.
Mr. De Quincey embraces eagerly the story that the
'Nature of Things' was written in the intervals of delirium, or, as he prefers to put it, in a delirious state ; he
is sure that he could have guessed as much from the poem,
which is all excitement and no lull, at the same time that
he admires the poet as the first of demoniacs. Professor
Sellar will not allow that even lucid intervals could have
produced the poem, and pronounces the poet to be not
only more characteristically Roman than any Latin writer
except Tacitus, but to be equalled in depth of human
sympathy and pathos by Homer alone among the ancients,
while in other respects he reminds his critic of Spinoza,
Pascal, and Milton. But, at any rate, we may carry
away impressions which, whether capable or not of being
combined into an intelligible whole, regarded singly are
full of depth, beauty, and truth. That fear of death for
which men, till the truth has made them free, are 'all their
lifetime subject to bondage,' has never been represented
with more terrible reality than in the lines near the beginning of the Third Book of the poem :—

> Et metus ille foras præceps Acheruntis agendus,
> Funditus humanam qui vitam turbat ab imo,
> Omnia suffundens mortis nigrore, neque ullam
> Esse voluptatem liquidam puramque relinquit.

What can be more striking in expression and in solemn
cadence than his picture of the degradation entailed by
violent and irregular passion ?—

Adde quod absumunt vires pereuntque labore ;
Adde quod alterius sub nutu degitur ætas ;
Labitur interea res et Babylonica fiunt,
Languent officia atque ægrotat fama vacillans.

Professor Sellar speaks justly of the power with which the
religious effect of the procession of the 'Great Goddess'
Cybele is impressed on the imagination :—

Ergo cum primum magnas invecta per urbes
Munificat tacita mortales muta salute.

The powerlessness of the healing art in the presence of
a mysterious pestilence is painted to the life in four
words :—

Mussabat tacito medicina timore.

We seem to see science, as impersonated by the physician,
generally so fertile in suggestion and so fluent in explanation, now reduced to inarticulate muttering. Such lines
as these are like the tolling of a bell ; continued for
a long time they would be oppressive and fatiguing ;
listened to at intervals, for a few minutes together, they
affect us powerfully. But there are not wanting longer
passages which can be perused with pleasure, the diffuseness of expression and the stately uniformity of cadence
answering to feelings which the author suggests and the
reader is glad to indulge. Such is the famous picture of
the fiend Superstition brooding over mankind, and the not
less famous Æschylean study that follows, the sacrifice of
Iphigenia. Such is the narration of the gradual origin of
society which occupies the latter half of the Fifth Book—
a long reach of disquisition, which, if occasionally dry and
barren, is generally rich and luxuriant. Such, above all
(for we need not run through the enumeration of beauties

which may be found in books of Latin extracts),[1] are the
two magnificent passages which respectively conclude the
Second and Third Books—the one treating of the decay
of the world, the other containing an expostulation with
man on the subject of the fear of death. The first,
though comparatively simple and unadorned, has a deep
and impressive melancholy to which we should find it
difficult to name a parallel. The second is much longer
and considerably more varied. There is elaborate reasoning, there is indignant remonstrance, addressed by Nature
herself to her recusant child, there is a muster-roll of all
the illustrious men who have submitted to death, there is
a bitterly sarcastic contrast of their greatness with the
contemptible littleness of the ordinary mortal who quarrels
with his doom. The effect of the whole recalls to us
those grand words in which Tacitus sums up the characteristics of a day of mourning, ' modo per silentium
vastus, modo ploratibus inquies,' an alternation of dreary
desolation with passionate sorrow.

As might be expected, Lucretius has not found many
translators. Single books or detached passages have been
occasionally attempted; but the only one of these fugitive
writers who need be mentioned is Dryden, who has left
us some specimens of harmonious reasoning, and coarse
though vigorous description. Of complete translations of
the poem there have been six, including that now before
us, three in verse and three in prose. Creech's (1682), in
heroic couplets, had a great reputation in its day, and is
not without merit; but though there is some masculine

¹ One such book, which we may recommend in passing to our readers,
has lately been published by Mr. St. John Thackeray, of Eton, under the
title of *Anthologia Latina*. It contains selections from Latin Poets, ranging
from Nævius to Claudian, and a few illustrative notes in Latin. The
passages are well chosen, and the appearance of the book is exceedingly
pretty, reminding us of such works as Mr. Palgrave's *Golden Treasury*.

writing in it, there is little grace or beauty, and a good
deal of triviality and vulgarity. Good's (1805–7) is an
attempt to make Lucretius speak in the blank verse of
Thomson and Akenside, the result being not a little feeble
verbiage and commonplace rhetoric, though the version, as
a whole, may be called tolerable. Busby's 'Didascalic
Poem' (1813), as he chose to call it, which might be
similarly characterised as an attempt to make Lucretius
talk like Dr. Darwin, was made the subject of some not
undeserved ridicule by our southern contemporary,[1] and is
still preserved in memory by the 'Architectural Atoms'
of the 'Rejected Addresses.' The prose versions are by
an anonymous author in the middle of the last century,
by Mr. Watson in Bohn's Classical Library, and by Mr.
Munro. The first we have seen, but have not within
call, and do not care to disinter; the second is a respectable specimen of its class, and might satisfy the ordinary
reader if there were none better. The excellence of
Mr. Munro's is the same as that which we have mentioned
as the excellence of his commentary—its great carefulness
and exactness. Perhaps it may occasionally disappoint
those who, knowing Lucretius only in select passages, take
up the translation in order to see how some favourite
poetical effect in the original is reproduced in English.
Mr. Munro has seen rightly that a translator of Lucretius
is the last who ought to sacrifice the whole to the parts;
that the poem ought really to be translated in the same
spirit as if it were a formal philosophical treatise, a particular nomenclature being preserved throughout, and
words which would suit the requirements of this or that
passage being unsparingly rejected if on consideration
they should appear unsuited for doing duty elsewhere.

[1] *Quarterly Review*, vol. xi. pp. 88–103.

He has laboured not for the many but for the few ; and the few, we feel assured, will thank him.   Meanwhile, we will venture to compare him and his brother translators in a single short passage, taken from that splendid peroration of the Third Book, to which we adverted a page or two back, rather for the sake of our readers, who may desire a little criticism in detail after so much general disquisition, than for the sake of the new translator, whose work, as we have just intimated, would be judged unfairly if judged in this way.   We select this particular passage, not merely for its force and impressiveness, but because it enables us to give a specimen of Dryden's version.   We may say, in passing, that we will not trouble our readers with Dr. Busby, who, though not, as in other passages, outrageously absurd, is feeble and ungrammatical :—

(Book iii. vv. 1045 *et seq.*)
Tu vero dubitabis et indignabere obire ?
Mortua cui vita est propo jam vivo atque videnti,
Qui somno partem majorem conteris ævi,
Et vigilans stertis nec somnia cernere cessas,
Sollicitamque geris cassa formidine mentem,
Nec reperire potis quid sit tibi sæpe mali, cum
Ebrius urgeris multis miser undique curis,
Atque animi incerto fluitans errore vagaris.

CREECH.

Then how darest thou repine to die, and grieve,
Thou meaner soul, thou dead e'en whilst alive,
That sleep'st and dream'st the most of life away ?
Thy night is full as rational as thy day :
Still vexed with cares, who never understood
The principles of ill nor use of good,
Nor whence thy cares proceed, but reel'st about
In vain unsettled thoughts, condemned to doubt.

DRYDEN.

And thou, dost thou disdain to yield thy breath,
Whose very life is little more than death?
More than one half by lazy sleep possest,
And when awake, thy soul but nods at best,
Day dreams and sickly thoughts revolving in thy breast.
Eternal troubles haunt thy anxious mind,
Whose cause and cure thou never hopest to find,
But still uncertain, with thyself at strife,
Thou wanderest in the labyrinth of life.

GOOD.

And dost thou murmur, and indignant die,
Whose life, while living, scarcely death exceeds?
Thou, who in sleep devourest half thy days,
And, e'en awake, who snorest, dreaming still,
And torturing all thy mind with vain alarms?
Thou, who lamentest oft, unknowing why,
Urged on, with fear intoxicated deep,
And in a maze of mental errors lost?

WATSON.

Wilt thou then hesitate and grudge to die, in whom, even while living and seeing, life is almost dead? thou, who wastest the greater part of existence in sleep, and snorest waking, nor ceasest to see dreams, and bearest a mind disturbed with empty terror; nor canst thou frequently discover what evil affects thee, when, stupified and wretched, thou art oppressed with numerous cares on all sides, and, fluctuating with uncertain thought, wanderest in error?

MUNRO.

Wilt thou then hesitate and think it a hardship to die? thou for whom life is well nigh dead while yet thou livest and seest the light, who wastest the greater part of thy time in sleep, and snorest wide awake, and ceasest not to see visions, and hast a mind troubled with groundless terror, and canst not discover often what it is that ails thee, when, besotted man, thou art sore pressed on all sides with a multitude of cares, and goest astray tumbling in a maze of mental error.

Our readers will see that Creech is not to be despised : he is not quite grammatical, but he is vigorous, and it is no fault of his that he has been eclipsed by Dryden. That great man is, as usual, easy and masterly. Of the last two lines of his original we think he might have made more than he has done. The metaphor, as we understand it, is not from a man wandering in a labyrinth, but from a ship without a pilot, which reels and staggers through the water, pressed and tossed by billows on all sides. Virgil, at any rate, that diligent student of the language of Lucretius, has borrowed the word 'fluitare' for the motion of Æneas' ship when deprived of her helmsman. Good is nearly valueless. Blank verse ought to be almost as close as prose, and he is far from close, while what he substitutes is no compensation for what he takes away. 'Indignant die' is not the same thing as 'indignabere obire.' 'Scarcely death exceeds' is a wretched dilution of 'mortua est prope.' 'Dreaming still and torturing all thy mind' represents as the same state two phrases of unsoundness which had better have been kept distinct. In the next line lamenting is substituted for being ill at ease. 'Urged on' is not 'urgeris ; ' and neither 'multis' nor 'undique' is given. Mr. Watson is very tolerable, though less good than Mr. Munro. 'Wastest,' by which both of them render 'conteris,' would have been a better equivalent for a less strong word, like 'teris.' We should prefer 'wearest away,' not as in itself more graphic than 'wastest,' but as less hackneyed, and so preserving its original outline more clearly. 'Geris,' which Mr. Watson renders 'bearest,' Mr. Munro extenuates into 'hast.' Perhaps he is right, as Lucretius constantly uses 'gerere' when he means no more than 'habere.' If we had only this passage to think of, we should be inclined to suggest 'bearest about with thee.' 'Stupefied and wretched' couples two words which Lucretius has not coupled. There is force in the order of the Latin: 'ebrius,' standing at the head of the line, gives the tone to the whole; 'miser' is little more than a qualifying adverb. For the rest, 'stupefied' seems to us rather better than 'besotted,' which has come to be appropriated to extreme folly, with scarcely a notion of bewilderment or unsteadiness. 'Staggering as from drink,' or 'drunken as with wine' would, we think, give the figure better. In the last line, whether we read 'animi' or 'animo,' we do not like Mr. Munro's 'mental error,' which turns into conventional prose what in Lucretius is graphic and poetical.

We must conclude. We doubt, as we have already intimated, whether even Mr. Munro's labours will make Lucretius popular, in that limited sense in which any Latin classic can be made popular. But we have no sort of doubt that his book will tell powerfully on English scholarship, and that English students of Latin literature will gladly resort to him for much which could not have been obtained from any English source, and something perhaps which even Germany might have failed to supply.

*THE STYLE OF LUCRETIUS AND CATULLUS AS
COMPARED WITH THAT OF THE AUGUSTAN
POETS.[1]*

Two years ago I wrote a review of the edition of
Lucretius recently published by my friend Mr. Munro.[2]
In the course of my criticism I ventured to protest
against an opinion, of which I thought I saw some traces
in one of the editor's Introductions, that the poets of
the last age of the Roman Commonwealth could fairly
be compared in point of art with their successors of
the Augustan period. His masterly work has since
reached a second edition : and in it he has done me the
honour to make an answer to my remarks. It appears
that there is a real question at issue between us ; and I
am glad to have had it put into a tangible shape for
discussion, and have been led to reconsider my reasons
for adopting a view which I still believe to be the true
one.

Perhaps it will be best for me to commence what I
have to say by quoting Mr. Munro's answer nearly *in
extenso.*

After observing that I find not only the rhythm, but
the style and language of his author to be immature,
prolix, incondite, he goes on :[3] 'That Lucretius is surpassed by Virgil in the rhythm and technical excellence
of his verse it would be foolish to deny ; but to me his
language appears inferior in no sense in which Cicero or

---

[1] This lecture, which was delivered at Oxford, March 0, 1807, is reprinted,
together with the Appendix, from the edition published in that year.
[2] See preceding Article.   [3] Vol. I. pp. 316, 317.

Cæsar may not be said to be inferior to Livy or Seneca. And in this belief I am glad to be confirmed by the Lambins and Scaligers of the sixteenth, the Goethes and Lachmanns of the nineteenth century. For Lucretius' sake I am not sorry to find Catullus put by his side and declared to be as much below Horace as Lucretius is below Virgil. Though Catullus' heroic poem was, I believe, one of his latest, I do not look on it or his elegiacs as the happiest specimens of his genius; but his lyrics, to my taste, are perfect gems, unequalled in Latin, unsurpassed in Greek poetry. Horace, when he wrote his epodes and earlier odes, was probably older than Catullus was when he died. Yet in the metres common to them both, in the iambic for instance and the glyconic, who will say that the former, with all his labour and care, has obtained the same mastery over them which Catullus displays, who would seem to have thrown them off at once without effort according as the *odi* or the *amo* constrained him at the moment to write? His language is as undefiled a well of Latin as that of Plautus, and is withal the very quintessence of poetry. To return to Lucretius, the reviewer finds about seven hundred brilliant lines in the whole poem: I find at least that number in the fifth book alone; and in these verses the highest efforts of his genius are to be sought for, not in the second or third book, impressive though they may be.' Mr. Munro then controverts an opinion which I am not at present concerned to vindicate, paralleling the work of Lucretius with the didactic compositions of the Alexandrian school, and ends by saying that even in those portions of the poem which at first may be somewhat dry and repelling, he, for one, discovers neither prolixity nor childishness, but rather, with Lachmann, a terse and manly simplicity.

What I have to prove, then, against my friendly antagonist is briefly this: that Lucretius is inferior to Virgil
not only in the technical structure of his versification, but
in style, and generally in poetical art; and similarly that
Catullus, as a complete and finished poet, is inferior to
Horace.   I say nothing about the native genius of each
writer: I only speak of the actual results attained by
each, my point being to characterise them, not as individuals, but rather as representatives of a period.   This
was the proposition laid down in the article of which I
have spoken; and this it is which I understand my friend
to traverse.

I do not feel sure at the outset what use I ought to
make of the admission that Virgil is superior to his predecessor in the management of the hexameter.   The
more I think of it, the less clear I feel how much such a
concession involves.   It is very hard, in analysing a poet,
to say what portion of the effect produced by his verses
is owing to the rhythm and what to the language.   The
two, in fact, are parts of one living organisation, acting
and reacting on each other.   It is possible, no doubt, to
think of words which, as words, would give pleasure to
readers of poetry, but which, either from their collocation
or perhaps in themselves, offend against our sense of
rhythm; but in practice we generally find that those
writers who are admired most for their choice of words
are admired also in the same proportion for the rhythmical
use which they make of their words.   So it is possible to
break up the order of the words in a passage from a
poem, and re-arrange them so that they shall make no
metre at all; but it does not follow from this that they
could be recombined into a different metrical form, so
that, while the versification should give us an increase or
a diminution of pleasure, the language should affect us in

the same way as before.   No amount of mere metrical manipulation, though the artist were Virgil himself, could transform a paragraph of Lucretius into a paragraph of Virgil.   Lucretius' solemn and uniform cadences suit the structure of his sentences: to set his language to another tune, you must recompose it and make it another language.   The structure of the sentence, again, and the choice of words naturally go hand in hand, and both are comprehended under the one term 'style.'   Now it is in this matter of style that, as I have said, I claim the superiority for Virgil; and as it seems to me to be inseparably connected with his acknowledged metrical success, I find it hard to discuss the one without taking advantage of the admission made about the other.   As, however, Mr. Munro, I presume, either does not recognise the connection, or, recognising it, thinks it possible that the same causes which operate favourably on style may operate less favourably on metre, or *vice versâ*, I must endeavour to isolate the question of style, and discuss the merits of Lucretius with reference to that, and that only.

I think it not impossible that a partial key to the difference between Mr. Munro's view and mine is to be found in the first sentence which I have quoted from him.   He there says that to him the language of Lucretius appears inferior to that of Virgil in no sense in which Cicero or Cæsar may not be said to be inferior to Livy or Seneca.   Holding the views which I do about the various stages of progress and decay in prose and poetical composition at Rome, I am a little surprised at the indiscriminate way in which, as it appears to me, these names are put together.   Two parallels are I suppose intended, the one of the two historians, the other of the two philosophical writers; but surely the width of the interval is an important element in the case, and the interval

between Cicero and Seneca, as writers of prose, is far
wider than that between Cæsar and Livy. Let that pass,
however; it may have been hastily said; it may have
been deliberately intended as a forcible way of expressing
the writer's conviction that the real decline of Roman
style is to be dated, not from the post-Augustan, but from
the Augustan era; that the so-called golden age was in
fact only silver-gilt. But what I wish to call attention to
is the intimation which the words seem to contain, that
poets and prose writers are to be judged by the same
standard. Lucretius is placed on a footing with Cicero;
and it is argued in effect that because the general consent
of sound criticism prefers the style of the latter to that
of the prose writers who have followed him, it must be
an unhealthy fastidiousness which would not accord to
the former in his own department a similar preference.
Here it is precisely that I am anxious to join issue. I
am disposed to think that a large portion of Lucretius'
poem, if stripped of metre, might pass muster among the
writings of Cicero. In other words, I believe it could
easily be reduced into clear, vigorous, rhetorical prose,
of a somewhat redundant and ornate character. It is
sound, pure, idiomatic Latin; but I venture to doubt
whether, except occasionally, it is poetry. That is the
point at issue: I do not dispute the goodness of the
language; what I say is, that it is good enough for a
prose writer, not good enough for a great poet. As I
have remarked elsewhere, I know no better distinction
between prose and poetry than that laid down by Coleridge as reported in his 'Table Talk,' though at first
sight it is apt to appear meagre and unsatisfying
enough. 'Prose is words in their right places; poetry,
the best words in their right places.' I will not enlarge
on this here; an excellent comment on it, by Coleridge
himself, may be found in the early chapters of the second

volume of his 'Biographia,' where he combats Wordsworth's celebrated thesis, that the language of poetry is
essentially the same with that of prose.   What I feel in
reading Lucretius then, is that his language in general
does not rise beyond a prose level ; he has striking
poetical images, more striking, it may be, considered
separately, than most of those which are to be found in
Virgil, but they are in a prose setting ; his enthusiasm,
always austere and genuine, is at times lofty and imaginative, but its effect is apt to be deadened by the
multitude of words in which it is conveyed.   This
redundance is not necessarily a vice in prose, where the
language is less choice, and every word is not expected
to stick in the memory.   But in verse it is the water
which dilutes the wine—the ivy which strangles the
tree round which it clings—the earth which makes the
lump of ore larger, but which must be removed by the
furnace before the pure metal can be obtained.

   And now let me justify what I have said by analysing
a passage or two from the 'De Rerum Natura' itself.   It
is the Fifth Book which Mr. Munro chooses to make the
battle-field ; and to the Fifth Book accordingly my extracts shall be confined.

   I take the opening lines.   They are, I think, a fair
specimen of Lucretius' manner, and they are to be found
in at least one of the works which profess to collect the
choicer passages of Roman poetry :—

> Quis potis est dignum pollenti pectore carmen
> Condere, pro rerum maiestate hisque repertis ?
> Quisve valet verbis tantum, qui fingere laudes
> Pro meritis eius possit, qui talia nobis
> Pectore parta suo quaesitaque praemia liquit ?
> Nemo, ut opinor, erit mortali corpore cretus.
> Nam si, ut ipsa petit maiestas cognita rerum,
> Dicendum est, Deus ille fuit, Deus, inclyte Memmi,
> Qui princeps vitae rationem invenit eam, quae

Nunc appellatur sapientia ; quique per artem
Fluctibus e tantis vitam tantisque tenebris
In tam tranquillo et tam clara luce locavit.

The chief thing, I think, which strikes us in considering these lines is their argumentative character. 'Who
can praise Epicurus worthily ? no mortal, for Epicurus
himself was more than a mortal, as the benefits he conferred on humanity show.' I cannot help thinking that
this savours rather of poetical rhetoric than of poetry ;
it is reasoning for reasoning's sake, where the forms of
reasoning at any rate were not called for. Virgil would
have conveyed the thought that the godlike sage needed
a god to praise him in a very different way. I do not
say that this argues an inferiority in poetical temperament,
but I say that it argues an inferiority in art. It is the
dialectician intruding into the poet's province, just as in
Plautus, and in the fragments of the early writers, the
grammarian is sometimes mixed up with the dramatist
or the satirist ; and it appears to me to be symptomatic
of a time when poetry is still immature. Examining the
lines in detail, I continue to find the same features.
There is a sameness in the repetition of 'pectore,' of
'rerum maiestate ' and ' maiestas rerum,' of ' pro maiestate '
and ' pro meritis.' The two first lines are repeated in
the three that follow, yet little seems to be gained by
thus presenting the thought in a twofold form. 'Mor-
tali corpore cretus ' is a piece of Lucretian commonplace, a formula which occurs from time to time in the
poem, just like the epic commonplaces which abound in
Homer, and do not displease us in him, because they
are felt to be characteristic of an early poet. And
what can be said of ' rationem vitae eam quae nunc
appellatur sapientia,' but that it is prose pure and simple,
where the words must wonder how, being as they are,

they ever got into metrical order?   On the other side,
all that can be alleged as marks of high poetical art are
the rapturous burst 'Deus ille fuit, Deus,' a pearl which
Virgil has judiciously transferred to his own treasury,
and the two last lines, though even there one may
question whether the language might not have been
refined a little more.   Some may wish to add the words
'carmen condere;' but Mr. Munro himself has shown
that the expression was an ordinary one at the time
when Lucretius wrote, common in prose as well as verse,
so that it is not to be compared to πυργώσας ρήματα
σεμνά, or 'build the lofty rhyme.'

I go on to the next paragraph :—

> Confer enim divina aliorum antiqua reperta ;
> Namque Ceres fertur fruges, Liberque liquoris
> Vitigeni laticem mortalibus instituisse :
> Cum tamen his posset sine rebus vita manere,
> Ut fama est aliquas etiam nunc vivere gentes
> At bene non poterat sine puro pectore vivi :
> Quo magis hic merito nobis Deus esse videtur,·
> Ex quo nunc etiam per magnas didita gentes
> Dulcia permulcent animos solatia vitae.

Here the spirit of prosaic reasoning is still more pronounced, and the traces of poetic colouring fainter.
Except for the expression 'liquoris vitigeni laticem,' the
passage might almost be transferred bodily into the
apology for Epicureanism in the 'De Natura Deorum.'
There is a flash of poetical feeling in the 'At bene non
poterat sine puro pectore vivi,' less, however, in the expression than in the thought; but the next line, with its
'Quo magis,' recalls us back to prose.   In the last two
lines, again, poetical feeling is struggling to find itself
words, but it scarcely attains to anything which a prose
style would reject as inappropriate.

The rest of the exordium is too long to quote; but if it were carefully analysed, I do not think it would be found seriously to interfere with the impression which the previous lines are calculated to make. The various labours of Hercules are indeed characterised in poetical language, but there is too great sameness in the manner of the enumeration; it should have been either shorter or more varied. Virgil has twice dealt with the same subject; in the one case, he condenses the more prominent exploits of the great demigod into three pregnant lines; in the other, his enumeration is as copious as that of Lucretius, but he varies the mode of expression with an art which has made that particular passage celebrated among critics as a masterpiece of poetical effect. So there is great dignity of thought, and some beauty of language, in the lines where Lucretius asks what must be the effect on human nature where the wilderness of the breast is left uncleansed. But the pervading fault of the whole passage is the vein of argumentation that runs through it. The form of the argument is prosaic; the grounds on which it is rested are puerile. Hercules is not so great a benefactor to the world as Epicurus, because a riddance from savage beasts is less important than a riddance from savage passions. So far so good; the thought is a striking one, the argumentative form is all that can be objected to. But why are the beasts the less evil of the two? Because the monsters which Hercules slew lived chiefly in out-of-the-way places, just as the noxious creatures with which the world still swarms are mostly confined to mountains, forests, and jungles, which people need not visit unless they like. Had there been no Hercules, mankind might have congregated in the less savage parts of the globe, and left the beasts to their own quarters. If this be not characteristic of an

immature period of poetical conception, I really do not
know what is.

To compare this with one of Virgil's greatest efforts,
the ' me vero primum,' for example, would obviously be
cruel, and, indeed, unfair.   But I will take a very short
passage from another part of the Second Georgic, and
try to exemplify by its help the points in which, as I
conceive it, the superiority of Virgil consists :—

> Nec minus interea fetu nemus omne gravescit,
> Sanguineisque inculta rubent aviaria baccis.
> Tondentur cytisi, taedas silva alta ministrat,
> Pascunturque ignes nocturni et lumina fundunt :
> Et dubitant homines serere atque impendere curam ?

Virgil has been occupying himself during the greater part
of the book with laying down rules for the rearing of
fruit-trees, especially the vine ; he now reminds the husbandman that there are other trees which in their degree
will repay cultivation.   How Lucretius would have done
this, the specimen we have had of his manner will enable
us easily to conjecture; but how does Virgil do it?   The
first line is little more than a brief statement of the fact
that other trees yield valuable produce as well as fruit-
trees proper; there is, however, a touch of imagination
in ' interea,' and in ' gravescit ;' while the precepts about
planting and dressing vines have been going on, all this
time the forest has been gradually bursting into fruitful
life, unheeded.   The next line, while professing to continue the general statement, which would have been
prosaic, really gives a typical example, that of the elder
or the arbute, with their crimson fruit.   We know how
Lucretius speaks of arbutes :—

> quae nunc hiberno tempore cernis
> Arbuta puniceo fieri matura colore :

where the fruit itself is characterised in picturesque language, but the way in which the mention of it is introduced is prosaic and matter of fact. But this is not all;
by the use of the word 'aviaria,' Virgil calls up another
thought, of an imaginative kind. There is nothing in
the context to lead us to think of the birds, but the
moment they are suggested, new lights seem to play
round us; we see that their presence is in keeping with
a state of nature and an absence of culture, while we
know that they will build and sing even in cultivated
trees, so that the reader is prepared beforehand to acquiesce in the injunction to cultivate when at last it
comes. And all this is done by a single word. Lucretius, writing in a different connection, talks of 'fron-
diferas domos avium;' had Virgil used so many words,
he would have destroyed the symmetry of the passage,
and made the hint less dexterous in making it broader.
Then come two lines on which I need not dwell, save to
point out the art with which the lowly lucerne, browsed
on by goats, is contrasted with the lofty pine forest, that
contrast being indicated by the one word 'alta,' while,
instead of a formal balance between 'cytisi' and 'pinus,'
'taedas,' the pinewood product, is put first in the clause,
so that the trees producing the torches can be spoken of
more generally, and, from a poetical point of view, more
impressively as 'silva alta.' After these typical instances,
the practical conclusion is introduced; but how is it introduced? With a 'quo circa' or 'quo magis,' or even
an 'ergo' or 'igitur?' No; these are good words in
their way, good enough even for Virgil elsewhere, but
not good enough for him here. He does not reason
with the husbandmen; he lifts up his hands wonderingly
at their supineness. 'Et dubitant homines serere atque
impendere curam?' In the face of all this, while the

vast capabilities of nature are hourly displayed before
them, men are still hanging back, doubting whether to
plant and bestow their pains. This, I contend, is high
art ; it is language really worthy of poetry. I see that
Ribbeck, in his recently published ' Prolegomena Critica,'
condemns this line ; it is not found in the text of the
Medicean, nor is it commented on by Servius, and
Ribbeck himself fancies that it is inconsistent with what
follows ; so he assigns it to an interpolator, and speaks of
the two other great MSS., the Palatine and Roman, as
' contaminated ' by it—' inquinati.' Contamination and
interpolation ! it would be well for the world and for
poetry if such contaminators and such interpolators were
more generally at work. Heyne thought very differently
of the merit of the line : ' Versus per se est praeclarus,'
and Heyne, though Virgilian criticism has advanced in
many respects beyond the point at which he left it
(in a hundred years it would be a shame if it had
not), was at any rate a man of judgment and poetical
feeling.

I will not quote the rest of the paragraph, though I
might do so with advantage. It would be easy to show
that what Ribbeck supposes to be an inconsistency is
really an additional proof of the art of the poet, who
substitutes a picture for an argument, and darts on from
point to point, varying the mode of expression, yet constantly enforcing the same conclusion, while critics and
logical reasoners have to follow him as they may.

> Et invat undantem buxo spectare Cytorum
> Naryciaeque picis lucos : iuvat arva videre
> Non rastris, hominum non ulli obnoxia curae.

This is not intended as a simple commendation of natural
products which spring up without the help of culture :

describing the moving train of the various seasons of
the year ; such are several portions of the long description of the origin and progress of human society, especially that grand outburst of feeling which tells us that
piety consists not in bowing the covered head to a stone,
and sprinkling the ground with the blood of four-footed
beasts, but in the power to contemplate all nature with
an untroubled soul. But these do not really touch the
question at issue. I have never denied, nobody has ever
denied, that the waste of didactic disquisition which
extends through the poem is relieved by many cases of
this sort, and that the Fifth Book can boast of an unusual
number of such resting-places for the mind ; my original
remarks expressly excepted them, and it is not of them
that I am now called to speak. Even of them I should
be inclined to say, that with all their greatness they show
obvious signs of an immature development of art : the
grandeur is too long drawn out, too uniformly solemn,
the grace and graphic beauty have an air of negligence
and rusticity : there is gold, but it is gold still encum-
bered with dross, not gold purified and refined. But it
is not of these that I have to speak. I am challenged
by the assertion that the language of the staple of Lucretius' poem is equal to that of any of Virgil's, that, of
the 1457 lines of which the Fifth Book consists, at least
700, nearly every other line, in fact, may be called brilliant ; and I have endeavoured to meet the challenge by
taking the first twenty lines of the book, a specimen, as
I conceive, certainly above the average, and showing, if
I mistake not, that scarcely one of these comes up to the
standard which the highest poetical art would require.
Say, if you please, that there is something in these lines
better than the perfection of art—that there is a charming simplicity, an engaging frankness, a pleasing, un-

studied freedom, a fresh, genuine unconventionality, and
what not. I do not question that. I do not question
either that to some moods of the mind such qualities
may appeal more forcibly than those which go along
with exquisite literary finish, just as to talk to children
may to some temperaments be pleasanter than to converse
with grown men: all I contend for is that the poetical
art which expresses itself in this way is not ripe but
unripe, not adult but adolescent. Manly, in one sense,
I may concede to my friend that it is: it is to a great
extent the language of ordinary life, which cares more
about general intelligibility than about absolute beauty:
but it is not manly in relation to that species of composition to which it professes to appertain: it is the manhood of prose, not the manhood of poetry.

In passing on to speak of Catullus and Horace, I confess
I feel less confident that I shall be able to substantiate
any case to the satisfaction of everyone. The considerations which it involves are subtler; they are less clear
to my own mind; I cannot hope to make them clear to
others by the simple application of two or three broad
strokes of the pencil. In the few remarks which I
hazarded about Catullus in the article over whose *corpus
vile* we are now contending, I certainly was thinking
of his hexameters and elegiacs rather than of his lyrics.
His hexameters and elegiacs, however, Mr. Munro virtually
gives up; and, of course, it must be owned that technically
they do not furnish a good subject for comparison with
anything in the writings of Horace. But it is not easy to
bring the two champions together on the lyric ground.
Catullus' lyric poems, I need not say, are chiefly hendeca-
syllables; and to find any hendecasyllabic parallel we
must pass over Horace altogether, and go on to Statius
and Martial, who are at least as far removed from the

point which I consider to be the acme of Roman poetical
composition on the one side, as Catullus is on the other.
Mr. Munro suggests that we should try the experiment on
the iambics and the glyconics; but to each of these there
is, I think, a valid objection. I certainly should not wish
to risk the claims of Horace on an examination of his
Epodes, which, though marked by many of the qualities
that distinguish his later works, would not, as I have
ventured to intimate elsewhere, if they stood alone, justify
the rank in lyric poetry which posterity in general has
been willing to accord him. As to glyconics, Horace has
only written them in combination with other metres; and
the principal glyconic poem of Catullus, the Epithalamium
of Junia and Mallius (so, according to Mr. Ellis, we are
to call them for the future, not Julia and Manlius), seems
to me to be too completely *sui generis* to admit of comparison. What I mean is this: the fault of Catullus, as
I conceive it, like that of Lucretius, is a certain redundancy, now tending to luxuriant ornamentation, now
to rustic simplicity; but in a poem like the Epithalamium
these qualities happen to be exactly in place. It is
written throughout in a style of which the diminutives
which abound in it (a characteristic feature these of
Catullus' diction) are a type and sample: there is a vein
of ὑποκορισμός, as the Greeks called it, running through
the piece, a petting, affectionate tone, which as little
bears to be criticised by ordinary rules as the 'Little
Language' of Swift's letters to Stella. I may add, too,
that the medium through which we regard a poem of
this kind is not altogether a transparent one; the
antiquity of the language gives it a distinct advantage,
making words appear graceful of which the modern
equivalents might possibly jar against a correct taste
just as the love poems which abound in the first division

of Mr. Palgrave's 'Golden Treasury' impress us in quite
a different way from that in which we should be affected
by similar thoughts similarly expressed by a poet of our
own time. When Herrick talks of

> A careless shoe-string in whose tie
> I see a wild civility,

we feel that it is natural and graceful: when Mr. Tennyson speaks of 'the least little delicate aquiline curve in a
sensitive nose,' almost the only blemish in what I venture
to think the most exquisite of his poems, it offends us, at
least it has always offended me, as too familiar. As, then,
I cannot take the iambic or glyconic poems as a means
of comparison, I will take the sapphic. Catullus has
produced but two of these; they are, however, among his
more distinguished performances; and one of them,
perhaps, will serve our purpose. I will quote the earlier
part of it:

> Ille mi par esse deo videtur,
> Ille, si fas est, superare divos,
> Qui sedens adversus identidem te
>   Spectat et audit
> Dulce ridentem: misero quod omnis
> Eripit sensus mihi: nam simul te
> Lesbia, aspexi, nihil est super mi
>   *   *   *   *
> Lingua sed torpet, tenuis sub artus
> Flamma demanat, sonitu suopte
> Tintinant aures, gemina teguntur
>   Lumina nocte.

This is a translation, it is true; but Catullus would not
have thought of making a translation unless it had
expressed his own feelings; he had no ambition, we may
be sure, to introduce to Roman readers Sappho's poem as
Sappho's; and, as a matter of fact, though the version is

a close one, it is sufficiently characteristic of its author.
I suppose it is generally admitted to be inferior to the
original; the only charm, indeed, which Catullus can be
said to have added to those which he has carried away
from the Greek is the second line, which is a graceful
ascent upon the first, and where the 'si fas est' is
eminently beautiful. Gaining this, he has lost what is of
more importance, the ἄδυ φωνείσας, which, in Sappho,
comes before the γιλαίσας ἰμερόεν; 'dulce ridentem'
has to do duty for smile and voice both. Throughout
the version there is an absence of any strikingly felicitous
expression, with the one exception which I mentioned
just now; compare, for instance, the commonplace
'lingua sed torpet' with Horace's 'Cur facunda parum
decoro Inter verba cadit lingua silentio?' while there are
words like 'identidem' and 'suopte,' which seem more
appropriate to prose than to poetry. The first, indeed,
he may have used for rhythmical reasons, to represent
the ἐνάντιός τοι of the Greek, though it is to be observed
that he has also employed it in his only other Sapphic
ode; for the second I fear not even this excuse can be
pleaded. How unlike this is to the language of Horace
we shall at once see, if we recollect the tumult that has
been made about the solitary place in his Odes where the
word 'cius' occurs; a word which, whether or no it is
actually found in Catullus, we may safely say would
never have brought suspicion upon the reading of any
line in which it had happened to appear. Lastly, in
point of rhythm (for when we are speaking of Catullus
rhythm may be brought into the question), there is an
unpleasant sameness between the sound of 'simul te' and
that of 'super mi,' ending two successive lines. Turn
now but for a single moment to Horace. I will not go

beyond the two lines of which Catullus' poem has doubtless reminded everyone:—

> Dulce ridentem Lalagen amabo,
> Dulce loquentem.

These lines, I suppose it will be admitted, have enjoyed
more fame even than their Greek original; and why?
Partly, doubtless, because Roman poetry is much more of
a household word with modern nations than Greek; but
is that all? I believe that a large part of their popularity
is due to the balanced and symmetrical form into which
they are cast.   In Sappho there is no attempt to preserve
a verbal or rhythmical balance between the sweet utterance and the charming smiles.   Each expression consists
of a participle in the genitive case constructed with an
adjective in the neuter gender ; but there the resemblance
ends.   The order of the words is not the same; they do
not occupy the same place in the verse.   Horace, on the
contrary, has aimed before all things at symmetry.   He
is not careful to mark any shade of difference that Sappho
may have intended between ἀδύ and ἱμερόεν; their
likeness is far more to him than their unlikeness.   The
same word is used for both, and it occupies the same
place in the two lines; and the correspondence of sound
between the two participles enhances the symmetrical
effect.   This, in fact, may be said to illustrate generally
the difference between Catullus and Horace as lyric
artists.   The Sapphic stanza of Catullus—and probably
the same remark might be extended to his other measures
—is modelled on the type of the Greek; he represents
Greek cadences ; the effects which he seeks are those
which are sought after in Greek poetry.   Horace has not
attempted to cope with Sappho and Alcaeus on their own
ground ; adopting their measures, he has at the same

time remodelled them; his cadences are his own; and
his language, far from representing their flowing Æolic,
where perhaps it may be said that half the charm consists
in the dialect, is terse, polished, and artistic. I fear he
was scarcely thinking of this when he said—

Líbera per vacuum posui vestigia princeps :
Non aliena meo pressi pede :

but the boast is one which in this sense he might have
made with justice. The same thing would be seen if we
were to compare Catullus and Ovid in their management
of the elegiac couplet. Catullus follows the Greek
structure; Ovid has introduced a structure of his own. I
will not now discuss which form is in itself the more
pleasing; perhaps some will consider that the practice of
successive generations of composers of Ovidian elegiacs
has settled that question. But even those who think it
would have been well if we had been taught to write
lines like ' Et mutam nequiquam alloquerer cinerem ' may
not be unwilling to admit that more art is shown in
framing a new type than in copying an old one. This is
the glory of the Augustan poets; in the province of
language and metre, at any rate, they were genuine
inventors; and if their works do not exhibit the exulting
strength of freedom, they realise more perfectly than
anything which went before them the grace and majesty
of law.

I am not so zealous a defender of my Augustan clients
as to contend that nothing was lost to Roman poetry by
this process of refinement. Something, I fear, must
always be lost in all changes, social and political as well
as literary; each phase has its characteristic charm, the
passing away of which leaves a blank not easily filled;
and a state of things which shall combine all excellences

is an ideal which we cannot even imagine as capable of being realised, εἰ μὴ ἴσως παρὰ τοῖς θεοῖς. Rules of writing, like rules of action, have necessarily a cramping tendency; in general they are not accepted till experience has shown that their absence leads to waste of power, delusion, and wrong-doing; they propose to foster excellence by excluding error; and they are consequently more concerned to prohibit everything that is wrong, than to legalise everything that is right. Perhaps the tendencies in Roman poetry which Virgil and his contemporaries set themselves to correct deserved a less severe check than they received; perhaps the diamond need not have lost so much of its original substance in order to be fashioned into a jewel. But no one, it seems to me, can justly refuse them the praise of having been the first to address themselves to the question how to endow the poetry of their country with appropriate language and appropriate metre. Ennius, indeed, formed a conception of the problem, and made an attempt, after his fashion, to solve it; but though his services as a pioneer are to be acknowledged with gratitude, the time at which he lived rendered it impossible that he should understand the real artistic capacities of his native tongue, or produce anything which in point of art should bear a moment's comparison with any Greek model. But the writers of the last age of the commonwealth seem almost to have allowed themselves to drift before the currents of their time, according as the influence of prose composition or of Greek poetry happened in each case to be the stronger. Lucretius complains of the poverty of his native language, but the complaint is made in the interest of science, not in that of poetry; of the need of a diction and a metre worthy of being compared with those of Greek masterpieces he does not

appear to be conscious. Catullus, at least in his hexameters and elegiacs, as Mr. Munro admits, treads closely
in the steps of the Alexandrine writers. The great
Augustan poets, on the other hand, so far as style and
metre are concerned, are singularly independent of
Greek influences. Their general conceptions, their types
of poetry, the subjects of their poems, are freely borrowed from Greek, and often from Alexandrine sources ;
they translate unhesitatingly from the Greek, and exhibit
the result as their own ; but when we come to the details
of execution, the thousand minutiæ of language and of
rhythm, they give abundant proof that, though they
have been on the watch for every opportunity to profit
by what Greek artists have done, they have thought out
the problem for themselves. Virgil's language, if borrowed at all, is borrowed not from any of his predecessors in pastoral, didactic, or epic poetry, from Theocritus,
or Hesiod, or Apollonius, but from Sophocles. His treatment of the hexameter is copied from no Greek model
whatever, whether Ionic or Alexandrine. Mr. Munro is
far too sweeping when he talks of Virgil as 'affecting'
the spondaic ending which, as he truly says, was in
vogue with the Alexandrians and their imitators. I have
not gone through the calculation ; but, judging from
Gossrau's Excursus on the Virgilian hexameter, and from
my own recollections, I should question whether thirty
instances can be produced out of the 9,890 lines of
which the 'Æneid' consists. I take up Apollonius, and I
find one or two spondaic endings in every page I look
at ; I take up Catullus, and I find at least twenty-seven
in 400 lines ; nay, I take up Homer, who lived before
Alexandrians and their mannerisms were thought of, and
I find nine or ten in the first 200 lines of the First Book
of the 'Iliad.' Virgil takes hints from all the masters of

hexameter rhythm that have preceded him ; but he binds
himself to none ; he considers the condition under which
the Roman hexameter can be perfected, and he produces
something, not Greek, not Alexandrine, but Roman. He
had evidently formed a strong conviction that, as a general rule, words of more than three syllables ought not
to be used at the end of a hexameter : and upon that
basis he constructed a poem of nearly ten thousand lines.
Possibly he may have had predecessors among his own
countrymen in carrying out this rule of exclusion ; one
such he would certainly seem to have had, a writer
who is not generally numbered among those who have
improved Roman poetry, I mean Cicero. But the con-
sensus of the classical authors of both nations was
undoubtedly the other way : those of Greece were
unanimous, those of Rome formed at any rate a majority : and to have succeeded in the face of all this
experience in introducing what was to all intents and
purposes a new national hexameter, is in itself sufficient
to establish Virgil's rank, not as a mere Alexandrine
copyist, but as an original artist. I am aware that on
this especial point I do not differ from my friend, who
has himself, in an eloquent sentence, done full justice to
the Virgilian hexameter ; ' that elaborate and complicated, yet exquisite perfection of rhythm,' as he truly
calls it, ' which is utterly different from the Homeric
movement, and yet appears as well adapted to the
Latin forms of speech as the other is to the Ionic.'
But he is a little inclined to mar the effect of his praise
by after thoughts and exceptions : he talks of conces-
sions to Greek rhythm and prettinesses in which Virgil
has indulged, but from which Lucretius is free : and he
evidently thinks that his favourite poet is so far the more
manly versifier of the two. To speak in this way is

really to be unfair to Virgil. His 'circumspicit Oriona' is not a concession to Alexandrine daintiness, any more than his 'simul hoc animo hauri' is a concession to Roman roughness: each, with him, is simply one of the innumerable experiments by the aid of which he works out the complex harmony of his verse: like the bee in Quintilian's simile, he imbibes the essences of all flowers and distils them into a perfect sweetness which does not exhibit the characteristic flavour of any. Criticism may identify the effects which he has taken from others; but criticism must admit that he has proved his right to them by the perfect appropriateness with which he has contrived to endow them.

I suppose that in strictness I am bound to complete my case by passing on to the poets of the silver age, and showing by a comparison of their style with that of Virgil and Horace that the Augustan period was in reality, as in common opinion it has always been considered to be, the crowning point of Roman poetical art. It would be easy to make the comparison: in fact, I attempted something of the kind three or four years ago on an occasion like this, when I spoke to you about Statius and the later epic poetry of Rome. But time will not allow of my doing so now: and I confess I venture to hope that what I have already said may have put the subject in such a light as to render the task a superfluous one. I mean to say that I trust my remarks may have tended to show that the line which, in my judgment, separates Lucretius from Virgil, and, in a less degree, Catullus from Horace, is not arbitrarily or capriciously drawn. I have pointed out that the question is not, as my friend appears to consider it, a question of the use of language, but a question of the use of language for the purposes of poetry. Whether the

Augustan age was an advance on the last age of the commonwealth in respect of prose composition is a point
which I am not concerned to rule one way or the other.
It is quite possible that the study of Alexandrine Greek
may have begun even then to tell unfavourably upon the
language of Rome: it is quite possible that prose was
being corrupted and enervated by the operation of the
same causes by which poetry was being purified and
refined. Of course, too, it must be admitted that the
golden age passed into the silver—that as Virgil succeeded Lucretius, so Lucan and Statius succeeded Virgil.
The laws of growth and decay in poetry, like those of
the development of national life, are a subject on which
we have doubtless much, very much to learn; but it
would be vain to deny that many of the signs which in
the writers of the silver age we recognise as symptomatic
of a period of decadence are directly traceable to causes
which were already at work in the Augustan era. Granting, however, to the full the connection of the conditions
of the two periods, what have we really conceded?
simply that rottenness comes after ripeness, that prime is
the harbinger of decline. At any rate, if Virgil and his
contemporaries are to be considered as already touched
by the canker, Lucretius will not profit by their condemnation. Pure model of perfect Latin idiom as he
may be, it is impossible to contend that his language
satisfies the conditions of the highest poetical art.
All that we shall then be able to say will be, that
Roman poetry never attained perfection at all: the year
had its spring, its autumn, and its winter, but it had no
summer.

I feel that I have been executing an ungracious task in
calling attention to the faults of writers whose essential
greatness I should myself be among the last to question.

Criticism in such cases can hardly fail to appear carping
and microscopic: and I have more than once been
reminded, during the process, of the examination which,
in the 'Frogs' of Aristophanes, Æschylus has to undergo
at the hands of his envious rival. But I may plead that
though the names which I have seemed to disparage are
great, those which I have endeavoured to vindicate are
greater; and that whatever may be the claims which an
illustrious poet has upon our deference, they cannot be
paramount to the duty which we owe to that truth of
critical judgment without which our sense of excellence
in poetry is a blind and unintelligent instinct.

––––––––––––

By way of Appendix, I subjoin a few remarks on another
point in controversy between Mr. Munro and myself, of
somewhat more limited interest.

In the article before mentioned I hazarded an opinion
that conjectural emendation had been less successfully
applied to the texts of Latin than to those of Greek
poets; a fact, if fact it be, which I inclined to attribute
not to the inferiority of the scholars who had attempted
the task, but to something in the nature of the task itself,
though I did not venture to say what that thing was. I
left the problem to be solved by those whose learning
and sagacity exceeded mine. Mr. Munro[1] denies the
existence of the fact; admitting its apparent truth, he
accounts for it by the length of time during which Latin
criticism has been prosecuted, as compared with Greek,
what looks new and wonderful in the case of the latter
language seeming commonplace in the case of the former;
Bentley, to the difference of whose success in dealing

––––––––––

[1] Postscript to second edition of *Lucretius*.

with Greek and Latin authors I had appealed in support
of my view, he thinks, would have succeeded better with
Lucilius than with Menander, worse with Sophocles than
with Horace, the difference which I had noted really
depending on the accident of his having taken up a Latin
author who did not need emending; Madvig, Ritschl,
and Lachmann, he contends, have done more for the
restoration of Latin fragments than any scholar with the
same opportunities has done for the restoration of Greek;
Lucretius, of whom I had especially spoken, depends
really on a single MS., and has already yielded to his
earlier editors a harvest of easy emendations quite equal
to all that the Porsonian school has done for the corrupter
plays of Æschylus and Euripides; while Lachmann,
besides eminent successes in 'the lower art of verbal
emendation,' has in many cases, by the combined force
of sagacity and industry, 'forced his way into the very
work-room of the poet,' so that it may be fairly asked
whether any Greek author similarly circumstanced has
been as fortunate in his editor as Lucretius has been in
Lachmann.

Now, I think the difference of opinion between Mr.
Munro and myself is partly due to his misapprehension
of my meaning. I was speaking throughout my remarks
of 'the lower art of verbal emendation,' not of anything
else, whether in itself more or less important; and I was
speaking of emendations, not of emenders.[1] The second
point I may dismiss at once, merely observing that I did
not intend to compare the individual labours of Lachmann
or Madvig with those of Porson or Elmsley, but the
aggregate of emendations of Greek poets with the aggre-

---

[1] It is true that I particularised Lachmann and Bentley; but the whole
tenor of my remarks will show that I instanced them merely as representatives of emendatory criticism in Greek or Latin.

gate of emendations of Roman poets : the first requires
a few words.

I repeat, then, that I intended my remarks to be confined strictly to verbal emendation, to that art which
restores not only the sense but the very words of the
author. This is an art which is more or less *sui generis* ;
it is fitful and occasional in its operations; with some
scholars it seems to depend on a peculiar conformation of
mind; with others it perhaps results from that practice
in Greek and Latin composition which, as Julius Hare
pointed out many years ago, gives English scholars an
advantage over the scholars of the Continent ; with others,
again, it comes in the later years of a life of study, as the
reward of a careful attention to the language of the
classical writers. Its results are sometimes valuable,
sometimes trifling ; sometimes, though important in themselves, they do not really imply any great merit in their
author, who has simply made a lucky guess ; at others,
they are the last spark which fires a long train laid by
learning and research ; but they have the one characteristic of certainty. I do not mean to say that many
plausible but untrue emendations are not made by
critics, and accepted by other critics ; what I do say is,
that it is the characteristic of a real emendation that, as
far as it goes, it shall restore not merely the meaning of
the author, but the actual words in which he expressed
the meaning. It is quite possible to put the sense of a
passage in a true light, but to leave the words uncertain.
A case in point is to be found in Æschylus' ' Agamemnon,'
vv. 764 foll. of Dindorf's edition. There it seems clear
that an antithesis is intended between the ancient wrong,
παλαία ὕβρις, and the later wrong to which it gives birth,
νεαρά or νία ὕβρις; it seems clear, too, though all scholars
have not seen it in that light, that the antithesis is intro-

duced in the words which are given in the MSS. as παρὰ
φάους κότον. But there certainty, or even high probability, ends: νία δ᾽ ἰφυσιν κόρον, though it restore sense
and metre, cannot be said to be more than plausible, as
it is just possible that the antistrophe may be corrupt;
while νία does not sufficiently account for παρά nor
ἰφυσιν for φάους, and there are other plausible emendations of κότον, if κότον is to be emended at all: then the
metre, and, consequently the text, of the next line is
uncertain; and, lastly, it is not clear whether μελαίνας
μελάθροισιν Ἄτας should stand, εἰδομέναν being changed
into εἰδόμενον, or whether μελαίνα . . . Ἄτα εἰδομένα is
not more likely to be the true reading. Thus, while
criticism has done much for the sense of this passage, it
has left the words nearly as they were. It has ascertained
the sort of words which Æschylus might have used: as
to the words which he actually did use we are still in the
dark. Why, in this particular case, the words should
remain intractable after the sense has yielded, is not
easy to say. Something, no doubt, is due to the choral
metre, which cannot always be established with certainty,
especially where, as here, some doubt hangs over the
antistrophe. The state of the MSS. of the ‘Agamemnon,’
too, has probably a good deal to do with it: the great
authority, the Medicean MS., is deficient in this part of
the play, which depends on two inferior copies, one of
them at least tampered with by the transcriber. These I
give merely as specimens of the causes which may have
contributed to a result, the complete account of which is
probably as insoluble a problem as the true reading of
the passage itself. One thing, however, is certain, that
the reason why the true reading of this passage has not
been recovered is not that the critics who have attempted
the task have been negligent or incompetent. And this

is precisely what I mean to assert with regard to the application of emendatory criticism to Latin. If I am right, as I still think I am, in supposing that it has been less successful there than in Greek, I gladly admit, what indeed I maintained from the first, that the cause of failure is to be sought, not in the critics, but in the subject-matter on which they have been engaged. At any rate, I hope I have now made my meaning clear, and shown the distinct and limited nature of the issue which it was my intention to raise. That criticism which restores the meaning of a passage while leaving the words doubtful is not emendatory in the technical sense, but interpretative. The triumphs of interpretative criticism form a much wider subject, with which I did not at all propose to deal. To institute a comparison between what has been done in interpreting Greek and what has been done in interpreting Latin is a task which would far exceed my modicum of knowledge, nor did I mean to hint, in the most distant way, that in that department Greek scholars had the slightest advantage. There, at any rate, as I expressed it in this very article, ' the battle is to the strong.'

Mr. Munro thinks that, in comparing the labours of the Porsonian school on the Greek drama with those of Lachmann on Lucretius, I am guilty of an injustice in the form of a practical anachronism. There are, he justly remarks, several stages in the emendation of the text of a classical author : the first critic gathers his fruit by hundreds, the second by tens, the third by units. The Porsonian critics, he contends, answer not to Lachmann, but to Lambinus, or Marullus, or both. ' Surely the emendations which a critic hardly now deigns to mention, such as *fera moenera*, out of *feram onera*; *vidi reddere*, out of *videre odore*; *suavi devinxit*, out of *sua videt vinxit*; *vera viai*, out of *ver aula; fuit umquam,* out of *fultum quam; uti risu tremulo,* out of *utiris ut aemulo; aevom vitamque,* out of *aevo multamque,* and hundreds such as these, equal all the manipulations of *αι* and *ι*, *η* and *ει*, and the like, which Porsonian critics have for two generations expended on such corrupt plays as the "Agamemnon," "Choephoræ," and "Bacchæ," which, therefore, may be brought into comparison with the manuscript text of Lucretius.' An inexperienced reader might suppose from this that the Porsonian critics were the first who attempted to restore the text of Æschylus and Euripides. As a matter of fact, I need not say that Æschylus and Euripides went through the earlier stages of emendatory criticism long before Porson was born; and it is to the changes introduced into their texts, in these earlier stages, that one would naturally compare the emendations of Lucretius by Marullus or Lambinus. I do not profess to go thoroughly into the matter: my knowledge of the minutiæ of Greek criticism is pretty much confined to Æschylus, and even that has suffered greatly from years of disuse; but I should have no difficulty in hazarding the assertion that at least two stages may be distinguished in the history of the text of Æschylus before the middle of the eighteenth century; the one represented by such men as Robortellus, Turnebus, and Victorius; the other, by such as Auratus, Canter, and Stanley. Of these, I think, it may be said, as Mr. Munro says of the two classes of Lucretian editors, that the first class counts its successes by hundreds, the second by tens. At any rate, there can be no doubt that what they accomplished between them is not to be despised. I will take a few instances from the first chorus of the 'Choephoræ,' not that I wish to risk my case on an examination of that single play, but that it happens to be the one which I know most intimately. I confine myself

to *bonâ fide* emendations of the text of the Medicean MS.,
leaving out those instances, of which there are not a few,
where corruptions introduced from a later MS., or from
the earliest editions, were afterwards removed by critical
ingenuity. v. 22 (ed. Dind.), ἔβην is Robortellus' correction
(I assume the identity of his MS. with the Medicean) of
ἔβη. v. 23, Arnald, a critic of the second period, restored
σὺν κτύπῳ for συνκύπτωι. v. 24, Stanley changed Φοινισ-
σαμυγμοῖς into Φοινίοις ἀμυγμοῖς. v. 26, δ᾽ ἰυγμοῖσι is
Canter's alteration of ἀοιγμοῖσι. v. 29, πρόστερνοι was
restored by Turnebus for πρόστελνοι. v. 38, Turnebus
changed ἔλαχον into ἔλακον. v. 45, μωμένα μ᾽ ἰάλλει,
Stanley; μωμέν ἀμιλλεῖ, MS. Med. v. 47, ἐκβαλεῖν,
Stanley; ἐκβάλλειν, MS. Med. v. 48, λύτρον, Canter;
λυγρόν, MS. Med. v. 56, φρενός, Victorius; φρένις, MS.
Med. v. 61, δίκας, Turnebus; δίκαν, MS. Med. v. 80,
πικρόν, Victorius; πικρᾶν, MS. Med. v. 83, παχνουμένη,
Turnebus; παχνουμένην, MS. Med. These changes are
most of them easy enough, and only one or two of them
reflect much credit on their inventor; but they will, I
think, show that the history of the text of Æschylus has
been not very unlike that of Lucretius, and that more
than one generation of editors had been required to place
the plays in a fairly readable condition before Porson and
the latter critics came.[1] Yet I doubt whether the criticism
of Lachmann and his successors has done as much for the
restoration of the actual words of Lucretius, as that of
Porson and his successors has done for those of Æschylus.
Take, for instance, Porson's διοσδότῳ γάνει (' Ag.' 1391),
τοῦδ᾽ ἄνοιγε ('Supp.' 321), εὑρεθέντα (ib. 401), δορυκανεῖ μόρῳ

---

[1] A comparison of the whole number of corruptions in the first 120 lines
of the *Choephorœ* and of those in the corresponding portion of the First Book
of *Lucretius*, as given respectively in the best MS., seems to show that the
former number is to the latter something like three to one.

(ib. 987); Hermann's ἐλπίδων (ib. 95), δύνασαι ('Cho.' 374), ἰηλεμιστρίας (ib. 424); Dindorf's καιρία ('Ag.' 1122); Franz's γᾶ χθονίων τε τιμαί (' Cho.' 399).[1] With regard to the value of the MS. authority for their respective texts, Æschylus and Lucretius seem to be nearly on a level. Dindorf and Cobet believe that all the MSS. of Æschylus are derived from the Med. MS.; and whether or no this is actually true, it is generally admitted that the other authorities for the several plays are comparatively of little value. This was what I had in my mind when, speaking of the MSS. of the different Latin poets whom Lachmann has edited, I risked the assertion, ' there are MSS. of each enough to stimulate critical ingenuity, not enough to supersede it.' I was thinking of the two authors with whom my own editorial experience has made me most familiar, Æschylus and Virgil, and I meant in effect that Lucretius is in the condition of the former, not of the latter. Perhaps I wrote carelessly; at any rate, I can assure Mr. Munro that I did not mean to contravene Lachmann's doctrine that all the MSS. of Lucretius are

---

[1] Mr. Munro asks 'to what play of Euripides does Porson or any of his followers restore whole verses with the same certainty as Lachmann gives back to Lucretius lines like " Effluat ambrosiae quad vere et nectari' linctus, Qua nil est homini quod amario' frondent esca?"' I confess I think that, estimated by Mr. Munro's own standard, Wellauer did at least as much for the text of Æschylus when he restored, in Supp. 184 foll., μιλανθὲς ἡλιό-στονον γένος τὸ γαῖον . . . Ζήνη . . Ἐφύσιθα. Those who went before him, following the corrupt readings ᾗ ἐνθεν-ον . . . τοὐγγαῖον, supposed the poet to be speaking of the Titans in Tartarus. Τὸν γαῖον had been previously conjectured by a writer in the *Quarterly Review*, but there is no reason to think that Wellauer knew of it. By the way, I think Mr. Munro should have mentioned, as Lachmann does, that 'frondent' had been already con-jectured by the 'Itali' for 'fronde ac.' This limits Lachmann's actual dis-covery to 'ambrosiae et nectari' linctus' in the first line, and 'esca' in the second. I have no wish to disparage either, or to detract from the merit of the happy thought of the parallel, Hom. *Od.* ix. 359; but I do not believe that anyone familiar with the achievements of Greek criticism would despair of finding something to equal their felicity.

ultimately traceable to one. Yet I venture to think that what I said is not inconsistent with Mr. Munro's own account of the MSS. of his author. The one MS. of Lucretius, to which all the rest are traceable, is not in existence; two copies, A and B, which were made from it immediately or mediately, exist at Leyden; fragments of one or two MSS., bearing a close resemblance to B, are preserved elsewhere; Poggio had a copy resembling A, which is now lost, and from it the remaining copies, sixteen or more, were derived. Now, if the original MS. existed, the copies would of course be worthless, except indeed in places where the original had suffered, subsequently to their transcription, by time or accident; as it is, most of them probably have their value, some more and some less, so far as it cannot be shown that they are copied from each other. Lachmann has apparently been able to determine with something like certainty what this archetypal MS. was like, the mode of writing, the number of lines in each page, &c.; but Mr. Munro does not consider it absolutely certain that even A was copied from it at first hand, without some intervening transcript. A, though generally far more correct than B, occasionally misses points which B hits, and both of them appear to be occasionally set right by the later copies, and that not always from critical conjecture. No doubt, as Mr. Munro says, all these aids merely help us to get at the reading of a single MS.; but this can scarcely be called a peculiar hardship. The students of Lucretius are not worse off than many of their neighbours; perhaps they may be even better off. Let us suppose that Dindorf and Cobet are right, and that the Medicean MS. is the one authority for the text of Æschylus. We do not know from what copy this MS. was transcribed: at any rate the copy is lost, like the archetype of the Lucretian MSS. Would it

not have been better for the student of Æschylus if,
instead of the Medicean and its subordinate MSS., they
had a number of MSS. more or less co-ordinate, all depending on a copy unknown?   They would then have
had several paths leading to the supposed lost MS.; now
they have only one.   It would almost seem as if the very
completeness of Lachmann's discovery had led his successors to take an unreal view of their position.   They
realise the existence of their lost archetype so vividly that
they habitually view the actually extant MSS. in their relation to it : and thus they speak of those copies in language
which, though not untrue in itself, may easily convey an
untrue impression to persons who wish to estimate the
MS. resources for the text of Lucretius in comparison
with those for the text of other authors.   Of course the
fact remains that an author, all of whose copies can be
traced to one archetype existent or non-existent, is probably in a worse condition than an author whose text has
several sources; though, before we can assert even this
positively, we must know something of the date of the
archetype and the history of the text.   It appears hard,
too, that when the archetype is known to have been a
faulty one, we should not possess even its faults at first
hand, but should have first to guess them out by the
help of yet more faulty transcripts, and then to decipher
the original text by their means.   Yet it is also true, if I
may return to the proposition which began the discussion,
that a certain amount of uncertainty is required to stimulate critical ingenuity.   Even now I am not without fear
that the statement I made in a note on a former page
may be turned against me, not indeed by Mr. Munro, but
by some other student of Lucretius, and that I may be
told that the reason why Æschylus has been more successfully restored than Lucretius is, that his MS. text is in a
worse state.

There is another point on which Mr. Munro mis-
apprehends my meaning. He thinks I am speaking of
emendations of Latin authors generally, not specifically of
emendations of Latin poets; and so he appeals to Madvig's
restorations of Livy, and Ritschl's corrections of inscriptions. Anyone who will favour me by looking at
the article in question will see that here, again, it was the
narrower issue that I meant to raise. The proposition
from which I start is contained in these words:—'No
scholar, so far as we are aware, for the last two centuries,
at least, has done for any Latin poet what Bentley did for
the fragments of Greek poetry, what Porson did for the
Greek drama.'¹ I then go into detail, and speak of
Bentley's Epistle to Mill, and emendations of Menander
as compared with his Horace and Manilius, and of Lach-
man's editions of Catullus, Propertius, and Lucretius.²
Afterwards, speaking generally, I talk of the results of
criticism as applied to Latin and Greek writers, of a new
critical edition of a Latin author, of the special impracticability of the text of Latin authors;³ but I do not suppose that I intended to introduce into the conclusion an
assertion obviously going beyond the original proposition
and the facts adduced in support of that proposition. At
any rate, I wish to be more guarded now. I have
myself next to no acquaintance with the textual criticism
of either Greek or Latin prose authors; and there is a
reason in the nature of the question itself which would
dispose me in any case to prefer dealing with the narrower
field. A prose author naturally suggests greater laxity
of emendation than a poet; the conditions under which
a word has to be supplied are far less accurately marked
out; if absolute literal conformity to the corrupt reading
is disregarded as too strict, as it must occasionally be, the

¹ p. 240.　　² Ib.　　³ p. 241.

o 2

sense is the only guide. Now I only profess to deal, as I
have explained repeatedly, with 'the lower art of verbal
emendation,' with that which restores, not the general
sense of the writer, but the very words in which it was
originally expressed; and therefore I may reasonably
decline to follow Mr. Munro into a field where the question between us cannot so satisfactorily be brought to the
test as in that in which we have hitherto been contending.
As to the fragments of Lucilius, which he instances as a
proof of Lachmann's success in emending Latin, I should
have no objection to accept his challenge, if it were given
in a less hypothetical way. 'Observe,' he says, 'the
masterly power with which Lachmann throughout his
Lucretius breathes life and meaning into the disjointed
members of Lucilius. Had he been spared for a few
months longer, he would have given us this author in
such a shape that no existing restoration of any fragmentary Greek writer would have borne a moment's
comparison with the work of Lachmann.' I have gone
through the fragments of Lucilius mentioned in Lachmann's
notes, and my general impression is, that though in dealing
with them he shows a vigour and ability markedly contrasting with the feebleness of Gerlach, and only occasionally paralleled by one or two earlier scholars like
Douza, he has made comparatively few restorations which
can be called certain. The whole number of his emendations is about forty; and of these there are, perhaps,
twelve which may fairly be styled more than probable,
though all of them are not of the same importance.[1]   Is

---

[1] There are forty-eight references to Lucilius in Lachmann's Index (he has
omitted one that he might have made, to p. 76 of his Commentary). Some
of them are to passages quoted but not amended; but, on the other hand, in
several of the pages referred to Lucilius is emended more than once. The
emendations which I should call successful are those contained in pp. 60
(Nonius 78), 70 (Non. 503), 82 (Non. 140), 116 (Non. 472), 170 (Non. 207,
id. 414), 188 (Non. 296), 212 (Serv. on Virg. G. iii. 159), 248 (Non. 459),

this a large proportion? It is true that we cannot say what Lachmann would have done, had he given us the whole of the remains of Lucilius; but we may reasonably suppose that he would not have inserted any of these emendations in a commentary on another author, if he had not himself set much store by it.

I hope I have now made my meaning sufficiently clear. A large part of the controversy between Mr. Munro and myself, I trust, is now set at rest already, by the explanation that I was speaking throughout of verbal emendation, and of that as applied to Latin and Greek poets, rather than to Latin and Greek authors generally. But there is still a good deal at issue between us; and knowing what I do of my friend's acquaintance with the subject, I cannot but fear that I may prove to have been mistaken. If, indeed, the question simply turned on the positive value of what has been done for Lucretius, I should think many times before I adventured my ignorance against his knowledge. But the question is a comparative one; and it is because I believe that justice has not been done to the other member of the comparison that I ask to be heard a second time.

276 (Non. 370), 320 (Non. 255), 400 (Velius Longus, 2227). There is a brilliant one, p. 413 (Non. 84); but where the data are so few we cannot talk of certainty.

EARLY ROMAN TRAGEDY AND EPIC POETRY.[1]

ROMAN TRAGEDY, more perhaps than any of the other
branches of Roman poetry, appears to have been an
exotic growth.   In comedy, for example, we see the
confluence of two distinct streams—the exuberance of
native pleasantry, welling out from the heart of a rustic
population in Fescennine verses and rude Atellane enter-
tainments, and the more regular course of the Athenian
drama, flowing on in an ever-widening, if not ever-deep-
ening channel, as it were in forgetfulness of the fountain-
head which it had left so long behind it ; and though the
torrent may seem to have been at once lost in the river,
yet we perceive that the great volume of waters must
have derived new elements of life and freshness.   Among
the Greeks, indeed, tragedy seems to have been evolved,
whether by Thespis or by his successors, from rudiments
as little calculated to excite pathos or deep emotion as
any of the Etruscan performances which the old Italians
loved ; but we feel that it is not in such embryo states
of being, equally capable, as far as we can see, of being
matured into one or the other of two distinct organisms,
that the actual type of either can be said to exist.   There
seems to have been nothing in the native institutions of
early Italy answering to the nucleus round which
Grecian tragedy gathered and clustered the Bacchic
chorus ; no depth of dithyrambic fervour, by entering
into which the population might have been led on to
conceive or appreciate a high and heroic argument.
Other conditions there may have been, no less adapted

---

[1] Reprinted from the *North British Review*, No. lxxxii.

to give the impulse required for the production of a
national tragedy; but these, if present, must have been
neutralised or retarded in their operation, so as to delay,
if not to postpone indefinitely, the set time of birth.
The same causes which prevented Rome from creating
tragedy for herself influenced her treatment of it when
adopted from without.   Greek tragedy, in its progress
from youth to manhood, was ever travelling further and
further from the East, ever losing sight more and more
of its Bacchic origin.   The chorus, which had once been
everything, was coming to be less and less ; dominant in
Æschylus; in Sophocles, occupying what may be thought
to be a just medium ; in Euripides, not indeed contract-
ing its dimensions, but frequently standing in no very
close relation to the business of the play, virtually a
mere relief between the acts ; in Agathon and his successors, attaining this consummation formally, as we
learn from Aristotle, who tells us that they were in the
habit of introducing ἐμβόλιμα or insertions, songs written
for no one play in particular, and therefore suiting any.
The next step in the development would obviously have
been to anticipate the course taken centuries after by the
modern drama, and discard the chorus altogether in
tragedy as well as in comedy—a result to which one at
least of the causes assigned for the cessation of the comic
chorus, the expense of training, might very well have
contributed ; if indeed we are not entitled to assert that
the step was actually taken, and with Quintilian and
Schlegel, to recognise in the new comedy of Menander
and Philemon the last phase of Athenian tragedy, the
Euripidean drama worked out to its completion.   It was
not in the genius of an imitative people to form such an
anticipation, any more than it was in the philosophy of
an uncritical age to perceive such an analogy.   The early

Roman inventors doubtless regarded the chorus as an integral part of the play they copied, and Horace, two centuries later, is as clear in requiring that it should be made relevant to the action as Aristotle himself; but the unreality of a Roman chorus must have made itself felt from the first. The Romans seem to have had no conception of that complex metrical variety, that 'linked sweetness, long drawn out,' and returning back upon itself, which characterise the structure of the Greek choral ode. To copy its metres in their manifold combinations would have been a prolongation of servile labour, from which even they would have recoiled, even supposing them to have thoroughly understood what they read; while they do not seem to have had anything analogous in the rude simplicity of their own poetical repertory. Horace appears to have regarded Pindar's dithyrambics as a mere inspiration, not bound by artistic rule, and therefore not to be attained by artistic practice; in the words of their common imitator, Cowley,

> Pindar is imitable by none,
> The Phœnix Pindar is a vast species alone:

yet modern science has discovered the laws of the Pindaric measure, and modern art, or modern genius, has produced odes of Pindaric complexity. So in the remains of the early Roman tragedians, when we pass beyond the common iambic or trochaic of the dialogue, we find only the simplest metres, anapæsts chiefly, with here and there a fragment of bacchiac or cretic, such as Plautus uses in the *canticum*, the recitative performed by a single voice to the sound of flute-music, and accompanied by gesticulation. Seneca, who is uniformly careful to allot to the chorus a respectable portion of each play, generally confines himself to anapæsts or some of

the simpler lyric metres, such as asclepiads, sapphics, or
glyconics; and in the two or three instances where he
attempts something more elaborate, by mixing them and
others together, the result is a curious piece of workmanship of the Chinese sort, not unlike the poem in which
an old grammarian has combined all the measures of
Horace—a composition which, if ever produced in the
theatre, for which Seneca's dramas were probably never
intended, would doubtless have issued in a mere medley
of discords. It is, in fact, what we know of the arrange-
ments of the Roman theatre which enables us to estimate
the self-confessed insignificance of the Roman chorus.
'The Roman orchestra,' we are told, 'contained no
Thymele, and was not destined for a chorus, but contained the seats for senators and other distinguished persons, which are called *primus subselliorum ordo.*' These
few words, which might perhaps be made the text for a
commentary on the differing spirit of the Greek and
Roman dramas, at any rate show that the day of the
old chorus was passed. Where there was no orchestra,
what place could there be for the variety of orchestral
motion and the fulness of orchestral harmony? How
could a chorus, compelled to share the stage with the
actors, preserve its ancient character of military symmetry, execute the grand movement of the Parodos, and
draw up in rank and file to chant the Stasimon? The
traditions of the dialogue could be conveyed from
country to country without injury; the traditions of
choric metre and choric gesture were precisely such as
were likely to perish in the attempt to transplant them,
if attempt there were.

Still, great as may have been the injury sustained by
the Roman drama from this humiliation of the chorus, it
is one which is but imperfectly brought home to the

modern reader. Even where the whole play has been
preserved, we may read it (in speaking of Seneca it
would be too much to say, enjoy it) in happy unconsciousness, for the most part, of the alterations which
its character must have undergone; much more when,
knowing that we have to deal with fragments, we are
disposed to think rather of what we find than of what
we miss. The fragments preserved from the dialogue of
Greek tragedy very greatly outnumber those which have
survived from the choral parts; a fact for which various
reasons may be adduced, such as the greater availability
of the former for most purposes of quotation, especially
where the quoter quotes from memory; and though it
cannot be used to invalidate what we have said about the
want of metrical variety in the Roman chorus, as if many
metres might have existed which quotation has not preserved, it at any rate prevents the student of one set of
fragments from feeling any strong sense of contrast when
he turns to examine the other.

Livius Andronicus is universally acknowledged to have
been the Thespis of Roman tragedy. Such a title indeed
would but imperfectly express the extent of his services
to the country of his adoption. With that ambidextrous
activity which is especially characteristic of an imitative
culture, he became also the Susarion of Roman comedy,
and perhaps the Homer of Roman poetry; the latter not
merely in virtue of his translation or reproduction of the
'Odyssey,' but as the first who is known to have written
a poetical work, as distinguished from that popular poetry
which may or may not have existed in the earlier days
of the city. A native of Tarentum, taken prisoner in
the Roman wars with Southern Italy, the slave, and
afterwards the freed man of M. Livius Salinator, whose

children he instructed, and whose name he bore when
enfranchised, he acquired the language of his conquerors
perfectly, and was thus able to interpret to them the
poetry of Greece, and create for them what they had
hitherto been without, and perhaps had hardly felt the
want of. The year 240 B.C. gives us the date of his first
acted drama, but we do not know whether it was a
tragedy or a comedy. The fragments of his tragedies,
the names of nine of which have come down to us,
amount to nearly forty lines. Like Thespis, he has had
forgeries attached to his name by unscrupulous or uncritical grammarians; but he has been so far more fortunate than his prototype, that posterity is able to form
a judgment of him from other data than these spurious
relics. The genuine fragments, indeed, though more
numerous, if not more pretentious than the forgery, are
scanty enough. Of the 'Achilles'—all his tragedies
appear to have been written on Greek subjects, if not
actually imitated from the Greek—only one line remains,
as also of the 'Ajax,' the 'Andromeda,' the 'Danae,'
and the 'Hermione;' of the 'Trojan Horse,' one line and
three words; of the 'Tereus,' not quite five lines. Fortune has been more kind to the 'Ægisthus,' which may
consequently be allowed a longer notice. Twelve lines
have been preserved, and they certainly tell us something
of the conduct of the play. There was a speech by a
herald or messenger, a narrative of the homeward voyage
of the Grecian fleet, answering apparently to that in the
'Agamemnon' of Æschylus, while in the fulness of its
details it perhaps approached more nearly to that in
the 'Agamemnon' of Seneca, to which it may have
supplied some hints. Like the latter, it seems to have
commenced *ab ovo*,

> Postquam Pergama
> Accensa, et præda per participes sequiter
> Divisa est,

after the burning of Troy and the partition of the booty.
Like the latter, it thought it worth while to notice the
gambols of the dolphins, Nereus' herd, with their flat
noses, about the sides of the vessels,

> Tum autem lascivum Nerei simum pecus
> Ludens ad cantum classem lustratur—

a picture which seems to have been a popular one, recurring, as we shall see, in Pacuvius, and which Æschylus,
at any rate, cannot be pretended to have anticipated,
though some recent critics have intruded it into his
description, not of the tempest in the Ægæan, but of the
course of the beacon.   An injunction apparently delivered
by Agamemnon to his slaves, to support Cassandra, and
lead her to the temple ; a single line speaking of the king
as engaged in solemn thanksgiving to heaven ; another
saying how he seated himself at the banquet, with Cly-
tæmnestra at his side, and his daughters occupying the
third place ; another describing him as dashing himself to
the ground in the agony of his death-wound, and an
inquiry, which may have been addressed to one of his
murderers, ' Jamne oculos specie lætavisti optabili ? '—
' Hast thou at length gladdened thy eyes with this desirable spectable ? '—complete our knowledge of the play.
It is worth mentioning that for all these fragments we are
indebted to Nonius, who, in the exercise of his calling,
quotes them not for their poetic beauty, but as authorities
for the use of certain words—*sequiter, lustror, pecus,* as
extending to other than quadrupeds, *proco, solemnitus,
juxtim, fligi, læto,* and *species.*   Similarly it is to Nonius,
Paulus, and Festus that we owe the very few fragments

which are quoted from unnamed plays of his. From them we learn that he indulged, as we might have expected, in Grecisms, which the genius of the language afterwards threw off, using *anclare*, or *anculare*, for ' to draw,' and speaking of a crag in no less than four passages by the name of *ocris*; that *dusmus* in his time stood for *dusmus* or *dumosus*; and that *quisquis* included the feminine as well as the masculine; that he talked of the stony heaps, ' struices saxeus,' along which Castalia tumbles, and applied *nefrens*—a word which, according to Varro, was used of young pigs—to the toothless infant into whose mouth its mother sheds the succour of her milk.[1] These are but faint and shadowy traces, a line here and there discernible in an effaced picture; but they may have their value for those whose curiosity has ever led them, as ours before now has led us, to search Johnson's Dictionary for extracts from an old author whose works happened at that time to be beyond their reach.

[1] Mommsen quotes this line, ' Quem ego nefrendem alui lacteam immulgens opem,' as a proof of his assertion that the language of Livius is harsh and quaint. It is, however, a tolerably close rendering of Æsch. *Cho.* 897, πρὸς ᾧ σὺ πολλὰ δὴ βρίζων ἅμα Οὔλωσιν ἐξήμελξας εὐτραφὲς γάλα, and may possibly have formed part of the *Ægisthus*, if that play, as is conceivable, included the death not only of Agamemnon, but of his murderers. There is nothing in the etymology of ' nefrens' (' ne-frendere,' virtually toothless) to show that it might not have been naturally applied to an infant; nor do grammarians speak of the use as a strange one; ' lacteam opem,' too, is quite in keeping with the style of earlier Latin poetry down to Lucretius and Catullus. Nor do the few lines preserved from Livius' *Odyssey* bear out Mommsen's contemptuous expressions, or warrant Mr. Sellar in calling it bald and prosaic, as compared, that is, with the remains of other early writers. Mommsen, who extols Nævius as far more original than Ennius, denies Livius any originality; in each case passing judgment without evidence. All that can be said is that Cicero thought Livius unreadable, and that we might probably think so too if he were extant, but that his few fragments impress us in much the same manner as those of his successor. Nævius, however, ought not to be judged apart from his comic remains, which are more lively and interesting than the relics of his epic and his tragedies.

The second of the Roman tragedians in order of time
was Nævius, who will come before us again in a later part
of this article as the predecessor, and, to some extent at
least, the rival of Ennius in epic poetry.   His first play,
tragedy or comedy we know not, is said to have been
represented B.C. 235, five years after the example was set
by Livius.   Our knowledge of his tragedies is rather
greater in actual extent than our knowledge of those of
Livius, nearly twenty of his lines having been preserved ;
but as they are distinctive rather of the age than of the
poet, they need scarcely detain us so long.   The names
of two of his plays—unfortunately they are mere names,
with but one line and three isolated words to support them—
the ' Clastidium,' and the ' Bringing up of Romulus and Remus,' are especially interesting as belonging to the class of
pretexta or *pretextatæ fabulæ*, plays on national subjects like
Æschylus' ' Persians,' or Phrynichus' ' Destruction of Mile-
tus,' or, to take an instance nearer home, the ' Histories ' of
Shakspeare—a class which might command our sympathies
more strongly than any other species of the drama, if the
data for our knowledge of it were not so scanty, or if it
did not seem to have filled a comparatively small space in
the minds of the Romans themselves.   The rest are on
Greek subjects, ' Andromache,' ' Danae,' another ' Trojan
Horse,' ' Hesiona,' ' Iphigenia,' and ' Lycurgus.'   Of these
the most important is the last, ' Lycurgus,' the remains of
which consist of more than thirty lines.   The quaintness
of one or two of the expressions has led Welcker to
suppose it to have been a mythological comedy, like the
' Amphitruo ' of Plautus ; but Ribbeck, with more veri-
similitude, pronounces the play to have been a tragedy,
occupying probably the same ground as the lost ' Edoni '
and ' Lycurgus ' of Æschylus, and answering in its general effect to the ' Bacchæ ' of Euripides.   We see the

Bacchants, 'thyrsigeræ Bacchæ Bacchico cum schemate,' carrying crested snakes high in the air, and ruining the tilled fields—*arva* being used as a feminine noun—wherever they tread. Lycurgus seems to command his servants, 'vos qui regalis corporis custodias agitatis,' to take these disturbers of the good order of his kingdom on a hunting expedition into the forest, where trees grow of their own will, not planted, 'ingenio arbusta ubi nata sunt, non obsita;' that when they get into his hunting-grounds they may be trapped themselves, and leave the light of day, like two-legged birds, by a snare. The victims apparently suspect him, and express their fear that in the thrill and rapture of the chase, 'in venatu vitulantes,' he will send them out of his forests with some savage vengeance as their guerdon, ' pœnis decoratas feris.' Bacchus, however, is captured and brought before the king, when an altercation ensues, of which two or three fragments have been spared, Lycurgus boasting of the wrath of his savage disposition, and the fierce ferocity of his spirit,' feri ingeni iram atque animi acrem acrimoniam,' and being warned not to set up his wrath in competition with the wrath of Liber. Further on we get a glimpse of the burning of the palace, the cross-beams far and wide all in a glow, and the whole building bursting and shining like a flower under the hand of Vulcan ; and we hear a voice calling loudly for King Lycurgus, the son of Dryas. Add to these one or two graphic expressions from his other plays, as where a child is bidden by a parent to store his words in his mind, as a vintager stores the grapes in his basket, or the mountains are called places where the winds are wont to break themselves, and one or two sayings which have had the good fortune to pass into household words, though their author may have been forgotten, ' male parta male dilabuntur,' ' lætus sum laudari me abs te, patre, a

laudato vivo,' and we shall know all that for our present
purpose we need to know of the tragedies of Nævius. If
it does not enable us to realise the 'immense chasm'
which Mommsen affects to perceive between his productions and the 'quasi-poetry of Livius,' it may at any
rate save us from the temptation of flying off under the
influence of an equally paradoxical reaction, and doubting
whether, if we possessed the entire works of both, we
should think that Nævius had made that advance on his
predecessor which he must have made, supposing him not
to have been essentially his inferior.

When we come to Ennius, we find the horizon of our
knowledge expand. The fragments mount up to about
four hundred lines, and we have better means of judging
of the plays from which they are taken, thanks to the
laudatory notices of his countrymen, as well as to the
greater fulness of the remains themselves. All of them,
with one doubtful exception, the 'Ambracia,' which some
regard as a *prætexta*, others as a comedy, were on the
stock subjects of Greek tragedy ; some of them ascertained
on external or internal evidence to have been translated
or adapted from dramas now extant, such as the ' Medea,'
the ' Hecuba,' and the ' Iphigenia ; ' others, including the
' Achilles,' the ' Achilles of Aristarchus,' the ' Ajax,' the
' Alcumæo,' the ' Alexander,' the ' Andromacha Æchmalotis,' the ' Andromeda,' the ' Athamas,' the ' Cresphontes,'
the ' Erechtheus,' the ' Eumenides,' the ' Ransoming of Hector '
(Hectoris Lustra), the ' Medea at Athens,' the ' Melanippe,'
the ' Phœnix,' the ' Telamo,' the ' Telephus,' and the ' Thyestes,' easily connected with Greek originals, surviving or
lost, by a more or less plausible conjecture. ' Who is
there,' asks Cicero, ' such an enemy, I might almost say
to the Roman name, as to reject or slight the " Medea " of
Ennius, or the " Antiopa " of Pacuvius, because he takes

pleasure in reading their originals in Euripides?' The
appeal to patriotic feeling may pass lightly by a modern
critic: still, there is an interest in seeing how the old
Romans attempted to render in their rough barbarian
tongue the productions of the most polished age of Athens
—an interest like that which we may feel in taking up a
translation of the 'Æneid' by a writer of Queen Mary's
day, or a version of the 'Pharsalia' by a poet of the
Commonwealth. The opening lines of Ennius's 'Medea'
(they may be found, along with their Greek original,
either in Mommsen or in Mr. Sellar) are abundantly characteristic. Euripides, very naturally, makes his nurse
first wish that the Argo had never passed the Symplegades,
and then, wandering back, wish that the timber for the
oars had never been cut down. This artful inartificiality
lay apparently too deep for the old Roman; he knew that
the cutting down of the timber was really an entire link
in the chain of causation, and to talk about it late, doubtless seemed to him a mere piece of poetical refinement, so
he chose to begin *ab ovo*. So there is great *naïveté* in
the way in which he introduces the Argo, explaining, for
the benefit of his countrymen, much in the style of an
early commentator or scholiast, that she was a vessel
bearing that name, and even taking the opportunity of
imparting a scrap of etymological information: 'Argo, so
called from the eminent Argives, who sailed in her.' The
same vein of rude formality, varied occasionally by some
quaint and forcible expression, runs through the other
fragments of the play, as when he turns the simple Κοριν-
θίαι γυναῖκες into 'Quæ Corinthum arcem altam habetis,
matronæ opulentæ, optimates,' or where Medea is made to
say that this day Creon has put into her hands the bolts
and bars, and enabled her to let loose her wrath—

Ille transversa mente mihi hodie tradidit repagula,
Quibus ego iram omnem recludam, atque illi perniciem dabo,
Mihi moerorem, illi luctum, exitium illi, exilium mihi.

Another fragment, containing the opening of the last
choral ode of the play, is interesting, as apparently affording an instance of what we remarked a few pages back,
the absence of any attempt to imitate the complexity of
the Greek choric metres :—

Juppiter, tuque adeo summe Sol, qui omnes res inspicis,
Quique lumine tuo maria, terram, cœlum contines,
Inspice hoc facinus priusquam fiat, prohibessis scelus.

Here the uncertainty of the text prevents our speaking
with confidence : but the matter appears to be only the
ordinary trochaic of the tragic dialogue. Of the fragments
of Ennius's remaining tragedies, the most considerable and
important are those which belong, by assumption or by
acknowledged title, to the 'Alexander' and the 'Andromacha Æchmalotis.' We know but little of the
structure of either play, except that both formed parts of
the tale of Troy, the scene of the first being apparently
laid during the siege, that of the second during the
capture. The first is supposed to have contained that
memorable speech of Cassandra, which, in whole or in
part, is more than once quoted by Cicero. ' Why does
madness flash from thine eye?' asks Hecuba of her
daughter : ' Where is thy maiden modesty?'

Sed quid oculis rabere visa es derepente ardentibus ?
Ubi illa tua paulo ante sapiens virginalis modestia ?

We know the Cassandra of Æschylus: let us hear the
Cassandra of Ennius :—

Mater, optumarum multo melior mulier mulierum,
Missa sum superstitiosis ariolationibus :
Namque Apollo fatis fandis dementem invitam ciet.

Virgines æquales vereor, patris mei meum factum pudet,
Optumi viri.　Mea mater, tui me miseret, mei piget.
Optumam progeniem Priamo peperisti extra me : hoc dolet :
Me obesse, illos prodesse, me obstare, illos obsequi !

And then, in the midst of her self-denunciation, the pro-
phetic frenzy comes upon her ; she sees the blood-red
firebrand which symbolised her brother's birth, and calls
on the Trojans to quench it :—

Adest, adest fax obvoluta sanguine atque incendio !
Multos annos latuit : cives, ferte opem et restinguite !
 Iamque mari magno classis cita
 Texitur : exitium examen rapit :
 Advenit, et fera velivolantibus
 Navibus complevit manus litora.

A later fragment, probably from the same speech, has
been copied by Virgil in the Sixth Book of the ' Æneid,'
as it is itself doubtless copied from a passage in the
' Agamemnon : '—

Nam maxumo saltu superabit gravidus armatis equus
. . . . qui suo partu ardua perdat Pergama.

So the address of Æneas to the visionary Hector is
taken almost verbally from a speech in which one of
the sons or daughters of the royal house apostrophises
the dead body :—

O lux Trojæ, germane Hector !
. . . . quid te ita contuo lacerato corpore,
Miser, aut qui te sic tractavere nobis respectantibus ?

The longest and most noticeable fragment of the ' Andromacha ' is in the same strain. The discrowned princess,
widowed wife, and bereaved mother, is recounting what
she has had to witness :—

Quid petam præsidi, aut exequar ? quove nunc
Auxilio aut exili aut fugæ freta sim ? .

> Arce et urbe orba sum.   Quo accedam? quo applicem?
> Quoi nec arae patriae domi stant, fractae et disjectae jacent,
> Fana flamma deflagrata, tosti alti stant parietes,
>   Deformati, atque abiete crispa.
>   O pater, O patria, O Priami domus,
>   Saeptum altisono cardine templum!
>   Vidi te, astante ope barbarica,
>   Tectis caelatis, lacuatis,
>   Auro, ebore instructum regifice.
>   Haec omnia vidi inflammari,
>   Priamo vi vitam evitari,
>   Jovis aram sanguine turpari.
>
> .   .   .   .
>
> Vidi, videre quod sum passa aegerrume,
> Hectorem curru quadrijugo raptarier,
> Hectoris natum de muro jactarier.

It is to these latter lines that the present Archbishop of
Dublin, in his work on Sacred Latin Poetry, refers for the
support of a theory that something like rhyme existed in
the early poetry of Rome.   Expressed in more general
terms, the view may perhaps be thought to receive confirmation not only from this passage, but from others
which we have quoted. These old fragments contain
many instances of similarity of sound, not only in the
ending but in the beginning of words, sometimes confined
to alliteration, sometimes passing into a jingle.   Precisely
the same thing occurs in Plautus, who abounds in jingles,
not amounting to puns, or even to plays on words.   The
first rude attempts at producing rhythmical symmetry of
language coincide with the first rude attempts at producing verbal wit. In their maturity they diverge widely;
in their infancy they seem closely to approximate.

We now come to two names which are probably the
greatest in the muster-roll of Roman tragic poets. Cicero,
indeed, seems to have felt as high an admiration for
Ennius as for his successors : but a reader of Horace

would infer that the enthusiasm of Roman critics and
Roman audiences was chiefly centred on Pacuvius and
Attius. Yet in the case of M. Pacuvius, at any rate, we
appear to be stepping back from comparative light into
comparative obscurity. The aggregate of his dramatic
remains, it is true, is somewhat larger than that of Ennius's :
but they consist chiefly of single lines, and so give us but
little opportunity of judging for ourselves of his poetical
characteristics. Meantime, one or two facts of his personal history are worth a passing notice. His life, which
was a long one, falls between the years 220 and 130 B.C.
He was connected with Ennius not merely by poetical
relationship, but by the ties of blood, being, according to
the most probable accounts, his sister's son, and about
twenty years his junior. In temperament as in genius, he
appears to have been a kind of Roman Sophocles, εὔκολος
μὲν ἐνθάδ', εὔκολος δ' ἐκεῖ. He took charge of his great
kinsman's funeral ; and many years later, when he had
himself retired from the scenes of his fame, to pass his old
age in his native Brundisium, his house and heart were
open to his young rival Attius, with whom he used, as we
shall see below, to converse freely on the subject of their
common pursuit. Though he had attained renown not
only as a poet, but as the painter of a picture esteemed
only second to the great masterpiece of Fabius Pictor, he
took leave of the world in an epitaph which, in its graceful modesty, is singularly contrasted with the arrogant
self-assertion of his brother poets, simply asking the
youthful reader to stop and read his memorial stone.
After catching this brief glimpse of the man, it is mortifying to find that our knowledge of his works is so scanty,
that we cannot judge whether Varro is right in quoting
his style as an instance of luxuriance, or Fronto, in a
later day, in characterising it as a uniform level ; what

are the grounds on which Cicero charged him with
speaking bad Latin in an age when, as he says, a good
style came to men by a sort of unconscious innocence ; or
in what respect he deserved the ambiguous epithet
'doctus' applied to him, whether from his acquaintance
with Greek, or from his acquaintance with his art, by the
connoisseurs not only of Horace's time, but of Quintilian's.[1]
His plays, so far as their names have come down to us,
amount to thirteen, the 'Antiopa,' the 'Judgment of the
Arms of Achilles,' the 'Atalanta,' the 'Chryses,' the
'Dulorestes,' the 'Hermiona,' the 'Iliona,' the 'Medus,'
the 'Niptra' or 'Ablutions,' a story partly taken from the
'Odyssey,' the 'Pentheus,' the 'Periboea,' and the 'Teucer,'
together with a *praetexta* named 'Paulus,' the subject of
which is conjectured to have been the Battle of Cannae.
Those of our readers who may happen to be familiar with
the fragments of Attic tragedy, will see that each of these
plays, with the exception, of course, of the last, must have
had a Greek prototype, after which it was probably
framed. But the remains themselves, as we have just
intimated, exist in too small portions to give us any sufficient notion of the manner in which the stories were
treated, or even of their own poetical value, considered
merely as isolated passages. Like the remains of Livius
and Naevius, they are in fact not so much fragments as
dust. Yet even there, perhaps, we may find something of
interest, if we single out four of these dramas from the
rest. We have already alluded to the warm eulogium
which Cicero more than once passes on the 'Antiopa ;'
but it should not be forgotten that there was another
Roman writer who looked upon that work of ancient art

---

[1] As usual, Mommsen discriminates him from Ennius, pronouncing that
though he 'polished more carefully, and aspired to a higher strain,' 'his
language appears more rugged, his style of composition pompous and pune-
tilious.'

with very different eyes.   It is on its unfortunate heroine,
and the sorrows whose pressure bolsters up her doleful
heart, that Persius vaunts the disgust which he feels at the
revival of a taste for obsolete poetry by the *dilettanti* of
his day; and the very deformities, the warts and ulcers,
which she is supposed to have contracted in the course of
her unwholesome captivity, are used to symbolise the
quaintnesses of language which are considered to disfigure the style of the old poet.   This diversity of judgment, however, tells us nothing about the character of the
play; it merely indicates a diversity of taste among the
judges, just as the same peculiar features which repel one
reader of our own Elizabethan drama attract another.
Of the fragments themselves, the most noticeable is one
quoted, though not *in extenso*, by Cicero, in the second
book of the 'De Divinatione,' as an instance of the obscurity with which a plain thing can be invested.
Amphion is speaking of a quadruped : slow-footed, field-
loving, low of stature, rough of skin, with a short head, a
snake's neck, a fierce look, with no entrails, and no
animal life, and yet with an animal's voice.   The
chorus of citizens tell him that he has guarded his
meaning with so strong a force of language, 'ita
sæptuosa dictione,' as effectually to exclude conjecture,
and that if he would be understood he must speak
plainly.   He then utters the name *tortoise*.   'Why
should not the harper have called it a tortoise at once,
instead of making such a mystery of it ?' asks Cicero
impatiently.   Where we have so few data, it would be
hazardous to attempt to answer the question ; but the
passage seems to be not a mere piece of circumlocution,
but a riddle, like that of the Sphinx, Amphion describing
his tortoise-shell lyre, not very consistently, partly by the
properties of the lion tortoise, partly as what it is when,
in the language of Shelley's version of Homer's 'Hymn to

Mercury,' 'the life and soul have been bored out of the
beast,' and it has been 'made to sing.' There is, in fact,
something in the humour with which the thought is
played with, which may remind us, as it was perhaps
intended to do, of the Homeric Hermes when he first
views the tortoise :—

> A useful godsend are you to me now,
>   King of the dance, companion of the feast,
> Lovely in all your nature! Welcome you
>   Excellent plaything! where, sweet mountain beast,
> Got you that speckled shell? Thus much I know,
>   You must come home with me and be my guest :
> You will give joy to me, and I will do
>   All that is in my power to honour you.
> Better to be at home than out-of-door :
>   So come with me ; and though it has been said
> That you alive defend from magic power,
>   I know you will sing sweetly when you're dead.

This parallel may console us for the utter absence of
anything salient in the few other remains of this once
celebrated play. The only one which calls for even a
passing notice is a line containing the expression 'flori
crines,' locks of bright bloomy hue, a reading which, if
the authority of Probus the grammarian is to be held
paramount, ought to take its place in a passage in the
Twelfth Book of the 'Æneid,' where we now read of the
yellow hair, *flori crines*, of the fair Lavinia. We pass on
to two plays which appear to have been connected in
subject, the 'Dulorestes' and the 'Chryses.' The title of
the former play, which seems to have been afterwards
borrowed by Varro for one of his 'Saturæ Menippeæ,'
'Agatho Dulorestes,' is still a perplexity to critics, who
cannot decide between Δολορίστης and Δουλορίστης,
Orestes practising a stratagem on Thoas, and Orestes

appearing, on some unspecified occasion, in the character
of a slave. The subject of the play was the same as that
of the 'Iphigenia in Tauris:' the brother and his friend
come to the Chersonese, where the sister is priestess, and
instead of being offered up by her as human sacrifices,
persuade her to elude her master and return with them.
Cicero more than once mentions the tumultuous applause
which invariably arose in the theatre during the thrilling
scene when the king has the two friends in his power, but
cannot tell which is Orestes, his intended victim, and each
asserts, drowning as it were the other's voice, that he is
the man; till at last, neither being able to prevail, they
entreat to be put to death together. 'It was a mere
histrionic fiction,' says he, 'yet the audience rose to their
feet and clapped.' With that exception, the remnants of
the play are quotations for mere lexicographical purposes,
made by Nonius, Festus, and Priscian, illustrating the use
of such words as *orbitudo, vanitudo, prolixitudo, temeri-*
tudo, fatiscor for *fatisco,* and *adjutor* for *adjuto.* The
only one to which we now refer is one of several
passages, in which the Roman writers as it were turn
commentators on their own language, and explain the
difference between *pigere* and *pudere*: ' Piget paternum
nomen, maternum pudet profari:' 'My father's name I
cannot tell for sorrow, my mother's for shame.' The
'Chryses' was a sequel to the 'Duloreotes,' and on the
Greek stage would doubtless have formed part of the
same tetralogy. The play was probably modelled on a
lost work of Sophocles, bearing the same name; the
story seems to have been preserved by Hyginus. The
fugitives, escaping from the Tauric Chersonese, take
refuge in the Isle of Chryse, known to all readers of the
First Iliad, as the home of the priest Chryses. Thither
they are pursued by Thoas, who requires their surrender.

But they have found a friend who can help them. Chryseis, so runs the post-Homeric legend, after her return to her father, was delivered of a son, who received his grandfather's name, and was brought up as the child of Apollo. He assists his new relatives against their enemy, and Thoas is killed. Yet here, as elsewhere, the fragments help us but little towards the story. The most memorable are one or two preserved by Cicero, on the subject of divination and physical philosophy; taken, it has been conjectured, from a dialogue between Orestes and the elder Chryses. One of these is a sneer at augury, such as the old poets were fond of indulging, the point being, that those who learn more from the inwards of others than from their own, ought to be heard rather than heeded :—

> Isti qui linguam avium intelligunt
> Plusque ex alieno jecore sapiunt quam ex suo,
> Magis audiendum quem auscultandum censeo.

Another speaks of the all-embracing sky as the source of all being :—

> Hoc vide, circum supraque quod complexu continet
> Terram
> Soliaque exortu capessit candorem, occasu nigret,
> Id quod nostri cælum memorant, Graii perhibent æthera :
> Quidquid est hoc, omnia animat, format, alit, auget, creat,
> Sepelit, recipit in sese omnia, omniumque idem est pater,
> Indidemque eadem quæ oriuntur, de integro æquo eodem
>   incidunt.

The last play we shall notice, the 'Niptra,' contains, as we have said, part of the history of Ulysses. It appears partly to have coincided with the end of the 'Odyssey,' partly to have carried on the narrative further. Like the 'Chryses,' it had its origin in a drama of Sophocles, the second title of which, Ὀδυσσεὺς ἀκανθοπλήξ, points to the post-Homeric part of the story. Ulysses arrives at his home, as in Homer, and is recognised by his nurse as she assists him in the bath. In lines which Gellius justly characterises as delightful, she invites the stranger to submit to those offices which she had so often paid to her old master :—

Cedo tamen pedem tuum lymphis flavis, flavum ut pulverem
Manibus isdem, quibus Ulyssi sæpe permulsi, abluam ;
Lassitudinemque minuam manuum mollitudine.

We may wonder at the notion of colour which chooses the same word, *flavus*—a mixture, so Fronto in Gellius lays down, of green, red, and white—to represent both the hue of the water that cleanses, and that of the dust that is cleansed, but it can be no surprise to us that the passage should have been thought graceful and pleasing. Another line apparently tells of the qualities which enable Euryclea to identify the wanderer with Ulysses :—

Lenitudo orationis, mollitudo corporis.

Afterwards, through what steps we know not, the story changes. Telegonus, the son of Ulysses by Circe, comes to Ithaca to seek his father, and wounds him ignorantly in a chance encounter, with a spear barbed with a fish-bone. 'He met our lance,' cries the wounded hero, 'with a noxious barbaric weapon, made of a strange shape, and put together by no skilful hand.' In the rest of the play we hear the complaints of the sufferer in his agony, reminding us of those of his old enemy Philoctetes, or of Hercules in the 'Trachiniæ.' 'Take me up gently,' he says,

Pedetentim ac sedato nisu,
Ne succussu arripiat major
Dolor.

And then, as the pain masters him, he shrieks aloud, and
begs to be left alone :—

> Retinete, tenete! opprimite ulcus,
> Nudate! heu miserum me, excrucior!
>   Operite, abscedite jamjam.
> Mittite : nam attrectatu et quassu
>   Sævum amplificatis dolorem.

Elsewhere, however, he rises superior to his anguish,
observing, when he is dying, that complaint is the natural
utterance for a man, lamentation for a woman; a contrast, Cicero seems to say, to the hero of Sophocles,
whose exclamations were less manly, or at any rate
were not met by the chorus in the same spirit of stoical
reproof.

The fragments of Pacuvius's nameless plays, though
not numerous, contain two passages of greater length
than any that are to be found among his other remains.
We will only quote one of them, the description of the
Greeks on their voyage home from Troy, to which we
alluded in speaking of Livius. At first they amuse themselves with looking at the fish that sport about the vessel;
but a storm soon gathers :

> Profectione læti piscium lasciviam
> Intuentur, nec tuendi capere satietas potest.
> Interea prope jam occidente sole inhorrescit mare,
> Tenebræ conduplicantur, noctisque et nimbum occæcal nigror,
> Flamma inter nubes coruscat, cœlum tonitru contremit,
> Undique omnes venti erumpunt, sævi existunt turbines,
> Fervit æstu pelagus.

But it is time to hasten to the last name on our
list.

Of the life of L. Attius we know less than that of his
predecessor, though he belonged to the next generation,

the date of his birth being B.C. 170, and survived into
the days of Cicero, who, as a young man, frequently
conversed with him. As a compensation for this slender-
ness of information, however, we have a clearer view of
his labours as an author, which appear to have been
nearly as various as those of Ennius, including not only
tragedies and *prætextæ*, but a historical epic like Ennius's,
with the same title, 'Annales,' and three prose works,
'Libri Didascalion,' apparently a history of poetry,
'Libri Pragmaticon,' and 'Parerga.' So, when we come
to his actual remains, we find that, as far at least as
mere quantity goes, time has dealt more kindly with him
than with his brethren, sparing us very nearly seven
hundred lines. It is in his relics alone that we find any
considerable fragment of a *prætexta*. He is known to
have written at least two plays of that description, the
'Æneadæ' or 'Decius,' and the 'Brutus,' the subject of
the last being the elder Brutus, the hero of the Regifuge,
though it is possible, as has been suggested, that he may
have intended to compliment another of the family,
D. Brutus, his own friend and patron. From the
'Brutus' Cicero has extracted two speeches, one of King
Tarquin recounting an alarming dream, the other of the
soothsayer giving the explanation. The king has
dreamed of a flock of sheep, from which he chose two
rams for sacrifice. He had slain one, when the other
ran at him, and butted him to the ground, and as he lay
there wounded, he saw the sun change his course and
move from left to right. This he tells in iambics; the
answer is in trochaics, and is not without interest, philosophical as well as poetical, attempting, as it does, to give
some sort of theory of dreams, which are said to arise
generally from natural causes, but which in some cases
are supernatural :—

Rex, quæ in vita usurpant homines, cogitant, curant, vident,
Quæque agunt vigilantes agitantque, ea si cui in somno ac-
    cidunt,
Minus mirum est; sed di rem tantam haud temere improviso
    offerunt.
Proin vide, ne quem tu esse hebetem deputes æque ac pecus,
Is sapientia munitum pectus egregie gerat
Teque regno expellat : nam id quod de sole ostentum est tibi,
Populo commutationem rerum portendit tibi,
Perpropinquam. Hæc bene verruncent populo! Nam quod
    dexterum
Cepit cursum ab læva signum præpotens, pulcherrime
Auguratum est rem Romanam publicam summam fore.

A curious story, whether authentic or no, is preserved
by Gellius, showing Attius's opinion of the character of
his own genius. We give it as translated by Mr. Sellar :—
‘ When Pacuvius, at a great age, and suffering from a
disease of long standing, had retired from Rome to Tarentum, Attius, at that time a considerably younger man,
on his journey to Asia, arrived at that town, and stayed
with Pacuvius. And being kindly entertained, and constrained to stay for several days, he read to him, at his
request, his tragedy of "Atreus." Then, as the story
goes, Pacuvius said that what he had written appeared
to him sonorous and elevated, but somewhat harsh and
crude. "It is just as you say," replied Attius ; "and in
truth I am not sorry for it, for I hope that I shall write
better in future; for they say that the same law holds
good in genius as in fruit. Fruits which are originally
harsh and sour afterwards become mellow and pleasant,
but those which have a soft and withered look, and are
very juicy at first, become soon rotten without ever
becoming ripe. It appears, accordingly, that there should
be left something in genius also for the mellowing influence of years and time."'

It would be interesting if we could verify this piece of self-criticism by an appeal to Attius's writings, and see whether his somewhat complacent anticipation can take rank as a fulfilled prediction. Here, however, as elsewhere, the state of our knowledge leaves us quite at fault. The names of no less than forty-five of his tragedies have been preserved—a number which, even if reduced, as a searching criticism would perhaps reduce it, by ten, will still be very considerable; but, except from Gellius' story, we appear to have no external means of ascertaining the time at which any of them were composed, and the remains themselves are not sufficiently speaking to give any evidence of their own age or youthfulness. We question, indeed—and here we are glad to find ourselves in agreement with Mr. Sellar—whether, to a modern apprehension, there is any sensible distinction between the style of Attius and his predecessor and critic; whether to one whose eyes were bandaged, the harsh fruit would not taste merely the same as the mellow; though Mommsen, of course, finds Attius's imitations 'more readable and adroit.' Each individual, doubtless, had critical stages in his own poetical life; each individual, doubtless, stood in some marked relation to his predecessors and successors, and to the other poets of his age. But at the point of view which we occupy, these minor differences between writer and writer, much more between a writer and himself, are no longer perceptible. Distance has done much to confound them; mediæval oblivion has all but swept away their very data. To us the old tragic poets are themselves but a single critical stage in the poetical life of their nation, their productions, one and all, impregnated by the same flavour of harshness, which was to find its season of mellowing, not in the lifetime of any one of

themselves, but in the ripe period of the Roman mind—
the Augustan era of Horace and Virgil.

But though we cannot compare the 'Atreus' of Attius
with its younger brothers and sisters, we have a few
glimmering lights which show us something of what it
was in itself. The savage nature of the hero is dwelt on
again and again by Cicero, with whom he is a type of
imperious cruelty—the gloomy tyrant of the Roman
stage. We are admitted to his confidence, and hear his
plans of vengeance against his brother, who has once
more roused the sleeping tiger within him :—

> Iterum Thyestes Atreum adtractatum advenit,
> Iterum jam aggreditur me et quietum exsuscitat :
> Major mihi moles, majus miscendum est malum,
> Qui illius acerbum cor contundam et comprimam.

The same or a similar speech contained the words which,
by frequent quotation, have passed into a proverb,
'Oderint dum metuant '—a sentiment which, says Seneca,
fathers itself at once on a contemporary of Sulla, but
which may also remind a modern reader of times nearer
to Seneca's own. But we are not left to think of Atreus
as a mere monster of cruelty ; we are bidden to recollect
that he is a man who has been deeply wronged as a
brother, a husband, and a king. He speaks of Thyestes
as one who was not content with seducing his wife ; he
lays stress on the adultery itself, as a crime especially
perilous in high places, and on the public evil to be
apprehended from any tampering with the royal stock ;
and he shows that his throne was menaced by the adul-
terous pair, who stole from him the golden lamb, the
heaven-sent Palladium of the kingdom. On the other
side we have the thoughts of Thyestes, by his own
showing, at least, even then a man more sinned against

than sinning, who by a stroke of tragic irony is represented as warning his children of the many snares that are laid for the good, and of the danger to a private man of sitting at meat with a king. We catch a glimpse of the bloody preparations for the feast; we hear the floor of heaven shaken with a sudden thunder-peal, 'tonitru turbida torvo;' Atreus tells the wretched father that he is himself his children's grave, and retorts the charge of broken faith by saying that there is no faith with the faithless; and then we listen to Thyestes as he recurs to the monstrous horror of the situation, a brother inducing a father to close his teeth on the flesh of his own sons, and asks what hope for the future there can be for one so steeped in pollution as himself:—

Egone Argivum imperium attingam aut Pelopia digner domo?
Quo me ostendam? quod templum adeam? quem ore funesto
alloquar?

Out of the remaining forty-four plays of Attius, we can afford only to pick an isolated fragment here and there.

Here is a specimen of that grammarian spirit which we have noted once or twice already in his predecessors, the spirit of men who feel themselves to be not only poets but writers, endeavouring to inform the heads of their countrymen as well as to move their hearts. Achilles is lecturing Antilochus on the difference between 'pervicacia' and 'pertinacia:'—

Tu pertinaciam esse, Antiloche, hanc praedicas:
Ego pervicaciam aio, et ea me uti volo:
Nam pervicacem dici me esse et vincere (vincier?)
Perfacile patior, pertinacem nil moror:
Haec fortes sequitur, illam indocti possident.
Tu addis quod vitio est, demis quod laudi datur.

In a single line we are told how to distinguish ' animus '
and ' anima : '—

Sapimus animo, fruimur anima : sine animo anima est debilis.

Here is a picture of the Argo, the first ship, drawn by
a shepherd who has seen it from a mountain :—

> Tanta moles labitur
> Fremebundo ex alto, ingenti sonitu et spiritu.
> Prœ se undas volvit, vortices vi suscitat :
> Ruit prolapsa, pelagus respergit, reflat.
> Ita dum interruptum credas nimbum labier,
> Dum quod sublime ventis expulsum rapi
> Saxum, aut procellis, vel globosos turbines
> Existere ictos undis concursantibus :
> Nisi quas terrestris pontus strages conciet ;
> Aut forte Triton fuscina evertens specus
> Subter radices penitus undanti in freto
> Molem ex profundo saxeam in cælum eruit.

The four following lines describe daybreak and its
occupations with a circumstantial minuteness which
in a modern poet would be tedious and ungraceful,
but in Attius is merely characteristic of antique simplicity :—

> Forte ante auroram, radiorum ardentum indicem,
> Cum e somno in segetem agrestes cornutos cient,
> Ut rorulentas terras ferro rufidas
> Proscindant, glebas molli ex arvo exsuscitent.

Lastly, here are some anapæsts from the ' Philoctetes,'
the first passage, an address to Ulysses, the second, part
of a description of Lemnos, the island of Vulcan :—

> Inclute, parva prodite patria,
> Nomine celebri claroque potens
> Pectore, Achivis classibus auctor,
> Gravis Dardaniis gentibus ultor,
>   Laertiade !

>   ·   ·   ·   ·   ·

Nemus expirante vapore vides,
Unde ignis cluet mortalibus olam
Divisus ; eum dictus Prometheus
Clepsisse dolo, pœnasque levi
Fato expendisse supremo.

In taking leave of these old tragedies, we will say a very few words on one point to which we have not yet adverted, the metre of the dialogue.

So far as we can follow Horace's not very intelligible account of the iambic trimeter, it would appear that he regarded it as having been gradually encroached upon by spondees, which, having been duly admitted into the first, third, and fifth of the six places in the verse, pushed their inroads further, so as to take possession of all but the last. Such a representation would not be true of the Greek iambic, which found no difficulty in keeping the spondees within bounds, though in the hands of the comic writers it was overrun by anapæsts ; but it may, perhaps, stand if we place together the experience of one language with the experience of another. Under the Romans, spondees seem to have asserted their title to the first five places of the trimeter from the very outset, and the result of the progress of tragic versification was not to extend (if indeed extension had been possible), but to contract their province, and to re-establish the Greek type substantially as it had existed in the days of Euripides. Perhaps it might be too much to say, that the iambic trimeter and trochaic tetrameter of early Roman tragedy are absolutely identical with those of Roman comedy ; yet they bear a strong resemblance to each other, not only as regards the nature of the fact admitted, but in the licenses of pronunciation allowed. Some of the lines which we quoted a short time back, 'Cœlo tamen pedem tuum lymphis flavis, flavum ut pulverem,' for instance, can only be received by an application of the Plautine and Terentian license, which makes 'meus,' ' tuus,' &c., monosyllables. The elision of the final 's,' though, of course, not peculiar to early dramatic poetry, points to the same thing, the assimilation of poetical recitations in those times to the ordinary pronunciation. The early Roman writers had doubtless no wish to confound tragedy and comedy, though they themselves produced either indifferently; they were not likely to have dreamed of the approximation between the two, which we mentioned at the opening of our remarks as having gradually taken place in Greece; but the accidents of their age and position led them unconsciously in the same direction, and their own imperfection as workmen prevented them from perceiving critically where they did not feel intuitively. Euripides, the chief agent in what may be called the secularisation of Greek tragedy, ventured on one occasion to break through the courtesies of scenic illusion, which ignore the spectators, and to make a tragic chorus address the audience in the name of the author of the play, after the manner of its comic counterpart. May we not recognise the same tendency in the custom which, as we learn from Horace and Quintilian, prevailed on the Roman stage, of closing tragedy and comedy alike with the emphatic *Plaudite?*

We must now return to Ennius, by far the greater part of our debt to whom still remains unpaid. As a tragedian he is only one among several, and not the greatest of the number: as an epic poet he filled a place in the minds of his countrymen somewhat analogous to, though of course not commensurate with, that occupied in Greece by Homer himself. However modern critics may adjust precedence among writers whose works they

have not read, there can be no question that he was
generally regarded by the Romans as the true founder
of their national poetry, 'the morning-star of song.'
Those who went before him he himself relegates to a
period when poetry had not yet been conceived of as an
art, 'when no one had scaled the crags of the Musea,
or was studious of speech;' and no attempt seems to have
been seriously made to disturb his verdict.   Cicero, perhaps the only ancient writer from whom a word can be
quoted in favour of Nævius as against his rival, is the
one whose voice is raised most consistently and emphatically to eulogise Ennius, our Ennius, the first of epic
poets; the man who celebrated our great ancestors, and
whom they in turn delighted to honour.   The title of the
second Homer, instanced by Horace as a specimen of
the criticism of his time upon Ennius, is a witness to the
admiration entertained for him by Lucilius.   Lucretius,
standing on the threshold of his own great poem, speaks
of Ennius as the first who brought from Helicon a
garland of unfading leaf to be had in renown among the
nations of Italy, and in questioning his doctrines declares
the verses in which they are enshrined to be eternal.
Propertius contrasts his own luxuriant ivy with the
austere laurels of Ennius; but such language is no more
than he bestows generally on writers whose subjects and
mode of treatment were severer than his own: and he
elsewhere tells of himself as having drunk at the same
spring with the father of verse, who rose from that
draught to sing of the Curii and Horatii, of the trophies
of Æmilius and the delays of Fabius, of the blow received at Cannæ, and the bowing of the will of heaven
by prayer, of the Lares that put Hannibal to flight, and
the geese that saved Capitolian Jove.   Ovid and Horace,
while impelled by a spirit perhaps of rivalry, perhaps

only of reasonable self-assertion, to contend that the old
bard's poems had no right to be regarded as the consummation of Roman art, are nevertheless not unwilling
to pay the homage demanded by so great a name, the
one conceding to the man of genius what he denies to
the artist, the other, in a passage whose apparent historical inaccuracy has been a standing difficulty to criticism, affirming that the fame of the African conqueror is
due not more to the burning of Carthage than to the muses
of Calabria. And though the sneer of Martial at those
who would read Ennius when they could read Virgil,
shows that the feud between the old and the new was
not confined to the Augustan age, we find that even in
the time of Gellius, an itinerant lecturer on Ennius, an
'Enniapista,' as he called himself, after the manner of
the Homeristæ, could command an audience, and that a
copy of the 'Annals,' of accredited authority, was procured at great expense, for the purpose of verifying the
reading of a single line. With such a chain of testi-
monials before him, a scholar may be excused if he
takes up the language of Scaliger, and complains, like
Priam, of the fortune of war which has destroyed the
hero of the family, and left so many of his less noble
brethren. We feel that for us the great year of Roman
poetry has lost its spring; and some sense of our loss
remains with us as we gaze on the meridian glow of
its fervid summer, or the hectic tints of its decaying
autumn.

Before we speak of the author and of the remains of
his works, the history of those remains deserves a few
words of notice. It is mortifying to think that a copy
of the poems of Ennius appears to have existed till
within a comparatively recent period. We cannot indeed
point to the precise part of the ocean where the vessel

went down, but we know where she was last spoken
with.   A catalogue of the date of the thirteenth century,
appended to a MS. of Statius in a library at Prague,
mentions copies of Ennius and Nævius; and a poet of
the same period, Alanus de Insula, a Scotchman, in his
'Anti-Claudianus,' talks of Ennius in his ragged plebeian
garb, thundering out the fortunes of Priam, as if his
knowledge of the old bard rested on something better
than hearsay.   It was an age when classical taste, which
had begun to show signs of life, again became nearly
extinct, the thick darkness which set in before the dawn;
and that it should willingly have let die an author whom
of all others Cicero would have struggled to save, is only
a single charge towards its condemnation.   At the revival of learning we hear only of the fragments of
Ennius; they began, however, to attract attention early
in the sixteenth century; and Ludovicus Vives, the
eminent Spaniard who taught Latin at Oxford, announced
a purpose of collecting and editing them.   The first who
actually performed that task were Robert and Henry
Stephens, in their collection of the 'Fragments of the
Ancient Latin Poets,' published at Paris in 1564.   Thirty-
six years later, a more elaborate edition was brought out
by an Italian, Hieronymus Columna, whose industry as a
collector of the fragments appears to have been sufficiently
praiseworthy, though unfortunately not equalled by his
sagacity in restoring their text or assigning to them their
probable places in the lost poems.   The next adventure
was at once more ambitious and less respectable.   Advantage was taken of the name of Ennius to propagate a
daring and ingenious forgery.   In 1595, Paulus Merula,
a Dutch jurisconsult, published at Leyden the fragments
of Ennius's 'Annals' in a corrected, rearranged, and en-
larged form, the main feature of his edition consisting of

some additional remains, recovered, as he professed, from
a treatise by L. Calpurnius Piso, addressed to the Emperor Trajan, 'On the Contents (continentia) of the
Ancient Poets.' This valuable repertory of quotations
had been examined by him, according to his statement,
in the library of St. Victor at Paris, where it had once
formed part of the same volume with a MS. of Lucan,
but had afterwards been separated from it; and now, he
declared, it was in great danger of being stolen.   On
examination, it appeared that the probability had become
a certainty; Piso's treatise had vanished, while the mutilated volume remained; and the latter part of the
discovery at any rate has apparently been accepted, even
by some recent critics, as an evidence of the general
truth of the story, though, when rigorously examined, it
seems not to be worth much more than the attestation of
the bricks in the chimney to Jack Cade's account of his
parentage.   Modern opinion appears to have decided
that Merula's anticipation was a prediction after the fact,
and that he was really both his own Piso and his own
Ennius; at the same time that we must confess with
Niebuhr that the forgery is executed with considerable
plausibility, and that the verses, if not such as Ennius
must have written, are such as he might have written.
After Merula, we find no name of any great importance,
real or fictitious, among the editors of Ennius, till we
come to Vahlen, whose edition we have already commemorated, and are glad once more to recommend to
our readers for carefulness in collecting the fragments,
labour in ascertaining their text according to the best
MSS. of the various authors who have preserved them,
and general good judgment in arranging them in their
places and establishing the main outlines of the lost
work.   Our own obligations to it have been very great,

and the sketch which we are about to give of the probable form and contents of Ennius's poems will be made up, we may say, exclusively from its materials.

First, however, we must briefly sketch the chief particulars that are known about the poet himself. The authorities for his history are rather various than copious; the fullest and in every way the most satisfactory being Cicero, whose notices have to be supplemented by the more equivocal testimony of later compilers, grammatical or historical.

Q. Ennius was born in the year B.C. 239, in the consulship of C. Mamilius Turrinus and Q. Valerius Falto, the year after poetry, as Cicero expresses it, had been introduced into Rome by the representations of the first drama of Livius Andronicus. His place of birth was Rudiæ (not Rudia), a village in the Calabrian hills; a fact established by the more or less distinct witness of various authors, including his own, as against Eusebius, who makes him to have been born at Tarentum. Calabria was formerly known as Messapia; and Ennius used to assert his descent from the eponymous hero Messapus, the 'Messapus equum domitor' of Virgil, who is said by Servius to have alluded to this claim in the passage of the Seventh Book of the 'Æneid' (vv. 698 foll.), where he introduces the followers of Messapus singing of their king as they marched, like long-necked swans. Silius Italicus represents him as serving in Sardinia under Manlius Torquatus, against the combined army of Sardinians and Carthaginians, at a time when he must have been about four-and-twenty; and, though the circumstances of the description are doubtless wholly due to that frigid imitator of Virgil, that seems no reason why the nucleus round which they cluster may not have been derived from a tradition of whatever value. Fifteen or twenty years

later he appears to have been still in Sardinia, if we may
trust the shadowy and somewhat conflicting authorities of
Cornelius Nepos and Aurelius Victor, from which we
gather that he then became connected with Cato, whether
during Cato's African quæstorship or Sicilian prætorship is
not clear, and was brought by him to Rome. In his
fifty-first year we find him attached to another eminent
man, Fulvius Nobilior, who took him with him on his
Ætolian campaign, and afterwards marked his recollection
of the companionship by making an offering to the Muses
out of the spoils of the victory. At a later period he
became a Roman citizen, through the instrumentality of
the son of Nobilior, who had been appointed a triumvir
for founding a colony, and availed himself of the opportunity to gratify his father's friend and his own. Meanwhile Ennius was living in a house on the Aventine, on
very restricted means, with the attendance of a single
female slave, reading with pupils Greek authors and his
own Latin compositions, and enjoying the intimacy of his
aristocratic friends, in particular of the family of the
Scipios. There he seems to have died, at the age of
seventy, of a complaint described as a disease of the
joints, probably gout—the result, it would appear, of that
habit of drunkenness, for which he is noted in the well-
known passage of Horace. The great Africanus ordered
his remains to be interred in his sepulchre, the famous
tomb of the Scipios; and there in the time of Livy were
to be seen three statues, those of the hero and of his
brother and of the poet whom they loved, standing
outside the gate of Capena.

Ennius used to say that he had three hearts, because
he knew three languages, Greek, Latin, and Oscan. The
expression is a fine one, though we must not interpret it
by our modern associations, remembering that with the

older Romans the heart was the seat of the intellect; and the boast which it symbolises is one which, if uttered with truth, might well be regarded as marking him out to be the father of Roman poetry, the man in whose capacious mind the language of Rome could take hold at once of the past and of the future, reaching out on the one hand to its early Italian cognate, and on the other to the great depository of foreign thought and feeling. Yet there were not wanting in his day men who, if they had chosen to adopt his metaphor, might have said of him that the Roman heart beat too feebly, the Greek too strongly. He lived at a time when the enthusiasm for Greek culture was forcing its way step by step against the exclusive national spirit, and the student of foreign training was perhaps in danger of being considered an enemy to his land's language. Cato, who, ' if we have writ our annals true,' had been Ennius's original patron, and who, according to a less probable part of the same story, condescended to learn Greek of him, afterwards attacked Fulvius Nobilior, with whose proceedings in Ætolia he had been in some way brought into contact, on the special ground that he had taken a poet with him into his province. The antagonism was not merely between the poetical Greek and the unpoetical Roman. There was an old school of poetry which had to yield to a new one; the Italian Camenæ were to give way to the Grecian Muses. Before Ennius appeared at Rome, Nævius the Campanian had been established there, and had obtained a name as a dramatic poet; but he had recently retired into banishment at Utica, if indeed he was not already dead. We know too little of his life or of his works to be justified in comparing him formally with his successor in poetical fame, though there are one or two faint traits which suggest the notion of a contrast. Both had seen

service in the army, Nævius having fought in the first
Punic War, as Ennius in the second ; but there the resemblance ceases.   Nævius was a plebeian, and stood by his
order, impugning the virtue of the great Scipio, and
telling the Metelli that they owed their repeated consul-
ships not to merit, but to destiny ; a license of tongue
which led, first to an imprisonment of sufficient length to
allow him to compose two of his dramas, and afterwards
to the exile in which he ended his days.   Ennius, as we
have seen, was the friend of the great, not necessarily
compromising his own independence, but willing to link
his name to theirs, and to include their praises in the
poems in which he celebrated the noble deeds of the
worthies of other times ; a type of the Roman author as
he was to be, a member of that fraternity which Horace,
many years later, could describe as absorbed in composition, and estranged from worldly cares, and Juvenal as
dependent on patronage, and labouring on in obscurity,
sustained by the hope of earning the ivy-wreath and the
bust.   As poets, they appear to have come into collision
in the field, not of the drama, but of the epic.   Their
tragedies, as we have seen, belong to the same school.
In the main, they are apparently translations or adaptations from the Greek ; Greek in their metre no less than
in their subject and treatment.   But in his exile Nævius
solaced his latest years by a composition of a different
kind, recording the stirring scenes of which he had
himself borne a part in a heroic poem on the first Punic
War.   The scope of the narrative is almost wholly
unknown to us, though it would seem not to have been
unmixed with Greek mythological legends ; but the
metre was at any rate national and Italian, the Saturnian
verse, ' the large utterance of the elder gods ' and demi-
gods of rural Italy ; in more historical times, the measure

of its ballad poetry, if it had any, and of what was
perhaps as yet its most elaborate composition in verse,
the 'Odyssey' of Livius Andronicus.   But when Ennius
entered the field with his national poem, which was to
surpass the ' Punic War,' both in the scope and magnitude
of its subject and in the skill of its treatment, he chose a
new metre, a long measure, as he calls it himself, the
Hexameter of Homer and the Grecian Epic ; and he is
known to have stigmatised the verses of his predecessor,
in a passage to which we have already alluded more than
once, as effusions like those of the old forest gods, made
by men who had never accomplished the ascent of the
true Parnassus.   He had not overrated the importance of
a change, which, it may be said without exaggeration,
was destined to revolutionise the whole structure of
Roman poetry.   Superficial observers are apt to treat
the influence of metre with comparative indifference, as
involving the mere outward form of poetry ; but a more
careful analysis will show that though the soul of verse
is doubtless originally separable from its body, the latter
is not a bare husk, to be assumed or thrown off at
pleasure, but a part of an organised whole, modified and
modifying in turn, and clinging to its partner with a
tenacious vitality, which criticism, in attempting to disentangle, is apt to destroy.   The language reacts on the
thought, which, in taking shape, is obliged to part with
something of its own, and accept something extraneous
and accidental ; and the metre exercises a similar constraint on the language, enforcing the substitution of one
word for another, and thus producing a still further
departure from the precise character of the conception
originally formed by the mind.   This second bondage
makes itself felt much more in ancient than in modern
metres, in proportion as the rule of quantity is more

scorchingly oppressive than the rule of accent. Probably
the hexameter itself was a more rigorous master to the
poet who accepted it than the Saturnian verse, which,
though it may not have dispensed with quantity, yet
seems to have admitted great varieties of structure; at
any rate, it must have been found sufficiently exacting,
even by those whom use or superior aptitude had taught
best to comply with its humours, as perhaps the experience of some of our readers may enable them to
understand. There is a work by a German scholar,
Köne, 'On the Language and Metre of the Roman Epic
Writers,' the object of which is to show that the introduction of the hexameter was an unfortunate innovation,
alien from the genius of the language, which had already
cast most of its words into moulds suited to other metres,
iambic or trochaic, and so tending of itself to produce an
unreal and artificial style, where words are distorted into
strange forms, or exchanged for inadequate synonyms,
where the grammatical proprieties of declensions and
tenses are sacrificed for metrical convenience, and rhythm
itself has to be violated in order to avoid unlawful sounds.
Without going to this length, or speculating whether the
Saturnian metre could have been made to bear the weight
which, at whatever cost of straining or even cracking,
was borne by the hexameter, we may still believe that
Ennius's innovation was, as we have said, little less than
revolutionary, and that in persuading the poets of his
country to submit to a new law, he was really exercising
an influence, unmistakeable, if not fully appreciable, on
the language and thought of succeeding generations.
The effect produced by the matter of his poetry, we must
be content to take mainly on trust; what he accomplished
by the form, we are able to estimate for ourselves.
Those who are most inclined to feel aggrieved at the

severity of the rule under which he laid his successors,
may be consoled by thinking that he appears to have
suffered from it himself, while the *naïve* directness of his
efforts to get relief, so unlike the artificial expedients of a
later day, may excite a smile, as when he makes a tmesis
which, as Servius, the commentator, truly says, though
tolerable in a compound word, is ' nimis asperum ' in a
simple, ' saxo *cere*-comminuit-*brum*,' or where, by a
dangerous extension of the figure apocope, he reduces
well-known substantives to monosyllabic crude forms,
' divum domus altisonum *cæl*,' ' replet te lætificum *gau*.'
It is the same even-handed justice which overtook the
Greek dithyrambic poet :—

> Οἵ τ' αὐτῷ κακὰ τεύχει ἀνὴρ ἄλλῳ κακὰ τεύχων.
> Ἡ δὲ μακρὰ 'ποβολὴ τῷ ποιήσαντι κακίστη.

Niebuhr confesses that, much as he likes the ' numeri '
and ' sales ' of Plautus, he cannot be pleased with the
hexameters of Ennius ; and certainly it seems difficult to
see how they could please anyone whose ear has been
accustomed to the cadence, we do not say of Virgil, but
of Lucretius or Catullus. They are, indeed, very similar
in structure, if not in their quantities, to a boy's first
attempts at school ; and, like some of the early poetry of
our own country, may seem to suggest a theory that the
progress of versifying in a nation is after all much the
same as in an individual. Yet it is through such rudimentary stages that excellence is at last attained ; and as
a student working with a model before him cannot hope
to attain perfection in a day, so the task of bringing that
model to perfection is not to be completed in a single
lifetime, but has to be elaborated by generations of
successive artists

But it is time that we should redeem our promise of

giving some account of the various works which Ennius
is known to have left behind him, so far as it is possible
to form an estimate of their character from the fragments
or other notices which have been preserved to us.   These
works, according to Vahlen, fall under nine heads, though
in the scantiness of our information even their number is
not placed beyond the reach of controversy.   First comes
the *opus magnum*—the 'Annals,' which were in eighteen
books; next his dramatic works, consisting of the tragedies
which we have already discussed, and two or three
comedies; six books of satires; some epigrams or inscriptions, three of which have come down to us; a poem
called 'Sota,' from the Sotadic verse in which it was composed; 'Protrepticus,' apparently a collection of precepts
in verse; 'Hedyphagetica,' a poem on eatable fishes;
'Epicharmus,' probably a poetical exposition of Pytha-
gorean philosophy; and, lastly, 'Euhemerus,' a translation of the sacred history of that well-known mythological rationaliser.   Of these, the first, the fragments of
which occupy about six hundred lines, out of an aggregate
of twelve hundred, is the only one which need occupy our
attention for any time; a very few words will suffice for
the rest.

The exordium of the 'Annals' appears to stand out
before us with tolerable distinctness.   Lucretius, at the
opening of his philosophical poem, Propertius in his vision
of Calliope, Virgil in the apparition of Hector to Æneas,
Persius in his 'Prologue,' and again in his celebration of
the bay of Luna, have all either imitated or referred to it.
After an invocation to the Muses by their two names,
Greek and Roman, Ennius gives an account of his calling
to the office of poet, possibly modelled after the proem to
Hesiod's 'Theogony'—how Homer appeared to him as
he lay sleeping on Mount Parnassus, and, shedding tears

of human saltness, unfolded to him the mysteries of
creation, and the divine origin of animal life. His own
soul, said the father of poetry, was now animating the
body of Ennius, having been transmitted from Euphorbus
to himself, from himself to Pythagoras, and from Pythagoras to a peacock. Ennius wakes from his sleep, and
proceeds to invite his countrymen to hear a description of
the harbour of Luna, where it is conjectured that he may
have dreamt this dream within a dream. Thence, by
what steps we know not, he passed to the subject of his
poem, the Annals of the Roman people. We catch brief
glimpses of the story of Æneas, his voyage to Italy, and
his interview with the King of Alba, 'rex Albai Longai,'
who seems to have held the same position in Ennius's version as Latinus holds in Virgil's. The three hundred years
of Alban sovereignty, so familiar to us from the 'Æneid,'
have no place in the legend which Ennius followed;
Æneas is himself the father of Ilia, the royal priestess
who gives birth to the founder of Rome. A continuous
fragment of seventeen lines is preserved by Cicero, in
which the Vestal, in verses of considerable beauty, relates
to her sister an alarming dream, how she was dragged by
a strong and beautiful being along willowy banks that
were strange to her, and, when left alone, sought in vain
for her sister, but found no path to support her, and how
her father appeared, and told her that she must first
endure sorrow, and afterwards fortune would come to her
from the river. A few scattered verses convey to us the
sequel of the tale, the birth and exposure of the twins,
their suckling by the wolf, their growth to manhood, and
the discovery of their parentage by Amulius. Another
fragment of twenty lines describes Romulus and Remus
waiting for the augury which was to decide their claims,
and the people looking on intently, as the spectators in

the circus watch for the consul's signal which is to let the
chariots go, when suddenly, after a night of expectation,
twelve sacred birds appear with the sunrise, and Romulus
knows that the throne is his. Again we have a few
isolated lines or parts of lines, from which we may glean,
as we best can, the story of the fratricide, the rape of the
Sabines, the partition of the empire with Tatius, and the
death of Romulus. We have a view, too, of the council
of the twelve gods,

> Juno, Vesta, Minerva, Ceres, Diana, Venus, Mars,
> Mercurius, Jovis, Neptunus, Vulcanus, Apollo,

sitting in heaven's two-gated banqueting-hall, where Juno
and Venus apparently plead against each other, as in the
Tenth Æneid, and the latter receives a promise from
Jove that Romulus shall be made one of themselves. The
only other fragment of importance in the First Book we
will venture to quote, as there is something in its melancholy monotone which accords well with the subject, the
lament of the Romans over their first king :—

> Pectora [fida] tenet desiderium, simul inter
> Sese sic memorant, O Romule, Romule die,
> Qualem te patriæ custodem di genuerunt !
> O pater, O genitor, O sanguen dis oriundum !
> Tu produxisti nos intra luminis oras.

These are sonorous lines ; but how much finer is the
lament of the Arcadians in Virgil over Pallas !

> O dolor atque decus magnum rediture parenti !
> Hæc te prima dies bello dedit, hæc eadem aufert,
> Cum tamen ingentes Rutulorum linquis acervos.

Of the next four books, from the Second to the Fifth
inclusive, only stray lines have come down to us. As it
were by flashes of lightning, we read of Numa's institu-

tions—a sufficiently dry catalogue—and of the sweet voice
of Egeria, 'suavis sonus Egeriai;' of the victory of
Horatius, and the murder of his sister; of Mettus Fuffetius,
the wretched man whose mangled limbs the vulture devoured among the thorns, and interred in a cruel sepulchre; of Ancus and his foundation of Ostia; of the arrival
of the first Tarquin; of the night which was the crisis of
the fate of Etruria, 'Hoc noctu filo pendebit Etruria tota;'
of 'the sixth king of four-cornered Rome' (such is the
solitary mention of the reign of Servius Tullius); of the
furious driving of Tullia's chariot; of the outrage on
Lucretia, who is supposed to look up to the starry heaven
and invoke the Lares; of Horatius Cocles leaping into
the Tiber; of the scaling of the walls of Anxur; of the
Samnite war, and the increased haughtiness of the Latins,
which is expressed by a lively image, 'aqua est aspersa
Latinia.'

The Sixth Book, which treated of the war with Pyrrhus,
or, as Ennius called him, Burrus, comes out in a somewhat clearer light. It opened with a line, of which the
first part has been copied by Lucretius, the last by Virgil,
'Quis potis ingentes oras evolvere belli?' The important
crisis seems to have been marked by another council of
the gods; but no trace has been preserved of their deliberations. One line records the well-known equivocal
oracle, 'Aio te, Æacida, Romanos vincere posse;' another
contains a reflection on the family of Æacus, perhaps by
the discontented Tarentines :—

> Stolidum genus Æacidarum :
> Bellipotentes sunt magis quam sapientipotentes.

Then we have the preparations at Rome, the proletariat
armed, sentries posted throughout the city, and the forest
trees hewn everywhere for timber, the last a passage

closely followed by Virgil in his accounts of the funerals
of Misenus and Pallas,—

> Incedunt arbusta per alta, securibus cadunt,
> Percellunt magnas quercus, exciditur ilex,
> Fraxinus frangitur, atque abies consternitur alta.
> Pinus procerae pervortunt : omne sonabat
> Arbustum fremitu silvai frondosai.

Next follow those lines, so familiar to every reader of
Cicero's 'Offices,' in which the King of Epirus restores the
captives unransomed, declaring that he will not make a
merchandise of war, but try out the question of sovereignty with the Romans by force of hand, and meanwhile
respect the freedom of those whose lives the fortune of
battle has respected.   Cineas is sent to Rome, but Appius
Claudius appeals to the better mind of his countrymen,
and the orator returns without the expected peace, and
makes report to the king.   Two lines on the supposed
self-devotion of the third Decius—a story which Cicero
is thought to have derived from Ennius—and one or two
probably referring to the operations at Beneventum, complete our knowledge of the Sixth Book.

The Seventh was probably devoted to the First Punic
War.   It is there that we find the sarcasm on Naevius's
poem, which, however, he admits to have preoccupied the
field, so that he proposes himself only to touch on the
period slightly.   But he seems to have taken occasion to
congratulate himself on his own happy daring, which led
him to unlock the sacred portals, adding that the blissful
vision of wisdom, 'Sophiam, sapientia quae perhibetur,'
is to be attained only by those who have begun to study.
A number of detached lines follow, some of them describing the practice of rowing, in reference, doubtless, to
the first naval armament of Rome, others seemingly from
speeches of generals encouraging their men, and one or

two giving a picturesque glimpse of external nature, the autumnal reddening of the leaves, and the appearance of the cypress and the box, 'Russescunt frundes, . . . longique cupressi Stant rectis foliis et amaro corpore buxum.' Among these there is one of much greater length, which claims especial notice. It is a description of a friend and counsellor of one of the generals, the sharer of his table and his conversation, and of the heap of his cares, 'rerum suarum congeriem,' with whom he used to confer when wearied by the day's fatigue in the broad forum and sacred senate, speaking boldly to him of things great and small, good and bad, and taking with him many a pleasure in public and in private; a man never led to commit a crime through levity or malice; learned, faithful, pleasing, eloquent, contented, knowing how to speak at the right moment, but sparing of his words; with a breast where many ancient things were buried, and a character which preserved both the old and the new.

> Scitus . . . multa tenens antiqua sepulta, vetustas
> Quem fecit mores veteresque novosque tenentem,
> Multorum veterum leges divumque hominumque;
> Prudenter qui dicta loquive tacereve possit:
> Hunc inter pugnas Servilius sic compellat.

We know nothing of Servilius but the name, while his marvellous friend is nameless; but Gellius, the preserver of the fragment, says on the authority of Ælius Stilo, that the poet intended to draw his own picture, doubtless as he appeared in Ætolia at the side of Fulvius Nobilior. As a portrait, perhaps, it hardly falls within our criticism; but we may be allowed to give it some praise as a painting.

After the Seventh Book the fragments again diminish, both in magnitude and in interest. The Eighth and Ninth were on the Second Punic War, but very little remains to show the way in which the subject was treated.

There are the lines about Discord bursting open the iron-bound gates of the war-god, which Horace quotes as a specimen of the epic style ; the lines on war which Cicero uses in his ' Pro Murena,' describing the triumph of violence—

> Pellitur e medio sapientia, vi geritur res,
> Spernitur orator bonus, horridus miles amatur ;

some single lines on a battle, probably Cannæ, dust flying and darts showering, and the Carthaginians ham-stringing the prisoners, a glimpse of yet another council of the gods, where Juno lays aside her enmity to Rome, and Jupiter promises that Carthage shall fall ; and the well-known eulogies on Cethegus and Fabius Cunctator, ' the choice flower of Rome, Persuasion's very marrow,' and ' the one man who saved the State by delay, caring more for men's lives than for their tongues.'

In the Tenth Book the Muse is invoked to sing of the exploits of the Roman generals in the war with King Philip of Macedon. Flamininus is troubled night and day, thinking how to penetrate into the enemy's country, when an Epirote shepherd, poor and honest, ' vir haud magna cum re sed plenus fidei,' accosts him in words applied by Cicero to another Titus, his friend Pomponius Atticus, and inquires what reward he may expect if he shall succeed in relieving him of his care. After this well-known fragment, the most noticeable is a simile of those lines about a hound giving tongue, applied, we may suppose, to the Romans tracking the foe :—

> Sicut si quando vinclis venatica velox
> Apta solet canis forte feram si nare sagaci
> Sensit, voce sua nictit, ululatque ibi acute.

The subjects of the two next books are not clearly ascertained. One fragment is supposed to refer to Flamin-

inus in Greece, another to a possible invective of Cato
against luxury in dress; but the only one of interest is a
couplet, imitated by Virgil in his Seventh Æneid, on the
inextinguishable vitality of the old Trojan stock :—

> Quæ neque Dardaniis campis potuere perire,
> Nec cum capta capi, nec cum combusta cremari.

The war with Antiochus is thought to have occupied the
Thirteenth and Fourteenth Books. Antiochus himself is
supposed to be speaking in one fragment, where he complains of having been misled by Hannibal; the rest are
general enough—a reflection on the trustworthiness of
soothsayers, a few scattered lines about ships sailing,
where the yellow sea is coupled with the green brine—a
propriety of colouring vindicated by Gellius—a word of
encouragement before a battle, and another of complaint
after defeat. Fulvius Nobilior is thought to have been
the hero of the next book, so that there at least the poet
would have spoken as an eyewitness; but the fragments,
though apparently pointing to the siege of Ambracia,
present nothing very tangible.

The Sixteenth, as we are told by Pliny, was added in
honour of T. Cæcilius Denter and his brother, personages
who figure very slightly in the history as we read it, but
whom Ennius seems to have extolled as models of valour.
The fragments are rather various than remarkable; we
may, however, specify three which speak of the slop-
ing mountains whence the night rises, of the night flying
with a girdle of constellations round her, and of the
torch of day setting and covering the ocean with a trail
of crimson light. The few remains of the Seventeenth
Book tell us vaguely of battle scenes; but there seems
reason to believe that it contained a tribute to the mag-
nanimity of a censor who, finding himself elected to-

gether with a personal enemy, sought a reconciliation on
the spot, that they might perform their joint work with
joint heart and soul.

The Eighteenth and last Book embraced the Histrian
War. There is a picture, studied after Homer's Ajax,
and itself reproduced in Virgil's Turnus, of a tribune defending himself against the Histrians, with darts raining
on his shield and helmet, and falling harmless and
shivered to the ground, with sweat streaming from every
pore, yet not a moment to take breath. But the interest
of the book, at least to us, must have centred in the
discourse about himself, in which the old bard seems to
have indulged in closing this his greatest poem. Even
now we may read with sympathy his boastful allusion
to his late enrolment among the citizens of the conquering city — 'Nos sumus Romani, qui fuimus ante
Rudini ;' we may be touched by the mention he appears
to have made of the year of his age in which he
wrote, bordering closely on the appointed term of man's
life ; and we may applaud as the curtain falls over
his grand comparison of himself to a victorious racer,
laden with Olympic honours, and now at last consigned
to repose :—

> Sicut fortis equus, spatio qui saepe supremo
> Vicit Olimpia, nunc senio confectus quiescit.

A very few words, as we have stated already, will
despatch what has to be said on the other works of
Ennius, numerous and varied as these appear to have
been. His strength was not supposed to lie in comedy ;
a poetical classification of the Roman comic writers,
quoted by Gellius, gives him the last place in a list of
ten, and that only in deference to his antiquity ; and,
accordingly, the whole number of fragments that has

come down to us amounts only to eleven lines, or parts
of lines, preserved simply as containing certain words,
and throwing no light on the nature of the pieces from
which they came.   The three titles which we possess are
'Ambracia,' which, as we have seen, may have been a
prætexta; 'Capuncula,' if the same is rightly restored, as
we should say, the Maid of the Inn, and 'Pancratiastæ,'
the Prize-fighters. Of Ennius's historical position as a
writer of satire we have no space to speak at length.
He seems to have been the first who gave satire its form;
its spirit of personal invective it did not receive till later.
We hear of as many as six books of his Satires; but the
actual remains are very slender, though sufficient to show
that he preserved that early characteristic of the 'Satura,'
a medley of metres. The most memorable of these books
would seem to have been the third, if it is rightly identified with a poem which he wrote in honour of Scipio.
The fragments which remain are partly personal, as where
he thanks himself in the name of mankind for giving
them to drink of the fiery wine of song drawn from his
heart :—

> Enni poeta salve qui mortalibus
> Versus propinas flammeos medullitus,

or where he tells us (if the line has been restored to its
right place) that he never writes poetry but when he has
the gout ; partly laudatory of his hero, who appeals for
a witness of his deeds to the broad and cultivated plains
of Africa, 'lati campi quos gerit Africa terra politos ;'
and in one case simply picturesque, describing a universal
hush in nature :—

> Mundus cæli vastus constitit silentio ;
> Et Neptunus sævus undis asperis pausam dedit :
> Sol equis iter repressit ungulis volantibus ;
> Constitere amnes perennes, arbores vento vacant.

A fragment about a slave, who annoys his prudent master
by his reckless laugh and wolfish appetite; four jingling
verses, telling a hoaxer that when the hoax does not
succeed, the hoaxer is hoaxed; a version, which, however, exists only in Gellius's prose, of Æsop's fable about
the lark and her young ones, and the well-known line
about the resemblance of the ape to man, 'Simia quam
similis, turpissima bestia, nobis,' comprise all that need
be noted in the rest of the Satires. The three 'Epigrams'
or Inscriptions, ten lines in all, we will quote entire.
The first is the famous epitaph on himself :—

> Aspicite, O cives, senis Enni imaginis formam !
>   Hic vestrum panxit fortia facta patrum.
> Nemo me lacrimis decoret nec funera fletu
>   Faxit.   Cur ?   Volito vivus per ora virum.

The second is on Africanus, the man to whom never
friend or foe could repay what he gave :—

> Hic est ille situs cui nemo civis neque hostis
>   Quivit pro factis reddere opis pretium.

The third is also on Africanus, into whose mouth it is
put :—

> A sole exoriente supra Mæotis paludes
>   Nemo est qui factis me æquiperare queat.
> Si fas endo plagas cœlestium ascendere cuiquam est,
>   Mi soli cæli maxima porta patet.

The three extant verses of the 'Sota' are not worth
dwelling on.   All that is known of the 'Protrepticus,' or
Collection of Precepts, consists of a single word 'pan-
nibus,' a variety for 'pannis,' the dative of 'pannus,'
and two lines and a half about a husbandman sepa-
rating tares from his wheat.   Of the 'Hedyphagetica,'
an imitation or translation of a once popular poem

by Archestratus of Gela, Appuleius has preserved us
eleven lines, describing various kinds of fish, and the
places where they are to be caught or bought, in
language which Horace may have had in his mind
when he wrote the dialogue between himself and
Catius. The title of the 'Epicharmus' is more promising: but the fragments come to but little. It was
written in trochaic tetrameters, and the philosopher himself seems to have been a speaker in it, if not the speaker
of the whole. Its chief utterances tell us that the body
is earth and the mind fire taken from the sun, and that
Jupiter is the air, comprising wind and clouds, rain and
cold, all which are rightly called Jupiter, 'quoniam
mortales atque urbes beluasque omnes juvat.' The extant remains of the 'Euhemerus' have descended to us
in prose; there is, however, reason to believe that it was
originally a poem, but that some later hand modernised
and transposed it; and it has been shown that a number
of trochaic tetrameters can be extracted from it without
much difficulty. The prose fragments, which, though
not numerous, are of considerable length, owe their
preservation to Lactantius. Whatever may have been
the case in their original state, in their present form they
do not possess much of the colour of poetry; in fact,
the language may be said to reflect the character of that
jejune mythology which it was intended to expound.

THE LATER ROMAN EPIC—STATIUS 'THEBAID.'[1]

THERE is no stronger attestation of the influence exercised
by Virgil on his country's literature than the large space
which the epic occupies in the poetry of post-Augustan
Rome. In Greece, after the cessation of that creative
activity which produced the poems of the Cycle and the
legends of Heracles, the epic muse found scarcely any
worshipper worthy of the name. For several centuries
the hexameter had the whole field to itself; but when
the territory was encroached upon by other settlers, the
ancient form of composition dwindled away, like an
aboriginal tribe in the presence of later civilisation.
While the spirit of Grecian song was pouring itself forth
in the lyric and the drama, the recollection of Homer
was continued only by a few faint echoes, scarcely
audible to contemporary ears, and wholly, or almost
wholly, lost to modern times; and though Apollonius
Rhodius is not, like Panyasis, Chœrilus, and Antimachus,
or his own Alexandrian brethren, Rhianus and Eupho-
rion, a mere name to us, we feel as we read him that
he would hardly have counted as an eminent poet,
among a poetical nation like the Greeks, in an age
where poetry was still fresh and vigorous. But in Rome
the case is far otherwise. As we pass from the golden
to the silver age, we are confronted by a body of epic
poetry which contains more than four times the bulk of
the 'Æneid.' The 'Pharsalia' of Lucan and the unfinished
'Argonautics' of Velarius Flaccus are indeed shorter than

[1] Reprinted from the *North British Review*, No. lxxix.

Virgil's poem; but the 'Thebaid' of Statius, taken together
with the fragment of the 'Achilleid,' is considerably longer,
and the 'Punic War' of Silius Italicus is nearly half as long
again.   These works, in fact, constitute about a third of
the extant classical poetry since the Augustan era.   Nor
have we any reason to think that they have been preserved to us by mere accident, while others, more worthy
of being kept alive, have been left to perish.   We may
not value these vast heroic efforts as we value some of
the less ostentatious performances of the same period,
the Satires of Persius and Juvenal, or the Epigrams of
Martial.   We may prefer, as we doubtless should prefer,
the 'Silvæ' of Statius to his 'Thebaid,' and argue that
the other three poets might have expended their powers
more profitably in attempts of a less ambitious nature.
But we cannot doubt that all four stood high in the
estimation of their own period, the period immediately
succeeding the acme of Roman culture: two of them
conspicuously so; and there is certainly some significance
in the fact that so much of the poetical power of a not
ungifted generation should have been consumed upon a
species of poetry which earlier and later ages, for very
various reasons, have been equally forward to extol, and
equally backward to cultivate.

Doubtless there were other influences which tended to
recommend the epic to the poets of Cæsarian Rome.   In
the days of the intellectual glory of Athens, the real
successors of Homer were to be found in the great
fathers of the drama.   To the public, the pleasure of
listening to a rhapsodist, however skilled, must have
been tame when compared with the charm of a dialogue
sustained by well-graced actors, relieved by orchestral
music, and set off by the accessories of scenery; while
the poet would naturally prefer a field of labour which,

independently of the confessed advantages of novelty and
popularity, might appear less interminable and more
diversified. But the drama, the tragic drama at any
rate, had never taken a thoroughly firm hold on Roman
soil; and it withered rather than flourished under the
imperial sunshine. The degradation of the chorus
stamped it from the first with the character of comparative insignificance; it was Greek tragedy shorn of one-
half of its glory. Already, in the time of Horace,[1] the
audience had begun to tire of the tragic dialogue, and
to care only for the splendour of the spectacle; and it
was not likely that under the successors of Augustus the
drama should compete advantageously with the shows
of the circus. The tragedy of Seneca was probably
unacted tragedy; and unacted tragedy, as the public
opinion of our own day tells us, is a plain confession of
weakness. But here was still a field for heroic poetry;
a wider one, it might seem, than it had enjoyed even in
Virgil's time. The poet of the 'Æneid' had read parts of
his work in the presence of the imperial family; but, if
we except a doubtful story of the recitation of his
'Eclogues,'[2] we do not know that he ever appeared before
a more general audience. But the atmosphere of imperial Rome was favourable to recitations; and it is
evident from Juvenal's language[3] that they formed a more
prominent feature in his experience than they had done
in that of Horace or Ovid. The same Satire which complains that they did not bring money, admits that they

---

[1] Horace, *Epistles*, Book ii. Ep. i. 187 foll.

[2] The story is that the *Bucolics* were so popular as to be recited repeatedly
on the stage, and that Cicero, being present on one of these occasions, pronounced the author 'Magnæ spes altera Romæ.' Cicero was killed before
Virgil lost his farm, so the whole may be a figment.

[3] Contrast the early part of the First and Seventh Satires of Juvenal with
such passages as Hor. Sat. I. iv. 23; Ep. I. xix. 37 foll.

brought fame. The poet might appear in his own person, and deliver his own verses, with no actor to intercept the rays of popular favour. The 'Thebaid,' as we learn from the famous passage in Juvenal, was received with rapture by a crowded assembly. The author himself, in a poem to a friend, speaks of the day when the representatives of Rome's great founders will come to hear his 'Achilleid.' We do not know what was the precise nature of the periodical contests for the crown of poetry, which formed so characteristic a feature of this, the silver age of Roman genius, and in which Statius was repeatedly successful; but we may well imagine that the poems submitted to competition would be of a more elaborate kind than the occasional pieces which make up the five books of the 'Silvæ.' The Roman Clio had not yet abandoned faith in her origin; she still strove to execute feats which might be worthy of a goddess. In a later age we find her contenting herself with minor epic excursions, like the 'Rape of Proserpine' of Claudian, while she sometimes condescends, with Ausonius, to compose catalogues of words and names for grammar-schools, and celebrate the conflicting powers of Yes and No. But at present she is confident in her strength, and even fonder of exhibiting it than when that strength was really at its height. The epigram is the amusement of her leisure moments; she may give days or weeks to the composition of a satire: but it is to poems like the 'Thebaid,' the product of the vigils of twelve long years, that she looks for enduring glory.[1]

The early Roman epic had been national in subject, if not in form. Nævius had sung of the great struggle

---

[1] See the concluding lines of the *Thebaid*:—

O mihi bissenos multum vigilata per annos
Thebai.

against Carthage; Ennius had recounted the annals of
the Roman people from the days of Romulus, if not
earlier; Hostius had commemorated the war with
Histria. The 'Æneid' is the glorification of the fore-
fathers of the imperial nation, who, though vanquished
in Phrygia, had been victorious in Italy. But the 'Æneid,'
though national in one of its aspects, is exotic in another.
It might be read by a Roman as a celebration of the
antiquarian glories of his country; it might be read as
a tale of the Homeric school, a sequel to the 'Iliad,' a
companion to the 'Odyssey.' It would naturally foster
the love, not only of Greek mythology in relation to the
history of Rome, but of Greek mythology as such; of
that wonderful body of legendary lore, by turns terrible
and pathetic, sublime and grotesque, which even in our
alien atmosphere has such a charm for the imagination of the boy, and for the intellect of the grown
man.   These two aspects combined in the 'Æneid,'
are found separately in the epics of the silver age.
Silius and Lucan choose national subjects; the one going
back on the traces of Nævius, and celebrating the Punic
Wars, the other treading on the scarcely extinguished
embers of civil discord, and telling the story of Pharsalia. Flaccus and Statius resort to the storehouse of
Grecian fable, which furnishes to the former the voyage
of the Argonauts, the subject selected by the Alexandrian poet, to the latter the first siege of Thebes, the
fertile theme of Athenian tragedy, and the life of Achilles,
that grand whole, of which only a part had been appropriated by Homer.

The choice of such a subject as the 'Thebaid' is itself
a significant one.   It was indeed not new to epic poetry;
it formed the subject of one of the poems of the Cycle,
the substance of which modern critics [1] have apparently

---

[1] See Mure, *History of Greek Literature*, vol. ii. pp. 269 foll.

been able to recover by the help of Pindar and Pausanias, though the extant fragments are but few; and it was revived some centuries later by Antimachus of Claros, whose enormous poem, twenty-four books of which were occupied in bringing the Seven Chiefs to Thebes, was listened to, Cicero tells us, by Plato, after all the other auditors had left the room, and is known to have been preferred by the imperial judgment of Hadrian to the works of Homer. Our associations with it are, of course, those of readers of Greek tragedy, in whose gallery of terrible imagery it forms so prominent a feature. There is reason to think, that as treated in the cyclic poem, it was without some of those revolting traits[1] which now characterise it; but whatever may have been the condition in which the tragic poets received it, there can be no doubt about the horrors which invested it when it left their hands. As handled by Æschylus and Euripides, it pleases more than it shocks; but it is only because we have submitted ourselves to the laws of that species of art, the object of which is to purge the passions by pity and terror. Just before Statius's time, Seneca, if we are right, as we well may be, in ascribing the Theban tragedy to him, has shown what might be made of the subject by a practised rhetorician who should simply abandon himself to the task of drawing out its horrible and loathsome details. Possibly by a recurrence to the ancient severity of treatment, it might have been made endurable as a subject for narrative poetry. But such self-restraint was foreign alike to the ambition of the poet and to the taste of his age. Statius appears to have been drawn to the subject, not in spite but in consequence of the features which would have repelled a sounder and more chastened judgment. He

[1] Such as the self-inflicted blindness of Œdipus.

wished to produce what, in language with which the
somewhat kindred experience of our own time has made
us familiar, would be called a work of the 'sensation'
school; and in the choice of means towards his end, he
certainly showed himself not injudicious.

It is of this poem that we intend to speak for the rest
of the present article. We shall give a critical account
in detail of the conduct of the story; we shall indicate
more briefly the principal characteristics of the poet's
style; and we shall mention one special point which
may seem to entitle him to the praise of incidental
success, even though the final verdict should be, as we
fear it will be, that the poem, as a whole, is an elaborate
failure.

The 'Thebaid' is contained in twelve books, the number
which the 'Æneid' had made classical; and the average
content of each is about the same as the average content
of the several books of the 'Æneid.' But it is made clear
at the very outset, that the spirit of Statius is not quite
the same as the spirit of Virgil. Instead of the modest
'cano' with which Virgil informs us of the subject of
his song, we are told that Pierian inspiration impels the
poet to sing of the strife of the brothers and the guilt of
Thebes. He asks rhetorically where he shall commence;
whether from the very first, the rape of Europa and the
voyage of Cadmus; and concludes that such a starting-
place would be too far off, and that he had better confine
himself to the family of Œdipus. He invokes his Cæsar,
Domitian, remembering that Virgil had invoked Augustus, but apparently forgetting that it was at the outset,
not of the 'Æneid,' but of the 'Georgics;' and then, after
another rhetorical inquiry, which of the invading heroes
he shall sing first, plunges into his subject. In the true
vein of Seneca, he introduces us at once to the blind

Œdipus, who, in the depth of his solitude at Thebes, raises the empty sockets of his eyes to heaven, strikes the ground with bloody hands, and implores the Queen of the Furies, by the recollection of his former deeds of horror, to avenge him on his undutiful children, and urge their congenial minds to some crime great enough to gladden their father. The Fury, to the loathsomeness of whose personal appearance full justice is done, makes her way to Thebes, and induces the two young kings to agree to a compact that they should reign alternately, the outgoing king leaving the country at the end of his year. Thebes, we are told, is but a poor kingdom,[1] yet the lust of sway is as strong in the two brothers as if they were striving for the empire of the world. Eteocles is the first to reign. The people feel some discontent at the arrangement, which they think, not without reason, has been made for the advantage of the brothers more than for their own. Jupiter calls a council, and announces his intention of taking vengeance on the two royal houses of Thebes and Argos for a long series of crimes. Juno puts in a word for Argos, but is sternly overruled, and Mercury is sent down to raise the ghost of Laius, who is to incite Eteocles to break the compact. Meantime Polynices, being excluded by the terms of the compact from Thebes, resolves, for some reason unknown, to visit Argos. He is represented as a veritable exile, without any companion to share his journey, which turns out to be an exceedingly rough one, through rain, wind, and thunder. He finds his way to the palace of Adrastus, the king of Argos, and has just taken shelter in the vestibule, when he is interrupted by another traveller in a similar plight. This is Tydeus, who has had to leave

---

[1] 'Pugna est de paupere regno' (Book i. 151), one of the very few expressions in Statius that have become in any way proverbial.

A A 2

his own home, Calydon, for having killed his brother. The strangers fight with fists, attempt to gouge each other, and would have drawn their swords if the noise had not awakened Adrastus, who separates them, takes them into his house, and entertains them. It is the night of a festival to Apollo, the institution of which is related by Adrastus in a long story, obviously modelled on Evander's narrative of the death of Cacus. A hymn to the great Sun-God concludes the book.

While this is going on, Laius is being conducted to earth by Mercury, not without envious gibes from his brother shades, who solace themselves with thinking that he will like his underground dwelling less for having been allowed a glimpse of daylight. On reaching Thebes, he takes the form of Tiresias, and appears to Eteocles in a vision, at the end of which he makes himself known. The scene then changes to Argos again. The morning after the storm, Adrastus makes a speech to his guests, and offers them respectively the hands of his two daughters, whom they had seen at the banquet of the previous night. They accept with thankfulness, and the double nuptials are celebrated with great pomp, which is, however, marred by one bad omen, the fall of a heavy shield from the roof of the temple of Pallas, just as the brides-elect are entering it by torchlight. The wedding festivities over, Polynices begins to sigh for Thebes; and eventually it is agreed that Tydeus, who has now come to be his firmest friend, should undertake the office of ambassador to Eteocles, and remind him that the year of royalty has expired. This duty he discharges in a speech which might have ruffled a more accommodating temper than that with which he has to deal. The king refuses to abdicate, basing his resolution on public grounds, as a change of rulers must be a bad thing for the nation; the ambassador breaks into a fury, denounces war, captivity, and death, and so leaves the presence. Eteocles determines to avenge himself on his audacious visitor, and posts fifty men in ambush along the road by which Tydeus has to travel. And now the poet has got his opportunity, and he uses it unsparingly. The scene is appropriate to a deed of impiety, being a defile overlooked by a rock—a place where the Sphinx once sat and tore her victims, and which cattle, and even birds of ill omen, avoid with horror. Tydeus is surprised by a dart, which strikes him, but does not draw blood; he vehemently calls on his adversaries to show themselves, springs on the fatal rock, and from that vantage-ground attacks the enemy with a fragment of stone, crushing four and making the rest retire. He comes down from the rock, and they soon assail him again; but he is more than a match for them; he keeps them off with his sword, receives their spears on his shield, and hurls the weapons back with deadly effect. Finally, he stands like Ulysses after the slaughter of the suitors, with all slain but a few unnerved wretches, who vainly beg for life, or attempt a feeble resistance. One of these, who happened to be innocent, is spared at the instance of Pallas, and sent back to Thebes to tell the tale. The conqueror ends the book with another hymn of praise, which this time is to Pallas.

The Third Book brings us back to Eteocles, who has passed a restless night, wondering that he does not hear of the death of Tydeus. In due time the unhappy survivor arrives, tells his tale, inveighs against his wicked master, and ends by stabbing himself. Eteocles refuses him burial; and the poet, with that zeal for freedom which so curiously characterises the courtiers of imperial Rome, delivers an enthusiastic eulogy on the man who dares boldly to confront a tyrant. The bodies of the other ambuscaders are brought home and buried, and there is more free speaking against Eteocles. Jupiter has been watching what has happened, and apparently thinking that Argos and Thebes are not sufficiently likely to quarrel already, sends for Mars, and bids him pay a visit to the Argives. Venus stops her lover as he is going, and pleads her affection for Thebes; he reassures her by a rough caress, hurting her, we are told, against his shield, and says that Fate must have its way, but that when the war has begun, he will bear hardly on Argos. And now we are called back to Tydeus, who reaches his father-in-law's home, and finding a council assembled, urges an immediate march on Thebes; to which Adrastus replies that he will think about it. After a week's deliberation, the Argive king resolves to find out the will of Heaven, and consults two prophets, Melampus and Amphiaraus. They agree to observe the flight of birds, and after a prayer to Jupiter, which reads like a philosophical apology for the practice of augury, are at last rewarded by an omen. They see an innumerable multitude of swans, which from their peaceful appearance they conclude to symbolise Thebes; these are attacked by seven eagles, of course the seven Argive chiefs, which in their turn meet with mysterious fates of various kinds, corresponding to the fates which actually await the doomed warriors. Statius, elsewhere minute even to tediousness, is here obscure and brief; he indemnifies us, however, by denouncing in his own person the passion for prying into futurity. Amphiaraus, being one of the seven intended chiefs, has discovered his own fate; and now, instead of telling what he knows, he buries himself in gloomy privacy, and keeps silence for twelve days. The war-fever rises, and Capaneus, one of the Argive magnates, threatens the augur, and throws contempt on his act. On this he

speaks, and in terms which, though somewhat enigmatical,
clearly announces coming ruin, warns his hearers to
abandon the expedition.   Capaneus retorts in a speech,
where, by a happy inconsistency of impiety, the gods are
alternately blasphemed and denied, and carries the people
with him.   Argia, the wife of Polynices, pays a midnight
visit to her father, and presses on him her husband's
claim.   He soothes her, and the book closes.

At the opening of the Fourth Book we find that a
second year has been spent in preparation, and that the
expected day has come at last.   The seven chiefs are
recounted in order, Adrastus himself, Polynices, Tydeus,
Hippomedon, Capaneus, Amphiaraus, Parthenopæus;
some of them apparently leaders of independent con-
tingents, others appointed to command tribes subject to
the Argive crown.   One or two incidents occur :—
Eriphyle, the wife of Amphiaraus, is bribed by a fatal
necklace, the property of the princess Argia, to induce
her husband to join the army; Atalanta, the mother of
Parthenopæus, parts with her son in words which show
that she does not expect to see him again.   The scene
shifts, and we are at Thebes, which has already heard
the rumour of invasion.   As at Argos, there is a wish to
explore the future ; and the blind Tiresias and his daughter Manto perform magical rites.   At last the infernal
world opens, and Manto is proceeding to describe the
commonplace features of it for her father's benefit, when
he tells her that he knows them already, and bids her
concentrate her attention on the spirits of Argos and
Thebes.   These accordingly pass in a somewhat tedious
review, when Tiresias, finding that a kind of second-sight
is given to him, singles out the ghost of Laius, and by a
mixture of threatening and encouragement extorts the
information that Thebes will conquer, that Polynices will

not gain the throne, and that Œdipus will have his will.
We leave the invaded, and return to the invaders, who
are on their march through the forest of Nemea. Bacchus,
the patron of Thebes, resolves to trouble them, and pre-
vails on the nymphs of the spot to dry up the rivers.
Burning with thirst, in their wanderings they meet with
Hypsipyle, the nurse of the child of Lycurgus, the king of
the country, and are guided by her to a small stream
which is still flowing.   Upon this they throw themselves
pell-mell, struggling for the water with a fury like that
of an army in action, and continuing to drink when it is
already foul and muddy.   Again the book is ended by a
sort of hymn, which on this occasion is addressed to the
god of the stream, by one of the chiefs from the middle
of the water.[1]

The Fifth Book contributes but little to the progress of
the poem.   Adrastus, wishing to show his interest in the
benefactress of his army, asks Hypsipyle who she is, and
hears a story in reply which occupies no less than 450
lines, more than half the book.   She was a noble lady of
Lemnos, and was living there with her father Thoas, when
Venus, deeming herself neglected by the Lemnian women,
made them first estrange themselves from their husbands,
and finally resolve to slaughter the whole male population
—a resolution which they accomplished on the occasion
of their husbands returning from an expedition against
Thrace.   Hypsipyle saved her father, who escaped to
Chios, under the guidance of his father, Bacchus; but
this act of splendid mendacity was not known, and the

---

[1] There is a difficult line in this part (v. 829), which is not cleared up by
such commentators as we have been able to consult:—

Hac sævisse tenus populorum incepta tuorum
Sufficiat.

Road 'in cœpta,' and all will be plain.

Lemnian ladies made her their queen. They were beginning to repent of their crime, when they were visited by the Argonauts, whom they first attempted to repulse, but finally fell in love with, Hypsipyle herself becoming the mother of twins by Jason. With the spring the Argonauts left them, and about the same time news arrived that Hypsipyle's father was alive. She fled, but fell in with pirates, who sold her to the master whose child she now nurses. This lengthy and irrelevant tale is told, like the story of the Thebaid itself, with much rhetorical indirectness; a good deal of effort is required to follow it; and whether it tired the hearers or no, it certainly tires the readers. However, if not important in one sense, it is important in another. While the nurse is telling her troubles, the infant is killed by a serpent, which the poet supposes to carry its sting in its tail. The serpent is attacked by the heroes, and killed by Capaneus, who expresses a hope that he may be slaying a favourite of the gods; the Nymphs and Fauns mourn for the reptile, and Jupiter is nearly avenging it by lightning. Hypsipyle is frantic at her loss, as is her royal employer, the child's father, who would have killed her on the spot, but for the interposition of the Argive chiefs, and the sudden appearance of her two sons, who happen just at that moment to have arrived at the palace in quest of their mother. This time the book is ended, not by a hymn, but by an oracular utterance from Amphiaraus, who tells the afflicted father and the Argives that the child's death was destined, but that, by way of compensation, it has been made a deity.

The Sixth Book has often been pointed to as a signal instance of Statius's want of judgment. Like the Twenty-third Iliad and the Fifth Æneid, it is taken up with funeral games celebrated by the heroes in honour of the

deified infant, as though the poet thought a book of
games a constituent part of an epic, and introduced it
without asking whether it was appropriate to the story or
not. A favourable critic of the last century, who published a translation of the book,[1] thinks it at once a
pleasing relief from the horrors of the story, and a
gentle introduction to the wars that are to come; an
opinion in which we do not think a continuous reader of
the poem will agree with him. A somewhat better vindication will be found in the fact that this celebration
seems to have formed part of the original Theban story,
being, in fact, the legendary account of the institution of
the Nemean games. But however the episode might have
fared in the hands of a more judicious poet, in those of
Statius it merely serves to distract us by a needless variety
of incident. The games are conducted by the Argives, the
father and mother simply abandoning themselves to wild
and furious grief. There is a chariot-race, in which Polynices drives his father-in-law's horse, the famous Arion, and
shares the fate of Phaethon, with whom he is compared.
There is a foot-race, which is disturbed, like that in
Virgil, by a trick, the second runner pulling the first
back by the hair; but they run again, and the author of
the foul play is fairly beaten. There is a throwing of
quoits, which affords no remarkable incident. There is a
boxing-match, where the gigantic Capaneus is confronted
by a cooler combatant, who baffles him, but whose life he
would apparently have taken had he not been appeased
by the prize. There is a wrestling-match, where Tydeus
throws an opponent of Herculean bulk, complacently
observing, as he takes the prize, how much more he
might have done had he not left so much of his blood on

---

[1] Harte, quoted by Malone in a note on Dryden's *Discourse on Epic
Poetry* (Dryden's Prose Works, vol. iv. p. 428).

the plains of Thebes. There was to have been a combat
with cold steel, had it not struck Adrastus that his chiefs
had better reserve their fury for the enemy than expend
it on each other. All the seven generals have now shown
some kind of superiority but Adrastus, who is accordingly
complimented by being asked to volunteer a display of
his strength or skill in shooting with the bow or hurling
the javelin. He shoots at an ash-tree in the distance; the
arrow hits the mark, but flies back to the place whence it
had been shot. The spectators assign it to natural causes;
but it is really a portent, signifying that he alone is to
return from the expedition.

The Seventh Book is much more business-like, not only
bringing the heroes to Thebes, but accomplishing one of
the chief events of the war. Jupiter, giving a nod which,
we are assured, adds sensibly to the burden of Atlas, sends
Mercury to stimulate Mars, who is to be told how the
Argives are waiting their time, and to have the option
given him of carrying on matters more vigorously, or
abandoning his office of war-god, and leaving the conduct
of the invasion to Pallas. Mars is found in his palace,
which is described after the manner of Ovid; and he is
not long in putting himself into motion. A false alarm is
raised, and the Argives are made to think that the
Thebans are advancing to meet them. Bacchus pleads to
Jupiter for Thebes, and complains that he is being sacrificed to his stepmother: Jupiter answers that he is not
influenced by Juno, but by the Fates, and that, though
the race of Œdipus must perish, Thebes itself is to be
respited. Eteocles prepares to defend the city, and
assembles his forces. Antigone appears on the walls, as
she does in the 'Phœnissæ' of Euripides, with an aged
attendant, whom she questions about such of the Theban
leaders as she does not know by sight. The old man

enters into a long rhetorical detail, which is, as usual,
obscure from want of simplicity, and breaks off weeping
at the thought of Laius, his ancient master. Eteocles
harangues his army, briefly and with some vigour. The
invaders march on, though forbidding portents spring up
along the whole line of their route; rivers flowing backward, showers of stones, oracles struck dumb, ghosts of
great criminals appearing, and weeping statues. The
Asopus swells as if to oppose their passage, but Hippomedon dashes into the stream, and the rest follow him.
When they reach Thebes, Jocasta insists on seeing Polynices, and produces a momentary impression, which, however, a fierce speech from Tydeus is sufficient to dispel.
The war is precipitated by an incident, evidently borrowed
from the Seventh Æneid of Virgil. There are two
tame tigers, which, having drawn the car of Bacchus in
the famous Indian campaign, are allowed to run loose,
and honoured with semi-divine observances. A Fury,
who is apparently in attendance on Mars, brings back
their savage nature; they attack the Argives, and are
pierced through and through with javelins, and driven to
Thebes. The sacrilegious author of their wounds is killed
in his turn, and the battle begins. Amphiaraus, the
doomed augur, performs prodigies of valour. In the
midst of them, his charioteer is killed, and Apollo takes
the vacant place, when a scene ensues, which Mr. Merri-
vale [1] justly characterises as a really fine one, though
overdrawn and overloaded. Apollo reveals himself, and
tells his votary that the hour of doom is come. Amphiaraus answers shortly and sadly. The earth is felt to
shake; a chasm opens at the horses' feet; and the augur
goes down alive into the depth in his chariot, with one
hand still on the reins, and the other on his weapon.

[1] *History of the Romans under the Empire.*

If Statius is able to draw a striking picture, he certainly is not able to leave it alone when drawn. The Eighth Book follows Amphiaraus down the chasm, and describes, at considerable length, the effect of his sudden appearance on the shades; how Pluto rises in gloomy wrath, but is appeased by the augur's prayers, and spares him as a lion is contented with trampling on a fallen foe. In the upper world, the lamentation is long and loud. The Argives spend the night in weeping, the Thebans in festivity. A new augur is appointed, who conducts his predecessor's funeral, and sings a rhetorical hymn to the earth. The battle recommences; and we have one of those enumerations of slaughter which are natural in Homer, scarcely tolerable in Virgil, and insufferable in a less simple and more ambitious writer, the chief actor being Tydeus. The daughters of Œdipus are exchanging their sorrows in their chamber, when young Atys, who had been plighted to Ismene, is borne into the palace, having received his death-wound from the terrible Ætolian. At last, a Theban, Melanippus, succeeds in striking down Tydeus, though he is struck down by him in return. Tydeus begs his comrades to bring him his enemy's head, and, after gloating on it, is impelled by the Fury to gnaw it to the brain, just as Pallas was coming with Jupiter's permission to make him immortal. The pure goddess veils her face with the Gorgon shield, flies away with loathing, and leaves her fiendish favourite to die.

The Ninth Book opens amid the horror of the Thebans and the grief of the Argives and Polynices, who speaks of Tydeus's last action as prompted by excess of friendship to himself. There is a fight over the body, which would have been rescued by Hippomedon, had not the Fury, who has an interest in Tydeus remaining unburied, raised a false alarm that Adrastus is in the hands of the enemy.

Hippomedon, finding himself baffled, mounts the dead
man's horse, and rides to the river Ismenus, where there
is a furious combat, like the Homeric combat at the Sca-
mander. The new Achilles, like his prototype, is in danger
of being overwhelmed by the river-god, whose grandson
he has killed. Juno begs that he may escape drowning,
and Jupiter assents ; but as soon as he has landed, he is
overpowered and slain. Three of the Argive chiefs have
now fallen, and a fourth is shortly to follow. The mother
of Parthenopæus, away in Arcadia, forebodes the death
of her son, and prays to her patroness, the huntress-
queen. Diana goes to Thebes, where Apollo consoles her
by telling her that he has himself had to lose his votary,
Amphiaraus : she resolves, however, to avenge her favourite's death, from whatever hand it may come. It is, as
our readers will have seen already, the story of Camilla
over again. The goddess does her best to make his career
a splendid one, filling his quiver with heavenly shafts, and
sprinkling him with ambrosia, which is to guard him
against every wound but the last fatal one. After he has
inflicted many deaths, she attempts to stop him from
going further, but in vain : and meantime Venus, who
has been viewing her interference with jealousy, sends
down Mars to order her away. Parthenopæus is struck
down, and expires with a rather touching address to his
mother, which closes the book.

Another night follows : as before, the Argives are
dispirited and the Thebans confident, insomuch that they
contemplate a night attack on the quarters of the enemy.
Meanwhile, the Argive matrons at home go in supplica-
tion to the temple of Pallas : and she resolves to trouble
the Thebans, though she feels that she cannot conquer
them. Accordingly, she sends down Iris to the cave of
Sleep, which is elaborately described, and incites that

drowsy power to fall on the hosts of Thebes, while the
Argives are to be kept wakeful. Adrastus is moved by the
advice of Amphiaraus's successor, who has been favoured
with a vision of Amphiaraus himself, to send out a small
band against the sleeping foe; and the new augur, with
two others, and a company of thirty men, offers himself
for the service. Not content with thus copying the
episode of Nisus and Euryalus, as Virgil copied that of
Ulysses and Diomed, Statius has chosen to remind us
yet more pointedly of the deeds and fate of the two
Trojan friends. The expedition has succeeded and is
retiring, when two members of it, Hopleus and Dymas,
companions respectively of Tydeus and Parthenopæus,
resolve to look for their leaders' bodies. They find them,
and are going off, each with his prize, when they are
discovered. Hopleus is killed: Dymas offers to forego
life and burial for himself, if his young chief may be
buried. He is offered his own life and the body of his
chief if he will tell what the Argives are intending; but
he will not sink to the level of the Homeric Dolon, and
stabs himself on the spot, Statius expressing a hope that
he and Hopleus will be welcomed as kindred spirits by
Euryalus and Nisus. The Argives make a furious assault on
the town, and the Thebans retire within the walls, which
they defend desperately. There are murmurs against
Eteocles, and Tiresias is bidden to tell the future. He
replies that Thebes may be saved by the death of the
youngest of the posterity of Cadmus. The goddess of
Virtue or Worth, a somewhat strange personage to introduce into a Greek legend, inspires Menœceus, the youngest
son of Creon, to offer himself willingly for his country.
Pretending to his father that he does not mean to comply
with the oracular voice, he mounts the walls, addresses
the gods, stabs himself, sprinkles the towers with his

blood, and falls, not to the earth, but into the arms of
Piety and Virtue, who waft his body gently down, while
his spirit ascends to heaven. And now the poet girds
himself to sing of the actions and death of Capaneus, and
invokes the aid of all the Muses at once. That tremendous warrior climbs the walls, torch in hand, breaks off
the battlements, and shatters Thebes with its own stones.
The gods are in confusion, glaring at each other on each
side of the throne of Jupiter. Capaneus dares them to
hinder him : the sky darkens, but he presses on, declaring
that the lightning will serve to rekindle his torch. A
thunderbolt strikes him, and he begins to burn, first his
crest, then his shield, and finally, his body ; yet he still
breathes defiance to heaven, and all but requires a second
bolt to extinguish him.

The death of Capaneus is felt to be a relief, not only
by the Thebans, but by the gods. They congratulate
Jupiter as they did after his victory over the giants, and
even the Thunderer feels respect for one who knew so
well how to hold his own. Far from being thrust down
to Tartarus, which we feel would have been his sentence
had he fallen into the hands of Virgil, he is received with
honour by the whole infernal world, and refreshes his
august spirit at the Stygian streams. Meantime, two of
the Furies agree to bring about a combat between the
brothers. Polynices challenges Eteocles, and Eteocles
accepts the challenge, after a quarrel with Creon, who
taunts him with cowardice. Various attempts are made
to stop the meeting : Jocasta flies to her son ; Antigone,
from the tower, calls to her brother ; Adrastus protests,
and finding himself unheeded, makes his way from the
field back to Argos ; the goddess of Piety comes down
and urges the two armies to interpose, but is driven from
the scene by the Fury, who shakes her serpents and

torches in her face. The combat is conducted like that
in the 'Phœnissæ' of Euripides, except that, in Statius,
Eteocles receives his death-wound first, and Polynices is
stabbed while leaning over him and taking his spoils.
Œdipus emerges from his cell, and insists on being taken
to the bodies. He repents of the curses he has invoked,
and says that natural piety has returned to him, which
he shows by wishing that he had his eyes back to be
pulled out again in sign of grief. Creon, who has succeeded
to the throne, with the insolence of an upstart monarch,
bids him leave Thebes. He replies indignantly, Antigone
submissively, and they are allowed to withdraw to
Cithæron. The Argives retire in confusion from the
Theban territory, and the Eleventh Book ends.

The story is now exhausted, and it is not easy to see
why the poet should have prolonged it, unless perhaps
in compliance with the practice of his predecessors. But
there is a class of readers who are curious to know the
sequel of every tale, who wish for a sixth act to 'Hamlet,'
and wonder what Edgar and Albany did after the death
of Lear: and it may gratify these to find that Statius
occupies a twelfth book with telling us that Creon buries
his son magnificently, Eteocles obscurely, and Polynices
not at all; that the widows of the Argive chiefs set out
for Thebes to beg their husbands' bodies, but, on hearing
of Creon's tyranny, turn aside to Athens, and implore the
aid of Theseus; that Argia, Polynices' wife, goes to
Thebes nevertheless, and is proceeding to lay out the
corpse when she falls in with Antigone, who had come
on the same errand; and that Theseus leads an army to
Thebes, conquers it with little or no resistance, and kills
Creon. The meeting of the husbandless wife and brother-
less sister is strikingly told, and might have been admired
had it occurred elsewhere: the conquering expedition of

Theseus is hurried over in a couple of hundred lines, as if it were a trifling episode. The poet himself seems to feel his mistake; he tells us that he cannot describe how the Argive ladies severally wailed their dead: it would be an extensive subject even for a new poem, and after his long voyage he wants to get into port. And so he takes leave of his work, which is already approved by Cæsar, and studied by the schoolboys of Italy, and will, he trusts, have an immortality of its own, though a less glorious one than that of the ' Æneid.'

Such is an outline of the principal work of a writer who, in the opinion of the elder Scaliger,[1] stands above all Greek and Roman epic poets, save Virgil alone; being superior to Homer in the quality of his verses, the number of his figures, the distribution of his characters, and the elaboration of his sentiments. To our readers, we fear, he will appear to have produced a medley of confused and exaggerated effects, crowding disproportioned incidents and overdrawn or underdrawn characters within the framework of a story, which may be a striking one, but which he did not invent, but borrow. He has been compared to Ovid, and with some justice, as both are apt to sacrifice taste to ingenuity, simplicity to show; but while Ovid, with all his faults, tells his tale excellently, Statius tells his indifferently. Nor can we agree with the praise which has been bestowed by two eminent critics, Mr. Hallam[2] and Mr. Merivale, on the structure of the ' Thebaid,' as though it had the advantage of other epic poems in unity and greatness of action. The March to Thebes is one thing, the Siege of Thebes another: the former interests us only as the preparation for the latter, and to spend half the poem on it is really to fall into the error of the writer, who, as we said earlier in this paper,

[1] Poetica.   [2] History of Literature of Europe.

could not despatch that part of his subject under twenty-four books. It may be true that the incidents of the march formed a recognised portion of the Theban legend, and could as little be dispensed with in a traditional exposition of the story as the incidents of the siege; but while we admit that there may be an excuse for the fault, we must not speak as if the fault had not been committed.

Our limits do not allow us to give our readers as adequate a notion as we should wish of the style of Statius. There is a family likeness among most, if not all, of the writers of the silver age; point, terseness, clever condensation, are characteristic of them all; their fault is a want of simplicity and repose. These characteristic features Statius may be said to exaggerate and distort. Everything with him is, so to say, of the second intention; thoughts are locked up in epigrams, facts in allusions. The great masters of this art were, we need not say, the writers of the corresponding period of Greek cultivation, the school of Alexandria. When Lycophron wants to describe Heracles, he speaks of him as one whom a dead man killed with swordless guile. But Statius is hardly less successful in darkening his meaning, when, at the outset of his poem, he says [1] he shall content himself with speaking of the arms of Aonia, and the sceptre fatal to two kings, the fury that stopped not after death, and the flames that waged fresh war on the funeral pile, and the royal deaths that found no burial, and the cities that were drained by alternate carnage. Some-

---

[1] Satis arma referre
Aonia, et geminis sceptram exitiale tyrannis,
Nec furiis post fata modum flammasque rebelles
Seditione rogi, tumulisque carentia regum
Funera et egestas alternis mortibus urbas.
                                Book i. 33 foll.

times, in interpreting him, we have to balance proba-
bilities between his love of the obscure and his love of
the horrible ; as when he tells us that the sons of Œdipus
trampled on their father's eyes as they fell from his head,[1]
and we are left in doubt whether he means what he says,
or whether it is merely his way of saying that the sons
insulted their father's blindness. But we shall exemplify
the qualities of his style best by analysing a very short
passage. He is speaking of the Fury as she appears on
earth: —[2]

> Centum illi stantes umbrabant ora cerastæ,
> Turba minor diri capitis : sedet intus abactis
> Ferrea lux oculis, qualis per nubila Phœbes
> Atracia rubet arte labor.

'A hundred uncoiled vipers shaded her brow, not half
the multitude of that terrible head : deep in her sunken
eyes sits an iron light, like as by Thessalian skill the
agony of Phœbe glares red through the clouds.' We
want our readers to observe the choice of the word
'cerastæ' for the common 'angues' or 'serpentes;' the
enigmatical expression 'turba minor,' signifying that the
snakes were innumerable, as one hundred was less than
half their number ; the boldness with which the light is
called 'ferrea,' iron-red, and made to sit in the eyes ; the
exaggeration of speaking of the eyes as 'abacti,' driven
away into the head ; the novelty of making the labour of
the moon look red, instead of the labouring moon herself ; and the use of the recondite word 'Atracian,' from
one of the tribes of Thessaly, for the ordinary word

---

[1] 'Natl, facinus sine more, cadentes calcavere oculos' (Book I. 238).
There is a similar doubt about verse 72, 'miseraque oculos in matre reliqui,'
which may only mean that Œdipus blinded himself at the time of his
mother's death.

[2] Book I. 103 foll.

'Thessalian.' We do not mean to say that most of these might not be paralleled from other poets, but we think it will be admitted that the allowance of strange expressions is large for three lines and a half.

It would be too much to say that the style of the silver age is essentially ill adapted to the production of broad pictorial effects in narrative. We are at once confronted by the fact that Tacitus, the most graphic historian of Rome, perhaps of any nation, belongs, not only by accident of birth, but by the quality of his genius, emphatically to the silver age. His narrative may indeed be called, as Mr. Carlyle's has been called in our own day, history read by flashes of lightning; but that vivid and fitful intensity leaves a more distinct as well as more powerful impression on the mind than the equable moonlight glow of Livy. But Tacitus is enabled to produce this effect by the presence of that stern self-restraint which accompanies power of the highest class. The flashes of his genius are no mere idle coruscations, but obey a fixed law which makes each subservient to a general result. But for this restraining principle, we should have not a history, but a series of epigrams. And this restraining principle is precisely what Statius wants. The consequence is that we have a narrative which is full of short cuts and compendious expedients, and at the same time incredibly tedious. We are always out of breath, and yet seem never to arrive at our journey's end. The paradox of the arguers against motion is realised, and progress is shown to be impossible by the infinite divisibility of the ground which has to be passed over. Let us contrast the narrative of the 'Thebaid' for a few moments with the narrative of the 'Æneid,' choosing a place in the two stories where they really come into competition, the description of the prize-fight

in the funeral games.   We must trust that our readers'
recollection will supply them with the details in Virgil's
account, while we endeavour to give them some notion
of those in the tale as told by Statius.

As soon as Adrastus has proclaimed that the boxing-
match is to begin, which he does by commending the
prowess shown in boxing as 'bellis et ferro proxima
virtus,' Capaneus rises like the Homeric Epeios or the
Virgilian Dares, puts the lead-weighted gauntlets on hands
as hard as they, and asks for an opponent, intimating
that he would rather have had a Theban, whom he might
fairly have killed, instead of being obliged to shed the
blood of a citizen.   Alcidamas, a young Spartan, rises at
last, to the surprise of all but his compatriots, who know
that he is a child of the palæstra, having been trained by
Pollux :

> Ipse deus posuitque manus et brachia finxit
> Materiam (suadebat amor): tunc sæpe locavit
> Cominus, et simili stantem miratus in ira
> Sustulit exultans, nudumque ad pectora pressit.

The passage is not altogether easy ; but we suppose the
meaning to be that Pollux had moulded the rudimentary
gristle of his young favourite into bone and muscle, had
stood up with him repeatedly, and had been so charmed
with his spirit and endurance as to catch him to his
breast and embrace him then and there.   Now let us
think of Virgil's notice of Dares' victory over Butes, or
Entellus's companionship with Eryx, and we shall be
better able to appreciate this unseasonable attempt to
interest us by minute word-painting in the antecedents
of a personage on whom the eye is only meant to rest for
a second or two.   Capaneus is indignant, scornful, and
affectedly contemptuous ; at length, however, his languid

sinews swell, and he stands up to fight. They confront
each other, the one like what Tityos would be if the
birds would suffer him to rise; the other so young as to
arrest the sympathies of the spectators, who tremble at
the prospect of seeing him bleed :—

> Quem vincl haud quisquam, sævo nec sanguine tingi
> Malit, et erecto timeat spectacula voto.

At first they are prudent and cautious, sparring rather
than hitting : 'explornnt cæstus hebetantque terendo.'
Alcidamas continues this Fabian policy, and keeps his
fury in reserve, 'differet animum:' Capaneus becomes
enraged, and expends both his hands recklessly : 'ambas
consumit sine lege manus.' The young Spartan has the
advantage, parrying his opponent's hits, while he sometimes goes into him (the word is Statius's own, 'intrat'),
like a wave breaking on a rock, and finally plants a
wound on his forehead. Capaneus hears the shout of
the spectators, but is unconscious that blood has been
drawn ; at last, however, he puts up his hand to his
brow, when the sight of the stains makes him more
furious than a wounded lion ; he rushes on Alcidamas,
who is driven before him, preserving his coolness nevertheless :—

> Non tamen immemor artis,
> Adversus fugit, et fugiens tamen ictibus obstat.

The mad effort soon exhausts them both, and they pause
to take breath ; and the poet takes breath too in a short
simile :—

> Sic ubi longa vagos lassarunt æquora nautas
> Et signo de puppi dato posuere parumper
> Brachia, vix requies, jam vox ciet altera remos.

The giant makes another rush, but his nimble adversary

first eludes him and then butts him over, 'sponte ruens
iuersusque humeris,' knocking him down again as he is
rising, till he is alarmed at his own success. The Argives
raise a shout which the shores and woods but faintly
echo; but Adrastus sees that Capaneus is not beaten,
but only made more dangerous, and interposes to prevent
murder from being done :—

> Ite, oro, socii, furit : ite, opponite dextras,
> Festinate, furit, palmamque et præmia ferte :
> Non prius effracto quam misceat ossa cerebro
> Absistet, video : moriturum auferte Lacona.

Tydeus and Hippomedon with some difficulty hold
Capaneus, telling him that he has conquered, and that it
is graceful to spare a vanquished foe who happens to be
an ally; but he thrusts aside the prize, and complains
that he is not allowed to beat the minion to a mummy,
and send him back thus to his patron. The Spartans
welcome their champion, and indulge in a distant laugh
at Capaneus's blustering ; and so the scene is ended.

We feel that this summary has done but little justice to
the real points of the narrative, which is at once far more
ingenious, and for that reason possibly more tedious, than
our plain prose can make it. Almost every line contains
some terse, pointed expression ; not a few of them are
distinguished by graphic and picturesque touches, which
we have been compelled to omit. Yet we cannot doubt
what the verdict will be, if we now call upon our readers
to decide between Statius and Virgil. The narrative in
the 'Æneid' reflects the simple majesty of the veteran
Entellus, rising modestly, only warming into passion, and
finally retiring from the victorious field with a tribute to
his patron, such as we can fancy Virgil paying to Homer.
In Statius all is noise, glare, and confusion, whether we

attempt to sympathise with the baffled giant whom failure
is turning into a fiend, or to join in the laugh with which
his threats are received by the backers of his young opponent. Yet it is not the absence of art which makes
Virgil what he is. Every line in him will bear examination; and every line will be seen upon examination to
have been made conducive to the purpose of the entire-
narrative. Take for instance the figure of Dares; he is
drawn with just sufficient definiteness to make him seem
as a foil to Entellus; beyond that we are not intended to
think of him either with sympathy or with aversion. He
is dragged away from the scene as any other beaten combatant might be, his plight being represented in words-
translated from the description of the Homeric Euryalus.
By a single word we are made to feel that his backers are
beaten as well as their champion; it is only after having
been *called*, ' vocati,' that they come and receive the prize
for him; over everything else a veil is drawn, and we are
not distracted by traits designed to individualise him or
them. ' Semper ad eventum festinat' might be said of
Virgil as truly as of Homer: but his haste is not hurry;
he sees the goal before him, and can wait till he
reaches it; he does not require to be always reassuring
himself by some small piece of immediate success, like the
hunters after applause complained of by Sir Walter Scott,
who, not content with running swiftly down the stream,
must needs taste the froth from every stroke of the oar.
He can be summary when he pleases; no writer more
effectively so; but he is not for ever calling our attention
to the fact by those short sharp jerks which make us feel
that the poet after all would have found his best employment in composing epigrammatic arguments for the several
books of his own work, and remind us that in another
generation or two the art of narrative composition at

Rome will culminate in such productions as Ausonius's Periochæ of the 'Iliad.'

But perhaps we shall give a better view of Statius, both in his weakness and in his strength, if we task the patience of our readers by quoting a passage *in extenso*. It is when Hypsipyle, after having been accosted by Adrastus, disclaims, like Nausicaa in the 'Odyssey' and Venus in the 'Æneid,' the divine character ascribed to her by her querist, and then guides him to the fountain, leaving the infant on the grass:—

> Dixit, et orantis media inter anhelitus ardens
> Verba rapit, cursuque animæ labat arida lingua.
> Idem omnes pallorque viros, flatusque soluti
> Oris habet : reddit demisso Lemnia vultu :
>   ' Diva quidem vobis, et si cælestis origo est,
> Unde ego ? mortales utinam haud transgressa fuissem
> Luctibus ! altricem mandati cernitis orbam
> Pignoris : at nostris an quis sinus, uberaque ulla,
> Scit deus : et nobis regnum tamen, et pater ingens.
> Sed quid ego hæc, femoaque optatis demoror undis ?
> Mecum age nunc, si forte vado Langia perennes
> Servat aquas : solet et rapidi sub limite cancri
> Semper, et Icarii quamvis juba fulgeret astri,
> Ire tamen.' Simul hærentem, ne tarda Pelasgis
> Dux foret, ah miserum vicino cespite alumnum,
> (Sic Parcæ voluere,) locat, ponitque negantem
> Floribus aggestis, et amico murmure dulces
> Solatur lacrimas : qualis Berecynthia mater,
> Dum circa parvum jubet exultare Tonantem
> Curetas trepidos : illi certantia plaudunt
> Orgia, sed magnis resonat vagitibus Ide.
>   At puer in gremio vernæ telluris, et alto
> Gramine, nunc faciles sternit procursibus herbas
> In vultum nitens ; caram modo lactis egeno
> Nutricem clangore ciens, iterumque renidens,
> Et teneris meditans verba illuctantia labris,
> Miratur nemorum strepitus, aut obvia carpit,

Aut patulo trahit ore diem : nemorisque malorum
Inscia, et vitæ multum securus inerrat.
Sic tener Odrysia Mavors nive, sic puer ales
Vertice Mænalio, talis per littora reptans
Improbus Ortygiæ latus inclinabat Apollo.

At first we seem to meet with nothing but misplaced
ingenuity. The thought of calling attention to the
parched tongues and panting breath of Adrastus and his
comrades might have occurred to Ovid, but would not
have occurred to Virgil, especially as the speech which
Adrastus has just delivered by no means reminds us of
the gasping utterance of physical distress, being, like all
Statius's speeches, epigrammatic and rhetorical. Nor is
Hypsipyle's reply expressed in the terms which would be
most appropriate to the comprehension of thirsty men.
To talk to persons in such a condition about the orphaned
nurturer of an intrusted pledge, who knows not whether
her own children have any breasts to suck, is to stipulate
that before receiving relief they shall guess an enigma.
Even when she comes to speak of water she cannot refrain
from astronomical and mythological details, Cancer and
the mane of the Icarian star. After this the description
becomes only pleasing and graceful; we are charmed with
the picture of the nurse laying down the child and soothing
its crying, and we do not resent the comparison to Cybele
and the infant Jupiter, though we feel it to be somewhat
ambitious. Virgil might have said this, or something like
this, just as before taking Cupid to Dido's palace he gives
us a momentary glimpse of Ascanius in Idalia. But with
the end of the paragraph Virgil would have stopped.
Statius, on the contrary, feels that his chance of displaying
his talent has come, and he will not forego it. Thus we
have the picture, an exceedingly pretty one, of the babe
propelling itself along the grass face foremost, crying for

its nurse, and then laughing and talking broken words, wondering at the forest noises, pulling to pieces what falls in its way, and taking in the breath of heaven through its parted lips. It is beauty out of place, but it is beauty still. The simile, or congeries of similes, that follows, is more questionable. After having heard of the infant Jupiter among the Curetes, we do not care to hear of the infant Mars in the snow, or the infant Mercury on the mountain-top; still less can we be said to require to have our apprehension assisted by the grotesque, if ingenious, portrait of the infant Apollo crawling along Delos, and nearly turning it over on its side.

When we examine the 'Thebaid' as a whole, we can only speak of it as a monument of misused power. It is only when we contemplate it in its parts that we see evidences of power directed towards an object, attaining to it, and resting in it. Every ingenious expression might be regarded in this way as a result gained: it is bad if viewed as a means; good if viewed as an end. But to criticise a work of art in this spirit is not to criticise at all; it is, in fact, to turn the ordered hierarchy of poetical creation into anarchy and chaos. There are, however, parts which are more capable than others of being regarded apart from the whole, even though we may feel that a censure on the poet is involved in the very act of so regarding them. The description of the infant which we have just quoted is one of these. But there are some which stand so completely in a class by themselves as to deserve a few words of separate commemoration. We allude to the similes of the poem. Two or three of them we have incidentally cited or referred to already; others will be familiar to the reader of Copleston's 'Prælectiones Academicæ,' where it is well remarked that their details, even when irrelevant, are often pleasing from their exceed-

ingly natural character. As parts of the narrative they
are sometimes felt to be excrescences : as pieces of independent description they are well worth studying. The
poet evidently liked them himself : he is never tired of
introducing them ; indeed, there is scarcely a page without
them. We will quote a very few of them, rendering them
more or less closely into English. Here is one from a
tiger:—[1]

> Qualis ubi audito venantum murmure tigris
> Horruit in maculas somnosque excussit inertes,
> Bella cupit, laxatque genas, et temperat ungues,
> Mox ruit in turmas natisque alimenta cruenta
> Spirantem fert ore virum : sic excitus ira
> Ductor in absentem consumit proelia fratrem.[2]

'As when a tigress, on hearing the horn of the hunters,
has bristled her spotted skin, and shaken off the sloth of
slumber, she yearns for battle, and eases her stiff jaws,
and trims her talons ; soon she rushes among the com-
panies, and carries off in her mouth a living man to feed
her savage whelps : so, stirred up with wrath, the prince
squanders deeds of arms on his absent brother.' The
Theban general is compared to a shepherd :— [3]

> Perspicuas sic luce fores et virgea pastor
> Claustra levat, dum terra recens : jubet ordine primos
> Ire duces, media stipantur plebe maritae :
> Ipse levat gravidas et humum tactura parentum
> Ubera, succiduasque apportat matribus agnas.

[1] Book ii. 128 foll.

[2] ' Horruit in maculas ' seems to mean no more than what we have made
it mean. Addison, however (*Spectator*, No. lxxxi.), applying it to the patches
worn in his day, says it is reported of the tigress that several spots rise in
her skin when she is angry, and quotes an imitation by Cowley—

> She swells with angry pride,
> And calls forth all her spots on every side.

[3] Book vii. 393 foll.

'Thus the shepherd opens at daybreak the transparent
door-work and the wattled enclosures, while there is freshness abroad on the earth; he bids the rams lead the way;
the mediate throng crowds on the ewes; with his own
hand he supports those heavy with young, and lifts the
udders which would else sweep the ground, and brings to
the mothers their dropping lambs.' Human as well as
animal life is made to furnish comparisons. The newly-
chosen successor of Amphiaraus reminds the poet of a
young Persian monarch:—[1]

> Sicut Achæmenius solium gentesque paternas
> Excepit si forte puer, cui vivere patrem
> Tutius, incerta formidine gaudia librat,
> An fidi proceres, ne pugnet vulgus habenis,
> Cui latus Euphratæ, cui Caspia limina mandet.
> Sumere tunc arcus ipsumque onerare veretur
> Patris equum, visusque sibi nec sceptra capaci
> Sustentare manu nec adhuc implere tiaram.

'Even as when the heir of Achæmenes succeeds to the
throne and the peoples that were his father's, himself a
mere boy, for whom it had been safer were his father still
alive, he wavers between the flutterings of joy and fear—
Can the nobles be trusted? Will the common herd rebel
against the yoke? To whom must he commit the
frontier of Euphrates? To whom the gates of the Caspian?
He is too modest to bend his father's bow or make his
father's steed feel his weight; he cannot think his hand
yet strong enough for the sceptre, or his brow large
enough for the tiara.' Following Virgil, he draws, as we
have seen, similes from mythology, but with a much less
sparing hand. The joy of Œdipus on emerging from his

---

[1] Book viii. 286 foll.

solitude is paralleled with that of Phineus when freed from his Harpy tormentors :—[1]

> Qualis post longæ Phineus jejunia pœnæ,
> Nil stridere domi volucres ut sensit abactas,
> Necdum tota fides, hilaris mensæque torosque
> Nec turbata feris tractavit pocula pennis.

'Even as Phineus, when his long penal fast was over, soon as he perceived the birds driven off, and no screeching at his doors, ere he wholly credited his bliss, handled gaily board and couch and winecups, unturmoiled by those fierce-flapping wings.' And there is surely some grandeur, if there is some exaggeration, in the comparison of the flight of Adrastus from Thebes to the first entrance of Pluto into his infernal realm,[2] a sort of anticipation of the Satan of Milton :—

> Qualis
> Demissus curru lævæ post præmia sortis
> Umbrarum custos mundique novissimus heres
> Palluit, amisso veniens in Tartara cælo.

'As when, dismounting from his car, after the award of the luckless lot, the warden of the shades, the last sharer of the world's inheritance, grew pale as he entered Tartarus, and felt that heaven was lost.'

Mr. Merivale has observed with much justice that Statius is a miniature painter employed by the caprice of a patron or his own unadvised ambition on a great historical picture. Such exaggerations as his are indeed the fruit of weakness quite as often as of ill-regulated strength. The commonplace aspects of a monstrous story may be seized by any quick apprehension, and reproduced by any fertile fancy: it is only high genius that can render them

---

[1] Book viii. 255 foll.   [2] Book xi. 443 foll.

human and credible.   Dryden[1] compares Statius to his
own Capaneus engaging the two immortals Virgil and
Homer, and reaping the fruit of his daring.   We would
rather compare him to his own Atys,[2] the plighted
husband of Ismene, who is slain by the mighty arm of
Tydeus.   The love of his Theban bride leads him into
war; he challenges the champion of the field, and falls at
the first shock; and he lies in death pale and bloody, yet
in the pride of youthful beauty and golden armour.

[1] 'Discourse on Epic Poetry,' prefixed to the Æneid.
[2] Book viii. 555 foll.

IN passing from the tragedians of the Roman Republic,
we feel that the gates of a heroic age are being closed
upon us. It is not merely that they, more fortunate than
their successors, though reduced to silence themselves,
found a Cicero to recount their triumphs : the less willing
testimony of Horace speaks sufficiently to the unrivalled
popularity which they enjoyed in the Augustan era ; and
the references made to them by later writers, scanty
as they are, seem to show that no tragic poet arose
after them whose authority was so generally recognised
by the critical taste of posterity. There is certainly no
one, of course with the exception of Seneca, of whose
works we know so much. We hear, indeed, the names of
many subsequent tragedians, but we hear scarcely anything more. A few of them are mentioned by Tacitus,
as having been in some way or other involved in the
history of the time ; a few of them find a place in the
Satires of Juvenal, to be ridiculed for their imbecility, or
pitied for their needy circumstances. Some were men
known in other walks of life, like Q. Cicero, Asinius
Pollio, and the Emperors Augustus and Nero ; others, like
Ovid, Lucan, and Statius, have left behind them more
durable monuments of their power and skill in poetry.
It may be that one kind of reputation has eclipsed the
other ; it may be that the author of one or two plays had
but a poor chance for posthumous fame as compared with

---

[1] Printed from the MS. of a Lecture delivered at Oxford in 1857.

the authors of thirty or forty.   But however it may be
accounted for, the fact is still there ; the accredited remains of these poets altogether do not amount to five and
thirty lines, and there are probably not more than four or
five on whose works contemporary or succeeding critics
have pronounced any opinion.

Of these ἀμένηνα κάρηνα, however, two at least seem to
have been of sufficient importance in their day to claim
a passing notice.   We know hardly anything of the plays
of Varius and Pomponius Secundus ; but the testimonies
of those who had an opportunity of reading them, induce
us to believe the first to have been really eminent, the
second more than respectable.

The name of L. Varius Rufus is familiar to all readers
of Virgil and Horace, who evidently regarded him as one
of the most illustrious members of their poetical brotherhood, the former not specifying the kind of poetry which
had won him his fame, the latter talking of him as an epic
writer, and (incidentally at least) an eulogist of Augustus.
Other authors, however, appear to have been more struck
with a single tragedy written by him on the well-worn
subject of ' Thyestes.'   ' The " Thyestes " of Varius,' says
Quintilian, ' may stand a comparison with any of the Greek
tragedies '—praise doubtless to be accepted with some
qualification, but sufficiently high nevertheless.   It is
mortifying to think that, as in the case of Ennius, we can
almost trace the casualty which took away from us the
means of judging for ourselves.   The play is lost, but
its title-page is still extant.   Nearly twenty years ago, a
scholium was printed from a Paris MS. of the eighth
century, which, if not actually forming part of a copy of
the play, was probably itself copied from one.   It opens
in the well-known manner, ' Incipit Thuestes Varii,' and
goes on with a sort of didascalia or historical notice,

'Lucius Varius cognomento Rufus Thyesten tragœdiam magna cura absolutam post Actiacam victoriam Augusti ludis ejus in scena edidit. Pro qua fabula sestertium deciens accepit.' The care bestowed on the composition of the tragedy—the occasion of its representation, namely, the rejoicings after the battle of Actium, and the remuneration received by the author, a million of sesterces —such are the facts which were intended to prepare us for a perusal. And now all that we actually possess of this elaborate and highly successful work is a couple of half lines, in which Atreus talks of his unspeakable injuries as forcing him to an unspeakable retaliation : ' Jam fero infandissima, jam facere cogor.' Possibly we may add to this morsel two anapæstic fragments, one of them quoted by a metrical writer, Marius Victorinus, to illustrate a strange theory about the stationariness of the Chorus in singing as symbolising the stationariness of the earth while the heaven is in motion ; the other, cited by an old commentator on Virgil's ' Eclogues,' apropos to Corydon's lamentation over his half-pruned vine. In any case it is not easy to see the ground of Niebuhr's criticism on the supposed characteristics of the play. ' I fear,' he says, ' that his manner was too declamatory, and that his " Thyestes" bore the same relation to the ancient Attic tragedian that Virgil's " Æneid " bears to the Homeric epics. This and all the later tragedies of the Romans were not, like those of Pacuvius and Attius, imitations of the Attic dramas, but were based upon the models of the Alexandrian period. The tragedies of what was called the " Pleias" were of a very different character from the ancient Attic tragedies ; and we may form a tolerably correct notion of them by looking at the productions of Seneca, which are not ancient Greek, and cannot be Roman. I would rather have had Varius' poem " De Morte " than his

tragedy.' No doubt it is likely that Varius, like Virgil,
may have had his eye on Alexandrian models, as well as
on the more ancient masterpieces of Greece. But is it to
such a spirit of imitation that the un-Homeric character
of the ' Æneid ' is mainly due, and not rather to the peculiarities of the author and to the impossibility of reproducing the Homeric epic in the Augustan age? and is
not the Augustan age more nearly parallel to the age of
Pericles than the last two centuries of the Republic, when
Pacuvius and Attius wrote? Of course it may be said of
a Roman poem on a Greek legend that it is not ancient
Greek, and cannot be Roman ; but a proposition like
this does not help us to bridge over the chasm which we
know separates Seneca from Virgil, and, we feel, may also
have separated him from Varius. Seneca, writing for no
stage but that of the study or the school, may have drunk
more or less deeply of the springs of Alexandrian rhetoric.
How far Varius did so is a question which must have
depended on the character of his own genius, and is hardly
soluble by a reference to the general features of the
period, which need not have been unfavourable to the
imitation of Sophocles or Euripides, as it certainly receives
no appreciable light from the fragment or fragments of
the ' Thyestes.'

Pomponius Secundus (the prænomen is variously given)
was a person of considerable distinction in his time, the time
of Tiberius, Caligula, and Claudius. He shared in the fall
of Sejanus, whose friend he had been, but lived to obtain
the consulship, and later still to gain a victory over the
barbarian Chatti, for which he received the triumphal
ornaments. Pliny the Elder was warmly attached to him,
and wrote his life in two books. Tacitus, who mentions
him more than once in his 'Annals,' in his dialogue on
orators, instances the reputation he enjoyed in life as a
proof that poetry confers at least as much distinction on

a man as eloquence. But the only definite judgment on his characteristics as a tragic poet, which has come down to us, is one reported by Quintilian, who calls him far the most eminent tragic writer with whom he had been contemporary, adding that the critics of a former generation thought him wanting in the pure tragic element, while acknowledging his erudition and poetical brilliancy. The few fragments which have been preserved from his plays will perhaps enable us to understand what is meant by the last-named qualities. His erudition seems to be proved by some peculiarities of language, which have caused him to be quoted by Charisius and Nonius—the use of *humile* as the ablative of *humilis*, the adoption of the orthography *omneis* in the accusative as distinguished from *omnes* in the nominative plural, the invention, if invention it were, of the word *notifico*, and the employment of *ascendibilis semita* as a poetical periphrasis for a scaling-ladder. These specimens of phraseology would lead us to suppose that he imitated the older tragedians, and the structure of the two lines which are extant, as remnants of his dialogues, iambic and trochaic, would confirm the supposition. Brilliancy is perhaps an exaggerated term to apply to the solitary piece of continuous writing which has been quoted from him—four anapæsts, not amounting to a complete sentence, on a harp which makes music with the woods and the meandering river, but they have certainly a poetical turn, in spite of some harshness of rhythm :—

> Pendeat ex humeris dulcis chelys,
> Et numeros edat varios quibus
> Adsonet omne virens late nemus
> Et tortis errans qui flexibus.

And now at last we may congratulate ourselves on having passed from conjectures to certainties—from frag-

ments short and far between to entire plays. Of the ten
tragedies bearing the name of Seneca, one, the ' Thebais,' or
' Phœnissæ,' is grievously mutilated. The last act lost, the
others headless or tailless, or both, and the intervening
choruses swept away—a reduction probably amounting
to one-half; but the remaining nine are complete, and
the total aggregate, 11,052 lines, gives us as ample an
opportunity as criticism could desire of judging of these,
the first and last surviving children of the Roman
Melpomene.

With respect, indeed, to the authorship of these plays,
there is still room for doubt and speculation. The MSS.
give them to Annæus Seneca, but the prænomen assigned
appears to fluctuate between Lucius and Marcus. The testimony of the ancient writers, again, is rather equivocal. The
' Medea,' the ' Troades,' the ' Hercules Furens,' the ' Hippolytus,' and the ' Thyestes,' are all quoted as Seneca's, the
first by Quintilian, the others by later authors, but without
any intimation that the poet is the same as the philosopher.
Sidonius Apollinaris, in the fifth century, expressly distinguishes them as different members of the same family,
in lines which show that if the generation in which he
lived had preserved the traditions of Roman biography,
it had, at any rate, lost those of Greek quantity :—

> Quorum unus colit hispidum Platona,
> Incassumque suum monet Neronem :
> Orchestram quatit alter Euripidis.

and a later witness, Paulus Diaconus, a contemporary of
Charlemagne, is quoted on the same side. On the other
hand, those who speak of Seneca the philosopher do not
mention that he wrote tragedies. But it is very possible
that the poetical studies of which Tacitus speaks as having
excited the jealousy of Nero, were no other than these

very plays; and though Quintilian, in reserving a conspicuous place for Seneca at the end of his well-known
chapter on the writers of Greece and Rome, merely instances poems among other proofs of his versatility, the
enumeration is too rapid and too casual for us to wonder
at the absence of any more formal notice of works which
the critic certainly did not put on a level with the best
dramas of his day.   The plays themselves, if I may trust
my own judgment, are such as we may well conceive to
have been written by the philosopher.   There is the same
sparkle and point, with the same deficiency of feeling and
reality—the same ambition of display, straining after exaggerated effects and delighting in high-flown sentiments
—the same combination, as Schlegel well puts it, of
tedious prolixity and conciseness passing into obscurity—
one common-place thought generating a hundred enig-
matic epigrams—which cannot but force itself on the
attention even of one whose acquaintance with the prose
works of Seneca is as slight as my own.   In the tragedies,
no less than in the epistles and moral treatises, we see
what it was which led the Emperor Caligula, who, if he
was a madman, was also sometimes a wit, to speak of
Seneca's style as sand without lime; what it was that
suggested to A. Gellius, on the authorities whom he quotes,
the happy expression ' ineptus inanisque impetus '—a
violent effort, without object or propriety.   Of course, it
is still possible that the poet and the philosopher may be
distinct, and that the internal evidence in favour of their
identity may be only a proof of family likeness, such as
certainly existed between Seneca and his nephew, the poet
Lucan ; but at any rate it may be said that there is no
conclusive argument which makes their identity incredible.   One of the plays, indeed, separated from the
rest by its subject, the ' Octavia,' actually introduces the

philosopher as one of its *dramatis personæ*, and there is
external ground for supposing that it may have been the
work of some other author, since it is not contained in
the oldest manuscript, the Florentine, while the style,
though certainly not unlike Seneca's, may perhaps, to a
minute observer, reveal some points of difference, apart
from those involved in the character of the play.   It is
not inconceivable in itself that Seneca, having followed,
and, as he possibly thought, surpassed the Greeks in nine
of his tragedies, chose for the tenth a subject more nearly
concerning himself, at once pleasing himself with the
thought of being the author of a *prætexta*, and satisfying
an impulse of another kind by the production of a work
which might seem as an apology for his connexion with
Nero; but it seems safe to conclude that in this instance,
and in this only, the work of some imitator of the philosophic tragedian may have been confounded by later judges,
critical or uncritical, with those of the philosophic tragedian
himself.   At any rate, there seems no reason, external or
internal, for dividing the authorship of the nine other
plays.   The extraordinary diversity of opinion which has
prevailed, especially among the earlier critics, with regard
to their merits, as compared with each other, is a thing
which, to my perception at least, is simply unaccountable.

Daniel Heinsius distributed the ten plays among no less
than five authors, giving the 'Troades,' 'Hippolytus,' and
'Medea,' which he considered the best, to the philosopher;
Lipsius thought he traced four authors, one of them being
the philosopher, another a still greater genius of the
Augustan age, but with him the 'Troades,' so far from
being one of the best, is contrasted with the 'Thebais,' his
first favourite, which Heinsius had placed nowhere.   Even
Bernhardy, supposing them to be the work of a rhetorical
school of writers, makes a marked distinction between

play and play, praising the 'Troades' for its powerful
though luxuriant rhetoric, and admitting that the 'Thyestes,' the 'Hippolytus,' and the 'Hercules Furens,' contain many excellent things, while he finds mere empty
prate in the 'Œdipus' and the 'Agamemnon,' and resolves the 'Hercules Œtæus' into wind and vapour.   I
confess it appears to me .that the same characteristics,
favourable or unfavourable, may be discovered in all. All
are written alike in that elaborate antithetical style, terse
in individual expressions, yet diffuse in its general effect,
which is the common property of the post Augustan
rhetorical school, both in prose and verse : in all alike the
sentiments are exaggerated, the passions swelled to
bursting, the horror which is involved in the catastrophe
drawn out into sickening detail : in all alike the dialogue
is declamatory or didactic, the choruses made up of commonplaces, moral or mythological—a caricature of the
Greek drama, in which uniformity of structure becomes
shapeless monotony, and simplicity of evolution passes
into the absence of all movement.

Of course you will not expect that I should verify this
criticism in detail by an examination of all the ten plays.
If you will allow me, however, I should be glad to single
out three of them of which I propose to give such an
account as may enable you to judge for yourselves what
their characteristics are.   It is difficult to make a choice ;
but I think I shall not do wrong if I name the ' Medea,'
the ' Thyestes,' and the ' Octavia '—the first, as offering
itself at once for comparison with one of the best known
of the Greek plays ; the second for the opposite reason,
as showing how Seneca can treat a subject which, though
often handled by the ancients, is untouched so far as our
imaginations are concerned ; the third, as exhibiting to
us the same powers, if they are the same, in yet another

field, and as affording, with all its drawbacks, the only specimen of a Roman drama or a Roman story.

You all remember the opening of the 'Medea' of Euripides, with what skilful indirectness we are informed of her wrongs, first by the conversation of her servants, and afterwards by her own agonized exclamations, uttered at intervals behind the scenes, and not intended for our hearing, till at last, when our minds have been sufficiently prepared, she appears herself on the stage, and we recognise not only the injured wife, but the woman of commanding intellect, dilating on the sufferings of her oppressed sex, and leading the Chorus to feel, even where she disclaims the thought, that their cause is the same as hers. Seneca, ignoring or disdaining such artificial approaches to our sympathies, attempts to take them by storm, by at once introducing his heroine, and that not as she would appear, comparatively self-controlled in the presence of others, but in all the abandonment of solitary passion. With a studied minuteness which may perhaps be excused as in keeping with the character of a practised enchantress, she invokes all the gods whom Jason's perfidy has made her friends, each by his proper mythological attribute. The goddess who taught Tiphys to navigate the Argo, and the mistress of the gloomy realms below, like herself, a ravished bride, but not, like herself, foully betrayed. She implores the Sun, her father, to lend her his chariot, that she may set the Isthmus of Corinth on fire, and make the two seas run into one; she recalls the crimes of her Colchian days, and declares that the deeds of a mother ought to outdo those of a maid, and that her divorce ought to be signalized no less than her marriage—

> Effera, ignota, horrida,
> Tremenda cœlo pariter ac terris mala,

Mens intus agitat; vulnera, et cædem, et vagum
Funus per artua.   Levia memoravi nimis.
Hæc virgo feci : gravior exsurgat dolor:
Majora jam me scelera post partus decent.
Accingere ira, teque in exitium para
Furore toto : paria narrentur tuis
Repudia thalamis.   Quo virum linquis modo ?
Hoc, quo secuta es.   Rumpe jam segnes moras :
Quæ scelere parta est, scelere linquenda est domus.

After fifty-five lines like these, a Chorus of Corinthian
women enters, to sing the epithalamium of Jason and
Creusa, an ode composed of asclepiads, glyconics, and
hexameters, not intermixed but successive, and consisting
of invocations like those in the preceding speech, only in
a different spirit, of compliments to the happy pair, she
being preferred to all Athenian and Spartan women,
he even to Bacchus, Apollo, Castor, and Pollux, and
allusions, not very apt, to the customs of a Roman
wedding.   In the Second Act we have 'Medea' again,
not alone, but with the nurse, her confidant, a personage
not unknown to the Athenian stage, but less frequent
there than in these tragedies, where he or she (for the
sexes vary) constitutes an ordinary, though not an indispensable, part of the play, an introduction owing partly
to the decreasing importance of the Chorus, which, while
preserving its fair numerical proportion so far as its odes are
concerned, bears but little share in the dialogue, partly
to the increasing taste for rhetoric which made it necessary that the chief speaker should have some recognised
person to draw out, if not to meet and rebut, his arguments.   Medea has heard the bridal song, and is thrown
into a fresh tempest of indignation ; she execrates Jason,
wishes he had a brother whom she could tear in pieces,
as she once tore in pieces her own for his sake, reminds
herself that he has a wife, and once more recalls the

slaughters through which she has waded ; then a change
of feeling succeeds, and she throws the whole blame on
Creon, who has broken the marriage tie with his sceptre,
and separated the mother from her children.   The nurse
attempts to restrain her by the general consideration (a
strange one, certainly, to think of here) that anger, when
loud, wastes itself, and that vengeance, to be effective, should
be silent.   An encounter of wits follows, in the course of
which occurs a passage often quoted to show both that
Seneca can say a striking thing, and that when he has
said it he cannot leave it alone.   The nurse has pointed
to Medea's forlorn condition :—

> Abiere Colchi : conjugis nulla est fides,
> Nihilque superest ossibus e tantis tibi.

She answers with a momentary flash of the sublime,
vanishing the next instant into rhetorical vapour :—

> Medea superest : hic mare et terras vides,
> Ferrumque et ignes et deos et fulmina.

While they are retorting on each other, the door
creaks, and Creon enters.   The dialogue which follows
is the first part of the play in which Seneca and Euripides come into direct competition.   The two scenes
substantially occupy the same ground, and both are
abundantly characteristic of their authors.   Euripides,
true to that conception of his heroine which makes her
character especially interesting to us, as embodying the
thoughts and feelings of the poet himself, puts into her
mouth a vindication of wise people against the suspicions
of their less advanced contemporaries ; Seneca seizes on
the opportunity thus, as he doubtless thought, left open to
allow Medea to plead her whole cause before Creon, as
the preserver of the Argo, and so the general bene-

factress of Greece. To help the afflicted, she urges on
Creon, is the one privilege which royalty can count on
securing as its own—it is the one recollection which
remains to her now in the wreck of all her queenly
state :—

> Solum hoc Colchico regno extuli,
> Decus illud ingens, gloriæ florem inclitum,
> Præsidia Achivæ gentis et prolem deûm,
> Servâsse memet. Munus est Orpheus meum,
> Qui saxa cantu mulcet et silvas trahit :
> Geminique munus Castor et Pollux meum,
> Satique Borea : quique trans Pontum quoque
> Summota Lynceus lumine immisso videt :
> Omnesque Minyæ : nam ducum taces ducem
> Pro quo nihil debetur : hunc nulli imputo :
> Vobis revexi ceteros, unum mihi.

All the rest she takes credit for, full credit—for
Orpheus, who can make the rocks follow him, for Castor
and Pollux, and the sons of Boreas, for Lynceus, whose
keen eyes can see beyond the Euxine, and all the
Minyæ; for Jason alone she claims no payment. The
upshot of the dialogue is the same in both cases; Medea
is allowed one day longer, a boon which in Euripides is
conceded to her reluctantly, in Seneca flung to her
haughtily, though she tells Creon she could do with less.
Seneca's Chorus, still taking no part in the action, sings
another song, on the voyage of the Argo, censuring, after
Horace, the boldness of the undertaking, enlarging on
the ignorance of the heavenly bodies which previously
prevailed, detailing the acts of seamanship which Tiphys
had to perform for the first time, the unfurling and
shifting of the sails and the like, contrasting the contented happiness of the golden age, recounting the
sufferings of the sailors for their presumption, their
encounters with Scylla and the Sirens, the last of whom,

nstead of leading away the Argonauts, were nearly led
away themselves by Orpheus, and at length concluding in a
very modern spirit about the present facilities of navigation, and the probability of finding out new countries—a
prophecy, so some have been pleased to regard it, of the
discovery of America, while others see in it merely a
historical allusion, couched in exaggerated language, to
the British expedition of Claudius. In the Third Act,
another scene with the confidant merely enables Medea
to utter · more rhetoric—to assure us that while the
revolutions of nature, which are carefully specified,
continue to go on, her rage shall remain unabated, more
terrible than Scylla, Charybdis, or Mount Ætna, with a
violence which neither torrent, nor stormy ocean, nor
fire, may restrain. Next comes an interview with Jason,
where again Seneca offers himself for comparison with
Euripides, though he has compressed into a single conversation what with his predecessor furnishes matter for
two, so that Medea in one and the same scene gives reins
to her passion as an injured wife, and with a sudden
accession of dissimulation, asks for reconciliation and
forgiveness—a transition which, whether natural or no,
could have become plausible only in the hands of a
more skilful artist.   The declaration, as usual, is tedious,
Medea taking pains to enumerate one by one the services
which she rendered Jason in Colchis; the dialogue is
smart enough. 'What charge can you bring against
me?' asks Jason. · 'Objicere crimen quod potes tandem
mihi?' 'Quodcunque fui' is her retort.

J.—Quid facere possim, eloquere.   M.—Pro me? vel
scelus.
J.—Hinc rex, et illinc.   M.—Est et his major metus,
Medea.

The scene being over, the Chorus, who, for anything we

know, may not have been present during the interview,
sings a Sapphic ode, pronouncing the rage of an injured
wife to be more vehement than the Danube, the Ister, or
the torrents of Mount Hæmus, and trusting that Jason
may be more fortunate than his fellow-voyagers, whose
untimely ends are severally recounted. The Fourth Act
is an Act of magical incantation, partly narrated by the
nurse, and partly performed by Medea herself on the
stage. Seneca has taken the circumstance of the presents
which are to be despatched to the rival bride, though he
has ignored the occasion for sending them, and seizes the
opportunity of showing his learning and his power of
accumulating horrors. The nurse goes through the whole
catalogue of evil agencies, the various deadly serpents, the
various noxious plants, all elaborately enumerated and
discriminated geographically. Medea evokes the tortured
ghosts from Tartarus, all of whom are to have a respite
from their sufferings that they may assist her, except
Sisyphus, who is Creon's father; she tells over her various
charms, each of which is a relic of some legendary horror;
she invokes Hecate, showing that all the proscribed rites
have been performed, the bloody turf pulled up, the brand
snatched from the funeral pile, the sepulchral fillet put
on, the branch of the Stygian tree waved. Once more
the Chorus sings, more briefly and more appositely than
usual, expressing their alarm at Medea's appearance,
though they take no notice of the proceedings in which
she has just been engaged, and wishing this last day of her
stay were well over. And now the Fifth Act brings the
crisis. If in the Fourth Act Seneca has been loquacious
where Euripides was silent, their mutual relations are
now reversed. Instead of that well-known description,
so fearful, yet so graceful, of the deaths of Creusa and
Creon, we hear briefly, in a dialogue which, for the first

and last time, is joined by the Chorus, that the royal pair
are destroyed ' fraude qua solent reges capi, Donis,' and
that the fire has consumed the palace, threatens the city,
and is not quenched but fed by water. It is then that
Medea, in the height of her triumph, after gloating on her
various crimes, past as well as present, is made to debate
with herself the question of killing her children. The
alternations of feeling are drawn somewhat after the
manner of Euripides, but condensed into rhetorical points,
and sometimes pushed into mere extravagance, as when
in the access of a fury-fit she wishes that, like Niobe, she
had fourteen children to be killed : ' Sterilis in poenas fui.'
Nor is there much nature in the supposed appearance of
the Furies, attended by her brother's spirit, who cries for
vengeance. Even after Jason appears, she hesitates ; she
has killed one child, but doubts about sparing the other.
Jason's entreaties decide her ; she tells him that if she
could have spared one, both might have been spared, and
that if there is any babe yet unborn, that shall be slain
too. At last she ends the suspense, throws down the
corpses, and flies away in her winged chariot, while Jason
cries after her that the heaven where she is soaring must
be uninhabited by gods.

> Per alta vade spatia sublimi aetheris :
> Tartara nullos esse, qua veheris, deos.

To furnish a suitable commencement to the 'Thyestes,'
the infernal world is thrown open, Tantalus being brought
up by Megaera, that he may excite his posterity to greater
atrocities. If it were ever desirable to put such machinery
into motion, a fitting occasion would certainly seem to be
furnished by a story, which, however treated, must, for
pure revolting horror, have surpassed any of the extant
themes of ancient tragedy ; yet if we compare the open-

ing of the 'Agamemnon' of Æschylus with that of the
'Agamemnon' of Seneca, where the spirit of Thyestes is
evoked to perform an office similar to that which is here
performed by the spirit of Tantalus, we can hardly doubt
that a poet of the old school would have devised some
more human introduction to a tale of human cruelty.
Æschylus does not shrink from the supernatural where, as
in the 'Eumenides,' it is involved in the very conception
of his subject; on the contrary, he wields it with a terrible
power which throws the mere human side of the narrative
into the shade; but for that very reason he does not put it
wantonly into requisition, wherever wickedness may seem
to require an external motive, or the crimes or wrongs of
the dead appear to make themselves felt by the living.
Euripides is perhaps less scrupulous; at least, there is some
resemblance between the appearance of Iris and Lytta,
the Frenzy-fiend, in the 'Hercules Furens,' and that of
Megæra and Tantalus here, though the Greek poet supplies no parallel to the rhetorical extravagances of the
Roman. Tantalus asks why he was summoned from his
ordinary punishment? whether to new tortures, such as
those of Sisyphus, Ixion, or Tityus, which he severally
characterises. When told of the work he is to do, he
attempts to escape, and offers to suffer any evil himself
rather than be the cause of fresh evil to others. But he
is sent into the palace, while his tormentor describes rhetorically the effect of his temporary presence on earth in
the drying up of the rivers and the ocean, the withering of
the trees, and the disorder of the sun. The Chorus, composed of aged Argives, pray that their country, the topo-
graphical features of which are touched at some length,
may be less stained by crime than in former generations,
and give a brief sketch of Tantalus's offence, and a more
elaborate picture of his punishment. The Second Act

introduces us to Atreus and a male confidant, or, as he is
called in the list of *dramatis personæ*, Satelles. Atreus
endeavours to rouse himself to vengeance by reproaching
himself for his inactivity, talks of a grand armed display,
and tries to think of some crime worthy of the occasion :—

> Age, anime, fac quod nulla posteritas probet,
> Sed nulla taceat : aliquod audendum est nefas
> Atrox, cruentum : tale, quod frater meus
> Suum esse malit. Scelera non ulcisceris,
> Nisi vincis.

The confidant counsels virtuous thoughts : Atreus replies
that virtuous thoughts are not for kings, and details his
injuries in a speech which may very probably have been
modelled on that fragmentary speech of the Atreus of
Attius, referred to in my former lecture, ending by asking
how Thyestes ought to be killed. 'Put him to the sword,'
suggests the confidant. This gives Atreus the opportunity
for a tyrannic utterance :—

> De fine pœnæ loqueris : ego pœnam volo :
> Perimat tyrannus lenis : in regno meo
> Mors impetratur.

No weapon, he declares, will serve against Thyestes, but
Thyestes himself. He gropes his way to a conclusion, led
on, he tells us, by a power not his own, while external
nature is showing signs of convulsion. Taking a hint,
which he duly acknowledges, from the story of Tereus, he
resolves that his brother shall be made to eat the flesh of
his own children ; and the vision, once presented, becomes
so clear to him that he wonders he can so long have been
blind to it. The acquiescent confidant inquires how Thyestes can be got into his brother's power, listens to an
explanation of ways and means, advises Atreus not to
employ his own sons as ambassadors to their uncle, or at

least not to admit them into the secret, and finally, of
course, promises secrecy, ' both for honour's sake and fear's
sake, but rather for honour's.' The Chorus, having by
some means or other heard that the family feud is composed, though unacquainted with Atreus' underlying plot,
sings some glyconics against the common view of the
attractions of royalty, and in support of the Stoical proposition that the real king is the king over himself. In
the Third Act, Thyestes is introduced, talking to his sons
about their uncle's proposal to share the kingdom with
him. Like the Thyestes of Attius, he is inclined to distrust the offer ; but the language which he uses could only
have come from a Stoic rhetorician. He prefers the humble life which he is leaving to a throne, says that a man is
a king when he has the power to die, and that to be able
to live without a kingdom is an enormous kingdom in
itself, and declares that before Atreus really loves his
brother the sea will touch the pole, the Ægean turn into
a cornfield, night give light to the world, water ally itself
with fire, death with life, the winds with the waves. Yet
a few assurances and a few fine sentiments from Atreus in
the next scene remove his fears, and he accepts his share
in the kingdom, after modestly declining it on the ground
of his own unworthiness. The Chorus, which has been
present at any rate during this scene, is equally credulous,
and takes occasion to comment on the marvellous strength
of natural affection, which has worked a change, to be
compared, as it is compared at great length, to the change
from a storm to a calm. The Fourth Act gives the one
only opportunity which here, as in the ' Medea,' they have
of entering into the dialogue. In a speech of more than
140 lines, only interrupted by a few interrogations and
exclamations, a messenger relates how Atreus has killed
his nephews and roasted their flesh. The place of the

butchery is elaborately described—a retired part of the palace, standing in a gloomy, haunted wood. We hear of the preparations for the deed, which have been constructed as if for a sumptuous sacrifice; we see Atreus unmoved by the prodigies with which nature is testifying her horror —the shaking of the building, the wine changed to blood, the weeping of the sacred ivory—yet doubting like a tiger where to make his first spring, while the victims, two young men and a boy, comport themselves heroically in prospect of their fate. 'O monstrous crime!' cries the Chorus, as they hear the details of the massacre. 'Are you horrified at this?' says the messenger; 'let the atrocity stop there, and it leaves him pure.' The Chorus, thus bidden to conjecture some worse barbarity, conjecture that he may have refused burial to the bodies, and given them to wild beasts. The messenger completes his tale by a recital of the horror that remains, describing the roasting and eating of the flesh with a loathsome minuteness. The Chorus, left alone to sing, concentrate their thoughts on the change of the sun's course, a subject which occupies them for nearly 100 lines; they describe the phenomenon and its accessories rhetorically, ransack mythology for every cause of it but the right one, and predict its effects on the mundane system, saying what will happen to each constellation. Atreus opens the Fifth Act with a triumphant soliloquy, which is broken off that we may listen to a song from Thyestes—a festal song, in which that unreasonable reveller at first tries to excite himself to conviviality by maxims about human fortune, but eventually passes into an account of his own involuntary perturbations and apprehensions. Atreus approaches, and places in his hands the cup in which the blood of the victims had been mixed in wine; but the portents increase, and Thyestes, more and more alarmed, asks for his children.

'You shall have them,' says Atreus, 'and they shall never part from you.' Every moment aggravates the father's distress, when at last he is told to open his arms and receive, not them but their heads. 'Do you recognise your children now?' 'I recognise my brother.'—'Natos ecquid agnoscis tuos?' 'Agnosco fratrem.' After resorting to mythological commonplaces to express his horror, Thyestes begs that he may have their bodies for burial, and once more receives an enigmatical answer: 'What is left of them you shall have; what is not left you have already.' When the truth is told him, he begs for a sword that he may rip open the stomach which has been so foully gorged, and in many sounding lines entreats the gods, not for his sake but for their own, to bring the world immediately to an end. Atreus, having used daggers, is ready to speak them. 'I know why you feel aggrieved; it is that you have been anticipated—not that you have partaken of this monstrous feast, but that you have not had the opportunity of giving it to me.' 'You will have your punishment from the gods,' returns Thyestes. 'And you yours from your children:'—

> *Thy.*—Vindices aderunt dei :
> His puniendum vota te tradunt mea.
> *Atr.*—Te puniendum liberis trado tuis.

Octavia, the heroine of the third play which I have selected, is the daughter of Claudius and wife of Nero; and the subject of the drama is her repudiation in favour of Poppæa, and subsequent removal to banishment and death. From the nature of the case, we are not called to sit down to a supper of horrors like those in the 'Thyestes' or 'Medea;' but the spirit which animates all three is substantially the same. Octavia herself commences with an anapæstic soliloquy: it is morning, and she wakes to

wail again, in strains more piteous than those of Halcyone,
Procne, or Philomele, for her own ill-starred marriage, and
the deaths of her mother Messalina and her father Claudius,
the emperor of the world and conqueror of Britain—a speech
seemingly modelled on the lamentations of Electra at her
first appearance in Sophocles. Her nurse enters and
soliloquises also, in iambics, on the instability of fortune
shown in the reverses of the family of Claudius, and on
the sufferings of Octavia in particular. The two then join
in what in a Greek play would be called a brief commatic
scene, ending in a regular iambic dialogue. Octavia talks
of her brother's ghost appearing in dreams, and invokes
her father's ; the nurse disparages her father for having
preferred his wife's son to his own, and enumerates the
tragedies which followed Claudius's marriage with Agrippina. The conversation then for a few lines is carried on
with that smartness of retort which Seneca loved. The
nurse consoles Octavia with the thought of her popularity :—

N.—Vis magna populi est.   O.—Principis major tamen.
N.—Respiciet ipse conjugem.   O.—Pellex vetat.
N.—Invisa cunctis nempe.   O.—Sed cara est viro.
N.—Nondum uxor est.   O.—Jam fiet, et genitrix simul.

The nurse bursts into an anapæstic consolation, com-
forting Octavia for her husband's unfaithfulness by the
example of Juno, to whom she is compared, not very de-
corously, as being at once the sister and consort of
Augustus. After a brief resumption of the dialogue, a
Chorus of Romans enter and sing an ode in which they
compassionate Octavia, whose incestuous marriage is dignified by the same comparison, recur to the old heroic
times of Rome, when great wickedness met with great
penalties, and are reminded by Tullia's parricide of the

recent matricide of Nero, the circumstances of which they
describe. The Second Act introduces Seneca, who indulges
in a soliloquy possibly such as he would himself have
delivered, but certainly as remote from ordinary nature
as any of the speeches which he has put into the mouth
of any of his fictitious characters. He expresses distrust
of his present prosperity; turns with sentimental regard to
his exile in Corsica, which we know historically to have
been distasteful to him; talks of the pleasure he then felt
in contemplating the mighty frame of the universe; thinks
it possible that Chaos may come again as an appropriate
termination to the crimes of the human race, and is describing at length the progress of society through the
well-known four ages, when he is interrupted by Nero.
The emperor, as he enters, despatches a prefect to take off
the heads of two nobles. Seneca remonstrates, and a war
of words follows, conducted at first in brief repartees,
through single lines and half-lines, afterwards by the more
cumbrous machinery of declamation and counter-declama-
tion. Seneca enlarges on Nero's distinguished position,
and the opportunities of doing good which it affords.
Nero replies that it would be madness not to guard his
position; that from neglect of salutary precautions Cæsar
fell a victim to Brutus; that Augustus shed blood
copiously in proscriptions, and crushed his rival Antony
without mercy, thus paving his own way to deification,
and that an example which had so glorious a result ought
to be followed. Seneca praises Octavia: Nero replies
that she hates him, and that he has found the idol of his
heart in Poppæa, who is superior to Venus, Juno, or
Minerva. Some discussion follows about Love, whom
Nero asserts to be the greatest of the gods, while Seneca
declares his deity to be a vulgar error, and reduces him
to a mere passion of the mind. After a second combat

of repartees, Nero breaks off the conversation impatiently, hoping that he may be allowed to do what Seneca disapproves, and fixing the next day for his new bridal. The Third Act succeeds, without any intervening Chorus. The spectre of Agrippina appears from the shades, to act, so she tells us, as torchbearer at this unhallowed wedding. She complains of her sufferings, something in the tone of Clytemnestra's ghost in the 'Eumenides,' and predicts that vengeance worse than the various forms of infernal punishment will overtake her son, whom she wishes she had killed while he was yet an infant. We then have a brief anapæstic scene between Octavia and the Chorus. She begs her friends not to incur the emperor's anger by grieving for her, and leaves the palace, hoping, rather than expecting, that her life may be spared. They ask where the old spirit of Rome has fled, and wish that violent hands may be laid on the new empress. In the Fourth Act, without any apparent reason, we have Poppæa herself brought on the stage, merely to discuss with her nurse (for she, too, has a nurse of her own to act as her confidant) an alarming dream which appeared to her on the bridal night. Her bridal train, she thought, had changed to a train of mourners, headed by the spectral Agrippina; as she followed them, the earth opened, and she fell into the chasm, at the bottom of which was her marriage bed; her former husband, Crispinus, advanced to embrace her, when Nero broke in upon them and buried his sword in her throat. The nurse, with a promptitude which supplies the want of ingenuity, immediately volunteers a favourable explanation of the various circumstances. As for Nero, and the bridal bed, of course it was natural that she should dream of them, having thought of them so much while awake. The train of mourners were mourning not for her but for

Octavia. The appearance of a personage like Agrippina
was a compliment. The bed in the infernal regions showed
that the marriage would rest on a permanent basis. The
burying of the sword in her throat was a sign that Nero's
sword would be kept in a sheath. Poppæa, without
criticising this notable interpretation, resolves to propitiate the gods by sacrifice. The Chorus, whose sympathies
for a time at least seem to have undergone a change, sing
some anapæsts in honour of Poppæa, preferring her beauty
to Europa's, Leda's, Danae's, or Helen's. A messenger
rushes in, announcing that there is a popular rising in
behalf of Octavia; but the Chorus, lately so warm in her
cause, take the news very calmly, and sing more anapæsts
about the hopelessness of resisting Love, who could subdue
Achilles and Agamemnon, and overturn the kingdom of
Priam. In the Fifth Act Nero enters, storming at the
disaffection of the populace, which is only to be put down
by sanguinary vengeance. The prefect announces that
the rising has been suppressed by the death of the ring-
leaders; the emperor answers that this is not enough—
more blood must be shed, and Octavia's the first. As
usual, the two speakers retort upon each other :—

> N.—Parere dubitas.   P.—Cur meam damnas fidem ?
> N.—Quod parcis hosti.   P.—Femina hoc nomen capit ?
> N.—Si scelera cœpit.   P.—Estne qui sontem arguat ?
> N.—Populi furor.   P.—Quis regere dementes valet ?
> N.—Qui concitare potuit.   P.—Haudquemquam reor.

The Chorus are now once more on the side of Octavia,
whom they regard as an instance of the dangers of popular
favour, and compare her fate with those of the Gracchi
and Drusus. She enters, inquiring why she is to be
dragged to death, and that a death in exile, and wishing
for the nightingale's song to bewail her fate, and for its

wings to escape it. They console her by reflections on
the immutability of destiny, and by the examples of other
unfortunate ladies of the Augustan family—Julia, Messalina, and the elder and younger Agrippina. She embraces
death; and they conclude the play by trusting that the
ship in which she is to travel may waft her away, a second
Iphigenia, from a bloody fate to an island of refuge :—

Lenes auræ, Zephyrique leves,
Tectam quondam nube ætheria
Qui vexistis raptam sævæ
Virginis aris Iphigeniam,
Hanc quoque tristi procul a pœna
Portate, precor, templa ad Triviæ !
Urbe est nostra mitior Aulis,
Et Taurorum barbara tellus :
Hospitis illic cæde litatur
Numen superum :
Civis gaudet Roma cruore.

I fear I may have detained you too long by this account
of works which, though not wanting in a certain kind of
ability, are chiefly remarkable for the gross and glaring
faults which they exhibit, insomuch that they might
almost seem to have been written in express contravention
of every rule laid down by Horace in his art of poetry as
essential to the composition of tragedy. Yet it is historically curious to observe the rhetorical spirit, which, as
Mr. Grote remarks, haunted the Athenian drama almost
from the first, thus attaining its final triumph in the destruction of all dramatic propriety, all tragic pathos: it
is historically curious also, though in a different way, to
see the life and feeling of the Rome of Claudius and Nero
clothing itself in the forms of Grecian legend, and to
associate Locusta with Medea, as we have already learnt
to associate Augustus with Æneas. And, perhaps, if we

look deeper, these tragedies may be found to have an interest for us which is not merely historical. No learned man of our own day is likely to maintain with the elder Scaliger that Seneca is equal to any of the Greeks in majesty, and in polish and elegance superior to Euripides : no popular dramatist is likely to produce imitations of Seneca on a modern stage, as was done by Corneille and even Racine. Still, if there be any tendency in any of the schools of poetry at the present time to sacrifice propriety to effect, the consistency of the whole to the brilliancy of the parts—to aim at producing rather lines to be quoted than works to be read—to dazzle the eyes with gaudy colouring, and fill the ears with the language of an ostentatious philosophy—to court applause by exaggerated sentiments, and seek the elements of grandeur in colossal wickedness and Titanic impiety, we may remember that characteristics like these are to be found in the tragedies of Seneca, and gather from the examination which we have been giving to the one hints for a right estimate of the other.

THE FABLES OF BABRIUS.[1]

THE name of Babrius is one which for the last hundred and eighty years has been gradually becoming more and more significant to students of antiquity. That he was a fabulist of one or other of the Greek classical periods, who wrote in choliambic verse, was already evident from a few fragments preserved by lexicographers and grammarians. But the first to make him more than a name was Bentley, in a dissertation on the supposed fables of Æsop, appended to the first draught of the immortal work on Phalaris. In reducing the father of fable to a mere shadow, he showed that some of the substance which had invested him really belonged to Babrius, whose half-corrupted choliambics might occasionally be traced through the prose versions of late paraphrasts. Tyrwhitt followed up the hint in a 'Dissertatio de Babrio,' published in 1776, detecting verses in a Bodleian MS. of the prose fables, and collecting all the remains of Babrius that were then extant. The publication, in 1809, of more prose fables belonging to an earlier version, from a Florentine MS., led to further choliambic discoveries, prosecuted in the first instance by Bishop Blomfield and Mr. Burges, though with different degrees of success, and afterwards by Sir George Lewis, whose *coup d'essai*, containing a collection of all the fables capable of entire restoration, appeared in 1832, in an elaborate paper in the Philological Museum. In 1835 a similar collection was published by a German scholar, Knoch, who appended the fragments, forming altogether a kind of variorum edition of all that had been written

[1] Reprinted from the *Edinburgh Review*, April 1861.

by or on Babrius up to that time. The year 1842 witnessed another discovery, much more important than
any—that of an actual MS. of Babrius, containing a
collection of fables supposed to have originally amounted
to about 160, but now consisting of 123 fables and two
short prefatory poems. The discoverer, M. Mynas, a
Greek, was employed by the French Government; and
accordingly the duty of giving the new-found treasure
to the world devolved on M. Boissonade, the patriarch
of French scholarship. Other editions soon followed;
and the list of editors or critics of Babrius now includes
the names of Dübner, Orelli, Baiter, Fix, Ahrens, Lachmann, Meineke, the Hermanns, Schneidewin, and Sir
George Lewis. In 1857 it was announced that M. Mynas
had made yet another discovery; and two years later
Sir George Lewis introduced to the public a Second
Part of Babrius, containing an independent collection
of ninety-four fables and a prefatory poem. As we
shall soon see, there are reasons for doubting whether
this Second Part affords a very favourable field for the
display of English scholarship; but, at any rate, it will
be apparent that to English scholarship Babrius has
already been greatly indebted. When he existed only in
a fragmentary form, English scholars were his most
felicitious restorers; and though when the MS. of the
First Part was discovered, there was no Porsonian school
in England to do the work of Lachmann and his friends,
producing by joint labour an amended text in a short
time, the accuracy, judgment, and fulness of information
displayed in Sir George Lewis's edition, embodying as it
does the chief results of continental cricitism, entitled it
to rank as the standard one.

The discovery of the First Part of Babrius made a
substantive addition to the treasures we already possess

in the remains of Greek poetical literature. Whatever the date of the fabulist—and dates of all kinds have been suggested, ranging from about 250 B.C. to as many years after the Christian era—he certainly wrote in a time when the echoes of classical poetry had not yet died out. In terseness, point, and eloquence he is, we think, equal to Phædrus, whom indeed he sometimes excels in treating the same subject. Let our readers compare the two following versions of an old favourite, ‘ The Fox and the Crow : ’—

> Qui se laudari gaudent verbis subdolis
> Sera dant pœnas turpes pœnitentia.
> Cum de fenestra corvus raptum caseum
> Comesse vellet, celsa residens arbore,
> Hunc vidit vulpes, dehinc sic occepit loqui :
> O qui tuarum, corve, pennarum est nitor !
> Quantum decoris corpore et vultu geris !
> Si vocem haberes, nulla prior ales foret.
> At Ille stultus, dum vult vocem ostendere,
> Emisit ore caseum, quem celeriter
> Dolosa vulpes avidis rapuit dentibus.
> Tum demum ingemuit corvi decoptus stupor.
>
> (Phædrus, book I. fab. 13.)

> Κόραξ δεδηχὼς στόματι τυρὸν εἱστήκει ·
> τυροῦ δ’ ἀλώπηξ ἰχανῶσα κερδῴη
> μύθῳ τὸν ὄρνιν ἠπάτησε τοιούτῳ ·
> κόραξ, καλαί σοι πτέρυγες, ὀξέη γλήνη,
> θνητὸς αὐχήν · στέρνον ἀετοῦ φαίνεις ·
> ὄνυξι πάντων θηρίων κατισχύεις ·
> ὁ τοῖος ὄρνις κωφὸς ἐσσὶ σοῦ κρώζεις !
> κόραξ δ’ ἐπαίνῳ καρδίην ἐχαυνώθη,
> στόματος δὲ τυρὸν ἐκβαλὼν ἐκεκράγει.
> τὸν ἡ σοφὴ λαβοῦσα κερτόμῳ γλώσσῃ,
> Οὐκ ἦσθ’ ἄφωνος, εἶπεν, ἀλλὰ φωνήεις.
> ἔχεις, κόραξ, ἅπαντα · νοῦς δέ σοι λείπει.[1]
>
> (Babrius, part I. fab. 77.)

[1] One of the prose versions points to another reading of the last line, which we should prefer as more humorous: ἔχεις, κόραξ, ἅπαντα· νοῦν μόνον

There is much quiet humour in the following, which
seem either to have suggested or to have been suggested
by Horace's 'Lusisti satis, edisti satis, atque bibisti:
Tempus abire tibi:'—

> Ζωμοῦ χύτρᾳ μῦς ἐμπεσὼν ἀπωμάστῳ,
> καὶ τῷ λίπει πνιγόμενος, ἐκπνίων τ' ἤδη,
> Βέβρωκα, φησί, καὶ πέπωκα, καὶ πάσης
> τροφῆς πέπλησμαι· καιρός ἐστί μοι θνήσκειν.
>
> (Fab. 60.)

We subjoin Mr. Davies's version, which, though somewhat deficient in freedom, is commendably close to the
original :—

> A mouse into a lidless broth-pot fell :
> Choked with the grease, and bidding life farewell,
> He said, 'My fill of meat and drink have I,
> And all good things ; 'tis time that I should die.'

The following, which is rather a poem than a fable,
touches the mythological history of the swallow and
the nightingale with an imaginative delicacy which may
remind our readers of Shakspeare's lines :—

> King Pandion, he is dead :
> All thy friends are lapped in lead.

> Ἀγροῦ χελιδὼν μακρὸν ἐξεπστήθη·
> εὗρεν δ' ἐρήμοις ἐγκαθημένην ὕλαις
> ἀηδόν' ὀξύφωνον· ἡ δ' ἀπεθρήνει
> τὸν Ἴτυν ἄωρον ἐκπεσόντα τῆς ὥρης.
> ἐκ τοῦ μέλους δ' ἔγνωσαν αἱ δύ' ἀλλήλας·
> καὶ δὴ προσέπτησάν τε καὶ προσωμίλουν.
> ἡ μὲν χελιδὼν εἶπε· Φιλτάτη, ζώεις ;
> πρῶτόν σε βλέπω σήμερον μετὰ Θρᾴκην.

ττήσαι. Such variations are not uncommon, the citations in Suidas occasionally differing so much from the text of the MS. of Babrius, as to indicate the existence of a different recension. For an instance in which
Phædrus's treatment of his subject is more successful than Babrius's, compare
Phædr. iii. 7, with Babr. part i. fab. 99.

ἀεί τις ἡμᾶς πικρὸς ἰσχίσεν δαίμων·
καὶ παρθένοι γὰρ χωρὶς ἡμεν ἀλλήλων.
ἀλλ᾽ ἐλθ᾽ ἐν ἀγρὸν καὶ πρὸς οἶκον ἀνθρώπων·
σύσηνος ἡμῖν καὶ φίλη κατοικήσεις,
ὅπου γεωργοῖς κοὐχὶ θηρίοις ᾄσεις·
ὕπαιθρον ὕλην λεῖπε, καὶ παρ᾽ ἀνθρώποις
ὁμόροφόν μοι δῶμα καὶ στέγην οἴκει.
τί σε δροσίζει πηκτὸς ἐννύχος στίβη,
καὶ καῦμα θάλπει, πάντα δ᾽ ἀγρότων τήκει;
ἄγε δὴ σεαυτήν, σοφὰ λαλοῦσα, μήνυσον.
τὴν δ᾽ αὐτ᾽ ἀηδὼν ὀξύφωνος ἠμείφθη·
"Εα με πέτραις ἐμμένειν ἀοικήτοις,
καὶ μή μ᾽ ὀρεινῆς ὀργάδος σὺ χωρίσῃς.
μετὰ τὰς Ἀθήνας ἄνδρα καὶ πόλιν φεύγω·
οἶκος δέ μοι πᾶς κἀπίμιξις ἀνθρώπων
λύπην παλαιῶν συμφορῶν ἀταξαίνει.

παραμυθία τίς ἐστι τῆς κακῆς μοίρης
λόγος σοφὸς καὶ μοῦσα καὶ φυγὴ πλήθους·
λύπη δ᾽ ὅταν τις οἷς ποτ᾽ εἰθενῶν ὤφθη
τούτοις ταπεινὸς αὖθις ὢν συνοικήσῃ.

                        (Fab. 12)

Far from men's fields the swallow forth had flown,
When she espied among the woodlands lone
The nightingale, sweet songstress. Her lament
Was Itys to his doom untimely sent.
Each knew the other through the mournful strain,
Flew to embrace, and in sweet talk remain.
Then said the swallow, ' Dearest, liv'st thou still?
Ne'er have I seen thee since thy Thracian ill;
Some cruel fate hath ever come between;
Our virgin[1] lives till now apart have been.
Come to the fields; revisit homes of men;
Come dwell with me, a comrade dear, again,
Where thou shalt charm the swains, no savage brood:
Dwell near men's haunts, and quit the open wood:
One roof, one chamber, sure, can house the two:
Or dost prefer the nightly frozen dew

[1] Mr. Davies here apparently mistakes the sense, which seems to be
' Even when we were maidens, we lived apart from one another.'

And day-god's heat? a wild wood life and drear?
Come, clever songstress, to the light more near.'
To whom the sweet-voiced nightingale replied:
' Still on these lonesome ridges let me bide,
Nor seek to part me from the mountain glen:
I shun, since Athena, man and haunts of men:
To mix with them, their dwelling-place to view,
Stirs up old grief, and opens woes anew.'
   Some consolation for an evil lot
Lies in wise words, in song, in crowds forgot.
But sore the pang when where you once were great
Again men see you, housed in mean estate.'

(Davies.)

We have heard that this First Part of Babrius has
been used as a class-book in one of our public schools,
and we really think the example might be worth following. The subject matter ensures that the thought will
be simple, while the language is just sufficiently difficult
and characteristic to give that exercise which constitutes
to a schoolboy one great advantage of a classical training. Some few forms of expression will require to be
unlearnt when the student comes to compose in Attic
Greek: but the general character of the style is classical
enough for all intents and purposes.

The Second Part purports to have been discovered
under much the same circumstances as the First. Each
professes to have been found in a monastery at Mount
Athos—whether in the same monastery we do not hear—
in each case the monks made a difficulty about parting
with their treasure, which accordingly reached Europe
only in the form of a transcript. The difficulty in the case
of the First, however, appears to have been only on the
score of expense; and this M. Mynas was able to
overcome in a subsequent visit, when he became the
purchaser of the original. Of the MS. of the Second

Part we hear only that the monks refused to part with
it, and that M. Mynas brought away a facsimile, which,
with the original MS. of the First Part, was sold by him
to the authorities of the British Museum, in August
1857. We understand that it was offered in the first
instance to the French Government, the purchasers of
the copy of the First Part, but that they disbelieved the
story of the second discovery, and refused to buy. Sir
George Lewis, however, as Mr. Davies tells us, had no
doubt that the copy was what it professed to be—made
from a genuine archetype. Genuine or not, it is admitted on all hands that the Second Part is of far less
value than the First. It professes to be not Babrius, but
Babrius spoiled. The whole collection, from first to last,
has passed through the hands of a 'diaskeunstes,' a scribbler who, apparently for his mere pleasure, has turned
classical Greek into a barbarous jumble, and good choliambics into a kind of political verse, as it is technically
called—lines having the requisite number of syllables,
but written with scarcely any regard to quantity; so that
nearly one half of the verses are shown by the metre
alone to have been such as Babrius never could have
produced. Such writers were not uncommon at various
periods during the decline of Greek literature, though
their function was more usually that of turning verse
into prose, or *vice versâ*, or one kind of recognised metre
into another. Still, even Babrius spoiled, if we could
be sure that we really possessed him, would be of some
literary value. He would scarcely give pleasure to the
student who reads Greek poetry for the love of it, nor
could we recommend him as a school-book; but he
would still have his place somewhat above those prose
versions which, no doubt, still conceal various Babrian
fables—the great point of superiority consisting partly

in traces of the Babrian manner, which could hardly be
obliterated, and partly in the certainty which we should
then have, and which in the case of the prose versions
is wanting, that each particular fable had a real Babrian
original.

Our own opinion is, we confess, strongly adverse to
the genuineness of these new fables. An attentive examination of them has led us to suspect that they are a
forgery, and that of a very recent date. It is not easy
to prove fabrication where the thing fabricated is, as we
have said, not Babrius himself, but Babrius barbarised,
and where the document to be appealed to is not an
original MS. but a copy, for the absolute accuracy of
which we have no definite guarantee. We believe,
however, that the evidences of spuriousness we have
discovered are neither few nor small. We can only
state them briefly and generally, leaving those who care
to pursue the subject to seek further details in an article
' De Babrii Fabularum Parte Secunda,' in the Rheinisches
Museum.[1]

First of all, we think it improbable that a new collection of ninety-four fables by Babrius should ever have
existed. By far the greater part of the fragments and
restored fables which were extant previous to 1842 are
comprised in the former collection, and those which
remain are no more than may well have been contained
among the forty additional fables which that collection
originally comprehended. Again, nearly half of the
verses of which the new fables consist are obviously
unmetrical, while a large portion of the remainder are
not such as a poet like Babrius is likely to have produced; yet of the actual fragments of Babrius which

---

[1] The article alluded to was written by Professor Conington, and is
printed in the appendix to vol. ii.

these fables embody few are altered at all, and not more
than two lines out of twenty-four rendered unmetrical.
Another most suspicious symptom is to be found in the
extraordinary coincidences between the text of these
new fables and Lachmann's conjectures on the fragments
and restored fables as appended to his edition. This can
only be estimated by those who will examine the matter
in detail; and therefore we will only say that Lachmann's
judgment is confirmed not only where he is probably
right, but where he is almost certainly wrong, or, at any
rate, where he has conjectured with scarcely any data to
go on. It should be observed that we have here the
twofold improbability that Lachmann should have restored the text of Babrius, and that the text of Babrius
should not have been altered by the barbarising ' dias-
keuastes.' Fourthly, while most of these fables closely
coincide with one or other of the prose versions (a thing
itself explicable on either hypothesis of genuineness or of
spuriousness), the remainder, with a single exception, are
copies more or less servile of fables occurring in such
writers as Aristophanes, Plutarch, Lucian, and Appian,
and included in the collections made by such scholars as
Di Furia and Cornes; whereas the genuine Babrius,
when telling the same fable as Lucian or Plutarch, takes
care to tell it in his own way. Lastly, the general
worthlessness of the fables is a strong reason for believing that they do not contain Babrius in any shape.
Besides the veritable fragments of Babrius, they contain
perhaps 100 lines which Babrius might have produced;
not one of these, however, seems to us so decidedly
stamped with his genius that it could not have been
produced as well by any clever writer of iambics, such
as are common enough in England, though possibly less
so in modern Greece. The treatment of the fables is

almost without an exception just up to the level of the
prose versions, and no more—another point of contrast
with the genuine Babrius, who frequently throws into
his fables poetical images, dramatic touches, and passages
of dialogue which the prose fabulists discard as unsuited
to their humbler purpose. On the whole, we cannot
doubt that these new fables are the work of a forger
who has turned the prose versions into choliambic lines,
occasionally good, but generally very indifferent or worse
than indifferent, and who, if he has not used the prose
collections by Di Furia or Coraes, has certainly been a
tolerably attentive student of Lachmann. At the same
time, we do not profess to account for all the phenomena
which the work presents. No one can do this who is
not prepared to identify the forger and trace his antecedents. But we see no difficulty in supposing that his
extraordinary command of unusual words—the chief point
which we have heard alleged in favour of the genuineness of the fables—may have arisen from a study of
ancient grammarians and glossarists, aided by a native
power of invention, while the better choliambics may
easily have been furnished to him by some more skilful
composer than himself. Forgery is an art, and a forger
would naturally provide himself with appliances for
practising his art with success. So a few obvious errors
which exist in the text of the fables may either have
been introduced accidentally in the process of transcription from a foul copy, or inserted deliberately to give an
air of genuineness. A forger who should be unable to
produce these and other plausible appearances would be
a very poor forger indeed.

It would be too much to wish that Sir George Lewis
may find leisure to enter into the controversy; but we
need not say that all scholars would be interested in

hearing the mature conclusions of one whose judgment
and learning have already done so much for Babrius.

Of Mr. Davies's version we have already spoken incidentally.   It is close and faithful, but wants facility.
Even where the individual lines are expressed with ease,
the effect of the whole is frequently that of too great
compression and slowness of movement.   The rhymes
are generally accurate, but there are a few instances like
beheld, held (p. 142), and in one place (p. 208) *broth* is
paired with *forth*.   Babrius would be nothing without
his style, and any want of grace or finish therefore is sure
to be noticed in his translator.

CRITICAL NOTES.[1]

τοιαῦτά φασι τὸν ἀγαθὸν Κρέοντα σοὶ
κἀμοί, λέγω γὰρ κἀμέ, κηρύξαντ' ἔχειν.

Soph. 'Antig.' 31, 32.

THIS passage seems to me capable of yielding a satisfactory sense without the need of having recourse to the construction proposed by Dr. Kennedy, which is, to say the least, an unusual one.

Let it be supposed that Antigone had said τοιαῦτά φασι τὸν ἀγαθὸν Κρέοντα σοὶ κηρύξαντ' ἔχειν. Everyone would have seen then that the use of σοι was perfectly obvious, indicating that faint notion of the concern of the party addressed, in the statement made so common in similar cases; why should we not go a step further, and conceive that having used, inadvertently as it were, a pronoun which, though not necessarily implying more than this faint notion of her sister's concern with Creon's doings, might yet, as it stood, be taken to mark Ismene as the party chiefly interested. The speaker corrects the probable misapprehension by immediately adding an emphatic mention of herself, ἐμοί, not μοι, to which he further calls attention in the following parenthesis, λέγω γὰρ κἀμέ? I, at least, see nothing far-fetched in such an explanation; and if there should appear to be anything of the kind, I believe it will be found to arise from the mere fact of an analysis having been attempted at all; an experiment which, if tried on any of the simpler forms of

[1] Reprinted from the *Classical Museum*, No. xiii.

ordinary conversation, would produce a similar effect of
apparent subtilty and refinement.

There is another passage in Sophocles, which might, I
think, be advantageously discussed by the readers of the
'Classical Museum.' It is from the 'Œdipus Tyrannus,'
44, 45 :—

> ὡς, τοῖσιν ἐμπείροισι καὶ τὰς ξυμφορὰς
> ζώσας ὁρῶ μάλιστα τῶν βουλευμάτων.

Most of the commentators, I believe, agree with Wunder
in making the general sense to be *consilia hominum pen-
dentium prosperum eventum habent*, τὰς ξυμφορὰς being
taken with τῶν βουλευμάτων, as in Thuc. i. 140, τὰς ξυμφορὰς τῶν πραγμάτων, where the Schol. renders ξυμφορὰς
by ἀποβάσεις. Not to mention that one would wish to
see ξυμφορὰς placed nearer to βουλευμάτων, an objection
doubtless capable of being obviated, but still not wholly
without force in a doubtful passage, the sentiment which
the words are made to convey appears to be a very flat
one. The Chorus had been exhorting Œdipus to suggest
some remedy if he should have chanced to derive any
from gods or men; and surely it is not very forcible
immediately to back this appeal by the remark, that experienced men are generally found to have the issues of
their counsels more prosperous; the power of καὶ being,
I suppose, that not only are their plans well formed, but
their success signal. My own suggestion, which I make
with considerable hesitation, is to separate ξυμφορὰς from
βουλευμάτων, and understand the latter as formed by
μάλιστα in the sense of μᾶλλον : 'Since I see that, with
men of experience, even casual knowledge is (often) more
effective than counsels of reason ;' a position at any rate
sufficiently to the purpose, and agreeing well with the
doubtful language held just before εἴτε του θεῶν φήμην

ἀκούσας εἴτ' ἀπ' ἀνῆρὸς οἶσθά του. Some may wish to take
ξυμφορὰς with βουλευμάτων as the *carnal part* of counsel,
but the other explanation seems less forced. It might
also be proposed to understand the passage, 'since I see
that, even with the experienced, our calamities are more
vigorous than what counsel can do,' were it not that καὶ
ought then rather to *have come before* τοῖσιν ἐμπείροισι.

And now, as this paper has already begun to assume a
miscellaneous character, I wish to be allowed to correct
two or three oversights—a specimen, I fear, of a much
larger number in my recently published edition of the
'Agamemnon.' However few, assuming your readers
may be acquainted with the work, I should be sorry to
stand accountable for any of the errors contained in it, in
the eyes even of a single individual, longer than I can
possibly help.

On 10, 11, I have raised the question, whether the
accusative absolute is not merely a figment of the grammarians. I ought at least to have marked off the cases
where the accusative occurs after ὡς in an apparently
absolute sense, though here writers seem agreed that the
words depend on some implied verb. The passage from
Plat. 'Gorg.' p. 495, c. quoted from Jelf (who treats it
especially from the instances with ὡς, though he supposes
ὡς ἴτεον to be put for ὡς ἔτερον οὖσαν), probably belongs
to this class, and so does not require the explanation I
have given.

In the note on v. 308, I inadvertently included ἵνα
among the illative particles which are found before the
optative with or without ἄν evidently with only a small
modification of the sense. I certainly did not mean to
prejudge the question against the commentators, who
contend that ἵνα, as a conjunction, is never found
with ἄν.

I retract also the qualified assent given in the note on
v. 601 to the doctrine that ἄν diminishes the contingency
of the optative.

Another position adopted by Haupt on v. 902, about
ἄν with the participle, appears to me now to be questionable in itself, and not required in this particular
passage.

The account given of οὐ and μή in a note on v. 491 is
not strictly accurate, asserting, as it does, too broadly,
that οὐ never denies with reference to anything that has
gone before. In such a passage as Eur. ' Bacch.' 271, 272,
θρασὺς δὲ δυνατὸς καὶ λέγειν οἷός τ᾽ ἀνὴρ κακὸς πολίτης γίγν-
εται νοῦν οὐκ ἔχων, the negative clause (as has been remarked to me by a friend) clearly does influence the sense
of the whole, indicating the reason why a confident man
becomes a bad citizen, *quippe qui mente careat*. This
passage may help us to amend our plea, and suggest that
the distinction between οὐ and μή in such cases is as
follows:—οὐ denies absolutely, though not always independently, as the denial may be put forward as the ground
of a proposition; μή gives a denial neither positive nor
independent, but checking the sentence as a hypothetical
condition; thus μή νοῦν ἔχων would mean 'if he has no
sense,' merely stating a possibility assumed solely for the
sake of supporting the truth of the previous declaration;
οὐ, as this word has even more than ordinary force, it is a
matter of fact denial, and something more; the confident
not only has not sense, but, by virtue of his confidence,
cannot have; μή, on the contrary, does not deny the
matter of fact at all; a confident man may or may not
have sense; indeed, it rather implies that in some cases
he has sense, by particularising the case of his not having
it as leading to a certain result. It will be safest then to
say, as a general rule, that οὐ denies always absolutely,

sometimes relatively too; μή, never absolutely, but always relatively. Thus there is no danger of confounding the two, even when both are relative, as the invariable presence of the absolute in οὐ will sufficiently distinguish it, as in the line above quoted, where *since* is very different from *if*. In the passage from the 'Agamemnon,' my version gives what I still hold to be the right rendering —'So let the bow shoot darts at us no more;' but the note is in error in assigning the meaning of *since* to μηκέτι rather than to οὐκέτι, and asserting that the use of the latter would necessarily have reduced the line to a mere ornamental addition.

I will conclude with a new explanation (as I believe) of a once much disputed passage in Horace, 'Ars Poetica,' v. 128.

'Difficile est propriè communia dicere: tuque Rectius Iliacum carmen diducis in actus Quam si proferres ignota indictaque primus.' The commentators have here been greatly perplexed. Horace speaks apparently of the difficulty of treating hackneyed subjects, adding, that, accordingly, it is better to dramatise the 'Iliad' than to attempt something entirely new. The contradiction between the two precepts is at once perceived. Some seek to remedy it by construing *tuque* as if it were *sed tu*: others, a considerable body, beginning, I believe, with Lambin, and ending with Orelli,[1] give an entirely new sense to *communia*, not that of hackneyed things, but precisely that of not-hackneyed things, things as yet untouched, and hence public property. It seems to me that the dilemma will vanish if we regard *ignota indictaque*

---

[1] It is not meant that all who take this view of *communia* agree in their general notion of its intention, *e.g.* Orelli does not refer it to *subjects*, but to *abstract qualities*, the individualising of which, in a human character, is supposed to be intruded by *propriè dicere*.

neither as opposed to nor identical with *communia*, but
as, in a sense, included under it, being, in fact, a method
of treatment, not a subject. The whole gist of the passage
will then be—It is hard to give freshness and individuality
to hackneyed subjects, and you had much better make up
your mind to the extreme of literal imitation than run the
opposite risk of offending the reader by any startling
novelty of handling; better decline the problem altogether
than produce a bad solution. This is premised as what
is to be done if the worst should come to the worst; then
follow some cautions to be observed by those who, in
spite of the difficulty, wish to maintain that 'Publica
materia privati juris erit,' &c., where the language is
clearly parallel to *propriè communia dicere*, a fact which
Orelli is compelled to deny. It is possible that others
may have given this interpretation, but I do not remember to have seen it anywhere.

I HAVE no special title to offer any remarks on the subject of Martial; but as, in looking through my friend Mr. Paley's interesting school edition of selected Epigrams, I have observed a number of places in which I am unable to agree with the interpretation given by him or his colleague, I venture to submit the questions at issue between us to the readers of this journal.

For the sake of convenience, I follow the numeration of the ordinary editions.

Book i. 26 (27). 5.
> Non haec Pelignis agitur vindemia praelis.

'This is not the common vintage squeezed in the presses of the Peligni.' Paley, and so the Delphin editor. Is there any other instance of this use of 'agitur?' If not, may it not be worth considering whether 'agitur' does not mean 'is in question,' 'Pelignis praelis' being a sort of ablative of origin, constructed with 'vindemia?'

i. 55. 14.
> Vivat et urbanis albus in officiis.

'*Albus*, as white as his own toga, viz., from paleness and ill-health or over-fatigue. This seems to be the sense of *albus* also in Pers. i. 16.' I have always taken 'albus' in the passage of Persius as denoting no more than the spruce get-up of the holiday reciter, and I think it would spoil the passage to give it any other sense. So here Martial, speaking of the blessings of a country life, impre-

cates a comic curse on his enemies, that they may always
live in full dress.

I. 70 (71). 15.

Nec propior quam Phoebus amet doctaeque sorores.

'*Propior*, more familiar as a friend, or one nearer and
dearer to Phoebus, lit. for Phoebus to love.' The Delphin
editor gives a choice between this interpretation and
another, connecting 'propior' with 'Phoebus.' Failing
a precise parallel to the former, I should prefer the latter,
taking 'propior amet' as nearly = 'propius amet,' or,
more strictly, 'amet ut propior amicus.'

I. 76 (77). 6.

Haec sapit, haec omnes fenerat una deos.

'*Fenerat deos*, lends money on security to the Gods,
like the *feneratores* or usurers. The construction is remarkable.' So remarkable, that I cannot believe it possible. The instances which Mr. Paley goes on to cite of
'fenare' used absolutely do not help us in the least. So
far as I see, 'fenerat deos' can only mean 'lends you the
gods on interest.' Martial doubtlessly means to say, as
Gronovius explains it, Minerva is the only god worth paying court to; get her, you get all the rest: and as money
is in question, he expresses this by saying not that she
gives you all the other gods, but that she lends you them
all at so much per cent.

I. 78 (79). 2.

Inque suos voltus serperet atra lues.

'*Suos*, of which it had taken possession.' I cannot
think this likely. The word must refer to Festus, who is
the main subject of the sentence, though he has not yet
been mentioned. There is a rival reading 'ipsos,' which,

from Schneidewin's 'Apparatus Criticus' appears to have
considerable authority.

I. 81.

> Sportula, Cane, tibi suprema nocte petita est :
> Occidit, puto, te, Cano, quod una fuit.

'On one Canus, who was so eager to obtain the client's
sportula that he sent to ask for it when *in extremis*, and
died of vexation for thinking it might be his last.' Surely
this is not the meaning of ' una.' Canus, as the Delphin
editor rightly says, wanted more shares than one, and died
of vexation when he only got one. I suppose the case
mentioned by Juvenal, i. 123 foll., of a man asking for a
second allowance for his absent wife, may throw some
light on the matter.

III. 23.

> Omnia cum retro pueris opsonia tradas,
> Cur non mensa tibi ponitur a pedibus?

'*A pedibus*, for the servants in attendance on their
masters. This is severe irony: for if the host would not
feed the masters, still less would he feed their slaves. . . . .
As the language has no article, *a pedibus* stands for τοῖς
πρὸς πόδας.' This is certainly not the natural interpretation of the words; and I do not see why it should be the
true one. The entertainer is constantly handing back
dishes to the slaves behind him, to be carried away.
Martial asks, would it not be simpler for him to have the
table put behind the guests instead of before them, as that
appears to be the destination of the dishes? It is a poor
joke enough : but such as it is, it seems an obvious one.
There is however another view of the epigram suggested
by a parallel which Salmasius (note in Delph. and Var.
edition of Martial) quotes from the Anthology (' Anth. Pal.'

ii. 11). The point of that epigram appears to be that a certain Epicrates, invited by the Epigrammatist to supper, brought with him a number of actors and dancers, to whom he handed the dishes from his host's table, πάντα διδοὺς ὀπίσω: whereupon the Epigrammatist remarks, εἰ δ' οὕτω τοῦτ' ἐστί, σὺ τοὺς δούλους κατάκλινον, Ἡμεῖς δ' αὐτοῦ σοὶ πρὸς πόδας ἐρχόμεθα, meaning, I suppose, that the host and other guests would like to change places with Epicrates' followers, so as to get the lion's share of the meal. Lucilius, the author of the epigram, lived in the time of Nero, so that Martial's may be an imitation intended to be taken in the same sense; though certainly no one on reading it would suppose it to be addressed to any but the giver of the entertainment. So understood, the epigram would coincide partially with Mr. Paley's view, though his conception of the irony is different, and in any case there is nothing to necessitate his construction of 'a pedibus.'

iii. 46. 5.

In turbam incideris, cuneos umbone repellet.

' *Umbone*, keeping up the metaphor, but meaning really *cubito*. . . . As Juvenal, iii. 243, says, "ferit hic cubito," so the sharp thrust of the elbow is here compared to the boss on the shield. Similarly Stat. "Theb." ii. 671, "clypeum nec sustinet umbo," and perhaps Suet. "Cæsar." § 68.' Whether this sense of ' umbo' can be supported, I do not feel sure; but the reading in the passage of Statius is far too uncertain to make it admissible as a parallel. Mr. Paley seems to waver between two opinions, one regarding the sense of ' elbow' as a technical one, the other supposing it to exist *pro hac vice* as part of a military metaphor.

Ib. v. 6.
> Invalidum est nobis ingenuumque latus.

'*Ingenuumque*: this is wittily added as if in disparagement, whereas it was the very thing that Candidus valued.
Cf. 544. 6.' On 544. 6 (x. 47. 6) we find '*Vires ingenuae*,
constitutional strength, ἰσχὺς ἐγγενής, σύμφυτος'. It is not
easy to make out from a comparison of these two notes
what is Mr. Paley's meaning here. The present line, as
my friend Mr. Pinder has pointed out to me, is closely
copied from Ovid, 'Tristia,' i. 5. 72, 'Invalidae vires in-
genuaeque mihi:' and these various passages, taken together with Martial vi. 11. 6, '*Non minus ingenua est et
mihi, Maree, gula*,' show that '*ingenuus*' has a special
sense of '*delicate*' as opposed to rude or robust.

Ib. vv. 11, 12.
> Ergo nihil nobis, inquis, praestabis amicus?
> Quidquid libertus, Candide, non poterit.

'*Quidquid*, &c. I will give you (*i.e.*, if you are deserving of it) what a libertus cannot, mutual friendship,
and the immortality of verse, he perhaps means to add.'
'The immortality of verse,' which I see is a notion also of
the Delphin editor, appears to me to spoil the humour of
the epigram. Martial complains that his friend exacts of
him physical exertions which have nothing to do with
friendship: and so he jocosely defines the duties of a friend
as exclusive of those which might be performed by a
friend's freedman.

III. 61.
> Esse nihil dicis quidquid petis, improbe Cinna:
> Si nil, Cinna, petis, nil tibi, Cinna, nego.

'A rebuke to one who was always asking some favour
as a mere trifle. You say it is nothing at all. Very well,
VOL. I.   F F

then, I will give you just what you ask.' Surely this
misses the point of the last line. Martial says, ' If what
you ask is nothing, in refusing it I refuse you nothing.'

lib. 63. 13.

Quid narras? hoc est, hoc est homo, Cotile, bellus?

' *Hoc*, &c. "Is this, and this also, a *bellus homo?*" So
τόσα καὶ τόσα is used of varied numbers or qualities.' In
τόσα καὶ τόσα, the καὶ is surely an important element.
We do not say 'such, such,' but 'such and such.' Is it
not safer to regard the repeated ' hoc est' as simply denoting impatience?

iv. 44. 7, 8.

Cuncta iacent flammis et tristi mersa favilla :
Nec superi vellent hoc licuisse sibi.

' *Nec*, &c. Not even the gods would wish that they had
the power to do this, viz., which some infernal agency has
done.' This is plausible enough ; but I am not sure that
there is not greater probability in the Delphin explanation ; ' hyperbolικῶς innuit poeta deos ipsos huius incendii
poenituisse.'

v. 10. 1, 2.

Seria cum possim, quod delectantia malo
Scribere, tu causa es, lector amice, mihi.

' *Delectantia*, viz., meipsum.   In the preceding epigram
he had said, "Non prosiut sane, nec tamen ista iuvant."'
Both expression and context seem to show that ' delectantia' means 'giving pleasure to others.' Comp. the
well-known line of Horace (' A. P.' 333), ' Aut prodesse
volunt aut delectare poetae.'

v. 18. 8.

Avidum vorato decipi scarum musco.

'*Scarum*, some unknown but highly-prized fish (Hor.

S. ii. 2. 22), which was caught by an inferior one used as a bait.' Are these last words intended as part of the explanation of the line? If so, is 'muscus' understood to be a fish? or is the implication that the 'scarus' swallows moss or sea-weed, supposing it to be a fish? I find no authority in the dictionary for calling 'muscus' a fish: and Brodaeus, whose conjecture 'musco' is, defends it by a reference to Athenaeus, where φύκια are spoken of as a bait. The MSS. reading is 'vorata...musca;' but 'musca' does not seem to mean a fish either.

v. 25. 11.

O frustra locuples, o dissimulator amici.

'*Amici*, perhaps *amice*. . . . The genitive seems to mean who disguise the character of a friend, *i.e.*, its true character. *Simulator*, one who feigns it, would suit the sense better: or perhaps, you who cheat your friend.' It appears to me better than all these to understand the words 'you who ignore your friend,' 'who pretend that he is not your friend.'

v. 30.

Laudatus nostro quidam, Faustine, libello
Dissimulat, quasi nil debeat : imposuit.

'On one whom the poet professes to have praised in his verses on purpose to get a legacy : but the man, he says, has deceived him, and pretends he was under no obligation.' What is there about a legacy here? Surely a present would be enough for the requirements of the epigram.

v. 38. 7, 8.

Unus cum sitis, duo, Calliodore, sedetis :
Surge : σολοικισμόν, Calliodore, facis.

Σολοικισμόν, a solecism in language, viz. " unus sumus."'

It can hardly be said that Calliodorus is responsible for 'unus sumus.' 'Unus sitis' is Martial's way of saying that the two brothers together only make up one 'eques.' I suppose he must mean that Calliodorus by his conduct practically says 'unus sedemus,' which would be grammatically objectionable, a thing by the way which 'unus sumus' or 'sitis' is not. I may add that the editor's conjecture in v. 3, 'Quadringenta seca qui dicit, σῦκα μερίζει' ('seca' after Rutgers), seems a happy one.

v. 39. 'A satire on fortune-hunters, such as Martial figures himself to be.' Surely the satire is intended to fall rather on the man who is always inspiring hopes in fortune-hunters by making fresh wills.

v. 62. 4.

Nam mea jam digitum sustulit hospitibus.

'*Digitum sustulit*: has been sold to my guests: *i.e.*, my guests have used it up just as if they had bought it at an auction. "Tollere digitum" means to make a bid.' This is one of two interpretations mentioned by the earlier commentators: but neither its original proposers nor Mr. Paley explain how the thing sold at an auction comes to be spoken of as a person who bids at an auction. I do not know whether there is sufficient authority for the other interpretation, which explains 'digitum tollere' of a gladiator confessing himself beaten, on the strength of a passage in Sidonius Apollinaris, Ep. v. 7, supported to some degree by the Scholiast on Persius v. 119: but it has at any rate the advantage of giving a consistent image.

v. 70. 0.

Frigus enim magnum synthesis una facit.

'*Frigus*, a chill to my genial feelings...The sense is, my *one* synthesis keeps me cool, and that in a double sense:

I have no fuss in changing, and no one cares about me.'
This appears to me quite to miss the point of the epigram.
Zoilus changes his dress eleven times in a single meal,
nominally because it is so hot, really to show how many
dresses he has. Martial answers the question why he,
who is Zoilus's guest, does not feel the heat equally:
because he has only one dress, and so has no object in
changing.

vi. 1. 3.

> Quem si terseris aure diligenti.

'*Terseris aure*: this is shortly put for "Quem si
diligenter audieris dum legitur, et terseris (spongia, *i.e.*
calamo)."' This is very involved. The allusion may be
to a sponge: but the sponge is a metaphorical one, viz.,
the ear itself. The words read pass through the ear,
and Martial supposes that they are refined as it were by
the physical process of so passing. Lucretius, vi. 119,
has 'aridus unde aures terget sonus' (comp. Persius, i.
107, where 'radere auriculas' is similarly used): Martial
speaks of the reciprocal action of the ear on that which
rubs against it.

vii. 27. 9, 10.

> Ad dominum redeas: noster te non capit ignis,
> Conturbator aper: villus esurio.

'*Vilius*, &c., it costs me less to starve at home, *i.e.* to
fare poorly and cheaply, than to accept a present involving so much cost. Cf. 269 (v. 78). 2.' In spite of the
parallel, the words seem more naturally to mean 'my
hunger will be satisfied at a cheaper rate,' I wish to eat at
a cheaper rate. Comp. Ovid, ex Ponto, i. 10. 10, 'Nil
ibi quod nobis esuriatur erit,' there will be nothing to
tempt my appetite.

vii. 44. 5.

Aequora per Scyllae magnus comes exulis isti.

'*Isti*, amico tuo.' This is a natural but unquestionable oversight. 'Isti' is for 'ivisti.' 'Percepsti' occurs a page or two later (vii. 56. 1), and Catullus has 'tristi.'

vii. 63. 5, 6.

Sacra cothurnati non attigit ante Maronis
Implevit magni quam Ciceronis opus.

'*Sacra*, &c. Silius did not take to writing poetry before he had read through Cicero, viz. to learn eloquence.' The meaning surely is that he did not imitate Virgil as a poet before he had performed the part of Cicero as a pleader. Silius's forensic triumphs are referred to in the following lines :—

viii. 37.

Quod Caietano reddis, Polycharme, tabellas,
    Milia te centum num tribuisse putas ?
Debuit haec, inquis. Tibi habe, Polycharme, tabellas,
    Et Caietano milia crede duo.

'Polycharmus wished to gain a great reputation for liberality by returning Caietanus his bond for 1,000 sesterces, when he found he could not pay the money. Martial says, that is nothing : if you want to be liberal really, keep your old bond, and lend him, which is as much as giving him, another 1,000. Cf. Ep. 65 and 506.' The general sense seems rightly explained, but the point of 'milia duo' appears to be missed. Polycharmus had lent 100,000, and now makes a merit of cancelling the bond. Martial says it will be a far greater kindness to lend Caietanus 2,000 more, a fiftieth part of the sum which you profess to give him. It is curious that in the notes to Ep. 506 (9. 102), to which we are referred

as a parallel, the sense of 'reddere tabellas,' if not mistaken, is so obscurely expressed that it could hardly have
been discovered from the words used, while in the present
note it is explained clearly enough.   This is probably one
of the inconveniences of divided authorship, traces of
which occasionally appear in the volume.   The latter
epigram, by the way, throws light on that now before us,
as there Martial says that, instead of having a bond for
400 cancelled, he should like 100 as a loan.

viii. 70. 7, 8.

Sed tamen hunc nostri scit temporis esse Tibullum
Carmina qui docti nota Neronis habet.

'Neronis : compared with Nero's verses, which are
keenly ridiculed by Persius, Sat. i., Nerva was the Tibullus
of our times.'   A different, and doubtless the true interpretation, is given in a note to a later epigram, ix. 26. 9,
10, 'Even young Nero, when he wrote verses, is said to
have hesitated to recite them to one whom he called his
Tibullus, Ep. 437 (8. 70). 7.'   No disparagement of Nero
seems to be intended in either epigram.   That Persius
ridicules Nero's verses in his first Satire is not a certain
fact, but a conjecture founded on a statement in the
Scholiast, which is balanced by a later statement that
some in the Scholiast's day said the lines were Persius's
own.

xi. 3 (4). 13.

Expectes et sustineas, Auguste, necesse est :
Nam tibi quod solvat non habet arca Iovis.

'Expectes: You, Augustus, must wait for a time and
forbear : for after paying Domitian, Jupiter will have
nothing left for you.'   Surely Domitian himself is the
Augustus spoken of.

ix. 31 (32).

Cum comes Arctois, &c.

I do not pretend to understand this epigram : but I would suggest that the goose had been a live one, that Velius had fixed on it as a victim before the war began, and had made it swallow a silver coin for each month, the eighth having already been swallowed before the news came that the war was over, and that the bird was then killed and perhaps stuffed, the coins being taken out and fastened to its beak. Vv. 5, 6 could hardly be understood except of a living bird : and ' extis condita ' can surely have but one meaning : while ' argento ' would naturally refer to the silver coin, in which the real value of the offering might be considered to consist. By the way, has Mr. Paley given the exact point of Vibius Crispus's famous answer to the question whether anyone was with Domitian, ' ne musca quidem,' ' i.e., to be transfixed with a pin ? ' I had always supposed it to be ' He is quite alone : not even a fly with him, for he has killed them all.'

ix. 51 (52). 7, 8.

Et si iam nitidis alternus venit ab astris,
    Pro Polluce mones Castora ne redeat.

' Et si iam, &c., and if now, by a compact like that between Castor and Pollux, he has come from the stars to take his turn with you on earth that you may take his in the sky, you act like a Pollux advising Castor not to return. You beg him to stay wholly on earth, declaring your readiness to resign life here for ever in his behalf.' I do not think this can be right. It assumes that Lucanus's brother has come down to the shades, whereas the point of the epigram lies in his being still alive : it talks of him as coming from the stars, whereas he would be coming from the earth : and it gives an unnatural sense to 'redeat.' The early commentators seem substantially right in their explanation. Lucanus is in the shades: Pollux has just arrived there to take the turn of Castor: Lucanus presents to Castor a higher ideal of brotherly devotion, and urges him not to go back to the sky in his brother's place, but remain where he is, as he himself is ready to do on *his* brother's account. Or 'alternus' may be Castor, who has just arrived, Pollux having gone at once: Lucanus seizes an early opportunity of impressing on him that when the next opportunity of change comes, he ought not to take advantage of it. In any case 'pro Polluce' goes with 'redeat.' A similar contrast between the affection of these two brothers and that of Castor and Pollux had already been drawn, Book i. Ep. 36.

ix. 52 (53). 1—3.

> Si credis mihi, Quinte, quod mereris,
> Natales, Ovidi, tuas Apriles
> Ut nostras amo Martias Kalendas.

' *Quod mereris* : this clause follows *amo tuas Apriles Kalendas.*' Is there any difficulty in taking the words, as the natural order suggests, after ' Si credis mihi,' 'if you believe an assertion which your desert warrants?'

ix. 64 (65). 8.

> Illi securus vota minora facit.

' *Illi* : to the original Hercules he offers prayers of less importance, when indifferent as to the result; or perhaps, without feeling anxious lest it should be refused.' The Delphin explanation seems better : 'quin Hercules non aegre feret a se minori deo peti minora quam a Domitiano deo maiori.'

ix. 74 (75).

'On a *cerea imago*, or bust of a young man, which

the father had represented as an infant, lest the real
likeness should awaken too keen regrets.   Ep. 487 (ix.
76 or 77) is on the same subject.'   This appears to be
the ordinary interpretation: but I see nothing in either
epigram to necessitate the supposition which it involves.
The most natural meaning would seem to be that a
picture (why are we to suppose it to be a 'cerea imago?')
had been painted of the youth while he was an infant,
but that after his death the father declined to have one
drawn of him as he had appeared in later years. ' Pictura '
in both epigrams I take not as a painting but as the art
of painting.   Comp. Book x. 33, where, as Mr. Paley
rightly says, we hear of a picture taken of Antonius as a
youth, which continued to be the only likeness of him,
though he lived long after.

ix. 06 (00).

> Vindemiarum non ubique proventus
> Cessavit, Ovidi: pluvia profuit grandis:
> Centum Coranus amphoras aquae fecit.

' Water is so much more valuable, in a season of
drought, than wine, that Coranus, a shrewd old vintner,
has made a hundred gallons of it.'   Can this be the
meaning?   Martial is not speaking of a dry, but of a wet
season, and his meaning seems to be that the rain has
not been altogether bad for the wine trade, as it has
enabled the vintners to adulterate their wine more freely.
The joke is not unlike one which is sometimes made in
dry seasons, that you can get no milk because the cows
and the pumps are both dry.   Book i. 56, which Mr.
Paley compares, is, as he says, on the same subject, but
the point is different, the season being described as so
wet that the vintners could not sell unadulterated wine
if they would: Book iii. 56 and 57, to which we are
also referred, are not parallel at all.

x. 17. 0.

Appia, quid facies, si legit ista Macer?

'*Ista* seems incorrect: it should rather be *haec*, these epigrams of mine. *Ista* should refer to *via Appia*, and then it would mean the *libelli mensorum*, which is against the sense.' There can be no doubt, I think, that ' iste ' is repeatedly used by Martial when there is no reference to any person supposed to be addressed. See Book i. 40 (41). 1; ib. 70 (71). 18 (where the explanation in Mr. Paley's note, that the book is speaking to the poet, cannot be true); iv. 49. 1, 10; vi. 76. 4.   In all these places ' hic ' might be substituted without altering the sense.   In later Latin I believe it is used without scruple for ' hic ;' and so we may suppose that the change in its meaning came in gradually.   At the same time there are passages in Augustan writers where it is exceedingly difficult to give it its usual force : Horace, Epist. i. 6. 67, 'Si quid novisti rectius istis Candidus imperti; si non his utere mecum :' Virg. 'Aen.' xi. 537, 'Neque enim novus iste Dianae Venit amor:' where to render ' iste ' ' this of which I am telling *you*' is simply to confess that the word is used improperly.   There is a later note in this edition, on Book xi. 2. 8, where Mr. Paley says ' iste ' is virtually equivalent to ' hic,' and appeals to the medieval usage, though he still tries to bring out the reference to a second person.

x. 57.

Argenti libram mittebas : facta selibra est,
Sed piperis. Tanti non emo, Sexte, piper.

' The patron's annual gift to his client has come down to half a pound (not of silver but) of pepper.   That, says the poet παρὰ προσδοκίαν, is not enough to buy—pepper with.'   Surely the point is that Martial pretends to

regard the half-pound of pepper as intended to be an
equivalent to the pound of silver, and says, 'I would
rather have the silver, for I am not accustomed to give
so much for my pepper as that.'

x. 58. 3.

> Et quod inhumanae Cancro fervente cicadae
>   Non novere nemus.

'*Inhumanae*, sulky, unlike others of their kind.' Is
it not rather meant as a constant epithet of the cicadas,
which make themselves troublesome by their noise where-
ever they are found?   (And so I see the Variorum
Commentary takes it.)

x. 65. 11.

> Nobis fistula fortius loquetur.

'*Fistula*, a doubtful reading. The MS. have *filia*. . . .
The sense may be, I cannot imitate such a squeaking voice:
my reed pipe could do that better than I.' I do not
know whose conjecture 'fistula' may be, as it is not
mentioned either in Schneidewin's 'Apparatus Criticus'
or in the Delphin and Variorum edition: but I should
imagine the author of it must have meant 'my windpipe
will utter louder sounds than that.'

x. 70. 5.

> Non resalutantes video nocturnus amicos.

'The sense is, at night I have to see friends who do
not come to return me the morning's call.' The reading
is not certain, the MSS. having 'nunc,' and 'non' being
a correction of Schneider's. If 'non' is right, the sense
seems to be, 'I get up at night to salute friends who
pay me no visit in return,' referring to the early hour at

which the morning 'salutatio' was made, like the well-
known lines of Juvenal, Sat. v. 19 foll. (comp. Book x.
82. 2). This, then, will be Martial's account of the
beginning of his day. The seventh line, 'Nunc ad luci-
feram signat mea gemina Dianam,' seems to refer to an
engagement between the early 'salutatio' and the 'prima
hora;' but whether it simply means 'I sign a document
by moonlight,' or 'I go at morning twilight to sign at
Diana's temple,' I do not venture to decide.

x. 73. 7, 8.

> A te missa venit : possem nisi munus amare,
>   Marce, tuum, poteram nomen amare meum.

'If I could not regard the gift, I could have regarded
the name of the donor, Marcus, which he holds in common
with myself.' So apparently the commentators : but the
sense scarcely seems inherent in the words. Can Antonius have had the name of Martial embroidered on the
toga?

x. 77.

> Nequius a Caro nihil unquam, Maxime, factum est,
>   Quam quod febre perit : fecit et illa nefas.
> Saeva nocens febris saltem quartana fuisset !
>   Servari medico debuit illa suo.

'The worst thing Dr. Carus ever did was that dying of
a fever. The fever too was greatly to blame : it should
at least have been an acute and painful quartan attack,
that the patient might have been reserved for his own
doctoring.' 'De Caro Medico' is the heading in the
ordinary editions. But what evidence is there that he
was a doctor at all? The natural sense is that he ought
not to have died so rapidly, but to have had a quartan

ague, that so he might have been killed by his doctor.
The notion that the patient was himself a doctor seems to
have depended on the reading ' illa ' in v. 4, which would
make no proper sense with 'servari.'   To understand
' medico suo ' ' his own doctoring ' seems impossible.
With this exception I agree with Mr. Paley against
Mr. Mayor, who supposes the poet to have wished that
Carus's fever, if not cured altogether, had been changed
into a quartan.   If it could be established that Carus
was himself a curer of quartans, which is the view of the
Delphin and Variorum commentators, we might restore
' illa,' which has the merit of answering to 'illa ' v. 2,
change ' servari ' into ' sanari,' and take the epigram as an
expression of genuine complimentary regret.

   xi. 3. 7.

At quam victuras poteramus pangere chartas,
   Quantaque Pieria praelia flare tuba,
Cum pia reddiderint Augustum numina terris,
   Et Maecenatem si tibi, Roma darent !

   ' More properly he should have said " quanta pangere-
mus si darent," or " poteramus pangere si dedissent," in
which latter case " reddidissent," an unmetrical form,
would have been required.'   ' Poteramus pangere ' is like
' poteras requiescere,' Virg. E. i. 80, ' poteras scribere,'
Hor. Sat. ii. 1, 16, denoting a contingency not really past,
so that there is nothing incongruous in its being followed
by ' darent.'   ' Reddiderint ' is perhaps less regular : if so,
I suppose it is to be accounted for as an aoristic use of
the perfect.

   xi. 40. 4.

Silius et vatem non minus ipse tulit.

   ' The reading tulit is obscure.   Lipsius proposed colit.

It seems to mean *sustulit*, raised, exalted.' I am surprised that Mr. Paley has not mentioned Barth's very plausible conjecture, 'netatem' for 'et vatem.' 'Aetatem' or 'vetustatem ferre' is a phrase for having a permanent value, the metaphor being apparently derived from wines. Thus the sense would be, Silius has earned immortality no less than Virgil. 'Colit,' on the other hand, requires the reading 'minor,' which has little or no MS. authority. Whether 'optatae,' v. 3, can stand in the sense of 'desideratae,' I do not know; nor yet whether 'numina,' the reading of one early and three late MSS., is worth substituting for 'nomina,' v. 2.

xi. 65. 6.

> Sexcentis hodie, cras mihi natus eris.

'The point is not very clear: either the absurdity of keeping *two* birthdays is meant, or the poet implies that he will keep it in his own peculiar way, *i. e.* with anything but good wishes, such as the others offer. Or thus; your second day's birth-day will do for your humble friends.' He seems rather to mean that he shall regard being asked alone as a compliment, which I see is Gruter's view.

xi. 70. 1, 2.

> Ad primum decima lapidem quod venimus hora,
> Arguimur lentae crimine pigritiae.

'He means, by a hyperbole, that he has been ten hours coming one mile.' Is there any occasion for so startling an assumption? May not the host simply have complained that though he only lived a mile out of town, Martial was an hour behind time?

xii. 92.

> Saepe rogare soles qualis sim, Prisce, futurus,
>   Si fiam locuples, simque repente potens.
> Quemquam posse putas mores narrare futuros?
>   Dic mihi, si fias tu leo, qualis eris?

'*Leo*: if you were to turn into a lion, you would devour the weaker. Possibly I might act like other *potentes* and *tyranni*, who do the same to their subjects.' Is not this treating a joke too seriously? Does Martial mean more than to ridicule the practice of asking what a person would do under such and such circumstances which are not his nor likely to be his?

A LIBERAL EDUCATION.[1]

This volume[2] is one of a class which has become rather a prominent feature in the literature of the day, the class of which the well-known 'Essays and Reviews' were perhaps the earliest, as they have certainly been the most conspicuous specimen. The type of the class may be described as a series of essays of moderate length, written with a polemical purpose by authors whose views of the general subject treated of are not indeed necessarily identical, but at any rate convergent. The 'Essays and Reviews' evoked various replies written on the same plan; the Ritualistic party has followed the example in the two volumes entitled 'The Church and the World.' Within the present year this mode of treatment has been extended to political questions; and we now see it applied to education. Like other literary varieties, it has its advantages and its disadvantages. Essays by various writers will, of course, want the unity, the compactness, the thoroughness which constitute the value of a systematic treatise; but they are more easily produced, they appeal to a wider if a more desultory circle of readers, they neutralise the evil of individual crotchetiness, they give play to special knowledge and special aptitude, and they create something of the effect in literature which in practical life is obtained by a party demonstration.

I hope in the following pages to sketch very briefly the contents of the volume, to examine some of the

[1] Reprinted from the *Contemporary Review*, January, 1868.
[2] *Essays on a Liberal Education.* London, Macmillan & Co., 1807.
VOL. I.   G G

particular opinions advanced, and to criticise its general
object. My own views differ considerably from many
of those expressed by the individual writers, nor have I
more than a limited sympathy with the polemical purpose which the book is intended to subserve; but there
is no reason why this should interfere with fair and
candid criticism, with the respect which the character
and position of the essayists demand, or the regard
which most of them claim from me as personal friends or
acquaintance.

The subjects treated of in the essays are sufficiently
various. Mr. Parker takes the History of Classical Edu-
cation; Mr. Henry Sidgwick, the Theory of Classical
Education; Professor Seeley, Liberal Education in Universities; Mr. Edward Bowen, Teaching by means of
Grammar; Mr. Farrar, Greek and Latin Verse Composition as a general branch of education; Mr. J. M.
Wilson, the Teaching of Natural Science in Schools;
Mr. Hales, the Teaching of English; Mr. Johnson, of
Eton, the Education of the Reasoning Faculties; Lord
Houghton, the present Social Results of Classical Education. Each writes with a more or less distinct purpose
of bringing about some practical reform. Mr. Parker's
essay, being historical, stands on a different ground from
the rest; yet he wants English taught in schools, modern
languages and natural science encouraged in the Universities, elementary mathematics made compulsory, the
education of passmen improved, and the study of Hebrew
introduced: Mr. Sidgwick wants Latin and Greek verse
and Greek prose to be abandoned in schools, natural
science, English, and French enforced, and the study of
Greek deferred, and in many cases discontinued; Mr.
Seeley wants to abate the idolatry of the Tripos at Cambridge; Mr. Bowen wants to have boys taught language
without systematic grammar; Mr. Farrar wants to abolish

Greek and Latin verse as a general engine of training;
Mr. Wilson wants to have a course of natural science
taught compulsorily at school; Mr. Hales wants to have
English taught at school before any other language is
learnt; Mr. Johnson wants to have the subjects now
taught at school so taught as to educate the reasoning
faculty, and in particular wants to have the French
language and literature studied systematically; Lord
Houghton's wants are less definite and detailed, but he
may be said generally to want a modern training as a
supplement to, if not as a substitute for, an ancient.
We begin to see already some of the advantages of this
mode of publication. The number of reforms proposed
would overweight a single essay, however extensive, and
injure the writer's chance of securing a hearing; while,
on the other hand, the repetition of the same demands
by different thinkers, such as those for the abandonment
of verses, the teaching of natural science, and the teaching of English, produces an effect which could hardly be
produced, unless under exceptional circumstances, by the
voice of a single pleader.

Perhaps it will be well that, before proceeding further,
I should indicate my own position with regard to the
whole question. My belief then is that what we want is
not the substitution of one theory of liberal education for
another, but an arrangement by which different theories
shall be allowed to subsist side by side. The prejudice
of which we require to be disabused is not faith in
classics as an exclusive training, but faith in any training
whatever as exclusive. It is the growth of free opinion
which is undermining the supremacy of the present
system; it is only by the suppression of free opinion
that any other system claiming to be universal can be
established. As I read the present volume, I find that

when the essayists advocate their favourite branches of
study, I can go along with them heartily, even where
my own knowledge is not sufficient to make my sympathy a very appreciative one. When they desire that
their studies shall be made compulsory, still more when
they attempt to discredit the studies advocated by others,
they seem to me to be venturing beyond their tether,
and I no longer listen to them with satisfaction. I
believe that there are many minds which do not require
the training into which it is proposed to force them: I
know that there is at least one which has derived great
and abiding profit from exercises which are described as
injurious and futile.

This premised, I will make a few remarks on the
several essays in detail.

Mr. Parker's, as I have already said, stands on a
different ground from the rest. It is not really a polemical one, though a few pages of polemical matter appear
at the end as the practical conclusion of a treatise which
is really historical. Even here the reforms desired are
registered statistically, rather than enforced argumenta-
tively: they are not examined, but proposed as things
which need examination so as to furnish a programme,
more or less exact, of the discussion which is to follow.
But the real value of the essay is as a digest of facts;
and here I can only wish that it had been longer and
fuller. Eighty pages out of less than four hundred are
certainly as much as could fairly be allotted to one
essayist out of nine; but eighty pages are scarcely sufficient for a history of the study of the classics and the
classical languages from the days of the fathers to the
present time. It is an unavoidable result of this brevity
that things are treated conjointly which one would have
been glad to see treated separately; that there is an

occasional oscillation of view between two aspects of the
subject. The history of classical teaching may be said
to have two parts, internal and external—the history of
its own development, of the changes through which it
has passed in the successive attempts to work it effectively, and the history of its foreign relations, of the
extent to which it has encroached on or been encroached
on by teaching of other kinds. Of these the latter
perhaps bears more closely on the general object of the
present volume, as it has undeniably grown in importance during the last century or two, and most markedly
during the last forty years. It is not surprising then
that Mr. Parker, in the latter part of his historical
sketch, should dwell on it almost exclusively, feeling, as
he doubtless does, that during the period in question the
course of home administration has depended a good
deal, though perhaps not as much as it might have done,
on considerations of foreign policy. Still, it would have
been interesting to hear what the history of classical
education in English schools and Universities has actually
been ; whether Eton has always cultivated Latin verses
with success ; how Greek scholarship was introduced from
Cambridge into Shrewsbury, and returned with interest
by Shrewsbury to Cambridge ; what classical teaching in
the Universities was like in the pre-examination period ;
and a number of other particulars, without which we
can hardly be said to know how we came to be what we
are. But the question after all is not whether we are
told as much as we should have asked, but whether the
narrator has told us what could best be comprised in the
limited space assigned to him ; and on this point I have
no desire to break a lance with Mr. Parker. Most
readers, I believe, will find much that he tells them both
new and interesting, and will be grateful to him for the

clear, pleasant, and unaffected style in which his facts are
communicated.

There is more true discussion in Mr. Sidgwick's essay
than in any of the others. He has decided views, but
on the whole he cannot be said to write like an advocate; and he is always thoughtful and suggestive. The
examination to which he subjects the different defences
that have been set up for the present classical system is
searching, and rarely unjust. No doubt the advantages
of Latin and Greek, as at present studied, have frequently been represented in far too sweeping language.
Yet, if the defenders of the classics would amend their
plea, and contend not that theirs is the only training
which will realise the objects they have in view, but that
it will realise them sufficiently, I do not see why they
should not still stand their ground. And I think Mr.
Sidgwick is inclined to be too exacting in demanding
a precise apportionment of means to ends. When he
says, 'Teaching the art of rhetoric by means of translation only is like teaching a man to climb trees in order
that he may be an elegant dancer,' his metaphor seems
to me rather to run away with him. Mental training is
not like bodily training: the muscles of the mind are
eminently sympathetic, and care bestowed on one will
often act immediately upon another. Besides, no one
supposes that a boy who is taught to translate will have
his rhetorical faculty insulated to that one point. He
will read some English at any rate for himself, and the
sharpening of his perceptions by translation will enable
him to read it profitably; and his tutor would probably
advise him, even for the sake of translation, to try to
catch the peculiarities of different English styles. So
again, when Mr. Sidgwick, correcting Dr. Moberly, says
that 'each language requires its own art of rhetoric,' he

says what is true in itself, but for the purpose of the
argument is only a refinement. Dr. Moberly probably
means little more than Mr. Sidgwick has just admitted,
that to master one style is a very great help to mastering
another. It is not necessary to maintain that Latin is a
unique skeleton key to language generally; all that
requires to be shown is that one or two languages must
be selected from the rest to act, as almost any literary
language may act, as skeleton keys, and that there are
special reasons for choosing Latin. Generally, I suppose,
the argument for teaching the classical languages may be
said to stand thus. It may be considered as granted—
Mr. Sidgwick, at any rate, grants it—that both language
and literature are important studies. To master either
completely, it would no doubt be necessary to know
many languages and literatures; but, practically, some
choice must be made. There are several candidates
awaiting the selection; and speaking roughly, any one
of them will give the linguistic and literary training
required. Thus the advantages belonging to the study
of language and literature belong implicitly to the study
of Latin and Greek, and it would probably be an interminable business to discuss the question of more or less.
What then are the reasons for preferring the classical
languages where so many are equal? Mainly these:
they are past, and they have exercised an enormous influence on the present. It may seem a paradox to prefer
a dead to a living language, or a dead to a living literature, *cæteris paribus*; but the cause is not far to seek.
Living languages and books written in them can take
care of themselves: if they are worth studying, they are
sure to be studied sooner or later. They lie about us:
if we leave our own country, we come at once into contact with them: we can attain them, if we please, with-

out schooling. But dead languages, if not learnt at school, will not be learnt at all, except by a mere handful of students: they are remote from us, and if the tradition of them is not kept up, the knowledge of them will be virtually extinguished. This is a ground for preference which every dead language has; but Greek and Latin have more. They are the only two languages possessing a literature which are inseparably entwined with ancient history, the only two which have profoundly influenced the life and genius of times far distant from their own. Hebrew is excluded by its particular circumstances: Sanskrit, the only other ancient language possessing a great literature, if it has influenced the history of later times, has, at all events, not influenced their historical consciousness. The student of Greek and Latin gains, in fact, one of the chief advantages which are gained from the study of history: I do not mean that he acquires a knowledge of events, though he does incidentally pick up some knowledge even of them, but that he realises the fact that there *is* a past of the world's history, that there have been states of society as cultivated as our own, but essentially different. 'I know not how it is,' says Mr. Matthew Arnold, 'but their commerce with the ancients appears to me to produce, on those who constantly practise it, a steadying and composing effect of their judgment, not of literary works only, but of men and events in general.' And, if we may pass for a moment from school, there can be no doubt that the professed scholar's work is essentially historical; in discovering the meaning of a word, or appreciating the genius of an author, he has to go through precisely the same processes that are practised by the historian who wishes to ascertain the reality or estimate the significance of an event. This is surely a great

combination of advantages, for which it would be difficult (I do not say impossible) to find a parallel in any
other study. 'Yes,' replies Mr. Sidgwick, 'but though
your training has many elements, each element is not (at
any rate, taken alone) the best thing of its kind, or the
thing we most want.' Here, as I have said before, he
seems to me too exacting, too refining: besides, the
words included in his parenthesis open a question which
is too important to be passed over so summarily. These
elements are not alone; they are combined in one and
the same study; and surely that is another advantage.
Boys, so far as my recollection serves me, are not creatures of very intellectual interests: if they can excel in
one or two things, it is about as much as you can hope.
It might be well to make them encyclopædic; it is more
practicable, as it seems to me, so to educate them that
one study shall do the work of many.

On some of Mr. Sidgwick's special points, the necessity of a knowledge of natural science, the uselessness of
verse composition, I shall have a word to say when I
come to other essayists, who press them more at length.
But there is one of his reforms which requires special
notice—the postponement of the study of Greek. He
thinks that 'if Latin (along with French and English)
was carefully taught up to the age of sixteen, speaking
roughly, a grasp of Greek, sufficient for literary purposes,
might be attained afterwards much more easily than is
supposed.' Now I do not say that there may not be a
large number of boys who had better not learn Greek at
all; all I wish is to guard against the seductive promise
of that word 'postponement.' A dead language which
is not learnt till the age of sixteen will, I fear, as a
general rule, not be learnt at all. There is something
in the mastering of grammar and dictionary difficulties

which naturally belongs to the earliest stages of instruction, when learning is more or less compulsory. A boy who is conscious of making real progress in one or two languages (I speak from my own school experience) will be the very person to resent most the drudgery of having to carry on, *pari passu*, the low, childish taskwork of another tongue. And if this is true of any language, it is true of Greek in a very high degree. The mere strangeness of the character has something repellent in it, so that even one who can read Greek pretty fluently (I speak not merely of what I felt as a boy, but of what I feel to this day) will often prefer, in reading an unfamiliar author, to read him with the help of a Latin translation. Then, again, the fact, noticed by Mr. Sidgwick in another connexion, that Greek has influenced modern languages so little, renders it specially difficult, and by consequence specially repulsive. Who that has groaned under the unfamiliarity of the German prefixes *an* and *mit*, *über* and *unter*, *ver* and *zer*, the force of which it requires such an effort to calculate beforehand, can doubt what annoyance a clever boy of sixteen would feel in constantly having to turn to his lexicon to satisfy himself about the effect of ἀνά, κατά, μετά, and παρά in composition? Altogether, I believe that there are few studies which it would be so easy to lose as that of Greek, few which it would be so hard to regain. What England would be if the knowledge of Greek were to fall into comparative desuetude, those whose experience has familiarised them from boyhood with the effect of the two studies combined can scarcely undertake to prophesy. Perhaps those who know less of England and more of France and Italy will find the prediction easier.

In what I have said, as in what I shall say hereafter, I

am anxious not to derogate in any way from the advantages of other studies to those whose circumstances or natural bent may happen to point in a different direction. My case is simply that classics, as at present taught, have a *locus standi* ; and that case, so limited, I do not think Mr. Sidgwick's arguments disprove.

Professor Seeley is less suggestive and less judicial than Mr. Sidgwick, but he is very interesting nevertheless. His complaint is that University education is becoming more and more mere training for examination : he wishes to see a more genial and natural love of learning for its own sake. This he thinks might exist if the examination were not made, as it is now, the central point of the system. A learned class, he contends, may also be a class of teachers. England, centuries ago, was known as the mother of ideas, and there is no reason why she should not be so again. Many University men would doubtless echo his aspirations, if only they could see any means of converting them into realities. His own suggestions are three, though he intimates that they do not exhaust the requirements of the case : the opening of College Fellowships in Cambridge to the whole University ; the re-organisation of the teaching system so that tutors should lecture not to men of their own college alone, but to all comers, and, in consequence, should be able to concentrate themselves on some particular study ; and the arrangement of the names in each class of every tripos, not by merit, but alphabetically. Unfortunately we in Oxford have two of Mr. Seeley's remedies, the first and the third, in full work as part of our institutions, and yet we are still, in the main, a University of examiners and examinees. The second is desired by many of us, and may not improbably be established before long in some form or other, if indeed it may not be said to be partially

existing already; but I fear that, even then, we shall be
a long way from the goal to which Mr. Seeley looks
forward.   Many other things would have to be brought
about before the Universities could become really learned
bodies.   The question of passmen is academically what
the question of a proletariat is socially and politically : as
long as it is left unsolved, it is an open wound.   The
college system, valuable if not invaluable for purposes of
discipline, tends directly to discourage learning ; the
wealth of the colleges makes them important, so that their
heads form a social aristocracy ; and yet a head of a
college is not necessarily a learned man.   Yet it can
hardly be said that the Universities in this respect do not
faithfully represent the feeling of the country, nor does
it seem likely that any legislative reform in Parliament,
be it what it may, will give us an aristocracy of
teachers.

On the subject of Mr. Bowen's essay, the desirability of
teaching language to boys without grammar, I have no
opinion to offer which would be of any value.   It is a
practical question to be solved by those who have had
practical experience.   In what he says about grammar
itself, his assertions seem to me far too sweeping and unqualified.   The laws of language are not fully contained
in grammar rules, but grammar rules are useful nevertheless to give form and stability to knowledge which
would otherwise be vague and fluctuating.   It is next to
impossible that a boy should read enough to make his
feeling for language a sufficient guide.   Nor is it, I
venture to maintain, any impeachment of the utility of
grammar (though Mr. Lowe, in his recent Edinburgh
address, appears to agree with Mr. Bowen in thinking so),
that it was not known at all by the oldest of the classical
writers, and only imperfectly known by the later.   I do

not see why a grammar-writer needs to be ' confounded
by the circumstance that Euripides wrote excellent Greek
without having heard of an optative mood,' when he reflects that there is an optative mood nevertheless, and
that those for whom he writes are not, like Euripides,
unconsciously speaking a living language, but consciously
learning a dead one. Here I am happy to believe that
I may claim the support of Mr. Sidgwick, who evidently
thinks it unreasonable when a French writer attacks
grammarians for introducing refinements which Bossuet
never knew, ' as if Virgil ever thought of a tertiary pre-
dicate, or Thucydides of the peculiar use of *ὅπως μή*.'
Mr. Bowen, however, is disposed to go further, and to
question the value of those qualifications which make up
what is called ' a beautiful scholar.' I will not follow him
there : the passage is too long to quote, and it is so rhetorically and (Mr. Bowen must forgive me when I say)
intemperately written, that it would be scarcely just to
an essay which is in many respects an interesting one to
bring it into prominence. I will only notice one matter
of fact about which Mr. Bowen's language might lead an
incautious reader to form a wrong impression. The
writers of dictionaries and grammars, he says, are sure to
attack a man of ability and conviction who, in expressing
himself on subjects of public importance, shows ignorance of the classics. ' A man of classical education,
we shall hear, would never have spoken of the " works "
of Thucydides.' The allusion, of course, is to a speech
made by Cobden some fifteen or sixteen years ago, in
which he was reported to have said that, to an Englishman
of the present day, there was more to be gained from a
single number of the ' Times ' than from the whole of the
historical works of Thucydides. Probably too much was
made of this lapse at the time when it was committed ;

and no one, of course, would now dream of quoting it
disparagingly against a great man. But the point was this :
Mr. Cobden was not borrowing an illustration from the
classics; he was depreciating them, as many thought,
rashly and unjustly ; and therefore it was fair argument,
as it was certainly tempting, to point out that the very
form of his depreciation showed that he could know but
little of what he was depreciating. A living great man
was made the object of criticism, but he had provoked it
by criticising a dead one.

It is not easy to discover whether one who, like myself,
believes in Greek and Latin verse as a training for some
boys, but quite admits that there are others to whom it is
unsuitable, has any ground of controversy with Mr. Farrar.
He apologises to classical scholars, who may have the
leisure and the inclination for such pursuits, for any strong
language which he may use about their favourite relaxation, and distinctly asserts that he has in view the case not
of the brilliant few, but of the mediocre multitude. Yet,
on the other hand, it appears to me that much that he
says is irreconcilable with this limitation, and can only be
interpreted on the supposition that his hostility to the
practice is internecine. He complains that ' there are
learned and able men who still cling to a system of verse-
teaching which bears to so many minds the stamp of
demonstrable absurdity;' asks why it is ' that no one,
either in or out of his senses, ever thinks of learning any
other language by a similar process;' ' cannot admit that
it teaches style even to a handful who become good
scholars;' ' deliberately and determinately repeats that in
this elegant trifling, success is often more deplorable than
failure;' appeals to periods in history where successful
cultivation of style produced frivolity and feebleness of
intellect; and ends by saying that ' we require the know-

ledge of *things*, and not of *words* ; of the truths which great men have to tell us, and not of the tricks or individualities of their style ; of that which shall add to the treasures of human knowledge, not of that which shall flatter its fastidiousness by frivolous attempts at reproducing its past elegancies of speech ; of that which is best for human souls, and which shall make them greater, wiser, better, not of that which is idly supposed to make them more tasteful and refined.'   These sentences (and no one who has read the essay will say that they misrepresent its spirit) surely apply not to the indiscriminate teaching of Latin and Greek verses, but to the teaching of them at all. To attempt to qualify them by interpolating in each of them, 'except in the case of the brilliant few,' would be not to explain, but to destroy their meaning.   In fact, Mr. Farrar seems to have made a promise which he has found himself unable to keep : he has undertaken to respect the liberty of a selected few ; but when he comes to introduce his reasonings, he finds them so clamorous and so cogent, that he is compelled to abandon even these privileged persons to their tender mercies, and to proclaim a war of extermination.

I must then accept Mr. Farrar's challenge, which has indeed already been given by Mr. Sidgwick, and declare that, whether in or out of my senses, I should be prepared to recommend the practice of verse-writing as a means of acquiring other languages, if they should have to be taught under the circumstances under which Latin and Greek are now taught at schools.   We take Latin and Greek (whether rightly or wrongly is not now the question) as typical languages, and apply to them a minuteness of study which we cannot afford to apply to others ; and part of this minute study is the practice of verse-composition.   And we choose verse-composition in particular,

because as a matter of fact we find that verse-composition
is suited to the capacities of young boys.   Mr. Johnson,
in a later essay, has done me the honour to refer with
approval to an opinion which I expressed to the Public
School Commissioners, to the effect that whereas a verse
is within the grasp of a boy's understanding, a prose
sentence is to him an impenetrable mystery.   This was
grounded on my vivid recollection of my own school days,
and also on the experience of some years at Oxford, during
which pupils were constantly bringing me composition in
verse and prose.   I have often amused myself by paralleling
individuals with nations, and noticing this comparatively
late appreciation of the capabilities of prose as a fact in
literature, as I had already observed it as a fact in
my own development.   Homer writes poetical narrative
when history is still unknown in Greece ; Hesiod versifies
didactics when there are no prose treatises on agriculture.
But further, I believe that a man (under favour of Mr.
Mill as well as of the two essayists) will appreciate the
artistic part of poetry better if he writes verses himself.
Here, again, I am stating what seems to me to be a conclusion from my own experience in the matter of English.
It may or may not be worth while to cultivate the habit,
but I cannot admit that it fails of its object.   As to the
extreme cases which Mr. Farrar mentions, boys saturating
themselves with Ovid in order to write elegiacs, no one is
concerned to defend them.   It is not desirable to be
thoroughly imbued with Latin erotic poetry ; but neither
is it necessary.   A literary police, I readily grant, is
needed for scholars, as it is for other people.   But to talk
broadly about ' a finical fine-ladyism of the intellect . . .
an exotic which flourishes most luxuriantly in the thin
artificial soil of vain and second-rate minds . . . the en-
thronement of conventionality, the apotheosis of self-

satisfaction,' as the kind of taste which Greek and Latin verse-writing tends to foster, is to talk unwarrantably and extravagantly. Such denunciations aggravate the mischief against which they are directed; they drive opponents into a defying and polemical attitude, and prevent them from candidly admitting that there are dangers in their study against which they, as sensible men, would wish to be on their guard.

I have not grappled with Mr. Farrar's argument from authority. My desire has been to record my own individual conviction, and so I have brought no compurgators with me, past or present. Yet I cannot help hoping that I might find some if it were necessary, though of course it is true that there are great names on the other side. Meanwhile, I think the moderate advocates of verse-composition may find some reason for reassuring themselves in the very violence of the storm which seems now to be setting in against them. Doubtless their party has in its time used expressions of unwarranted contempt in speaking of studies of a different kind; and it is no more than retribution that they should 'hear themselves as many things as they have said of others.' But Nemesis is just, and a limit must exist somewhere. There cannot be much more to be said against their study, and then, perhaps, the tide will turn.

I now come to an essay which I have read in some respects with more interest than any other in the volume; I mean Mr. Wilson's. It may not be as thoughtful as one or two others, but it is decidedly the most inspiring. The gem of the whole paper is contained in a few pages, where he gives an account of his own method of teaching botany to a class of boys by what he truly calls a *maieutic* process, drawing out intelligence before communicating knowledge, and only imparting formulas where the pupil's

mind has come absolutely to yearn for some principle
under which to combine its facts. Even those who are
ignorant of natural science must feel, on reading these
pages, that they are in the presence of a really
eminent teacher, who could hardly fail to exercise a
powerful influence on any mind of decent capacity with
which he might be brought into contact. Perhaps I may
be allowed to mention the effect which their perusal had
on myself. It did not make me feel that natural science
ought to be taught in schools less restrictedly than it is ;
that I was already prepared to concede. It did not make
me feel that natural science ought to be made a part of
every boy's education ; that I fear I shall always be disposed to question. But it set me thinking whether the
method employed so successfully in teaching natural
science might not be applied to other things in which I
happen to be more interested—whether Mr. Bowen's view
of teaching language without grammar, to which I was
not previously inclined, might not have some portion of
truth in it.

What more I have to say must unhappily be confined to
the point on which I differ from Mr. Wilson, the necessity
of compelling all boys to undergo a course of scientific
instruction. I believe to a considerable extent in what
Mr. Wilson ' holds to be a pestilent heresy '—' a theory of
education in which boys should learn nothing but what
they show a taste for.' I should not myself put it quite
so nakedly ; and I should be ready to have my theory
modified (which does not mean set aside) by the practical
experience of schoolmasters. What I think then is, that
boys who have a decided taste for any intellectual study
recognised as forming a part of school education ought to
be allowed to indulge it, to the total neglect of some
studies, and the partial neglect of others. The Platonic

Socrates lays down (whether he is always consistent with himself on this, any more than on other subjects, I really do not know) that ' no trace of slavery ought to mix with the studies of the free-born man ; for the continual performance of bodily labour does, it is true, exert no evil influence upon the body ; but, in the case of the mind, no study, pursued under compulsion, remains rooted in the memory.'[1] Probably many instances might be quoted to disprove this last statement ; but I am sure there is a great deal of truth in it. ' Male parta male dilabuntur :' what we take no interest in learning we are commonly glad to forget. The real thing, it seems to me, is to strengthen the love of knowledge where it exists, and lead it on continually to fresh acquirements, seeking corrections for one-sidedness where I believe they may generally be found, in ever widening and deepening views of the study itself. There will always be outlying subjects to which the student will have some affinity, and these he may easily be led to pick up : a boy with classical tastes, e.g., will, as a general rule, with a little encouragement, take kindly to English literature. On the other hand, there will be studies to which a boy of this kind will be apt to feel a natural repugnance ; witness what I may almost call the hereditary feud between classics and mathematics. I do not say that it may not be possible, by a long and elaborate course of training, to soften these antipathies ; I do not say that it may not be in some cases desirable to do so ; but, after all, some choice must be made, and there are many things of which the majority of cultivated men must, each in his own sphere, be content to remain in ignorance. I am ready to include Latin and Greek among these, as regards one type of men, destined to one course in life. I do not see why I may not include

---

[1] Plato, *Republic*, book vii. p. 5.36 (Davies and Vaughan's translation).

natural science as regards another. One class need not know the Greek name for the liver, or the Latin for the spleen; another class need not know where the liver or the spleen is, unless, unhappily, the information should be brought home to them in a practical shape. Some physical facts the literary man will require for the conduct of ordinary life, and he will get them; some facts about antiquity the scientific man will require in order to understand the condition of things about him, and he will also get them. For these purposes, as well as for purposes of social intercourse, the broad sheet of the 'Times' newspaper will supply sufficient common ground. For purposes of mental culture, apart from professional exigencies, each will find ample means of refreshment in his own and cognate studies.

But it is said that classical men need a scientific education. Mr. Parker tells us that men of science make the complaint which Erasmus made of the scholars of his day: 'Incredibile quam nihil intelligat litteratorum vulgus.' Mr. Faraday, to a paper of whose he refers, spoke strongly to the Public School Commissioners of the delusions entertained by cultivated persons on matters of which no one can be a judge without having had a scientific training. 'Up to this very day there come to me persons of good education, men and women quite fit for all that you expect from education; they come to me, and they talk to me about things that belong to natural science, about mesmerism, table-turning, flying through the air, about the laws of gravity; they come to me to ask me questions, and they insist against me, who think I know a little of those laws, that I am wrong and they are right, in a manner which shows how little the ordinary course of education has taught such minds.' No one will defend these injudicious querists, who go to consult the oracle and then argue against the response given ; though I suppose it might be asked whether their belief in their illusions is likely to have done them much harm, apart from leading them, as it apparently did, to violate good taste. But I will meet the complaint by a counter bit of experience. In 1853, not long after table-turning came into vogue, I was acquainted with a person who had no scientific knowledge, but occupied himself chiefly with the study of Greek plays. He heard of table-turning, and became rather interested in it. He tried it himself in a miniature form, which at that time was fashionable among beginners, the turning of a hat. The hat turned readily. He had endeavoured to observe his own movements while the process was going on, but found that the very act of thinking of his fingers' ends gave him a sensation as if his fingers' ends did not belong to him, so that he could not tell whether they were imparting any motion to the hat, much less whether the fingers' ends of his neighbours were imparting any. He resolved to suspend his judgment until some physical philosopher should speak. In two or three weeks one did speak, and that was Mr. Faraday himself, in a well-known letter to the 'Times.' My friend was satisfied, and troubled himself very little about table-turning afterwards. What led him to so sane a conclusion? It was simply that he was just then beginning to take a firm hold of his own subject, and, in consequence, to understand the authority which special knowledge imparts to its possessor.

But, granting that it is possible for non-scientific persons to avoid forming or propounding rash judgments on scientific subjects by attending to the simple rule of minding one's own business, is there nothing of importance to all educated men, to appreciate which a knowledge of science is absolutely necessary? My readers will have anticipated that I am going to speak of a matter far graver than any I have touched on yet, the issue now pending between science and revelation. Mr. Parker presses this point in a few words; Mr. Wilson more at length. The latter thinks that no one can meet the question properly in whose mind religious and scientific ideas have not been allowed to grow up side by side. Now, it is important at starting to ascertain to whom or what the duty of coming to a conclusion on this is owing. Is it to religion or to science? Clearly to the former. I do not say that we have no duties to science: we all of us have duties to it; those who are led to it by natural bent or circumstances are bound to cultivate it; those who are not so led are bound to treat it with respect, and to refrain from rash and ignorant comments on it. But that belongs to the part of the argument with which we have been engaged for the last page or two, not to the part which we are now considering. The new claim advanced for science rests on another duty, our duty to religion. Science and religion are in apparent conflict, and therefore it concerns all religious men to entertain some opinion on a struggle which may affect religion. It is a question whether we are all bound to be scientific; there is no question, among those with whom I desire to class myself, that we are all bound to be religious. I am not advocating any sectarian view; I admit freely that all truth comes from God, and that religion may be injured, not merely by questioners who start difficulties, but by answerers who, ignore them. I am only anxious to put the matter, as regards those who recognise religion, on its true basis. What we have to inquire, then, is, how may our duty to religion in this matter be satisfied? Is it due to religion that all those of us who are capable of acquainting themselves with scientific

truth should try to do so ?   Let us consider what the points
at issue between science and religion are.   Two of those
most prominently canvassed are the truth of the Mosaic
account of the creation, and the credibility of the Gospel
miracles.   Would the breach that exists with regard to
matters like these be healed by a general diffusion of
scientific knowledge?   Some have thought that a profounder investigation of science would remove the
apparent contradictions which now trouble so many minds.
It may be so; but is this likely to result from a more
general diffusion of scientific education?   If it is necessary
to dig deeper than the science of the present day, will not
such digging be carried on by the few rather than by the
many?   On the other hand, might there not be a danger,
if science were more diffused among educated men, that
those who are zealous for religion would broach superficial theories of reconciliation or confutation, such as
readily commend themselves to partial knowledge, while
they could not have occurred to honest ignorance ?   Surely
the present aspect of the controversy tends to show that
men require, for their own peace, at any rate, not instruction in natural science, but views drawn from a philosophy of another kind ; views which, while accepting the
statements of science, if need be, at its own estimate,
shall suggest other considerations unknown to science,
and produce in the mind, not, perhaps, intellectual satisfaction, but at any rate a contented acquiescence in imperfect light, as a condition at once warranted by fact
and recommended by analogy.   If, as I believe, our conclusion must be, as religious men alive to the controversies
of our time, that while, on the one hand, there are many
unsolved difficulties, on the other there are realities lying
beyond the range of those difficulties, why are we bound
to engrave the difficulties deeply on our minds, so that,

turn where we will, they may always confront us? Why
is it necessary that every cultivated man should be able
to appreciate from his own experience the full strength of
the resistance which scientific habits of mind oppose to
the reception of supernatural interference? No one pretends that the dispute is really to be decided on that
issue; it is merely one of various elements in the question;
and till all cultivated men are so educated as to appreciate
all the elements of the question thoroughly, it is worse
than vain, it is mischievous, to press on religious grounds
the claims of any single element to special study. No
doubt the study of evidences is the proper work of the
ablest of the clergy, and of such of the laity who feel that
from circumstances they are best able in that way to
serve their generation; but it should be really thorough
study, neither one-sided nor superficial. What others
have to do is, not to solve the problem for the world, but
to appreciate its conditions, which will be one way of
solving it for themselves.

After all, I fear Mr. Wilson will still be unconvinced.
He will not allow literary men to argue from their own
mental experience that they do not need a scientific
training; and that, I am afraid, is at bottom the argument which is really powerful with all of us   I will
only entreat him to believe that, though a literary student
may not use his faculty of natural observation when he
is out of doors, his mind is not necessarily idle or un-
occupied; he may have thoughts which are worth having
in themselves, and which he could not have if his attention
were otherwise engaged.

The three remaining essays need not detain us so long.
The matters for controversy which they open have been
partially anticipated; and generally they may be said to
be less controversial than most of their predecessors. Two

of them, moreover, are comparatively short, those by Mr. Hales and Lord Houghton. Lord Houghton's acts as a sort of *l'envoy*, not going into detail, but enforcing the general doctrine of making education more modern on social grounds. Like everything which comes from him, it is elegantly and gracefully written, and, standing as it does at the end of the list, it enables us to close the volume with a sense of artistic finish. Mr. Hales, on the other hand, devotes himself to a special point, the teaching of English in schools, which he thinks ought to be made the basis of all other linguistic and literary training. Mr. Sidgwick had already pressed the same thing, though I am not sure whether he would entirely agree with Mr. Hales on all matters of detail. Their view would have my warm sympathy if I could be quite sure of its feasibility. No one will deny that a knowledge of the English language and literature is an essential part of the literary training of an Englishman. Other modern languages he may neglect with more or less of impunity; but to neglect his own would be absolutely suicidal. The only question is whether room can be found for it in the classical part of the present school curriculum. I am assuming that Greek and Latin are to be retained as portions of the early training of boys educated in that department; and I should be inclined to add to them German, for the reason which I hinted in a former page, that, while it is all-important as a key to modern learning, it is comparatively difficult to pick up later, and therefore ought, I think, to be mastered in those early years which are naturally associated with intellectual drudgery. With three languages on hand, I confess I doubt whether even a clever boy would find room for the systematic study of a fourth, even though that fourth be his own. On the other hand, knowledge of English can always be picked

up : a boy's ignorance of his own language is not that
kind of ignorance which offers resistance to the acquirement of knowledge, and much may be done without
direct teaching to make a clever boy a good English
scholar. Let me say, by the way, that I scarcely agree
with Mr. Sidgwick when he declares that he wishes the
' occasional and irregular training' which boys now get
' to be made as general and systematic as possible.' One
of the complaints against the increasing exactingness of
modern education is, that it allows boys no time for
reading. Doubtless, now that athletic tastes have become
so absorbing, masters may be jealous of leaving more
leisure than necessary at a boy's disposal ; yet I think
most would feel it to be a pity that a pupil should receive
the whole of his intellectual impressions through the
medium of his form-master or his private tutor. That
English should be taught to those whose training is not
intended to be classical, I readily admit ; and if in a
bifurcated school any crumbs from the well-furnished
table in the modern department could be made to fall to
the classical boys without entailing the necessity of their
sitting through every meal, it would be a real point
gained. While I am on the subject, I may note that, the
absence of any Professor of English is one of the most
patent wants of the English Universities. An Anglo-
Saxon chair may throw light on the ' divine fore-time ' of
the language ; a Poetry chair may do something for parts
of the literature ; but a more systematic cultivation of the
subject is needed, and it is a discredit that Oxford and
Cambridge should make no attempt to supply it.

Mr. Johnson's essay comes near Mr. Sidgwick's for
suggestiveness and thought, if it is not quite equal to it.
Perhaps its effect is injured to some extent by the form
into which a good deal of it is thrown. There is an auto-

biographical element in it; it professes to record the
writer's experiences as a schoolmaster; and this is not unfrequently done in a tone of cynical self-depreciation. The
result is that, though we have much light, the light is not
always quite dry. The same vein of individuality appears
occasionally in the illustrations with which he sets forth
his arguments. Like most of his colleagues in this volume,
he pleads for physical science; and one of the considerations he advances is the value which the classical writers
whom we admire attached to the study. ' It is painful to
enumerate all that we leave unnoticed; the " natural
questions" which a Seneca would have asked, which we,
the distant heirs of Seneca, either slight or dread. We
force our pupils to say in Latin verse, that sounds to me
almost as the voice of the Fairy Queen summoning the
rhymer, " Happy is he who hath been able to learn the
causes of things, why the earth trembles, and the deep
seas gape ;" and yet we are not to tell them. Virgil
humbly grieved, but we grieve not, that we cannot reach
these realms of wonder. . . . What would Lucretius have
thought of men who knew, or might know, such things,
and were afraid to tell the young of them, for fear of
spoiling their perception of his peculiarities? How would
Ovid flout at us if he heard that we could unfold the
boundless mysteries contained in his germinal saying, "All
things change, nothing perishes," and passed them by to
potter over his little ingenuities!' Surely it is misleading
to talk in this way of the ancients, as though their circumstances were precisely the same as our own. Knowledge was in their days far less extensive and multifarious
than it is now, and the principle of a division of studies
was in consequence much less recognised. An ancient
student was necessarily more ambitious in his range of
inquiry than a modern student either can or ought to be.

Then there are special circumstances attaching to each of the different writers named. It is difficult to understand why we are bound to follow in the steps of Seneca; he is not one of the authors who have made our knowledge of classical literature what it is to us; and the mere fact that he writes in Latin and was encyclopædic is hardly a reason why those who read Latin should be encyclopædic also. Virgil, if I read him rightly, did not so much wish to be a natural philosopher, which he might have been, as to be the poet of natural philosophy; nor is it clear, even so, what his wish means. It may be a graceful way of deprecating comparison with Lucretius, to whom the whole passage is an allusion: it may be a despairing aspiration after the inward satisfaction supposed to be given by Epicurean belief or disbelief. As for Lucretius, the 'nature of things' had a terrible reality to him; his creed was bound up with his physical theory. It would certainly be strange if anyone should read through his poem for the sake of noting his peculiarities without attempting to understand his philosophy; but is this often done? My own experience would lead me to think that hardly any who are not prepared to enter into his philosophy read him continuously, and that those who wish to observe his peculiarities as a writer read only certain parts of his poem, those, namely, which contain least of natural science. Ovid's case is diametrically opposite: whatever he may have thought of his 'germinal saying,' it is in no sense a sample of his poetry; and those who, instead of trying to develop its meaning, devote their time to his prettinesses of expression, do no more than he apparently wished them to do. Is a reader of Pope's 'Essay on Man' bound to study the philosophy, which is probably second-hand as well as second-rate, rather than the diction and versification, which are really what give the poem its character?

But I must not follow Mr. Johnson further into details, though I should have liked to put him on his defence for his statement that 'the monstrous fatuities which disfigure Æschylus are condemned by the clear head of an Aristophanes, and can be proved to be bad;' an unmeasured way of talking, from which even Mr. Sidgwick is not quite free. A dissection of an illustration takes up more room than the illustration itself; and the more an essayist has to say, the more a reviewer is obliged to say in answering him. I will only add, then, briefly, that I cordially agree with Mr. Johnson's object, the education of the reasoning faculties of boys, and think that he has been very successful in showing in how many ways it may be done without outstepping the ordinary limits of a classical and literary training. To his plan of teaching French systematically to his classical pupils I incline to demur, for the reason I gave a page or two back in speaking of Mr. Hales's essay. Three languages seem to me the utmost that a boy can profitably pursue at once; and French is not, like German, a language which it is difficult to acquire at a later period.

I should be sorry if it were supposed that I wished the foregoing pages to be accepted as an adequate examination of the contents of this volume. To examine it thoroughly would require a volume of at least twice its bulk, and a writer far more versed in educational questions than I am. All that I have attempted to do is to follow the example of the Parliamentary orator (was it Mr. Cobden?) who said it was his habit to step out and join the debate when he saw it coming by his door. The thread which runs through my criticism is, as I have said already, a belief that the question before us is not how to frame a new theory of liberal education which shall supersede the old, but how to construct a system which shall give scope for different theories, adapted to different circumstances. We are not likely to convince each other; we have no right to silence or ignore each other; it remains that we should tolerate each other. How a toleration may best be organised is a question which I leave to those who are more accustomed to grapple with details. The adoption of bifurcation in all our larger schools would seem to be a natural way of meeting the want in its earlier stages: to satisfy it in a later period it would probably be necessary that the Universities should recognise from the first that distinction of studies which is now conceded, sparingly and with hesitation, in the latter part of an academical career.

The following note is reprinted from the *Contemporary Review*, April 1868, page 631, where it appeared as a correction to the article republished Vol. I. p. 479 :—

On further consideration, I see reason to alter the opinion expressed in pp. 410, 411 of this *Review* about the meaning of the words in the Prayer of Humble Access. I said there that the revisers of 1552 altered the prayer in one or two verbal points only, from which I inferred that the construction which we should have put on the prayer, as it stands in the Liturgy of 1549, is the true construction now. I have since perceived that one of the alterations, and that occurring in the very clause in question, is more than verbal. In 1549, the clause ran, 'so to eat the flesh of Thy dear Son Jesus Christ, and to drink His blood, in these holy mysteries.' In 1552, the last four words were omitted, as is still the case. It has been suggested to me that the reason of their removal was the change made at the same time of the position of the prayer, which formerly stood after the Prayer of Consecration, the expression, 'these holy mysteries' not being strictly applicable before consecration has taken place. But the friend who makes the suggestion admits that it may be urged, on the other side, that the words 'this holy sacrament' are retained in the Invitation, the place of which was similarly changed in 1552, an inconsistency of practice which he attributes to oversight. It appears to me more likely that the revisers of 1552 omitted the mention of the holy mysteries from a wish not to determine exactly whether the reception of the Body and Blood was involved in the reception of the elements, or generally in the whole act of Eucharistic worship, of which the reception of the elements forms a part. This opinion is strengthened by the fact that the very same omission is made in a later prayer, that which is now the alternative prayer after the Communion. The beginning of that prayer originally stood, 'Almighty and ever living God, we most heartily thank Thee for that Thou hast vouchsafed to feed us in these holy mysteries with the spiritual food of the most precious Body and Blood of Thy Son our Saviour Jesus Christ.' Now we read 'for that Thou dost vouchsafe to feed us, who (which, 1552) have duly received these holy mysteries, with the spiritual food' &c. One reason of making the alteration, of course, was the transfer of the condition of due reception, which, in 1549, was attached to the second part of the sentence, that speaking of the 'virtus sacramenti,' to the first part, where the 'res sacramenti' is spoken of (a point, by the way, which has apparently escaped the annotator, who, in warning us that 'duly' is the English word for 'rite,' and so applies to all who have received, is as inconsistent with the language of the prayer of 1549 as he is consistent with its doctrine); but, taking the changes in the two prayers together, I cannot doubt that the revisers were influenced by a further reason, and preferred, as I have said, to use words not making the

THE ANNOTATED BOOK OF COMMON PRAYER
ON THE COMMUNION SERVICE.[1]

THERE are few things, it seems to me, by which theologians can do better service than by commenting carefully and judiciously on our doctrinal formularies. While we have doctrinal standards, questions will constantly arise about the compatibility of particular opinions, held by individuals or sections of the Church, with the true meaning of those standards; and there can be no better way of ascertaining that meaning than by close and scrupulous commentaries, drawing out the sense of the original by the same rigorous method of interpretation which is daily being applied with success to the study of ancient literature. Such works, so executed, would be of the highest use with reference to the legal decision of questions like those which are now vexing the Church : not only would they be quoted by advocates, but they might materially assist lay judges; nay, it is scarcely too much to say that they might contribute greatly to remove the unsatisfactoriness which even persons least inclined to undermrate the advantages of lay courts of appeal will admit to be inherent in the decision of theological issues by unprofessional authority. And, putting controversy out of sight, I may be allowed to say that no class of books would be more interesting to students like myself, who know by experience the value of accurate exposition, and desire to see the work which they are attempting to do for others in one department done for themselves in another.

[1] Reprinted from the *Contemporary Review*, March 1868.

Accordingly, it was with much pleasure that I noticed the appearance of the 'Annotated Prayer-Book.'[1] From the names associated with it, I presumed that I should find in it many points ruled otherwise than I should myself be likely to rule them; but I felt that this, if fairly and candidly done, need not interfere with my deriving much valuable instruction, and I reflected that interpreters of a different school might not have had that sustaining enthusiasm for the subject which is the best guarantee for work being performed well and thoroughly. I naturally turned to that part of the work which may be said to be the keystone of the whole, the Communion Office. I can scarcely say how much I have been disappointed. I have as little title as I have wish to dispute the learning there displayed; but it seems to me to be applied almost throughout, not to candid exposition, but to polemical pleading. I propose to establish this by an examination of this portion of the commentary in detail; and I am anxious to appeal to my friend, Mr. Meddl, who is one of the authors of it, on behalf of those principles of just criticism which I cannot believe that he himself undervalues.

The fault of the commentary (here, as elsewhere, I am speaking exclusively of the commentary on the Communion Office) appears to me to be that it is written on a theory. Now, there is scarcely any subject on which, as I venture to think, the intrusion of theory requires to be so jealously watched as in that of interpretation. We come to our work as learners, expecting to find out from the words of the document what the meaning of the document is; and it is only when the words have quite failed

---

[1] *The Annotated Book of Common Prayer*, Part II. London: Rivingtons, 1866. I have not been able to collate the first edition (that which I have had before me) with the second; but so far as I have glanced at the latter, it seems (at least in the part with which I am concerned) substantially unaltered. J.C.

to give us light that we can have any right to resort to
hypothesis. Of course I do not mean to say that there
will not be some cases where the use of hypothesis is
justifiable and necessary; but they will be comparatively
few, unless, which is not likely to occur, the general language of the document is confessedly perplexed and difficult. In such cases, no doubt, collateral considerations,
involving more or less of theory, will come in. But to
view the whole subject in the light of theory is simply to
prejudge it; to profess to institute an examination, yet
to take the most effectual means of rendering that examination nugatory.

The theory of the annotators, which appears, I think,
plainly in the Introduction to the Communion Office, is
the substantial identity of the Eucharistic doctrine contained in the English office with that of the various liturgies which it superseded. No one will dispute the right
to hold such an opinion, if it is supported by facts. But
it is evident that one chief class of facts on which it must
rest is that furnished by the Communion Office itself, and
that therefore those facts must not be explained by the
theory. Yet that this is what is attempted will, I think,
be plain as we go on to examine the commentary in
detail. One conspicuous instance meets us in the Introduction itself (p. 154) :—

Although, however, the change in the position of the words
of oblation has tended to obscure the meaning of the service,
it cannot for a moment be supposed that the revisers of our
Liturgy in 1552 were so exceedingly and profanely presumptuous as to wish to suppress the doctrine of the Eucharistic
sacrifice. There were probably some unfortunate temporary
reasons (such as the unscrupulous tyranny of ignorant and
biassed rulers) which induced them to make such a change as
would save the doctrine, while it left the statement of it more

open than before; and they probably thought it better to consult expediency to a certain extent than to run the risk of such an interference as would have taken the Prayer-Book out of the hands of the Church, and moulded it to the meagre faith of Calvinistic Puritans.

The writer then goes on to mention that some eminent divines, such as Andrewes and Overall, used to alter the order *proprio motu*, and to express, if I understand him rightly, his regret that this unauthorised mode of redressing what is conceived to be wrong has not been practised since the last revision. Now, without stopping to remark on the want of moderation shown in speaking of a course which, whether it was historically adopted or not, would have accorded with the belief of many of the writer's fellow-churchmen at the present day, as ' exceedingly and profanely presumptuous,' I think there can be no doubt that we have here an illegitimate use of hypothesis. We are told that a certain thing cannot have been intended, because the writer feels that it ought not to have been intended. This, it is obvious, can only be a legitimate consequence on the supposition that the framers of the Liturgy of 1552 would certainly have agreed with the writer in repudiating that interpretation of their action which he deprecates. Yet we know that Cranmer was one of the principal agents in framing that Liturgy, and it is admitted that at the time of framing it he had already, as Dr. Pusey has expressed it in his book on the Real Presence, ' gone over to the Swiss school.' I do not allege this fact as proving that the alteration made by the framers is to be interpreted in a certain way, but as showing that to interpret it in that particular way would not be in itself monstrous. It is still open to contend that Cranmer did not impress his own view on the Liturgy, but that can only be supported by an examination of the formu-

lary itself. The writer, it is true, goes on to give positive
reasons why the alteration cannot have the effect imputed
to it. These I shall have substantially to deal with afterwards; at present, I will only say that they would have
lost nothing in the estimation of candid men if they had
not been preceded by an attempt to put opponents summarily out of court.

I proceed to the commentary.

The first note, one of several on the title, runs thus :—

The title of this office in the Prayer-Book of 1549 was 'The
Supper of the Lord, and the Holy Communion, commonly
called the Mass.' It is evident that the Reformers did not
see any reason why this sacrament should not still be commonly
called 'the mass,' but the name soon dropped out of use after
the introduction of the vernacular into Divine service, and it was
not printed as a third title in 1552, or in any subsequent
Prayer-Books.

The 'evidence,' I suppose, depends on the assumption
that the Reformers, having once used the word 'mass'
after breaking with Rome, are not likely to have seen any
objection to it subsequently. The more ordinary argument would be that as they dropped the word they saw
some objection to it. Nor does it appear why the mere
adoption of the vernacular in the service should have led
to the disuse of the old name. The word 'mass' was, to
all intents and purposes, a thoroughly vernacular word,
and continued so. But it had become associated with
the ante-Reformation service, from which, rightly or
wrongly, the reformed one was supposed essentially to
differ; and this will sufficiently account for its coming to
be abandoned as a popular term in connection with the
new Liturgy. It may at least be said that if the framers of
1552 had been more anxious than those of 1549 to separate themselves from the ante-Reformation use (whether

or not this be conceded as a fact), the abandonment of the word 'mass' would have been as important a step in that direction as any that was likely to occur to them.

The next note begins, 'As the name "mass" was used after the introduction of the Reformed office, so that of "Lord's Supper" was used before,' a fact of which proofs are then adduced. This is of course intended to leave the notion on the reader's mind that the two words were considered to be perfectly indifferent so far as the issues of the Reformation were concerned. I will merely ask, Is this fair?

We now come to a very important and indeed cardinal point: the entire omission of the word 'altar' in the Liturgy of 1552 and the subsequent revisions. The fact is of course frankly admitted by the annotator, who endeavours to account for it :—

The motive was the necessity of (·1) disabusing the minds of the people of the gross and superstitious notions with reference to the Eucharistic sacrifice . . . . which had gradually grown up during the latter centuries of the mediæval period, and (2) of bringing back into its due prominence the truth of the doctrine of communion. The consequence of this (it is added) has been the partial obscuration of the sacrificial aspect of the Holy Eucharist, and the almost exclusive concentration of popular belief on its communion aspect.

Here it is implied, if not expressly intimated, that though the Reformers abandoned the word 'altar,' they did so for merely temporary reasons, and did not abandon the thing. It may be so; yet surely candour ought to have admitted that the abandonment furnishes a formidably strong argument to the supporters of the opposite view, and that so serious a change in language could not be made without committing the Church that accepted it. Far from allowing this, the annotator simply concerns himself to prove, from

the Bible and from general theological considerations, that
the table is an altar, prefacing his argument by saying
that 'only those ignorant of theology can maintain that
there is any contradiction between the two.' The answer,
of course, is that many persons (rightly or wrongly) have
thought otherwise, that the framers of the Liturgy seem
to agree with them, and that it is the sense of the Liturgy
which is the question at issue. Two other statements are
made, with the intention of proving that the Church of
England holds the doctrine of the altar; that the word is
still retained throughout in the form for the Coronation of
the Kings and Queens of England in Westminster Abbey,
and is used throughout the office of Institution of Ministers
into Parishes or Churches, set forth in the General Convention of the American branch of the English Church in
1804 and 1808. It is difficult to see what argument can
be based on the language of a formulary which does not
appear to have been ever accepted either by Parliament
or by Convocation, and which, being used only four or five
times in a century, would naturally escape a thorough
controversial revision, or on the words of a document
adopted by a sister, but independent Church.

The next note, on the 'fair white linen cloth,' is much
more satisfactory in its mode of argumentation, though its
conclusion is, I think, a doubtful one. It remarks justly
that to understand the force of a law, we must understand
the meaning which was given to its words at the time
when it was imposed; says that 'fayre' is translated
'pulcher, venustus, decorus, bellus,' in the 'Promptorium
Parvulorum,' and that of the seventeen meanings assigned
to the word in Johnson's Dictionary, only one, that
answering to 'pulcher,' is found in the English Bible, the
notion of cleanliness being expressed by 'clean' or
'pure;' and concludes that 'a fair white linen cloth'

must mean a white linen cloth rendered beautiful by ornamentation. It is somewhat singular that in examining the use of the word in the English Bible the annotator should have passed over one passage, Zechariah iii. 5 : 'Let them set a fair mitre on his head.' I am no Hebraist, and cannot say what the force of the word in the original may be; but when I find the LXX. rendering κίδαριν καθαράν, the Vulgate 'cidarim mundam,' and a writer so unlikely to be swayed by LXX. or Vulgate traditions as De Wette, 'einen reinen Bund,' I can have little doubt what our translators meant. It seems to me also that an annotator trained in a stricter school of interpretation would have selected, as crucial instances of the use of 'fair,' passages where it might conceivably mean 'clean,' but, as a matter of fact, does not, not combinations like 'fair colours' and 'fair jewels,' where the meaning 'clean' is out of the question. No one doubts that 'fair' can mean 'beautiful,' and in connection with colours and jewels it can scarcely mean anything else. On the other hand, such an annotator would probably have remarked that 'fair' in the sixteenth century, as well as our own day, was constantly used in antithesis to 'dark,' so that 'fair white' may well be an intensified expression like 'spotless white;' and again, that it has also been for centuries contrasted with 'foul,' which then, as now, had a technical sense in connection with linen. I am only indicating such considerations as happen to occur to me, and such as would have been in place, in default of better, in commenting on an ancient author; but, of course, what is wanted is to adduce passages from authors of the sixteenth century where the words 'fair white' are found together, especially in connection with an article like linen; and the only book which is at hand to supply the defects of my reading,

Clarke's 'Concordance to Shakspeare,' furnishes me with none such.[1]

Passing over one or two other notes on the rubric, where the expression 'north side' is made the occasion for introducing facts and directions about altar curtains, and also the whole of the commentary on the early part of the Communion Service, in which, as was to be expected, not much controvertible matter occurs, I come to the Offertory. Here the annotator quotes the rubric of 1549, which runs as follows:—

> Then shall the minister take so much bread and wine as shall suffice for the persons appointed to receive the Holy Communion, laying the bread upon the corporas, or else in the paten, or in some other comely thing prepared for that purpose; and putting the wine into the chalice, or else in some fair or convenient cup prepared for that use (if the chalice will not serve), putting thereto a little pure and clean water, and setting both the bread and wine upon the altar.

He then proceeds:—

> The substance of this rubric is retained in that which immediately precedes the Prayer for the Church Militant, and its significance was heightened in the revision of 1661 by the introduction of the word 'oblation' into that prayer. The rubric and the words of the prayer together now give to our liturgy as complete an oblation of the elements as is found in the ancient offices.

Now, considering that the existing rubric merely says, 'And when there is a communion, the priest shall then

---

[1] Since writing the above, I have met with a passage which confirms one of my surmises. Queen Elizabeth, in a letter to Parker and others dated January 22, 1500-1, speaks of 'the unclean or negligent order and spare-keeping of the house of prayer . . . . by appointing unmeet and unseemly tables with foul cloths for the communion of the sacraments.' (Correspondence of Parker, Parker Society, p. 133.)

place on the table so much bread and wine as he shall think sufficient,' we may fairly argue that whatever special significance there may be in its words is due, not to the words themselves, but to the prayer which follows them. It would be perfectly open to a Church which knew nothing of any sacrificial doctrine that the elements should be placed on the table by the priest, and at that particular time of the service. The fact that from 1552 to 1661 no direction existed on the subject, does not show that the direction had any higher object than decency or supposed convenience. Hickes, who agrees with the annotator in his view of its significance, complains that it had been 'almost never observed in cathedral or parochial churches:' 'I say almost never, because I never knew or heard but of two or three persons, which is a very small number, who observed it;' a fact scarcely to be accounted for, if it had been recognised from the first as having a doctrinal bearing. The meaning of the word 'oblations' is certainly a very difficult and doubtful question. No one can deny that, taken in connection with liturgical history, the word itself naturally suggests the notion of an offering of the elements; nor would I wish to give anything short of its due weight to the consideration that the Caroline divines who introduced it are likely to have wished to enforce that view. Yet there is at least equal force, I think, in the considerations adduced by Canon Robertson ('How shall we Conform to the Liturgy?' pp. 206. foll., second edition),' that the distinction between alms for the

---

' To the instances there quoted add Bishop Wren's *Orders and Directions*, No. xviii. (Cardwell's *Documentary Annals*, vol. ii. p. 205): 'That the holy oblations, in such places where it pleaseth God at any time to put into the hearts of His people by that holy action to acknowledge His gift of all they have to them, and their tenure of all from Him, and their debt of all to Him, be received by the minister standing before the table at their com-

poor and offerings for Church purposes was a common
one in the seventeenth century, and that other alterations
corresponding to this distinction were made by the same
Caroline revisers in several of the rubrics. It might be
added, that had Eucharistic oblation been intended, we
should have expected it to be made a more prominent
feature in the prayer, though to this it may be replied
that the revisers, under all the circumstances, would
naturally be content with a minimum of alteration. On
the whole, it is perhaps safest to conclude with Canon
Robertson that both senses were intended, if indeed it be
not nearer the truth to say that a word was chosen in
which various parties might unite, though attaching different senses to it. It is scarcely necessary to observe that,
even if Eucharistic oblations alone be intended, this does
not close the question of doctrine, as many persons not
agreeing with the annotators in their full sacrificial view
have, nevertheless, held that the elements may be offered
to God as His gifts. I will only add an expression of
regret that no trace of any attempt to compare antagonistic views on this very difficult point should be found in
the notes before us.

The next note I have to notice is that which deals with
the commemoration of the faithful departed at the end of
the Church Militant Prayer. The annotator first says :—
' In commemorating the departed at the time of celebrating the Holy Eucharist, the Church of England simply
does as every known Church has done from the earliest
age in which its liturgical customs can be traced.' He
then quotes or refers to the Liturgies of St. James, St.

ing up to make the said oblation, and then by him to be reverently presented
before the Lord, and set upon the table till the service be ended.' Wren
was an intimate friend of Laud, and in perfect accordance with him, as Dr.
Cardwell says, in matters of faith and discipline.

Mark, St. Clement, and St. Chrysostom, in each of which prayers are distinctly made for the dead. He concludes as follows :—

> It will thus be seen how great a deviation it would be from primitive Christianity to omit all mention of the deceased members of Christ, at the time when celebrating the great sacrament of love by which the whole Church is bonded together. And it must be considered as a great matter for thankfulness that in all the assaults made on the Liturgy of the Church of England by persons holding a more meagre belief in things unseen, the providence of God has preserved the prayer for the whole Church, departed as well as living, in the Prayer for the Church Militant.

The meaning of these sentences, as may be gathered by comparing them with a passage in the Introduction, p. 156, is this : The mention of the dead is made in the sentence at the conclusion of the prayer, where we bless God's name for the departed, and pray that we may follow their good examples ; but this is linked on to the actual prayers for the dead contained in the earlier Liturgies, by the expression occurring afterwards in what is sometimes called the Prayer of Oblation (the Prayer for the Church Militant is mentioned by mistake), ' that . . . . . we and all Thy whole Church may obtain remission of our sins, and all other benefits of His passion.' In the note on the passage in the Prayer of Oblation it is said :—

> The double supplication is here to be noticed. The prayer is that (1) we and (2) *all Thy whole Church,* and it is also that we may obtain remission of our sins, and that all Thy whole Church may receive *all other benefits* of His passion. The latter phrase looks towards the ancient theory of the Church, that the blessed sacrament was of use to the departed as well as to the living. It is a general term used by men who were fearful of losing all such commemoration, if inserted broadly and openly, but yet feared lest no gate should be left

open by which the intention of such commemoration could
enter.

Now, if the two prayers are to be taken in connection
with each other, there is one important point to be noted.
In 1549 the Prayer for the Whole State of Christ's Church
was not limited to the Church Militant on earth, but contained petitions for the dead as well as for the living.
This fact would naturally govern the sense of the words,
'Thy whole Church,' occurring in the Prayer of Oblation.
But with the alteration in the Prayer for the Whole State
of Christ's Church the case is altered. The sense of the
words in the Prayer of Oblation, if not governed differently,
is at any rate left ungoverned. In themselves the words
'whole Church' have no determinate meaning. Whether
they are taken in the widest possible sense, or in a more
or less restricted one, must depend on the nature of the
case. In the Authorised Version of the New Testament,
where they occur three times,[1] their sense is more or less
restricted. The question, then, whether or not in the
Prayer of Oblation they apply to the dead, depends on
the previous question whether the use of the Church of
England recognises prayers for the dead. They do not
interpret that use, but are interpreted by it. Meantime
it is curious that the annotators, who refer in their Introduction to the words in the Prayer for the Sovereign,
'have mercy on the whole Church,' do not quote a passage from another prayer where the parallel is more
complete, the conclusion of the Prayer for the Parliament.
That prayer, as is shown in the first part of the present
work, is based on a fast-day prayer, perhaps by Laud,
where, as in our form, 'these and all other necessaries'
are asked 'for them, for us, and Thy whole Church.'

---

[1] Acts xv. 22; Rom. xvi. 29; 1 Cor. xiv. 23.

Laud's private opinions of course are of no value in authoritative interpretation ; but if he was the author of the Fast-day Prayer, it is likely enough that he intended his words to convey a sense which, as the annotator shows, Cosin, following Andrewes, wished to fix on the words now in question.   But whether or not this sense be under the circumstances an admissible one in the present case, it is, as the annotator allows, rather latent than patent in the words as they stand in the present service ; and it is rather surprising that the writer of the Introduction to the Liturgy, taking this passage in connection with that in the Prayer for the Church Militant, should say that, ' if the language used is more concise than formerly,' when the dead were distinctly prayed for, ' it cannot be said to be less comprehensive.'

The Exhortations open the question whether the formularies of the Church of England contemplate frequent or infrequent communions. So far as cathedrals, collegiate churches, and colleges go, the question is settled by the rubric at the end of the Communion Service, which enjoins celebration at least every Sunday.   The writer of the Introduction goes further, and (it is difficult to say on what evidence, except the practice of the unreformed Church and some notices in the Liturgy of 1549) pronounces ' regular Sunday celebrations of the Holy Communion ' to be ' the undoubted rule for every Church.' The annotator admits that ' the tone of the rubric and the Exhortations is plainly fitted to a time of infrequent communions,' but contends that this probably was owing to temporary reasons.   There is more plausibility in this argument here than in other cases where it is applied to prove that the framers of the Liturgy held doctrines the expression of which they chose to omit, as the rubrics at the end of the service evidently imply that what the framers feared was the paucity of communicants.   Yet it would have been better if the view had not been enforced by a questionable piece of interpretation. 'The rubric does not seem to enjoin their constant use, but to require this form of exhortation to be used at those times when the minister thinks it necessary to "give warning," that is, to exhort his people, respecting "the celebration of the Holy Communion."' It would not be easy to persuade an ordinary reader that 'to give warning' is likely to mean anything else than 'to give notice;' and if he happens to be a student of Shakspeare, he will know that the expression in this sense was as familiar in the sixteenth and seventeenth centuries as it is now. Yet this sense is not even named in the note. Turning back, however, to a note on the earlier rubric before the sermon, I find the word 'warning' quoted apparently in its ordinary sense, so that there may be a difference of opinion on the matter between the annotators themselves.

In the note on the Prayer of Humble Access, the hypothesis of 'some temporary influence or danger' is again employed to account for the change in the position of the prayer, which the annotator, in common with Archbishop Laud, whom he quotes, appears to regret. My chief object, however, in referring to this prayer, is to make an admission which, it seems to me, candour requires, though the annotator himself has forborne to claim it explicitly. I believe it to be the one part of our present Communion Office where words occur which, understood in their natural and obvious sense, not only admit, but assert the doctrine of an objective presence. When we pray that we may 'so eat the flesh of Christ and drink His blood that our sinful bodies may be made pure and our souls washed,' we necessarily imply that we might eat the flesh and drink the blood with a different result. We imply, in short, what is contended for by Archdeacon Denison and Dr. Pusey with reference to the Twenty-ninth Article. And this was doubtless the intention of the original authors of the prayer, which is substantially the same as that in the Liturgy of 1549. Why the revisers of 1552, altering the prayer in one or two verbal points, left it intact in this respect, though in other parts of the service they seem to have wished to remove the traces of the doctrine in question, is a point on which I do not seek to offer an hypothesis. It is of more importance to estimate what consequences are involved in the admission which, as I have said, I feel bound to make. That the more definite and dogmatic part of the formularies ought to interpret (for purposes of Church conformity) the less definite and dogmatic seems only reasonable, though I am of course aware that it has been much questioned. Looking to Art. XXIX., I will only say, without entering into the question in detail, for which this is hardly the place, that its natural meaning seems to me to deny that our Lord is present in the elements to the good and the wicked alike. On the other hand, apart from controversy, there appears to me nothing in the words of the prayer which need jar on the feelings of a worshipper who believes that the presence is confined to the faithful. 'Lex supplicanti, lex credendi,' so far as it is true, surely applies to the general character of our prayers, not to the logical implication of each expression. Still, when a dogmatic issue is raised, I feel that the words I speak of ought to be allowed their full weight in determining what is the mind of the Church of England on the subject; nor should I think it just if a divine of an opposite school to that of the annotators were simply to dismiss the question by saying that the words were doubtless retained merely for temporary reasons, and that con-

sequently they need not be taken into account in forming
a conclusion. If we wish (as for purposes of Church
conformity we must wish) to form a conception of the
general doctrine of the Church of England on a given
point, we cannot avoid the responsibility of deciding
which of two apparently antagonistic statements must
give way to the other; but it is not the less incumbent
on us, before making the decision, to give each its distinct
force, as explained according to the natural rules of
language.

With regard to the precise force of the words used by
the priest in delivering the elements, there will of course
be difference of opinion, according to the view taken
of the effect of the act of consecration. The effect of
the substitution of the words ' take and eat,' &c., for ' the
Body,' &c., made by the revisers of 1552, can scarcely
be misunderstood. The Elizabethan Reformers joined
the two forms of delivery together, for which they are
commended by L'Estrange, whom the annotator quotes,
and apparently by the annotator himself. But it will
hardly be contended that the combination does not leave
it open to those whose convictions so require to understand the first part of the words of delivery as a prayer
that through the medium of the elements about to be
received the spiritual blessing of communion may be
conferred, without being committed to any belief in a
change having passed on the elements by virtue of the
prayer of consecration. We must remember, what the
annotator does not bring out with sufficient definiteness in
his text and notes, though by printing the Liturgy of
1549 in an Appendix he enables the reader to verify the
matter, that the most important words in the prayer of
consecration do not stand now as they did in 1549. Then
the prayer was that the bread and wine might be sanctified

so as to become to the recipients the Body and Blood ; now
it is that the congregation, receiving the bread and wine,
may be partakers of the Body and Blood,—words which,
it is evident, admit a wider latitude of dogmatic belief.

I now come to one or two notes on minor points.

The direction in the rubric to deliver the elements to
the people ' in order ' is explained : ' *i.e.*, first to the men
and then to the women, according to the practice in the
best-ordered churches.' This is an endeavour, of which
there are many in the book, to combine the office of a
Directorium with that of a Commentary, a union of functions which I think does not conduce to scrupulous care
in commenting. So the words ' in their hands ' are explained in accordance with a direction of St. Cyril,
that the bread is to be taken, not in the fingers, but in
the palm of the right hand ; no mention being made of
the fact, which a commentator would naturally have
thought more germain to his province, that the words
are a substitute for a direction in a rubric of 1549, according to which the communicants were to receive the
sacrament of Christ's body in their mouths.

In commenting on the direction to ' place what remaineth of the consecrated elements reverently on the Lord's
table,' the annotator argues that the word ' reverently,'
occurring as it does among a number of rubrics which
have been greatly cut down from their original fulness,
must point to a belief in an actual change of the elements.
' Were the elements sacred only so far as they were partaken of, there could be no reason for specially directing
the priest to place what remaineth *reverently* on the Lord's
table, for no more reverence to them would be needed
than that respect which is shown for everything used at
the Holy Communion.' I should have thought that a
church just emerging from the Puritan period (the rubric

was added in 1661) might naturally have used the word without necessarily implying any such further meaning as is supposed. The annotator himself in the Appendix reprints the Presbyterian Office with reluctance, calling it a ' presumptuous and irreverent parody of the Liturgy ;' and whether or not the Caroline bishops would have expressed themselves as strongly about that particular form of ritual, they must have been cognisant of much undoubted irreverence which might well call for a single word of warning even from men disposed to be sparing in their injunctions.

I have already adverted to the remarks in the Introduction on the alteration of the position of the Prayer of Oblation. It is now time to speak of that part of the argument which depends not on general presumption, but on a consideration of the service itself. The first assertion in the Introduction, that the act of consecration, apart from any express words of oblation, is itself an act of sacrifice, is felt by the annotator not to be absolutely conclusive ; in fact, it begs the question. A further reason for regarding the scope of the prayer as not substantially altered by its change of position, is that the remainder of the consecrated elements has just been replaced on the table, so that of them at any rate an oblation may be made.[1] Yet, to one looking at the question dispassionately, it would seem strange that a Church that wished to enforce the doctrine of Eucharistic oblation should solemnly offer, not the elements as a whole, but that part of them which may happen to be left over in the event of the priest having consecrated more than is sufficient. Accordingly, the change is re-

---

[1] I have taken this argument as it stands in the Introduction ; whether it is quite identical with that in the note, which is somewhat less definitely expressed, I am not sure.

gretted; and we are told, as in the Preface, that Bishop
Overall disregarded it, and Bishop Cosin thought it accidental. This last supposition the annotator regards with
some favour, though it would seem in the last degree
unlikely that the revisers of 1552, or any other period,
would acquiesce, in a matter of such importance, in what
they must have known to be a printer's error.[1] Would
not a commentator on an ordinary text have thought it
worth his while to mention that there was another interpretation which at any rate had the merit of taking the
prayer as it stands, to the effect that by the Eucharistic
sacrifice is meant the whole act of worship, and by the
oblation an oblation of ourselves? It is not pretended
that this would have exhausted the meaning of the words
as they were originally used in the Liturgy of 1549; but
the question is whether the change in the position of the
prayer does not naturally limit and modify the meaning.

I have now only to notice the note about the Declaration on Kneeling. It lays stress, justly enough, on the
fact that the revisers of 1661, in reviving it after a century of disuse, did so with a change in the wording of
one part, 'corporal presence' being substituted for 'real
and essential presence.' I quite agree with Dr. Pusey[2]
that 'it is a paradox to say that while the reformers of
the rubric deliberately ejected what its framers deliberately inserted, it is all one as if they had not ejected it
and substituted another word:' that indeed is precisely
what I have been urging throughout with respect to the
changes introduced in the successive revisions. The
change of the words no doubt removes the denial of a real
and essential presence. Whether it affects the declara-

---

[1] We know as a fact that Cranmer was ordered to correct such printer's
errors as actually occurred. (Introduction to *Annotated Prayer-Book*,
p. 31.)

[2] *Real Presence the Doctrine of English Church*, p. 322.

tion in any way is a different question.   For we are told
in the declaration not only what kneeling does not import,
but what it does import.   The order to kneel, it is said, 'is
well meant, for a signification of our humble and grateful acknowledgment of the benefits therein' (in the sacrament) 'given to all worthy receivers, and for the avoiding
of such profanation and disorder in the Holy Communion
as might otherwise ensue.'   This, however, touches a
question which the annotator does not raise, the question
of Eucharistic adoration.   Meanwhile I would only observe that, in accepting Mr. Perry's view that the original
declaration of 1552 was probably intended merely as a
protest against the doctrine of transubstantiation, and the
low notion of a carnal presence which had come to be
the interpretation too commonly put on the phrase ' real
and essential presence,' the annotator differs from Dr.
Pusey, who says,[1] ' They who first framed the sentence
moulded it carefully to exclude the Real Presence altogether.'

I have ventured to maintain that the radical fault of
this commentary is its having been written under the
influence of a theory, that theory being the substantial
identity of the Eucharistic doctrine, as contained in the
present Liturgy, with that of its various predecessors.   It
may be said, however, that we have distinct warrant for
assuming this identity at the very point where the breach
of continuity has been alleged to be most patent, the
substitution of the Liturgy of 1552 for that of 1549.
The Act of Parliament establishing Edward's Second
Prayer-Book declares the first to be ' a very godly order,
agreeable to the Word of God and the primitive Church,
very comfortable to all Christian people desiring to live
in Christian conversation, and most profitable to the state

[1] *Real Presence the Doctrine of English Church*, p. 322.

of the realm;' and speaks of the doubts about the manner of using it as having arisen 'rather by the curiosity
of the ministers and mistakers than of any other worthy
cause.' Such an argument, however, if it proves anything, proves too much. The Elizabethan Act of Uniformity endorses the Second Prayer-Book of Edward,
minimizing the changes made in it, and saying in particular of the Liturgy that two sentences only are added:
but would it be fair to contend from this mode of speech
that the two sentences in question, those added in the
form of the delivery of the elements, are of no importance? If it be said that the words in Edward's Act of
Uniformity are stronger, it may be replied that the
charges then made were much more extensive. 'Qui
s'excuse, s'accuse:' the Parliament which issued the
Second Book was the same that had issued the First
Book, and it would scarcely have proclaimed the fact
that the two books seriously differed from each other.
Besides, the argument is two-edged: while some use it to
prove that the Second Book means no less than the First,
others use it to prove that the First Book means no more
than the Second, which is indeed said in this very Act of
Parliament to 'explain and make it fully perfect." After
all, the question is not what may be inferred about the
meaning of our formularies from the brief and general
words of an Act of Parliament, but what the formularies,
naturally interpreted, witness about themselves. Whatever the Parliament of 1552 thought about the First

---

' The case appears to stand thus. As a question of reason, it would seem
that the more explicit document should interpret the less explicit. As a
question of authority, the later ought to interpret the earlier. But it is
only the presumed authority of the Parliament of 1552 which would lead us
to interpret either document by the other; therefore, if we are to entertain
such considerations at all, we must go by authority, not by reason.

Book weighs but little against the fact that they superseded it.[1] Ἐν τῷ λέγειν καινήν, πεπαλαίωκεν τὴν πρώτην.

My object in making these remarks has been to register a protest—a temperate one, I would hope—against what I cannot but regard as an unsatisfactory mode of commenting on the Prayer-Book. I admit readily that there is room in the Church of England for more doctrinal schools than one; and that being so, it is necessary that each school should have a theory for reconciling its own belief with the formularies. But this, it seems to me, is a separate question from the interpretation of the formularies, and ought to be kept distinct. Let us first interpret the formularies according to the strict rules of interpretation; let us then consider what degree of license may be fairly claimed in each particular case by members of a Church which has never been without parties, and has passed at different times under the more especial influence of one or other of them. Even as interpreters we might often disagree; but we should profit increasingly by each other's labours, and we should learn to recognise more thoroughly the common ground on which we stand.

---

[1] If Parliament were to enact that certain formularies, imposed by its authority, were to be understood in a certain sense, that sense would be imperative, even if it did not happen to be the natural one. But a legislature is hardly likely to go to this length; and nothing short of it would interfere with the original duty of ascertaining what the formularies mean from what they say.

BISHOP FORBES ON THE ARTICLES.[1]

I LATELY commented in this Review on some unsatisfactory, because inexact and arbitrary, interpretations of the Communion Service.[2] I now wish to call attention to a series of explanations of the Thirty-nine Articles,[3] which appears to me to be open to a similar objection.

It would not seem to be very difficult to lay down generally what is required in a commentary on the Articles. They should be interpreted, like any other statement of opinions, according to the natural meaning of the words, taken in significant connection with each other, with their context, and, in case of doubt, with the rest of the document, recourse being had, where it may be needful, to the theological history of the time, and specially to the writings of the framers of the Articles, and of others who are known to have sympathised with them. This is the way in which the true sense of a document of the kind is likely to be ascertained; and it would seem obvious, as I have said, that it is to be employed in the present case. The meaning of the Articles being thus arrived at, it is a separate, though of course a very important, task to estimate the bearing of their meaning on the general doctrine of the Church of England, to harmonise apparently conflicting results, and to obtain a view of the mind of the Church on the various points on which questions may be raised. There is again a third inquiry which also has its place, though of an inferior and subordinate kind. There

---

[1] Reprinted from the *Contemporary Review*, July 1868.
[2] See preceding Article.
[3] *An Explanation of the Thirty-nine Articles*, by A. P. Forbes, D.C.L., Bishop of Brechin. Oxford: Parker, 1807–1808.

are different schools within the Church of England, which
in one form or other have existed for the last three centuries, if not for a longer period; and as it is not only
possible but likely that no one of them exactly expresses
the mind of the Church on all doctrinal points, it is natural
to inquire what limits of divergence may be allowed to
each in the case of this or that matter of belief.   This is
of course a casuistical question depending on many minute
considerations; but it is of consequence to the whole body
of churchmen, as well as to the particular section concerned, not only that it should be entertained, but that it
should be determined fairly and reasonably.   These, it is
plain, are distinct tasks; and though the temptation may
be great to confuse them in practice, I believe it is in
proportion as they are kept distinct that each is likely to
be satisfactorily performed.

　If these remarks are true, it seems evident that a work
which, like Bishop Forbes's, professes to explain the
Articles on a particular theory commits a fundamental
mistake.   The interpretation of the Articles requires no
theory, and admits none.   Particular passages may be
doubtful, and with reference to them these or those external considerations may be legitimately employed; but
to interpret the whole in the light of an external theory
is self-condemnatory.   As English churchmen, we may be
bound, as Bishop Forbes thinks we are, to hold what is
called the Catholic theory of belief.   If the Articles express that theory, they will say so when interrogated by
the ordinary methods of inquiry.   Protestant tradition
may have encrusted them; but there are recognised,
though it may be slow, methods of removing all such en-
crustations.   If the Articles, fairly interpreted, are not
Catholic, it may still be possible, by taking them in connection with other statements of the Church's belief, to

produce on the whole a Catholic result. If this again
cannot be made out, it is open to contend that there are
certain limits beyond the strict line of the formularies
within which Catholic opinion has a standing-ground in
the Church of England. But no supposed duty to Catholic
truth can warrant us in explaining the Articles in any
other sense than that which may appear on detailed examination to be the sense of the Articles themselves.

But it will be right to expound Bishop Forbes's theory
somewhat more fully before proceeding to comment on
his practice. This is indeed not so easy as it may appear
at first sight, as, though he expressly states that he has a
theory, the precise nature of it is not so much to be found
explicitly stated in any one passage of his work as to be
collected from several. I am not sure that I altogether
comprehend it : I am not sure that he is in these different
passages absolutely consistent with himself ; but I believe
that in what I am going to say I shall not far misrepresent him.

Bishop Forbes seems to arrive at his mode of interpreting the Articles, so to say, by a sort of double route. It
is with him a question of duties ; of duty to the Articles
themselves, and of duty to Catholic belief. To the first
he evidently attaches comparatively little importance. The
Articles are an uninspired document, and there is a *primâ
facie*, though it may be unavoidable, hardship in requiring
assent to them. Clergymen and others are bound to them
simply because they have subscribed them : the obligation
is to be interpreted legally, and the document itself to be
construed with a legal literalness which takes the text
sentence by sentence, and does not trouble itself with deductions and implications. ' The plain literal and grammatical sense, interpreted by the hardest legal head, is all
that we have to do with in accepting the text : and as

regards the inferences, we have nothing whatever to do
with them.'[1] The duty to the Articles being thus discharged, another duty begins. The obligations of Catholic
truth require that the Articles should be understood in a
Catholic sense, and it is to this that the legal interpretation is calculated to pave the way. The one creates the
vacuum (it is Bishop Forbes's own image applied to legal
interpretation in another connection[2]); the other comes
and fills it. Our right to regard the Articles in this light
is strengthened by historical considerations, by a view of
the Elizabethan age, when they were tendered to the
acceptance of a clergy oscillating between old and new
beliefs, and by a reference to the disputes of the Caroline
period, when the literal and grammatical sense was maintained by the king and the bishops, and denounced by
the Puritans as Jesuitical and Arminian.

Such, so far as I am able to ascertain it, is Bishop
Forbes's theory; and yet, as I have intimated already, I am
not sure that I have exhibited it rightly. Perhaps he is not
altogether consistent with himself in what he says about
his own canon of interpretation. He claims to be bound
by the literal sense of the Articles; yet he seems to admit
that those whose historical position he defends as the true
one, the Catholic party in the Elizabethan age of the
Church, imported into them preconceived notions foreign
to their letter, just as he says is now done by Low Churchmen.[3] So there is something not easily explicable in his
comment on the Royal Declaration. ' The Caroline
bishops knew very well what they were doing; so did the
Puritans. No wonder that these latter sought to stigma-

---

[1] Vol. ii. p. 805.

[2] 'The object of lawyers, according to the principle of acquitting one
criminated if possible, is to evacuate the meaning of terms whereby the
Church has defined and guarded the faith.'—Vol. ii. p. 700.

[3] Vol. i. p. xxi.

tise the sense' enjoined by the Declaration ' as Jesuitical
and Arminian. The instinct of Puritanism was naturally
aroused; the Declaration was the enunciation of the
Catholic sense of the Articles; Tract XC. and the Eiren-
icon are legitimate outcomes of the King's Declaration.'[1]
Now, if the contention of the Caroline bishops is rightly
represented by the Declaration, it was not for a bare literal
lawyer's sense, but for a meaning variously described as
' the true, usual, literal meaning,' ' the plain and full meaning,' ' the literal and grammatical sense' — for that, in
short, for which most clergymen, of whatever party, would
contend in the present day. The Puritans thought the
reformed formularies required yet further reformation, and
so gave the High Churchmen the advantage of appearing
as defenders of the *status quo*. But Bishop Forbes seems
to imply that there was more in the controversy than this
—that the struggle was really for a Catholic or non-
Catholic sense. If this was so, I think that the Puritans,
whose strong language in the discussions on the question
is generally contrasted unfavourably with the moderation
of their opponents, had really some justification for their
vituperative epithets. On the whole, I cannot feel certain
whether Bishop Forbes conceives himself to be interpreting the Articles naturally or not.[2] The best hypothesis I
can form is that which I have given above, that he first
interprets them like a lawyer, in order that he may after-

[1] Vol. I. p. xl.

[2] His account of his own relation to the Articles is as follows :—' I can
sign them myself in "the literal and grammatical sense," that is, taking
sentence by sentence as a lawyer would do; and when the plain and full
meaning alluded to in the Declaration is doubtful, I supplement any deficiency by the interpretation of the other subscriptions which I have made and
the documents I am bound to : so that not having the necessity to call in to
my aid more than the most moderate help of such laws of explanation as all
men practically need in the interpretation of every oath, obligation, pledge,
or subscription, I feel that I am in the position of being able to come to a
pretty impartial opinion on the subject of relaxation.'—Vol. i. pp. viii., ix.

wards interpret them as a Catholic divine; but I cannot
say how far he consciously realises to himself this twofold
process.

Possibly, in one respect, Bishop Forbes's theory may
appear to have something in common with the principles
of interpretation laid down at the beginning of this paper.
He remarks that ' it is very difficult now to throw oneself
into the mind of the framers of the Articles at their last
revision,' intimating that this is what we ought to do if
we wish to approach them properly. It is, indeed, a duty
which a judicious commentator would not only admit, but
enforce. But I do not think Bishop Forbes equally satisfactory in his way of acting on it. What he does is to
show at some length, and by various proofs, that a large
portion of the nation and the clergy was Catholic at the
time of Elizabeth's accession, and to argue that, as only a
few of the clergy refused the Articles, the remainder of
the Catholic party must either have been consciously dis-
honest, or must have submitted in a Catholic sense. Now
if it can be proved or made probable that the Articles, or
any portions of them, were worded in a particular way in
order to conciliate this section of the Church, the fact is,
of course, important with reference to the interpretation
of the document in whole or in part. Bishop Forbes
does attempt this in a few places in the body of his commentary: in these cases, of course, due weight ought to
be given to the argument. But simply to argue that
because such and such persons signed such and such statements, therefore the statements must have a sense corresponding to the belief of the signers, is surely very insecure
reasoning at best. If the Articles were an undeciphered
inscription, such evidence as to their meaning might be
acceptable for want of better. As it is, to interpret the
Articles by the supposed conviction of the Catholics who

originally signed them, rather than by their own words,
is something like the task imposed on the hero of mythology, of hitting an object which he was only allowed to
see as reflected in a vessel of oil. In their proper place
these considerations have their importance. They affect
not the interpretation of the Articles, but what I have
called the casuistical question of the license to be allowed
to schools of opinion in the Church, over and above the
ascertained meaning of the formularies. In an inquiry
like that, Shakspeare and Machyn's 'Diary' may be tendered in evidence to prove that half the people of England
were Catholic at the time when the Articles were originally
imposed. But the poet and the London citizen will
scarcely help us to ascertain what the framers of the
Articles meant by the terms in which they expressed their
own and the Reformed Church's belief.

Another thing still remains to be noticed before I
examine Bishop Forbes's commentary in detail. He declares that 'the Articles have suffered from being always
treated controversially,' and accordingly proposes to turn
them 'from transitory controversies of the sixteenth
century to those immutable truths which have been taught
in the Church and by the Church in all ages.' Two important things are here assumed; that certain controversies
are transitory, and that certain truths are immutable. If
it should prove that the controversies assumed to be
transitory are still being waged on substantially the same
grounds as in the Elizabethan age, and that the truths
assumed to be immutable are propositions which one party
in the Church, and that one especially attached to the
Articles, regards as more than questionable, I think we
shall not doubt that this mode of dealing with the Articles
is really as controversial as that which it professes to
supersede, while it has the disadvantage of using the

Articles for a purpose which is, to say the least, not that which they were intended to serve. 'For example,' he says, 'the Romish doctrine of pardons, alluded to in Article XXII., was a perversion of the belief and practice of the penitential discipline of the Church. It shall be my duty to show what that penitential discipline was, and so of the rest.' Is Bishop Forbes, however, quite sure that, in distinguishing between the truth and the perversion, he is drawing the line exactly where the Church of England would draw it? In his exposition of that part of the Article he makes no attempt to define the doctrine of the English formularies, or even to construct a catena on the subject from the writings of English divines : he casually mentions the address at the beginning of the Commination Service ; but the bulk of his comment consists of a brief historical sketch, embracing the early Church, the mediæval Church, and the decisions of the Council of Trent, the canon by which truth is distinguished from error being nowhere defined or stated. Few things, indeed, are likely to strike a reader more than the absence of reference to Anglican authority in a work purporting to be a constructive exhibition of Anglican doctrine. A chain of English divines is at best only a secondary and subsidiary witness to the teaching of the Church of England, but it would seem to be more in place in a commentary on the Articles than extracts from schoolmen or from modern Roman Catholics.

Descending from generalities to details, I must beg to confine myself almost entirely to Bishop Forbes's exposition of the anti-Roman Articles. They, it is needless to point out, are the real test of the canon of interpretation which he adopts. Even of these I shall not notice all.

The first five Articles I pass over *sicco pede*, merely

stopping for a moment to note a single point. In pur-
suance of his design of explaining the Articles constructively, Bishop Forbes seizes the opportunity presented by
the words of the Second, ' in the womb of the Blessed
Virgin, of her substance,' to enforce at some length the
honour due to the Virgin.   The same thing is done later at
greater length in a more singular connection, in the process
of commenting on Article XV., ' Of Christ alone without
Sin,' where we are first assured that the Virgin and some
of the saints are exceptions to the language of the Article,
and then instructed in the true view of the dignity of the
Mother of our Lord.   This, it is hardly necessary to say,
is not commenting on the Articles, but supplementing and
correcting them.   Nor can it be said that these supple-
ments and corrections are derived from other portions of
the teaching of the English Church.   In the exposition of
the Second Article, indeed, a passage speaking honourably
of the Virgin is quoted from a sermon of Latimer's—one of
the very few cases in which an English divine is appealed
to at all in the work : in the other place references are
made to two passages in the Prayer-Book, and two in
the Homilies.   Of these, Latimer's is of course merely an
individual authority, while Bishop Forbes would himself
contend that the sanction given to the Homilies by
Article XXXV. cannot be taken as extending to all their
details : the passages from the Prayer-Book speak of our
Lord as ' born of a pure Virgin,' words which it is a mere
assumption to interpret of freedom from sin, and of His
being ' made very man of her substance, and that without
spot of sin,' where our Lord's nature would seem to be
specially distinguished from His mother's in respect of
sinlessness.   No notice meanwhile is taken of the facts,
surely significant ones, that, with the exception of this
incidental mention of the Virgin in the Second Article,
the Articles are completely silent about her, and that in

the Collects for the two festivals associated with her name, that name is omitted altogether, the event commemorated being regarded simply in its relation to Christ.

The Sixth and Twentieth Articles resemble each other so much in the ground they traverse that it seems natural to treat them together. Yet, though connected, they are by no means identical. The Sixth is confined to the truth taught, but says nothing about the teacher, who may be an individual or a Church. It simply denies that the teacher, whoever he may be, has any right to enforce any doctrine as necessary to salvation which is not to be found in or collected from Scripture. The Twentieth recognises the Church as an expounder of Scripture, declares that it may not expound Scripture contradictorily, or teach anything contravening it, and repeats the prohibition against enforcing anything beyond Scripture as of necessity to salvation. I think, then, that a commentator anxious for clearness of exposition would have reserved what he had to say on the teaching power as much as possible for his explanation of the Twentieth Article. Bishop Forbes, however, treats the two questions together, and we may as well follow him in doing so. Apparently fearing that the Sixth Article, if left alone, would be misunderstood, he supplies the requisite correction :—

It (the Article) says nothing against the acceptance of whatever the Church proposes for our belief, because whatsoever is so proposed to us must rest ultimately on the authority of Scripture, of which the Church is the guardian and the expounder. All that it seeks to protect the faithful against is the enforcement on them, as requisite to salvation, of individual opinions, which, being without the authentication of Church authority, have consequently no Scriptural authority.

This is constructive explanation, certainly. A cautious expositor would have remarked, 'Nothing is said here about the office of the Church as a teacher.' Bishop

Forbes tells us that nothing is said derogatory to the office of the Church as a teacher, because, in fact, nothing can be said, the teaching of a doctrine by the Church being the only criterion we have of knowing whether it is contained in Scripture. All that is forbidden is the unscriptural teaching of individuals; and even that is not to be tested by Scripture, but by the authority which is the criterion of Scriptural doctrine, the Church. Now this may be the meaning of the Article, but it can hardly be said to lie on its surface, much less to be expressed in its title, ' The sufficiency of the Holy Scriptures for salvation ;' and considering how many persons, not only at the present day, but at the time of the Reformation, were in the habit of attaching a different and (according to Bishop Forbes) erroneous meaning to the words, ' sufficiency of Scripture,' it seems a little inconsiderate in the framers of the Article not to have expressed their mind on the matter more clearly. Meantime, it is strange that Bishop Forbes, after saying that *all* that the Article seeks to protect the faithful against is the enforcement of unauthorised opinions by individuals, proceeds in the very next sentence to say that the Article would condemn any accretive development by the Church which would add to the substance of the faith. The Article then is to guard us not merely against what individuals may do, but against what the Church may do. But why not say this plainly at the outset? If the Article is to be explained constructively, let us know what is involved in its constructive teaching. Does it mean that when the Church professes that its doctrine is contained in or deducible from Scripture, the doctrine is to be accepted; but that when it professes to be teaching an accretive development, the development is to be rejected? It can scarcely mean anything else ; for if the individual

is to be the judge whether a doctrine is a deduction or
an accretion, the whole of Bishop Forbes's exposition falls
to the ground. On the whole, I interpret Bishop Forbes's
interpretation of the Article to mean that the Article is
addressed not to the individual, but to the Church in its
teaching capacity, recognising the power of the Church,
but warning it to be careful how it exercises that power.
If the Church neglects the warning, and teaches as a
deduction what is really an accretion, individuals, it
would seem, must accept it without interposing their own
judgment.[1]

I do not mean, of course, to maintain that the doctrine
of the framers of the Articles on this subject is clear and
unembarrassed. They nowhere assert the right of the
individual to judge whether the teaching of the Church is
scriptural or not. But the persistence with which they
insist upon the Scripture as the rule of faith, and the
emphasis with which they deny that the Church has any
right to add to or contradict it, are hardly consistent in
moral effect, whatever they may be in logic, with Bishop
Forbes's constructive doctrine that the individual can
only know that a thing is scriptural from the fact of its
being taught by the Church. To borrow an illustration
of his own, a charter given by a king to his subjects,
which dwelt repeatedly and emphatically on his possible
violations of duty, would hardly leave on their minds the
impression that they had no right in any case to judge
whether such a violation had been committed.

I go to Article X. Here Bishop Forbes begins his
comment thus :—

This is one of the instances in which the title of the Article
does not correspond accurately with its contents. In the
Article there is no direct assertion of the free will of man, nor

---

[1] See vol. I. p. 101, where this seems to be explicitly asserted.

definition of its meaning, though it is implied in its very
limitation. The Article ought really to be termed, 'Of the
Necessity of Divine Grace.'

This criticism is only applicable if we accept Bishop
Forbes's view of the doctrine of the Church of England
on the subject of Free Will.   He asserts that men in their
natural condition have free will, and censures Luther for
denying it.   If he is right, the Article certainly does seem
to be rather strangely drawn up.   But if we suppose that
the framers of the Article did not hold Bishop Forbes's
doctrine, the difficulty vanishes.   Let the Article be understood to mean that man in his natural state has no
effectual free will for good, but that such a free will can
only be given to him by the grace of God, and the title 'Of
Free Will' is seen to be appropriate enough.   I do not
say that the Article goes to the full length of the
Lutheran doctrine, or that Bishop Forbes does not satisfy
its meaning when he says, 'No one by his natural powers
can obtain actual grace, or the beginning of spiritual life.'
But I think that his adoption of a form of thought confessedly different from that which found favour with the
reforming divines has prevented him from seeing the plain
intention of the Article.

In the Thirteenth Article, again, Bishop Forbes takes
exception to the title.   'It would be correct,' he says, 'if
it were worded, "Of some Works before Justification."'
No doubt the title does present a difficulty.   A person
may cordially agree with the Article that 'works done
before the grace of Christ and the inspiration of His
Spirit are not pleasant to God, forasmuch as they spring
not of faith in Jesus Christ,' and yet hesitate to affirm the
same of 'Works before Justification.'   The case of the
heathen is one which the framers of the Article might
reasonably decline to deal with : the case of Cornelius they
might fairly have been expected to consider.   There would

be no difficulty in admitting that Cornelius had faith in Christ, according to the proposition laid down in the Seventh Article: there would be considerable difficulty in maintaining that he was justified in the theological sense. How the framers of the Article would have dealt with the difficulty, had their attention been drawn to it, I do not pretend to say, but I do not think they would have agreed with Bishop Forbes in introducing the word ' some' into their title, and thus practically stultifying the title itself. The question of the authority of the titles of the Articles is one which will meet us again when we come to Article XXIX. I do not think they are to be forced into agreement with the meaning, real or supposed, of the body of the Articles which they respectively precede; but there can be no doubt that individual subscribers may be allowed the benefit of any difference which may appear to exist between a doctrine as stated in the Article and a doctrine as stated in the title. It needs no general theory of subscription, Catholic or Puritan, to make us realise the fact that those to whom the Articles were originally tendered must have been allowed that latitude; for it is only what would be allowed in the present day in case any new set of Articles were proposed to the acceptance of members of the Church. But this, as I have already insisted, is a question not of explanation, but of that adjustment of opinions which comes in after explanation has done its work.

The Seventeenth Article affords a very conspicuous instance of Bishop Forbes's method of interpretation. He gives an interesting sketch of the history of the Predestinarian controversy, showing how the circumstances of the Reformation tended to divert men's thoughts from the security offered by their connection with the Church to some more personal and individual ground of confidence.

He contrasts the extreme language of Calvin with the
more guarded expressions of the Article, and observes
that as a matter of fact the Article never satisfied the
Puritans. Thus he prepares the way for his own explanation, which is that ' God's predestination is bestowed
on every baptized Christian.' How much is assumed in
this I need not point out. A student of the Articles will
be tempted to ask the question whether Bishop Forbes
can really have read through the Article on which he
comments. The very first sentence of the Article tells
us that the counsel of God in predestination is secret to
us, and that those who are so chosen by God are brought
to everlasting salvation ; whereas baptismal predestination
is a known, visible thing, and need not be finally effectual.
What makes the matter stranger is that Bishop Forbes,
in a note, calls attention to the fact that the words ' licet
prædestinationis decreta sint nobis ignota ' occurred in
Edward VI.'s Articles, but were erased by Parker. He
perceives the relevancy of this omission to his view of the
Article, but does not notice that the equivalent words,
' suo consilio nobis quidem occulto,' are still retained.[1]
He fortifies his interpretation by saying that ' no interpretation of this Article can be the right one which is
at variance with the statements in Articles XXI., V., and
XI.,' where it is asserted that the offer of salvation is
made to all. No one, of course, will deny that these
Articles do present a difficulty, as compared with the
Article before us ; but the difficulty is not one which the
framers of the Articles made, but which they found in
the Bible, and to assume that it must be solved in Bishop
Forbes's way is, as I have just said, to assume a great deal.

---

[1] The author of the letter supposed to be by Bishop Geste (see below)
wishes to strike out these words, but on grounds different from Bishop
Forbes's interpretation. See Parry, *Declaration on Kneeling*, pp. 195 foll.

Meanwhile it is important to notice that Bishop Forbes here distinctly asserts the principle that the Articles are to be interpreted by each other—*i. e. not*, as he says in the Epistle Dedicatory, 'taking sentence by sentence as a lawyer would do.'

In the comment on the Nineteenth Article there is a singular piece of verbal explanation. Quoting the words, ' As the Church of Jerusalem, Alexandria, and Antioch have erred, so also the Church of Rome hath erred, not only in *their* living and manner of ceremonies, but also in matters of faith,' he proceeds to say : ' The emphatic word here is *their*. It refers to the human side of the Church, or rather to the individuals in the Church who do not live up to the graces bestowed on them.' Has Bishop Forbes read the Latin article, which he prints on the same page with the English ? If so, he must have seen that the framers were so careless as to omit this emphatic word altogether when writing in another language. 'Sicut erravit Ecclesia Hierosolymitana, Alexandrina, et Antiochena, ita et erravit Ecclesia Romana, non solum quoad agenda et cærimoniarum ritus, verum in his etiam quæ credenda sunt.' Surely it is unnecessary to state that *their* must be understood (whether idiomatically or not is another question) of the four Churches spoken of, each of which is declared to have erred in the ways described.

I now come to the Articles which bear most on the controversies of the present day—those on the Sacraments. On these Bishop Forbes is more copious than on most of the others, and his reviewer must be more copious also.

The latter part of Article XXV. says, 'The sacraments were not ordained of Christ to be gazed upon, or to be carried about, but that we should duly use them.' Bishop Forbes's comment is :—

In this sentence the stress is on the words, 'were not ordained of Christ to be,' &c. The Article does not say that the things spoken of may not be done, but that they were not *the* objects for which Christ ordained them. Had they been, they could not have been laid aside without sin. Being of ecclesiastical, not of Divine institution, they were mutable, not immutable. What it affirms is strictly historically true.

Those who attend to the language of the Articles on the Sacraments will have little doubt that the reason why the institution of Christ is dwelt on is because that, in the judgment of the framers, was the one thing of paramount importance. The five so-called 'Sacramentals' are rejected in this very Article, because they have not any visible sign or ceremony *ordained of God*: the two Sacraments are called Sacraments ordained of Christ: 'Christ's ordinance' and 'Christ's institution and promise' are put prominently forward in Article XXVI. as the basis on which sacramental efficacy rests: Infant Baptism is enjoined in Article XXVII. as most agreeable with the institution of Christ: Article XXX. prescribes the administering of the Communion in both kinds on the ground of Christ's ordinance and commandment. Besides, the words of the passage before us are sufficient to show that the framers of the Article intended to disparage those uses of the Sacrament which Bishop Forbes thinks indifferent or laudable. What else can be the meaning of saying, ' were not ordained of Christ to be gazed upon, &c., *but that we should duly use them* ? '[1] The inference surely is, that other applications of the Sacrament are not legitimate. Again, on Bishop Forbes's hypothesis, what is the error against which the statement in the Article is levelled? Did anybody ever assert that the Sacraments

---

[1] A contemporary comment on these words is supplied by Bishop Gesta, Treatise against Private Mass, pp. 123, 124 of Dugdale's *Life of Geste*, a reference which I owe to Mr. Sedley Taylor's pamphlet.

were ordained of Christ for either of the purposes first named? Bishop Forbes himself answers the question in the words immediately following those which I have quoted. 'By carrying the Sacraments about, we are probably to understand the procession of the Corpus Domini. *No person in his senses would say that this was ordained of Christ.*' Would any person in his senses think of formally denying what no one in his senses would assert? It is true that the Tridentine decrees distinguish between the facts of Christ's institution and the ulterior purposes and variations which the Church has introduced. The former they admit, as they could not avoid doing; the latter they assert as holding good nevertheless. But the admission would be a barren truism without the subsequent assertion; and to supply the assertion *ex ingenio* is an effort of constructive exposition which sound interpretation will hardly warrant.

The five so-called 'Sacramentals' are defended by Bishop Forbes, including Extreme Unction, 'the last Pleiad,' as he calls it, 'of the Anglican firmament.' But as his defence does not lead him to wrest the language of the Articles, though he thinks it 'awkward and embarrassed,' and also 'unfortunate,' it does not come within the scope of this paper to criticise it. We may even note with satisfaction that he says, 'For the right interpretation of the Article we need but these simple principles :—1. That the framers did not mean to contradict the Homilies, which they praised; 2. That the writers, both of the Articles and of the Homilies, did not use carefully guarded language without a meaning.' The solidarity between the Articles and Homilies is asserted in too unqualified a manner, such as I cannot think Bishop Forbes himself would maintain in the case of other doctrinal statements; but the principle of inter-

preting the Articles by other writings of the Reformation
period is within certain limits a true one, while it is
undoubtedly different from that 'interpretation by the
hardest legal head,' which is elsewhere advocated.

The Twenty-sixth Article is made the subject of an
unauthorised comment. After stating the error against
which the Article is generally understood to be directed,
Bishop Forbes proceeds :—

> This led on to another error at the time of the Reformation.
> The efficiency of the Sacraments was held no longer to depend
> on the interior disposition of the minister. Not the beneficial
> effect only, but the reality also of the Sacrament, was held to
> depend on the interior disposition, the faith of him to whom
> the Sacrament was administered. Our Article condemns both
> these notions. It lays down that the Sacraments have an
> objective value in virtue of their institution. Sacraments ' be
> effectual because of Christ's institution and promise,' therefore
> they do not depend on the state of the recipients.

Whether this is the doctrine of the Church of England,
we shall see when we come to Article XXIX. All that
is at present necessary to say is, that it is not expressed
or implied in the Article before us. All that the Article
does is to deny that the effect of the Sacraments is
hindered by the unworthiness of the ministers, as it does
in the title. It is a mere assumption to argue that
because it is Christ's institution and promise that makes
the Sacraments effectual, therefore they do not depend
on the state of the recipient. In fact, Bishop Forbes
has to introduce a distinction between reality and bene-
ficial effect, of which the Article gives no hint. The
more natural inference from the Article certainly would
be, that the Sacraments by Christ's institution only take
effect in the case of such as rightly and by faith receive

them. But this question, as I said, is better reserved for Article XXIX.

In treating the Twenty-eighth Article, Bishop Forbes contends that the Church of England does not really negative the authorised Roman doctrine of transubstantiation.

It is self-evident (he says) that the English Article does not go directly against the Council of Lateran—(1) Because the term 'transubstantiatio' is a subordinate part of the Lateran Canon ; (2) because . . . . even of the statement in which it occurs, our Article does not even touch upon the most important part—the change '*into* the substance of the body and blood of Christ ;' (3) because there is ground to think that two entirely distinct meanings, and those not having the slightest bearing upon one another, have been given to the word 'substance.'

Without wishing to cavil about words, I would remark that a conclusion like this, depending upon three propositions, none of which would be admitted without argument, cannot be called 'self-evident.' As to the propositions themselves, it is sufficient to say, on the first, that whether the word 'transubstantiatio' be prominent or not in the Lateran Canon, Bishop Forbes agrees that it was used there with the special object of condemning Berengar, who had brought the word 'substance' into the controversy, while there is no doubt that, however understood, it was the received term at the time of the framing of the Articles to express the Roman doctrine. The second depends on the fact that the Article originally defined transubstantiation as the change of the substance of bread and wine into the substance of Christ's body and blood, and that the last eight words were afterwards omitted. It is possible that this may

have been done with an object, as we know that Bishop
Geste, the reviser, if not the framer, of this Article, was
anxious to conciliate those who held a high sacramental
doctrine; it is possible, also, that the change may have
been adopted to assimilate the English Article to the
Latin, which simply has 'panis et vini transubstantiatio.'
What gain could arise from the omission to anyone
accustomed to strictness of thought it would be difficult
to see: the change of substance must imply a change
into some other substance, in whatever way the word
' substance' is understood. The real weight of the argument lies in the third proposition, the allegation that
the framers of the Articles understood the word ' substance' in a different sense from that which it bears in
the decrees of the Roman Church. According to Bishop
Forbes, the word has two entirely different meanings,
the one metaphysical and technical, the other physical
and popular; and it is in this latter sense that the
framers of our formularies understand it when they condemn transubstantiation. The argument is one which
has recently been put with considerable plausibility by
the author of the 'Kiss of Peace,' and answered in a
learned and elaborate pamphlet by Mr. Sedley Taylor.
Whether the controversy is yet exhausted I cannot say,
but there can be no doubt that it is not so easy of
decision as Bishop Forbes appears to think. Mr. Taylor
has shown that Cranmer and Geste, in arguing against
transubstantiation, recognised the distinction between
substance and accident, and reasoned on that basis. He
has also answered by anticipation one or two of the
special points on which Bishop Forbes relies, the points
themselves having previously been raised in the ' Kiss of
Peace.' He shows that the 'Declaration on Kneeling'
furnishes no presumption that its authors understood

substance in the popular sense, and that Bishop Geste
himself, while recognising the distinction between substance and accidents, brings the very same objection
against transubstantiation as is brought in the Article,
that it 'overthroweth the nature of a sacrament.' If
Bishop Forbes wishes to establish his position, he must
adduce some further evidence than that which Mr.
Taylor has disposed of. Meantime it is strange to see
Bishop Forbes going further in one respect than Dr.
Newman went in Tract XC. Dr. Newman, when he
wrote the tract, thought that the doctrine condemned in
the Article as having 'given occasion to many super-
stitions,' was exemplified in the story of the appearance
of blood in the chalice to St. Odo, and in that of the
child seen during administration by St. Wittekundus.
Bishop Forbes takes a distinction :—

> It would not be superstitious to believe that, as in the case at
> Bolsena (assuming the circumstance to be true), our Lord
> attested the truth of His presence in the sacrament by an
> appearance of blood ; but it would be superstitious to believe
> that that appearance was physical—that it was our Lord's
> blood, and as such to be received. And so it would be super-
> stitious to believe that those appearances of Christ as a little
> child in the sacrament, which have from time to time been
> vouchsafed to God's servants, was the actual body of our Lord
> in its natural condition.

I do not mean to say that Bishop Forbes's explanation is
inconsistent with Dr. Newman's argument, which is that
what the Article condemns is the notion of a carnal
presence ; but I think that the scrupulousness which
refuses at once to surrender these stories is scarcely
in unison with the spirit in which the Article was
written.

Bishop Forbes says, 'one cannot exaggerate the im-

portance of the words *given*, *taken*, and *eaten*,' in the
third paragraph of this Article. By 'importance' he
must mean importance with a view to the establishment
of a particular interpretation : for the general purposes
of the Article it is obvious that they require to be
estimated with just the same accuracy, neither more nor
less, as the other expressions in the Article which are
not confessedly mere expressions of course. They are,
undoubtedly, somewhat fuller than might have been expected, and for this fulness an interpreter must, of course,
seek a reason. Dean Stanley [1] finds it in a wish to accu-
mulate terms out of which Romanist, Lutheran, Zuinglian,
and Calvinist might take their choice. Dr. Hawkins [2]
says, 'the point of the argument is in the words, "only
after a heavenly and spiritual manner : " and without
asserting that the body of Christ is "given " at all, the
Article declares that, whether regarded as " given," or
" received," or " eaten," in any case it is only after a
heavenly and spiritual manner.' While Dr. Hawkins is
right in his view of the main thought of the sentence,
I think he makes rather too little of the word
'given.' The Article, it seems to me, does commit itself
to the statement that the Body is given, though only as
an *obiter dictum*. But what does 'given' mean? Is it
more than a correlative to 'taken and eaten?' Those
who believe that what the priest distributes is in all
cases our Lord's body may, of course, use the word, but
so may those who believe that it is so only to the
faithful. The only opinion which, it seems to me, the
word does not favour is that which, as I said in the postscript to my paper on the Communion Office, seems to
have dictated some of the alterations made by the

---

[1] *Letter to Bishop of London on Subscription*, p. 14.
[2] *Notes upon Subscription*, p. 26.

revisers of 1552, viz., that the act of communion is not
connected with the actual reception of the elements;
so that the insertion of the word may be compared with
the changes made in the Communion Office by the
Caroline revisers.   There is some doubt about the precise theological position of Geste, the framer of this part
of the Article.   His opinions on the Eucharist are to be
gathered from his Treatise against the Prevee (Privy or
Private) Masse, published 1548, from some notes on the
Prayer-Book sent to Burghley, apparently undated, from
a letter to Burghley on this very Article, dated December
22, 1566, and from another letter to the same person, on
various passages in the Articles, without a signature, but
apparently in his handwriting, and supposed to be
written in May, 1571.   If the two first documents stood
alone, his leanings would seem to be Protestant: if we
had only the last two, we should suppose that he held
a high sacramental doctrine.[1]   On the particular point
before us, however, there is no necessary contrariety in
his statements.   His letter of 1566 asserts that the words
' after a heavenly and spiritual manner *only*,' as used by
him, ' did not exclude the presence of Christ's body in
the Sacrament, but only the grossness and sensibleness
in the receiving thereof.'   In his treatise he had said,
' that we as materially and truly, though not grosslier
(grossly or ?) sensibly, but ghostly receive and eat Christ's
body and drink His blood as we do the foresaid ' (the
bread and wine).   But what we are concerned with,
after all, is the meaning he expressed in the Article, re-
collecting, as we must, that he would naturally choose

---

[1] He is contrasted with some other bishops as having preached in defence
of the real presence by a Roman Catholic controversialist of the time
(Dorman's *Disproof of M. Nowell's Reproof*, Antwerp, 1565, pp. 52a, 103a,
a rare book, to which my attention was directed by Mr. Sedley Taylor, if
indeed I ought not rather to name Mr. H. R. Droop, to whom he refers).

terms which, while conveying his own view, would be accepted by his episcopal brethren. That meaning I believe to be that which I have stated above, an assertion of the connection of our Lord's presence with the elements, excluding the notion of a carnal presence, but not entering further into definition on the matter. For such further definition we must look to the next Article.

On the concluding sentence of the Article, Bishop Forbes repeats what he had said on Article XXV., that the Article does not prohibit the practices mentioned, but merely says that they are no part of Christ's institution. Accordingly, he sketches the history of the several practices, much as a commentator on Article XXV. might sketch the history of Infant Baptism, and ends by saying, ' It is unnecessary to go into the question of the worship of Our Lord in the Sacrament, after the exhaustive treatise of John Keble, τοῦ μακαρίτου, to which the reader is referred.' If this is constructive exposition, it is so in the sense of building up again the things which the Reformers destroyed.

We now come to the chief battle-ground of the Eucharistic doctrine in the Articles, Article XXIX. There can be little doubt that it was regarded as such at the time when it was put forth. It originally formed part of the revised Articles of 1563; but it was omitted when they came to be published in that year, and it did not finally take its place till 1571. There is a letter, from Parker to Burghley,[1] implying that difficulties were felt regarding it ; and another, supposed to be by Geste, also to Burghley, begging that it may not be adopted,[2] ' be-

---

[1] Parker's Correspondence (Parker Society), p. 381.

[2] Perry, *Declaration*, p. 200. The passage is further important, as showing how the writer understood the expression afterwards introduced into the Catechism, ' reception by the faithful.'

cause it is quite contrary to the Scripture and to the doctrine of the Fathers.' As to its object, I do not see that there can be any reasonable doubt. The question whether the wicked receive the body of Christ, or not, was a very common one at the Reformation, as anyone who will look at the works of the Reformers may see. It was, in fact, one of the tests applied by the Romanists in their examinations of the accused Reformers at the time of the Marian persecution, the question of Adoration being another. It is one of the principal subjects discussed by Cranmer in his controversy with Gardiner. There was no dispute that the wicked did not receive the 'virtus Sacramenti;' whether they received the 'res Sacramenti,' or merely the 'signum Sacramenti,' was the point at issue. Article XXV. speaks only of the 'virtus Sacramenti.' Article XXVIII. touches on the 'res Sacramenti' when it says that the mean whereby the body of Christ is received and eaten in the Supper is faith, but does not go into the question. The present Article deals with the question, and deals with it as it was dealt with (I believe) by the Reformers generally, denying that the wicked receive more than the 'signum.'

Such seems to me the natural explanation of the Article: now let us see what Bishop Forbes has to allege against it. He first asserts that the reception of the 'res Sacramenti' by the wicked is required by the language of St. Paul in the First Epistle to the Corinthians. To this it can only be said that many expositors do not feel the necessity of so understanding St. Paul's words, and that there is no evidence that the Reformers felt it. He appeals to expressions in the Communion Office, ' receive *the same* unworthily,' ' unworthily receiving *thereof*,' ' receive *it* unworthily,' the reference to Judas, the reference to St. Paul's language, the words in the Prayer of Humble Ac-

cess, and those in the second Post-Communion Prayer.
As to the first three passages, no one doubts that good
and bad alike receive the Communion, in the sense in
which the word is ordinarily understood—*i.e.*, the consecrated elements.[1] The reference to Judas, like that
to St. Paul, proves no more than that the Reformers,
like the sacred writers, looked upon unworthy reception
as an act of profanation which would be followed by
punishment; which, again, is not in dispute. The other
two passages were discussed in the postscript to my previous paper. Bishop Forbes then urges the words about
unworthy reception at the end of Article XXV. They
have reference, as I said just now, to the 'virtus Sacramenti.' As to any argument based on the adoption of
St. Paul's words, it must of course stand or fall with the
interpretation of those words. He next comes to the
words of the present Article. The Fathers, he says,
generally assert that the wicked, in some sense, do receive the body of Christ—*i.e.*, they receive the 'res Sacramenti.' St. Augustine, in other passages than that
quoted in the Article, admits such a reception; therefore, the passage quoted must be understood in that
sense. This is rather a proof that the framers of the
Article *ought* to have meant a certain thing than that
they *did* mean it. Further, he appeals to the words, 'yet
are they in nowise partakers of Christ.' 'To be a par-
taker of Christ is the language of St. Paul. Our Article
uses St. Paul's language in St. Paul's meaning. No one
ought to attempt to maintain that our Article uses the
words of Holy Scripture in a non-Scriptural sense.' This
is a hazardous canon to lay down, especially for one who

---

[1] This question was raised at the time of the Reformation, and answered
by the Protestants much as I have answered it. See Redman in Foxe, vol.
vi. pp. 200 foll. ed. 1846, quoted by Perry, *Declaration*, p. 20.

believes, with Bishop Forbes, that the Church is the one interpreter of Scripture. Surely the question of the meaning of the words of Scripture in themselves is distinct from the question of the meaning attributed to them in a formulary of the Church where they are quoted. In interpreting an Article, at any rate, we are to interpret its applications of Scripture by themselves, not by our views of Scripture. In the present case, however, I suspect the discrepancy is one of Bishop Forbes's own creation. The Article says that the wicked are *in no wise* partakers of Christ, neither beneficially nor in the sense of partaking of the 'res Sacramenti.' The implication would seem to be, that to allow that they are partakers of Christ, though only to their condemnation, is to allow too much. I do not advance this as a certain interpretation, but as a highly probable one; agreeing as it does not only with the title of the Article, but with its whole tenor. That the wording may at the same time have been so formed as to give a *locus standi* for those who, like the author of the letter ascribed to Bishop Geste, did not sympathise with the Article is of course possible. But, urges Bishop Forbes, we happen to know over and above that the scriptural meaning was the meaning of the framer of the Article. How do we know this? From Archbishop Parker's letter to Burghley, in which he says that he is still advisedly of opinion concerning St. Augustine's authority 'concerning so much wherefore they be alleged in the Article.' This must mean that, though the words would not prove that the wicked do not receive the 'res Sacramenti,' they are enough to prove that the wicked do not receive the 'virtus Sacramenti.' Now all that we happen to know is that Burghley, for some reason unstated, objected to St. Augustine's authority as alleged in the Article, and that

Parker maintained that it was sufficient for the purpose
for which it was alleged. The nature of Burghley's objection and the purpose of the Article, as conceived by
Parker, we must supply from conjecture.[1] From the
letter itself (which Bishop Forbes does not give entire) it
would seem that Burghley was, so to say, the spokesman
of some men who ' varied ' from the doctrine of the Article. The only objections which we know to have been
taken at the time are those contained in Geste's (?) letter
to Burghley, so that the probability would appear to be
that these are referred to. Strype assumes without doubt
that they came from the Papists. The reference to St.
Augustine certainly creates a difficulty on Bishop
Forbes's hypothesis: *primâ facie* it unquestionably seems
to deny that the ' res Sacramenti ' is received by the
wicked. Why should Parker have adduced it at all, on
the supposition that such was not his meaning, when, as
Bishop Forbes tells us, and as Gardiner had shown in his
work against Cranmer, there are other passages in St.
Augustine which would have expressed his real intention
unquestionably ? As to the antithetical structure of the
Article, which Bishop Forbes urges in support of his
view, it proves nothing. The logical opposition is between partaking of Christ and eating the sign or sacrament of so great a thing. Nor is he more fortunate in his
attempt to rebut the evidence which the title of the Article bears to its meaning. If, indeed, as he asserts, the
grammatical structure of the words of the Article would
not admit the meaning expressed in the title, the title, as

---

[1] I am aware of the argument founded by Dr. Pusey (*Real Presence the
Doctrine of English Church*, pp. 276 foll.) on the passages of Prosper to
which Parker refers: but it does not seem to me to overbalance the general
probability on the other side. What I am concerned to maintain is merely
that Parker's letter has not that decisive value which Bishop Forbes attributes to it.

I said some pages ago, could not be allowed to overbear
the Article.   But I shall be surprised if anyone who has
followed this discussion agrees with Bishop Forbes that
the words of the Article will not grammatically bear the
meaning that the wicked do not eat the body of Christ.
Such a meaning may be contrary to the sense of Scripture, contrary to the teaching of the Fathers, but contrary to the words of the Article most assuredly it is not.

The only other comments which I have occasion to
notice are those on Articles XXXI. and XXXII.

Bishop Forbes maintains that the Eucharist is a com-
memorative sacrifice, available for the dead as well as for
the living, and that the Thirty-first Article does not contradict this.   He asserts, first, that it is a sacrifice ; and,
secondly, that it is available as aforesaid.   The first he
proves, as usual, from the Fathers, and then quotes Sir
William Palmer and the Bishop of Exeter to show that it
is reconcilable with the Article.   What the Article is
likely to have meant is a question which he does not consider, though, as we have seen, he is not indisposed to
raise it in other cases.   He does, however, indirectly pass
judgment on this question, when, after speaking of the
testimony of the early Church, he says, ' It is probable
that the English Reformers were not conversant with the
Eastern Liturgies ; otherwise we cannot conceive how
they could have preferred the Second to the First Book
of Edward, or have rested content with the emendations
at the beginning of the reign of Elizabeth.'   With reference to the extent of the efficacy of the Eucharist, he
quotes the passage from the Post-Communion Prayer discussed in my former paper, ' we and all thy whole
Church,' which he says ' many English divines have applied, without blame,' to those in the intermediate state,
and states that ' the Church of England has judicially

ruled in her supreme tribunal that prayer for the dead is
not unlawful.' The remainder of his comment is chiefly
devoted to showing that the doctrine of a continuing
Eucharistic sacrifice is not inconsistent with the doctrine
of the one oblation of Christ once offered, not that the
Church of England does not consider it inconsistent. Yet,
in an explanation of Anglican formularies, the latter
would have seemed the point chiefly to be laboured.

In the Thirty-second Article Bishop Forbes lays stress
on the title. In 1553 it ran, 'The state of single life is
commanded of no man by the word of God;' in Latin,
'Cœlibatus ex verbo Dei præcipitur nemini:' in 1571 it
was changed into, 'Of the Marriage of Priests,' 'De Con-
jugio Sacerdotum.' The change extends to the body of
the Article: in 1553 the obligation to celibacy was denied
of the clergy alone, the liberty of all other men being left
to be inferred; now it is denied of the clergy as of other
Christian men: in 1553 the heading spoke of a 'præ-
ceptum,' the Article of a 'mandatum;' now the two are
combined: lastly, the present heading introduces the important word 'sacerdotum.' How Bishop Forbes should
think 'the marked contrast of the clergy with other Christian men an observable thing,' is not easy to see. The
simple account of the matter is that the clergy, who had
been excepted from the liberty to marry under the old
religion, are now declared to be excepted no longer.
The original Article said the same thing, but it said it
awkwardly, stating, as it were, the major premiss of the
syllogism in the title, the conclusion in the Article itself.
As for the combination of mandate and precept, it removes any question that might arise on the interchange-
able use of the two words, while it makes the cogency
of the rule of celibacy more stringent, and, by conse-

quence, the exemption from it more complete. Any significance that there may be in the assertion that bishops,
presbyters, and deacons are all in some sense 'sacerdotes,'
I have no wish to ignore. Only it should be recollected
that the more is made of the word, the more force is
given to the Article. In whatever sense the English clergy
are priests, in that sense it is true that their sacerdotal
character leaves them free to marry or not as they like.
Before I leave the question of the heading, I would remind Bishop Forbes that Article XXIX. is also one of those
which had their titles revised. Originally it stood in the
Latin, 'Impii non manducant Corpus Christi in usu Cœnæ;'
afterwards it was altered into, 'De manducatione Corporis
Christi, et impios illud non manducare.' Is no argument
as to the meaning of the Article to be founded on the fact
that, while the title was altered, the words which it is
sought to deprive of their strict meaning were retained?
In the latter part of his comment on the present Article,
Bishop Forbes maintains that by leaving the choice of a
married or single life to the conscience of each person,
clerical or lay, it really implies that the question is not
free to the individual. This is of course true; not so the
corollary Bishop Forbes draws from it, that the very circumstances of the clergy make them more responsible in
the matter than the laity, or that 'the Church of England
leans to the celibate,' though 'it does not enjoin it.'[1] I
do not say that the Article lays any burden on those who
wish to decide their individual case on what may be called
professional grounds; but it expressly declines to bias their
judgment.

[1] This seems to be made out from the Marriage Service, which speaks of
those who have not the gift of continence. But what the Marriage Service
says it says to all; and any opinion that the clergy have a special duty in
the matter, whether an admissible one or not, is at any rate a private one.

A few words on the comment on the Ratification will bring me to the end of what I have to say.

The Articles (says Bishop Forbes) are primarily a State document, made ecclesiastical by the acceptance of the two Convocations in 1562 and 1571. . . . . One treats them very differently from the decrees of a Provincial Synod of the Church of England. Convocation . . . . is not a Council in the strictly ecclesiastical sense.[1] . . . . It only binds the conscience as a result of subscription.

I do not object to this view of our duty to the Articles, though I dissent from the remarks that follow (remarks to which I have already adverted), that subscription only binds us to the plain literal and grammatical sense, interpreted by the hardest legal head. But there are two questions which I am desirous to ask. Is it nothing in Bishop Forbes's estimation that the Articles, as we have them, though enacted by Parliament, were framed by the bishops? Is it nothing in Bishop Forbes's estimation, as a Scotch bishop, that the Articles were accepted by the Convention or Synod of Laurencekirk?

I have spoken of Bishop Forbes's work as what it professes to be—an explanation of the Articles. If it were possible to regard it in any other light, it would be easy to do justice to its merits. It contains much interesting theological argument, and many sketches of the history of doctrines, presented in a lively if somewhat desultory manner, and occasionally relieved by illustrations and quotations which will please the literary reader. The spirit in which he writes is earnest, and the tone which he adopts towards opponents in general conciliatory. It

---

[1] He calls it, however, a Synod, in the Chronological Table prefixed to Vol. I.

is as an exegetical work that it has come before me; whether I have estimated it justly as such I leave others to judge.

In conclusion, I have to say that I am not ignorant that other writers have maintained many of Bishop Forbes's interpretations on substantially the same grounds; but I have thought it better to deal with his work alone, being as it is the most complete and systematic exposition of a certain theory of the Articles, than to extend the field of controversy further.

END OF THE FIRST VOLUME.

LONDON: PRINTED BY
SPOTTISWOODE AND CO., NEW-STREET SQUARE
AND PARLIAMENT STREET